# JOHN SANDFORD

## THREE COMPLETE NOVELS

*Also by John Sandford*

MIND PREY
NIGHT PREY
WINTER PREY
SILENT PREY

# JOHN SANDFORD

THREE COMPLETE NOVELS

RULES OF PREY

SHADOW PREY

EYES OF PREY

G. P. PUTNAM'S SONS
NEW YORK

G. P. Putnam's Sons
*Publishers Since 1838*
200 Madison Avenue
New York, NY 10016

Library of Congress Cataloging-in-Publication Data

Sandford, John, date.
[Selections.   1995]
Three complete novels / John Sandford
p.   cm.
ISBN 0-399-14007-7
Contents: Rules of prey—Shadow prey—Eyes of prey.
1. Davenport, Lucas (Fictitious character)—Fiction. 2. Private
investigators—Minnesota—Minneapolis—Fiction. 3. Detective and
mystery stories, American. 4. Minneapolis (Minn.)—Fiction.
I. Sandford, John, Rules of prey.   II. Sandford, John, Shadow prey.
III. Sandford, John, Eyes of prey.   IV. Title.
PS3569.A516A6   1995                94-33362 CIP
813'.54—dc20

Printed in the United States of America

10   9   8   7   6   5   4   3   2   1

*Book design by Patrice Sheridan*

# Contents

# RULES OF PREY

# 1

A rooftop billboard cast a flickering blue light through the studio windows. The light ricocheted off glass and stainless steel: an empty crystal bud vase rimed with dust, a pencil sharpener, a microwave oven, peanut-butter jars filled with drawing pencils, paintbrushes and crayons. An ashtray full of pennies and paper clips. Jars of poster paint. Knives.

A stereo was dimly visible as a collection of rectangular silhouettes on the window ledge. A digital clock punched red electronic minutes into the silence.

The maddog waited in the dark.

He could hear himself breathe. Feel the sweat trickle from the pores of his underarms. Taste the remains of his dinner. Feel the shaven stubble at his groin. Smell the odor of the Chosen's body.

He was never so alive as in the last moments of a long stalk. For some people, for people like his father, it must be like this every minute of every hour: life on a higher plane of existence.

The maddog watched the street. The Chosen was an artist. She had smooth olive skin and liquid brown eyes, tidy breasts and a slender waist. She lived illegally in the warehouse, bathing late at night in the communal rest room down the hall, furtively cooking microwave meals after the building manager left for the day. She slept on a narrow bed in a tiny storage room, beneath an art-deco crucifix, immersed in vapors of turpentine and linseed. She was out now, shopping for microwave dinners. The microwave crap would kill her if he didn't, the maddog thought. He was probably doing her a favor. He smiled.

The artist would be his third kill in the Cities, the fifth of his life.

The first was a ranch girl, riding out of her back pasture toward the wooded limestone hills of East Texas. She wore jeans, a red-and-white-checked shirt, and cowboy boots. She sat high in a western saddle, riding more with her knees and her head than with the reins in her hand. She came straight into him, her single blonde braid bouncing behind.

The maddog carried a rifle, a Remington Model 700 ADL in .270 Winchester. He braced his forearm against a rotting log and took her when she was forty yards out. The single shot penetrated her breastbone and blew her off the horse.

That was a killing of a different kind. She had not been Chosen; she had asked for it. She had said, three years before the killing, in the maddog's hearing, that he had lips like red worms. Like the twisting red worms that you found under river rocks. She said it in the hall of their high school, a cluster of friends standing around her. A few glanced over their shoulders at the maddog, who stood fifteen feet away, alone, as always, pushing his books onto the top shelf of his locker. He gave no sign that he'd overheard. He had been very good at concealment, even in his youngest days, though the ranch girl didn't seem to care one way or another. The maddog was a social nonentity.

But she paid for her careless talk. He held her comment to his breast for three years, knowing his time would come. And it did. She went off the back of the horse, stricken stone-cold dead by a fast-expanding copper-jacketed hunting bullet.

The maddog ran lightly through the woods and across a low stretch of swampy prairie. He dumped the gun beneath a rusting iron culvert where a road crossed the marsh. The culvert would confuse any metal detector used to hunt for the weapon, although the maddog didn't expect a search—it was deer season and the woods were full of maniacs from the cities, armed to the teeth and ready to kill. The season, the weapon cache, had all been determined far in advance. Even as a sophomore in college, the maddog was a planner.

He went to the girl's funeral. Her face was untouched and the top half of the coffin was left open. He sat as close as he could, in his dark suit, watched her face and felt the power rising. His only regret was that she had not known that death was coming, so that she might savor the pain; and that he had not had time to enjoy its passage.

The second killing was the first of the truly Chosen, although he no longer considered it a work of maturity. It was more of . . . an experiment? Yes. In the second killing, he remedied the deficiencies of the first.

She was a hooker. He took her during the spring break of his second year, the crisis year, in law school. The need had long been there, he thought. The intellectual pressure of law school compounded it. And one cool night in Dallas, with a knife, he earned temporary respite on the pale white body of a Mississippi peckerwood girl, come to the city to find her fortune.

The ranch girl's shooting death was lamented as a hunting accident. Her parents grieved and went on to other things. Two years later the maddog saw the girl's mother laughing outside a concert hall.

The Dallas cops dismissed the hooker's execution as a street killing, dope-related. They found Quaaludes in her purse, and that was good enough. All they had was a street name. They put her in a pauper's grave with that name, the wrong name, on the tiny iron plaque that marked the place. She had never seen her sixteenth year.

The two killings had been satisfying, but not fully calculated. The killings in the Cities were different. They were meticulously planned, their tactics based on a professional review of a dozen murder investigations.

The maddog was intelligent. He was a member of the bar. He derived rules.

*Never kill anyone you know.*

*Never have a motive.*

*Never follow a discernible pattern.*

*Never carry a weapon after it has been used.*

*Isolate yourself from random discovery.*

*Beware of leaving physical evidence.*

There were more. He built them into a challenge.


He was mad, of course. And he knew it.

In the best of worlds, he would prefer to be sane. Insanity brought with it a large measure of stress. He had pills now, black ones for high blood pressure, reddish-brown ones to help him sleep. He would prefer to be sane, but you played the hand you were dealt. His father said so. The mark of a man.

So he was mad.

But not quite the way the police thought.

He bound and gagged the women and raped them.

The police considered him a sex freak. A cold freak. He took his time about the killings and the rapes. They believed he talked to his victims, taunted them. He carefully used prophylactics. Lubricated prophylactics. Postmortem vaginal smears on the first two Cities victims produced evidence of the lubricant. Since the cops never found the rubbers, they assumed he took them with him.

Consulting psychiatrists, hired to construct a psychological profile, believed the maddog *feared* women. Possibly the result of a youthful life with a dominant mother, they said, a mother alternately tyrannical and loving, with sexual overtones. Possibly the maddog was afraid of AIDS, and possibly—they talked of endless possibilities—he was essentially homosexual.

Possibly, they said, he might *do something* with the semen he saved in the prophylactics. When the shrinks said that, the cops looked at each other. Do something? Do what? Make Sno-Cones? What?

The psychiatrists were wrong. About all of it.

He did not taunt his victims, he comforted them; helped them to *participate*. He didn't use the rubbers primarily to protect himself from disease, but to protect himself from the police. Semen is evidence, carefully collected, examined, and typed by medical investigators. The maddog knew of a case where a woman was attacked, raped, and killed by one of two panhandlers. Each man accused the other. A semen-typing was pivotal in isolating the killer.

The maddog didn't save the rubbers. He didn't *do something* with them. He flushed them, with their evidentiary load, down his victims' toilets.

Nor was his mother a tyrant.

She had been a small unhappy dark-haired woman who wore calico dresses and wide-brimmed straw hats in the summertime. She died when he was in junior high school. He could barely remember her face, though once, when he was idly going through family boxes, he came across a stack of letters addressed to his father and tied with a ribbon. Without knowing quite why, he sniffed the envelopes and was overwhelmed by the faint, lingering scent of her, a scent like old wild-rose petals and the memories of Easter lilacs.

But she was nothing.

She never contributed. Won nothing. Did nothing. She was a drag on his father. His father and his fascinating games, and she was a drag on them. He remembered his father shouting at her once, *I'm working, I'm working, and you will stay out of this room when I am working, I have to concentrate and I cannot do it if you come in here and whine, whine* . . . The fascinating games played in courts and jailhouses.

The maddog was not homosexual. He was attracted only to women. It was the only thing that a man could do, the thing with women. He lusted for them, seeing their death and feeling himself explode as one transcendent moment.

In moments of introspection, the maddog had rooted through his psyche, seeking the genesis of his insanity. He decided that it had not come all at once, but had *grown.* He remembered those lonely weeks of isolation on the ranch with his mother, while his father was in Dallas playing his games. The maddog would work with his .22 rifle, sniping the ground squirrels. If he hit a squirrel just right, hit it in the hindquarters, rolled it away from its hole, it would struggle and chitter and try to claw its way back to the nest, dragging itself with its front paws.

All the other ground squirrels, from adjacent holes, would stand on the hills of sand they'd excavated from their dens and watch. Then he could pick off a second one, and that would bring out more, and then a third, until an entire colony was watching a half-dozen wounded ground squirrels trying to drag themselves back to their nests.

He would wound six or seven, shooting from a prone position, then stand and walk over to the nests and finish them with his pocketknife. Sometimes he skinned them out alive, whipping off their hides while they struggled in his hands. After a while, he began stringing their ears, keeping the string in the loft of a machine shed. At the end of one summer, he had more than three hundred sets of ears.

He had the first orgasm of his young life as he lay prone on the edge of a hayfield sniping ground squirrels. The long spasm was like death itself. Afterward he unbuttoned his jeans and pulled open the front of his underwear to look at the wet semen stains and he said to himself, "Boy, that did it . . . boy, that did it." He said it over and over, and after that, the passion came more often as he hunted over the ranch.

Suppose, he thought, that it had been different. Suppose that he'd had playmates, girls, and they had gone to play doctor out in one of the sheds. *You show me yours, I'll show you mine. . . .* Would that have made all the difference? He didn't know. By the time he was fourteen, it was too late. His mind had been turned.

A girl lived a mile down the road. She was five or six years older than he. Daughter of a real rancher. She rode by on a hayrack once, her mother towing it with a tractor, the girl wearing a sweat-soaked T-shirt that showed her nipples puckered against the dirty cloth. The maddog was fourteen and felt the stirring of a powerful desire and said aloud, "I would love her and kill her."

He was mad.

When he was in law school he read about other men like himself, fascinated to learn that he was part of a community. He thought of it as a community, of men who understood the powerful exaltation of that moment of ejaculation and death.

But it was not just the killing. Not anymore. There was now the intellectual thrill.

The maddog had always loved games. The games his father played, the games he played alone in his room. Fantasy games, role-playing games. He was good at chess. He won the high-school chess tournament three years running, though he rarely played against others outside the tournaments.

But there were better games. Like those his father played. But even his father was a surrogate for the real player, the other man at the table, the defendant. The real players were the defendants and the cops. The maddog knew he could never be a cop. But he could still be a player.

And now, in his twenty-seventh year, he was approaching his destiny. He was playing and he was killing, and the joy of the act made his body sing with pleasure.

The *ultimate game*. The *ultimate stakes*.

He bet his life that they could not catch him. And he was winning the lives of women, like poker chips. Men always played for women; that was his theory. They were the winnings in all the best games.

Cops, of course, weren't interested in playing. Cops were notoriously dull.

To help them grasp the concept of the game, he left a rule with each killing. Words carefully snipped from the Minneapolis newspaper, a short phrase stuck with Scotch Magic tape to notebook paper. For the first Cities kill, it was *Never murder anyone you know*.

That puzzled them sorely. He placed the paper on the victim's chest, so there could be no doubt about who had left it there. As an almost jocular afterthought, he signed it: *maddog*.

The second one got *Never have a motive*. With that, they would have known they were dealing with a man of purpose.

Though they must have been sweating bullets, the cops kept the story out of the papers. The maddog yearned for the press. Yearned to watch his legal colleagues follow the course of the investigation in the daily news. To know that they were talking to him, about him, never knowing that he was the One.

It thrilled him. This third collection should do the trick. The cops couldn't suppress the story forever. Police departments normally leaked like colanders. He was surprised they'd kept the secret this long.

This third one would get *Never follow a discernible pattern*. He left the sheet on a loom.

There was a contradiction here, of course. The maddog was an intellectual and he had considered it. He was careful to the point of fanaticism: he would leave no clues. Yet, he deliberately created them. The police and their psychiatrists might deduce certain things about his personality from his choice of words. From the fact that he made rules at all. From the impulse to play.

But there was no help for that.

If *killing* were all that mattered, he didn't doubt that he could do it and get away with it. Dallas had demonstrated that. He could do dozens. Hundreds. Fly to Los Angeles, buy a knife at a discount store, kill a hooker, fly back home the same night. A different city every week. They would never catch him. They would never even *know*.

There was an attraction to the idea, but it was, ultimately, intellectually sterile. He was developing. He wanted the *contest*. Needed it.

The maddog shook his head in the dark and looked down from the high window. Cars hissed by on the wet street. There was a low rumble from I-94, two blocks to the north. Nobody on foot. Nobody carrying bags.

He waited, pacing along the windows, watching the street. Eight minutes, ten minutes. The intensity was growing, the pulsing, the pressure. Where was she? He needed her.

Then he saw her, crossing the street below, her dark hair bobbing in the mercury-vapor lights. She was alone, carrying a single grocery bag. When she passed out of sight directly below him, he moved to the central pillar and stood against it.

The maddog wore jeans, a black T-shirt, latex surgeon's gloves, and a blue silk ski mask. When she was tied to the bed and he had stripped himself, the woman would find that her attacker had shaven: he was as clean of pubic hair as a five-year-old. Not because he was kinky, although it did feel . . . *interesting*. But he had seen a case in which lab specialists recovered a half-dozen pubic hairs from a woman's couch and matched them with samples from the assailant. Got the samples from the assailant with a search warrant. Nice touch. Upheld on appeal.

He shivered. It was chilly. He wished he had worn a jacket. When he left his apartment, the temperature was seventy-five. It must have fallen fifteen degrees since dark. God damn Minnesota.

The maddog was not large or notably athletic. For a brief time in his teens he thought of himself as lean, although his father characterized him as *slight*. Now, he would concede to a mirror, he was puffy. Five feet ten inches tall, curly red hair, the beginnings of a double chin, a roundness to the lower belly . . . lips like red worms. . . .

The elevator was old and intended for freight. It groaned once, twice, and started up. The maddog checked his equipment: The Kotex that he would use as a gag was stuffed in his right hip pocket. The tape that he would use to bind the gag was in his left. The gun was tucked in his belt, under the T-shirt. The pistol was small but ugly: a Smith & Wesson Model 15 revolver. He'd bought it from a man who was about to die and then did. Before he died, when he offered it for sale, the dying man said his wife wanted him to keep it for protection. He asked the maddog not to mention that he had purchased it. It would be their secret.

And that was perfect. Nobody knew he had the gun. If he ever had to use it, it would be untraceable, or traceable only to a dead man.

He took the gun out and held it by his side and thought of the sequence: grab, gun in face, force on floor, slap her with the pistol, kneel on back, pull head back, stuff Kotex in mouth, tape, drag to bed, tape arms to the headboard, feet to baseboard.

Then relax and shift to the knife.

The elevator stopped and the doors opened. The maddog's stomach tightened, a familiar sensation. Pleasant, even. Footsteps. Key in the door. His heart was pounding. Door open. Lights. Door closed. The gun was hot in his hand, the grip rough. The woman passing . . .

The maddog catapulted from his hiding place.

Saw in an instant that she was alone.

Wrapped her up, the gun beside her face.

The grocery bag burst and red-and-white cans of Campbell's soup clattered down the wooden floor like dice, beige-and-red packages of chicken nibbles and microwave lasagna crunched underfoot.

"Scream," he said in his roughest voice, well-practiced with a tape recorder, "and I'll kill you."

Unexpectedly, the woman relaxed against him and the maddog involuntarily relaxed with her. An instant later, the heel of her foot smashed onto his instep. The pain was unbearable and as he opened his mouth to scream, she turned in his arms, ignoring the gun.

"Aaaiii," she said, a low half-scream, half-cry of fear.

Time virtually stopped for them, the seconds fragmenting into minutes. The maddog watched her hand come up and thought she had a gun and felt his own gun hand traveling away from her body, the wrong way, and thought, "No." He realized in the next crystalline fragment of time that she was not holding a gun, but a thin silver cylinder.

She hit him with a blast of Mace and the time stream lurched crazily into fast-forward. He screeched and swatted her with the Smith and lost it at the same time. He swung his other hand and, more from luck than skill, connected with the side of her jaw and she fell and rolled.

The maddog looked for the gun, half-blinded, his hands to his face, his lungs not working as they should—he had asthma, and the Mace was soaking through the ski mask—and the woman was rolling and coming up with the Mace again and now she was screaming:

"Asshole, asshole . . ."

He kicked at her and missed and she sprayed him again and he kicked again and she stumbled and was rolling and still had the Mace and he couldn't find the gun and he kicked at her again. Lucky again, he connected with her Mace hand and the small can went flying. Blood was pouring from her forehead where it had been raked by the front sight on the pistol, streaming from the ragged cut down over her eyes and mouth, and it was on her teeth and she was screaming:

"Ass*hole*, ass*hole*."

Before he could get back on the attack, she picked up a shiny stainless-steel pipe and swung it at him like a woman who'd spent time in the softball leagues. He fended her off and backed away, still looking for the gun, but it was gone and she was coming and the maddog made the kind of decision he was trained to make.

He ran.

He ran and she ran behind him and hit him once more on the back and he half-stumbled and turned and hit her along the jaw with the bottom of his fist, a weak, ineffective punch, and she bounced away and came back with the pipe, her mouth open, her teeth showing, showering him with saliva and blood as she screamed, and he made it through the door and jerked it shut behind him.

". . . ass*hole* . . ."

Down the hall to the stairs, almost strangling in the mask. She didn't pursue, but stood at the closed door screaming with the most piercing wail he'd ever heard. A door opened somewhere and he continued blindly down the stairs.

At the bottom he stripped off the mask and thrust it in his pocket and stepped outside.

Amble, he thought. Stroll.

It was cold. Goddamn Minnesota. It was August and he was freezing. He could hear her screaming. Faintly at first, then louder. The bitch had opened the window. The cops were just across the way. The maddog hunched his shoulders and walked a little more quickly down to his car, slipped inside, and drove away. Halfway back to Minneapolis, still in the grip of mortal fear, shaking with the cold, he remembered that cars have heaters and turned it on.

He was in Minneapolis before he realized he was hurt. Goddamn pipe. Going to have big bruises, he thought, shoulders and back. Bitch. The gun shouldn't be a problem, couldn't be traced.

Christ it hurt.

# 2

The counterman was barricaded behind a wall of skin magazines. Cigarettes, candy bars, and cellophane sacks of cheese balls, taco chips, pork rinds, and other carcinogens protected his flank. Next to the cash register, a rotating stand was hung with white buttons; each button carried a message designed to reflect each individual purchaser's existential motif. *Save the Whales—Harpoon a Fat Chick* was a big seller. So was *No More Mr. Nice Guy—Down on Your Knees, Bitch*.

The counterman wasn't looking at it. He was tired of looking at it. He was peering out the flyspecked front window and shaking his head.

Lucas Davenport ambled out of the depths of the store with a *Daily Racing Form* and laid two dollars and twelve cents on the counter.

"Fuckin' kids," the counterman said to nobody, craning his neck to see further up the street. He heard Lucas' money hit the counter and turned. His basset-hound face tried for a grin and settled for a wrinkle. "How's things?" he wheezed.

"What's going on?" Lucas asked, looking past the counterman into the street.

"Couple of kids on skateboards." The counterman had emphysema and his clogged lungs could manage only short sentences. "Riding behind a bus." Whistle. "If they hit a manhole cover . . ." Suck wind. "They're dead."

Lucas looked again. There were no kids in the street.

"They're gone," the counterman said morosely. He picked up the *Racing Form* and read the first paragraph of the lead article. "You check the sale table?" Wheeze. "Some guy brought in some poems." He pronounced it "pomes."

"Yeah?" Lucas walked around to the side of the counter and checked the ranks of battered books on the table. Huddled between two hardback surveys of twentieth-century literature he found, to his delight, a slim clothbound volume of the poetry of Emily Dickinson. Lucas never went hunting for poetry; never bought anything new. He waited to find it by chance, and surprisingly often did, orphan songs huddled in collections of texts on thermoelectrical engineering or biochemistry.

This *Emily Dickinson* cost one dollar when it was printed in 1958 by an obscure publishing house located on Sixth Avenue in New York City. Thirty years later it cost eighty cents in a University Avenue bookstore in St. Paul.

"So what about this pony?" Gurgle. "This Wabasha Warrior?" The counterman tapped the *Racing Form*. "Bred in Minnesota."

"That's what I think," Lucas said.

"What?"

"Bred in Minnesota. They should whip its ass down to the Alpo factory. Of course, there is a silver lining . . ."

The counterman waited. He didn't have the breath for repartee.

"If Warrior gets any kind of favorite-son action," Lucas said, "it'll push up the odds on the winner."

"That'll be . . ."

"Try Sun and Halfpence. No guarantee, but the numbers are right." Lucas pushed the *Emily Dickinson* across the counter with the eighty-cent sticker price and five cents tax. "Let me get out of the store before you call your book, okay? I don't want to get busted for conspiracy to tout."

"Whatever you say." Suck. "Lieutenant," the counterman said. He tugged his forelock.

Lucas carried the *Emily Dickinson* back to Minneapolis and parked in the public garage across from City Hall. He walked around the wretchedly ugly old pile of liverish granite, across another street, past a reflecting pool, and into the Hennepin County Government Center. He took an escalator down to the cafeteria, bought a red apple from a vending machine, went back up and out the far side of the building to the lawn. He sat on the grass between the white birch trees in the warm August sunshine and ate the apple and read:

. . . but no man moved me till the tide
Went past my simple shoe
And past my apron and my belt
And past my bodice too,
And made as he would eat me up
As wholly as a dew

Upon a dandelion's sleeve
And then I started too.

Lucas smiled and crunched on the apple. When he looked up, a young dark-haired woman was crossing the plaza, pushing a double baby carriage. The twins were dressed in identical pink wrappings and swayed from side to side as their mother strutted them across the plaza. Mama had large breasts and a small waist and her black hair swung back and forth across her fair cheeks like a silken curtain. She wore a plum-colored skirt and silky beige blouse and she was so beautiful that Lucas smiled again, a wave of pleasure washing through him.

Then another one walked by, in the opposite direction, a blonde with a short punky haircut and a revealing knit dress, tawdry in an engaging way. Lucas watched her walk and sighed with the rhythm of it.

Lucas was dressed in a white tennis shirt, khaki slacks, over-the-calf blue socks, and slip-on deck shoes with long leather ties. He wore the tennis shirt outside his slacks so the gun wouldn't show. He was slender and dark-complexioned, with straight black hair going gray at the temples and a long nose over a crooked smile. One of his central upper incisors had been chipped and he never had it capped. He might have been an Indian except for his blue eyes.

His eyes were warm and forgiving. The warmth was somehow emphasized by the vertical white scar that started at his hairline, ran down to his right eye socket, jumped over the eye, and continued down his cheek to the corner of his mouth. The scar gave him a raffish air, but left behind a touch of innocence, like Errol Flynn in *Captain Blood*. Lucas wished he could tell young women that the scar had come from a broken bottle in a bar fight at Subic Bay, where he had never been, or Bangkok, where he had never been either. The scar had come from a fishing leader that snapped out of a rotting snag on the St. Croix River and he told them so. Some believed him. Most thought he was covering something up, like a bar fight East of Suez.

Though his eyes were warm, his smile betrayed him.

He once went with a woman—a zookeeper, as it happened—to a nightclub in St. Paul where cocaine was dealt to suburban children in the basement bathrooms. In the parking lot outside the club, Lucas encountered Kenny McGuinness, who he thought was in prison.

"Get the fuck away from me, Davenport," McGuinness said, backing off. The parking lot was suddenly electric, everything from gum wrappers to discarded quarter-gram coke baggies springing into needle-sharp focus.

"I didn't know you were out, dickhead," Lucas answered, smiling. The zookeeper was watching, her eyes wide. Lucas leaned toward the other man, hooked two fingers in his shirt pocket, and gently tugged, as though they were old companions trading memories. Lucas whispered hoarsely: "Leave town. Go to Los Angeles. Go to New York. If you don't go away, I'll hurt you."

"I'm on parole, I can't leave the state," McGuinness stammered.

"So go to Duluth. Go to Rochester. You've got a week," Lucas whispered. "Talk to your dad. Talk to your grandma. Talk to your sisters. Then leave."

He turned back to the zookeeper, still smiling, McGuinness apparently forgotten.

"You scared the heck out of me," the woman said when they were inside the club. "What was that all about?"

"Kenny likes young boys. He trades crack for ten-year-old ass."

"Oh." She had heard of such things but believed them only in the way she believed in her own mortality: a faraway possibility not yet requiring examination.

Later, she said, "I didn't like that smile. Your smile. You looked like one of my animals."

Lucas grinned at her. "Oh, yeah? Which one? The lemur?"

She nibbled her lower lip. "I was thinking of a wolverine," she said.

If the chill of his smile sometimes overwhelmed the warmth of his eyes, it didn't happen so frequently as to become a social handicap. Now Lucas watched the punky blonde turn the corner of the Government Center, and just before she stepped from sight, look back at him and grin.

Damn. She had known he was watching. Women always knew. Get up, he thought, go after her. But he didn't. There were so many of them, all good. He sighed and leaned back in the grass and picked up *Emily Dickinson*.

Lucas was a picture of contentment. More than a picture.

A photograph.


The photograph was being taken from the back of an olive-drab van parked across South Seventh Street. Two cops from internal affairs worked in sweaty confinement with tripod-mounted film and video cameras behind one-way glass.

The senior cop was fat. His partner was thin. Other than that, they looked much alike, with brush-cut hair, pink faces, yellow short-sleeved shirts, and double-knit trousers from J. C. Penney. Every few minutes, one of them would look through the 300mm lens. The camera attached to the lens, a Nikon F3, was equipped with a Data Back, which had a battery-operated clock programmed for accuracy through the year 2100. When the cops took their photographs, the precise time and date were burned into the photo frame. If necessary, the photograph would become a legally influential log of the surveillance subject's activities.

Lucas had spotted the pair an hour after the surveillance began, almost two weeks earlier. He didn't know why they were watching, but as soon as he saw them, he stopped talking to his informants, to his friends, to other cops. He was living in a pool of isolation, but didn't know why. He would find out. Inevitably.

In the meantime, he spent as much time as he could in the open, forcing the watchers to hide in their hot, confining wagon, unable to eat, unable to pee. Lucas smiled to himself, the unpleasant smile, the wolverine's smile, put down *Dickinson* and picked up the *Racing Form*.

"You think the motherfucker is going to sit there forever?" asked the fat cop. He squirmed uncomfortably.

"Looks like he's settled in."

"I gotta pee like a Russian racehorse," said the fat one.

"You shouldn't of drank that Coke. It's the caffeine that does it."

"Maybe I could slide out and take a leak . . ."

"If he moves, I gotta follow. If you get left behind, Bendl will get your balls."

"Only if you tell him, asshole."

"I can't drive and take pictures at the same time."

The fat cop squirmed uncomfortably and tried to figure the odds. He should have gone as soon as he saw Lucas settle on the lawn, but he hadn't had to pee so bad then. Now that Lucas might be expected to leave, his bladder felt like a basketball.

"Look at him," he said, peering at Lucas through a pair of binoculars. "He's watching the puss go by. Think that's why we're watching him? Something to do with the puss?"

"I don't know. It's something weird. The way it come down, nobody sayin' shit."

"I heard he's got something on the chief. Lucas does."

"Must have. He doesn't do a thing. Wanders around town in that Porsche and goes out to the track every day."

"His jacket looks good. Commendations and all."

"He got some good busts," the thin cop admitted.

"Lot of them," said the fat man.

"Yeah."

"Killed some guys."

"Five. He's the number-one gunslinger on the force. Nobody else done more than two."

"All good shootings."

"Press loves him. Fuckin' Wyatt Earp."

"Because he's got money," the fat man said authoritatively. "The press loves people with money, rich guys. Never met a reporter who didn't want money."

They thought about reporters for a minute. Reporters were a lot like cops, but with faster mouths.

"How much you think he makes? Davenport?" the fat one asked.

The thin cop pursed his meager lips and considered the question. Salary was a matter of some importance. "With his rank and seniority, he probably takes down forty-two, maybe forty-five from the city," he ventured. "Then the games, I heard when he hits one, he makes like a cool hundred thou, depends on how well it sells."

"That much," said the fat one, marveling. "If I made that much, I'd quit. Buy a restaurant. Maybe a bar, up on one of the lakes."

"Get out," the thin one agreed. They'd had the conversation so often the responses were automatic.

"Wonder why they didn't bust him back to sergeant? I mean, when they pulled him off robbery?"

"I heard he threatened to quit. Said he didn't want to go backwards. They decided they wanted to keep him—he's got sources in every bar and barbershop in town—so they had to leave him with the rank."

"He was a real pain in the butt as a supervisor," said the fat man.

The thin man nodded. "Everybody had to be perfect. Nobody was." The thin man shook his head. "He told me once that it was the worst job he ever had. He knew he was messing up, but he couldn't stop. Some guy would goof off one inch and Davenport would be on him like white on rice."

They stopped talking for another minute, watching their subject through the one-way glass. "But not a bad guy, when he's not your boss," the fat cop offered, changing direction. Surveillance cops become expert at conversational gambit. "He gave me one of his games, once. For my kid the computer genius. Had a picture of these aliens, like ten-foot cockroaches, zinging each other with ray guns."

"Kid like it?" The thin cop didn't really care. He thought the fat cop's kid was overly protected and maybe even a fairy, though he'd never say so.

"Yeah. Brought it back into the shop and asked him to sign it. Right on the box, Lucas Davenport."

"Well, the guy's no couch," said the thin one. He paused expectantly. A minute later the fat one got it and they started laughing. Laughing doesn't help the bladder. The fat cop squirmed again.

"Listen, I gotta go or I'm gonna pee down my leg," he said finally. "If Davenport takes off for somewhere besides the shop, he'll have to get his car. If you're not here when I get back, I'll run get you outside the ramp."

"It's your ass," said his partner, looking through the long lens. "He just started the *Racing Form*. You maybe got a few minutes."

Lucas saw the fat cop slip out of the van and dash into the Pillsbury Building. He grinned to himself. He was tempted to stroll away, knowing the cop in the van would have to follow and strand the fat guy. But it would create complications. He would rather have them where he was sure of them.

When the fat cop got back, four minutes later, the van was still there. His partner glanced over at him and said, "Nothing."

Since Lucas hadn't done anything yet, the photos they took had never been developed. If they had been, they would have found that Lucas' middle finger was prominent on most of the slides and they might have decided that he had spotted them. But it didn't matter, since the film would never be developed.

As the fat cop scrambled back into the van and Lucas sprawled on the grass, paging through the poetry again, they were very close to the end of the surveillance.

Lucas was reading a poem called *The Snake*, and the fat man was peering at him through the lens of the Nikon when the maddog killer did another one.

# 3

He had first talked to her a month before, in the records department of the county clerk's office. She had raven-black hair, worn short, and brown eyes. Gold hoop earrings dangled from her delicate earlobes. She wore just a touch of scent and a warm red dress.

"I'd like to see the file on Burhalter-Mentor," she told a clerk. "I don't have the number. It should have been in the last month."

The maddog watched her from the corner of his eye. She was fifteen or twenty years years older than he was. Attractive.

The maddog had not yet gone for the artist. His days were colored with thoughts of her, his nights consumed with images of her face and body. He knew he would take her; the love song had already begun.

But this one was interesting. More than interesting. He felt his awareness expanding, reveled in the play of light through the peach fuzz of her slender forearm. . . . And after the artist, there had to be another.

"Is that a civil filing?" the clerk asked the woman.

"It's a bunch of liens on an apartment complex down by Nokomis. I want to make sure they've been resolved."

"Okay. That's Burkhalter . . ."

"Burkhalter-Mentor." She spelled it for him and the clerk went back into the file room. She's a real-estate agent, the maddog thought. She felt his attention and glanced at him.

"Are you a real-estate agent?" he asked.

"Yes, I am." Serious, pleasant, professional. Pink lipstick, just a touch.

"I'm new here in Minneapolis," the maddog said, stepping a bit closer. "I'm an attorney with Felsen-Gore. Would you have a couple of seconds to answer a real-estate question?"

"Sure." She was friendly now, interested.

"I've been looking around the lakes, down south of here, Lake of the Isles, Lake Nokomis, like that."

"Oh, it's a very nice neighborhood," she said enthusiastically. She had what plastic surgeons called a full mouth, showing a span of brilliantly white teeth when she smiled. "There are lots of houses on the market right now. It's my specialty area."

"Well, I'm not sure whether I want a condo or a house . . ."

"A house holds its value better."

"Yeah, but you know, I'm single. I don't really want to hassle with a big yard . . ."

"What you really need is a bungalow on a small lot, not much yard. You'd have more space than you would in an apartment, and you could sign up for a lawn service for thirty dollars a month. That'd be cheaper than the mainte-nance fee on most condos, and you'd maintain resale value."

The maddog got his file and waited until she got a photocopy of the liens. They drifted together along the hall to the elevators and rode down to the first floor.

"Well, hmm, look, in Dallas we had this thing, it was called the multiple list, or something like that?" said the maddog.

"Yes, multiple listing service," she said.

"So if I were to drive around and find a place, I could call you and you could show it to me?"

"Sure, I do it all the time. Let me give you my card."

Jeannie Lewis. He tucked her card into his wallet. As soon as he turned away and stepped out of her physical presence, he saw the artist again, her face and body as she walked through the streets of St. Paul. He hungered for her, and the real-estate agent was almost forgotten. But not quite.

For the next week, he saw the card each time he took his wallet out of his pocket. Jeannie Lewis of the raven hair. A definite candidate.

And then the fiasco.

He woke the next morning, bruised and creaking. He took a half-dozen extra-strength aspirin tablets and carefully twisted to look at his back in the bathroom mirror. The bruises were coming and they would be bad, long black streaks across his back and shoulders.

The obsession with the artist was broken. When he got out of the shower, he saw a strange face in the mirror, floating behind the steamed surface. It had happened before. He reached out and wiped the mirror with a corner of his towel. It was Lewis, smiling at him, engaged in his nudity.

Her office was in the south lake district, in an old storefront with a big window. He drove the neighborhood, looking for a vantage point. He found it on the parking boulevard kittycorner from Lewis' office. He could sit in his car and watch her through the storefront window as she sat in her cubicle, talking on the telephone. He watched her for a week. Every afternoon but

Wednesday she arrived between twelve-thirty and one o'clock, carrying a bag lunch. She ate at her desk as she did paperwork. She rarely went back out before two-thirty. She was stunning. He best liked the way she walked, using her hips in long fluid strides. He dreamt of her at night, of Jeannie Lewis walking nude toward him across the desert grass. . . .

He decided to collect her on a Thursday. He found a nice-looking home on a narrow street in a redeveloping neighborhood six blocks from her office. There were no houses directly across the street from it. The driveway was sunken a few feet into the lawn, and stairs led behind a screen of evergreens to the front door. If he rode with Lewis to the house and she pulled into the driveway, and he got out the passenger side, he would be virtually invisible from the street.

The house itself felt empty. He checked the cross-reference books used by investigators at his office, found the names of the neighbors. He called the first one in the book and got a nosy old man. He explained that he would like to make a direct offer for the house, cutting out the real-estate dealers. Did the neighbor know where the owners were? Why, yes. Arizona. And here's the number; they're not due back until Christmas, and then only for two weeks.

Scouting the neighborhood, the maddog found a small supermarket across from a Standard station a few blocks from the house.

On Thursday, he packed his equipment into the trunk of his car and wore a loose-fitting tweed sport coat with voluminous pockets. He checked to make sure Lewis was in, then drove to the supermarket, parked his car in the busy lot, and called her from a pay phone.

"Jeannie Lewis," she said. Her voice was pleasantly cool.

"Yes, Ms. Lewis?" said the maddog, pronouncing it "miz." His heart was thumping against his ribs. "I ran into you in the clerk of court's office a month ago. We were talking about houses in the lakes area?"

There was a moment's hesitation at the other end of the line and the maddog was afraid she had forgotten him. Then she said, "Oh . . . yes, I think I remember. We went down in the elevator together?"

"Yes, that's me. Listen, to make a long story short, I was cruising the neighborhood down here, looking, and I had car trouble. So I pulled into a gas station and they said it would be a couple hours, they've got to put in a water pump. Anyway, I went out to walk around and I found a very interesting house."

He glanced at the paper in his hand, with the address, and gave it to her. "I wonder if we might set up a time to look at it?"

"Are you still at that Standard station?"

"I'm at a phone booth across the street."

"I'm not doing anything right now and I'm only five minutes away. I could stop at the other realtor's, they're only two minutes from here, pick up the key, and come and get you."

"Well, I don't want to inconvenience you . . ."

"No, no problem. I know that house. It's very well-kept. I'm surprised it hasn't gone yet."

"Well . . ."

"I'll be there in ten minutes."

It took fifteen. He went into the supermarket, bought an ice-cream bar, sat on a bus bench next to the phone booth, and licked the ice cream. When Lewis arrived, driving a brown station wagon, she recognized him at once. He could see her teeth as she smiled at him through the tinted windshield.

"How are you?" she asked as she popped open the passenger-side door. "You're the attorney. I remembered as soon as I saw your face."

"Yes. I really appreciate this. Have I introduced myself? I'm Louis Vullion." The maddog killer pronounced it "Loo-ee Vul-yoan," though his parents had called him "Loo-is Vul-yun," to rhyme with "onion."

"Glad to meet you." And she seemed to be.

The drive to the house took three minutes, the woman pointing out the advantages of the neighborhood. The lakes close enough that he could jog down at night. Far enough away that he wouldn't be bothered by traffic. Schools close enough to enhance the resale value of the house, should he ever wish to sell it. Not so close that kids would be a problem. Enough stability in the housing that neighbors knew each other and strangers in the neighborhood would be noticed.

"The crime rate around here is quite low compared to other neighborhoods in the city," she said. Just then a jet roared low overhead, going in for a landing at Minneapolis–St. Paul International. She didn't mention it.

Vullion didn't mention it either. He listened just enough to nod at the right places. Deeper inside, he was going through his visualization routine. This time, he couldn't mess it up, as he had with the artist.

Oh, yes, he'd assumed the blame for that one; there was no shirking it. He'd erred and he had been lucky to escape. A one-hundred-thirty-pound woman in good shape could be a formidable opponent. He would not forget that again.

As for Lewis, he couldn't foul it up. Once he attacked, she had to die, because she'd seen his face, she knew who he was. So he'd practiced, as best he could, in his apartment, hitting a basketball hung from a hook in the bathroom door. Like it was a head.

And now he was ready. He'd tucked a gym sock filled with a large Idaho baking potato into his right jacket pocket. The bulge showed, but not much. It could be anything, an appointment book, a bagel. A Kotex pad, the tape, and a pair of latex surgeon's gloves were in his left pocket. He would touch nothing that would take a fingerprint until he had the gloves on. He thought about it, rehearsed it in his mind, and said, "Oh, yes?" at the right spots in Lewis' sales talk.

And as they drove, he felt his awareness expanding; realized, with a tiny touch of distaste, that she probably smoked. There was the slightest odor of nicotine about her.

When they pulled into the driveway, his stomach began to clutch just as it had with the artist and the others. "Nice place from the outside, anyway," he said.

"Wait'll you see inside. They've done a beautiful treatment of the bath-rooms."

She led the way to the front door, which was screened from the street by evergreens. The key opened the door, and they pushed in. The house was fully furnished, but the front room had the too-orderly feeling of long-prepared-for absence. The air was still and slightly musty.

"You want to wander around a minute?" Lewis looked up at him.

"Sure." He glanced at the kitchen, strolled through the front room, walked up three stairs to the bedroom level, looked in each room. When he came back down, she was clutching her purse strap in front of her, examining with some interest a crystal lamp on the fireplace mantel.

"How much are they asking?"

"A hundred and five."

He nodded and glanced toward the basement door at the edge of the kitchen.

"Is that the basement?"

"Yes, I believe so."

When she turned toward the door, he took the sock out of his pocket. She took another step toward the basement door. Swinging the sock like a mace, he slammed the Idaho baker into the back of her head, just above her left ear.

The blow knocked her off her feet and Vullion dropped on her back and slammed her again. This one was not like the bitch artist. She was an office worker with no strength in her arms. She moaned once, dazed, and he grabbed the hair on the crown of her head and wrenched her head straight back and shoved in the Kotex. He pulled on his gloves, took the tape from his side pocket, and quickly wrapped her head. As she finally began to struggle against him, he rolled her over, crossed her wrists, and taped them. She was beginning to recover, her eyes half-open now, and he dragged her up the stairs into the first bedroom and threw her on the bed. He taped her arms first, to the head-board, then her legs, apart, to the corner posts of the bed.

He was breathing hard but he could feel the erection pounding at his groin, the excitement building in his throat.

He stepped back and looked down at her. The knife, he thought. Hope there's a good one. He went down to look in the kitchen.

On the bed behind him, Jeannie Lewis moaned.

# 4

The Twin Cities' horse track looks like a Greyhound bus station designed by a pastry chef. The fat cop, no architecture critic, liked it. He sat in the sun with a slice of pepperoni pizza in his lap, a Diet Pepsi in one hand and a portable radio in the other. He took the call on the portable just before the second race.

"Right now?"

"Right now." Even with the interference, the voice was unmistakable and ragged as a bread knife.

The fat cop looked at the thin one.

"Christ, the fuckin' chief. On the *radio*."

"His procedure is fucked." The thin cop was eating the last of a hot dog and had dribbled relish down the front of his sport coat. He brushed at it with an undersize napkin.

"He wants Davenport," said the fat one.

"Something must have happened," said the thin one. They were outside, on the deck. Lucas was on the blacktopped patio below, two sections over. He lazily sprawled over a wooden bench directly in front of the tote board and thirty feet from the dark soil of the track. A pretty woman in cowboy boots sat at the other end of the bench drinking beer from a plastic cup. The two cops went up the aisle to the top of the grandstand, down the staircase, and pushed through a small crowd at the base of the steps.

"Davenport? Lucas?"

Lucas turned, saw them, and smiled. "Hey. How're you doing? Day at the races, huh?"

"The chief wants to talk to you. Like right away." The fat cop hadn't thought of it until the last minute, but this could be hard to explain.

"They pulled the surveillance?" Lucas asked. His teeth were showing.

"You knew about it?" The fat cop lifted an eyebrow.

"For a while. But I didn't know why." He looked at them expectantly.

The thin cop shrugged. "We don't know either."

"Hey, fuck you, Dick . . ." Lucas stood up with his fists balled, and the thin cop took a step back.

"Honest to Christ, Lucas, we don't know," said the fat one. "It was all hush-hush."

Lucas turned and looked at him. "He said right now?"

"He said right now. And he sounded like he meant it."

Lucas' eyes defocused and he turned toward the track, staring sightlessly across the oval to the six-furlong starting gate. The jockeys were pressing their horses toward the gate and the crowd was starting to drift down the patio to the finish line.

"It's the maddog killer," Lucas said after a moment.

"Yeah," said the fat cop. "It could be."

"Has to be. Goddammit, I don't want that." He thought about it for another few seconds and then suddenly smiled. "You guys got horses for this race?"

The fat cop looked vaguely uneasy. "Uh, I got two bucks on Skybright Avenger."

"Jesus Christ, Bucky," Lucas said in exasperation, "you're risking two dollars to get back two dollars and forty cents if she wins. And she won't."

"Well, I dunno . . ."

"If you don't know how to play . . ." Lucas shook his head. "Look, go put ten bucks on Pembroke Dancer. To win."

The two cops looked at each other.

"Really?" said the thin one. "This is a maiden, you can't know . . ."

"Hey. It's up to you, if you want to bet. And I'm staying for the race."

The two internal-affairs cops looked at each other, looked back at Lucas, then turned and hurried inside to the nearest betting windows. The thin one bet ten dollars. The fat one hesitated, staring into his wallet, licked his lips, took out three tens, licked his lips again, and pushed them across the counter. "Thirty on Pembroke Dancer," he said. "To win."

Lucas was sprawled on the bench again and had started a conversation with the woman in the cowboy boots. When the surveillance cops got back, he moved down toward her but turned to the cops.

"You bet?" he asked.

"Yeah."

"Don't look so nervous, Bucky. It's perfectly legal."

"Yeah, yeah. It ain't that."

"Have you got a horse?" The woman in the cowboy boots leaned forward and looked down the bench at Lucas. She had violet eyes.

"Just a guess," Lucas said lazily.

"Is this, like, a private guess?"

"We've all got a couple of bucks on Pembroke Dancer," Lucas said.

The woman with the violet eyes had a *Racing Form* on the bench beside her, but instead of looking at it, she looked up at the sky and her lips moved silently and then she turned her head and said, "She had a terrific workout at six furlongs. The track was listed as fast but it probably wasn't that good."

"Hmm," said Lucas.

She looked at the tote board for a few seconds and said, "Excuse me, I gotta go powder my nose."

She left, hurrying. The fat cop was still licking his lips and watching the tote board. The odds on Pembroke Dancer were twenty to one. Three other horses, Stripper's Colors, Skybright Avenger, and Tonite Delite, had strong races in the past three weeks. Pembroke Dancer had been shipped in from Arkansas two weeks earlier. In her first race she finished sixth.

"What's the story on this horse?" asked the fat cop.

"A tip from a friend." Lucas gestured over his shoulder with his thumb, up toward the press box. "One of the handicappers got a call from Vegas. Guy walked into a horse parlor a half-hour ago and bet ten thousand on Pembroke Dancer to win. Somebody knows something."

"Jesus. So why'd he lose his last race so bad?"

"She."

"Huh?"

"She. Dancer's a filly. And I don't know why she lost. Might be anything. Maybe the jock was dragging his feet."

The tote board flickered and the odds on Pembroke Dancer went up to twenty-two to one.

"How much you bet, Lucas?" the fat cop asked.

"It's an exacta. I wheeled Dancer with the other nine horses. A hundred each way, so I have nine hundred riding."

"Jesus." The fat man licked his lips again. He had another twenty in his wallet and thought about it. Across the track, the first of the horses was led into the gate and the fat cop settled back. Thirty was already too much. If he lost it, he'd be lunching on Cheetos for a week.

"So you got anything good?" asked Lucas. "What was this thing about Billy Case and the rookie?"

The fat cop laughed. "Fuckin' Case."

"There was this woman lawyer," said the thin one, "and one day she looks out her office window, which is on the back of an old house that they made into offices. The back of her office looks at the back of the business buildings on the next street over. In fact, it looks right down this walkway between these buildings. At the other end of this walkway there's a fence with a gate in it, like blocking the walkway from the street. So you can't see into the walkway from the street. But you can see into it from this lawyer's office, you know? So anyway, she looks down there, and here's this cop, in full uniform, getting his knob polished by this spade chick.

"So this lawyer's watching and the guy gets off and zips up and he and the spade chick go through this gate in the little fence, back onto the street. This lawyer, she's cool, she thinks maybe they're in love. But the next day, there's two of them, both cops, and the spade chick, and she's polishing both of them. So now the lawyer's pissed. She gets this giant camera from her husband, and the next day, sure enough, they're back with another chick, a white girl this time. So the lawyer takes some pictures and she brings this roll of Kodachrome in to the chief."

The first of the horses was guided into the back of the gate and locked. The woman with the violet eyes got back and settled at the end of the bench. The thin cop rambled on. "So the chief sends it down to the lab," he said, "and they're only like the best pictures anybody ever took of a knob-job. I could of sold them for ten bucks apiece. So the chief and the prosecutors decide there's some problem with the chain of evidence and we wind up in this lawyer's office with a video unit. Sure enough, here they come. But this time they got both the spade chick and the white chick. This is like in Cinemascope or something. Panavision."

"So what's going to happen?" Lucas asked.

The fat one shrugged. "They're gone."

"How much time did they have in?"

"Case had six years, but I don't give a shit. He had a bad jacket. We think he and a security guard was boosting stereos and CD players out of a Sears warehouse a few months back. But I feel sorry for the rookie. Case told him this was how it's done on the street. Gettin' knob-jobs in alleyways."

Lucas shook his head.

"Right on the street, in daylight," said the fat cop.

The last horse was pushed into the back of the gate, locked, and there was a second-long pause before the gate banged open and the announcer called "They're all in line . . . and they're off, Pembroke Dancer breaks on the outside, followed by . . ."

Dancer ran away from the pack, two lengths going into the turn, four lengths at the bottom of the stretch, eight lengths crossing the wire.

"Holy shit," the fat cop said reverently. "I won six hundred bucks."

Lucas stood up. "I'm going," he said. He was staring at the tote board, calculating. When he was satisfied, he turned to the other two. "You coming behind? I'll drive slow."

"No, no, we're all done," said the fat cop. "Thanks, Lucas."

"You ought to quit now," said Lucas. "The rest of these races are junk. You can't figure them. And, Bucky?"

"Yeah?" The fat cop looked up from his winning ticket.

"You won't forget to tell the IRS about the six hundred?"

"Of course not," the cop said, offended. Lucas grinned and walked away and the fat cop muttered, "In a pig's eye." He looked at his ticket again and then noticed that the woman with the violet eyes was hurrying after Lucas. She caught him just before he got inside, and the fat cop saw Lucas grin as they walked together into the building.

"Look at this," he said to the thin cop. But the thin cop was looking at the tote board and his lips were moving quietly. The fat cop looked at his partner and said, "What?"

The thin cop put up a hand to hold off the question, his lips still moving. Then they stopped and he turned and looked after Lucas.

"What?" said the fat cop, looking in the same direction. Lucas and the woman with the violet eyes had disappeared.

"I don't know much about this horse-race bullshit," said the thin cop, "but if I'm reading the tote board right, this exacta payoff, Davenport took down twenty-two thousand, two hundred and fifty bucks."

The office of the chief of police was on the first floor of City Hall, in a corner. Windows dominated the two walls that faced the street. The other two walls were covered with framed photographs, some in color, some in black and white, stretching back in time to the forties. Daniel with his family. With the last six Minnesota governors. With five of the last six senators. With a long and anonymous chain of faces that all looked vaguely the same, faces that took up space at chicken dinners for major politicians. Directly behind the chief was the shield of the Minneapolis Police Department and a plaque honoring cops who had been killed in the line of duty.

Lucas sprawled in the leather chair that sat squarely in front of the chief's desk. He was surprised, though he tried not to show it. It had been a while since anything surprised him, other than women.

"Pissed off?" Quentin Daniel leaned over his glass desktop, watching Lucas. Daniel looked so much like a police chief that a number of former political enemies, who were now doing something else, made the mistake of thinking he got the job on his face. They were wrong.

"Yeah. Pissed off. Mostly just surprised." Lucas did not particularly like Daniel, but thought he might be the smartest man on the force. He would have been surprised—again—to know that the chief thought precisely the same about him.

Daniel half-turned toward the windows, his head cocked, still watching.

"You can see why," he said.

"You thought I did it?"

"A couple of people in homicide thought you were worth looking at," said Daniel.

"You better start at the beginning," Lucas said.

Daniel nodded, pushed his chair away from his desk, stood up, and wandered to a wall of photographs. He inspected the face of Hubert Humphrey as though he were looking for new blemishes.

"Two weeks ago, our man made a run at a St. Paul woman, an artist named Carla Ruiz," he said as he continued his inspection of Humphrey's face. "She managed to fight him off. When St. Paul got there, the sergeant in charge found her looking at a note. It was one of these rules he's leaving behind."

"I haven't heard a thing about this Ruiz," Lucas said.

The chief turned and drifted back to his chair, no hurry, his hands in his pockets. "Yeah. Well, this sergeant's a smart guy and he knew about the notes in the first two killings. He called the head of St. Paul homicide and they put a lid on it. The only people who know are the St. Paul chief and his chief of homicide, the two uniforms who took the call, a couple of people in homicide here, and me. And the artist. And now you. And every swingin' dick has been told that if this leaks, there'll be some new foot beats out at the landfill."

"So how'd it point to me?" Lucas asked.

"It didn't. Not right away. But our man dropped his gun during the fight with the artist lady. The first thing we did was print it and run it. No prints—checked everything, including the shells. We had better luck on the ownership. We ran it down in ten minutes. It went from the factory to a gun store down on Hennepin Avenue, and from there to a guy named David L. Losse—"

"Our David L. Losse?"

"You remember the case?"

"Shot his son, said it was an accident? Thought somebody was breaking into the house?"

"That's him. He fell on a manslaughter, though it was probably a straight-out murder. He got six years, he'll serve four. But there's still an appeal floating around. Because of the appeal, the evidence was supposedly up in the property room. We went up and looked. The gun is gone. Or it was gone, until the killer dropped it."

"Shit." Things had disappeared from the property room before. Five grams of cocaine became four. Twenty bondage magazines became fifteen. As far as Lucas knew, this was the first time a gun had gone missing.

"You had access to the evidence room a couple of times. During the Ryerson case and during that hassle over the Chicago burglary gang. We cross-referenced everything we had from the killings and the witness. Times, places, the artist's description. We could eliminate as suspects all the women who had access to the room. We could eliminate cops who were confirmed on-duty when the killings took place. People have been killed or attacked in all three shifts . . . Anyway, we got it down to your name, basically. You're the right size. Nobody ever knows where you're at. You're a games freak and this guy is apparently playing some kind of game. And the gun came out of the property room. I never really thought you were the one, but . . . you see how it went down."

"Yeah, I see," Lucas said sourly. "Thanks a lot."

"Hey, what would you have done?" Daniel asked defensively.

"Okay."

"Now we know you're clean," the chief said. He leaned back in his chair, stretched, and crossed his legs. " 'Cause our man did another one. Four to six hours ago. We figure it was just about the time you were sitting out on the lawn eating that apple."

Lucas nodded. "Where's this one?"

"Down by Lake Nokomis. Just west of the lake, up in those hills."

"Can you contain it?"

"No." Daniel shook his head. "This is three. If we tried to contain it, we'd be leaking like a rusty faucet by tomorrow afternoon. That'd cause more trouble than if we go out front with it. I've already called a press conference for nine o'clock tonight. That'll give the TV stations time to make the ten-o'clock news. I want you to be here. I'll outline the killings, appeal for help, all that. And I'm assigning you to the case, full-time."

"I don't want it," said Lucas. "Homicide bores me. You walk around all day talking to civilians who don't know anything. There are other guys do it better. And I got a lot of stuff going on this crack business. I got a half-dozen guys picked out—"

"Yeah, yeah, yeah, that's absolutely fuckin' wonderful, but the media is going to hang us all by our balls if we don't get this freak," Daniel said, cutting Lucas off in mid-sentence. "You remember back a few years when those two women got killed in the parking ramps? Like two, three weeks apart, different guys? Pure coincidence? You remember how the media went out of their minds? You remember how the TV stations were having seminars on self-defense? How they had reports every night on progress? You remember all that?"

"Yeah." It had been a nightmare.

"This is going to be worse. Those guys in the parking ramps, we grabbed one the same day, we got the other one a couple days after he did it. We still got hysteria. This guy, he's killed three, attacked another one, raped them and stabbed them, and he's still on the loose."

Lucas nodded and rubbed his jaw with his fingertips. "You're right. They'll go berserk," he admitted.

"Guaranteed. This doesn't happen in the Twin Cities. So fuck the crack. I want you on this thing. You'll work by yourself, homicide will work parallel. The media'll like that. They think you're some kind of fuckin' genius."

"What does homicide think about me working on it?" Lucas asked.

"A couple of guys will be moaning about it, because they always do, but they'll go along. Besides, I don't care what they think. Their asses aren't on the line. Mine is. I come up for new term next year and I don't need this sitting on my back," Daniel said.

"I've got full access?"

"I talked to Lester. He'll cooperate. He really will." Lucas nodded. Frank Lester was the deputy chief for investigations and a former head of robbery-homicide.

"I'll want to talk to this artist," Lucas said.

Daniel nodded. "The woman doesn't have a pot to piss in. We had to get her a phone two days after she was attacked. Just in case the guy comes back after her. Here's her number and address." He handed Lucas a slip of paper.

Lucas tucked the slip in his pants pocket. "They're processing this Nokomis killing now?"

"Yeah."

"I better get down there." He stood and started for the door, stopped and half-turned. "You really didn't think I did it?"

Daniel shook his head. "I've seen you around women. I didn't think you could do that to them. But I had to know for sure."

Lucas started to turn away again, but Daniel stopped him.

"And, Davenport?"

"Yeah?"

"Be here for the press conference, okay? Dress just like that, the tennis shirt and the khakis. You got any jeans? Jeans might be better. Those whatdaya call them, acid jeans?"

"I could change on the way back. I got some stone-washed."

"Whatever. You know how that TV puss goes for the street-cop routine. What's your title again?"

"Office of Special Intelligence."

The chief snapped his fingers, nodded, and scrawled "OSI" on his desk pad. "See you at nine," he said.

Jeannie Lewis lay on the narrow bed with her hands bound up over her head, where they were taped to the headboard. A look of inexpressible agony held her face, her mouth locked open by the Kotex pad stuffed between her jaws, her eyes rolled so far back that nothing but the whites could be seen beneath the half-closed lids. Her back was arched from the pressure of the bonds, the nipples of her small breasts pointing left and right, nearly white in death. Her ankles were bound to the opposite corners at the foot of the bed, but she had managed to roll her thin legs inward, a final effort to protect herself. The knife still protruded from the top of her abdomen, just below the sternum, its handle almost flat against her stomach. It had been slipped in at an acute angle, to more directly penetrate the heart without complications of bone or muscle.

"Pushed it in and wiggled it," said the assistant medical examiner. "We can tell more after the autopsy, but that's what it looks like. Just a little entry slit, but a lot of damage around the heart."

"Professional?" asked Lucas. "A doctor?"

"I wouldn't go that far. I don't want to mislead you. But it's somebody who knows what he's doing. He knows where the heart is. We want to leave the knife in place until we get downtown and take some pictures, X rays, but from the look of the handle, I'd say it's about the most efficient knife for the work. Narrow point, sharp, rigid blade, fairly thin. It'd slip right in."

Lucas stepped over to the bed and looked at the knife handle. It was smooth, unfinished wood. "County Cork Cutlery" was branded on the wood.

"County Cork Cutlery?"

"Forget it. There's a whole drawer full of it, out in the kitchen."

"So he got it here."

"I think so. I did the first woman he killed, Lucy What's-her-name. He did her with a plastic-handled knife, nothing like this one."

"Where's the note?"

"In the baggie, over on the chest of drawers. We're sending it to the lab, see if they can print it."

Lucas stepped over to the chest and looked at the note. Common notebook paper. Even if there were six pads of it in a suspect's home, it would prove nothing. The words were cut from a newspaper and fastened to the paper with Scotch tape: *Never carry a weapon after it has been used*.

"He lives by those rules," the medical examiner said. "He didn't even pull the knife out, much less carry it anywhere."

"Note looks clean."

"Well, not quite. Hang on a second," the medical examiner said. He peeled off the plastic gloves he was wearing, replaced them with a thinner pair of surgeon's gloves, opened the baggie, and slipped the note halfway out.

"See this kind of funny half-circle under the tape?"

"Yeah. Print?"

"We think so, but if you look, you can see there's no print. But it's sharply defined. So I think—" he wiggled his fingers at Lucas— "that he was wearing surgeon's gloves."

"That says doctor again."

"It could. It could also say nurse, or orderly, or technician. And since you can buy the things at hardware stores, it could be a hardware dealer. Whoever he is, I think he wears gloves even when he's sitting at home making these notes. So now we know something else: he's a smart little cocksucker."

"Okay. Good. Thanks, Bill."

The medical examiner eased the note back in the bag. "Can we take her?" he asked, tilting his head at Lewis' body.

"Fine with me, if homicide's finished." A homicide cop named Swanson was sitting at a table in the kitchen, eating a Big Mac, fries, and a malt. Lucas stepped into the doorway of the bedroom and called across to him. "I'm done. Can they take her?"

"Take her," Swanson said around a mouthful of fries.

The medical examiner supervised the movement, with Swanson ambling over to watch. They pulled the bag over her head, carefully avoiding the knife, and lifted her onto a gurney.

Like a sack of sand, Lucas thought.

"Nothin' under her?" asked Swanson.

"Not a thing," said the medical examiner. They all looked at the sheets for a moment; then the medical examiner nodded at his assistants and they pushed the gurney out the bedroom door.

"Lab's coming through with a vacuum. They haven't printed the furniture yet," Swanson said. What he meant was: Don't touch anything. Lucas grinned. "They'll take the sheets down for analysis."

"I don't see any stains."

"Naw, they're clean. I don't think there's any hair, either. Took a close look, but she didn't have any broken fingernails, didn't look like anything balled up underneath them, no skin or blood."

"Shit."

"Yeah."

"I want to poke around out here a little. Anything critical?"

"There's the potato . . ."

"Potato?"

"Potato in a sock. It's out in the living room." Lucas followed him into the living room, and Swanson used his foot to point under a piano bench. There was an ordinary argyle sock with a lump in one end.

"We think he hit her on the head with it," Swanson said. "First cop in saw it, peeked inside, then left it for the lab."

"Why do you think he hit her with it?" Lucas asked.

"Because that's what a potato in a sock is for," Swanson said. "Or, at least, it used to be."

"What?" Lucas was puzzled.

"It's probably before your time," Swanson said. "It used to be, years ago, guys would go up to Loring Park to roll the queers or down Washington Avenue to roll the winos. They'd carry a potato with them. Nothing illegal about a potato. But you put one in a sock, you got a hell of a blackjack. And it's soft, so if you're careful, you don't crack anybody's skull. You don't wind up with a dead body on your hands, everybody looking for you."

"So how'd the maddog know about it? He's gay?"

Swanson shrugged. "Could be. Or could be a cop. Lots of old street cops would know about using a potato."

"That doesn't sound right," Lucas said. "I never heard of an *old* serial killer. If they're going to do it, they start young. Teens, twenties, maybe thirties."

Swanson looked him over carefully. "You gonna detect on this one?" he asked.

"That's the idea," Lucas said. "You got a problem?"

"Not me. You're the only guy I ever met who detected anything. I have a feeling we're gonna need it this time."

"So what do the other homicide guys think?"

"There a couple new guys think you're butting in. Most of the old guys, they know a shit storm's about to hit. They just want to get it over with. You won't have no trouble."

"I appreciate that," Lucas said. Swanson nodded and wandered away.


Lewis had been found in the back bedroom by another real-estate agent. She'd had a midafternoon appointment, and when she didn't show up, the other agent got worried and went looking for her. When Lucas had arrived, pushing through the gloomy circle of neighbors who waited beside the house and on the lawns across the street, Swanson briefed him on Lewis' background.

"Just trying to sell the house," he concluded.

"Where are the owners?"

"They're a couple of old folks. The neighbors said they're down in Phoenix. They bought a place down there and are trying to sell this one."

"Anybody gone out to Lewis' house yet?"

"Oh, yeah, Nance and Shaw. Nothing there. Neighbors said she was a nice lady. Into gardening, had a big garden out back of her house. Her old man worked for 3M, died of a heart attack five or six years ago. She went to work on her own, was starting to do pretty good. That's what the neighbors say."

"Boyfriends?"

"Somebody. A neighbor woman supposedly knows him, but she hasn't been home and we don't know where she is. Another neighbor thinks he's some kind of professor or something over at the university. We're checking. And we're doing all the usual, talking to neighbors about anybody they saw coming or going."

"Look in the garage?"

"Yeah. No car."

"So what do you think?"

Swanson shrugged. "What I think is, he calls her up and says he wants to look at a house, he'll meet her somewhere. He tells her something that makes her think he's okay and they ride down here, go inside. He does her, drives her car out, dumps it, and walks. We're looking for the car."

"Anybody checking her calendars at her office?"

"Yeah, we called, but her boss says there's nothing on her desk. He said she carried an appointment book with her. We found it and all it says is, 'Twelve-forty-five.' We think that might be the time she met him."

"Where's her purse?"

"Over by the front door."

Now, wandering around the house, Lucas saw the purse again and stooped next to it. A corner of Lewis' billfold was protruding and he eased it out and snapped it open. Money. Forty dollars and change. Credit cards. Business cards. Lucas pulled out a sheaf of plastic see-through picture envelopes and flipped through them. None of the pictures looked particularly new. Looking around, he saw Swanson standing by the bedroom door talking to someone out of sight. He slipped one of the photos out of its envelope. Lewis was shown standing on a lawn with another woman, both holding some kind of a plaque. Lucas closed the wallet, slid it back in the purse, and put the photograph in his pocket.

It was cold when he left the murder scene. He got a nylon jacket from his car, pulled it on, and sat in the driver's seat for a moment, watching the bystanders. Nobody out of place. He hadn't really thought there would be.

On the way back to the station, he crossed the river into St. Paul, stopped at his house, changed into jeans, and traded the nylon jacket for a blue linen sport coat. He thought about it for a few seconds, then took a small .25-caliber automatic pistol and an ankle holster from a hideout shelf in his desk, strapped it to his right ankle, and pulled the jean leg down to cover it.

The television remote-broadcast trucks were stacked up outside City Hall when Lucas got back to police headquarters. He parked in the garage across the street, again marveled at the implacable ugliness of City Hall. He went in the back doors and down to his office.

When he'd been removed from the robbery detail, administration had to find a place to put him. His rank required some kind of office. Lucas found it himself, a storage room with a steel door on the basement level. The janitors cleaned it out and painted a number on the door. There was no other indication of who occupied the office. Lucas liked it that way. He unlocked it, went inside, and dialed Carla Ruiz' phone number.

"This is Carla." She had a pleasantly husky voice.

"My name is Lucas Davenport. I'm a lieutenant with the Minneapolis Police Department," he said. "I need to interview you. The sooner the better."

"Jeez, I can't tonight . . ."

"We've had another killing."

"Oh, no. Who was it?"

"A real-estate saleslady over here in Minneapolis. The whole thing will be on the ten-o'clock news."

"I don't have a TV."

"Well, look, how about tomorrow? How about if I stopped around at one o'clock?"

"That'd be fine. God, that's awful about this other woman."

"Yeah. See you tomorrow?"

"How'll I know you?"

"I'll have a rose in my teeth," he said. "And a gold badge."

*    *    *

The briefing room was jammed with equipment, cables, swearing technicians, and bored cops. Cameramen negotiated lighting arrangements, print reporters flopped on the folding chairs and gossiped or doodled in their notebooks, television reporters hustled around looking for scraps of information or rumor that would give them an edge on the competition. A dozen microphones were clipped to the podium at the front of the room, while the tripod-mounted cameras were arrayed in a semicircle at the rear. A harried janitor fixed a broken standard that supported an American flag. Another tried to squeeze a few more folding chairs between the podium and the cameras. Lucas stood in the doorway a moment, spotted an empty chair near the back, and took a step toward it. A hand hooked his coat sleeve from behind.

He looked down at Annie McGowan. Channel Eight. Dark hair, blue eyes, upturned nose. Wide, mobile mouth. World-class legs. Wonderful diction. Brains of an oyster.

Lucas smiled.

"What's going on, Lucas?" she whispered, standing close, holding his arm.

"Chief'll be here in five minutes." ·

"We've got a newsbreak in four minutes. I would be *very* grateful if I knew what was going on in time to call it in," she said. She smiled coyly and nodded at the cables going out the door. The press conference was being fed directly to her newsroom.

Lucas glanced around. Nobody was paying any particular attention to them. He tilted his head toward the door and they eased outside.

"If you mention my name, I'll be in trouble," he whispered. "This is a personal two-way arrangement between you and me."

She colored and said, "Deal."

"We've got a serial killer. He killed his third victim today. Rapes them and then stabs them to death. The first one was about six weeks ago, then another one a month ago. All of them in Minneapolis. We've been keeping it quiet, hoping to catch him, but now we've decided we have to go public."

"Oh, God," she said. She turned and half-ran down the hallway toward the exit, following the cables.

"What'd you tell that bitch?" Jennifer Carey materialized from the crowd. She'd been watching them. A tall blonde with a full lower lip and green eyes, she had a degree in economics from Stanford and a master's in journalism from Columbia. She worked for TV3.

"Nothing," Lucas said. Best to take a hard line.

"Bull. We've got a newsbreak in . . ." She looked at her watch. "Two and a half minutes. If she beats me, I don't know what I'll do, but I'm very smart and you'll be very, very sorry."

Lucas glanced around again. "Okay," he said, pointing a finger at her, "but

I owed her one. If you tell her I leaked this to you too, you'll never get another word out of me."

"You're on," she said. "What is it?"

Late that night, Jennifer Carey lay facedown on Lucas' bed and watched him undress, watched him unstrap the hideout gun.

"Do you ever use that thing, or do you wear it to impress women?" she asked.

"Too uncomfortable for that," Lucas lied. Jennifer sometimes made him nervous. He felt she was looking inside his head. "It comes in handy. I mean, if you're buying some toot from a guy, you can't be packing a gun. They figure you for a cop or maybe some kind of nutso rip-off psychotic, and they won't serve, won't deal. But if you got a hideout in a weird place and you need it, you can have it in their face before they know what you're doing."

"Doesn't sound like Minneapolis."

"There are some bad folks around. Anytime you get that much money . . ." He peeled off his socks and stood up in his shorts. "Shower?"

"Yeah. I guess." She rolled over slowly and got off the bed and followed him into the bathroom. The print pattern from the bedspread was impressed on her belly and thighs.

"You could've brought McGowan home, you know," she said as he turned on the water and adjusted it.

"She's been coming on to me a little," Lucas agreed.

"So why not? It's not like you're bored by the new stuff."

"She's dumb." Lucas splashed hot water on her back and followed it with a squirt of liquid bath soap from a plastic bottle. He began rubbing it across her back and butt.

"That's never stopped you before," she said.

Lucas kept scrubbing. "You know some of the women I've taken out. Tell me a dumb one."

Jennifer thought it over. "I don't know them all," she said finally.

"You know enough of them to see the pattern," he said. "I don't go out with dummies."

"So talk to me like a smart person, Lucas. Did this killer torture these women before he killed them? Daniel was pretty evasive. Do you think he knows them? How does he pick them?"

Lucas turned her around and pressed his index finger across her lips.

"Jennifer, don't pump me, okay? If you catch me off guard and I blurt something out and you use it, I could be in deep trouble."

She eyed him speculatively, the water bouncing off his chest, his mild blue eyes darkened with an edge of wariness.

"I wouldn't use it before I told you," she said. "But you never blurt anything out. Not that you didn't plan to blurt out. You're a tricky son of a bitch, Davenport. I've known you for three years and I still can't tell when you're lying. And you play more goddamn roles than anyone I've ever met. I don't even think you know when you're doing it anymore."

"You should have been a shrink," he said, shaking his head ruefully. He cut the water off and pushed open the shower door. "Hand me that big towel. I'll dry your legs for you."

A half-hour later, Jennifer said hoarsely, "Sometimes it gets very close to pain."

"That's the trick," Lucas said. "Not going over the line."

"You come so close," she said. "You must have gone over it a lot before you figured out where to stop."

Two hours later, Lucas' eyes clicked open in the dark. Somebody was watching. He thought about it. The ankle gun was in the desk . . . Then Jennifer poked him, and he realized where it was coming from.

"What?" he whispered.

"You awake?"

"I am now."

"I've got a question." She hesitated. "Do you like me more than the others or are we all just meat?"

"Oh, Jesus," he groaned.

"Say."

"You know I do. Like you better. I can prove it."

"How?"

"Your toothbrush? It's the only one in the bathroom cabinet besides mine."

There was a moment of silence and then she snuggled up on his arm. "Okay," she said. "Go to sleep."

# 5

For the first twenty rings he hoped it would stop. He got out of bed on the twenty-first and picked up the receiver on the twenty-fifth.

"What?" he snarled. The house was cold and he was naked, goose bumps erupting on the backs of his arms, his back, and his legs.

"This is Linda," said a prim voice. "Chief Daniel has called a meeting for eight o'clock sharp and you're to be there."

" 'Kay."

"Would you repeat that, Lucas?"

"Eight o'clock in the chief's office."

"That's correct. Have a good morning." She was gone. Lucas stood looking at the receiver for a moment, dropped it onto the hook, yawned, and wandered back to the bedroom.

The clock on the dresser said seven-fifteen. He reached over to Jennifer, swatted her on the bare butt, and said, "I gotta get out of here."

"Okay," she mumbled.

Still naked, Lucas padded back down the hallway to the living room, opened the front door a crack, made sure nobody was around, popped the screen door, and got the paper off the porch. In the kitchen, he shook some Cheerios into a bowl, poured on milk, and unfolded the paper.

The maddog led the front page, a double-deck headline just below the *Pioneer Press* nameplate. The story was straightforward and accurate as far as it went, with no mention of the Ruiz woman. The chief hadn't talked about survivors. Had lied, in fact—had said the only known attacks by the killer were the three that produced deaths. Nor had he mentioned the notes.

There was a short, separate story about Lucas' involvement in the investigation. He would work independently of homicide, but parallel. Controversial. Killed five men in line of duty. Commendations. Well-known game inventor. Only cop in Minnesota who drove a Porsche to work.

Lucas finished the story and the Cheerios at the same time, yawned again, and headed down to the bathroom. Jennifer was staring at herself in the medicine-cabinet mirror and turned her head when he came in.

"Men have it easy when it comes to looks, you know?"

"Right."

"I'm serious." She turned back to the mirror and stuck her tongue out. "If anybody at the station saw me like this, they'd freak out. Makeup all over my face. My hair looks like the Wolf Man's. My ass hurts. I don't know . . ."

"Yeah, well, let me in there, I have to shave."

She lifted an arm and looked at the dark stubble in her armpit. "So do I," she said morosely.


Lucas was ten minutes late for the meeting. Daniel frowned when he walked in, and pointed at the empty chair. Frank Lester, the deputy chief for investigations, sat directly opposite him. The other six chairs were occupied by robbery-homicide detectives, including the overweight head of the homicide division, Lyle Wullfolk, and his rail-thin assistant, Harmon Anderson.

"We're working out a schedule," Daniel said. "We figure at least one guy ought to know everything that's going on. Lyle's got his division to run, so it's gonna be Harmon here."

Daniel nodded at the assistant chief of homicide. Anderson was picking his teeth with a red plastic toothpick. He stopped just long enough to nod back. "A pleasure," he grunted.

"He won't be running you, Lucas, you'll be on your own," Daniel said. "If you need to know something, Harmon'll tell you if we got it."

"How'd it go with the media this morning?" Lucas asked.

"They're all over the place. Like lice. They wanted me on the morning show but I told them I had this meeting. So then they wanted to shoot the meeting. I told them to go fuck themselves."

"The mayor was on," said Wullfolk. "He said we had some leads we're working on and he'd expect to get the guy in the next couple of weeks."

"Fuckin' idiot," said Anderson.

"Easy for you to say," Daniel said gloomily. "You're civil service."

"You got some ink," said Anderson, squinting at Lucas.

Lucas nodded and changed the subject. "What about the weapon from the property room?"

Anderson stopped picking his teeth. "We run a list," he said. "We got thirty-four people, cops and civilians, who might of took it. There are probably a few more we don't know about. Found out the fucking janitors go in there all the time. I think they're smoking some of the evidence. Everybody says he's clean, of course. We got IAD looking into it."

"I want to talk to them, the thirty-four people," Lucas said. "All at once. In a group. Get the union guy in here too."

"For what?" Wullfolk asked.

"I'll tell them that I want to know what happened to the gun, and the guy that tells me, I won't turn him in. And that the chief will call off the IAD investigation and nothing more'll happen. I'm going to tell them that if nobody talks to me, we'll go ahead with the shoo-flies and sooner or later we'll find out who it is and then we'll prosecute the son of a bitch on accessory-to-murder and throw his ass in Stillwater."

Anderson shook his head. "I wouldn't buy it, if I was the guy."

"You got a convincer?" asked Daniel.

Lucas nodded. "I think so. I'll outline how the interrogation will go and I'll tell them that I won't read them their rights or anything else, so even if they are prosecuted, the whole thing would be entrapment and the case would be thrown out. I think we could build it so the guy would buy it."

Anderson and Daniel looked at each other, and Anderson shrugged. "It's worth a try. It could get us something fast. I'll set something up for late afternoon. Try to get as many as I can. Four o'clock?"

"Good," Lucas said.

"We've set up a data base in my office, we got a girl typing everything in and printing it out. Everybody working it gets a notebook with every piece of paper we develop, every interview," Anderson said. "We'll go over everything we know about these people. If there's a connection or a pattern, we'll find it. Everybody's supposed to read the files every night. When you see something, tell me. We'll put it in the file."

"What do we have so far?" asked Lucas.

Anderson shook his head. "Not much. Personal data, some loose patterns, that sorta shit. Number one was Lucy Bell, a waitress, nineteen years old. Number two was a housewife, Shirley Morris, thirty-six. Number three was the artist that fought him off, Carla Ruiz. She's thirty-two. Number four was this real-estate woman Lewis, forty-six. One was married, the other three were not. One of the other three, the artist, is divorced. The real-estate woman was a widow. The waitress was a rock-'n'-roller, a punk. The real-estate lady went to classical-music concerts with her boyfriend. It goes like that. The only pattern seems to be that they're all women."

Everybody thought about it for a minute.

"What's the interval between murders?" asked Lucas.

"The first one, Bell, was July 14, then Morris was on August 2, nineteen days between them; then the next was Ruiz on August 17, fifteen days after Morris; then Lewis on August 31, fourteen days later," said Anderson.

"Getting shorter," said one of the cops.

"Yeah. That's a tendency with sadistic killers, if he is one," said Wullfolk.

"If they start coming faster, he'll be doing them off the top of his head, not so careful-like," said another of the cops.

"We don't know that. He may be picking them out six months ahead of time. He may have a whole file of them," Anderson said.

"Any other pattern to the days?" asked Lucas.

"That's one thing, they're all during the week. A Thursday, a Tuesday, a Wednesday, and another Wednesday. No weekends."

"Not much of a pattern," Daniel said.

"Anything about the women?" asked Lucas. "All tall? All got big tits? What?"

"They're all good-looking. That's my judgment, but I think it's right. All have dark hair, three of them black—the Bell girl, who dyed hers black, Ruiz, and Lewis. Morris' hair was dark brown."

"Huh. Half the women in town have blonde hair, or blondish," said one of the other detectives. "That might be something."

"There are all kinds of possibilities in this stuff, but we gotta be careful, because there's also coincidence to think about. Anyway, look for those patterns. I'll make a special list of patterns," Anderson said. "Bring in your notebooks every afternoon and I'll give you updates. Read them."

"What about the lab, they sittin' on their thumbs, or what?" asked Wullfolk.

"They're doing everything they can. They're running down the tape he used to bind them, they're sifting through the crap they picked up with the vacuum, they're looking at everything for prints. They haven't come up with much."

"If any of these notebooks get to the media, there are going to be some bodies twisting in the wind," said Daniel. "Everybody understand?"

The cops all nodded at once.

"I don't doubt that we're going to spring some leaks," Daniel said. "But nobody, *nobody* is to say anything about the notes the killer is leaving behind. If I find somebody leaks to the media on these notes, I'll find the son of a bitch and fire him. We've been holding it close to our chests, and it's going to stay that way."

"We need a surefire identifier that the public doesn't know about," Anderson explained. "They knew they had the Son of Sam when they looked through the window of his apartment and saw some notes like the ones he'd been sending to the cops and the media."

"There's going to be a lot of pressure," Daniel said. "On all of us. I'll try to keep it off your backs, but if this asshole gets one or two more, there'll be reporters who want to talk to the individual detectives. We're going to put that off as long as we can. If we get to the point where we've got to do it, we'll get the attorney in to advise you on what to say and what not to say. Every interview gets cleared through this office in advance. Okay? Everybody understand?"

The heads bobbed again.

"Okay. Let's do it," he said. "Lucas, hang around a minute."

When the rest of the cops had shuffled out, Daniel pushed the door shut.

"You're our pipeline to the media, feeding out the unofficial stuff we need in the papers. You drop what we need on one of the papers and maybe one TV station as a deep source, and when the others come in for confirmation, I'll catch that. Okay?"

"Yeah. I'm a source for people at both papers and all the TV stations. The biggest problem will be keeping them from figuring out I'm sourcing all of them."

"So work something out. You're good at working things out. But we need the back door into the media. It's the only way they'll believe us."

"I'd just as soon not lie to anybody," Lucas said.

"We'll cross that bridge when we come to it. But if you gotta burn somebody, you burn him. This is too heavy to fool around with."

"Okay."

"You got an interview with that artist?"

"Yeah. This afternoon." Lucas looked at his watch. "I've got to close down my net and get back here by four. I better get moving."

Daniel nodded. "I got a real bad feeling about this one. Homicide won't catch the guy unless we get real lucky. I'm looking for help, Davenport. Find this son of a bitch."

\* \* \*

Lucas spent the rest of the morning on the street, moving from bars to pay phones to newsstands and barbershops. He talked to a half-dozen dope dealers ranging in age from fourteen to sixty-four, and three of their customers. He spoke to two bookies and an elderly couple who ran a convenience mail drop and an illegal switchboard, several security guards, one crooked cop, a Sioux warrior, and a wino who, he suspected, had killed two people who deserved it. The message was the same for all of them: I will be gone, but, I trust, not forgotten, because I will be back.

Freezing the net worried him. He thought of his street people as a garden that needed constant cultivation—money, threats, immunity, even friendship—lest the weeds of temptation begin to sprout.


At noon Lucas called Anderson and was told that the meeting had been set.

"Four o'clock?"

"Yeah."

"I'll see you before that. Talk it over."

"Okay."

He ate lunch at a McDonald's on University Avenue, sharing it with a junkie who nodded and nodded and finally fell asleep in his french fries. Lucas left him slumped over the table. The pimple-faced teenager behind the counter watched the bum with the half-hung eyes of a sixteen-year-old who had already seen everything and was willing to leave it alone.

Ruiz' warehouse studio was ten minutes away, a shabby brick cube with industrial-style windows that looked like dirty checkerboards. The only elevator was designed for freight and was driven by another teenager, this one with a complexion as vacant as his eyes and a boombox the size of a coffee table. Lucas rode the elevator up five stories, found Ruiz' door, and rapped on it. Carla Ruiz looked out at him over the door chain and he showed her the gold shield.

"Where's the rose?" she asked. Lucas had the shield in one hand and a briefcase in the other.

"Hey, I forgot. Supposed to be in my teeth, right?" Lucas grinned at her. She smiled back a small smile and unhooked the chain.

"I'm a mess," she said as she opened the door. She had an oval face and brilliant white teeth to go with her dark eyes and shoulder-length black hair. She was wearing a loose peasant blouse over a bright Mexican skirt. The gun-sight gash on her forehead was still healing, an angry red weal around the ragged black line of the cut. Bruises around her eyes and on one side of her face had faded from black-and-blue to a greenish yellow.

Lucas stepped inside and pocketed the shield. As she closed the door he looked closely at her face, reaching out with an index finger to turn her chin up.

"They're okay," he said. "Once they turn yellow, they're on the way out. Another week and they'll be gone."

"The cut won't be."

"Look at this," Lucas said, tracing the scar line down his forehead and across his eye socket. "When it happened, this wire fishing leader was buried right in my face. Now all that's left is the line. Yours will be thinner. With some bangs, nobody'll ever see it."

Suddenly aware of how close they were standing, Ruiz stepped back and then walked around him into the studio.

"I've been interviewed about six times," she said, touching the cut on her forehead. "I think I'm talked out."

"That's okay," said Lucas. "I don't work quite like the other guys. My questions will be a little different."

"I read about you in the paper," she said. "The story said you've killed five people."

Lucas shrugged. "It's not that I wanted to."

"It seems like a lot. My ex-husband's father was a policeman. He never shot his gun at anybody in his whole career."

"What can I tell you?" Lucas said. "I've been working in areas where it happens. If you work mostly in burglary or homicide, you can go a whole career without ever firing your gun. If you work in dope or vice, it's different."

"Okay."

She pulled a dinette chair out from a table and gestured at it, and sat on the other side. "What do you want to know?"

"Do you feel safe?" he asked as he put his briefcase on the table and opened it.

"I don't know. They say he got in by slipping the locks, so the landlord put on all new locks. The policeman who was here said they're good. And they gave me a phone and I have a special alarm code for 911. I just say 'Carla' and the cops are supposed to come running. The station is just across the street. Everybody in the building knows what happened and everybody's looking for strangers. But you know . . . I don't feel all that safe."

"I don't think he'll come back," Lucas said.

"That's what the other cops, uh, the other policemen said," she said.

"You can call us cops," Lucas said.

"Okay." She smiled again and he marveled at her even white teeth. She wasn't pretty, exactly, but she was extraordinarily attractive. "It's just that I'm the only witness. That scares me. I hardly go out anymore."

"We think he's a real freak," said Lucas. "A freak-freak, different from other freaks. He seems to be smart. He's careful. He doesn't seem to be running out of control. We don't think he'll come back because that would put him at risk."

"He seemed crazy to me," Ruiz said.

"So talk about it. What did he do when he first came after you?" Lucas asked. He thumbed through his copy of her interviews with St. Paul and Minneapolis homicide detectives. "How did it work? What did he say?"

For forty-five minutes he carefully led her through each moment of the attack, back and forth until every split second was covered. He watched her face as she relived it. Finally she stopped him.

"I can't do this much more," she said. "I was having nightmares. I don't want them to come back."

"I don't want them to either, but I wanted to get you back there, living through it. Now I want you to do one more thing. Come here."

He closed his briefcase and handed it to her. "These are your groceries. Start at the door and walk past the pillar."

"I don't—"

"Do it," Lucas barked.

She walked slowly back to the door and then turned, her arms wrapped around the briefcase. Lucas stepped behind the pillar.

"Now walk past. Don't look at me," he said.

She walked past and Lucas jumped from behind the pillar and wrapped an arm around her throat.

"Uhhh . . ."

"Do I smell like him? Do I?"

He eased up on his arm. "No."

"What? What'd he smell like?"

She turned into him, his arm still over her shoulder. "I don't . . . he had cologne of some kind."

"Did he smell like sweat? Perspiration? Were his clothes clean or did they stink?"

"No. Like after-shave, maybe."

"Was he as big as I am? Was he strong?" He pulled her tight against his chest and she dropped the briefcase and turned into him, beginning to struggle. He let her struggle for a moment and then she suddenly relaxed. Lucas tightened his grip further.

"Shit," she said and she fought and he let her go, and she turned into him, her eyes wide and angry. "Don't do that. Stay away." She was on the edge of fear.

"Was he stronger?"

"No. He was softer. His hands were soft. And when I relaxed, he relaxed. That's when I stamped on his instep."

"Where'd you learn that?"

"From my ex-husband's father. He taught me some self-defense things."

"Come here."

"No."

"Come here, goddammit."

She reluctantly stepped forward, afraid, her face pale. Lucas turned her again and put his arm around her neck without tightening it.

"Now, when he had you, he said something about not screaming or he'd kill you. Did he sound like this?" And Lucas tightened his grip and pulled her high, almost off her feet, and said hoarsely, "Scream and I'll kill you."

Ruiz struggled again and Lucas said, "Think," and let her go, pushing her away. He walked away until he was near the door. Ruiz had her hands at her throat, her eyes wide.

"New Mexico," she said.

"What?" Lucas felt a spark.

"I think he might be from New Mexico. It never occurred to me until now, but he *didn't* sound quite like people up here. It wasn't the words. It's not an accent. It's almost, like, a *feeling*. I don't think you'd even notice it, if you weren't thinking about it. But it was like back home."

"You're from New Mexico?"

"Yes. Originally. I've been up here six years."

"Okay. And you said he smelled like cologne. Good cologne?"

"I don't know, just cologne. I wouldn't know the difference."

"Could it have been hair oil?"

"No, I don't think so. I think it was cologne. It was light."

"But he didn't stink? Like he was unwashed?"

"No."

"He was wearing a T-shirt. You said he was white. How white?"

"Really white. Whiter than you. I mean, I'm kind of brown, you're tan-white, he was real white."

"No tan?"

"No. I don't think so. That's not my impression. He was wearing those gloves and I remember that his skin was almost as white as the gloves were."

"You said when you were talking to the St. Paul police that he was wearing athletic shoes. Do you know what kind?"

"No. He just knocked me down and I was getting up and I remember the shoes and the little bubble thing on the side . . ." She stopped and frowned. "I didn't tell the other officers about the bubble thing."

"What kind of bubble thing?"

"Those transparent bubble things, where you can look inside the shoe soles?"

"Yeah. I know. Do you go down to St. Paul Center much?"

"Sometimes," she said.

"If you've got the time, walk over this afternoon and look at the shoes, see if there's anything like it. Okay?"

"Sure. Jeez, I didn't think . . ."

Lucas took out his badge case, extracted a business card, and handed it to her. "Call me and let me know."

They talked for another ten minutes, but there was nothing more. Lucas made a few final notes on a steno pad and tossed the pad and the investigation notebook back in his briefcase.

"You scared me," Ruiz said as Lucas closed the case.

"I want to catch this guy," Lucas said. "I figured there might be something you wouldn't remember unless you walked through it again."

"I'll have nightmares."

"Maybe not. Even the worst ones fade after a while. I won't apologize, considering the situation."

"I know." She plucked at the seam of her skirt. "It's just . . ."

"Yeah, I know. Listen, I've got to make a call, okay?"

"Sure." She walked back to a stool next to a loom and sat on it, her hands resting between her legs. She was subdued, almost depressed. Lucas watched her as he dialed the information operator, got the number for St. Anne's College, hung up, and redialed the new number.

"Think about something else entirely," he said to her across the room.

"I try, but I can't," she said. "I just keep going over it in my head. My God, he was right in here . . ."

Lucas held up a hand to stop her for a moment. "Psychology department. . . . Thanks. . . . Sister Mary Joseph. . . . Tell her Detective Lieutenant Lucas Davenport . . ." He glanced at Carla again. She was staring fixedly out the window.

"Hello? Lucas?"

"Elle, I've got to talk to you."

"About the maddog?" she asked.

"Yeah."

"I was halfway expecting you to call. When do you want to come?"

"I'm in St. Paul now. I've got to be over in Minneapolis for a meeting at four, I was hoping you could squeeze me in now."

"If you come right this minute, we can walk down to the ice-cream store. I've got a faculty meeting in forty-five minutes."

"I'll see you in front of Fat Albert Hall in ten minutes."

Lucas dropped the phone back on the hook.

"You going to be okay?" he asked as he headed for the door. "I was a little rough . . ."

"Yes." She continued to stare out the window and he paused with his hand on the bolt.

"Will you check downtown for me? About those shoes?"

"Sure." She sighed and turned toward him. "I've got to get out of here. If you can wait a minute, I'll get my purse. You can walk me out of the building."

She was ready in a moment and they rode the old elevator down to the first floor. The elevator operator had plugged a set of headphones into his boombox, but the sound of heavy metal leaked out around the edges.

"That shit can sterilize you," Lucas said. The operator didn't respond, his head continuing to bob with the pounding beat of the music.

"This elevator guy . . ." Lucas said when they got off the elevator. There was a question in his voice.

"No chance," Carla said. "Randy's so burned out that he can barely find the right floors. He could never organize an actual attack on somebody."

"All right." He held the door for her and she stepped out on the sidewalk.

"It's nice to be out," she said. "The sunshine feels great." Lucas' car was parked a block toward Town Center and they strolled together along the sidewalk.

"Listen," she said when he stopped beside the Porsche. "I get over to Minneapolis once a week or so. I show in a gallery over there. If I stopped in some morning, could you let me know how things are going? I'd call first."

"Sure. I'm in the basement of the old City Hall. You just leave your car—"

"I know where you are," she said. "I'll see you. And I'll call you this afternoon, about the shoes."

She walked off down the sidewalk and Lucas got in the car and started it. He watched her through the windshield for a moment and she looked back and smiled.

"Hmph," he grunted. He rolled down the street until he was beside her, pulled over, and rolled down the passenger-side window.

"Forget something?" she asked, leaning over the window.

"What kind of music do you listen to?"

"What?" She seemed confused.

"Do you like rock?"

"Sure."

"Want to go see Aerosmith tomorrow night? With me? Get you out of your apartment?"

"Oh. Well. Okay. What time?" She wasn't smiling but she was definitely interested.

"Pick you up at six. We'll get something to eat."

"Sure," she said. "See you." She waved and stepped back from the car. Lucas made an illegal U-turn and headed back toward the Interstate. As he pulled away, he glanced in his rearview mirror and saw her looking after him. It was silly, but he thought he felt their eyes touch.

Sister Mary Joseph had grown up as Elle Kruger on the near north side of Minneapolis, a block from the house where Lucas was born. They started grade school the same autumn, their mothers walking them down the cracked sidewalks together, past the tall green hedges and through the red brick arches of St. Agnes Elementary. Elle still ran through Lucas' dreams. She was a lovely slender blonde girl, the most popular kid in the class with both the pupils and the teachers, the fastest runner on the playground. At the blackboard, she regularly thrashed the class in multiplication races. Lucas usually finished second. In the spelldowns, it was Lucas who won, Elle who finished second.

Lucas left St. Agnes halfway through fifth grade, after the death of his father. He and his mother moved down to the south side and Lucas started at public school. Later, at a hockey tournament, he was warming up, swinging down the ice, and he stopped on the opponents' side of the rink to adjust his skates. She was there in the crowd, with a group of girls from Holy Spirit High. She had not seen him, or not recognized him in his hockey gear. He stood transfixed, appalled.

It had been six years. Other girls, gawky as she had been beautiful, had blossomed. Elle had not. Her face was pitted and scarred by acne. Her cheeks, her forehead, her chin were crossed with fiery red lines of infection. The small part of her face free of scarring was as coarse as sandpaper from attempts at treatment.

Lucas skated away, around the rink toward the home bench, Elle's face bobbing in his mind. A few minutes later, the players for the two teams were introduced and he skated out to center ice, his name booming from the public-address system, unable *not* to look, and found her grave eyes following him.

After the match he was clumping toward the tunnel to the locker rooms when he saw her standing on the other side of the barricade. When their eyes met her hand came up and fluttered at him and he stopped and reached across the barrier and took her hand and said, "Can you wait for me? Twenty minutes, outside?"

"Yes."

He drove her home after a tour of southern and western Minneapolis. They talked as they had when they were children, laughing in the dark car. At her house, she hopped out and ran up to the porch. The light came on, and her father stepped out.

"Dad, do you remember Lucas Davenport, he used to live down the street?"

"Sure, how are you, son?" her father said. There was a sad edge to his voice. He asked Lucas in and he sat for another half-hour, talking to Elle's parents, before he left.

As he walked out to the curb, she called him from her bedroom window on the second floor of the house, her head backlit against the flowered wallpaper.

"Lucas?"

"Yeah?"

"Please don't come back," she said, and shut the window.

He heard from her next a year and a half later, a week before graduation. She called to tell him that she was entering a convent.

"Are you sure?"

"Yes. I have a vocation."

Years later, and two days after Lucas had killed his first man as a police officer, she called him. She was a shrink of sorts, she said. Could she help? No, not really, but he would like to see her. He took her to the ice-cream shop. Professor of psychology, she said. Fascinating. Watching minds work.

Did she have a vocation? Lucas wondered. Or was it her face, the cross that she bore? He couldn't ask, but when they left the shop she took his arm and smiled and said, "I have a vocation, Lucas."

A year later, he sold his first game and it was a hit. The *Star-Tribune* did a feature story about it and she called him again. She was a game player, she said. There was a games group at the college that regularly got together . . .

After that, he saw her virtually every week. Elle and another nun, a grocer and a bookie, both from St. Paul, a defense attorney from Minneapolis, and a student or two from St. Anne's or the University of Minnesota made up a regular war-gaming group. They met in the gym, played in an old unused room off what had been a girls' locker room. They furnished the room with a half-dozen chairs, a Ping-Pong table for the gaming maps, a used overhead light donated by a pool parlor, and a bad stereo that Lucas got on the street.

They met on Thursdays. They were currently working through Lucas' grandest creation, a replay of the Battle of Gettysburg that he would never be able to sell commercially. It was simply too complex. He'd had to program a portable computer to figure results.

Elle was General Lee.

Lucas parked the Porsche just down the hill from Albertus Magnus Hall and walked through the falling leaves up the hill toward the entrance. As he reached the bottom of the steps, she came out. The face was the same; so were the eyes, grave and gray, but always with a spark of humor.

"He can't stop," she told him as they strolled down the sidewalk. "The maddog falls into a category that cop shrinks call the sadistic killer. He's doing it for the pleasure of it. He's not hearing commands from God, he's not being ordered by voices. He's driven, all right, but he's not insane in the sense that he's out of control. He is very much in control, in the conventional sense of the word. He is aware of what he's doing and what the penalties are. He makes plans and provides for contingencies. He may be quite intelligent."

"How does he pick his victims?"

She shrugged. "Could be a completely adventitious encounter. Maybe he uses the phone book. But most likely he sees them personally, and whether he realizes it or not, he's probably picking a type. There may well have been an encounter of some kind when he was young, with his mother, with a female friend of his mother's . . . somebody whose sexual identity has become fixed in his mind."

"These women are small and dark—dark hair, dark eyes. One is a Mexican-American . . ."

"Exactly. So when he encounters one of these types, she somehow becomes fixed in his mind. Why it's that particular one, when there are so many possibilities, I just don't know. In any case, after he's chosen her, he can't escape her. His fantasies are built around her. He becomes obsessive. Eventually . . . he goes after her. Acts out the fantasies."

At the ice-cream parlor, she ordered her usual, a hot-fudge with a maraschino cherry. A few of the customers glanced curiously at them, the nun in her black habit, the tall, well-dressed male who was so obviously her friend. They ignored the passing attention.

"How long would it take him to fix on a particular woman? Would it be an instantaneous thing?"

"Could be. More likely, though, it would be some kind of encounter. An exposure, a conversation. He might make some kind of assessment of her vulnerability. Remember, this may be a very intelligent man. Eventually, though, it goes beyond his control. She becomes fixed in his mind, and he can no more escape her image than she can escape his attack."

"Jesus. Uh, sorry."

She smiled at him. "You just didn't get enough of it, you know? If you'd stayed at St. Agnes for another two, three years, who knows? Maybe it'd be Father Davenport."

Lucas laughed. "That's a hair-raising thought," he said. "Can you see me running the little ankle-biters through First Communion?"

"Yes," she said. "In fact, I can."


The phone was ringing when Lucas got back to his office. It was Carla. She thought the shoes on the maddog were the Nike Air model, but she was not sure which variation.

"But the bubble thing on the sole is right. There wasn't anything else like it," she said.

"Thanks, Carla. See you tomorrow."

Lucas spent ten minutes calling discount shoe stores, getting prices, and then walked up the stairs to the homicide office. Anderson was sitting in his cubbyhole, looking at papers.

"Am I set on the meeting?" Lucas asked.

"Yep. Just about everybody will be there," Anderson said. He was a shabby man, too thin, with nicotine-stained teeth and small porcine eyes. His necktie was too wide and usually ended in the middle of his stomach, eight inches above his belt. His grammar was bad and his breath often smelled of sausage. None of it meant much to his colleagues. Anderson had a better homicide-clearance rate than any other man in the department. On his own time he wrote law-enforcement computer-management programs that sold across the country. "There'll be four missing, but they're pretty marginal anyway. You can talk to them later if you want."

"What about the union?"

"We cooled them out. The union guy will give a statement before you talk."

"That sounds good," Lucas said. He took out his notebook. "I've got some stuff I want to get in the data base."

"Okay." Anderson swiveled in his chair and punched up his IBM. "Go ahead."

"He's very light-complexioned, which means he's probably blond or sandy-haired. Probably an office worker or a clerk of some kind, maybe a professional, and reasonably well-off. May have been born in the Southwest. New Mexico, like that. Arizona. Texas. May have moved up here fairly recently."

Anderson punched it into the computer and when he was done, looked up with a frown. "Jesus, Davenport, where'd you get this?"

"Talking to Ruiz. They're guesses, but I think they're good. Now. Have somebody go around to the post offices and pull the change-of-address forms for anybody coming in from those areas. Add Oklahoma. Everybody who moved into the seven-county metro area from those places."

"There could be hundreds of them."

"Yeah, but we can eliminate a lot of them right off the bat. Too old, female, black, blue-collar, originally from here and moving back . . . Besides, hundreds are better than millions, which is what we got now. Once we get a list, we might be able to cross-reference against some other lists, if we get any more."

Anderson pursed his lips and then nodded. "I'll do it," he said. "We got nothing else."


They met in the same room where the press conference had been held the night before, thirty-odd cops and civilians, an assistant city attorney, three union officials. They stopped talking when Lucas entered the room.

"All right," he said, standing at the front. "This is serious. We want the union to talk first."

One of the union men stood, cleared his throat, looked at a piece of paper, folded it, and stuck it back in his coat pocket.

"Normally, the union would object to what's going to happen here. But we talked it over with the chief and I guess we've got no complaint. Not at this point. Nobody is being accused of anything. Nobody's going to be forced to do anything. We think for the good of the force that everybody ought to hear what Davenport's going to say."

He sat down and the cops looked back at Lucas.

"What I'm going to say is this," Lucas said, scanning the crowd. "Somebody took a piece out of the property room. It was a Smith, Model 15. From the David L. Losse box. You remember the Losse case, it was the guy who lit up his kid? Said it was an accident? Went down on manslaughter?" Several heads nodded.

"Anyway, it was probably somebody in this room who took it. Most of the people with access are here. Now, that gun was used by this maddog killer. We want to know how he got it. We don't think anybody here is the maddog. But somebody here, somehow, got this gun out to him."

Several cops started to speak at the same time, but Lucas put up his hand and silenced them.

"Wait a minute. Listen to the rest of it. There might be any number of reasons somebody thought it was a good idea to take the piece. It's a good gun and maybe somebody needed a backup piece. Or a piece for his wife, for home protection, and it got stolen. Whatever. The maddog gets his hands on it. We're looking for the connection.

"Now, the chief is going to put IAD on it and they're going to be talking to every one of you. They're not going to do anything else until they find out what happened."

Lucas paused and looked around the room again.

"*Unless,*" he said. "Unless somebody comes forward and tells me what happened. I give you these guarantees. First, I don't tell anybody else. I don't cooperate with IAD. And once we know, well, the chief admits there'd be no reason to really push the investigation. We got better things to do than chase some guy who took a gun."

Lucas pointed at the assistant city attorney. "Tell them about the punishment ruling."

The attorney stepped toward the center of the room and cleared his throat. "Before the chief can discipline a man, he has to give specific cause. We've ruled if the cause is alleged criminal wrongdoing, he has to provide the same proof as he would in court. He is not allowed to punish on a lesser standard. In other words, he can't say, 'Joe Smith, you're demoted because you committed theft.' He has to prove the theft to the same standards as he would in court—actually, for practical purposes, he has to get a conviction."

Lucas took over again.

"What I'm saying is, you call me, tell me where to meet you. Bring a lawyer if you want. I'll refuse to read you your rights. I'll admit to entrapment. I'll do anything reasonable that would kill my testimony in court. That way, even if I talked, you couldn't be punished. And I won't talk.

"You guys know me. I won't burn you. And we've got to catch this guy. I'm passing out my card, I've written my home phone number on the back. I want everyone to put the card in his pocket, so the guy who needs it won't be out there by himself. I'll be home all night." He handed a stack of business cards to a cop in the front row, who took one, divided the rest in half, and passed them in two directions.

"Tell them the rest of it, Davenport," said the union man.

"Yeah, the rest of it," said Lucas. "If nobody talks to me, we push the IAD investigation and we push the murder investigation. Sooner or later we'll identify the guy who took the gun. And if we have to do it that way . . ."

He tried to pick out each face in the room before he said it: ". . . we'll find a felony to hang on it. We'll put somebody in Stillwater."

An angry buzz spread through the group.

"Hey, fuck it," Lucas said, raising his voice over the noise. "This guy's butchered three women in the worst way you could do it. Go ask homicide if you want the details. But don't give me any brotherhood shit. I don't like this any better than you guys. But I need to know about that piece."


Anderson caught him in the hall after the meeting.

"What do you think?"

Lucas nodded down the hallway, where a half-dozen of his cards littered the floor.

"Most of them kept the cards. I've got nothing to do but go home and wait."


# 6

---

Bats flicked through his head, bats with razor-edged wings that cut like fire. Monsters. Kill factor low, but they were virtually transparent, like sheets of broken glass, and almost impossible to see at night in the thorn brush outside the dark castle . . .

Lucas looked up at the clock. Eleven-forty. Damn. If the cop who took the gun was planning to call, he should have done it. Lucas looked at the phone, willing it to ring.

It rang. He nearly fell off his drawing stool in surprise.

"Yes?"

"Lucas? This is Jennifer."

"Hey. I'm expecting a call. I need the line open."

"I got a tip from a friend," Jennifer said. "He says there was a survivor. Somebody who fought off the killer. I want to know who it was."

"Who told you this bullshit?"

"Don't play with me, Lucas. I got it solid. She's some kind of Chicana or something."

Lucas hesitated and realized a split second later that his hesitation had given it away. "Listen, Jennifer, you got it, but I'm asking you not to use it. Talk to the chief first."

"Look. It's a hell of a story. If somebody else gets onto it and breaks it, I'd feel like an idiot."

"It's yours, okay? If we have to break her out, we'll get you in first. But the thing is, we don't want the killer to start thinking about her again. We don't want to challenge him."

"C'mon, Lucas . . ."

"Listen, Jennifer. You listening?"

"Yeah."

"If you use this before you talk to the chief, I'll find some way to fuck with you. I'll tell every TV station in the world how you fed the name and address of an innocent woman to a maddog killer and made her a target for murder and rape. I'll put you right in the middle of the controversy, and that means you'll lose your piece of it. You'll be doing dog-sled stories out of Brainerd."

"I heard he hit her in her apartment, so he already knows—"

"Sure. And after about a week of argument, that'd probably come out too. In the meantime, the local feminists would be doing a tap dance on your face and you wouldn't be able to get a job anywhere east of the Soviet Union."

"So fuck you, Lucas. When can I talk to Daniel?"

"What time you want him?"

"Nine o'clock tomorrow morning."

"I'll call him right now. You be down there at nine."

He dropped the phone in its cradle, looked at it for a second, picked it up, and dialed Daniel's home phone. The chief's wife answered and a moment later put Daniel on the phone.

"You got him?" He sounded like he was talking around a bagel.

"Yeah, right," Lucas said dryly. "Go stand on the curb in front of your office and I'll drop him off in twenty minutes. If I'm late, don't worry, I'll be along. Just wait there on the curb."

The chief chewed for a minute, then said, "Pretty fuckin' funny, Davenport. What do you want?"

"Jennifer Carey just called. Somebody told her about Ruiz."

"Shit. Wasn't you, was it?"

"No."

"Somebody told me you were puttin' the pork to the young lady."

"Jesus Christ . . ."

"Okay, okay. Sorry. So what do you think?"

"I shut her mouth for the time being. She's coming down to your office to see you tomorrow. Nine o'clock. I'd like to hold her off Ruiz for at least a couple of days. But if somebody tipped her, it's going to get out."

"So?"

"So when she sees you tomorrow, tell her to hold off a couple of days and then we'll set up an interview for her, if Ruiz will go along. Then, if Ruiz is willing to go along, we'll set up an interview for six o'clock in the evening and let Jennifer tape it for the late news. While I'm over there with her, you can call a press conference for eight o'clock or eight-thirty. Then I bring Ruiz over, we let the press yell at her for twenty minutes or so, and they get tape for ten o'clock."

"Carey'll be pissed if we burn her."

"I'll handle that. I'll tell *her* that you wouldn't go for an exclusive break, but she's the only TV station with a personal interview. The other stations will have nothing but press-conference stuff. Then we'll tell the *other* stations that Carey had a clean tip, had us against the wall, but because you're their friend, you decided to go with a press conference. That way, everybody owes us."

"How about the papers? They're out of it."

"We let them sit in on the interview with Carey so they can drop in long profiles. They won't publish until the next morning anyway, so Jennifer still gets the break. I'll feed it to the two papers as special treatment from you. I'll let them know that the even-handedness could change if we start having trouble with them."

"Okay. So tomorrow morning I'll see Carey at nine o'clock, put her off, maybe feed her a tidbit. We can work all the rest out later, in detail."

"See you tomorrow."

"Don't forget the meeting."


When he got off the phone, Lucas rubbed his eyes and bent over the drawing table again. He read penciled numbers from a list on a yellow legal pad, cranking them through an electronic desk calculator. A near-empty coffee cup sat at the top of the table. He took a sip of the oily remnant and grimaced.

Lucas wrote games. Role-playing fantasies, Civil War historical reconstructions, combat simulations from World War II, Korea, Vietnam, Stalingrad, Battle of the Bulge, Taipan, the Punch Bowl, Bloody Ridge, Dien Bien Phu, Tet.

The games were marketed through a New York publisher who would take all he could create, usually two a year. His latest was a role-playing fantasy adventure. They were the best moneymakers but the least intrinsically interesting.

He looked at the clock again. Twelve-ten. He walked over to the sound system, picked out a compact disc, slipped it in the player, and went back to the numbers as Eric Clapton started on "I Shot the Sheriff."

The fantasy game's story line was complicated. An American armored platoon was fighting in the Middle East at some unspecified time in the near future. The platoon got word that a tactical nuke was headed toward it and dug in the best it could.

At the instant of expected detonation, there was an intolerable flash and the platoon found itself—complete with M3 tanks—in Everwhen, a land of water and fens and giant oaks. Where magic worked and soulless fairies danced in the night.

The whole thing tended to give Lucas a headache. Every fantasy game in the world, he thought, had a bunch of computer freaks with swords wandering around Poe-esque landscapes with red-haired freckled beauties with large breasts.

But it was money; and he had a responsibility to the prepubescent intellectuals who might someday buy his masterpiece, the Grove of Trees. He thought about Grove for a minute, the Gettysburg game he was perfecting in the weekly bouts at St. Anne's. Grove required an IBM computer and a separate, dedicated game room, along with teams of players. It took two nights just to set up the pieces. As a game it was impractical and unwieldy. But fascinating.

He tapped the pencil against his teeth and stared sightlessly over the drawing table. On the fifth night of the game, Jeb Stuart was still out of touch with Lee, riding far to the east around the Union army that was slowly crawling north toward Gettysburg. That had happened in the actual conflict, but this time, in the game, Stuart—in the person of the St. Paul grocer—was moving more aggressively to close the gap and could reach Gettysburg in time to scout the good ground south of town.

In the meantime, Lee's order of battle had been shuffled. As he closed through the mountains toward Gettysburg, Pickett's division was in the lead and was hunting for bear. Even if Reynolds—a university student—got there ahead of Stuart, and Reynolds managed to stay alive, as he hadn't in the original fight, Pickett's aggressiveness might push him aside and allow the Confederates to take the hills at the end of Cemetery Ridge or even the entire ridge. If he did, then the gathering Union forces would have to choose between an offensive battle or retreating on Washington. . . .

Lucas sighed and wrenched his mind back to Everwhen, which was, naturally, under attack by the forces of evil. The armored platoon had been called in by a good wizard who planned to introduce a new element to what had been a losing war: technology. Once signed up with the forces for good, the armored platoon would march on the cloud-veiled castle of the Evil One.

The story was not particularly original. Working the details into a logical game was an ordeal.

Like the M3 tanks. Where did they get fuel and repairs? Magic. How did the platoon acquire magical talents? By valiant deeds. Save a virgin from a dragon and the magic quotient goes up. If the dragon kicks your ass, it goes down.

The creatures of Everwhen were a troublesome problem. They had to be dangerous, interesting, and reasonably original. They also had to be exotic, but familiar enough to be comprehensible. The best ones were morphologically related to familiar earth creatures: lizards, snakes, rats, spiders. Lucas spent dozens of winter evenings sitting in his leather chair in the den, a yellow pad on his lap, dreaming them up.

The slicers were one of them. A slicer was a cross between a bat and a razor-edged plate of glass. Slicers attacked at night, slashing their targets to pieces. They were too stupid to be affected by magic, but were easy enough to kill with the right technology. Like shotguns.

But how would you even see them? Okay. Like bats, they used a kind of sonar. With the right magic, the platoon's radios could be tuned to it. Could you get them all? Maybe. But if not, there were hit points to be worked out. So many hit points, and a character died. Lucas had to take care not to kill off the characters too easily. The players wouldn't stand for it. Nor could the game be too simple. It was a matter of walking the line, of luring the players deeper and deeper into the carefully crafted scenarios.

He worked hunched over the drawing table in a pool of light created by the drafting lamp, hammering out the numbers, drinking coffee. When Clapton started on "Lay Down, Sally" he got up and did a neatly coordinated solo dance around the chair. Then he sat down, worked for fifteen seconds, and was back up with "Willie and the Hand Jive." He danced in the dark room by himself, watching the song time counting down on the digital CD clock. When "Hand Jive" ended, he sat down again, called up a file on his IBM, read out the specs, and went back to the numbers after an almost unconscious glance at the clock. Twelve-fifteen.

Lucas lived in a three-bedroom ranch home, stone and cedar, across Mississippi Boulevard and a hundred feet above the river. When the leaves were off the trees in the fall and winter, he could see the lights of Minneapolis from his living room.

It was a big house. At first, he worried that it was too big, that he should buy a condominium. Something over by the lakes, where he could watch the singles out jogging, skating, sailing.

But he bought the house and never regretted it. He paid $120,000 for it, cash, in 1980. Now it was worth twice that. And in the back of his head, as he pushed into his thirties and contemplated the prospect of forty, he still thought of children and a place for them.

Besides, as it turned out, he quickly filled up the space. A beat-up Ford four-wheel-drive joined the five-year-old Porsche in the garage. The family room became a small gym, with free weights and a heavy bag, and a wooden floor where he did kata, the formal exercises of karate.

The den was converted to a library, with sixteen hundred novels and nonfiction works and another two hundred small volumes of poetry. A deep leather chair with a hassock for his feet, and a good light, were the main furnishings.

For those times when reading didn't appeal, he'd built in a twenty-five-inch color television, videotape player, and sound system.

Tools, laundry appliances, and outdoor sports gear were stored in the basement, along with a sophisticated reloading bench and a firearms locker. The locker was actually a turn-of-the-century bank safe. An expert cracksman could open it in twenty minutes, but Lucas didn't expect any expert cracksmen to visit his basement. A snatch-and-run burglar wouldn't have a chance against the old box.

Lucas owned thirteen guns. His daily working weapon was a nine-millimeter Heckler & Koch P7 with a thirteen-shot clip. He also carried, on occasion, a nine-millimeter Beretta 92F. Those, and the small ankle gun, were kept on a concealed shelf in his workroom desk.

The basement locker contained two Colt .45 Gold Cups, both further customized by a Texas gunsmith for combat target competition, and three .22's, including a Ruger Mark II with a five-and-a-half-inch bull barrel, a Browning International Medalist, and the only nonautomatic, a bolt-action Anschutz Exemplar.

In the bottom of the locker, carefully oiled, wrapped, and packaged, were four pistols he'd picked up on the job. Street guns, untraceable to anyone in particular. The last weapon, also kept in the locker, was a Browning Citori over-and-under twenty-gauge shotgun, the upland version. He used it for hunting.

Of the rest of the house, the two smaller bedrooms actually had beds in them.

The master bedroom became his workroom, with a drawing table, drafting instruments, and the IBM. There were two walls of books on weapons and armies—on Alexander and Napoleon and Lee and Hitler and Mao, details of Bronze Age spears and Russian tanks and science-fiction fantasies that discussed seeker-killer shells, rail guns, plasma rifles, and nova bombs. Ideas that he would weave into the net of a game. The slicers flitted through Lucas' mind like splinters as he worked over the drawing table, hammering out the numbers.

When the phone rang, he jumped. It seldom rang; few people had the number. Thirty-odd more this evening, he thought, laying his pencil on the table. He glanced at the clock: twelve-twenty-two. He stepped across the room, turned down the CD player, started the tape recorder he'd attached to the receiver, and picked up the extension.

"Yes?"

"Davenport?" A man's voice. Middle-aged, or a little past it.

"Yeah."

"You taping this?" Vaguely familiar. He knew this man.

"No."

"How do I know that?"

"You don't. What can I tell you?"

There was a pause; then the voice said, "I took the Smith, but I want to talk to you about it face-to-face."

"Let's do it now," said Lucas. "This is a very heavy situation."

"The deal is like you said this afternoon?"

"That's right," Lucas said. "It won't go any further. No comebacks."

There was a pause; then, "You know that taco joint across I-94 from Martin Luther College?"

"Yeah?"

"Twenty minutes. And, goddammit, you come alone, you hear?"

Lucas made it in eighteen. The restaurant parking lot was empty. Inside, a lone diner stared out a window as he nursed a cup of coffee over the cardboard remains of his meal. An employee was mopping the floor and turned to watch Lucas come in. The countergirl, probably a student from the university, smiled warily.

"Give me a Diet Coke," Lucas said.

"Anything else?" Still wary. Lucas realized that in his leather bomber jacket, jeans, and boots, with a day-old beard, he might look threatening.

"Yeah. Relax. I'm a cop." He grinned, took the badge case out of his shirt pocket, and showed it to her, and she smiled back.

"We've had some problems here," she said.

"Holdup?"

"Last month and the month before. Four months ago it was twice. There are some bikers around."

When the cop came in, Lucas recognized him instantly. Gray-haired, wearing a lightweight beige jacket and brown slacks. Roe, he thought. Harold Roe. Longtime cop. Must be near retirement.

Roe looked around, stopped at the counter, got a coffee, and walked over.

"You it?" Lucas asked.

"You wearing a wire?"

"No."

"If you are, you're entrapping me."

"I admit it. If I am, I'm entrapping you. But I'm not."

"Read me my rights."

"Nope."

"Hmph. You know, this is all horseshit," Roe said, taking a sip of his coffee. "If they put you on the witness stand, you might tell a whole 'nother story."

"Won't be any witness stand, Harry. I could walk out of here right now, go to Daniel, say 'Harry Roe is the man,' and the IAD would put together a case in three days. You know how it goes, once they got a starting point."

"Yeah." Roe looked around wearily and shook his head. "Jesus, I hate this."

"So tell me."

"Not much to tell. I figured that piece was cold. Never show up in a million years. There was this guy down the block, Larry Rice was his name, I grew up with him. He was a maintenance man for the city. I used to see him around City Hall all the time. You probably seen him yourself. Heavyset guy with a limp, always wore one of those striped train-engineer hats."

"Yeah, I remember him."

"Anyway, he was dying of some kind of cancer, little bit by little bit. It was working its way up his body. First he couldn't walk, then he couldn't control his bowels, like that. His wife was working and he was at home. One day these neighborhood punks came in and took the TV and stereo right out from in front of him. He had this wheelchair, but he couldn't fight them. He couldn't identify them, either, because they were wearing paper sacks on their heads. . . . Assholes is who they were."

"So you got him the gun?"

"Well, his wife came over after this happened, and asked my wife if I had an extra gun. I didn't. I'm no gun freak—sorry, I know you're into guns, but I'm not."

"That's okay."

"So I went up there to the property room and I knew about the gun because I worked on the case. I figured there was no way in hell it would ever be needed for anything."

"And you took it."

Roe took a sip of his coffee. "Yep."

"So this Rice guy . . ."

"He's dead. Two months ago."

"Shit. How about his wife?"

"She's still out there. After the meeting this afternoon, I went over and asked her about the gun. She said she didn't know where it was. She looked, but it was gone. She said the last couple of weeks before he died, Larry sold a whole bunch of personal stuff to get money for her. He was afraid he wouldn't leave anything. She said when he died, he left about a thousand bucks behind."

"She doesn't know who got the gun?"

"No. I asked her how he sold the stuff and she said he just sold it to people he knew, friends and so on. He had a little sign in the window, she said, but he didn't advertise it or nothing. People might see the sign walking by on the sidewalk, but that was all." Roe passed a slip of paper across the table. "I told her you'd want to see her. Here's her address."

"Thanks." Lucas drained the last of his Coke.

"Now what?" asked Roe.

"Now nothing. If you've been telling the truth."

"It's the truth," Roe said levelly. "I feel like a piece of shit."

"Yeah, it's a bummer. It won't go any further than this table, though I suppose if we ever need Mrs. Rice to testify, somebody could figure it out. But it won't come to anything."

"Thanks, man. I owe you."

Roe left first, relieved to get away. Lucas watched his car pull out of the parking lot, then got up and strolled past the counter.

"You mind if I make a comment?" he asked the countergirl.

"No, go ahead." She smiled politely.

"You're too pretty to be working in this place. I'm not hustling you, I'm just telling you. You're an attraction. If you stay here, sooner or later you're going to catch some bad news."

"I need the money," she said, her face tense and serious.

"You don't need it that bad," he said.

"I have two more years at the university, one year for my bachelor's and nine more months for my master's."

Lucas shook his head. "If I knew your parents, I'd call them. But I don't. So I'm just telling you. Get out of here. Or get on the day shift."

He turned and started away.

"Thanks," she called after him. But he knew she wouldn't do anything about it. He stepped outside, considered the problem for a minute, and went back in.

"How many tacos could you rip off without anyone knowing about it? I mean, every night. A couple of dozen?"

"Why?"

"If you gave a cup of coffee and a free taco to every patrol cop who came in, say, from ten o'clock at night to six in the morning, you'd have cops around, or arriving or leaving, most of the night. It'd give you some cover."

She looked interested. "We wouldn't have hundreds of cops or anything, would we?"

"No. On a heavy night, maybe twenty or thirty."

"Shoot," she said cheerfully. "The owner has trouble keeping people working here. He's kind of desperate. I don't think I'd have to steal them. I think he'd say okay."

Lucas took out a business card and handed it to her. "This is my office phone. Call me tomorrow. If the boss says okay, I'll get the word out about the free coffee and tacos. I'll tell both towns, you'll have cops coming in from all over the place."

"I'll call tomorrow," she said. "Thanks really a lot."

Lucas nodded and turned away. If it worked out, he'd have another source on the street.

*   *   *

When Lucas designed his games, he laid them out on sheets of heavy white drawing paper, twenty-two by thirty inches, so he could draw the logical connections between the elements. The visual representation helped him to avoid the inconsistencies that drew sophomorically scathing letters from teen-age gamers.

Back at the house, he got four sheets of paper, carried them to the spare bedroom, and pinned them to the wall with push-pins. With a wide-tip felt pen he wrote the name of one victim at the top of each sheet: Bell, Morris, Ruiz, Lewis. Beneath the names, he wrote the dates, and under the dates, what he hoped were relevant personal characteristics of the victims.

When he finished, he lay back on the bed, propped his head on a pillow, and looked at the wall charts. Nothing came. He got up, put up a fifth one, and wrote "Maddog" at the top of it. Under that he wrote:

Well-off: Wears Nike Airs. Clean clothes. Cologne. Convinced real-estate saleswoman that he could afford expensive home.
May be new to area: Has accent, wore T-shirt on August night.
May be from Southwest: Ruiz recognized accent.
Office job: Soft hands & body, arms white. Not a fighter.
Fair skin: Arms very pale. Probably blond.
Sex freak? Game player? Both? Neither?
Intelligent. Leaves no clues. Wears gloves even when preparing notes, loading shells in pistol.

He thought a moment and added. "Knew Larry Rice?"

He peered at the list, and reached out and underlined "real-estate sales-woman" and "Knew Larry Rice?"

If he was new to the area, maybe he really was looking for a house, and met Lewis that way. It would be worth checking area real-estate offices.

And he might have known Larry Rice. But that worked against the proposition that he was new to the area—if Rice had been dying of cancer, that would presumably take some time, and he wouldn't be making many friends along the way.

A hospital? A doctor in a hospital? It was a possibility. It would account for the maddog's delicate touch with the knife. And a doctor would have the soft hands and body, and would be well-off. And doctors, especially new ones, were mobile. All of these women could have been to a doctor. . . .

He walked back to the library and took down a volume on the history of crime and paged through it. Doctors as murderers had a whole section of their own.

Dr. William Palmer of England killed at least six and maybe a dozen people for their money in the mid-nineteenth century. Dr. Thomas Cream killed half a dozen women with botched abortions and poison in Canada, the U.S., and England; Dr. Bennett Hyde killed at least three in Kansas City; Dr. Marcel Petiot murdered at least sixty-three Jews whom he had promised to smuggle out of Nazi-occupied France; Dr. Robert Clements of England killed his four wives before he was caught. The "torture doctor" of Chicago, who had studied medicine but never quite became a doctor, killed as many as two hundred young women who had been attracted to the city by the 1893 World's Fair. The worst of the bunch, of course, were the Nazis. Medical men associated with the death camps had killed thousands.

The list of doctors who had killed only one or two was lengthy, including several celebrated cases in the United States since the 1950's.

Lucas shut the book, thought about it, and looked at his watch. Two-thirty. Far too late to call. He paced and looked at his watch again. Fuck it. He went into the workroom, got his briefcase with Carla Ruiz' phone number, and called. She answered on the seventh ring.

"Hello?" Half-asleep.

"Carla? Ruiz?"

"Yes?" Still sleepy, but suspicious now.

"This is Lucas . . . the detective. I'm sorry to wake you up, but I'm sitting here looking at some stuff and I need to ask you a question. Okay? Are you awake?"

"Uh, yes."

"When was the last time you saw a doctor and where was it?"

"Uh, gee . . ." There was a long silence. "A couple of years ago, I guess. A woman at the clinic over on the west side."

"You're sure that was the last? No visits to hospitals, nothing like that?"

"No."

"How about with a friend, just stopping by, visiting?"

"No. Nothing like that. I don't think I've been in a hospital since, well, my mother died, fifteen years ago."

"Know any doctors socially?"

"A few come to the gallery, I guess. I don't really know any personally. I mean, I've talked to some at openings and so on."

"Okay. Look, go on back to bed. I'll talk to you tomorrow. And thanks."

He dropped the phone back on the hook. "Shit," he said aloud. It was possible, but a long shot. He made a mental note to check the gallery for regular patrons who were doctors. But it didn't sound good.

He looked at the charts for a few more minutes, yawned, turned out the light, and headed for his bedroom. The guy was smart. Nuts, but smart. A player? Maybe.

Maybe a player.

# 7

Lucas edged into the briefing room, late again.

"Where the fuck you been?" Daniel asked angrily.

"Up late," Lucas said.

"Sit down." Daniel looked around the room. A half-dozen detectives peered into their working notebooks. "To sum up, what we got is about three hundred pages of reports that don't mean diddly-squat. Am I wrong? Somebody tell me I'm wrong."

Harmon Anderson shook his head. "I don't see anything. Not yet. It might be in there, but I don't see it."

"What about this stuff that you got, Lucas?" asked one of the detectives. "Is it reliable?"

Lucas shrugged. "Yeah, I think so. There're a lot of guesses in there, but I think they're pretty good."

"So what?" said Daniel. "So we're looking for a medium-sized white guy who works in an office. That cuts it down to a half-million guys, not including St. Paul."

"Who recently moved up here from the Southwest," said Lucas. "That cuts out another 499,000 guys."

"But that could be bullshit. Probably is," Daniel snorted.

"We might know a little more in a couple of hours," Lucas said. Daniel raised an eyebrow. "The gun guy called last night. I know where the gun went."

"Well, Jesus!" Daniel exploded.

Lucas shook his head. "Don't get your hopes up." He explained how the gun got to Larry Rice and that Rice was dead. "His wife told my man that she doesn't know where the pistol went. Probably sold. Could have been stolen, I suppose."

"Okay, but it's something," said Daniel. "He had the gun for what, six months? And he probably sold it to somebody he knew."

Daniel pointed at Anderson. "Your best man. Best interrogator. Put him on her. We squeeze every goddamned drop out of her. Everybody her old man saw in the last six months. She must know most of them. The killer should be on the list."

"I'm talking to her this afternoon," Lucas said, looking at Anderson. "One o'clock. Your man could meet me there, we'll go in together."

"So are we going to get the name of the guy who took the piece?" asked Daniel.

Lucas shook his head. "No. I swore. You could probably break it out of Rice, if you want, but you really don't want to know. He was doing a kindness. He's a pretty good guy."

Daniel looked at him for a minute and nodded. "Okay. But if it becomes relevant . . ."

"You might be able to break it out of Rice," Lucas repeated. "You won't get it from me."

There was a moment of silence; then Daniel let it go. "We've got another problem," he said. "Somebody fed a story to Jennifer Carey that we have an attack survivor. I'm going to talk to her in ten minutes and try to put her off. Anybody know anything about who tipped her off?"

Nobody answered.

"We can't have this," Daniel said.

One of the detectives cleared his throat. "I might, uh, have an idea about that."

"What?"

"She shot that documentary on St. Paul cops, the one that ran on PBS? She's got sources over there you wouldn't believe."

"Okay. Maybe that's it. So now, we don't talk to St. Paul cops any more than we have to. Be polite, but . . ." He groped for a word. "Reserved." He looked around. "Anything else?"

Lucas opened his notebook and looked at a short list on the back page.

"I'd like to find out about doctors. Did any of these women see the same guy? Ruiz' doctor is a woman, but there may be a few male docs going through her gallery. She could have been picked up there, and we ought to check."

"We can check that," said Anderson.

"How about those change-of-address cards?"

"That's a problem," Anderson said. "We called the post office and they don't have cards for incoming people. Only people moving out. So if we want to check change-of-addresses for people coming to the Cities, we'd have to take the Cities and all the suburb names and go to every post office in the Southwest and check them."

"They're not computerized?"

"Nope. It's done at the local post offices."

"Dammit." Lucas looked at the chief. "What'd it take to check all the major cities down there, ten guys for three weeks? Something like that?"

"Three months is more like it," said Anderson. "I looked in the phone book and there are about eighty post-office branches just in the Minneapolis area, and that doesn't include St. Paul and the St. Paul suburbs. So then I looked at a map and the major cities we'd have to check, and I figure maybe two thousand post offices to cover just the bigger cities. And at each one, we'd have to check for all the different cities and suburbs up here. We'd be lucky if a guy could do three or four a day, even with good cooperation from the post offices."

"Maybe we could work through the post office," Daniel suggested. "Get a list of all the post offices, work out some kind of form they could fill out, and mail it to them. Explain how important it is, call all these places to make sure they're doing it . . ."

"If we did it that way, we could maybe do it with a couple, three guys full-time," said Anderson.

"They wouldn't have to be cops," Daniel said. "Work up a form and I'll talk to the post office. I'll send a couple of clerks over there to handle it."

"Driver's licenses," said one of the detectives.

"What?"

"If he just moved in, he probably had to get a new driver's license. They make you surrender your old one when you move in. The Public Safety people over at the state should have a record."

"Good," said Daniel. "We need that kind of thinking. Check that."

The detective nodded.

"Anything else?" he asked. "Lucas?"

Lucas shook his head.

"All right," said Daniel, "let's do it."


"Detective Davenport."

Lucas turned and saw her walking down the hall, Carla Ruiz, a smile on her face.

"Hi. What are you doing over here?"

She wrinkled her nose. "Divorce stuff. When I moved out of the house, my ex-husband was supposed to sell it and give me half the money. He never sold it and we're trying to get him moving."

"Unpleasant."

"Yeah. It just drags things out. I've been over here a half-dozen times. I'm tired of it."

"Got time for a cup of coffee?" Lucas asked, tilting his head toward the cafeteria.

"Ah, no, I guess not." She glanced at her watch. "I've got to be in the judge's chambers in twelve minutes."

"I'll walk you down to my corner," Lucas said. They fell in together and started toward the tunnel that led to the county courthouse. "Sorry about that weird call last night."

"That's okay. This morning I almost thought it was a dream. Did it help?"

"Oh, I guess. I was thinking maybe a doctor did it. Maybe all the women had the same doctor or something. You just about eliminated that possibility."

"Bet that made you happy," she said, smiling again.

"It's early," he said. They walked along for a minute and Lucas said, "We might have a problem. Involving you."

"Oh?" She was suddenly serious.

"One of the television stations got a tip about you. A reporter, Jennifer Carey, is in talking to the chief right now. She wants an interview."

"Is he going to give her my name?"

"No. He's going to put her off, but it can't hold up. Carey's got good sources over in St. Paul. Sooner or later, she'll find out, and she'll harass the hell out of you."

"So what do we do?"

"We've been thinking it might be better to give her an interview and then give the rest of the stations a press conference with you. Get it over with. That way, we can control it. You won't have people hitting you by surprise."

She thought it over, her face downcast.

"I don't trust those people. Especially TV."

"Carey's about the best of them," Lucas said. "She's a friend of mine, to tell you the truth. I didn't tell her about you, though. I don't know where she got the information. Maybe from St. Paul."

"Would she really be okay?"

"She'd probably do the most sensitive job. After it was done, we'd get you out of town for a few days. When everything cooled off, you could slide back in quietly and probably be okay."

"Can I think about it?" Carla asked.

"Sure. The chief will probably call you about it."

"If I went out of town, would the city pay? It's not like I'm rich."

"I don't know. You could ask the chief. Or if you want to, you can stay in my cabin. I've got a place on a lake up north, in Wisconsin. It's a pretty place, quiet, out-of-the-way."

"That might be okay," she said. "Let me think."

"Sure."

There was a long moment of silence which Lucas broke by asking, "So how long have you been divorced?"

"Almost three years. He's a photographer. He's not a bad guy. He even has some talent, but he doesn't use it. He doesn't do anything. He just sits around. Other people work, he sits. One of the reasons I'm so anxious to get the money out of the house is that it was my money."

"Ah. Good reason."

"I'm looking forward to Aerosmith tonight," she said, "I mean, if it's still on."

"Sure it's on," Lucas said. He stopped at a branching corridor. "I turn here. See you at six?"

"Yes. And I'll think about the TV thing." She walked on, half-turned to wave, and kept going. Nice, he thought as he watched her go.

*　　*　　*

Mary Rice was not very bright. She sat slumped on a kitchen chair, looking nervously at Lucas and Harrison Sloan, the second detective assigned to talk to her. Sloan had the ingratiating manner of a vacuum-cleaner salesman.

"It's very essentially important that we get a complete list from you," he purred, scooting his chair an inch closer to Rice's. He looked like a gynecologist on an afternoon soap opera, Lucas decided. "We would like to get a calendar or something, so we could figure out week by week and day by day who your husband saw."

"I won't tell you the man who gave me the gun," she said, her lower lip quivering.

"That's okay. I talked to him last night and that's all worked out," Lucas assured her. "We do need to know everybody else."

"There aren't very many. I mean, we never had a lot of friends, and then one or two of them died. When Larry got his cancer, some of the others stopped coming around. Larry had to wear this bag come out of his side, you know . . ."

"Yeah," said Lucas, wincing.

"There'll still be quite a few people," said Sloan. "Mailmen, neighbors, any doctors or medical people who came here . . ."

"There was only a nurse," she said.

"But those are the kind of people we're looking for."

Lucas listened for a few more minutes as Sloan worked to relax her, then broke in.

"I have to leave," he told Rice. "Detective Sloan will stay and chat with you, but I have a couple of quick questions. Okay?" He smiled at her and she glanced at Sloan and then back and nodded.

"I'm looking for a white man, probably about my size, probably works in an office somewhere. He might have an accent, kind of southwestern. Kind of cowboy. Probably well-to-do. Does that jog anything in your memory? Do you remember anybody like that?"

She frowned and looked down at her hands, at Sloan, and then around the kitchen. Finally she looked back at Lucas and said, "I don't remember anyone like that. All our friends are white. There haven't been any colored people in here. Nobody with a lot of money that I know of."

"Okay," Lucas said, an impatient edge to his voice.

"I'm trying to remember," she said defensively.

"That's okay," Lucas said. "Did your husband have people here that you didn't know about?"

"Well, he put a sign in the window for some things he wanted to sell. He had some of those little doll things he brought back from the war against the Japs. Those little carvings? Somebody bought those. He got five hundred dollars for fifteen of them. They were real cute things. Like little pigs and rats, all curled around."

"You don't know who that was, who bought them?"

"Oh, I think so. I got some kind of receipt somewhere."

She looked vaguely around the kitchen again.

"Did you ever see the man who bought them?"

"No, no, but I think he was older. You know, Larry's age. I got that idea."

"Okay. Try to find that receipt and give it to Detective Sloan. Was there anybody else?"

"The mailman would stop and talk, he's a younger fellow, maybe forty. And a young fellow came out from the welfare. We weren't on welfare," she said hastily, "but we had some medical assistance coming . . ."

"Sure," said Lucas. "Listen, I'm going to run. We appreciate any cooperation you can give Detective Sloan."

Lucas went out through the kitchen door, let it close behind him, and walked down the steps. As he passed the kitchen window he heard Rice say, ". . . don't like that fellow so much. He makes me nervous."

"Quite a few people would agree with you, Mrs. Rice," Sloan said soothingly. "Can I call you Mary? Detective Davenport is . . ."

"Pushy," said Rice.

"Lot of people would agree with you, Mary. Look, I really hope we can work together to catch this killer . . ."

Lucas smiled and walked out to his car, opened the door, looked inside for a moment, then shut it and walked back to the house.

Inside, Sloan and Rice were looking at a steno pad on which Sloan had written a short list of names. They both looked up when Lucas came back in.

"Could I use your telephone?" Lucas asked.

"Yes, it's right . . ." She pointed at the wall.

Lucas looked in his notebook, dialed and got Carla Ruiz on the second ring.

"This is Lucas. How many times were you in the courthouse on the divorce?"

"Oh, four or five. Why?"

"How about before you were attacked? Right before, or when?"

"Let me go get my purse. I keep an organizer . . ."

He heard the receiver land on the table and looked over at Rice.

"Mrs. Rice, this guy from welfare. Did you have to go down to the county courthouse to see him, or did he come out here, or what?"

"No, no, Larry was disabled when we found out he could get some medical, so this fellow came out here. He came out twice. Nice boy. But I think Larry knew him from before, from work."

"That's a county job. I thought your husband worked for the City of Minneapolis."

"Well, he did, but you know, people go back and forth all the time, between City Hall and the courthouse. Larry's job, he knew everybody. Every time something went wrong, they called him because he could fix anything. He used to see . . . the police officer who gave us the gun down in the cafeteria."

Ruiz was back on the line.

"I was over there three weeks and four weeks before," she said.

"Before you were attacked."

"Yes."

"Thanks. Listen, see you at six, but try to remember everybody you saw in the courthouse, okay?"

"Got something?" asked Sloan when Lucas hung up the phone.

"I don't know. You got the phone number where this Lewis woman worked, the real-estate office?"

"Yeah, I think so." Sloan got out his project notebook, ran down the list, and gave Lucas the number. He dialed and got the office manager and explained what he wanted.

". . . So did she go down there?"

"Oh, sure, all the time. Once a week. She carried a lot of the paperwork for us."

"So she would have been down there before she was killed?"

"Sure. You people have her desk calendars, but she hadn't taken any vacation in the couple of months before she died, so I'm sure she was down there."

"Thanks," Lucas said.

"Well?" said Sloan.

"I don't know," Lucas said. "Two of the women were in the courthouse shortly before they were attacked. Even the woman from St. Paul, and it wouldn't be that common for somebody from St. Paul to be over in the Hennepin County courthouse. And Mr. Rice was there all the time. It would be a hell of a coincidence."

"One of the other women, this Bell, the waitress-punker, was busted out at Target on Lake Street for shoplifting. It wasn't all that long ago. I remember that from our notebooks," Sloan said. "I bet she went to court down there. I don't know about the Morris woman."

"I'll run Morris," Lucas said. "It could be something."

"I got her house number, maybe her husband's there," Sloan said. He flipped open his notebook and read out the number as Lucas dialed. Lucas let it ring twenty times without an answer, and hung up.

"I'll get him later," Lucas said.

"Want me to check on this welfare guy?"

"You might take a look at him," Lucas said. He turned to Rice. "Did the welfare worker have an accent of any kind? Even a little one?"

"No, not that I remember. I know he's from here in Minnesota, he told me that."

"Damn," said Lucas.

"Could be a Svenska," said Sloan. "You get some of those Swedes and

Germans from out in central Minnesota, they still got an accent. Maybe this Ruiz heard the accent and thought it was something like southwestern."

"It's worth a look," Lucas said.


At the office, he called Anderson and got Morris' husband's office. He answered on the first ring.

"Yes, she did," he said. "It must of been about a month before . . . Anyway, she used to work out at a health club on Hennepin Avenue, and about once a week she'd get a parking ticket. She'd just throw it in her glove compartment and forget about it. She must have had ten or fifteen of them. Then she got a notice that they were going to issue a warrant for her arrest unless she came down and paid and cleared this court order. So she went down there. It took most of a day to get everything cleared up."

"Was that the only time she was down there?"

"Well, recently. She might have been other times, but I don't know of any."

When he finished with Morris, Lucas called the clerk of court and checked on Lucy Bell's appearance date on the shoplifting charge. May 27. He looked at a calendar. A Friday, a little more than a month before she was killed.

So they had all been in the courthouse. The gun had come from City Hall, through a guy who hung around the courthouse. Lucas walked down the hall to Anderson's office.

"So what does it mean?" Anderson asked. "He's picking them up right here?"

"Picking them out, maybe," Lucas said. "Three of them were involved in courts and would have court files. Our man could be researching them through that."

"I'll check on who pulled the files," Anderson said.

"Do that."

"So what do you think?" Anderson asked.

"It was too easy," Lucas said. "This cat don't fall that easy."


Aerosmith was fine. Lucas sat back in his seat, watching with amusement as Carla bounced up and down with the music, turning to him, laughing, reaching a fist overhead with the other fifteen thousand screaming fans to shake it at the stage. . . .

She asked him up for coffee.

"That's the most fun I've had since . . . I don't know, a long time," she said as she put two cups of water in the microwave.

Lucas was prowling the studio, looking at her fiber work. "How long have you been doing this?" he asked.

"Five, six years. I painted first, then got into sculpture, and then kind of drifted into this. My grandmother had a loom, I've known about weaving since I was a kid."

"How about this sculpture?" he asked, gesturing at the squidlike hangings.

"I don't know. I think they were mostly an effort to catch a trend, you know? They seemed okay at the time, but now I think I was playing games with myself. It's all kind of derivative. I'm pretty much back to straight weaving now."

"Tough racket. Art, I mean."

"That isn't the half of it, brother," she said. The microwave beeped and she took the cups out, dumped a spoon of instant gourmet coffee into each cup, and stirred.

"Cinnamon coffee," she said, handing him a cup.

He took a sip. "Hot. Good, though."

"I wanted to ask you something," she said.

"Go."

"I was thinking I did pretty well when I fought this guy off," she said.

"You did."

"But I'm still scared. I know what you said the other night, about him not coming back. But I was lucky the first time. He wasn't ready for me. If he comes back, I might not be so lucky."

"So?"

"I'm wondering about a gun."

He thought about it for a minute, then nodded.

"It's worth thinking about," he said. "Most people, I'd say no. When most people buy a gun, they instantly become its most likely victim. The next-most-likely victims are the spouse and kids. Then the neighbors. But you don't have a spouse or kids and you're not likely to get in a brawl with your neighbors. And I think you're probably cool enough to use one right."

"So I ought to get one?"

"I can't tell you that. If you do, you'd be the most likely victim, at least statistically. But with some people, statistics are nonsense. If you're not the type of person to have stupid accidents, if you're not careless, if you're not suicidal or think a gun's a toy, then you might want to get one. There is a chance that this guy will come back. You're the only living witness to an attack."

"I'd want to know what to get," Carla said. She took a sip of coffee. "I couldn't spend too much. And I'd want some help learning to use it."

"I could loan you one, if you like, just until we get the guy," Lucas said. "Let me see your hand. Hold it up."

She held her hand up, fingers spread, palm toward him. He pressed his palm against hers and looked at the length of his finger overlap.

"Small hands," he said. "I've got an older Charter Arms .38 special that ought to fit just about right. And we can get some semiwadcutter loads so you don't get too much penetration and kill all your neighbors if you have to use it."

"What?"

"Your walls here are plaster and lath," Lucas explained. He leaned back and rapped on a wall, and little crumbs of plaster dropped off. "If you use too powerful a round, you'll punch one long hole through the whole building. And anybody standing in the way."

"I didn't think of that." She looked worried.

"We'll fix you up. You live about a hundred yards from the St. Paul police indoor range. I shoot over there in competition. I could probably fix it to give you a few lessons."

"Let me sleep on it," she said. "But I think so."

When he was leaving, she closed the door except for a tiny crack and said as he started down the hall, "Hey, Davenport?"

He stopped. "Yes?"

"Are you ever going to ask me out again?"

"Sure. If you're willing to put up with me."

"I'm willing," she said, and eased the door closed. Lucas whistled on his way to the elevator, and she leaned against the door, listening to the sound of him and smiling to herself.

Late that night, Lucas lay in the spare bedroom and looked at the charts pinned to the wall. After a while he stood and wrote at the bottom of the killer's chart, "Hangs around courthouse."

# 8

He was delighted by the newspapers.

He knew he shouldn't save them. If a cop saw them . . . But then, if a cop saw them, here in his apartment, it would be too late. They would know. And how could he not save them? The inch-high letters were a joy to the soul.

The *Star-Tribune* had SERIAL KILLER SLAYS 3 CITIES WOMEN. The *Pioneer Press* was bigger and better: SERIAL KILLER STALKS TWIN CITIES WOMEN. He liked the word "stalks." It reflected a sense of a continuing process, rather than a historical one; and work that was planned, instead of random.

Purely by chance, on the night the story broke, he saw a nine-o'clock newsbreak promoting it. The station's top reporter, a tall blonde in a trench coat, rapped the harsh word "murder" into a microphone set up outside City Hall. An hour later, he taped TV3's ten-o'clock news report, which replayed key parts of the press conference with the chief of police.

The conference was chaotic. The chief was terse, straightforward. So were the first few questions. Then somebody raised his voice, cutting off a question from another reporter, and the whole conference reeled out of control. At the end, newspaper photographers were standing on chairs in front of the television, firing their strobes at the chief and the half-dozen other cops in the room.

It took his breath away. He watched the tape a half-dozen times, considering every nuance. If only they'd run the whole press conference, he thought; that would be the responsible thing. After thinking about it for a moment or two, he called the station. The lines were busy and it took twenty minutes to get through. When he finally did, the operator put him on hold for a moment, then came back to tell him there were no plans "at the present time" to run the entire conference.

"Might that change?" he asked.

"I don't know," she said. She sounded harassed. "It might. About a million people are calling. You oughta check the *Good-Morning Show* tomorrow. If they decide to run it, they'll say then."

When he got off the phone, the maddog got down on his knees with the VCR instructions and figured out how to program the time controls. He'd want to tape all the major newscasts from now on.

Before he went to bed, he watched the tape one last time, the part with Lucas Davenport. Davenport had been shown in a brief cut, sitting cross-legged in a folding chair. He was wearing jeans and an expensive-looking sport coat. Called the smartest detective on the police force. Working independently.

He got up early for the *Good-Morning Show*, but there was nothing but a rehash of the news from the night before. Later, when he was reading the morning papers, he found a short sidebar on Lucas Davenport in the St. Paul paper, with a small photograph. Killed five people? A *games* inventor? Wonderful. The maddog examined the photo closely. A cruel jawline, he decided. A hard man.


The maddog could barely work during the day, impatiently rushing through the stack of routine real-estate and probate files on the desk before him. He spent a few more minutes with two minor criminal cases he was also handling, but finally pushed those aside as well. The criminal cases were his favorites, but he didn't get many of them. The maddog was recognized in the firm as an expert researcher; but it was already being said that he would not work well before a jury. There was something . . . wrong about him. Nobody said it publicly, but it was understood.

The maddog lived alone near the University of Minnesota, in one of four apartments in a turn-of-the-century house that had been modernized and converted to town houses. He rushed home after work, hurrying to catch the six-o'clock news. There was no more hard information, but TV3 had news crews out all over the city getting reaction from people in the street. The people in the street said they weren't scared, that the police would get him.

A cop in a squad car revealed that he signed himself "maddog," and the newscasters picked it up. The maddog liked it.

After the news, he spent an hour cleaning and squaring his meticulously neat apartment. He usually watched television at night or rental movies on his VCR. That night he couldn't sit still. Eventually he went downtown, from bar to bar, cruising the crowds. He saw a James Dean-wannabe at a fashionable disco, a young man with long black hair and wide shoulders, a T-shirt under a black leather jacket, a cruel smile. He was talking to a girl in a short white dress that showed her legs all the way to her crotch and from the top down almost to her nipples.

*You think he's dangerous,* he thought of the woman, *but it's all a charade. I'm the dangerous one. You don't even see me in my sport coat and necktie, but I'm the one. I'm the One.*

It was time to begin again. Time to begin looking. The need would begin to work on him. He knew the pattern now. In ten days or two weeks, it would be unbearable.

So far he had taken a salesgirl, a housewife, a real-estate agent. How about one out of the pattern? One that would really mess with the cops' minds? A hooker, like in Dallas? No need to hurry, but it was a thought.

He was drifting along, deep in thought, when a voice called his name.

"Hey, Louie. Louie. Over here."

He turned. Bethany Jankalo, God help him. One of the associates. Tall, blonde, slightly buck-toothed. Loud. And, he'd been told, eminently available. She was on the arm of a professorial type, who stood tall, sucked a pipe, and looked at the maddog with disdain.

"We're going to the *Mélange* opening," Jankalo brayed. She had a wide mouth and was wearing fluorescent pink lipstick. "Come on. It's a lot of laughs."

Jesus, he thought, and she's an attorney.

But he fell in with them, Jankalo running her mouth, her escort sucking his pipe, which appeared to be empty and made slurping sounds as he worked it. Together they walked down a block, to a gallery in a gray brick building. There was a small crowd on the walk outside. Jankalo led the way through, using her shoulders like a linebacker. Inside, middle-aged professionals carried plastic glasses of white wine through the gallery while staring blankly at the canvases that lined the eggshell-white walls.

"Who dropped the pizza?" Jankalo laughed as she looked at the first piece. Her escort winced. "What a bunch of shit."

*    *    *

Some of it was not.

The maddog did not know about art; wasn't interested in it. On the walls of his office, he had two duck prints, taken from the annual federal waterfowl stamps. He'd been told they were good investments.

But now his eyes were opened. Most of the work was, indeed, very bad. But Larson Deiree did riveting nudes posed against bizarre situational backdrops. Their contorted bodies caught in explicitly sexual offerings, the recipients of the offers, men in overcoats and broadbrimmed hats and wing-tip shoes, their faces averted, shown as alienated strangers. Power transactions; the women as unequivocal prizes. The maddog was fascinated.

"Have a wine and a cracker, Louie," Jankalo said, handing him a glass of pale yellow fluid and a stack of poker-chip-size crackers.

"Sort of like 'I argued before the Supreme Court in my Living Bra,' huh?" she asked, looking at the Deiree painting behind him.

"I . . ." The maddog groped for words.

"You what?" Jankalo said. "You like that?"

"Well . . ."

"Louie, you're a pervert," she said, her voice so loud it was virtually a shout. The maddog glanced around. Nobody was paying any attention. "That's my kind of man."

"I like it. It makes an argument," the maddog said. He surprised himself. He didn't think in those terms.

"Oh, bullshit, Louie," Jankalo shouted. "He's just hanging some snatch out there to hype the sales."

The maddog turned away.

"Louie . . ."

He thought about killing her. All in an instant, he thought about it.

It would have a certain artistic spontaneity to it. It would, in a way, follow the maxim that he not establish a pattern, because it would not be calculated and planned. And it would be amusing. Jankalo, he didn't doubt, would largely cooperate, right up to the moment the knife went in. He felt a stirring in his groin.

"Louie, you can be such an asshole," Jankalo said, and walked away. She had said, *Louie, you're a pervert . . . my kind of man*. An offer? If so, he'd let it dangle too long. She was headed back to her professor. The maddog was not good in social situations. He took a bite of cracker and looked around, straight into the eyes of Carla Ruiz.

He looked away.

He did not want to catch her eye. The maddog believed that eye contact was telling: that she might look him in the eye and suddenly *know*. They had, after all, shared a considerable intimacy.

He maneuvered so that he could watch her from angles, past others. The cut on her forehead looked bad, the bruises going yellow. The maddog was still badly bruised himself, green streaks on his back and one arm.

Maybe he should come back on her.

No. That would violate too many rules. And the need to do her had passed.

But it was tempting; for revenge, if nothing else, like the farmgirl he'd blown off the horse. The thought of killing made him tingle, pulled at him, like a nicotine addict who had gone too long between cigarettes.

The need would grow. Better start doing research Monday. At the latest.

# 9

Jennifer Carey was staring at him in the dark again.

"What?" he asked.

"What, what?"

"You're staring at me."

"How do you know I'm staring? You're looking the other way," she said.

"I can feel it." Lucas lifted his head until he could see her. She was sitting up, looking down at him. The thin autumn blanket had fallen around her hips and the flickering candle gave her skin a warm pink glow.

"I'm thirty-three," she said.

"Oh, God," he groaned into his pillow.

"I'm taking a leave of absence from reporting. I'll work half-time, producing. Do some free-lance writing."

"You can starve that way," Lucas said.

"I've got money saved." Her voice was level, almost somber. "I've been working since I was twenty-one. I've got that fund from my folks. And I'll still be half-time with the station. I'll be okay."

"What's this about?"

"It's about the old biological clock," she said. "I've decided to have a baby."

Lucas didn't say anything, didn't move. She grinned. "Ah, the nervous bachelor, already scouting escape routes."

There was another long moment of silence. "That's not it," he said finally. "It's just kind of sudden. I mean, I really like you. Are you bailing out? Should I be asking who the lucky guy is?"

"Nope. See, I figured you might not be interested in cooperating with my little plan. On the other hand, from my point of view, it's not that often you meet a guy who is intelligent, physically acceptable, heterosexual, *and* available. I decided I'd have to take things in my own hands, if you know what I mean."

Lucas was on his back staring at the ceiling. Looking down at him, she saw his stomach muscles tighten, and his chest lifted off the bed as though he were levitating, his head coming up, eyes wide.

"Jennifer . . ."

"Yeah. I'm pregnant."

He flopped back on the pillow.

"Oh."

She laughed. "You can be one of the funniest men I know."

"Why is that?"

"I tried to figure out what you'd say when I told you. I thought of everything except 'Oh.' "

He sat up again, his face deeply serious. "We ought to get married. Like tomorrow. I can fix the blood tests—"

She laughed again. "Yo. Davenport. Wake up. I'm not getting married."

"What?"

"Just a few minutes ago you said you liked me, not loved me. For one thing. Besides, I don't want to marry you."

"Jennifer . . ."

"Listen, Lucas. I'm touched by the offer. I wasn't sure you'd make it. And you'd make a wonderful father. But you'd make an awful husband and I couldn't put up with that."

"Jennifer . . ."

"I thought it out."

"What about me, goddammit?" he said. He threw off the blanket and knelt over her, his heavy fists in tight balls, and she dropped flat, suddenly, for the first time afraid of him. "It's my kid too. Right? I mean, it *is* mine?"

"Yes."

"And I don't want my kid being a little fuckin' bastard."

"So what are you going to do, beat me into marriage?"

He looked down at his balled fists and suddenly relaxed. "No, of course not," he said softly. He flopped down beside her.

"Look. I'm going to have the kid," she said. "If you don't want anyone to know he's yours, that's okay. If you don't mind, I'd love to have you around to help. I'll be here in the Cities. I assume you will be too."

"Yeah."

"So we'll really be together."

"No. Not sharing a bed every night. Look, I'm going to tell you. I'm going to spend the next nine months—"

"Seven months."

"—seven months trying to convince you to marry me. If you won't, what would you say about moving in here?"

"Lucas, this house is a men's club. You've got everything but spittoons."

"Listen, I'll tell you what . . ."

"Lucas, we've got months to figure out the exact arrangements. And right now I feel kind of horny again. Something about your reaction. It was much nicer than I expected."

A few minutes later she said, "Lucas, you're not paying attention."

And a few minutes after that she gave up. "It's like trying to make love with a rope. A short rope. No offense."

He didn't laugh. He said, "Jesus Christ, I'm going to have a kid." And then he reached over and placed a hand on her stomach. "I've always wanted a kid. Maybe two or three." He looked at her. "You don't think it could be twins, do you?"

The next morning, Jennifer was peering at herself in the mirror over the bathroom sink and Lucas stopped by the door and looked at her.

"Doesn't show," he said.

"In a month it will," she said. She turned her face to him. "I want the interview with that Chicana chick."

"The chief—"

"I don't care about the chief. I got some more background on her, and I'll go with what I've got unless you set something up. Tonight, tomorrow."

"I'll check."

She looked back in the mirror and stuck her tongue out. "This is going to be weird," she said.

The shower was running when Lucas finished dressing. He hurried in to the kitchen telephone, found Carla's phone number in his pocket directory, and dialed. The shower stopped just as the phone was answered.

"Carla? This is Lucas."

"Yes, hi. What's going on?"

"We're getting some fierce pressure for an interview with you. The woman from TV3, Jennifer Carey, has a leak somewhere. She knows some things about you and it's only a matter of time before somebody tracks you down. It might be better if we went ahead and gave her an interview while we can control things a bit."

There was a moment of silence.

"Okay. If you think so."

"It'll be in the afternoon or early evening. I'll get back to you."

"Should I pack a suitcase?"

"Oh . . . yeah. You want me to go to the chief for a hotel, or you want to try the cabin?"

"How about the cabin? I like the lakes."

"Pack a bag. We'll go up tonight."

Lucas hung up and redialed, calling Daniel on his direct line.

"Linda? I need to talk to the chief."

"He's pretty busy, Lucas. Let me ask."

"Jennifer Carey says she's going with the story about the survivor."

"Hang on."

Jennifer walked down the hall, rubbing her wet hair with a bath towel, and got a bagel out of the refrigerator.

Lucas covered the phone's mouthpiece with the palm of his hand. "Something's happening," he said.

She stopped chewing. "What?"

"I don't know."

Jennifer pulled out a kitchen chair and lowered herself into it as Linda came back on the line. "I'm switching you in," the secretary said.

Daniel was on a second later. "Lucas? I was about to call. You better get down here."

"What's happening?"

"Sloan interviewed this Rice woman about the gun?"

"Yeah, I was there for some of it."

"She mentioned a welfare guy. Sloan put that with your idea that he picks his victims in the courthouse and did some checking. This welfare guy fits a lot of the profile. He's gay. He's in the right age and size slot. And listen to this: he's into art. Sloan was greasing one of the women from the welfare office, got her talking about Smithe, and she was saying what a waste this guy is. Big, good-looking, but she said she went to an opening and saw him there with his boyfriend. Sloan checked with the Ruiz woman. She was at the opening. It was a week before she was hit."

"Damn." Lucas thought for a moment. "I don't know."

"What?"

"Hang on a second. Jennifer Carey is sitting here." Lucas put his hand over the mouthpiece again. "Go on back to the bathroom and shut the door."

"Hey . . ."

"Don't give me any trouble, Jennifer, please? This is a private conversation. We'll have to work out some rules, but right now . . ."

"All right." She stood and flounced out of the room and down the hall, and he heard the door close behind her.

He took his hand off the mouthpiece.

"I sent her back to the bathroom. She's pissed . . . There, the door closed. I'll tell you what, chief, it seems awfully easy. The guy is too smart to be caught that quick. And a week is a pretty short time to check her out."

"Sure, but we only caught him through a freak accident. He didn't plan to lose the gun."

"Then why didn't the brass have prints on them? He used gloves to load the son of a bitch."

"Sure, but I bet he didn't know where the gun came from—that we could trace it. And he is gay. All the shrinks say he will be."

Lucas thought about it. "That's a point," he admitted. "Okay. It sounds like he's worth a check."

"We don't want to fuck up. I think we're going to want you to . . . develop some intelligence on him."

"Okay." Daniel wanted him to bag the guy's house. "Listen, Carey wants to talk with Ruiz. I think I should set it up. It'll keep her off this other thing."

"What does Ruiz think?"

"She seems to be willing. Or I could talk her into it. We could set it up just the way we talked about. That'd keep all the newsies busy while we work on Smithe."

"Do it. And get down here. We're going to meet at ten."

"Come on out," he hollered. He stepped into the hallway and noticed the bathroom door was open. He walked swiftly to the bedroom and pushed the door open. Jennifer was screwing the mouthpiece back on the phone.

"I needed one more minute," she said. It wasn't an apology.

"Goddammit, Jennifer," Lucas said in exasperation.

"I don't take orders about news stuff. Not from cops," she said, tightening the mouthpiece and replacing it on the receiver.

"We gotta work something out," he said, hands on his hips. "What'd you hear?"

"You've got a suspect. He's gay. That's all. And about Ruiz."

"You can't use it."

"Don't tell me—"

"You might think that listening on my private line is something that a real hard news broad would do, but your lawyers wouldn't think it's so cute. Or the station, after they thought about it. The state news council might have a few words about it too. And to tell you the truth, I kind of think this gay guy might not be the right one. If he's not, and you constructively identify him, he'll be the new owner of the station after the libel suit."

"I'll think about it."

"Jennifer, if we're going to have a kid together, we can't play mind games anymore. I've got to trust you. On the cases I'm working on, you only use what I say is okay."

"I don't make that kind of deal."

"You better start or we're going to have trouble. We'll both be sitting around afraid to talk to each other. Besides, it only applies to the cases I'm working on."

She thought it over. "We'll figure something out," she said noncommittally. "I won't cover for you. If I come up with a tip from another source, I'll use it."

"Okay."

"It won't be so much of a problem when I start producing," Jennifer said. "I'll be concentrating on longer-range stuff. Not police stuff."

"That'd be better for both of us. But what about this thing? Will you hold off for now?"

"What about this Ruiz woman?"

"I already called her, while you were in the shower. She says she'll do it. We should be able to set something up for tonight. You heard Daniel, he says to go ahead."

Jennifer thought it over and finally nodded. "Okay. Deal. I'll hold off on the suspect as long as you promise that I get the first break. If there's a break."

"I promise you'll share it."

"God damn, Lucas . . ."

"Jennifer . . ."

"This is going to be hard," she said. "Okay. For now. I'll give you notice if I think I have to change my mind."

He nodded. "I'll call Ruiz again and set up a specific time."


"The guy's name is Jimmy Smithe," Anderson told him as they walked down the hall to the meeting room. "I pulled his personnel file out of the computers and ran it against the psychological profile the shrinks put together and the information we developed. There are some matches."

"How about misses?" Lucas asked. "Does he come from the Southwest?"

"No. As far as I can tell, he was born and raised here in Minnesota, went to the University of Michigan, worked in Detroit for a while, spent some time in New York, and came back here to take a job in welfare."

"You run his sheet?"

"Nothing serious. When he was seventeen the Stillwater cops gave him a ticket for possession of a small amount of marijuana."

"What's his rep with welfare?"

"Sloan says it's pretty good. Smithe is gay, all right, doesn't hide it, but he doesn't flaunt it either. He's smart. He gets along with other people in his department, including the guys. He's up for a promotion to supervisor."

"I don't know, man. He doesn't sound tight enough."

"He's there physically. And we can put him with two people."


When Lucas and Anderson arrived, Daniel was talking to the other eight cops in the room.

"I don't want the word to get out of this group," he said. "We've got to take a close look at this guy without anybody knowing."

He poked a heavy finger at Sloan.

"You hit the neighborhood. Tell them it's a security investigation for a job offer with the department. If we need to back it up, I'll come up with some bullshit about a liaison officer between police and the gay community on AIDS and other problems. What the police can do to help, sensitivity training, all that. They ought to buy it."

"Okay." Sloan nodded.

"Actually, that's not a bad idea," Lucas said.

"We've got enough gays of our own without going outside," Daniel said. He poked a finger at Anderson. "Find out everything you can and cross-check it with the other victims. We've got him with Ruiz. See if we can match up somewhere else.

"Now, you guys," he said to the other six detectives, "are going to watch every move he makes. Two guys all the time, round the clock. Overtime, no problem. You see an eighty-year-old society lady getting gang-banged, you call it in and forget it. You never take your eyes off this motherfucker. You got that? Smithe is the *only* priority. And I want fifteen-minute checks on location. Call it in to Anderson during the day, the duty officer at night."

"My husband's going to love this," one of the women cops muttered.

"Fuck your husband," said Daniel.

"I'd like to," said the cop, "but people keep putting me on nights."

When the meeting broke, he asked Lucas to stay behind.

"You got the Ruiz thing fixed?"

"Yeah. I talked to her just before I came in. We'll do it tonight, at her place. Six o'clock. She's willing, if it'll help, and it'll cool out Carey."

"I hope your dick isn't getting you in trouble with that woman."

"It's under control," Lucas said. "I'll tip the papers and the TV people that you'll be calling a press conference. And I'll talk to the papers about doing their interviews at the same time Carey does hers. We'll be back over here for the press conference at nine. Afterward, I'm going to head up to my cabin for a couple of days. I've got some time coming."

"Jesus, this isn't such a good time for a vacation."

"I've got things covered. I'll leave my number with the shift commander if you need me."

"Okay, but tonight prep Ruiz for making some kind of appeal for coopera- tion, will you? You know the stuff." Daniel leaned back in his chair, put one foot on his desk, looked at his wall of photographs, and changed the subject. "You know what we need."

"Yeah."

"I'll tell Anderson to give you location checks. We already know he lives alone. It's a little house down by Lake Harriet."

"Not far from where Lewis worked. The real-estate woman."

"We thought of that," Daniel said. "He didn't buy the house from her agency, though."

"Look. Don't get too far out front on this thing, okay? I mean you personally," Lucas said. "If there's a leak to the press, tell them that you're looking at a guy, but you think it's thin."

"You don't believe it?"

"I've got a bad feeling."

"Can you get something going this afternoon? That might tell us something."

"I'll give it a shot."

Nobody said anything about a bag job.

From his office, Lucas called the newspapers and television stations and tipped friends that Daniel would be calling a press conference. He talked separately to assignment editors from both papers and suggested that they keep a soft-touch reporter around late, that there'd be a good next-day story breaking around six o'clock.

That done, he got Smithe's address and phone number from Anderson and found the house on a city map. He knew the neighborhood. He thought about it for a minute, pursing his lips, then opened the bottom drawer of his desk, reached far into the back, and found the lock rake. It was battery-operated, roughly the same shape but only half the size of an electric drill, with two prongs sticking out where the drill bit would have been. One prong was bent, the other straight. Lucas unscrewed the butt cap, reversed the batteries into working position, and squeezed the trigger. The picks rattled for a second and he released the pressure and sighed.

Smithe's house was tan stucco with a postage-stamp lawn. Fifteen-foot-tall junipers flanked the concrete steps that led to the front door. There were only occasional people on the quiet streets around the house. Lucas cruised by twice, then drove out to a street phone.

"Anderson."

"This is Davenport. Where's Smithe?"

"Just had a call. He's at his desk."

"Thanks."

Next he dialed Smithe's number and let it ring. After the thirtieth ring he took a pair of wire cutters from the glove compartment, looked around, nipped off the receiver, and dropped it on the floor of the car. If the receiver was gone, there was little chance that a passerby would manually disconnect the phone.

The Porsche was too noticeable to park outside Smithe's house. Lucas dropped it a block away and walked down the street, the pick in his jacket pocket. A kid was pedaling a bike along the street and Lucas slowed and let him pass. At Smithe's house he turned in and walked straight up to the steps without looking around.

He could hear the phone ringing from the porch. The lock was an original, from a door that was probably installed in the fifties. The pick took it out in less than a minute. Lucas pushed the door open with his knuckles and stuck his head inside.

"Here, boy," he called. He whistled. Nothing. He stepped inside and pushed the door shut.

The house was still and smelled faintly of some chemical. What? Wood polish? Wax. Lucas cruised quickly through the ground floor on a preliminary survey, stopping only to lift the ringing phone, silencing it.

The living room was sparsely but tastefully furnished with an overstuffed couch-and-chair set and a teardrop glass coffee table from the fifties. The kitchen was a pleasant, sunny room with yellow tiles and a half-dozen plants perched on the counter near the window. There was a bathroom with a cast-iron tub, a small bedroom with a double bed pushed into a corner, an empty chest of drawers, and a desk and chair, apparently used as an office and a guest bedroom. He checked the drawers in the desk and found bills, financial statements, and copies of income-tax returns.

The master bedroom had been converted into a media room, with a set of five-foot-tall speakers and a twenty-seven-inch television facing a long, comfortable couch. One wall of the media room was lined with photos. Smithe stood next to a smiling older couple that Lucas assumed were his parents. Another photo showed him with two other men, all showing a strong family resemblance, probably his brothers; they were dressed in high-school wrestling uniforms, flexing their biceps for the camera. There was a picture of Smithe throwing hay off a rack with his father. Smithe with a diploma. Smithe with a male friend on the streets of New York, arms wrapped around each other's waists.

Where's the bedroom? Lucas went down the hall, found the stairs going up. The bedroom ran the whole length of the house and featured a king-size bed still rumpled from the night before. Jeans, underwear, and other pieces of clothing were scattered around on chairs. A bookcase held a few books, mostly science fiction, and a small selection of gay skin magazines. Lucas looked at the chest of drawers. Keys, cologne, a money clip with the insignia of Ducks Unlimited, a small jewelry box, a photo of Smithe with another man, both bare from the waist up, arms around each other's shoulders.

Lucas pulled open the top drawer. Prophylactics. Two boxes, one of lubricated, the other nonlubricated, both boxes about half-empty. He took one of the lubricated variety and dropped it in his pocket. Ran through the rest of the drawers: a bundle of letters from a man named Rich, fastened together with a rubber band. Lucas looked at two: chatty letters from an ex-lover. No threats, no recriminations.

Checked the closet. Athletic shoes, five pairs. Adidas, Adidas, Adidas, Adidas, and Adidas. No Nike Airs. Down the stairs, into the bathroom. The medicine chest had four bottles of prescription drugs: two penicillin, one of them expired, a weak painkiller, a tiny bottle of ophthalmological ointment.

Through the kitchen, the basement stairs, and down. Basement unfinished. A gun rack with three shotguns. The back room: weights. A full set, with an elaborate weight bench. Pictures of weight lifters in full grease, pumped and flexed. A handmade exercise chart, with checks next to the days of the week when each exercise was completed. He didn't miss often.

Back out to the main room. A chest of drawers. More guns? Lucas ran through it, nothing but tools. Up the stairs, through the living room. Two nice drawings, both in charcoal, nudes of long sinuous women. Glanced at the watch: in nine minutes now.

Into the office. Pulled out drawers. Financial records, letters. Nothing interesting. Brought up IBM computer. Loaded Word Perfect. Loaded files disks. Letters, business correspondence. Smithe worked at home. Nothing like a diary.

Last check. Looked at the photos in the media room again. Happy, Lucas thought. That was what he looked like.

Checked watch. Seventeen minutes. And out.


He stopped at Daniel's office.

"What?" Daniel looked harassed.

Lucas dipped into his pocket, took out the packaged ring of the prophylactic, tossed it on the desk. Daniel looked down without touching it, then back up.

" 'Share,' " he read from the pack. He looked up at Lucas. "The notebooks have a list that the lab made up, the rubbers that use the kind of lubricant they found in the women."

"Yeah."

"This one on it?"

"Yeah."

"God damn. We got anything we can make a warrant with?"

"It'd be thin."

Daniel reached out and pushed an intercom button.

"Linda, get Detective Sloan for me. Detective Anderson down in homicide should be able to reach him. I want to talk to him right away."

He took his finger off the button and looked at Lucas. "Any problems out there?"

"No."

"I don't want you on TV for the next few days. Stay out of sight at this press conference just in case somebody saw you on the street."

"Okay. But I got in clean."

"Christ, if this is the guy, we're going to look good. Out in Los Angeles they can chase these guys for years, and some of them they never catch." Daniel ran his fingers through his hair. "It's gotta be him."

"Don't think like that," Lucas said urgently. "Think cool. When we pick somebody up, the media's going to go berserk. If it's not him, you'll be dangling from a tree limb. By your balls. Especially with the gay politics around here."

"All right, all right," Daniel said unhappily. He swung one hand in the air as though brushing away gnats. The phone rang and he snatched it up.

"Yeah. We've been waiting." He looked at Lucas and mouthed "Sloan." "Did you ever check that list of houses Lewis sold? . . . Yeah. How many? . . . What about dates? . . . Huh. Okay. Stay with that, pick up any more you can find. Talk to her boyfriend, see what bars they went to, any that we might cross with Smithe. . . . Yeah. We might be going for a warrant. . . . What? . . . Wait a minute."

Daniel looked up at Lucas.

"Sloan says the garbage pickup is tomorrow. He wants to know if he should grab the garbage if Smithe brings any out."

"Good idea. It's not protected; we don't need a warrant. If we find anything in it, that could build the warrant for us."

Daniel nodded and went back to the phone. "Grab the garbage, okay. And good work. . . . Yeah." He slammed the phone back on the hook.

"Lewis sold a house the next block over. Seven weeks before she was killed."

"Oh, boy, I don't know—"

"Wait, listen. Sloan's been talking to people out there. Smithe is a jogger and he jogs down that same block almost every summer evening. Right past the house she sold."

"That's weak."

"Lucas, if we get one more thing, anything, I'm going in for a warrant. We've got Laushaus on the bench, he'd give us a warrant to search the governor's underwear. With the governor in it."

"It's not getting the warrant I'm worried about. I'm worried about the reaction."

"I'll handle it. We'll be careful."

Lucas shook his head. "I don't know. I've got a feeling that everybody's starting to run in one direction." He glanced at his watch. "I've got to make some calls on the Ruiz interview. Take it easy, huh?"


Lucas talked to an assignment editor at the *Pioneer Press:*

"Wally? Lucas Davenport."

"Hey, Lucas, how's the hammer hangin'?"

"Wonderful expression, Wally. Where'd you hear that?"

"I thought the pigs talked like that. Excuse me, I meant cops. Just trying to be friendly."

"Right. You got one of your hacks who can meet me on the front porch of the St. Paul cop shop, say about six o'clock?"

"What's up?"

"Well, to tell you the truth, we got a survivor from a maddog attack and we're going public."

"Whoa. Hold on."

There was a series of muffled exclamations on the other end of the line, then a new voice, female. Denise Ring, the city editor.

"Lucas, this is Denise. Where'd this woman come from?"

"Hey, Denise. How's the hammer hangin'?"

"What?"

"Wally just asked me how the hammer was hangin'. I thought it was newspaper talk."

"Fuck you, Lucas. And fuck Wally. What's with this survivor?"

"We got one. We held back, because we needed to talk to her a lot. But Jennifer Carey found out about it—"

"From you?"

"No. I don't know where she heard it. St. Paul cops, I think."

"You're sleeping with her."

"Jesus Christ, does everybody read my mail?"

"Everybody knows. I mean, we figured it was just a matter of time. She was the last available woman in town. It was either her or you'd have to start dating out-state."

"Look, Denise, you want this story or what?"

"Yeah. Don't get excited."

"Jennifer said she was going public, whether we cooperated or not, so we talked to the survivor and she said she'd be willing to make an appeal. Jennifer wanted it exclusive, but Daniel said no. Said to call you and the *Star-Tribune*, so that's what I'm doing."

"Six o'clock? Cammeretta will be there. How about art?"

"Send a photographer. Jennifer will have a camera."

"Is that what this press conference is about at nine?"

"Yeah. The survivor'll be talking in public to the other stations, but you and TV3 and the *Strib* will have the exclusive stuff from the six-o'clock meeting."

"Not exclusive for us. Jennifer will have it first."

"But not as much—"

"And the *Strib* will be there with us."

"But I'm sure you'll do it better."

"We always do," Ring said. "Okay. Six o'clock. What'd you say her name was?"

Lucas laughed. "Susan B. Anthony. Wait. Maybe I got that wrong. I'll know for sure at six."

"See you then," Ring said.

Lucas tapped the cut-off button, redialed the *Star-Tribune*, gave the assignment editor the same story, and then called Carla.

"You'll be there, right?" She sounded worried.

"Yeah. I'll come over about five and we'll talk about what you want to say. Then when it's time, I'll walk over to the station and get them. That'll be about six. It'll be Jennifer Carey from TV3, a cameraman, two newspaper reporters, and two newspaper photographers. I know all of them and they're pretty good people. We'll break it off about seven. Then we'll go out for something to eat and come over here to Minneapolis for the press conference. We can talk about that on the way over."

"Okay. I'm going to do my hair. What else?"

"Wear a plain blouse. Not yellow. Light blue would be good if you've got one. Jeans are fine. Stay away from the makeup. Just a touch of lipstick. Jennifer's pretty good. You'll do fine."


"I'm Jennifer Carey. How are you?"

"I'm fine. I see you on the news . . ."

Lucas watched them talk as Jennifer's cameraman, the two newspaper reporters, and the two photographers looked curiously around the studio. Jennifer was watching Carla's face closely, gauging her reactions, smiling, encouraging her to talk.

"Okay, listen, guys," Jennifer said finally, turning to the newspaper people. "Why don't we do it this way. I need camera time, so why don't we have Carla tell her story for you guys and we'll film that, and you can get your pictures. That'll let Carla get what she wants to say in mind. Then we'll do our interview."

"I'll want to stay around for your interview," said the *Star-Tribune* reporter. The *Pioneer Press* reporter nodded.

"No problem, but no breaking in."

Lucas watched as the two newspaper reporters extracted the story from Carla. She relaxed under the friendly attention, becoming almost ebullient as she told how the killer had fled for his life. After fifteen minutes Lucas called for a time-out.

"We've got to make the press conference at nine o'clock," he said to Jennifer. "You better get started."

"We'd like to get you to walk through it, just show us where the guy grabbed you, and what happened from there. Use it for the art, the pictures," said one of the newspaper photographers.

Carla re-created it, starting from the door, a mime of a woman carrying groceries and then suddenly attacked. As she walked about, becoming increasingly animated, the photographers danced around her, their strobes flickering like lightning.

When they were done, Jennifer led her through it again, acting the part of the attacker. When that was done, the two women sat and chatted, the cameraman taking frontal and reverse shots of both, with facial close-ups.

"Okay. Is there anything we missed?" asked Jennifer. She glanced at her watch.

"I don't think so," said Carla.

"We all done, guys?" she asked the other reporters. They both nodded.

"Okay, I'm shutting it down," Lucas said. "Nobody gets back in for a last word. If you think of anything you *must* have, get it from your guys at the press conference. Okay? Everybody cool?"

He ushered them out five minutes later.

"What do you think?" he asked Carla after they were gone.

"It was interesting," she said, her eyes bright.

"Yeah, well, the press conference will be different. Lots of very quick questions, maybe nasty. Don't mention this interview or the other stations will go crazy. By the time they see TV3, we want you out of sight."


On the way to the press conference, Carla said, "How long have you known Jennifer Carey?"

He glanced across at her. "Years. Why?"

"She stood in your space. And you didn't notice. That usually means . . . intimacy at some level."

"We've been friends for a long time," Lucas said neutrally.

"Have you slept with her?"

"We don't know each other well enough to talk about that kind of thing," he said.

"Sounds like a big *yes* to me," she said.

"Jesus."

"Hmm."


The press conference was short, loud, and finally nasty. The chief spoke after Carla.

"Do you have any suspects?" one reporter shouted.

"We are checking all leads—"

"That means no," the reporter shouted.

"No, it doesn't," Daniel said. Lucas winced.

"Then you *do* have a suspect," a woman called.

"I didn't say that."

"You want to tell us what you're saying? In short words?"

An hour after the press conference, whipping north along I-35 in Lucas' Porsche, Carla was still hyper.

"So you'll have tapes of Jennifer's interview?"

"Yeah, the recorder's set. You can look at them when you get back."

"It sure went downhill after the chief called that guy a jerk," Carla said.

Lucas laughed. "I loved it. The guy *was* a jerk. But it chilled out Daniel, too. That's good. He'll be more careful."

"And you're not going to tell me about the suspect?"

"Nope."

It was a three-hour drive to Lucas' cabin. They stopped at a general store to stock up on groceries and Lucas chatted with the owner for a minute about fishing. "Two large last week," the owner said.

"How big?"

"Henning, the doctor, the row-troller? He got one forty-eight and a half inches off the big island in those weeds. He figured thirty-two pounds. Then some guy on the other side of the lake, tourist from Chicago, I think he was fishing out of Wilson's, took a twenty-eight-pounder."

"Henning release it?"

"Yeah. He says he's not keeping anything unless there's a chance it'll go forty."

"Could be a long wait. There aren't that many guys in the North Woods with a forty-pound musky on the wall."

"It's beautiful," Carla said, looking out at the lake.

"Doesn't hurt to have the moon out there. It's almost embarrassing. It looks like a beer ad."

"It's beautiful," she repeated. She turned back into the cabin.

"Which bedroom should I take?" He pointed her back to the corner.

"The big one. Might as well take it, since I won't be here. There's a bike in the garage, it's a half-mile out to the general store, three miles into town. There's a boat down at the dock. You ever run an outboard?"

"Sure. I used to go north with my husband every summer. One thing he could do was fish."

"There are a half-dozen rods in a rack on the porch and a couple of tackle boxes under the glider, if you want to try some fishing. If you go off the point out there, around the edges of the weed bed, you'll pick up some northern."

"Okay. You going back right now?"

"In a little while. I'll stick the food in the refrigerator and then I'm going to have a beer and sit out on the porch for a while."

"I'm going to get changed, take a shower," Carla said.

Lucas sat on the glider and kept it gently swinging, his feet flexing against the low window ledge below the screen. The nights were getting cool and there was just enough wind to bring in the scent and the sound of the pines. A raccoon crossed through the yard light of a neighboring cabin, heading back toward the garbage cans. From the other way, a few lots down the lake, a woman laughed and there was a splash. From the cabin behind him, the shower stopped running. A few minutes later, Carla came out on the porch.

"You want another beer?"

"Mmm. Yeah. One more."

"I'm going to have one."

She was wearing a pink cotton robe and rubber shower shoes. She brought back a Schmidt and handed it to him, sat next to him on the glider, and curled her legs beneath her. Her hair was wet and the drops of water glistened like diamonds in the indirect light from the windows.

"A little cool now," she said. "You ever come up here in winter?"

"I come up here every chance I get. I come up in the winter and ski, cross-country. There are trails all over the place. You can ski for miles."

"Sounds great."

"You're invited," Lucas said promptly.

As they talked he could feel the warmth coming off her, from the shower.

"Are you getting cold?"

"Not yet. Maybe in a few minutes. Right now it feels fresh." She turned and leaned backward, her head on his shoulder. "It doesn't seem like a cop ought to have a place like this. I mean, a drug-and-vice guy with a Porsche."

"Doctor's orders. I got so I was doing nothing but work," he said. He eased an arm behind her shoulder. "I'd be on the street all day and sometimes half the night, then I'd go home and work on my games. I'd get so cranked I couldn't sleep even when I was so tired I couldn't walk. So I went in to see the doc. I thought I ought to get some legal downers and he said what I really needed was a place not to work. I never work up here. I mean, never money-work. I chop wood, fix the garage, work on the dock, all that. But I don't money-work."

"Guess what?" Carla said.

"What?"

"I don't have a goddamn thing on under this robe." She giggled a beer giggle.

"Jeez. Absolutely buck naked, huh?"

"Yep. I figured, why not?"

"So can I consider this an official pass?"

"Would you rather not?"

"No, no, no no no." He leaned forward and kissed her on the jaw just below her ear. "I was desperately figuring my chances. I'd been such a nice guy all along, it seemed sort of crass to suddenly start hustling."

"That's why I decided to come on to you," she said. "Because you weren't rushing me like some guys."

Much later in the night, she said, "I've got to sleep. I'm really starting to feel the day."

"Just one thing," he said in the dark. "When we went through that routine up in your apartment the first time I interviewed you, you said the guy who jumped you felt softer than me. You still think that?"

She was silent for a moment, then said, "Yes. I have this distinct impression that he was a little . . . not porky, but fleshy. Like there was fat under there and that he wasn't terribly muscular. I mean, he was a lot stronger than I am, but I only weigh a little over a hundred pounds. I don't think he's a tough guy."

"Shit."

"Does that mean something?"

"Maybe. I'm afraid it might."

Early the next morning Lucas walked out to his car, fished under the seat, and retrieved a Charter Arms .38 special revolver in a black nylon holster and two boxes of shells. He carried them back to the house.

"What's that?" Carla asked when he brought it in.

"A pistol. You thought you might need one."

"Hmm." Carla closed one eye and squinted at him with the other. "You brought it up with you, but didn't bring it out last night. That suggests you expected to stay over."

"A subject which does not merit further exploration," Lucas declared with a grin. "Get your shoes on. We've got to take a hike."

They went into the woods across the road from Lucas' cabin, followed a narrow jump-across stream that eventually became a long damp spot, then turned into a gully that led into the base of a steep hill. They came out on a grassy plateau facing a sandy cutbank.

"We'll shoot into the cutbank," Lucas said. "We'll start at ten feet and move back to twenty."

"Why so close?"

"Because if you're any further away, you ought to run or yell for help.

Shooting is for close-up desperation," Lucas said. He looked around and nodded toward a downed log. "Let's go talk about it for a minute."

They sat on the log and Lucas pulled the pistol apart, demonstrated the function of each piece and how to load and unload it. He was clicking the brass shells into the cylinder when they heard a chattering overhead. Lucas looked up and saw the red squirrel.

"Okay," he whispered. "Now, watch this."

He pivoted slowly on the log and lifted the weapon toward the squirrel.

"What are you going to do?"

"Show you what a thirty-eight will do to real meat," Lucas said, his eyes fixed on the squirrel. The animal was half-hidden behind a thick limb on a red pine but occasionally exposed its entire body.

"Why? Why are you going to kill it?" Carla's eyes were wide, her face pale.

"You just don't know what a bullet will do until you see it. Gotta stick your fingers in the wounds. Like Doubting Thomas, you know?"

"Hey, don't," she commanded. "Come on, Lucas."

Lucas pointed the weapon at the squirrel, both eyes open, waiting.

"Hit the little sucker right between the eyes, never feel a thing . . ."

"Lucas . . ." Her voice was up and she clutched at his gun arm, dragging it down. She was horrified.

"You look horrified."

"Jesus Christ, the squirrel didn't do anything . . ."

"You feel scared?"

She dropped her arm and turned cold. "Is this some kind of lesson?"

"Yeah," Lucas said, turning away from the squirrel. "Hold on to that feeling you had. You felt that way for a squirrel. Now think about unloading a thirty-eight into a human being."

"Jesus, Lucas . . ."

"You hit a guy in the chest, not through the heart, but just in the chest and you'll blow up his lungs and he'll lie there snorting out this bright red blood with little bubbles in it and usually his eyes look like they're made out of wax and sometimes he rocks back and forth and he's dying and there's not a thing that anybody can do about it, except maybe God—"

"I don't want the gun," she said suddenly.

Lucas held the weapon up in front of his face. "They're awful things," he said. "But there's one thing that's even more awful."

"What's that?"

"When you're the squirrel."

He gave her the basics of close-in shooting, firing at crude man-size figures drawn in the sand of the cutbank. After thirty rounds she began hitting the figures regularly. At fifty, she developed a flinch and began to spray shots.

"You're jerking the gun," Lucas told her.

She fired again, jerking the gun. "No I'm not."

"I can see it."

"I can't."

Lucas swung the cylinder out, emptied it, put three shells in random chambers, and handed the pistol back to her.

"Shoot another round."

She fired another shot, jerking the weapon, missing.

"Again."

This time the hammer hit an empty chamber and there was no shot, but she jerked the pistol out of line.

"That's called a flinch," Lucas said.

They worked for another hour, stopping every few minutes to talk about safety, about concealment of the gun in her studio, about combat shooting.

"It takes a lot to make a really good shot," Lucas told her as she looked at the weapon in her hand. "We're not trying to teach you that. What you've got to do is learn to hit that target reliably at ten feet and at twenty feet. That shouldn't be a problem. If you ever get in a situation where you need to shoot somebody, point the gun and keep pulling the trigger until it stops shooting. Forget about rules or excessive violence or any of that. Just keep pulling."

They fired ninety-five of the hundred rounds before Lucas called a halt and handed her the weapon, loaded with the last five rounds.

"So now you'll have a loaded gun around the house," he said, handing it to her. "You carry it back, put it where you think best. You'll find that it's kind of a burden. It's the knowledge that there's a piece of Death in the house."

"I'll need more practice," she said simply, hefting the pistol.

"I've got another three hundred rounds in the car. Come out here every day, shoot twenty-five to fifty rounds. Check yourself for flinching. Get used to it."

"Now that I've got it, it makes me more nervous than I thought it would," Carla said as they walked back to the cabin. "But at the same time . . ."

"What?"

"It feels kind of good in my hand," she said. "It's like a paintbrush or something."

"Guns are great tools," Lucas said. "Incredibly efficient. Very precise. They're a pleasure to use, like a Leica or a Porsche. A pleasure in their own right. It's too bad that to fulfill their purpose, you've got to kill somebody."

"That's a nice thought," Carla said.

Lucas shrugged. "Samurai swords are the same way. They're works of art that are complete only when they're killing. It's nothing new in the world."

As they crossed the road back to the cabin, she asked, "You've got to go?"

"Yeah. I've got a game."

"I don't understand that," she said. "The games."

"Neither do I," Lucas said, laughing.

*   *   *

He took his time driving back to the Twin Cities, enjoying the countryside, resolutely not thinking about the maddog. He arrived after six, checked Anderson's office, found that he had gone home for the evening.

"Sloan's still out somewhere," the shift commander said. "But nobody's told me to look for anything special."

Lucas left, changed clothes at home, stopped at a Grand Avenue restaurant in St. Paul, ate, and loafed over to St. Anne's.

"Ah, here's Longstreet, slow as usual," Elle said. Even as General Robert E. Lee she wore her full habit, crisp and dark in the lights of the game room. A second nun, who wore conventional street dress and played the role of General George Pickett, was flipping through a stack of movement sheets. The attorney, Major General George Gordon Meade, commander in chief of the Union armies, and the bookie, cavalry commander General John Buford, were studying their position on the map. A university student, who played General John Reynolds in the game, was punching data into the computer. He looked up and nodded when Lucas came in. The grocer, Jeb Stuart, had not yet arrived.

"Talking game-wise," the bookie said to Lucas, "you've got to do something about Stuart. Maybe take him out as a playable character. He keeps getting loose, and when he gets word to Lee, it changes everything."

Lucas relaxed and started arguing. He was in his place. The grocer arrived ten minutes later, apologizing for his tardiness, and they started. The battle went badly for the Union. Stuart was getting scouts back to the main force, so Lee knew the bluecoats were coming. He concentrated on Gettysburg more quickly than had happened in historical fact, and Pickett's division—marching first instead of last—brushed aside Buford's cavalry, pressed through the town, and captured Culp's Hill and the north end of Cemetery Ridge.

They left it there. Late that evening, as they sat around the table talking over the day's moves, the attorney brought up the maddog.

"What's happening with this guy?" he asked.

"You looking for a client?" asked Lucas.

"Not unless he's got some major bucks," the attorney said. "This is the kind of case that will stink up the whole state. But it's interesting. It could be a hard case for you to make, actually, unless you catch him in the act. But the guy who gets him off . . . he's going to smell like a buzzard."

"Some of the people playing *this* game have noticed a buzzardlike odor," the grocer said. He was feeling expansive. He was rehabilitating old J.E.B. Stuart, making him a hero again.

The lawyer rolled his eyes. "So what's happening?" he asked Lucas. "You gonna catch him?"

"Not much progress," Lucas said, peeling a chunk of cold pizza out of a greasy box. "What do you do with a fruitcake? There's no way to track him. His mind doesn't work like an ordinary crook's. He's not doing it for money. He's not doing it for dope, or revenge, or impulsively. He's doing it for pleasure. He's taking his time. It might not be quite at random—we've found a few patterns—but for practical purposes, they don't help much. Like the fact that he attacks dark-haired women. That's maybe only thirty or forty percent of the women in the Cities, which sounds pretty good until you think about it. When you think about it, you realize that even if you eliminate the old women and the children, you're talking about, what, a quarter-million dark-haired possibilities?"

The bookie and the grocer nodded. The other nun and the student chewed pizza. Elle, who had been fingering the long string of rosary beads that swung by her side, said, "Maybe you could bring him in to you."

Lucas looked at her. "How?"

"I don't know. He fixates on people and we know the type. But if you put out a female decoy, how would you know he'd even see her? That's the problem. If you could get a decoy next to him, maybe you could pull him into an attack that you're watching."

"You've got a nasty mind, Sister," the bookie said.

"It's a nasty problem," she answered. "But . . ."

"What?" The lawyer was looking at her with a small smile on his face.

"Interesting," she said.

# 10

"Daniel's hunting for you." Anderson looked harassed, teasing his thinning blond hair as he stepped through Lucas' office doorway. Lucas had just arrived and stood rattling his keys in his fist.

"Something break?"

"We might go for a warrant."

"On Smithe?"

"Yeah. Sloan spent the night going through his garbage. Found some wrappers from rubbers that use the same kind of lubricant they found in the women. And they found a bunch of invitations to art shows. The betting is, he *knows* this Ruiz chick."

"I'll talk to the chief."

*       *       *

"Where have you been?" Daniel asked.

"My cabin. I ditched Ruiz up there," Lucas said.

Daniel snapped his fingers, remembering. "That's right. Dammit. I didn't know she was going with you. How come your cabin?"

Lucas shrugged. "She would only give the interview if we could get her away afterward. This seemed simpler than trying to get the city to keep her in a hotel."

Daniel's eyes narrowed; then he gave Lucas a tiny nod. "So what is it, three hours up there?"

"Yeah."

"Okay. We're going to turn you back around. We want you to show her a photo spread, see if she can pick out Smithe. Take the chopper up."

"Anderson said you're going for a warrant," Lucas said.

"Maybe. Once we knew what we were looking for, we had Sloan go through the garbage scrap by scrap. Sure enough, he found some wrappers from those Share rubbers. So we got him with Rice, we know he's been at the same art shows as Ruiz, and he very well might have seen Lewis. Then this punk chick, she hung out at the clubs off Hennepin, mixing it up with the gays on the streets, he could have bumped into her there. And we got the lubricant, and the opportunity to meet them here in the courthouse. And he's gay. Depending on what you get, we could go for it. We've got Laushaus ready to sign whatever we need."

"We could find twenty guys who fit the same pattern."

"What's your problem with this, Davenport?" Daniel asked in exasperation. "You've taken guys down on one-tenth of what we got."

"Sure. But I knew I was right. This time we might be wrong. All we've got is the easy stuff, and nothing else. I think he's a workout freak; Ruiz said the attacker was soft. This guy's a native Minnesotan; Ruiz said he has a southwestern accent. Ruiz says the guy wears Nike Air shoes; he didn't have any Nike Airs in his closet. Eight pairs of shoes, but no Nike Airs."

"There's the rubber."

"That's the only thing, and that's not definitive."

"He knows guns."

"Not handguns. There wasn't a handgun in the place."

"Listen, just get up there with the pictures," Daniel said. "They've got a package for you down at the lab."

"Will you make the call on the warrant? Or you going to let homicide do it?"

"I've been pretty deep in this," Daniel said. "I wouldn't want to shove the responsibility off on somebody else."

"Let homicide make the call," Lucas urged. "They'll do what you want, but you'll be able to change your mind if there's a problem. And something else. Maybe you ought to suggest that they keep the warrant in their pocket. Ask the guy to come in, get him a lawyer, tell him that you have the warrant, and then if he can come up with anything that cools the case, you just pitch the warrant and shake his hand."

"He might not go for that."

"Man, I'm getting real bad vibes from this thing."

"We got people being killed," Daniel said. "What if we're right and we just let it go and he gets another one?"

"Put a heavier net around him. If he tries, we've got him."

"What if he waits for three weeks? Have you seen the television? It's like the Ayatollah and the hostages. 'Day Fifteen of the Maddog's Reign of Terror.' That'll be next."

"Goddammit, chief . . ."

Daniel waved him off. "I'll think about it. You get up there and show the mugs to Ruiz. Call back and tell us what she says."


Lucas tried to call Carla from the station and from the airport, but there was no answer.

"Get her?" asked the pilot.

"No. I'll find her when we get up there."

The chopper cut the travel time to the cabin to less than an hour, sweeping across the high-colored hardwood forests and the transition zone into the deep green of the North Woods. The pilot dropped the aircraft beside a road intersection three hundred yards out from the cabin, and he and Lucas walked in with the manila envelopes full of photos. Carla was waiting by the back porch.

"I was out in the boat and I heard the helicopter. I couldn't think of anybody else that it might be for. What happened?" She looked curiously from one to the other.

"We want you to look at some pictures," Lucas said as they went inside. He gestured at the pilot. "This is Tony Rubella. He's the helicopter pilot but he's also a cop. I'm going to record the interview."

Lucas put his tape recorder on the table, said a few test words, ran the cassette back, and listened until he was satisfied that it was working. Then he started it again and read in the time, date, and place.

"Conducting the interview is Lucas Davenport, lieutenant, Minneapolis Police Department, with Officer Anthony Rubella, Minneapolis Police Department. Interviewee is Miss Carla Ruiz of St. Paul. Carla Ruiz is well-known to Officer Davenport as the victim of an attack in her residence by a man believed to have committed a series of murders in the city of Minneapolis. We will show Ruiz a photo array of twelve men and ask if she recognizes any of them."

Lucas dumped a dozen photographs on the table, all of young men, all shot on the street, all vaguely similar in appearance, size, and dress. Eleven of them were cops or police-department clerical personnel. The twelfth was Smithe.

Lucas arranged them in a single row and Carla leaned over them and studied the faces.

"I know this guy for sure," she said, tapping one of the cop photos. "He's a cop. He works off-duty as a security guy at that grocery store at the bottom of Nicollet."

"Okay," Lucas said for the recorder. "Miss Ruiz has identified one photo as a man she knows and she says she believes he is a police officer. Our data indicate that he is a police officer. I am asking Miss Ruiz to turn the photograph over, to mark it with the capital letter A, and to sign her name and put the date below it. Miss Ruiz, will you do that now?"

Carla signed the photo and went back to the display. "This guy looks familiar," she said, tapping the photo of Smithe. "I've seen him on the art scene, you know, openings, parties, that sort of thing. I don't know why, but I've got it in my head that he's gay. I think I might have been introduced to him."

"Okay. Are you sure about him?"

"Pretty sure."

"Okay. Miss Ruiz has just identified the photograph of Jimmy Smithe. I will ask Miss Ruiz to mark that photograph on the back with a capital letter B and sign her name and the date."

Carla signed the second photo and Lucas asked her to look at the photo spread again.

"I don't see anybody else," she said finally.

"I am now showing Miss Ruiz seven additional photographs of Jimmy Smithe and asking her if she confirms her identification of him in the random spread."

Carla looked at the second group of photos and nodded.

"Yes. I know him."

"Miss Ruiz has confirmed that she knows the suspect, Jimmy Smithe. She has also added details, such as she believes him to be homosexual and that he frequents art galleries and that she may have been introduced to him. Miss Ruiz, does anything else come to mind about Mr. Smithe?"

"No, no, I really don't know him. I remember him because he's handsome and I got the impression that he's intelligent."

"Okay. Anything else?"

"No."

"Okay. That concludes the interview. Thank you, Miss Ruiz." He punched the button on the tape, ran it back, listened to it, then took the cassette out of the recorder, put it back in its protective box, and slipped it into his pocket.

"Now what?" Carla asked.

"I've got to use the phone," Lucas said. He went straight through to the chief.

"Davenport? What?"

"She knows him," Lucas said. "Picked him out with no problem."

"We're going to take him."

"Listen. Do it my way?"

"I don't know if we can, Lucas. The media's got a smell of it."

"Who?"

"Don Kennedy from TV3."

"Shit." Kennedy and Jennifer were professional bedmates. "Okay. I'll be back in an hour and a half. When are you taking him?"

"We were waiting for your call. We've got a couple guys here and we'll get the surveillance people. He's working at his desk over in the county building. We're just going to walk over and get him."

"Who made the call? To make the bust?"

There was a pause. Then, "Lester."

"Outstanding. Stay with that."

Daniel hung up and Lucas turned to Rubella. "Get the chopper cranked up. We've got to get back in a hurry."

When Rubella was gone, he took Carla's hands.

"They've got a case against this guy, but I don't like it. I think they're making a mistake. So just sit tight, okay? Watch the evening news. I'll call every night. I'll try to get back up here in a couple of days, if things cool down."

"Okay," she said. "Be careful." He kissed her on the lips and jogged down the dusty track after Rubella.


The flight back to the Cities and the drive from the airport took two hours. Anderson was sitting at his desk, his feet up, staring distractedly at a wall calendar when Lucas arrived.

"Where've you got him?" Lucas asked.

"Down in interrogation."

"His lawyer in there?"

"Yeah. That could be a problem."

"Why's that?"

" 'Cause it's that asshole McCarthy," Anderson said.

"God damn." Lucas ran his hands through his hair. "The usual bull?"

"Yeah. The little dickhead."

"I'm going down there."

"Chief's down there."


"We're not getting anything out of him." Daniel was leaning on the wall outside the interrogation room. "That prick McCarthy won't let him say a word."

"He smells a good one," Lucas said. "If this goes to trial and he gets Smithe off, he can quit the county and make some real money in private practice."

"So what're you going to do?" Daniel asked.

"I'm going to be a good guy. A real good guy. And I'm going to get mad and read off McCarthy."

"Not too much. You could jeopardize what we got."

"Just plant a seed of doubt."

Daniel shrugged. "You can try."

Lucas took off his jacket, loosened his tie and mussed his hair, took a deep breath, and went through the door at a jog. The interrogators, the lawyer, and Smithe were seated around a table and looked up, startled.

"Jesus. Sorry. I was afraid I'd miss you," Lucas said. He looked down at McCarthy. "Hello, Del. You handling this one, I guess?"

"Does the pope shit in the woods?" McCarthy was a short man in a lumpy brown suit. His dishwater-blond hair swelled out of his head in an Afro, and muttonchops swept down the sides of his square face. "Is a bear a Catholic?"

"Right." Lucas looked at the interrogators. "I've been cleared by Daniel. You mind if I ask a few?"

"Go ahead, we ain't gettin' anywhere," said the senior cop, swirling an oily slick of cold coffee in a Styrofoam cup.

Lucas nodded and turned to Smithe. "I'll tell you up front. I was one of the people who questioned the survivor of the third attack. I don't think you did it."

"Is this the good-guy routine, Davenport?" asked McCarthy, tipping his chair back and grinning in amusement.

"No. It's not." He pointed a finger at Smithe. "That was the first thing I wanted to tell you. The second thing is, I'm going to talk for a while. At some point, McCarthy here might tell you to stop listening. You better not—"

"Now, wait a minute," McCarthy said, bringing the chair legs down with a bang.

Lucas overrode him. "—because how can it hurt just to listen, if you're not admitting anything? And your lawyer's priorities are not necessarily the same as yours."

McCarthy stood up. "That's it. I'm calling it off."

"I want to hear him," Smithe said suddenly.

"I'm advising you—"

"I want to hear him," Smithe said. He tipped his head at McCarthy while watching Lucas. "Why aren't his priorities the same as mine?"

"I don't want to impeach the counselor's personal ethics," Lucas said, "but if this goes to trial, it'll be one of the big trials of the decade. We just don't have serial killers here in Minnesota. If he gets you off, he'll have made his name. You, on the other hand, will be completely destroyed, no matter what happens. It's too bad, but that's the way it works. You've been around a courthouse long enough to know what I'm talking about."

"That's enough," said McCarthy. "You're prejudicing the case."

"No I'm not. I'm just prejudicing your job in it. And I won't mention that again. I'm just—"

McCarthy stepped between Lucas and Smithe, his back to Lucas, and leaned toward Smithe. "Listen. If you don't want me to represent you, that's fine. But I'm telling you as your lawyer, right now, you don't want to talk—"

"I want to listen. That's all," Smithe said. "You can sit here and listen with me or you can take a hike and I'll get another attorney."

McCarthy stood back and shook his head. "I warned you."

Lucas moved around to where Smithe could see him again.

"If you've got an alibi, especially a good alibi, for any of the times of the killings, you better bring it out now," Lucas said urgently. "That's my message. If you've got an alibi, you could let us go to trial and maybe humiliate us, but you'd have a hard time working again. There'd always be a question. And there'd always be a record. You get stopped by a highway patrolman in New York and he calls in to the National Crime Information Center, he'll get back a sheet that says you were once arrested for serial murder. And then there's the other possibility."

"What?"

"That you'll be convicted even if you're innocent. There's always a chance that even with a good alibi, the jury'd find you guilty. It happens. You know it. The jury figures, what the hell, if he wasn't guilty, the cops wouldn't have arrested him. McCarthy here can tell you that."

Smithe tipped his head toward McCarthy again. "He told me that as soon as I started dealing in alibis, you'd have guys out on the street trying to knock them down."

Lucas leaned on the interrogation table. "He's absolutely right. We would. And if we can't, I guarantee you'd be back on the street and nothing happens. Nothing. You haven't been booked yet. You never would be. Right now, we've got a good enough case to pick you up, maybe take it to trial. I don't know what these guys have been telling you, but I can tell you that we can put you with two of the victims and a third guy who is critical to the case, and there's some physical evidence. But a good alibi would knock the stuffing out of it."

Smithe went pale. "There can't be. Physical evidence. I mean . . ."

"You don't know what it is," Lucas said. "But we have it. Now. I suggest you and Mr. McCarthy go whisper in the hallway for a couple of minutes and come back."

"Yeah, we'll do that," McCarthy said.

They were back in five minutes.

"We're done talking," McCarthy announced, looking satisfied with himself.

Lucas looked at Smithe. "You're making a bad mistake."

"He said—" Smithe started, but McCarthy grabbed him by the arm and shook his head no.

"You're playing the weak sister," McCarthy said to Lucas. "From what you've said, there're only two possibilities: You've got no case and you're desperate to make one. In which case you won't book him. Or you've got a case, in which case you'll book him no matter what we say and use what he says against him."

"McCarthy, a fellow out in the hall called you a dickhead," Lucas said wearily. "He was right. You can't even see the third possibility, which is why we're all sweating bullets."

"Which is?"

"Which is we got a good case that feels bad to a few of us. We just want to *know*. We've got pretty close to exact times on two of the attacks, real close on a third. If Mr. Smithe was out of town, if he was talking to clients, if he was in the office all day, he'd be in the clear. How can it hurt to tell us now, before we book—"

"You're just afraid to book because of what will happen if you're wrong."

"Goddamn right. The department will look like shit. And Smithe, not incidentally, will take it right in the shorts, no offense."

"Now, what the fuck does that mean?"

"He knows I'm gay," Smithe said.

"That's a prejudicial remark if I ever—"

"Fuck it," said one of the interrogators. "I don't want to hear any more." He stalked out of the room and a minute later Daniel stepped in.

"No deal?" he asked Lucas.

Lucas shrugged.

"No deal," said McCarthy.

"Take him upstairs and book him," Daniel told the remaining interrogator.

"Wait a minute," said Smithe.

"Book him," Daniel snarled. He stormed out of the room.

"Good work, McCarthy, you just built your client a cross," Lucas said.

McCarthy showed his teeth in what wasn't quite a smile. "Go piss up a rope," he said. They left in a group—Smithe, McCarthy, and the interrogation cop. As they went, the cop turned to Lucas.

"You know the difference between a skunk dead on the highway and a lawyer dead on the highway?"

"No, what?"

McCarthy turned his head.

"There's skid marks in front of the skunk," the cop said. Lucas laughed and McCarthy bared his teeth again.


"Look at them down there, like lice on a dog," Anderson said gloomily, exploring his gums with a ragged plastic toothpick. On the street below, television cameramen, reporters, and technicians were swarming around the remote-broadcast trucks parked outside City Hall.

"Yeah. Looks like Lester is going to have a full house," Lucas said. Jennifer's head bobbed through the swarm, headed toward the entry below them. "Got to run," Lucas said.

He caught her just inside the entrance, dragged her protesting through the halls to his office, pushed her into the desk chair, and closed the door.

"You tipped Kennedy about the gay. You told me you wouldn't."

"I didn't tip him, Lucas, honest to Christ."

"Bullshit, bullshit, bullshit," Lucas stormed. "You guys have washed each other's hands before, I've seen you do it. As soon as Daniel told me that Kennedy had the tip, I knew it was from you."

"So what are you going to do about it, Lucas? Huh?" She was angry now. "This is what I do for a living. It's not a fuckin' hobby."

"Great goddamn way to make a living."

"Better than renting yourself out as a stormtrooper."

Lucas put his fists on his hips and leaned close to her face. She didn't back off even a fraction of an inch. "You know what you did to get a break on a story? You pushed the department into booking an innocent man, which will probably kill the guy. He's in the welfare department surrounded by women and they'll never trust him again, no matter what anybody says. He's a suspect, all right, but I don't think he did it. I was trying to get them to go easy, but your fuckin' tip pushed them into picking him up."

"If they don't think he did it, they shouldn't pick him up."

Lucas slapped himself on the forehead. "Jesus. You think all the questions are easy? Smithe might be guilty. He might not be guilty. I might be wrong about him, and if I am and if I talked the department into letting him go, he might go right back on the street and butcher some other woman. But I might be right and we're destroying the guy, while the real killer is planning to rip somebody else. All we needed was a little time, and you snooped on a private conversation out of my house."

"And?"

Lucas turned cool. "I've got to make some basic decisions about whether to talk to you at all."

"I didn't really need to hear that phone call at your place," Jennifer said. "I would have gotten it anyway. I've got sources here you wouldn't believe. I don't need you, Lucas. I might just tell you to go fuck yourself."

"I'll take the risk. I can't put up with spying. I am considering—considering —calling a lawyer and having him call your general manager to tell him how you got the information and threatening to file suit against the station for theft of proprietary information."

"Lucas—"

"Get out of here."

"Lucas . . ." She suddenly burst into tears and Lucas backed a few steps away.

"I'm sorry," he said, miserably. "I just can't . . . Jennifer . . . stop that, goddammit."

"God, I'm a wreck, my makeup. I can't do this press conference. . . . God . . . can I use your phone?" She poked at her face with a tissue. "I want to call the station, tell them to let Kathy Lettice take it. God, I'm such a mess . . ."

"Jesus, stop crying, use the phone," Lucas said desperately.

Still sniffling, she picked up the phone and dialed. When it was answered, her voice suddenly cleared. "Don? Jen. The guy's name is Smithe and he works for welfare—"

"Goddammit, Jennifer!" Lucas shouted. He grabbed the phone, twisted it out of her hand, and slammed it on the hook.

"I cry good, don't I?" she asked with a grin, and she was out the door.

"Davenport, Davenport," Daniel moaned. He gripped handfuls of hair on the side of his head as he watched Jennifer finish the broadcast.

". . . called by some the smartest man in the department, told me personally that he did not believe that Smithe is guilty of the spectacular murders and that he fears the premature arrest could destroy Smithe's burgeoning career with the welfare department . . ."

"Burgeoning career? TV people shouldn't be allowed to use big words," Lucas muttered.

"So now what?" Daniel asked angrily. "How in the hell could you do this?"

"I didn't know I was," Lucas said mildly. "I thought we were having a personal conversation."

"I told you that your dick was going to get you in trouble with that woman," Daniel said. "What the hell am I going to tell Lester? He's been out there in front of the cameras making his case and you're talking to this puss behind his back. You cut his legs out from under him. He'll be after your head."

"Tell him you're suspending me. What's bad? Two weeks? Then I'll appeal to the civil-service board. Even if the board okays the suspension, it'll be months from now. We should be able to put it off until this thing is settled, one way or another."

"Okay. That might do it." Daniel nodded and then laughed unpleasantly, shaking his head. "Christ, I'm glad that wasn't me getting grilled. You better get out of here before Lester arrives or we'll be busting him for assault."

At two o'clock in the morning the telephone rang. Lucas looked up from the drawing table where he was working on Everwhen, reached over, and picked it up.

"Hello?"

"Still mad?" Jennifer asked.

*"You bitch*. Daniel's suspending me. I'm giving interviews to everybody except you guys, you can go suck—"

"Nasty, nasty—"

He slammed the receiver back on the hook. A moment later the phone rang again. He watched it like a cobra, then picked it up, unable to resist.

"I'm coming over," she said, and hung up. Lucas reached for it, to call her, to tell her not to come, but stopped with his hand on the receiver.


Jennifer wore a black leather jacket, jeans, black boots, and driving gloves. Her Japanese two-seater squatted in the driveway like red-metal muscle. Lucas opened the inner door and nodded at her through the glass of the storm door.

"Can I come in?" she asked. She was wearing gold-wire-rimmed glasses instead of her contacts. Her eyes looked large and liquid behind the lenses.

"Sure," he said awkwardly, fumbling with the latch. "You look like a heavy-metal queen."

"Thanks loads."

"That was a compliment."

She glanced at him, looking for sarcasm, found none, peeled off the jacket, and drifted toward the couch in the living room.

"You want a coffee?" Lucas asked as he closed the door.

"No, thanks."

"Beer?"

"No, I'm fine. Go ahead, if you want."

"Maybe a beer." When he got back, Jennifer was leaning back on a love seat, her knee up on the adjacent seat. Lucas sat on the couch opposite her, looking at her over a marble-topped coffee table.

"So what?" he said, gesturing with the beer bottle.

"I'm very tired," she said simply.

"Of the story? The maddog? Me?"

"Life, I think," Jennifer said sadly. "The baby was maybe an attempt to get back."

"Jesus."

"That little scene with you today . . . God, I don't know. I try to put a good face on it, you know? Gotta be quick, gotta be tough, gotta smile when the heavy stuff comes down. Can't let anybody push you. Sometimes I feel like . . . you remember that little Chevrolet I had, that little Nova, that I wrecked, before I bought the Z?"

"Yeah?"

"That's how my chest feels sometimes. All caved in. Like everything is still hard, but all bent up. Crunched, crumbled."

"Cops get like that."

"Not really. I don't think so."

"Look, you show me a guy on the street for ten or fifteen years—"

She held up a hand, stopped him. "I'm not saying it's not tough and you don't get burned out. Awful stuff happens to cops. But there are slow times. You can take some time. I never have time. If things get slow, for Christ's sake, I've got to *invent* stuff. You show me a slow day, where a cop might cruise through it, and I'll show you a day when Jennifer Carey is out interviewing some little girl who got her face burned off two months ago or two years ago because we had to have something by six P.M., or else. And we don't have time to think about it. We just do it. If we're wrong, we pay later. Do now, pay later. What's worse, there aren't any rules. You don't find out until later if you're right or wrong. Sometimes you never find out. And what's right one day is wrong the next."

She stopped talking and Lucas took a swig of beer and watched her. "You know what you need?" he said finally.

"What? A good fuck?" she asked sarcastically.

"I wasn't going to say that."

"Then what?"

"What you need is to leave the job for a while, get married, move in here."

"You think being a housewife is going to fix things?" She looked almost amused.

"I didn't say housewife. You said housewife. I was going to suggest that you move in here and not do a fuckin' thing. Take a class. Think things over. Take a trip to Paris before the kid gets here. Something. That argument this afternoon, those fake tears, my God, that's so tough it's not human."

"The tears weren't fake," she said. "The alibi was, afterward. I was thinking, I couldn't break down and cry on the job. Then I got home, and I thought, why not? I mean, I'm not stupid. You gave me that little lecture about Smithe, you think I don't know I might have hurt him? I admit it. I might have hurt him. But I'm not sure. I'm—"

"But look at what you're putting yourself through the wringer for. You got the name out to Kennedy, and for what? A ten-minute lead on the other reporters? Christ . . ."

"I know, I know all that. That's why I'm over here. I'm screwed up. I don't know that I'm wrong, but I'm not sure that I'm right. I'm living in murk and I can't stop."

Lucas shook his head. "I don't know what to do."

"Well." She took her leg off the love seat. "Could you come over and sit next to me for a minute?"

"Um . . ." Lucas stood up, walked around the table, and sat down next to her.

"Put your arm up around my shoulder."

He put his arm around her shoulder and she snuggled her face into his chest.

"You ready for this?" she asked in an oddly high-pitched, squeaky voice.

He tried to pull back and look down at her, but she clung to him. "Ready for what?"

She pressed her face against him even more firmly, and after a few seconds, began to weep.

No sex, she said later. Just sleep. He was almost asleep when she said quietly, "I'm glad you're the daddy."

# 11

Louis Vullion did not laugh.

Home late the night of the announcement, he neglected to look at his videotapes and learned of the arrest the next morning in the *Star-Tribune*.

"This is not right," he said, transfixed in the middle of his living room. He was wearing pajamas and leather slippers. A shock of hair stood straight up from his head, still mussed from the night.

"This is *not right,*" he hissed. He balled up the paper and hurled it into the kitchen.

"These people are idiots," the maddog screamed.

He turned to the tapes and watched the announcement unfold, his rage growing. Then the face of Jennifer Carey, with her statement that the game inventor, the lieutenant, Lucas Davenport, disagreed, thought they had the wrong man.

"Yes," he said. "Yes."

He ran the tape back and played it again. "Yes."

"I should call him," he said to himself. He glanced at the clock. "No hurry. I should think about it," he said.

Don't make a mistake now. Could this be a ploy? Was the gamesman setting him up? No. That simply wasn't possible. The game was free-form, but there were *some* rules; Davenport, or the other cops—whoever—wouldn't dare permit this man, this gay, to be crucified as part of a ploy. But why was he arrested? Except for the gamesman, Davenport, the police seemed confident that they had a case. How could this mistake happen?

"So stupid," the maddog said to the eggshell-white walls. "They are so fucking dumb."

He couldn't think of anything else. He sat at his desk and stared blindly at the papers there, until his shared secretary asked if he was feeling unwell.

"Yes, a little, I guess; something I ate, I think," he told her. "I've got the Barin arraignment and then I think I'll take the rest of the work home. Something closer to the, ah, facilities."

Barin was a teenage twit who had drunk too much and had driven his car into a crowd of people waiting on a corner to cross a street. Nobody had been killed, but several had been hospitalized. Barin's driver's license had been suspended before the latest accident, also for drunken driving, and he had served two days in jail for the last offense.

This time, it was more serious. The state was in the throes of an antidrinking campaign. Several heretofore sacred cows, for whom the fix would have routinely been applied only a year before, had already done jail time.

And Barin was an obnoxious little prick attached to a large and foul mouth. His father, unfortunately, owned a computer-hardware company that paid a substantial retainer to the maddog's firm. The father wanted the boy to get off.

But the boy was doomed. The maddog knew it. So did the rest of the firm, which was why the maddog had been allowed to handle the trial. Barin would serve three to six months and possibly more. The maddog would not be blamed. There was nothing to be done. The senior partners were patiently explaining that to the father, and the maddog, already indemnified against failure, secretly hoped the judge would sock the little asshole away for a year.

The arraignment was the last of the morning. The maddog arrived early and slipped onto a back bench in the courtroom. The judge was looking down at a young girl in jeans and a white blouse.

"How old are you, Miss Brown?"

"Eighteen, judge."

The judge sighed. "Miss Brown, if you are sixteen, I would be distinctly surprised."

"No, sir, I'm eighteen, three weeks past—"

"Be quiet, Miss Brown." The judge thumbed through the charge papers as the prosecuting and defense attorneys sat patiently behind their tables. The girl had large doe-eyes, very beautiful, but her face was touched with acne and her long brown hair hung limply around her narrow shoulders. Her eyes were her best point, the maddog decided. They were frightened but knowing. The maddog watched her as she stood shifting from foot to foot, casting sideways glances at her public defender.

The judge looked over at the prosecutor. "One prior, same deal?"

"Same deal, Your Honor. Eight months ago. She's been home since then, but her mother threw her out again. The caseworker says her mom's deep into the coke."

"What are you going to do if I let you out, Miss Brown?" the judge asked.

"Well, I've made up with my mom and I think I'm going to earn some money so I can go to college next quarter. I want to major in physical therapy."

The judge looked down at his papers and the maddog thought he might be trying to hide a smile. Eventually he lifted his head, sighed again, and looked at the public defender, who shrugged.

"Child protection?" the judge asked the prosecutor.

"They sent her to a foster home the last time, but the foster mother wouldn't have her after a couple of days," he said.

The judge shook his head and went back to reading the papers.

She was quite a sensual thing in her own way, the maddog decided, watching her nervously lick her lips. A natural victim, the kind who would trigger an attack by a wolf.

The judge at last decided that nothing could be done. He fined her one hundred and fifty dollars on a guilty plea to soliciting for prostitution.

Barin, the twit, showed up just as the case was being disposed. An hour later, when the maddog walked back to the clerk's office, the Heather Brown file was in the return basket. He slipped it out and read through it, noted that she was picked up on South Hennepin. Heather Brown's real name was Gloria Ammundsen. She had been on the street for a year or more. The maddog noted with interest in a narrative section that she had offered the arresting officer a variety of entertainments, including bondage and water sports.

The maddog took his extra work home, but couldn't get anything done. He made a quick supper—sliced ham, fruit, a half-squash. Still agitated, he went out to his car and drove downtown, parked, and walked. Through Loring Park, where the gays cruised and broke and rebroke in their small groups. Over to Hennepin Avenue, and south, away from town. Punks on the street, watching him pass. One kid with a mohawk and dirty black jacket, unconscious on a pile of discarded carpet outside a drugstore. Skinheads with swastikas tattooed on their scalps. Suburban kids hanging out, trying to look tough with cigarettes and black makeup.

A few hookers. Not too obvious, not flagging down cars, but there along the streets for anyone who needed their services.

He looked at them carefully, walking by. All young. Thirteen, fourteen, fifteen, he thought. Fewer sixteen, even fewer eighteen. Very few older. The older ones were the quick-blow-job-in-the-doorway sort, dregs so battered by the street, so unable to get inside, to a sauna, a back room, that they were little more than wet, mindless warm spots in the night, open to any sort of abuse that happened along.

He spotted Heather Brown outside a fast-food restaurant. Most of the hookers were blonde, either natural or bottle. Heather, with her dark hair, reminded him of . . . Who? He didn't know, though it seemed a shadow was back there in his memory. In the night, away from the fluorescent lights of the courtroom, she was prettier.

Except for her eyes. Her eyes had been alive in the courtroom. Out here they had the thousand-yard stare found in battle-fatigue cases. She wore a black blouse, a thigh-length black leather skirt, open-toed high heels, and carried an oversize black bag. Her body, her face, *said* something to him. Her *look* called to him.

"Whoa," she said as he approached and slowed down. "What's happening?"

"Just out for a stroll," he said pleasantly.

"Nice night for it, officer." Her green eye shadow had been applied with a trowel.

The maddog smiled. "I'm not a cop. In fact, I won't even try to pick you up. Who knows, *you* might be. A cop, I mean."

"Oh, sure," she said, cocking a hip so her short skirt rode up.

"Have a good one," he said.

"Ships passing in the night," she said, already looking down the street past him.

"But if I were to come back some night, do you usually go out for your walks around here?"

She turned and looked at him again, the spark of interest rekindled. "Sure," she said. "This is kind of my territory."

"You got a place where we could go?"

"What for?" she asked cautiously.

"Probably a half-'n'-half, if it doesn't cost more than fifty. Or maybe you'd know something more exciting."

She brightened up. He'd made the offer, mentioned a specific act and money, so he wasn't a cop.

"No problem, honey. I know all kinds of ways to turn a boy on. I'm here most every night but Thursday, when my man takes me out. And Sunday, 'cause there's no action."

"Fine. Maybe in a night or two, huh? And you got a place we can go?"

"You got the cash, I got the crash," she said.

"What's your name?"

She had to think about it for a minute. "Heather," she said finally.


"You are making a mistake," the maddog said. He paced the living room. "It's got to be a mistake."

But it was tantalizing. He looked at the personnel directory on the table. Davenport, Lucas. The number. It would be a mistake, but how? Get him at home, late at night, he'd be off guard. No automatic tape to record the voice.

He thought about it and finally wrote the number on a piece of paper, went back out to the car, drove a mile to a phone booth, and dialed. The phone at the other end rang once. It was answered by a baritone voice, absolutely clear. No sleep in it.

"Detective Davenport?"

"Yeah. Who's this?"

"An informant. I saw the story on television last night, your dissent from the actions of your superiors, and I want you to know this: you're absolutely right about the maddog killer. The gay man is not him. *The gay is not him.* Do you get that?"

"Who is this?"

"I'm not going to tell you that, obviously, but I know that you have arrested the wrong man. If you ask him about leaving the notes, he won't know about them, will he? He won't know that you should never kill anyone you know. Never have a motive. Never follow a discernible pattern. You should do something to remedy this miscarriage or I'm afraid that you will be severely embarrassed. The maddog will demonstrate this man's innocence sometime in the near future. Did you get all that, lieutenant? I hope so, because it's all I have to say. Good-bye."

"Wait—"

The maddog hung up, hurried to his car, and drove away. In a block he started to giggle with the excitement of it. He hadn't anticipated the surge of joy, but it was there, as though he'd survived a personal combat. And he had, in a way. He had touched the face of the enemy.

# 12

Lucas was sitting at the drafting table, a printout of the rules for Everwhen on the tabletop. He rubbed his late-night beard, thinking. The notes. The guy knew the notes. And the accent was there, and it was right. Barely perceptible, but it was there. Texas. New Mexico.

He picked up the phone and dialed Daniel.

"It's Davenport."

The chief was unconscious. "Davenport? You know what time it is?"

Lucas glanced at his watch. "Yeah. It's twelve minutes after two in the morning."

"What the fuck?"

"The maddog just called me."

"What?" Daniel's voice suddenly cleared.

"He quoted the notes to me. He had the accent. He sounded real."

"Shit." There was a five-second pause. "What'd he say?"

Lucas repeated the conversation.

"And he sounded real?"

"He sounded real. More than that. He sounded pissed off. He'd seen Jennifer's piece, about how I didn't think Smithe did it. He wants me to set things straight. Man, he wants the *credit*."

There was a long silence. "Chief?"

Daniel moaned. "So now we got Smithe in jail and the maddog is about to rip another one."

"We've got to start backing away from Smithe. Go butter up the public defender tomorrow. McCarthy is sucked on Smithe's neck like a lamprey. If we can get him off, maybe we can talk some sense to the guy about giving us an alibi. If he does—if he gives us anything—we can turn him loose."

"If he doesn't?"

"I don't know. Keep trying to work something out. But if the guy who called me is real, and I'd bet my left nut on it, then I suspect Smithe will come up with something. He's had some time in Hennepin County now, and you know that place."

"Okay. Let's do it that way. God, the first appearance was fourteen hours ago, and we're already doing a two-step. I'll talk to the PD tomorrow and see if there's a deal somewhere. You stop at homicide in the morning and make a statement on the phone call. The preliminary hearing is Monday? If we're going to move, we ought to do it before then. Or the maddog may do it for us. That'd be a real turd in the punch bowl, wouldn't it?"

"The guy usually hits at midweek," Lucas said. "This is Thursday morning. If he follows the pattern, he'll do it tonight or wait until next week."

"He said 'the near future' on the phone?"

"Yeah. It doesn't sound like he was ready to go. But then, he could be . . . dissembling."

"Good word."

"He started it. I'm sitting here trying to remember the exact words he used, and he used some good ones. 'Dissent' and 'miscarriage.' Maybe some more. He's a smart guy. He's had some education."

"Glad to hear it," Daniel said wearily. "Fuck it. I'll talk to you tomorrow."


When he got off the phone, Lucas couldn't focus on the game and finally left it. He wandered out to the kitchen, got a beer from the refrigerator, and turned out the light. As the light went out, a yellow-and-white rectangle caught his eye and it meant something. He took a step down the hallway, frowned, stepped back, and turned on the light. It was the cover on the phone book.

"Where'd he get my number?" Lucas asked aloud.

Lucas was unlisted.

"The goddamn office directory. It has to be."

He picked up the phone and dialed Daniel again, but the line was busy. He put the phone back on the hook, paced for one minute by his watch, and dialed again.

"What, what?" The chief was snarling now.

"It's Davenport again. Just had an ugly thought."

"Might as well tell me," Daniel said in vexation. "It'll add color to my nightmares."

"Remember back when you had me under surveillance? Thought it might be a cop, and you had a couple of reasons?"

"Yeah."

"This just occurred to me. The guy called me at home. The only place my number is listed is in the office directory. And that Carla identified one of the pictures she had seen as a cop . . ."

"Uh-oh." There was another long silence; then, "Lucas, go to bed. I got Anderson out of the sack to tell him about the call. I'll call him again and tell him about this. We can figure something out tomorrow."

"We'd look like idiots if Carla fingered the guy in our lineup and we ignored it."

"We'd look worse than that. We'd look like criminal conspirators."

The phone rang again and Lucas cracked his eyelids. Light. Must be morning. He looked at the clock. Eight-thirty.

"Hello, Linda," he said as he picked up the phone.

"How'd you know it was me, Lucas?"

"Because I have a feeling the shit hit the fan."

"The chief wants to see you now. He says to dress dignified but get down here quick."

Daniel and Anderson were huddled over the chief's desk when Lucas arrived. Lester was sitting in a corner, reading a file.

"What's happened?"

"We don't know," Daniel said. "But the minute I walked in the door, the phone rang. It was the public defender. Smithe wants to talk to *you*."

"Great. Did you say anything about the call last night?"

"Not a thing. But if he's ready to alibi, maybe we can find a way to dump the whole thing on McCarthy . . . something along the lines of Smithe decided to cooperate and with his cooperation we were able to eliminate him as a suspect. We could come out smelling like a rose."

"If we can eliminate him," Anderson said.

"What about this cop?" Lucas asked "The one Carla picked out?"

"I came down last night after the chief called," Anderson said. "I pulled the rosters. He was on duty when Ruiz was attacked, with a partner, up in the northwest. I talked to his partner and he confirms they were up there. They took a half-dozen calls around the time of the attack. We went back and checked the tapes, and he's on them."

"So he's clear," said Lucas.

"Thank Christ for small favors," Daniel said. "You better haul ass over to the detention center and talk to Smithe. They're waiting for you."

McCarthy and Smithe waited in a small interrogation room. The decor was simple, being designed to repel bodily fluids. McCarthy was smoking and Smithe sat nervously on a padded waiting-room chair, rubbing his hands, staring at his feet.

"I don't like this and I'm writing a memorandum to the effect," McCarthy spat as Lucas walked in.

"Yeah, yeah." He looked at Smithe. "Could I ask you to stand up for a minute?"

"Wait a minute. We wanted to talk—" McCarthy started, but Smithe waved him down and stood up.

"I hate this place," he said. "This place is worse than I could have imagined."

"Actually, it's a pretty good jail," Lucas said mildly.

"That's what they tell me," Smithe said despondently. "Why am I standing up?"

"Flex your pecs and stomach for me."

"What?"

"Flex your pecs and stomach. And brace yourself."

Smithe looked puzzled, but dropped his shoulders and flexed. Lucas reached out with his fingers spread and pushed hard on Smithe's chest, then dropped his hand and pushed on his stomach. The underlying muscles felt like boards.

"You work out?"

"Yeah, quite a bit."

"What's this about?" McCarthy asked.

"The woman who survived. The killer grabbed her from behind, wrapped her up. She said he felt kind of thick and soft."

"That's not me," Smithe said, suddenly more confident. "Here, you turn around."

Lucas turned and Smithe stepped behind him and wrapped him up. "Get loose," Smithe said.

Lucas started to struggle and twist. He had enough weight to move Smithe around the floor in a tight, controlled dance, but the encircling arms felt almost machinelike. Try as he might, he couldn't break loose.

"Okay," Lucas said, breathing hard.

Smithe released him. "If I had her, she wouldn't get loose," Smithe said confidently. "Does that prove anything?"

"To me it does," Lucas said. "It wouldn't convince a lot of other people."

"I saw that thing on television, about you believing me," Smithe said. "And I can't handle this jail. I decided to take a chance on you. I have an alibi. In fact, I've got two of them."

"We could do all of this at the preliminary," McCarthy said.

"That's four days away," Smithe said sharply. He turned to Lucas. "If my alibis are good, how soon do I get out?"

Lucas shrugged. "If they're good and we can check them, we could have you out of here this afternoon."

"All right," Smithe said suddenly. "Mr. McCarthy brought my calendar in. On the day Lewis was attacked, that afternoon, I was doing in-service training. Started at nine o'clock in the morning and went straight through to five. There were ten people in the class. We all ate lunch together. That wasn't long ago, so they'll remember.

"And on the day Shirley Morris was killed, the housewife? I got on a plane for New York at seven o'clock that morning. I have the plane tickets and a friend took me out to the airport, saw me get on the plane. I've got hotel bills from New York, they have the check-in time on them. Morris was killed in the afternoon, and I checked in during the afternoon. I bet they'll remember me, too, because when I went up to my room with the bellhop, he pulled back my sheet and there was a rat under it and the guy freaked out. I freaked out. This is supposed to be a nice hotel. I went down to the desk and they gave me a new room, but I bet they remember that rat. You can check it with phone calls. And Mr. McCarthy has the bills and plane tickets at his office."

"You should have told us," Lucas said.

"I was scared. Mr. McCarthy said . . ." They both turned and looked at McCarthy.

"It was too much all at once. You were grilling him, everybody was running around yelling, we had to cool out or we could make a mistake," McCarthy said.

"Well, we sure made a mistake doing it this way," Smithe said. "My family knew I was gay, my parents and my brothers and sisters and a few friends back home, but most people in my high school didn't, most of the people around the home place . . ."

He suddenly sat down and started to sob. "Now they all know. You know how hard it'll be to go back to the farm? My home?"

McCarthy stood up and kicked his chair.


In the lobby of the detention center, Lucas stopped at a phone and made a single call.

"Lucas Davenport," he said. "Can you meet me someplace discreet? Quickly?"

"Sure," she said. "Name the place."

He named a used-book store on the north side of the loop. When she arrived, he thought how out-of-place she looked. With her perfect hair and faultless makeup, she wandered through the stacks like Alice in Wonderland, stunned by the presence of so many baffling artifacts. Annie McGowan. Pride of Channel Eight, the Now Report.

"Lucas," she whispered when she saw him.

"Annie." He stepped toward her and she reached out with both hands, as though she expected Lucas to take her in his arms. He instead took her hands and pulled her close to his chest.

"What I'm going to tell you now must be kept a secret. You must give me journalistic immunity or I can't tell you," he said, glancing back over his shoulder. *Introduction to Method Acting 1043, two credits.*

"Yes, of course," she blurted. Her breath smelled like cinnamon and spice.

"This gay fellow arrested for the maddog murders? He didn't do it," Lucas whispered. "He has two excellent alibis that are being checked out even as we speak. He should be released late this afternoon. No one, but no one, knows this outside the police department, except you. If you wait until three-thirty or so, you can probably catch his attorney—you know McCarthy, the public defender?"

"Yes, I know him," she said breathlessly.

"You can catch him outside the detention center, signing Smithe out. Better stake the place out around three o'clock. I don't think it could happen earlier than that."

"Oh, Lucas, this is enormous."

"Yeah. If you can keep it exclusive. And I'll give you another tip, but this also has to come from 'an informed source.' "

"What?"

"These women were supposedly raped, but nobody ever found any semen. They think the killer may be using some kind of . . . foreign object because he's impotent."

"Oh, jeez. Poor guy."

"Uh, yeah."

"What kind of object?"

"Uh, well, we don't know exactly."

"You mean like one of those huge rubber cocks?" The words came tripping out of her perfect mouth so incongruously that Lucas felt his chin drop.

"Uh, well, we don't know. Something. Anyway, if you handle this right and protect me, I'll have more exclusive tips for you. But right now I've got to get out of here. We can't be seen together."

"Not yet, anyway," she said. She turned to go, and then stepped back.

"Listen, when you call me at the station, they'll know who my source is if you keep leaving your name. I mean, if you can't get me."

"Yeah?"

"So maybe we should use a code name."

"Good idea," Lucas said, dumbfounded. He took a card from his wallet, wrote his home phone number on the back of it. "You can call me at the office or at home. I'll be one place or the other when I call you. When I call, I'll say 'Message for McGowan: Call Red Horse.' "

"Red Horse," she whispered, her lips moving as she memorized the phrase. "Red Horse. Like the horse in chess?"

More like the fish, the red horse sucker, Lucas thought. McGowan stepped forward another step and kissed him on the lips, then with a flash of black eyes and fashionable wool coat was gone down the stacks.

The store owner, an unromantic fat man who collected early editions of Mark Twain's *Life on the Mississippi*, appeared in the dim aisle and said, "Jesus, Lucas, what're you doing back there, squeezin' the weasel?"


Lucas stopped at Daniel's office and outlined Smithe's alibis. Together they went to the homicide division and outlined them to Lester and Anderson.

"I want everybody off everything else, I want this checked right now," Daniel said. "You can start by going over to the welfare office, see about this in-service training. That'll give us a quick read. Then look at these tickets, make a few calls. If it all checks, and I bet it will, we'll set up a meeting with the prosecutor's office. For like one o'clock, two o'clock. Decide what to do."

"You mean drop the charges," Lester said.

"Yeah. Probably."

"The press'll eat us alive," Anderson said.

"Not if we play it right. We tell them that Davenport was the only guy Smithe would trust, told him the stories, Davenport came to us, and we realized our mistake."

"Sounds like a lead balloon to me," Lester said.

"It's all we got," Daniel said. "It's better than having McCarthy shove it down our throats."

"Christ." Lester's face was gray. "I made the call. They're going to be all over me. The fuckin' TV."

"Could be worse," Daniel said philosophically.

"How?"

"Could be me."

Lucas and Anderson started laughing, then Daniel, and finally Lester smiled.

"Yeah, that'd be un-fuckin'-thinkable," Lester said.

*    *    *

Lucas spent the rest of the morning in his office, talking to contacts around the Cities. Nothing much was moving. There were rumors that somebody had been killed at a high-stakes poker game on the northeast side, but he'd heard a similar rumor three weeks earlier and it was beginning to sound apocryphal. Several hundred Visa blanks had hit the Cities and were working through the discount stores and shopping centers; some heavy-hitting retailers were upset and were talking to the mayor. There was a rumor about guns, automatic weapons going out-country through landing strips in the Red River Valley. That was a weird one and needed checking. And a strip-joint owner complained that a neighboring bar was putting on young talent: "It ain't fair, these girls ain't old enough to have hair on their pussy. Nobody else is gettin' any business, everybody's down at Frankie's." Lucas told him he'd look into it.

"It all checks," Daniel said. "We faxed a photo out to New York, had the cops run it over to the hotel, and the bellhop remembers him and remembers the rat. He couldn't remember the exact date, but he remembers the week it was in. It's the right week."

"How about the in-service?"

"Checks out. That's the clincher, because there isn't any question about it. As soon as we asked the question, word was all over welfare that we fucked up. It'll be all over the courthouse by tonight."

"And?"

"We've got a meeting with the prosecutor and the public defender at two o'clock," Daniel said. "We're going to recommend that all charges be dismissed. We'll have a press conference this evening."

"He's going to sue our butts," Anderson said.

"We'll ask for a waiver," Daniel said.

"No chance," said Lucas. "The guy is freaked." He looked at the chief. "I don't think I ought to show at the press conference."

"That might be best."

"If anybody asks, you can tell them I'm on vacation. I'm going to take a couple of days off and go up north."

Lucas left City Hall at three and wandered down to the detention center, stopping only to pick up a box of popcorn. Annie McGowan and a cameraman were outside the center, waiting. Lucas sat on a bus bench a block away, and a half-hour later saw McCarthy walk out of the center with Smithe right behind. They were with two older people, a man and a woman, whom Lucas recognized as Smithe's parents from the photos in his house. McGowan was on them in a flash, and after a bit of milling around, they apparently agreed to a brief on-camera interview. Lucas balled up the empty popcorn bag, tossed it under the bench, and smiled.

"Press conference at seven," Anderson said, spotting Lucas in the hall.

"I've got something going tonight," Lucas said. "And I'm trying to hide out for a while."

Before leaving, he made arrangements for backup with the patrol division and headed home in time for the six-o'clock news. McGowan looked wonderful as she delivered her scoop. After two minutes of videotaped interview outside the detention center, the cameras cut back to McGowan in the studio.

"Now Report Eight has also learned that police believe the real killer is sexually impotent and the women may actually have been raped using some kind of blunt object because he is incapable of raping them himself."

She turned to the anchorman and smiled. "Fred?"

"Thanks for that exclusive report, Annie . . ."

Lucas turned to Channel Four. The last story of the broadcast was a recap of McGowan's, obviously stolen: "We have just learned that Jimmy Smithe, who was arrested in the investigation of the multiple murders of three Twin Cities women, has been released and that police apparently now believe him to be innocent of the crimes . . ."

Jennifer was on the phone five minutes later.

"Lucas, did you feed her that?"

"Feed who what?" Lucas asked innocently.

"Feed McGowan the Smithe release?"

"Has he been released?"

"You jerk, you better be wearing your steel jockstrap the next time I'm over, because I'm bringing a knife."

Late that evening, he cruised Lake Street in an unmarked departmental pool car, watching the night walkers, the drinkers, the hookers, looking for any one of a dozen faces. He found one just before ten.

"Harold. Get in the car."

"Aw, lieutenant . . ."

"Get in the fuckin' car, Harold." Harold, a dealer in free-market pharmaceuticals, got in the car.

"Harold, you owe me," Lucas said. Harold weighed a hundred and thirty pounds and was lost in his olive-drab field jacket.

"What do y' want, man?" he whined. "I haven't been talking to anybody . . ."

"What I want is for you to go into Frankie's and do some light drinking. On me. But light. Wine, beer. I don't want you hammered."

"What's the bad part?" Harold asked, suddenly looking perkier.

"They're going to put some young puss up on the bar. Real young. When they do, I want you to walk out and tell me. I'll be up the block. You come out as soon as she starts, hear? Not two minutes later, just as soon as she starts." He handed Harold a ten.

"Ten? You want me to stay in there drinkin' on ten?" he complained.

Lucas gripped the front of Harold's field jacket and shook him once. "Listen, Harold, you're lucky I don't charge you for the privilege, okay? Now, get your lame ass in there or I'm going to rip your fuckin' face off."

"Jesus, lieutenant . . ." Harold got out, and Lucas slumped in the seat, watching the passersby. Most were drinking or already drunk. A few drug cases walked by. A pimp and one of his string; Lucas knew him, and put his head down further, his hand up to block a view of his face. The pimp never looked toward him. A pusher, a pusher, a fat-faced boy who might just have come in from the country, and a drunk salesman. He watched the parade for a half-hour before Harold eased up to the car.

"There's one on and she's real young," he whispered.

"Okay. Take off." Harold vanished. Lucas used the radio to make a prearranged call for patrol backup, pulled on a tweed shooting hat and a pair of windowpane glasses, got out of the car, locked it, and headed down the street to Frankie's.

Frankie's smelled of old beer and cheap wine. The front room, next to the street, was empty except for two unhappy-looking women sitting across from each other in a red leatherette booth. The bartender was wiping glasses and casually watched Lucas pick his way through the empty tables to the entry arch into the back room.

The back room was jammed, thirty or forty men and a half-dozen women in a cloud of cigarette smoke, clapping to the rock music that poured out of a jukebox. The girl was dancing on the bar, stripped down to a tiny brassiere and a pair of translucent blue underpants. Lucas shouldered his way through the crowd and spotted Frankie himself behind the bar, pushing out plastic glasses of beer as fast as the tap would pour them. Lucas tilted his head up at the girl. Eleven? Twelve? She did a bump and reached behind her back with one hand, her teeth biting her lower lip in a semiprofessional grin. She was feeding off the crowd's enthusiasm. With another bump, she popped the brassiere and slowly peeled it off, carefully covering her tiny breasts with her forearms as she did it. After a few more bumps she tossed the brassiere behind the bar and switched into a new dance, her exposed breasts bobbing in the flashing ceiling lights.

"Bottoms, bottoms, bottoms," the crowd was chanting, and the girl hooked her thumbs in the top of the pants and after coyly pulling them down an inch here and an inch there, turning, bending, peering out between her legs, she stood and slid them off, her back to the audience, and then turned to finish the dance.

And the bartender from the front screamed, "There're cops outside."

"Take off," yelled Frankie. As the crowd broke for the two doors, he reached up and grabbed the nude girl by the ankle. Lucas lurched forward and got his gun out, his elbows on the bar, and poked the muzzle of the weapon into Frankie's cheek.

"Don't make me have an accident, Frank," he said. "This weapon has a very light trigger pull." Frankie froze. Three uniformed cops ran in from the front, pressing customers to the wall as they passed. A dozen Ziploc bags of cocaine and crack hit the floor. Lucas looked up at the girl. "Get down," he said.

She leaned over and carefully spat in his face.

"So what happened to her?" Carla asked.

They sat on the edge of the dock, their feet hanging over the water. It was an hour before sunset and they had just walked down to the dock from the firing range in the woods. The afternoon was cool and quiet, the violet hue of the sky reflected in the water. Three hundred feet out, a musky fisherman was working a surface lure around the edges of a submerged island. The water was as flat as a tabletop and they could hear the paddle-wheel chop-chop-chop of the lure as the fisherman retrieved it.

"We dropped her off with child protection," Lucas said. "They'll try to figure out who her parents are, get her back there. Two weeks from now she'll run away again and start hooking or dancing or whatever. At her age, it's the only kind of job she can get."

"What about Frankie?"

"We wrote him up for everything we could think of. We'll get him on some of them, felonies. He'll do some time, lose his liquor license."

"Good. They ought to . . . I don't know. A twelve-year-old."

Lucas shrugged. "The average age of the hookers out on the street is probably fourteen. By sixteen they're getting too old. The younger they are, the more money they make; it's what the johns want. Young stuff."

"Men are such perverts," Carla said, and Lucas laughed.

"What do you want to do, go fishing or go inside and fool around?" he asked.

"I've already been fishing," she said, wrinkling her nose at him.

# 13

The maddog's secretary served as the office's rumor-central. That might have helped him in office politics—if he had taken part in office politics—but he did not relate well to his secretary. He dealt with her with his eyes averted. He was aware of the habit and struggled to correct it, to look straight at her. He was unsuccessful and had taken to staring at the bridge of her nose. She knew that he was not looking into her eyes.

The situation was made more difficult by her appearance. She was far too pretty for the maddog. She had made it clear soon after his arrival that she would not welcome an approach. In his own way, he was grateful. If she had snared him, if she had been Chosen, she would have to die and that would violate one of the principal rules: Never kill anyone you know.

When he came into the office, three other women were clustered around her, talking.

"Did you hear, Louis?" One of the women in the cluster was speaking to him. Margaret Wilson was her name. She was an attorney who specialized in personal-injury law, and though she was not yet thirty, was rumored to be one of the best-paid attorneys in the office. She had hazel eyes, large breasts, and heavy thighs. She laughed too much, the maddog thought; actually, she frightened him a bit. He stopped.

"Hear what?" he asked.

"That gay guy they arrested, that they thought was the maddog killer? He's not the one."

"Yes. I saw it on the news last night. That's too bad. I thought they had him," the maddog said, struggling to keep his voice level. The police press conference, the portions he'd seen on TV3, had delighted him. He took another step toward his office.

"They say he can't get it up," said Wilson.

He stopped again, confused. "Pardon?"

"Channel Eight, Annie McGowan? The reporter with the short dark hair-bob like the ice skater What's-her-name? She talked to somebody in the police. They say he's impotent and that's what's driving him to do it," she said. Was she taunting him? There seemed to be an element of challenge in her tone.

"Well, they were wrong about the homosexual . . ." the maddog started tentatively.

"It's all that pop psychology," the maddog's secretary said scornfully. "Everybody else says he rapes them. If he can't get it up, how does he . . . ?"

"They never found any semen," said Wilson. "They think he uses something."

All the women looked at each other, and the maddog said, "Well," and went into his office and shut the door. He stood there, just for a second, suffused with rage. Impotence? Uses something? What were they talking about?

There was a burst of laughter from outside, and he knew they were laughing about him. Uses something. Probably like old Louis there, I wonder what Louis uses? they were saying. They didn't know who he was, what he was; they didn't know the power. And they were laughing at him.

He walked to his desk, dropped his briefcase, sat down, and stared at the duck print on the wall. Three mallards coming into a cattail swamp at dusk. The maddog stared at it without seeing it, the rage growing. There was another burst of laughter from beyond the door. If he'd had a pistol with him, he would have stepped into the hallway and killed them all.

He left the office at eleven-thirty and drove home to watch the noon news. He watched TV3 by preference, believing that what little dignity was allotted to news coverage by television could best be found there.

But he might have to change channels if this McGowan had special sources. He left his car in the driveway and hurried inside. He was a little early and had time to make a cup of hot soup before the news came on. He sat in the overstuffed chair in the living room sipping the salty hot concoction, and when the news came up, McGowan's was the lead story. It was apparently a rehash of the night before, with tape of McGowan interviewing the homosexual on the steps of the county jail and later repeating the impotence story. Her pretty, clear face was intent with the seriousness of her information; as the camera closed in on her face for the last shot, the maddog felt himself stir, even as the anger began to rekindle. He controlled it, breathing hard, and punched off the television. Annie McGowan. Her face hung in the bright afterimage of the television screen. She was an interesting one. Better than the blonde on TV3.

The morning copy of the *Star-Tribune* was still on the kitchen table. He checked it again. There was a large story on the release of Smithe, but there was no reference to the impotence allegations.

Why would the police tell McGowan that he was impotent? They must know he was not. They must know that it was wrong. Could it be an attempt to draw him out? Something to deliberately anger him? But that was . . . crazy. They would do anything to avoid angering him. Wouldn't they?

He went back to work, the anger still roiling his mind. There was a temptation to find Heather, to take her immediately. But not yet, he decided as he sat with his books and his yellow pads. He could feel the strength building, but it had not reached the urgency that guaranteed the kind of transcendent experience he had come to require. To kill Heather now was to strike at the cops, but it would do something . . . unpleasant to his need for her. It would be, he thought, premature, and therefore disappointing. He would wait.

The maddog worked through the weekend, feeling the need for the girl developing, blossoming within him.

He enjoyed himself. The office was empty on Saturday afternoon and Sunday, leaving him alone, as he preferred to be. And he'd found an interesting case. Since it would go to trial, he would not handle it, but the senior trial attorney had passed it down through the assignment system, asking for research.

The defendant was named Emil Gant. He had been harassing his ex-wife and her current boyfriends. He followed them, exchanged words with them, finally threatened violence. The threats were believable. Gant was on parole, having served thirty months of a forty-five-month prison term on a conviction of aggravated assault. The woman was worried.

The current charge came after Gant was caught in his ex-wife's garage. The woman was in her house alone, at night. A neighbor saw Gant sneak in through an open door. The neighbor called the woman, the woman called 911, and the cops arrived in less than a minute. Gant was found hiding behind a car.

Once he would have been charged with lurking. That charge no longer existed. He couldn't be charged with assault because he hadn't assaulted anyone. He couldn't be charged with breaking and entering, because he hadn't broken into the garage. He was finally charged with trespassing.

Actually, the prosecutors didn't much care what he was charged with. A conviction on any charge would send Gant back to Stillwater State Prison for the remaining fifteen months of his original forty-five-month term.

But the maddog, studying the state trespassing law, found a tidy little loophole. The law had been designed to deal with hunters who were trespassing on farms without permission, not with criminal harassment. Nobody wanted to arrest thousands of hunters every fall. Most of them were voters. So the trespass laws had some special provisions.

Most important, the trespasser had to be warned and given a chance to leave—and refuse, or substantially delay—before the act of trespass was complete. The maddog looked over the police reports. Nobody had said anything to the man before the cops arrived. He was never given a chance to leave.

The maddog smiled and started writing the brief. This would never go to trial: Gant had not completed the basic elements of the crime under Minnesota law. So he had been caught hiding in a private garage just before midnight? So what? Nobody told him to go away. . . .

The maddog left the brief on his secretary's desk before he left the office Sunday afternoon. On Monday morning he happened to get on an elevator with the chief trial attorney and his assistant. They nodded to the maddog and turned their backs on him, watching the numbers change.

Halfway up the assistant cleared his throat. "Got something for you on that Gant case," he said.

"Oh yeah?" Olson was a sharp dresser. Gray suits, paisley ties, big white teeth in an easy grin. "I thought I already put a stamp on that turkey and mailed him back to Stillwater."

"Not quite, O wise one," the assistant said. "I got to thinking about the state trespass law and came in over the weekend to look it up. Sure enough. There's a provision in there . . ."

The assistant then related, paragraph by paragraph, the maddog's research. Olson was laughing by the time they got to the skyway level and he slapped the assistant on the back and crowed, "God damn, Billy, I knew there was a reason I hired you."

The maddog stood thunderstruck at the back of the car. Neither of the others noticed. In a half-hour, he was in a rage. He couldn't go to Olson and claim the work as his own. That would seem petty. The assistant would claim he simply had similar ideas.

It had always been like this. He had always been ignored. The rage fed the need for the girl. It built like a thunderhead, and he went home, the need crawling in his blood.

Heather Brown was back on the block. She wore a short leather skirt and a turquoise blouse open to her belt. Glass beads dangled over her thin freckled chest; a headband pinned back her hair.

The maddog walked down the sidewalk toward her, his eyes running over her body. He was most carefully dressed; more carefully dressed than for any of the other killings, because this pickup would be in public and might well be witnessed.

The maddog wore jeans and boots, a red nylon athletic jacket, and a billed John Deere hat. He was slightly out of place on Hennepin. Not enough to be outrageous, but enough that his clothes might stick in somebody's mind. He was a farmer, clear and simple. In a crowd of farmers, he would fit without the slightest wrinkle, he thought, as long as he kept his mouth shut.

He had cut a hole through the back seam of the jacket pocket and a long wicked blade from Chicago Cutlery nestled in the lining.

"Heather," he said as he approached. He glanced around. The nearest person was a black man sitting on a bus bench across the street. He turned away from the man. Heather had been looking past him and her eyes snapped back.

"How are you, honey?"

"I talked to you the other night . . ."

"I don't remember you."

"I offered fifty for a half-'n'-half . . ."

"Oh, yeah." She tipped her head in bemusement. "You look a lot different."

The maddog looked down at himself, nodded, and changed the subject. "You said you might come up with something more exciting, if I could get the money."

"You get the money?"

"I got a hundred."

"So what you got in mind, cowboy?"

*    *    *

The motel was pleasingly decrepit. Heather went into the office, got a key, and returned a minute later. Inside, the maddog looked around the room, sniffed. Disinfectant. They must spray the place, he decided. The bathroom was tiny, the floor was missing tiles, the bedspread was thin and badly worn.

"Why don't we get the money out of the way first?" Heather Brown asked.

"Oh, yes. A hundred?" The maddog took the bills out of his pants pockets and tossed them on the dresser. Five twenties. "And if we can really do . . . you know . . . I've got another fifty."

"Hey, I like you, guy," she said with a bright smile. "Why don't we just go in here and discuss it while we take a little shower."

"Start it, I'll be right there," he said. He started taking off his jacket, and when she stepped into the bathroom, took the knife out of his pocket and slipped it under the bed.

The shower was agonizing. She carefully washed his penis, and when nothing happened, said, "Have a little trouble there?" She frowned, a wrinkle between her eyes. The impotent ones weren't the worst of the trade, but certainly slowed down the turnover.

"No, no, no, not if we can . . ."

She had silk scarves in her handbag, four of them, one for each wrist and ankle.

"Don't tie them too tight," she said. "Just looping them is enough."

"I can do this," he said through his teeth. He tied her feet first, one out to each corner at the foot of the bed, then her hands, out to the sides, tied to the sideboards.

"How we doing, honey?"

"Fine," he said, turning toward her. He had a half-erection now, his penis standing away from his body.

"If you want to bring it up here for a minute, I can help you out," she offered.

"No, no, I'm fine; but I want to use a rubber . . . I'm sorry . . ."

"No, that's good," she said encouragingly. He turned and picked his jacket up off the floor, found a rubber, ripped it out of the package, and unrolled it on himself. Then he took the Kotex from the same pocket and lay down beside her.

"Open wide," he said.

Sensing that something was wrong, she tried to sit up, opened her mouth, perhaps to scream, and the maddog grabbed her by the sides of the throat and squeezed and pushed her down on the bed. She flopped, twisting her shoulders, struggling against the binding scarves. As he squeezed and squeezed, her mouth opened wider, and she managed to force out a moan, not loud enough to attract attention in a motel like this, and then he forced the Kotex into her mouth, stuffing it in.

When it was in, he covered her mouth with one hand and fished in the pocket of the jacket with the other, found his gloves and slipped them on, one at a time. The girl watched him, still bucking against the scarves, her eyes wide and terrified now. When the gloves were on, he took his tape from the other pocket and wrapped it twice around her head and across the gag. Next he checked the bonds again; they were holding nicely.

"Look at it now," he said to the girl, kneeling over her. "That's the real thing. And they tried to say I was impotent."

She had stopped struggling and shrank back on the bed, watching him.

"So now we'll have a little fun," he said. He found the knife under the bed, took it out, and showed it to her, the steel blade shimmering in the lamplight. "It won't hurt too much; I'm very good at this," he said. "Try to keep your eyes open when it goes in; I like to watch the eyes," he said.

She looked away, and there was suddenly a smell in the room and he looked down at her pelvis and realized that she had wet herself.

"Oh, for Christ's sake," he said. But he was delighted. She'd wet herself in fear. She knew the power.

But he wouldn't rape her now. The thought of lying in cold urine was distasteful. And rape wasn't necessary, anyway. The maddog stretched out beside her, reached over and kissed her gently on the cheek as she strained away from him. "It'll just take a second," he said. She began frantically jerking her arms against the bonds. He laid the point of the knife just below her breastbone and felt the orgasm rising up within him as he pressed the knife up and in. The girl's eyes opened, straining, straining, and then the light went out and it all stopped for her. The maddog peered into her eyes as the light faded, felt the waves of the orgasm receding and the pressure lifting off his mind.

It had gone very well, he thought. Very well.

He stepped back from the bed and looked at her. Not pretty, he thought, but there was something beautiful in her attitude. He stripped off the rubber and tossed it in the toilet and flushed and began to get dressed, stopping frequently to look at his work. Inside, he rejoiced.

When he was dressed, he took a last long look, reaching out to stroke her cooling leg, and started toward the door.

"Whoops," he said aloud. "Can't forget the note." He fished it out of his jacket pocket and dropped it on her body.

Outside, it was a beautiful crisp fall night. He walked across the blacktopped parking lot, risking a quick glance toward the motel office. The clerk was visible inside the window, the blue light of a television bathing his face. He didn't look out. Keeping his head carefully averted, the maddog walked down the sidewalk and around the corner, where he pulled off the jacket and hat. He rolled the jacket with the hat inside and tucked it under his arm. He turned another corner and was at his car. He climbed inside and tossed the jacket on the floor of the car. If anybody had seen him get in the car, it would not have been a man in a red jacket wearing a billed hat.

He drove six blocks back toward the loop and stopped at a bar. A police car, flashing red lights but without a siren, sped past down Hennepin while he had the first drink. He nursed it, then nodded at the bartender for a refill. When he came out, an hour had passed since he'd left the motel room.

"Another unnecessary risk," he told himself. "I won't drive by, though. Only close enough to watch."

From a traffic signal a block away, he could see at least four police cars at the motel. As he waited for the light to change, a television truck rolled up to the motel and a dark-haired girl got out of the passenger side. He recognized her at once, Annie McGowan, the woman who said he was impotent.

A car horn sounded from behind and he glanced in the rearview mirror and then at the traffic signal, which had turned green. He turned the corner and pulled over to the curb. McGowan was talking to a cop and the cop was shaking his head. A group of people walked down the sidewalk past the maddog's car, attracted by the police lights and the television truck.

The maddog was tempted to join them, but decided against it. Too risky; he'd taken risks enough. Besides, there was enough of a glow from the killing that he should go home where he could relax and enjoy it. A long hot bath, close the eyes, and rerun the part where the light went out in Heather Brown.

# 14

It had been one of the best weekends of the year, with warm days and crisp, cold nights. Brilliant color lingered in the woods, and the faint scent of burning birch logs hung in the air.

"We've got at least another week for the leaves. Maybe two," Carla said. A stand of maples on the north end of the lake was a flaming orange. "Too bad you don't have more maples."

"I thought about that when I bought the place," Lucas said. "I didn't want maples. They're pretty, but I wanted the pines. They give the place a North Woods feel. A little further south, down in the maples and oaks, it feels like farm country."

They drifted along the shoreline, working the bucktail lures around emergent weeds, docks, and fallen timber. "There are some people who'd say it's already too late for bucktails, but I don't hold with that. And they're more fun to throw," Lucas said.

In three hours of casting they caught five northern pike and had two musky follows.

"Bad day for musky, huh?" Carla said as they headed back to the dock.

"Hate to tell you this, but that was a good day. Two follows is all right. Lots of days, you don't see any."

"Great sport."

"Don't have to fool around with cleaning any fish, anyway," he said with a grin.

"When do I have to leave here?" she asked.

"What do you mean, *have to leave?*"

"I assume that the hot pursuit by the television people will have tapered off by now. I could go back. But jeez, you know, I've been living in that studio with a hot plate. I hate to go."

"Hey, stay a month if you want," Lucas said. "I've got to come up in two or three weeks and pull the dock out. After that, there won't be much to do until the freeze and the snow comes in."

"I accept," Carla said, laughing. "Maybe not a month, but for a couple of more weeks. You don't know how much of a break this is for me. I brought up a couple of drawing pads and some pastels and I'm having a great time."

"Good. That's what the place is for."

She looked over at him. "I'm glad you could stay an extra day. It's quiet here all the time, but on Saturday and Sunday there are a few people around. Today we had it to ourselves. It's kind of special on the weekdays."

After dinner, Lucas started a fire in the fireplace, dragging in birch logs cut the previous fall. When the fire was going, they sat on the couch and talked and watched television and then a rental movie, *The Big Chill.*

Toward the end of the movie Lucas started working on her blouse buttons. When the phone rang, he had her blouse off and she was straddling his hips, tickling him. He looked up at her and said, suddenly somber, "I don't want to answer. He's killed somebody else."

Carla stopped giggling and half-turned and reached out to grab the receiver and thrust it at him. He looked at it for a second and then reluctantly took it.

"Davenport," he said, sitting up.

"Lucas," said Anderson, "we've got another one."

"Shit." He looked at Carla and nodded.

"You better get down here."

"Who is it?"

"A hooker. We've got a street name, that's all. Heather Brown. Maybe fifteen. Knife, just like the others. The note's there."

"I don't know her. You check on Smithe?"

"Yeah, he's up at the family farm. We figure she was done around seven o'clock. A TV crew followed him up to the farm. They did some film at six. He's still up there. He's out of it."

"How about the girl's pimp?"

"We're looking for him. That's one reason we need you down here—we need you to look at her, see if you recognize her, shake down some of her people."

"Vice working it?"

"Yeah. They know her, but they haven't come up with anything yet."

"Where was it?"

"Down on South Hennepin. Randy's."

"Yeah, I know it. Okay, I'll be down as soon as I can."


He hung up and turned to Carla, who was slipping into her blouse. He reached out and pressed a palm against one of her breasts.

"I've got to go," he said.

"Who was it?" Her voice was low, depressed.

"A hooker. In a hot-bed hotel. It's the guy, all right, but it's kind of . . . weird. It sounds almost spontaneous. And it's the first time he's gone near a hooker." He hesitated. "I've got a favor to ask you, but I don't want you to take it the wrong way."

She wrinkled her forehead and shrugged. "So ask."

"Could you take a walk down to the dock for a few minutes?"

"Sure . . ."

"I've got to make a phone call, and . . ." He gestured helplessly. "It's not that I don't trust you, but it would be best if I was talking in private. Sometimes I do things that are considered mildly outside the law. If there were ever a grand jury . . . I wouldn't want you to perjure yourself or even think you had to."

She smiled uncertainly. "Sure. So I take a walk. No problem."

"It feels like a problem," Lucas said, running his hands through his hair. "Every time I get into this situation with a woman, they think I don't trust them."

"You've been in it a lot?" she asked.

"A couple of times. Drives me crazy."

"Okay. So you're a cop."

She picked up one of his long-sleeved flannel shirts that she'd been wearing in the cool evenings and smiled at him. "Don't worry about it, for God's sake. I'll be down at the dock, just call when you're done."

He watched her go down the steps and along the path through the front yard, and a moment later saw her silhouette against the dark water as she stepped out on the dock. He picked up the phone and dialed.

"I need to talk to Annie McGowan immediately. This is an emergency."

"Can I tell her who's calling, please?"

"Tell her Red Horse."

A moment later McGowan was on the line. "Red Horse?"

"Annie, there's been another killing. Have you heard yet?"

"No." Her voice was quick, excited. "Where's it at?"

"It's a hooker at Randy's Motel, down on Hennepin. Young girl. Her street name was Heather Brown. We've got people on the scene right now, you better get a crew up there. And let me give you one more piece of information about him, that our shrinks worked out. The chief and the other detectives will probably try to deny it, because they don't want this kind of sensitive information getting out, but we were expecting him to kill a hooker."

"Jeez, why?"

"Our shrinks think the guy is probably so ugly, so unattractive to women that not only can't he get it up, he can't get a woman on his own, either. One probably contributes to the other. We don't know that it's appearance, though. Maybe it's body chemistry or something. You know, maybe he's got like world-class body odor."

"Wow."

"Yeah, you get the idea. Really repellent, like a human lizard. I wouldn't give this to anybody, but I liked the way you blended my last tip, about the impotence, into your story. Now that he's killed the hooker, I think maybe this last piece of information will give the Now Report viewers some exclusive insight into the mind of a serial murderer, you know."

"This is really heavy, Luca . . . uh, Red Horse. Let me get this stuff going and I'll get back to you. Are you at home?"

"No. I'm way up north, three hours away. I'm about to start back, I'll get there just before midnight. I'll be at my house, probably, sometime after one o'clock, and I'll be up until three or so. If you have to call, call then."

"Okay. Thanks, Red Horse."


Carla was on the dock, wrapped in the flannel shirt.

"You going?"

"Yeah."

"I'll walk you up to your car."

"I wanted to spend more time," he said.

"So come back."

"If I can." He wrapped his arms around her and kissed her and she clung to him for a moment, then broke away and turned to the cabin. Lucas dropped into the Porsche, brought it around in a circle, and headed back to the Cities.


Driving at speed on the narrow roads of the North Woods thrilled him, but he usually did it in the daytime. At night the roadside timber seemed to step in, to press closer to the road. He overran his headlights, brush and phone poles flicking in and out of his vision without leaving time for thought.

Thirty miles out, just across the Minnesota border, he passed a roadside rest and the red lights came up behind him as a highway-patrol car burst onto the road.

Lucas wrenched the car to the shoulder and climbed out with his badge case in his hand. The patrolman was already on the road, one hand on his weapon, the other holding a long steel flashlight.

"I'm a Minneapolis cop making an emergency run back to the Cities," Lucas said as he walked toward the patrolman, extending the badge case. "Lieutenant Lucas Davenport. The maddog killer just ripped a hooker, a little girl. I'm trying to get back."

"Uh-huh," the patrolman said. He looked at the badge case and ID card with his light, then flashed it momentarily in Lucas' face.

"If you can call your dispatcher and have them patch you through to our dispatch—"

"I've seen you on TV," the patrolman said. He handed the badge case back. "I'm not going to give you a ticket, but a word to the wise, okay? I clocked you at eighty-three miles an hour. If you drive from here to the Interstate at fifty-five instead of eighty-three, it'll cost you an extra two minutes. If you drive at eighty-three and you hit a deer or a bear, you'll be dead. You're lucky you haven't hit one already. They're really moving right now. You hit a big old sow-bear broadside with that car, it'd be like hitting a brick wall."

"Right. I'm just sort of freaked out."

"Well, cool off," said the patrolman. "I'll call up ahead, tell the guys on the Interstate that you're trying to make up a little extra time. Keep it under a hundred and they won't hassle you, once you get on the Interstate."

"Thanks, man." Lucas headed back to his car.

"Hey, Davenport."

Lucas stopped with the door half-open. "Yeah?"

"Get that cocksucker."

The motel was a shabby single-story L-shaped building with a permanent hand-painted vacancy sign. There were a half-dozen squad cars and four television trucks parked in front when Lucas rolled in. He saw Jennifer and, further down the street, Annie McGowan, both with cameramen. Lucas squeezed the Porsche between two squad cars, got out, locked it, and started toward the yellow tape that blocked the motel driveway.

"Lucas."

"Hey, Jennifer . . ."

"You son of a bitch, you fed her another one."

"Who?"

"You know who. McGowan." Jennifer turned her head to glare down the street at the other woman.

"I did not," Lucas lied. "I was up north at my cabin, for Christ's sake."

"Well, somebody's feeding her select stuff. She's laughing up her sleeve at the rest of us."

"That's the way it goes in the news biz, huh?" He crouched and slipped under the tape. "Give me a call tomorrow, I'll see if I can get something for you."

"Hey, Lucas, you're not still angry? About the Smithe thing?"

"We have to talk," he said. "We have to figure out some kind of arrangement. You off tomorrow night?"

"Yeah, sure."

"So I'll take you to dinner somewhere private. We'll work something out."

"Great." She smiled and he turned and saw Anderson standing in a crowd outside the motel manager's office.

"So what?" he asked, taking Anderson by the sleeve.

"Come on down and take a look." He led the way toward the rear of the motel.

"Who found her?"

"The night clerk," Anderson said, glancing back. "The girl'd stop by and rap on the window when she was coming and going. She rapped going in, but never came back out. After a while, he kind of stuck his head out and says he saw this crack of light around her door. The killer apparently didn't pull it all the way shut when he left. That made the clerk curious and he walked down and knocked. And there she was."

"Did he see the killer? The clerk?"

"Uh-uh. He says he didn't see anybody."

"This clerk, is it Vinnie Short?"

"I don't know his name," Anderson said. "He's short, though."

Heather Brown was bound like the others, but unlike the others, her arms were stretched out at right angles to her body, as though she'd been crucified. The handle of the knife protruded from her chest under her breastbone. Her head was turned to one side, her eyes and mouth open. Her tongue stuck out, obscenely pale. She had long narrow scars on her thighs, white against her too-even machine tan.

"I don't know her," Lucas said. A vice officer walked in. "You know her?" Lucas asked.

"Seen her around a few times, she's been on the street a couple years," the vice cop said. "She used to be over on University, in St. Paul, but her old man OD'd on crank and she disappeared for a while."

"You're talking about Louis the White?"

"Yeah. See the scars on her legs? That was Louis' trademark. Used to beat them with coat hangers. Said it never took more than twice."

"But he's dead," said Lucas.

"Eight months ago. Good riddance. But I'll tell you something. His girls did the specialty tricks. Golden showers, bondage, spanking, like that. So this guy may have known her. The way she's tied up . . . it'd be hard to tie somebody up like that if she wasn't cooperating."

"You guys don't know who's running her now?"

"Nope. Haven't seen her around for a while," said the vice cop.

"We've talked to the night clerk but he claims he doesn't know anything about her," Anderson said. "Said she's been around two, three weeks. She'd come into the office, pay for the room, leave. She'd take a room for the night, bring two or three guys back, knock on the window when she was coming and going. She'd remake the bed herself."

"How much did she pay for the room?"

"I don't know," the vice cop said. "I could check."

"Usually it's one guy, one rent. They don't usually take them for the night. Not if the motel knows what's going on."

"This guy knows," said the vice cop.

"It's Vinnie Short?"

"Yeah."

"We have a long relationship. I'll go talk to him," Lucas said. He looked around the room again. "Nothing, huh?"

"Not much. The note."

"What'd it say?"

" 'Never carry a weapon after it has been used.' "

"Son of a bitch. He's not leaving us much."

Anderson wandered out. Lucas looked at the body again, then picked up Brown's bag and looked through it. A cheap plastic billfold contained fifteen dollars, a driver's license, a social-security card, and a half-dozen photos. He pulled the clearest one out of the billfold and let it fall to the bottom of the bag. In a side pocket he found two twists of plastic. Cocaine.

"Got a couple quarter-grams here," he said to the vice cop. "You inventoried her purse yet?"

"Not yet."

"Stick your head out the door and call Anderson, will you?"

When the cop stepped outside, Lucas pocketed the photograph from the billfold and snapped the billfold shut.

"Yeah?" Anderson stepped back inside.

"Got some toot. Better get a property bag around this purse before it goes away."

Vincent Short was short. He also had long, thinning red hair and thought he looked like Woody Allen. He didn't know nothing. He scratched his head and shook it, and scratched his head some more. The dandruff flakes fell like snow on his black turtleneck shirt. Two vice cops were standing around looking at him when Lucas came in. Short looked up and paled.

"Lieutenant," he said nervously.

"Vincent, my friend, we need to talk," Lucas said cheerfully. He looked around at the vice cops. "Could I have a private talk with this guy? We're old pals."

"No problem," said one of the cops.

"Say, you find the girl's registration card?"

"Yeah, right here."

One of the vice cops handed it to him and Lucas glanced at the total charge. Thirty dollars. "Thanks. See you around."

When they were gone, Lucas turned to Short, who was shrinking back in his chair.

"Maybe we ought to go back in the office where we can talk," he suggested.

"You fuck, Davenport—" Short started to cry.

Lucas leaned over his chair and spoke in kindly tones. "Vincent, you know who the girl's pimp is. Now, you've got to decide, are you more scared of him? Or more scared of me? And let me give you a hint. We're working on a multiple killer here. My ass is on the line. So you should definitely be more scared of me."

"You fuck—"

"And maybe you should think about what the boss is going to say when he finds out you rented a room to a hooker, all night, for thirty bucks. You must have been getting a little on the side, huh? Maybe a little pussy, maybe a little kickback? Huh, Vincent?"

"You fuck . . ."

Lucas glanced out the windows toward the street. Nobody was looking in. He reached down and grabbed the flesh between Short's nostrils between a thumb and forefinger and drove his thumbnail into it. Short arched his head as though he were being electrocuted and dragged at Lucas' hand with his, but Lucas hung on and pressed his other thumb into Short's throat below his Adam's apple so he couldn't scream. They struggled for a few seconds and then Lucas let go and backed off, and Short doubled up in the chair, his face buried in his hands, a long groan squeezing from his mouth.

Lucas leaned over him and wiped his fingers on Short's shirt, his face close to Short's.

"Who's her pimp?" Lucas asked quietly.

"Aw, c'mon, Davenport."

"If you think that hurt, I've got a couple more in places you wouldn't even believe," Lucas said. "Don't show, either."

"Sparks," he mumbled. His voice was almost inaudible. "Don't tell him I told you."

"Who?"

"Jefferson Sparks. She works for Sparks."

"Sparky. God damn." Lucas patted Short on the shoulder. "Thanks, Vincent. The police appreciate the cooperation of our citizens."

Short looked up at him, his eyes rimmed with red, tears running down his cheeks.

"Get out of here, you fuck."

"If this isn't right, if it's not Sparky, I'll be back," Lucas promised. He smiled at Short. "Have a nice day."

Outside, they were moving the body, wheeling it out into the flaring lights of the TV cameras. The vice cops were standing in a small group by the sidewalk, watching, when Lucas walked up.

"Your old pal tell you anything?"

"She worked for Jefferson Sparks," Lucas said.

"Sparky," one of the cops said enthusiastically. "I do believe I know where he's staying."

"Pick him up," said Lucas. "Soliciting or something. We'll talk to him down-town tomorrow morning."

"Sure."


Anderson was talking to the medical examiner. When he finished, he walked over to Lucas, shaking his head.

"Nothing?" asked Lucas.

"Not a thing."

"You're dragging the neighborhood for witnesses?"

"Got guys all over the place. Won't know anything until tomorrow."

"We got a name on the pimp," Lucas said. "Vice is going to look for him. Probably have him tomorrow."

"I hope he's got something," Anderson said. "This is getting old."


Lucas worked on his game for half an hour, editing the scenarios. It was the worst part of the job. The finishing touches were never done. With the murder of Heather Brown, he couldn't focus on the work.

He quit at two o'clock, ate a cup of strawberry yogurt, checked the doors, and turned out the lights. He had been in bed for ten minutes when the doorbell rang. Crawling out of bed, he tiptoed into the workroom so he could look out a window down the length of the house to the front door.

The doorbell rang again as he peeked out. Annie McGowan, alone in the streetlight, self-conscious as she waited by the door. Lucas sat down with his back to the wall, staring into the dark room. Jennifer was pregnant. Carla was waiting at the cabin. Lucas loved women, new women, different women.

Loved to talk to them, send them flowers, roll around in the night. Annie McGowan was stunning, a woman with the face of Helen and what promised to be an exquisite body, pink nipples, pale, solid flesh.

And she was dumb as a stump. Lucas thought about it, pinching the bridge of his nose.

Outside, Annie McGowan waited, and after another minute turned away from the house and started back toward her car. Lucas stood up and peered through a crack between the curtain and the wall as she opened the car door, hesitated, looked back at the house. The window opened vertically, with a crank. His hand was on the crank and it would take only a second to open it, call out to her before she got away. He didn't move. She slid into the driver's seat, pulled the door shut, and backed out of the drive.

In another second she was gone. Lucas walked back to the bedroom, lay down, and tried to sleep.

Visions of Annie . . .

# 15

Lucas' office door was open and the vice cop ambled in and plopped down in one of the extra chairs.

"Sparky's gone," he said.

"Damn. Nothing's coming easy," Lucas said.

"We found his place, down on Dupont, but he split last night," the vice cop said. "The guy who lives upstairs said Sparky came home about midnight, threw his shit in the car, and took off with one of his ladies. Said it didn't look like he was coming back."

"He knew about Brown," said Lucas, leaning back and planting his feet on the desktop.

"Yeah. Looks like."

"So where'd he go?"

The vice cop shrugged. "We're asking around. He's got a couple of other women. We've heard they're working a sauna out on Lake Street. Used to work at a place called the Iron Butterfly, but that's closed now. So we're looking."

"Relatives?"

"Don't know."

"When did we last have him in?" Lucas asked.

" 'Bout a year ago, I guess. Gross misdemeanor, soliciting for prostitution."

"He do time?"

"Three months in the workhouse."

"File upstairs?"

"Yeah. I could get it."

"Never mind," Lucas said. "I'm not doing anything. I'll walk over and take a look."

"We'll keep looking for him," the vice cop said. "Daniel's all over our backs."


Lucas flipped the lock on his office door and was pulling it closed when the phone rang. He stepped back inside and picked it up.

"Lucas? This is Jennifer. Are we going out tonight?"

"Sure. Seven o'clock?" An image of Carla flashed into his mind, her back arched, her breasts flattened, her mouth half-open.

Carla Ruiz.

Jennifer Carey, pregnant. "Yeah, that'd be fine. Pick me up here?"

"See you at seven."


The maddog was waiting for files in the clerk's office when Lucas walked in. The maddog recognized him immediately and forced himself to look back at the file he was holding. Lucas paid no attention to him. He walked through the swinging gate, behind the service counter, and across the room to the supervisor's cubicle. He stuck his head in the door and said something the maddog couldn't quite make out. The supervisor looked up from her desk and laughed and Lucas went in and perched on the edge of her desk.

The detective had an easy way about him. The maddog recognized and envied it. The files supervisor was an iron-girdled courthouse veteran who had seen one of everything, and Davenport had her fluttering like a teenage girl. As he watched, Lucas suddenly turned and looked at him and their eyes touched briefly. The maddog recovered and looked down at the file again.

"Who's the dude at the counter?" Lucas asked.

The supervisor looked around him at the maddog, who dropped the file in the return basket and headed for the door. "Attorney. Can't remember the firm, but he's been around a lot lately. He had that Barin kid, you know, that rich kid who drove into the crowd . . ."

"Yeah." The maddog disappeared through the door and Lucas dismissed him. "Jefferson Sparks. Bad guy. Pimp. I need the latest on him."

"I'll get it. You can use Lori's desk. She's out sick," the supervisor said, pointing at an empty desk behind the business counter.

Sparks had three recent files, each with a slender sheaf of flimsies. Lucas read through them and found a half-dozen references to the Silk Hat Health Club. He picked up the phone, called vice, and asked for the detective he had talked to that morning.

"Is the Silk Hat still run by Shirley Jensen?" he asked when the detective came on the line.

"Yup."

"I find the name in a couple of places in Sparky's file. Could that be where his women are working?"

"Could be. Come to think of it, Shirley used to do the books on the Butter-fly."

"Thanks. I'll run out there."

"Stay in touch."

Lucas hung up, tossed the files in the return basket, and glanced at his watch. Just after noon. Shirley should be working.

The Silk Hat was a black-painted storefront squeezed between a used-clothing store and a furniture-rental agency. The neon sign in the window said "Si k Hat t ealth Club" and the glass in both the window and door had been painted as black as the siding. There was a small wrought-iron door light over the door and a wise guy had spray-painted it red. Or maybe not a wise guy, Lucas thought. Maybe the owner.

Lucas pushed through the door into a small waiting room. Two plastic chairs sat on a red shag carpet behind a coffee table. A fish tank full of guppies perched on the sill of the blacked-out window. There were a half-dozen well-thumbed copies of *Penthouse* magazine on the coffee table. The chairs were facing a six-foot-long business counter that looked like it might have been stolen from a doctor's office. A door beside the counter led into the back of the store.

As Lucas stepped into the waiting room, he heard a buzzer sound in the back, and a few seconds later a young woman in a low-cut black dress stepped up behind the counter. She was chewing gum, and a june-bug tattoo was just visible on the swell of her left breast. She looked like Betty Boop but smelled like Juicy Fruit.

"Yah?"

"I want to talk to Shirley," Lucas said.

"I don't know if she's here."

"Tell her Lucas Davenport is waiting and if she doesn't get her fat ass out here, I'm going to fuck the place up."

The woman looked at him for a second, working her jaw until the gum snapped. She was not impressed. "Pretty tough," she said laconically. "I got a guy here you might want to talk to. Before you fuck the place up."

"Who?"

She looked him over and decided he might recognize the name. "Bald Peterson."

"Bald? Yeah. Tell him to get his ass out here too," Lucas said enthusiastically. He reached under his jacket and took out the P7 and the woman's eyes widened and she put up her hands as though to fend off a bullet. Lucas grinned at her and kicked the front panel of the counter and it splintered and he kicked it again and the woman turned and started running toward the back.

"Bald, you cocksucker, come out here," Lucas shouted into the back. He reached across the counter, grabbed the bottom side of the top sheet and pulled and it came up with a groan and he let it go and he kicked the front panel again and a piece of board broke off. "Bald, you motherfucker . . ."

Bald Peterson was six and a half feet tall and weighed two hundred and seventy pounds. He had had a minor career as a boxer, a slightly bigger one on the pro wrestling tour. Some people on Lake Street were sure he was psychotic. Lucas was sure he was not. Bald had attacked Lucas once, years before, when Lucas was still on patrol. It happened in a parking lot outside a nightclub, one-on-one. Bald used his fists. Lucas used a nine-inch lead-weighted sap wrapped in bull leather. Bald went down in six seconds of the first round. And after he went down, Lucas used his feet and a heavy steel flashlight and broke several of the bones in Bald's arms, most of the bones in his hands, the lower bones in both legs, the bones in the arches of his feet, his jaw, his nose, and several ribs. He also kicked him in the balls a half-dozen times.

While they were waiting for the ambulance, Bald woke up and Lucas gripped him by the shirt and told him that if he ever had any more trouble with him, he would cut off his nose, his tongue, and his dick. Lucas was suspended for investigation of possible use of excessive force. Bald was in the hospital for four months and a wheelchair for another six.

If Bald had been psychotic, Lucas thought, he would have come after Lucas with a gun, a knife, or, if he was really crazy, with his fists, as soon as he could walk. He didn't. He never looked at Lucas again, and walked wide around him.

"Bald, you dickhead . . ." Lucas shouted. He kicked the front panel of the desk and it caved in. There was a clattering on a back stairs and he stopped kicking and Shirley Jensen hurried up the hallway toward the counter. Lucas put the P7 away.

"You asshole," Jensen yelled.

"Shut up, Shirley," Lucas said. "Where's Bald?"

"He's not here."

"The other cunt said he was."

"He's not, Davenport, I mean, Jesus Christ on a crutch, look at this mess . . ." Jensen was in her late forties, her face lined from years of sunlamps, bourbon, cigarettes, and potatoes. She was a hundred pounds overweight. The fat bobbled under her chin, on her shoulders and upper arms, and quivered like jelly beneath her gold lamé belt. Her face crinkled and Lucas thought she might cry.

"I want to know where Sparky went."

"I didn't know he was gone," she said, still looking at the wreckage of the counter.

Lucas leaned forward until his face was only four inches from her nose. Her

Pan-Cake makeup was cracking like a dried-out Dakota lake bed. "Shirley, I'm going to tear this place up. My neck is on the line with this maddog killer, and Sparky might have some information I need. I'm going to wait here . . ." He looked at his watch, as though timing her. "Five minutes. Then I'm coming over the counter. You go find out where he is."

"Sparky knows something about the maddog?" The idea startled her.

"That was one of his girls who got ripped last night. The maddog's starting on hookers. It's a lot easier than scouting out the straights."

"Don't kick my counter no more," Shirley said, and she turned and waddled down the hallway and out of sight.

A few seconds later the front door opened and Lucas stepped back and away from it. A narrow man with a gray face, thin shoulders, and a seventy-dollar suit stepped inside, blinked at the ruined counter, and looked at Lucas.

"Jeez, what happened?"

"There's a police raid going on," Lucas said cheerfully. "But if you just want to exercise, you know, like push-ups, and drink some fruit juice, that's okay. Go on back."

The narrow man's Adam's apple bobbed twice and he said, "That's okay," and disappeared out the door. Lucas shrugged and dropped into one of the plastic chairs and picked up a *Penthouse*. *"I didn't believe things like this really happened,"* he read, *"but before I tell you about it, maybe I should describe myself. I'm a junior at a big midwestern university and the coeds around here say I'm pretty well-equipped. A girlfriend once measured me out at nine inches of rock-hard—"*

"Davenport . . ." Shirley emerged from the back.

"Yeah." He dropped the magazine on the table.

"Don't know where he is exactly, what hotel," she said, "but it's like in Cedar Rapids, some downtown hotel—"

"Iowa?"

"Yeah. He trolls through there a couple of times a year, Sioux City, Des Moines, Waterloo, Cedar Rapids. So one of his girls says he's down there, she don't know exactly the place, but she says it's a hotel downtown."

"Okay." Lucas nodded. "But if he's not there . . ."

"Fuck you, Davenport, you broke my desk."

Jennifer liked the flowers. Each table had two carnations, one red and one white, in a long-necked vase. The restaurant was run by a Vietnamese family, refugees who left a French restaurant behind in Saigon. The old man and his wife financed it, their kids ran the place and cooked, the in-laws worked the tables and bar and cash register, the ten-year-old grandchildren bused the tables and washed up.

"The big problem with this place," Jennifer said, "is that it's about to be discovered."

"That's okay," Lucas said. "They deserve it."

"I suppose." Jennifer looked at the red wine in her glass, watching the light reflections thrown through the venetian blinds from the street. "What are we going to do?" she asked after a moment of silence.

Lucas leaned back in his chair and crossed his legs. "We can't go on like this. You've really hammered me. Daniel knows about our relationship, and every time something breaks in the press, he's looking at me. Even if it's Channel Eight."

"I'm done reporting, at least for now," she answered. She tilted her head and let her hair fall away from her face, and Lucas' eyes traveled around the soft curve of her chin and he thought he was in love.

"Yeah, but if you get a lead . . . tell me you won't feed it to one of your pals," he said.

Jennifer sipped the wine, set the glass on the table, ran her finger around its rim, and suddenly looked up into his eyes. "Did you sleep with McGowan?"

"Goddammit, Jennifer," Lucas said in exasperation. "I did not. Have not."

"Okay. But I'm not sure about you," she said. "Somebody's feeding stuff to her, and whoever he is, he's tight with the investigation."

"It's not me," Lucas said. He leaned forward and said, "Besides, the stuff she's getting . . ." He stopped, bit his lip. "I could tell you something, but I'm afraid you'd quote me and really louse me up."

"Is it a story?" she asked.

Lucas considered. "It could be, maybe. It'd be pretty unusual. You'd be cutting on McGowan."

Jennifer shook her head. "I wouldn't do that. Nobody in TV does that. It's too dangerous, you'd set off a war. So tell me. If it's like you say, I swear nobody will hear it from me."

Lucas looked at her a minute. "Really?"

"Really."

"You know," he said casually, as though it were of no importance, "I've threatened to stop talking to you in the past, but there were always reasons to get together again. I could always find a way to excuse what you did."

"That's big of you."

"Wait a minute. Let me finish. This time, you've made a direct promise. No ifs, ands, or buts. If it gets out, I'll know where it had to come from. And I'll know that we won't have any basis to trust each other. Ever. Even with the kid. I'm not playing a game now. This is real life."

Jennifer leaned back, looked up at the ceiling, then dropped her eyes to him. "When I was a teenager, I made a deal with my father," she said slowly. She looked up. "If something was really important and he had to know the truth of it, I would tell him the truth and then say 'Girl Scout's honor.' And if he wanted to tell me something and emphasize that it was important and he wasn't kidding or fibbing, he'd say 'Boy Scout's honor' and give me the Boy Scout sign. I know it sounds silly, but we never broke it. We never lied."

"And you won't tell . . ."

"Girl Scout's honor," she said, giving the three-finger sign. "Jesus, we must look ridiculous."

"All right," Lucas said. "What I was going to tell you is this. I don't know where McGowan's information is coming from, but most of it is completely wrong. She says we think the guy is impotent or smells bad or looks weird, and we don't think any of that. It's all courthouse rumor. We think she's probably getting it from some uniform out on the periphery of the investigation."

"It's all bull?" Jennifer asked, not believing.

"Yep. It's amazing, but that's the truth of the matter. She's had all these great scoops and it's all bullshit. As far as I know, she's making it up."

"You wouldn't be fibbing, would you, Davenport?" She watched him closely and he stared straight back.

"I'm not," he said.

"Did you sleep with McGowan?"

"No, I did not," he said. He lifted his hand in the three-fingered Scout sign. "Boy Scout's honor," he said.

She toyed with the stem of her wineglass, watching the wine roll around inside. "I've got to do some thinking about you, Davenport. I've had some . . . passions before, for other men. This is turning into something different."

They slept in the next morning. Jennifer was reading the *Pioneer Press* and Lucas was cooking breakfast when the phone rang.

"This is Anderson."

"Yeah."

"A cop from Cedar Rapids called. They busted Sparky for conspiracy to commit prostitution, and they've got—"

"Conspiracy to what?"

"Some kind of horseshit charge. He said their county attorney will kick their ass when he finds out. They'll have to tell him this afternoon, before the end of business hours. We got you on a plane at ten. Which gives you an hour to get out to the airport. Ticket's waiting."

"How long does it take to drive?"

"Five, six hours. You'd never make it, not before they have to tell the county attorney. Then they'll probably have to turn Sparky loose."

"All right, all right, give me the airline." Lucas wrote the details on a scratch pad, hung up, and went to tell Jennifer.

"I won't ask," she said, grinning at him.

"I'll tell you if you want. But I'd need the Girl Scout's oath that you won't tell."

"Nah. I can live without knowing," she said. She was still grinning at him. "And if you're going to fly, you might want to break out the bourbon."

The airline that flew between Twin Cities International and Cedar Rapids was perfectly reliable. Never had a fatal crash. Said so right in its ads. Lucas held both seat arms with a death grip. The elderly woman in the next seat watched him curiously.

"This can't be your first time," she said ten minutes into the flight.

"No. Unfortunately," Lucas said.

"This is much safer than driving," the old woman said. "It's safer than walking across the street."

"Yes, I know." He was staring straight ahead. He wished a stroke on the old woman. Anything that would shut her up.

"This airline has a wonderful safety record. They've never had a crash."

Lucas nodded and said, "Um."

"Well, don't worry, we'll be there in an hour."

Lucas cranked his head toward her. He felt as though his spine had rusted. "An hour? We've been up pretty long now."

"Only ten minutes," she said cheerfully.

"Oh, God."

The police psychologist had told him that he feared the loss of control.

"You can't deal with the idea that your life is in somebody else's hands, no matter how competent they are. What you have to remember is, your life is always in somebody else's hands. You could step into the street and get mowed down by a drunk in a Cadillac. Much more chance of that than a plane wreck."

"Yeah, but with a drunk, I could see him coming, maybe. I could sense it. I could jump. I could get lucky. Something. But when a plane quits flying . . ." Lucas mimed a plane plowing nose-down into his lap. "Schmuck. Dead meat."

"That's irrational," the shrink said.

"I know that," Lucas said. "I want to know what to do about it."

The shrink shook his head. "Well, there's hypnotism. And there are some books that are supposed to help. But if I were you, I'd just have a couple of drinks. And try not to fly."

"How about chemicals?"

"You could try some downers, but they'll mess up your head. I wouldn't do it if you have to be sharp when you get where you're going."

The flight to Cedar Rapids didn't offer alcohol. He didn't have pills. When the wheels came down, his heart stopped.

"It's only the wheels coming down," the old woman said helpfully.

"I know that," Lucas grated.

Lucas cashed the return portion of the plane ticket.

"You'll take a loss," the clerk warned.

"That's the least of my problems," Lucas said. He rented a car that he could drop back in Minneapolis and got directions to the police station. The station was an older building, four-square concrete, function over form. Kind of like Iowa, he thought. A cop named MacElreney was waiting for him.

"Carroll MacElreney," he said. He had wide teeth and an RAF mustache. He was wearing a green plaid sport coat, brown slacks, and brown-and-white saddle shoes.

"Lucas Davenport." They shook hands. "We appreciate this. We're in a bind."

"I've been reading about it. Sergeant Anderson said you don't think Sparks did it, but might know something? That right?"

"Yeah. Maybe."

"Let's go see." MacElreney led the way to an interview room. "Mr. Sparks is unhappy with us. He thinks he's been treated unfairly."

"He's an asshole," Lucas said. "You find his girl?"

"Yeah. Kinda young."

"Aren't they all?"

Sparks was sitting on one of three metal office chairs when Lucas followed the Cedar Rapids cop into the room. He's getting old, Lucas thought, looking at the other man. He had first seen Sparks on the streets in the early seventies. His hair then had been a faultless shiny black, worn in a long Afro. Now it was gray, and deep furrows ran down Sparks' forehead to the inside tips of his eyebrows. His nose was a flattened mess, his teeth nicotine yellow and crooked. He looked worried.

"Davenport," he said without inflection. His eyes were almost as yellow as his teeth.

"Sparky. Sorry to see you in trouble again."

"Whyn't you cut the crap and tell me what you want?"

"We want to know why you left town fifteen minutes after one of your ladies got her heart cut out."

Sparks winced. "Is that what—"

"Don't give me any shit, Sparky. We just want to know where you dumped the knife." Lucas suddenly stopped and looked at MacElreney. "You gave him his rights?"

"Just on the prostitution charge."

"Jesus, I better do it again, let me get my card . . ." Lucas reached for his billfold and Sparks interrupted.

"Now, wait a minute, Davenport," Sparks said, even more worried. "God damn, I got witnesses that I didn't do nothin' like that. I loved that girl."

Lucas eased his billfold back in his pocket.

"You see who did it?"

"Well, I don't know . . ."

Lucas leaned forward. "I personally don't think you did it, Sparky. But you gotta give me something to work with. Something I can take back. These guys from vice want to hang you. You know what they're saying? They're saying, sure, he might not be guilty of this. But he's guilty of everything else and we can get him for this. Dump old Sparky in Stillwater, it'd solve a lot of problems. That's what they're saying. They found some coke in your lady's purse, and that doesn't go down too well either . . ."

Sparks licked his lips. "I knew that bitch was holding out."

"I don't care about that, Sparky. What'd you see?"

"I seen this guy . . ."

"Let me get my recorder going," Lucas said.

Sparks had a crack habit that was hard to stay ahead of. On the night Heather Brown was killed, he had been sitting on a bus bench across the street, waiting for her to produce some money. He had seen her last date approach her.

"Wasn't it pretty dark?"

"Yeah, but they got all them big blue lights down there."

"Okay."

There was nothing particularly distinctive about the maddog. Average height. White. Regular features, roundish face. Yeah, maybe a little heavy. Went right to her, there didn't seem to be much negotiation.

"You think she knew him?"

"Yeah, maybe. But I don't know. I never saw him before, and she was on the street for a while. Wasn't a regular. At least, not while she was with me."

"She still doing the rough trade?"

"Yeah, there was a few boys would come around." He held his hands up defensively. "I didn't make her. She liked it. Get spanked a little. Good money, too."

"So this guy. How was he dressed? Sharp?"

"No. Not sharp," Sparks said. "He looked kind of like a farmer."

"A farmer?"

"Yeah. He had one of them billed hats on, you know, that got shit wrote on the front? And he was wearing one of those cheap jackets like you get at gas stations. Baseball jackets."

"You sure this was her last date?"

"Yeah. Had to be. She went to the motel and I went off to get a beer. The next thing I knew was the sirens coming down the street."

"Farmer doesn't sound right," Lucas said.

"Well . . ." Sparks scratched his head. "He didn't look right, either. There was something about him . . ."

"What?"

"I don't know. But there was something." He scratched his head again.

"You see his car?"

"Nope."

Lucas pressed, but there wasn't anything more.

"You think you'd recognize him?"

"Mmm." Sparks looked at the floor between his feet, thinking it over. "I don't think so. Maybe. I mean, maybe if I saw him walking down the street in the night with the same clothes, I'd say, there, that's the motherfucker right there. But if you put him in a lineup, I don't think so. I was way across the street. All there was, was those streetlights."

"Okay." Lucas turned off his recorder. "We want you back in the Cities, Sparky. You can run your girls. Nobody will hassle you until we get this turkey. When we locate him, we'd like you around to take a look. Just in case."

"You ain't gonna roust me?"

"Not if you stay cool."

"All right. How about this bullshit charge here?"

MacElreney shook his head. "We can process you out in ten minutes if Minneapolis doesn't want you."

"We don't want him," Lucas said. He turned back to Sparks. "But we do want you back in the Cities. If you start trolling the other Iowa cities on your route, we'll roust you out of every one of them. Get back up to Minneapolis."

"Sure. Be a relief. Too much corn down here for the likes of me." He glanced at MacElreney. "No offense."

MacElreney looked offended.


Lucas had unlocked the door of the rental car when MacElreney shouted at him from the steps of the police station. Sparks was right behind him and they walked down the sidewalk together.

"I thought of what was weird about that dude," Sparks said. "It was his haircut."

"His haircut?"

"Yeah. Like, when they walked away from me toward the motel, he took his hat off. I couldn't see his face or anything, only the back of his head. But I remember thinking he didn't have a farmer haircut. You know how farmers always got their ears stickin' out? Either that, or it looks like their old lady cut their hair with a bowl? Well, this guy's hair was like *styled*. Like yours, or like a businessman or a lawyer or doctor or something. Slick. Not like a farmer. Never seen a farmer like that."

Lucas nodded. "Okay. Blond guy, right?"

Sparks' forehead wrinkled. "Why, no. No, he was a dark-haired dude."

Lucas leaned closer. "Sparky, are you sure? Could you make a mistake?"

"No, no. Dark-haired dude."

"Shit." Lucas thought it over. It didn't fit. "Anything else?" he asked finally.

Sparks shook his head. "Nothin' except you're getting old. I remember when I first knew you, when you beat up Bald Peterson. You had this nice smooth face like a baby's ass. You gettin' some heavy miles."

"Thanks, Sparks," Lucas said. "I needed that."

"We all be gettin' old."

"Sure. And I'm sorry about your lady, by the way."

Sparks shrugged. "Women do get killed. And it ain't like there's no shortage of whores."

The drive back took the rest of the day. After a stop near the Iowa line for a cheeseburger and fries, Lucas put the cruise control on seventy-five and rolled across the Minnesota River into Minneapolis a little after eight o'clock. He dropped the rental car at the airport and took a taxi home, feeling grimy and tight from the trip. A scalding shower straightened out his bent back. When he was dressed again, he got beer from the refrigerator, went down to the spare bedroom, put the beer can on the floor next to the bed, and lay back, looking at the five charts pinned to the wall.

Bell, Morris, Ruiz, and Lewis. The maddog. The dates. Personal characteristics. He read through them, sighed, got up, pinned a sixth sheet of paper to the wall, and wrote "Brown" at the top with his Magic Marker.

Hooker. Young. Dark hair and eyes. The physical description was right. But she was killed in a motel, after being picked up on the street. All the others had been attacked in private places, their homes or apartments, or, in Lewis' case, the empty house she was trying to sell.

He reviewed the other features of the Brown murder, including her appearance in court. Could the maddog be a lawyer? Or even a judge? A court reporter? How about a bailiff or one of the other court personnel? There were dozens of them. And he noted the knife. The maddog brought it with him for this killing. Chicago Cutlery was an expensive brand, and it was widely sold around the Twin Cities in the best department and specialty stores. Could he be some kind of gourmet? A cooking freak? Was it possible that he bought the knife recently and that a check of stores would turn up somebody who'd sold a single blade to a pudgy white guy?

*    *    *

Lucas looked at the notes on the maddog chart. That he was well-off, that he could be new to the area. Up from the Southwest. Office job. Sparks had confirmed that he was fair-skinned. The business about the dark hair was a problem; Carla was sure that he was very fair, and that suggested lighter hair. There were some black-haired Irish, and some Finns would fit the bill, but that seemed to be stretching. Lucas shook his head, added "dark hair?" At the end of the list he wrote "Expensive haircut. Dark hair? Wig? Wears disguises (farmer). Gourmet?"

He lay back again, his head propped up on a pillow, took a sip of beer, held the can on his chest, and read through the lists again.

*Rich man, poor man, beggar man, thief, doctor, lawyer, Indian chief. Cop.*

He glanced at his watch. Nine-forty-five. He got off the bed, the beer still in his hand, walked back to the workroom, and picked up the telephone. After a moment's hesitation he punched in the number for Channel Eight.

"Tell her it's Red Horse," he said. McGowan was on the line fifteen seconds later.

"Red Horse?"

"Yeah. Listen, Annie, this is exclusive. There was a witness on the street near the Brown killing. He actually saw the maddog. Says he looked like a farmer. He was wearing one of those hats with the bills on them, like seed hats? So it's possible that he's driving in from the countryside."

"A commuter killer?"

"Yeah, you could say that."

"Like he commutes to the Twin Cities to murder these women, then goes back home, where he's just another farmer picking potatoes or whatever?"

"Well, uh, we think maybe he's a pig farmer. This guy, the witness, brushed past him, wondered what this farmer-looking dude was doing with a chick like Brown. Anyway, he said there was a kind of odor hanging about him, you know?"

"You mean . . . pig shit?"

"Uh, pig manure, yes. That kind of confirms what we thought before."

"That's good, Red Horse. Is there any chance we can get this guy on camera?"

"No. No chance. If something happens to change that, we'll let you know, but we're keeping his identity a secret for now. If the maddog found out who he is, he might go after him."

"Okay. Let me know if that changes. Anything else?"

"No. That's it."

"Thanks, Red Horse. I mean, I really, really appreciate this."

There was a moment of silence, of pressure. Lucas fought it.

"Uh, yeah," he said. "See you."

# 16

A pig farmer?

The maddog raged through his apartment. They said he was a pig farmer. They said he smelled like pig shit.

He had trouble focusing.

The real issue. He had to remember the real issue: somebody had seen him and remembered the way he dressed. Had they seen his face? Was an artist working on circulars? Would they be plastered around the courthouse in the morning? He gnawed on a thumbnail, pacing. Pain flashed through his hand. He looked down and found he had ripped a chunk of nail out, peeling it away from the lobster-pink underskin. Blood surged into the tear. Cursing, he stumbled to the bathroom, found a clipper, tried to trim the nail, his hand shaking. When it was done, his thumb still throbbing, he wrapped it with a plastic bandage and went back to the television.

Sports. He ran the videotape back and watched Annie McGowan deliver her scoop. Pig farmer, she said. Commuter killer. Smells of pig manure, may explain his inability to attract women. He punched the sound and watched only the picture, her black hair with the bangs curled over her forehead, her deep, dark eyes.

Now she stirred him. She looked like . . . who? Somebody a long time ago. He stopped the tape, rewound it, ran it again, with the sound muted. She was Chosen.


McGowan.

Research would be needed, but he had time. She was a good choice for several reasons. She would be satisfying; and she would teach a lesson. He was not One to laugh at. He was not One to be called a pig farmer. The Cities would be horrified; nobody would laugh. They would know the power. Everybody: they would know it. He paced rapidly, circling the living room, watching McGowan's face, running the tape back, watching again. A fantasy. A lesson.


A lesson for later. There was another Chosen. She moved through his sleep and his waking vision. She *moved*; she did not walk. She lived less than two long blocks from the maddog. He had seen her several times, rolling down the sidewalk in her wheelchair. An auto accident, he learned. She was an undergraduate at the university when it happened. She had been streaking through the night with a fraternity boy in his overpowered sports car. His neck snapped with the impact when they hit the overpass abutment, her back was shattered by a seat frame. Took an hour to get her out of the car. Both newspapers reported the accident.

But she came back, and both newspapers did feature stories about her return.

Graduated from the school of business, started law. A woman in law; they were all over the place now. She had a backpack hung from the side of her machine to carry her books. She rolled the chair with her own arms, so she'd be strong. Lived by herself in an apartment on the back of a crumbling house six blocks from the law school.

The maddog had already scouted the apartment. It was owned by an old woman, a widow, who lived in the front with a half-dozen calico cats. A student couple lived upstairs. The cripple lived in back. A ground-level ramp allowed her to roll right into the kitchen of the three-room unit. The news clips said she valued her singleness, her independence. She wore a steel ring on a chain around her neck; it had belonged to the boy killed in the wreck. She said she had to live for both of them now. More clips.

The maddog had done his research in the library, finding her name in the indexes, reading the stories on microfilm. In the end, he was certain. She was Chosen.

If he had the chance to take her. But he had been seen. Recognized. What would the morning bring? He paced for an hour, round and round the apartment, then threw on a coat and walked outside. Cold. A hard frost for sure. Winter coming.

He walked down the block, down the next, past the cripple's house. The upper apartment was lit up. The lower one, the old lady's, was dark. He continued past and looked back at the side of the house; the cripple's window was also dark. He glanced at his watch. One o'clock. She was top of the class, the news clips said. He licked his lips, felt the sting of the wind against his wet mouth. He needed her. He really did.


He continued his walk, across the street, down another block, and another. The vision of the cripple rolling through his mind. He had been seen. Would his face be in the papers the next day? Would the police get a call? Might they be getting a call now? They could be driving to his apartment now, looking for him. He shivered, walked. The cripple floated up again. Sometime later, he found himself standing in front of a university dormitory. A new building, red brick. There was a phone inside. Davenport.

The maddog walked into the dormitory in a virtual trance. A blonde coed in a white ski-team sweatshirt glanced at him as she went through the door into the inner lobby, past the check-in desk. The phone was mounted on a wall opposite the rest rooms. He pressed his forehead against the cool brick. He shouldn't do it. He groped in his pocket for a quarter.

"Hello?"

"Davenport?" He sensed a sudden tension on the other end.

"Yeah."

"What is this game? What is this pig thing?"

"Ah, could you—?"

"You know who this is; and let me warn you. I've chosen the next one. And when you play games, you anger the One; and the Chosen will pay. I'm going to go look at her now. I'm that close. I am looking." The words, in his own ears, sounded pleasantly formal. Dignified.

He dropped the receiver back on the hook and walked back through the empty outer lobby, pushed through the glass doors. Pig farmer. His eyes teared and he bent his head and trudged toward home.

The walk was lost in alternating visions of the Chosen and McGowan and quick cuts of Davenport in the clerk's office, his face turning toward him, looking at him. The maddog paid no attention to where he was going, until he unexpectedly found himself standing outside his apartment. His feet had found their own way; it was like waking from a dream. He went in, began to take off his coat, hesitated, picked up the phone book, found the number, and dialed the *Star-Tribune*.

"City desk." The voice was gruff, hurried.

"When do the papers come out?"

"Should be on the street now. Anytime."

"Thanks." The phone on the other end hit the hook before the word was fully out of his mouth.

The maddog went out to his car, started it, drove across the Washington Street bridge into the downtown. There were two green newspaper boxes outside the *Star-Tribune* building. He pulled over, deposited his quarters, and looked at the front page: MADDOG A HOG FARMER? TV STORY SAYS "YES."

The story was taken directly from McGowan's news broadcast. A brief telephone interview with the chief of police was appended: "I don't know where she got the information, but I don't know anything about it," Daniel said. He did not, however, deny the possibility that the killer was a farmer. "Anything is possible at this point," he added.

There was no sketch. There was no description.

He went back to his car, sat in the driver's seat, and paged quickly through the paper. There was another story about the killings on page three, comparing them to a similar string of killings in Utah. Nothing more. He turned back to the front page.

Hog farmer, it said.

He would not permit it.

# 17

Daniel leaned far back in his chair, the eraser end of a yellow pencil pressed against his lower teeth, watching Sloan. Anderson and Lester slumped in adjacent chairs. Lucas paced.

"What you're saying is, we got nothing," Daniel said when the detective finished.

"Nothing we can use to bag the guy," Sloan said. "When we find him, we've got information we can use to pin him down. We could even run him by Jefferson Sparks, see if he rings a bell. But we don't have anything to point at him."

"What about driver's licenses? Did we get that?"

Anderson shook his head. "They don't track incoming state licenses by individual names."

Lucas paced at the perimeter of the room. "What about those post offices?"

"We're getting some returns. Too many of them. We've had a hundred and thirty-six moves so far, covering the past two years, and we've only heard from post offices covering maybe a tenth of the population we're looking at. If that rate holds up, we'll get about fourteen hundred names. We're also finding out that the most likely moves are young single males. Probably a third of them in that category. That's something like five hundred suspects. And all of it rests on the idea that the guy's maybe got an accent."

"And if he moved here three years ago, instead of in the last two, we're fucked anyway," said Daniel.

"But it's something," Lucas insisted. "How many of the ones that you have so far are single males? Assuming that's what we want to look at?"

"Thirty-eight of the hundred and thirty-six. But some of those apparently moved here with women or moved in with a woman after they got here, or are old. We've had a couple of guys doing a quick scan of the names, and there are about twenty-two that fit all the basic criteria: young, single, male, unattached."

"White-collar?" asked Lucas.

"All but two. People don't move here for blue-collar jobs. There are more jobs in Texas, and less cold," Anderson said.

"So what are we talking about?" Daniel asked.

"Well, we're talking about checking these twenty-two. We should be able to eliminate half or better, just walking around. Then we'll focus tighter on the rest of them. 'Course, we'll have new names coming in all the time."

"Lucas? Anything else?"

Lucas took another turn at the back of the room. He had talked to Daniel the night before about the phone call from the maddog, and told the others at the start of the meeting. He'd taped the call. He was taping all calls now. First thing in the morning, he'd taken a copy of the tape to the university and tracked down a couple of linguists to listen to it.

They had called Daniel during the meeting: Texas, one of them said. The other was not quite so certain. Texas, or some other limited sections of the Southwest. The eastern corner of New Mexico, maybe, around White Sands. Oklahoma and Arkansas were out.

"His accent has a strong overlay of the Midwest," the second linguist said. "There's this one line, 'I'm going to go look at her now.' If you listen closely, break it down, what he really says is 'I'm-unna go look at her now.' That's a midwesternism. Upper Midwest, north central. So I think he's been here awhile. Not so long that he's completely lost his southwestern accent, but long enough to get an overlay."

"Ah," Lucas said. The detectives were looking at him curiously. "Last night, I was watching Channel Eight. McGowan comes on and she has this piece about the pig farmer. So the maddog calls forty-five minutes later. I checked with the *Pioneer Press* and the *Star-Tribune* to see what time the first editions came out—they both carried follows on the McGowan story. None of them were out when the maddog called."

"So he saw it on TV," Anderson said.

"And I've been thinking about McGowan," Lucas said. "She fits the type the maddog's been going after . . ."

"Ah, Jesus Christ," Daniel blurted.

"There was something about that call. There's something special about this 'chosen' one he talks about. I feel it."

"You think he might go after McGowan?"

"He's watching her on TV. And physically, she fits his type. And she's had all these weird stories. The guy seems to want the attention, but from his point of view, everything she's been saying is negative. He talks about being the 'one' and she says he's impotent and smells bad and farms pigs. Last night, he was pissed."

"That's it," Daniel said, his face flushed. "I want a watch on McGowan, twenty-four hours."

"Jesus, chief—" Anderson started.

"I don't care how many guys it takes. Break some of them out of uniform if you have to. I want guys on her during the day and I want a watch on her house at night."

"But delicately," Lucas said.

"What?"

"She's our chance to grab him," Lucas said. He put up his hands to stop interruptions. "I know, I know, we've got to be careful. Not take any chances with her. I know all that. But she might be our best shot."

"If you're right, he might be looking at her right now," Lester said. "Right this minute."

"I don't think he'll try during the day. She's always around people. If he tries, it'll be at night. When she's on her way home or at her home. He could break into her house during the day and wait for her. We should cover that possibility."

"You've thought about this," Daniel said, his eyes narrowing.

Lucas shrugged. "Yeah. Maybe I've got my head up my ass. But it seems like a chance, just like when you put a watch on me."

"Okay," Daniel said. He turned and pressed an intercom lever. "Linda, call Channel Eight and tell them I want to talk to the station manager urgently." He let the intercom go and said, "Lucas, stay a minute. Everybody else, let's get going on the basics. Start processing the list of guys who moved in. It won't do any good if he's really been here for a while, but we've got to check. Anderson, I want you to go back over every note we've got, see if we're missing anything we should have covered."

As the others drifted out of the room, Lucas slouched against a wall, staring at the rug.

"What?" Daniel said.

"This guy is nuts in a different way than I thought. He's not a straight, cold killer. There's something else wrong with his head. The way he was talking about the 'one' and the 'chosen.'"

"What difference does it make?"

"I don't know. Could make it harder to outguess him. He might not react like we expect him to."

"Whatever," Daniel said dismissively. "I wanted to ask you about something else. Where is McGowan getting this crap she's putting on the air?"

Lucas shook his head. "Probably a uniform who's just close enough to the investigation to pick up some stuff, but not close enough to get it right."

"So you're in Cedar Rapids yesterday and it's the first time anybody said the word 'farmer' in the whole investigation. The next thing I know, she's on the air saying the maddog is a farmer."

"Saying *pig farmer*. There's a difference. Whoever's feeding her is cutting the killer up. Sparks doesn't even think the maddog is a farmer. I don't either. I stopped on the way back and called in what Sparks said, so Anderson could get it in the data base. After that? Who knows. There's a leak, but it's all twisted up."

"Okay," said Daniel. He was suspicious, Lucas thought. More than suspicious. He knew, and was talking for the record. "I'm not going to ask you anything else about this coincidence. But I would remark that if somebody is playing a game, it could be a dangerous one."

"We're already playing a dangerous game," Lucas said. "The maddog's not giving us any choice."

Lucas spent the afternoon on the street, touching informants, friends, contacts, letting them know he was alive. A Colombian had been in town, supposedly to negotiate a four-way cocaine wholesaling net to cover the metro area. It would be run by three men and a woman, each with separate territories and responsibilities. If any of them tried to make a move on somebody else's territory, the Colombian would cut off the troublemaker's supply.

Lucas was interested. Most of the cocaine in the Twin Cities was in weights of three ounces or less, bought on the subwholesale level from Detroit and Chicago, and, to a lesser extent, Los Angeles. There had been rumors of direct Colombian connections before, but they never materialized. This had a different feel to it. He pushed his informants for names, promising money and immunity in return.

There were more rumors of gang activity, recruitments of local chapters out of Chicago and Los Angeles. Gang growth was slow in the Cities. Members were systematically harassed by the gang squads in both towns and were sent to prison so often, and for so long, that any kid with an IQ above ninety stayed away from them.

Indians on Franklin Avenue were talking about a woman who either jumped or was thrown off the Franklin Avenue bridge. No body had shown up. Lucas made a note to call the sheriff's river patrol.

He was back at his desk late in the afternoon when McGowan called.

"Lucas? Isn't it wonderful?" she bubbled.

"What?"

"You know about this thing with the maddog? They're setting up surveillance around me?"

"Yeah, I knew the chief was going to get in touch."

"Well, I agreed to the surveillance, but only if we could tape parts of it. You know, we'll cooperate and everything, but once in a while, when it's natural, we'll get a camera in the house and get some tape of me cooking or sewing or something. They're going to set up a surveillance post across the street and another one behind the house. They'll let a camera come up and shoot the cops watching my house with their binoculars and stuff." She was more than excited, Lucas thought. She was ecstatic.

"Jesus, Annie, this isn't a sporting event. You'll be covered, of course, but this guy is a maniac."

"I don't care," she said firmly. "If he comes after me, the story will go network. I'll be on every network news show in the country, and I'll tell you what—if I get a chance like that and I handle it right, I'll be out of here. I'll be in New York in six weeks."

"It's a nice idea, but death would be a nasty setback," Lucas said.

"Won't happen," she said confidently. "I've got eight cops, twenty-four hours a day. No way he'll get to me."

Or if he got to her, there was no way he'd escape, Lucas thought. "I hope they're setting you up with some sort of emergency alarm."

"Oh, sure. We're working that out right now. It's like a beeper and I wear it on my belt. I never take it off. As soon as I hit it, everybody comes running."

"Don't get overconfident. Carla Ruiz never saw him coming, you know. If she hadn't been worried about going out on the street alone and if she hadn't been carrying that Mace, she'd be dead."

"Don't worry, Lucas. I'll be fine." McGowan's voice dropped a notch. "I'd like to see you, you know, outside of work. I was going to mention something, but now, with twenty-four-hour surveillance . . ."

"Sure," he said hastily. "It wouldn't be good if the chief or even your people found out how close we are."

"Great," she said. "I'll see you, good old Red Horse."

"Take care of yourself."


Detectives from narcotics, vice, and sex set up the direct surveillance, backed by out-of-uniform patrolmen who were assigned unmarked cars on streets adjacent to McGowan's. Lucas stayed away the first night, when the posts were established. Too many cops, too much coming and going, would draw attention from the neighborhood. The second night he went out with a vice cop named Henley.

"You ever seen her place?" Henley asked.

"No. Pretty nice?"

"Not bad. Small older house across the street from Minnehaha Creek. Two stories. Lot and a half. There's a big side yard on the east with a couple of apple trees in it. There's another house on the west, maybe thirty feet between them, all open. Must have set her back a hundred thou."

"She's got some bucks," Lucas said.

"Face like hers on TV, I believe it."

"She said you're on both sides?"

"Yeah. We've got a place directly across the street in front and one across the alley in back," Henley said. "We're watching from the attics in both places."

"We renting?"

"The guy on the Minnehaha side didn't want any money, said he'd be happy to do it. We told him we could be there a couple months, he said no problem."

"Nice guy."

"Old guy. Retired architect. I think he likes the company. Lets us put stuff in the refrigerator, use the kitchen."

"How about in back?"

"That's an old couple. They were going to give us the space, but they looked like they were hurting for money, so we rented. Couple hundred bucks a month, gave them two months. They were happy to get it."

"Funny. That's a pretty rich neighborhood," Lucas said.

"I was talking to them, they're not doing so good. The old man said they lived too long. They retired back in the sixties, both had pensions, they figured they were set for life. Then the inflation came along. Everything went up. Taxes, everything. They're barely keeping their heads above water."

"Hmmp. Which one are we going to?"

"The architect's. We park on the other side of the creek and walk across a bridge. We come up behind a row of houses along the water, then into the back of his house. Keeps us off the street in front of the place."

The architect's house was large and well-kept, polished wood and Oriental rugs, artifacts of steel and bronze, beautifully executed black-and-white etchings and drypoints hung on the eggshell walls. The vice cop led the way up four flights of stairs into a dimly lit, unfinished attic space. Two cops sat on soft chairs, a telephone by their feet, binoculars and a spotting scope between them. A mattress lay on the floor to one side of the room. Beside it, a boombox played easy-listening music.

"How you doing?" one of the cops asked. The other one nodded.

"Anything going on?" Lucas asked.

"Guy walked his dog."

Lucas walked up to the window and looked out. The window had been covered from the inside with a thin, shiny plastic film. From the street, the window would appear to be transparent, the space behind it unoccupied.

"She home?"

"Not yet. She does the ten-o'clock news, cleans up, usually goes out for something to eat. Then she comes home, unless she has a date. For the next couple of weeks, she's coming straight home."

Lucas sat down on the mattress. "I think—I'm not sure—but I think if he hits her, he'll come after dark but before midnight. He's careful. He won't want to walk around at a time when people will notice him, but he'll want the dark to hide his face. I expect he'll try to get in the house while she's gone and jump her when she comes back. That's the way he did it with Ruiz. The other possibility would be to catch her right at the door as she's going in. Sap her, push her right inside. If he did it right, it would look like he was meeting her at the door."

"We thought he might try some kind of con," said one of the surveillance cops. "You know, go up to the door, say he's a messenger from the station or something. Get her to open the door."

"It's a possibility," Lucas said. "I still like the idea—"

"Here she comes," said the cop at the window.

Lucas got up and half-crawled, half-walked to the window and looked out. A red Toyota sports car pulled up to the curb directly in front of McGowan's house, and a moment later she got out, carrying a shopping bag. She self-consciously didn't look around and marched stiffly up to the house, unlocked the door, and went inside.

"In," said the first surveillance cop. The second shone a miniature flashlight on his wristwatch and counted. Thirty seconds. A minute. A minute and a half. A minute forty-five.

The phone rang and the first surveillance cop picked it up.

"Miss McGowan? Okay? Good. But keep the beeper on until you go to bed, okay? Have a good night."


"You coming up every night?" Henley asked casually.

"Most nights, midweek. For three hours or so, nine to midnight or one o'clock, like that," Lucas said.

"You do it for too long, you wind up brain dead."

"And if the surveillance doesn't do it, this fuckin' elevator music will," Lucas said. The easy-listening music still oozed from the boombox.

One of the surveillance cops grinned and nodded at his partner. "Compromise," he said. "I like rock, he can't stand it. He likes country and I won't listen to all that hayseed hillbilly tub-thumping. So we compromised."

"Could be worse," Henley chipped in.

"Not possible," Lucas said.

"Ever listen to New Age?"

"You win," Lucas conceded. "It could be worse."


"Oh, God damn, folks, she's doing it again."

"What?" Lucas crawled off the mattress toward the window.

"We thought maybe she didn't realize there's a crack in the curtains," the cop said. His partner had his binoculars fixed on McGowan's house and said, "C'mon, babee." Lucas nudged the first cop away from the spotting scope and peered through it. The scope was focused on a space in the curtains on a second-story window. There was nothing to see at first, then McGowan walked through a shaft of light coming from what Lucas supposed was a bathroom. She was brushing her hair, her arms crossed behind her head. She was wearing a pair of white cotton underpants. Nothing else.

"Look at that," whispered the cop with the binoculars.

"Give me the fuckin' things," said Henley, trying to wrench them away.

"Goddamn one-hundred-percent all-American TV-reporter pussy," the surveillance cop said reverently, passing the binoculars to the vice cop. "You think she knows we're watching?"

She knows, Lucas thought, watching her face. It was flushed. Annie McGowan was turned on. "Probably not," he said aloud.

Five days of surveillance produced nothing. No suspicious cars checked her home, no approaches on the street. Nothing but falling leaves and cold winds rattling the tiles on the architect's roof. The curtain never closed.

"Red Horse?" It was midday and Lucas was calling from his home.

"Yeah, Annie. This is no hot tip, but I was out in the neighborhoods and noticed something you might be interested in. One of the women's business clubs is going to hear a lecture from a university shrink about—I'm reading this from a flier—'the relationship between sexual-social inadequacy and antisocial activity, with comments about the serial killer now terrorizing the Twin Cities.' That sounds like it could be good. Maybe you'd want to get a camera over to see this guy before he gives his speech."

"That sounds pretty relevant. What's the name?"

"Lucas?" It was Jennifer, a little breathless.

"Jennifer. I was going to call. How are you feeling?"

"I'm getting a little queasy in the morning."

"Have you seen a doctor?"

"Jesus, Lucas, I'm okay. It's only morning sickness. I just hope it doesn't get much worse. I almost lost my breakfast."

"With the breakfasts you eat, I believe it. You've got to get off that eggs-and-sausage and butter-toast bullshit. It'll kill you even if it doesn't give you morning sickness. Your cholesterol is probably six hundred and eight. Buy some oatmeal or some Malt-O-Meal. Get some vitamins. I can't figure out why you don't weigh two hundred pounds. For Christ's sakes, will you—?"

"Yeah, yeah, yeah. Listen, I didn't call you for culinary advice. This is an official call. I've been hearing strange rumors. That something heavy is happening with the maddog. That you know who he is and that you're watching him."

"Absolutely wrong," Lucas said flatly. "I can't prove it, obviously, but it's not true."

"I won't ask you for Boys Scout's honor, because that's personal and this is an official call."

"Okay, listen, as the woman who is carrying my kid, I don't want you to run around and get exhausted, okay? So on a purely personal basis, I tell you, Boy Scout's honor, we've got no idea who he is."

"But you're doing something?"

"That's an official question. I can start lying again."

Jennifer laughed and Lucas felt cheered. "I read you like an open book," she said. "I bet I find out what's going on within, say, a week."

"Good luck, fat lady."


Anderson and Lucas were talking in Lucas' office when Daniel edged in. He had never seen Lucas' office before. "Not bad," he said. "It's almost as big as my closet."

"There's a trick wall and it opens into a full-size executive suite, but I only do it when I'm alone," Lucas said. "Don't want to make the peons jealous."

"We were going over the case," Anderson said, looking up at the chief. "It's been ten days since the maddog's last hit. If the shrinks are right, he should be coming up on another one. Probably next week."

"Christ, we gotta do something," Daniel said. He was wringing his hands and Lucas thought he had lost weight. His hair was uncharacteristically mussed, as though he had forgotten to brush it before he left home. The maddog was bearing him down.

"Nothing on the McGowan thing?" he asked.

"Nope."

"Lucas. Tell me something."

"I don't have anything specific. We might be able to cool the media. I'm thinking that we should release some information about him. Something that would make it harder for him to pick up his victims."

Daniel paused. "Like what?"

"A flier listing the type of woman he goes after—dark hair, dark eyes, young to middle-aged, attractive. Then maybe a few hints about him. That he's light-complected, dark-haired, a little heavy, maybe recently moved in from the Southwest. That he dressed like a farmer at least once, but that we believe him to be a white-collar worker. Appeal to women who fit the type, and who feel approaches from men like that, and ask them to call us."

"Christ, you know how many calls we'd get?" Anderson asked.

"Can't be helped," Lucas said. "But we're not getting anywhere, and if he takes another one next week . . . We'd be better off if the press thought we were doing something about it."

Daniel pursed his lips, staring blankly at the pebbled plaster on Lucas' office wall. Eventually he nodded. "Yes. Let's do it. At least we're doing something."

"And maybe call an alert for next week," Lucas suggested. "Put a lot of extra cops on the street. Let the media know about it, but ask them not to publish. They won't, and it'll make them feel like they're in on something."

"Not bad," Daniel admitted with a wintry smile. "And after it's over, we can all go on television and debate media ethics, whether they should have cooperated with the cops."

"You got it," said Lucas. "They love that shit."

*    *    *

Lucas called her from a street phone.

"Red Horse?"

"Listen, Annie, Daniel has ordered Anderson—you know, from robbery-homicide?—he's ordered him to make up a list of characteristics for both the victims and the maddog killer and release it to the media. Probably sometime this afternoon. Some of them are already well-known, but some of them were confidential up to this time."

"If I can get it in ten minutes, I can make the noon report."

"I can't give you all of it, but we think he's fairly new to the area. We don't think he's been here more than a few years and that he moved in from the Southwest."

"You mean like Worthington, Marshall, down there?"

"No, no, not southwest Minnesota, the southwestern United States. Texas, probably. Maybe New Mexico. Like that. Daniel will make it official that he was seen in farmer clothes, just like you had it. But now they think it might be a disguise and that he's really white-collar."

"Great. Really great, Red Horse. What else?"

"There'll be more on the list, but that's the best stuff. And listen, before you put it on the air, call Anderson and ask him about it. He'll tell you. He's in his office now." He gave her Anderson's direct line. "Thanks. I'll see you on the air in fifteen minutes."


Midafternoon. Lucas was suffering post-luncheon *tristesse*, and sluggishly picked up the phone.

"Lucas?"

"How're you feeling, Jennifer?"

"What's going on with McGowan?"

"Jennifer, goddammit—"

"No, no, no. I'm not asking you if you screwed her. You already gave me Boy Scout's honor on that. What I want to know is, what's going on with McGowan and the surveillance? Why are the cops watching her?"

Lucas hesitated before answering, and instantly knew he had made a mistake.

"Ah. You *are* watching her," Jennifer crowed.

"Jennifer, remember when I asked you to talk to the chief before you did anything on Carla Ruiz? I'm asking you to talk to him again."


Evening. The sun went down noticeably early now. The summer was gone. Lucas waited outside the door of Daniel's office. He had been waiting fifteen minutes when Daniel came in from the outside.

"Come in," he said. He pulled off his topcoat and tossed it on the couch. "I'm asking you straight out. Did you tip Jennifer Carey on the surveillance?"

"Absolutely not. She's got her own sources. She called me and I sent her to you."

Daniel poked a finger at him. "If I find out otherwise, I'll kick your ass."

"It wasn't me. What happened when she called?"

"I called the station manager, got him with Carey in a meeting, and read them the riot act. Carey started on this media-ethics trip and the station manager told her to shut up. Said he wasn't going to have his station blamed if a star from another station was murdered by the maddog."

"So that's it?"

"They wanted equal access with Channel Eight. They're going to take a camera into her house over the weekend, when nothing's happening, shoot some film of McGowan ironing shirts or something. We'll let them in the surveillance post for a few minutes. Just the once."

"And they hold the film until we catch him?"

"That's the deal."

"Not a bad deal," Lucas said approvingly. "What did Jennifer have to say about it?"

"She was unhappy, but she'll go along. She'll produce the McGowan interview. Some kid's reporting it," Daniel said. "To tell you the truth, I think she's a little jealous. I think she wishes it were her, not McGowan."


"Do you remember that awful poem you wrote to me when we first started going out? About having my baby?"

"That wasn't so awful," Lucas said, propping himself on one elbow. There was a little edge to his voice. "I thought it was rather intricate."

"Intricate? It sounded like a bad teenage rock-'n'-roll song from 1959."

"Look, I know you don't particularly like my—"

"No, no, no. I loved it. I kept it. I have it taped to the pull-out typewriter tray on my desk, and about once a week I open it and read it. I just read it today, and I was thinking: Well, I really am having his baby."

Lucas pressed his ear to Jennifer's bare midriff.

"Am I supposed to be hearing anything yet?"

"Are you listening really closely?"

"Yeah." He pressed down harder.

"Well, if you listen very closely . . ."

"Yeah?"

"You can probably hear that Budweiser I had before bed."

*   *   *

Lucas arrived at the lake in time to watch the sun go down Saturday evening. Carla was gone on the bike, but arrived a half-hour later with a small bag of groceries and a bottle of red wine. Lucas spent Saturday night and Sunday, and most of Sunday night at the cabin. At two in the morning he kissed Carla on the lips and drove back to the Cities, hitting his own bed a little after five. He was late for the project meeting again.

"Whatever happened to the list of people we got from the Rice woman?" Lucas asked. Monday morning in the chief's office. Half the detectives looked out of focus, tired from another weekend's overtime. "You know, when we were checking about the maddog's gun and who bought it from her husband?"

"Well, we checked everybody she could remember," said Sloan, who had done the Rice interview.

"Nothing?"

"We didn't actually interview everybody. We checked them. If they were way off the profile, we let it go. You know, women, old men, boys, we let them go. We did interviews with everybody that might come close to the profile, and came up dry. We were going to go back to the rest, but everything slowed down when Jimmy Smithe started to look good. Everything got thrown on that."

"We should go back for interviews with everybody," Lucas said, turning to Daniel. "We know that goddamn gun is critical. Maybe somebody bought it and resold it. I say we check women, boys, old men, everybody."

"Get on it," Daniel told Anderson. "I assumed it was done."

"Well . . ."

"Just get it done."

Lucas sat on the attic floor.

"Wednesday. I didn't think we'd make it to Wednesday," said the surveillance man. "He's overdue."

"Cold in here," Lucas said. "You can feel the wind coming through."

"Yeah. We keep the door open but there aren't any heating vents. We're thinking about bringing up a space heater."

"Good idea."

"Thing is, downtown doesn't want to pay for it. And we don't want to get stuck for the money."

"I'll talk to Daniel," Lucas said.

"Car coming," said the second surveillance man.

The car rolled slowly down the street, paused beneath them, and then kept going, around the corner.

"Get the plate?"

"Guy at the end of the street's doing that, one of the cars. He's got a starlight scope."

A radio sitting beside the mattress suddenly burped.

"Get him?" the surveillance man asked.

"Yeah. Neighbor."

"He slowed down outside her house."

"Guy's sixty-six, but I'll note it," said the radio voice.

"How's it going?"

"Cold," the car man said.

They went back to waiting.

"Action stations," the surveillance man said twenty minutes later. "I get the scope."

Lucas watched through binoculars. McGowan was wearing a frothy pink negligee and tiny matching bikini pants. She moved back and forth behind the eight-inch gap in the curtain, more tantalizing than any professional stripper.

"She's gotta know," the surveillance cop said.

"I don't think so," Lucas said. "I think she's just so used to that gap in the curtains that she doesn't notice—"

"Bullshit. Look at that, when she stretches. She's showing it off. But she never shows all of it. She walks around without a bra, but you never catch her without her pants, even when she's been in taking a shower. She's teasing us. I say she knows . . ."

They were still arguing about it when the maddog did the cripple.

# 18

The maddog got a flier at the county clerk's office, a piece of pink paper handed to him as he walked out the door. He read it as he stood in front of the bank of elevators.

There was no attempt at a drawing and no real description. They said he was white-collar, possibly connected with the Hennepin County Government Center or Minneapolis City Hall. Fair-skinned. Southwestern accent, possibly Texas. Once seen dressed as a farmer, but that was probably a disguise.

The maddog folded the paper and stood watching the lights on the elevator indicator. When it came, he stepped inside, nodded to the other two occupants, turned, and stared at the door. He hadn't thought that he might have an accent. Did he? In his own ears, he sounded like everybody else. He *knew* talking to Davenport would be a mistake. Now he might pay for it.

The maddog's mind slipped easily into the legal mode. What could they make of it? So he had an accent. Hundreds of people did. He was white-collar. So was most of Minneapolis. He frequently passed through the Government Center. So did ten thousand people a day, some with business in the Center, some passing through in the skyways. A conviction? No chance. Or little chance, anyway. Some leeway must be given for the vagaries of juries. But would he take a jury? *That* was something to be contemplated. If they got him, he could ask for a nonjury trial. No judge would convict him on what they had on the flier. But what else did they have? The maddog bit his lip.

What else?

As he worried, the need for another was growing. The law student's face floated before him, against the stainless-steel doors. He was so taken with the vision of her that when the doors opened, he started, and the woman standing beside him glanced at him curiously. The maddog hurried off the elevator, through the skyways, and back to his office. His secretary was out somewhere. As he passed her desk, he saw the corner of a pink slip of paper under a file folder. He paused, glanced around quickly, and pulled it out. A flier. He pushed it back in place. Where was she?

He went inside his office, dropped his briefcase beside the desk, sat down, and cupped his face in his hands. He was still sitting like that when there was a tentative knock at the door. He looked up and saw his secretary watching him through the vertical glass panel beside the door. He waved her in.

"Are you okay? I saw you sitting like that . . ."

"Bad day," the maddog said. "I'm just about done here. I'm going to head out home."

"Okay. Mr. Wexler sent around the file on the Carlson divorce, but it looks pretty routine," she said. "You won't have to do anything on it before the end of the week anyway."

"Thanks. If you don't have anything to do, you might as well take the rest of the day," he said.

"Oh. Okay," she said brightly.

On the way out to his car, he thought about the innocent conversation. He had said, "Bad day." He had said, "I'm just about done here, I'm going to head out home." That's what he thought he had said. Had his secretary heard, "Bay-ed day-ee"? Had she heard "Ah'm" instead of "I'm"? Was "head out" a Texas expression, or did they use that here?

Did he sound like Lyndon Johnson?

At his apartment, the maddog looked in the freezer, took out a microwave dinner, set the timer on the oven, and punched the Start button. His face was reflected in the window of the microwave. Lips like red worms. His hand slipped into his coat pocket and encountered the flier. He took it out and read through it again.

The victims, it said, were a type. Dark eyes, dark hair. Attractive. Young to middle-aged.

He thought about it. They were right, of course. Maybe he should take a blonde. But blondes didn't appeal. The pale skin, the pale hair. Cold-blooded people. And he didn't want anyone old. That was distasteful. Old women would know too much about their own deaths. His women should be confronting the prospect for the first time.

I won't change, he thought. No need to, really. There were better than a million women in the Twin Cities. Probably a quarter of a million fit his "type." A quarter-million prospective Chosen women. From that point of view, the description of a "type" was meaningless. The police wouldn't have a chance. He felt a surge of confidence: the whole thing was meaningless. Having been fought off by one woman, having been seen at the Brown killing by another witness, he realized the police had less than he had expected. If they were telling everything.

The microwave beeped at him and he took the dinner out and carried it to the table. If they catch me, he thought as he ate the lonely meal, I could use the microwave defense. Like the guy who claimed he was driven crazy by excess sugar from an overdose of Twinkies. The Twinkie defense; his would be the Tater-Tot defense. He speared one of the potato nubbins and peered at it, popped it in his mouth.

Tonight, he thought. I can't wait any longer.


He called the cripple's house a little after six but there was no answer. He called again at seven. No answer. At eight there was an answer.

"Phyllis?" he asked in his highest-pitched voice.

"You must have the wrong number." It was the first time he'd heard her voice. It was low and musical.

"Oh, dear," he said. He sounded dainty in his own ears; like anything but a killer. He gave her a number with one digit different from her own.

"That's the wrong number," she said. "I'm five-*four*-seven-six."

"Oh. I'm sorry," he said, and hung up. She was home.

He prepared carefully, the excitement growing but under control. A hunter's excitement, a hunter's joy. He would wear his best tweed sport coat, the black cashmere overcoat, with black loafers. Snap-brim felt hat.

The overcoat had big pockets. They would take the potato—the potato had worked so well last time. He went to the closet, took a Kotex pad out of the box he'd bought three months before. Tape. Latex gloves under his leather driver's gloves. A scarf would partially cover the bottom of his face, giving him more protection against recognition: this was new, after all, a collection in his own neighborhood. Had to be ready to abort, he thought. If anyone sees me outside her door, forget it.

Knife? No. She'd have one.

When he was ready, he went through the side door into the attached garage, got in the car, punched the button on the remote garage-door opener, backed into the street, closed the garage, drove two blocks, and parked the car. He reached into the back seat and got a brown business envelope, opened the flap, and looked inside. A half-dozen forms, procured from a bin on the first floor of the Government Center. Applications for employment.

As he walked down to the door, the excitement became almost unbearable. I am coming, he prayed, I am coming for the Chosen; the One is coming. He felt the cold wind on his face and exulted in it, the smell of the Northwest, the expectant winter.

He walked briskly to her house, a businessman on business, and without breaking step turned down her sidewalk. The door had four small panes set in the center, just at head height, partly covered by a small curtain. He looked into her kitchen. She was not in sight. The maddog rapped on the door.

And waited. Rapped again. A noise? Then he saw her, rolling down the linoleum floor in her wheelchair. Not a wealthy woman, but such a face; such a fresh face, for one who had been so badly injured. An optimist.

She half-opened the inner door, left the outer one closed.

"Yes?"

"Miss Wheatcroft? I am Louis Vullion, an attorney with Felsen-Gore. I'm on the Minnesota Bar Association scholarship committee." He reached under his coat, took out a business card, opened the outer door, and handed it to her. She looked at it and said, curiously, "Yes?"

He held up the brown envelope. "I was just talking to Dean Jensen at the law school. Actually, I was over there picking up applications for the Felsen Legal Residencies and Dean Jensen said you must have neglected to submit yours. Either that, or it was lost?" He waved the brown envelope at her, started to fumble out the white application forms.

"I don't know about that," she said. "I never heard of them."

"Never heard of them?" The maddog was puzzled. How could she not have heard of them? "I'm sorry, I assumed all the top students knew about the residencies. They pay so well, and, you know, you probably get more experience in top-level personal injury and tort. They're at least as sought after as the clerkships, especially since they pay so well."

She hesitated, looked at his face, his clothes, the brown envelope, the business card. "Maybe you better come in, Mr. . . ."

"Vullion," he said, stepping inside. "Louis Vullion. Nasty night, isn't it?"

\*    \*    \*

This one was different. Comfortable, almost. He took almost twenty minutes to kill her, lying nude beside her on her bed, the rubber firmly protecting him from seminal disclosures. He needed it. He came once as he worked on her and again when he finally slipped the knife under her breastbone and her back arched and she left him.

And he felt sleepy, looking at her, and laid his head upon her breast.


Cold. Stiff. He sat up, looked around. My God, he had been asleep. Panic gripped him and he looked down at her cooling body and then wildly around the room. How long? How long? He glanced at his watch. Nine-forty-five.

He stood, tore off the rubber, flushed it. His body was covered with blood. He stepped into the tiny bathroom, turned on the shower, and rinsed himself. He kept the latex gloves on; he didn't want to leave prints. Not now. Not in his finest hour so far.

When he'd cleaned off most of the blood, he stepped out of the shower but left it to run. If he'd lost any hair in the shower, the water might wash it down the drain. He picked up a towel, then put it down. Hair again. He dried himself with his undershirt, and when he was reasonably dry, he stuffed the shirt in his coat pocket. Thinking about hair had made him paranoid. He had continued shaving his pubic hair, but he feared the loss of hair from his chest or head. He got his roll of tape, made a loop around his hand, and blotted the bed where he'd been lying. When he was finished, he looked at the tape; there were small hairlike filaments stuck to it, and what might have been one or two black pubic hairs, the woman's. Nothing red, nothing of his. He stuffed the tape in his coat pocket with the damp shirt, stepped into the bathroom, turned off the shower, and dressed.

When he was ready, he looked around, took stock. Still wearing the latex gloves. Sport coat, overcoat, hat, scarf, driving gloves. Was he forgetting anything? The business card. He found it on the floor. That was everything. Leave the sock and potato on the floor. Drop the note on her chest: *Isolate yourself from random discovery*. Ready. He patted her on the tummy and left.

He stepped out, walked down the sidewalk and around the house, stripping off the latex gloves as he walked. The old woman's apartment was dark. There was a light upstairs, in the third apartment, but nobody at the window. He walked briskly down the sidewalk, and, as he passed under a streetlight, noticed a dark stain on the back of one hand. He hesitated, looking at it. Blood? He touched it to his tongue. Blood. Sweet. He passed no one on the street on the way to his car. He opened it, climbed in, and drove.

Out to I-94. Pressure behind his eyes. He was going to do it. Telephone on a pole, outside a Laundromat. One guy inside, reading a newspaper while his clothes went around in the dryer. It was a mistake before, it would be a mistake again. But he needed it. He needed it like he needed the women. Someone to talk to. Someone who might understand. The maddog pulled in to the Laundromat phone, dialed Davenport's house.

And got an answering machine. "Leave a message," Davenport's voice said tersely, without identifying itself. There was a beep. The maddog was disappointed. It was not the same as human contact. He touched his tongue to the spot of blood on the back of his hand, savored it, then said, "I did another one."

The line stayed open and he wet his lips.

"It was lovely," he said.

# 19

"It was lovely."

Lucas listened a second time, the despair growing in his chest.

"Motherfucker," he whispered.

He ran the tape back and played it again.

"It was lovely."

"Motherfucker." He sank down beside the desk, put his elbow on it, propped his forehead up with his hand. He sat for three minutes, unable to think. The house huddled around him, dim, protective, quiet. A car rolled by in the street, its lights tracking across the wall. Rousing himself, he called Minneapolis and asked for the watch commander.

"Nothing here," he was told. St. Paul said the same. Nothing in Bloomington. There were too many suburbs to check them all. And Lucas thought it likely that the maddog had killed one in Lucas' own jurisdiction. It was a contest now. Explicitly.

"Lucas?" Daniel's voice had an ugly edge to it.

"I got a call. He's says he's done another one."

"Sweet bleedin' Jesus," Daniel said. In the background Lucas heard Daniel's wife ask if there had been another one, and where.

"I don't know where," Lucas said. "He didn't tell me. He just said it was lovely."

They found the law student two days later, in the late afternoon. She rarely missed class. When she was gone the first day, her absence was noted, but not investigated. When she missed the second day with no word from her, no excuse, a friend called her apartment but got no answer. At dinnertime the friend stopped and saw the light in the back. She knocked, peered through the window, saw a rubber grip handle of the wheelchair protruding from the bedroom doorway. Worried, she went to the old woman, who brought her keys. Together they found the Chosen.

"I was afraid the maddog had killed her," the friend wept when the first cops arrived. "I thought of it on the way over. What if the maddog's taken her?"


"Red Horse?"

"Annie, there's another one," Lucas said. He gave her the name and address. "Over by the university. A law student, crippled. Name Cheryl—"

"Spell it."

"Wheatcroft, C-h-e-r-y-l W-h-e-a-t-c-r-o-f-t. There have been a bunch of newspaper stories about her, I think, in the *Strib*."

"I can look. We've got an on-line library."

"Look in the *Pioneer Press* too. She was a senior, right at the top of her class. Her folks are here; they live over on the east side of St. Paul. Nobody else knows about it yet, but everybody's going to find out pretty soon. There are about a million cops in the street, going in and out. And the medical examiner. We're attracting neighbors and students. But if you get a crew over here fast, you should catch the parents coming out."

"Five minutes," she said, and hung up.


"Cheryl Wheatcroft," Daniel said. He stood in the kitchen, hatless, coatless, angry. "What did she do to deserve this, Davenport? Did she sin? Did she fornicate in the nighttime? Did she miss Mass on Sunday? What did she fuckin' do, Davenport?"

Lucas looked away from the outburst, tried to deflect it with a question. "What'd they show her folks?"

"Her face. That's all. Her mother wanted to see the rest of her, but I told her old man to get her out of here. He was almost as bad as the old lady, but he knew what we were talking about, he got her out. That TV camera was right in their faces. Jesus Christ, those people are animals, the fuckin' TV people are as bad as the fuckin' maddog."

The homicide detectives moved around the apartment with their heads down, as though with poor posture they might somehow avoid Daniel's wrath. The talk was in whispers. It continued in whispers after Daniel left. When he went out the door, the TV cameras across the street caught his face and held it. For the next week, his profile, frozen in anguish like a block of Lake Superior ice, was used to promo the nightly news on Channel Eight.

Lucas stayed at the scene while the technicians processed it. "Is there anything out of the pattern?" he asked the medical examiner.

The chief examiner was on the scene in person. He turned his eyes on Lucas and gave him a tiny nod. "Yeah. He butchered her. The other ones, it was surgical. Go in, kill. This one, he cut apart. She was alive for most of it."

"Sex?"

"You mean did he rape her? No. Doesn't look like it. She has numerous stab wounds over the pelvic area, up into the vaginal opening, the rectum, then across the anterior aspect of the pelvis—"

"The what?"

"The front, the front, right up her front. It looks like . . . Mother of God . . ." The medical examiner ran his hands through his graying hair.

"Sam . . ."

"It looks like he was trying to find where the pain started. She has a case full of medical records, and from what I can tell, the spinal event that crippled her was relatively high. Above the hip, below the breasts. She would have lost the superficial . . . Jesus, Lucas, this is freaking me out. Can't you wait for the reports?"

"No. I want to hear it."

"Well, when you have a spinal accident, you lose varying amounts of muscular control and the super . . . the feeling in your lower body. The loss ranges from minor disability to total paralysis, where you lose everything. That's what happened to her. But depending on where the damage happens to the spine, you lose superficial sensory . . . you lose the feeling over different areas. We're talking about the pain. And it looks like he was systematically working up her body, trying to find where it began."

"What about all the stab wounds in the vaginal area?"

"I was about to say, that doesn't fit with the other pattern of wounds. That appears to be sexual. And it's not uncommon when there's a sexual motivation behind a murder. There was also substantial flensing of the breasts—"

"What? Flensing?"

"He was skinning her. I think he stopped when he realized she was dying. That's when he finally put the knife in, so he could do it himself. Kill her."

"Jesus God."

The technicians tramped in and out. Lucas poked through the cripple's possessions, found a small collection of graduation pictures tucked in the top drawer of her chest. She was wearing a black gown and mortarboard, tassel to the left. He slipped the picture in his pocket and left.


Lucas was awake when the newspaper hit his screen door. He lay with his eyes closed for a moment, then gave up and walked out to retrieve it.

A double-deck headline spread across the page. Beneath it a four-column color photograph dominated the page, a shot of the covered body being rolled out to the medical examiner's wagon on a gurney. The photographer had used a superwide lens that distorted the faces of the men pushing the gurney. HANDICAPPED, the headline said. TORTURE, it said. Lucas closed his eyes and leaned against the wall.

The meeting started angry and stayed that way.

"So there's nothing substantial?" They were gathered in Daniel's office—Lucas, Anderson, Lester, a dozen of the lead detectives.

"It's just like the others. He left us nothing," said Anderson.

"I'm not going to take this kind of answer anymore," Daniel suddenly shouted, smashing the top of his desk with his hand, staring at Anderson. "I don't want to hear this bullshit about—"

"It's not bullshit," Anderson shouted back. "It's what we got. We got nothing. And I don't want to hear any shit from you or Davenport about any fuckin' media firestorms—that's the first fuckin' thing you said when we came in: what about the fuckin' media? Fuck the fuckin' media. We're doing the best we fuckin' can and I don't want to hear any fuckin' shit about it. . . ." He turned and stomped out of the room.

Daniel, caught in mid-explosion by Anderson's outburst, slumped back in his chair. "Somebody go get him back," he said after a minute.

When Anderson came back, Daniel nodded at him. "Sorry," he said, rubbing his eyes. "I'm losing it. We've got to stop this dirtbag. We gotta get him. Ideas. Somebody give me ideas."

"Don't cut the surveillance on McGowan," Lucas said. "I still think that's a shot."

"She was all over the place out at the Wheatcroft scene," one of the detectives said. "How'd she know? She was there a half-hour before the rest of the media."

"Don't worry about it," Daniel snapped. "And I want the surveillance on her so tight that an ant couldn't get to her on his hands and knees. Okay? What else? Anything? Anybody? What's happening with the follow-up on the people who might have gotten the gun from Rice?"

"Uh, we got an odd one on that," said Sloan. "Rice was over in Japan right after World War II and he brought back these souvenirs, these little ivory-doll kind of things? Net-soo-kees? Anyway, he told some guy about them, a neighbor, and the neighbor told him about this gallery that deals in Oriental art. This guy from the gallery comes over and he buys these things. Gave Rice five hundred dollars for fifteen of them. We got the receipt. I went over to talk to the guy, Alan Nester's his name, he's over on Nicollet."

"I've seen his place," said Anderson. "Alan Nester Objets d'Art Orientaux. Ground floor of the Balmoral Building."

"Pretty fancy address," said Lucas.

"That's him," said Sloan. "Anyway, the guy wouldn't give me the time of day. Said he didn't know anything, that he only talked to Mr. Rice for a minute and left. Never saw any gun, doesn't know about the gun."

"So?" asked Daniel. "You think he might be the guy?"

"No, no, he's too tall, must be six-five, and he's real skinny. And he's too old for the profile. Must be fifty. One of those really snotty assholes who wear those scarves instead of ties?"

"Ascots?"

"Whatever, yeah. I don't think he's the guy, but he was nervous and he was lying to me. He probably doesn't know anything about the maddog, but there's something he's nervous about."

"Look around, see what you can find out," Daniel said. "What about the other people?"

"We've got six more to do," he said. "They're the least likely ones."

"Do them first. Who knows, maybe somebody'll jump up and bite you on the ass." He looked around. "Anything else?"

"I've got nothing," Lucas said. "I can't think. I'm going out on the street this afternoon, catch up out there, then I'm going up north. I'm not doing any good here."

"Hang around for a minute, will you?" Daniel asked. "Okay, everybody. And I'm sorry, Andy. Didn't mean to yell."

"Didn't mean to myself," Anderson said, smiling ruefully. "The maddog is killing us all."

"Anderson doesn't want to talk about the media," Daniel said, rapping the pile of newspapers on his desk. "But we've got to do something. And I'm not talking about saving our jobs. We could see some panic out there. This might be routine in Los Angeles, but the people here . . . It just doesn't happen. They're getting scared."

"What do you mean by *panic*? People running in the streets? That won't happen. They'll just hunker down—"

"I'm talking about people carrying guns in public. I'm talking about a college kid coming home from the U when his parents don't expect him, in the middle of the night, and having the old man take off his head with the family Colt. That's what I'm talking about. You're probably too young to remember when Charlie Starkweather was killing people out in Nebraska, but there were people walking around in the streets of Lincoln carrying shotguns. We don't need that. And we don't need the National Rifle Association cranking up its scare campaign, a gun in every house and a tank in every garage."

"We should talk to the publishers and the station managers or the station owners," Lucas said after a moment's reflection. "They can *order* the heat turned down."

"Think they'll do it?"

Lucas considered for another moment. "If we do it right. Media people are generally despised, but they're like anybody else: they want to be loved. Give them a chance to show that they're really good guys, they'll lick your shoes. But it's got to come from you. Like, top guy to top guy. And maybe you ought to take the deputy chiefs with you. Maybe the mayor. That'll flatter them, show them that you respect them. They're going to ask some stuff like, 'You want us to censor ourselves?' You've got to say, 'No, we don't. We just want to *apprise* you of the dangers of public panic; we want you to be *sensitive* to it.' "

"Do I have to *share* those thoughts with them?" Daniel asked sarcastically.

Lucas pointed a finger at him. "Quit that," he said harshly. "No humor. You're dealing with the press. And yeah, say *share*. They talk like that. 'Let me share this with you.' "

"And they'll buy it?"

"I think so. It gives the newspapers a chance to be responsible. They can do that because they aren't making any money off the deal anyway. You don't get more advertisers because you're carrying murder stories. And they don't care much about short-term circulation gains. They can't sell those, either."

"What about the TV?"

"That's a bigger problem, because their ratings *do* shift, and that *does* count. Christ, I think I read in the paper last week that the sweeps are coming up. If we don't cut some kind of a deal with TV, they'll go nuts with the maddog stuff."

Daniel groaned. "The sweeps. I forgot about the sweeps. Jesus, this is supposed to be a police department. We're supposed to catch crooks, and I sit here sweating about the ratings sweeps."

"I'll get the names of everybody you want to talk to," Lucas said. "I'll give them to Linda in an hour. With phone numbers. Best to call them directly. Then they think you know who they are."

"Okay. One meeting? Or two? One for the papers and one for the TV?"

"One, I think. The TV people like to be in the same discussions with the newspaper guys. Makes them feel like journalists."

"What about radio?" Daniel asked.

"Fuck radio."

Anderson propped himself in Lucas' office doorway.

"Something?"

"He may drive a dark-colored Thunderbird, new, probably midnight blue," he said with just the mildest air of satisfaction.

"Where'd that come from?" Lucas asked.

"Okay. The medical examiner figured she was killed sometime Wednesday night or Thursday morning. We know she was alive at seven o'clock because she talked on the telephone with a friend. Then a guy who lives across the

street works on the night shift, he got home at eleven-twenty and noticed that
her light was still on. He noticed because she usually went to bed early."

"How's he know that?"

"I'm getting to it. This guy works a rotating shift out at 3-M. When he was
working the day shift, seven to three, he used to see her going down the
sidewalk when he left for work. One time he asked her why she got up so early,
and she said she always did, it was the best time of day. She couldn't work at
night. So he noticed the light. Thought maybe she had a big test."

"And . . ."

"So we think she was dead then. Or dying. Then, about ten o'clock—we're
not exact on this time, but within fifteen minutes either way—this kid was
walking up toward his apartment and he noticed this guy walking down the
sidewalk on the other side of the street. Going the same way. Middle height.
Dark coat. Hat. This is the street that runs alongside Wheatcroft's house. Anyway, they walk along for a couple of blocks, the kid not paying attention. But
you know how you keep track of people when you're out at night on foot?"

"Yeah."

"It was like that. They walk for a couple of blocks and the guy stops beside
this car, this Thunderbird. The kid noticed it because he likes the car. So the
guy unlocks it, climbs in, and drives away. When the kid hears about Wheatcroft, he thinks back and it occurs to him that this guy was kind of odd. There
were a million parking places on the street around there, and it was cold, so
why park at least two or three blocks from wherever you're coming from?"

"Smart kid."

"Yeah."

"So did you look at him?" Lucas asked.

"Yeah. He's okay. Engineering student at the U. He's got a full-time live-in.
The guy across the street looks okay too."

"Hmph." Lucas rubbed his lip.

Anderson shrugged. "It's not a major clue, but it's something. We're checking insurance records on Thunderbirds, going back three years, against people
who transferred policies up here from somewhere else. Like Texas."

"Luck."

The meeting was held the next day at midmorning in a *Star-Tribune* conference room. Everybody wore a suit. Even the women. Most of them had leather
folders with yellow legal pads inside. They called the mayor and Daniel by their
first names. They called Lucas "lieutenant."

"You're asking us to censor ourselves," said the head of the *Star-Tribune*
editorial board.

"No, we actually aren't, and we wouldn't, because we know you wouldn't
do it," Daniel said with a treacly smile. "We're just trying to *share* some con-

cerns with you, point out the possibility of general panic. This man, this killer, is insane. We're doing everything we can to identify and arrest him, and I don't want to minimize the . . . the horribleness—is that a word?—of these crimes. But I would like to point out that he has now killed exactly five people out of a population of almost three million in the metropolitan area. In other words, your chances of dying in a fire, being murdered by a member of your own family, being hit by a car, to say nothing of your chances of dying from a sudden heart attack, are much more significant than your chances of encountering this killer. The point being, news coverage that produces panic is irresponsible and even counterproductive—"

"Counterproductive to what? You keeping your job?" asked a *Star-Tribune* editorialist.

"I resent that," snapped Daniel.

"I don't think it was entirely appropriate," the paper's publisher commented mildly.

"He doesn't have to worry about it anyway," said the Minneapolis mayor, who was sitting at the foot of the table. "Chief Daniel is doing an excellent job and I intend to reappoint him to another term, whatever the outcome of this investigation."

Daniel glanced at the mayor and nodded.

"We have a problem here," said the station manager for TV3. "This is the most intensely interesting story in the area right now. I've never seen anything like it. If we deliberately deemphasize the coverage and our colleagues over at Channel Eight and Channel Six and Channel Twelve don't, we could get hurt in terms of ratings. We don't have newspaper circulation counts to go by, the ratings are our lifeblood. And since we're the top-rated station—"

"Only at ten; not at six," interjected the Channel Eight manager.

"And since we're the overall top-rated station," the TV3 manager continued, "we have the most to lose. Frankly, I doubt our ability to work out any kind of agreement that everybody would hold to. There's too much in the balance."

"How about if me and a bunch of other cops went through the force man by man and told them how a particular station was hurting us with their coverage? How about if we asked each and every cop, from the watch commanders on down, not to talk to that station? In other words, shut down one station's contacts with the police force. Froze you out. Would that have an impact on ratings?" asked Lucas.

"Now, that's a dangerous proposition," said the representative from the St. Paul papers.

"If we get some media-generated panic, *that's* a dangerous proposition," Lucas said. "If some kid who's living in the dorm comes home from the university at night unexpectedly, and his old man blows him away because he thinks it's the maddog, whose fault is that going to be? Whose fault for building up the fear?"

"That's not fair," said the TV3 manager.

"Sure it is. You just don't want it to be," Lucas said.

"Calm down, lieutenant," the mayor said after a moment of silence. He looked down the table. "Look, all we're asking you to do is not to hammer so hard. I timed Channel Eight last night, and you gave more than seven minutes to this case in four separate segments. In terms of television news, I think that's overkill. There almost *weren't* any other stories. I'm just suggesting that everybody look at every piece of coverage and ask, 'Is this necessary? Will this really build ratings? And what if Chief Daniel and the mayor and the City Council and the state legislators get really angry and start talking about the irresponsible press and mentioning names? Will that help ratings?' "

"Bottom line, then, you're saying don't make us mad," said the news director from Channel Twelve.

"Bottom line, I'm saying, 'Be responsible.' If you're not, you could pay for it."

"That sounds like a threat," said the news director.

The mayor shrugged. "You take a dramatic view of things."


As they went through the lobby on the way to the street, Daniel looked at the mayor.

"I appreciate that thing about the reappointment," he said.

"Don't go out and celebrate yet," the mayor said through his teeth. "I could change my mind if you don't catch this asshole."

# 20

The two days between the taking and the discovery of the body had been days of delicious anticipation. The maddog relaxed; he smiled. His secretary thought him almost charming. Almost. Except for the lips.

The maddog ran the tapes over and over, watching McGowan report from the Wheatcroft scene.

"This is Annie McGowan reporting from the scene of the latest in the series of killings by the man called maddog," she said, her lips making sensual O's. "Minneapolis Police Chief Quentin Daniel himself is inside this house just three blocks from the University of Minnesota campus. It was here that a crippled law student, Cheryl Wheatcroft, celebrated as one of the best minds of her law-school class, was tortured, stabbed to death, and sexually mutilated by a man police say is little better than a wild beast . . ."

He liked it. He even liked the "wild beast." The "pig farmer" was gone, forgotten. He reveled in the papers, read the stories over and over, lay on his bed and reran the memory of Wheatcroft dying. He masturbated, the face of Annie McGowan growing prominent in his visions.

The media reaction built through the weekend, culminating in three pages of coverage in the Minneapolis Sunday paper, a smaller but more analytical spread in the St. Paul paper. On Monday, the coverage died. There was almost nothing, which puzzled him. Burnt out already?

That afternoon, he went to the county recorder's office and politely introduced himself as a lawyer doing real-estate-tax research. He showed them his card and they instructed him in the use of computerized tax files. McGowan? The names ran up the computer monitor: McGowan, Adam, Aileen, Alexis, Annie. There she was. A sole owner. Nice neighborhood.

The computer gave him square footages, prices. He would need more research. He went from the computer files to the plat books and looked at the neighborhood maps.

"If you need aerial photos, you'll find them in those cases over there," said the clerk, smiling pleasantly. "They're filed the same way."

Aerial photos? Fine. He looked them over, picking out McGowan's house, noting its relationship to the neighboring houses, the garden sheds, the detached garage. He traced the alley behind the house with a fingertip. If he walked in from the north side, he could approach from the alley and go straight to the back door, pop it, and go in. If he came in early enough, when he knew McGowan was on the air, he would have a chance to explore it. What if there was another occupant? Easy enough to find out; that was what the telephone was for. He would call night and day, while she was working, looking for a different voice; he knew hers so well now. Maybe she had a roommate. He thought about that, closed his eyes. He could do a double. Two at the same time.

But that didn't feel right. A taking was personal, one-to-one. It was to be shared, not multiplied. Three's a crowd.

The maddog left the recorder's office and walked through another glorious fall day to the library, to the crime section, and began pulling out confessional books by burglars. They were intended, their authors said, to help homeowners protect their property.

From a different perspective, they were also a short course in burglary. He had studied a couple of them before he went into Carla Ruiz' studio. They helped. The maddog believed in libraries.

He thumbed through the books, picked the four best that he hadn't read. As he walked out of the stacks, past rows of books on crime and criminals, the name "Sam" caught his eye. Son of Sam. He had read about Sam, but not this particular book. He took it.

Outside in the sunshine, the maddog took a deep breath and watched the people scurrying by. Ants, he thought. But it was hard to take the thought too seriously. The day was too good for that. Like early spring in Texas. The maddog was not unaffected.

The burglary books gave him material for contemplation; the Sam book, even more.

Sam should not have been caught, not when he was.

On his last mission, as the maddog thought of it, he had shot a young couple, killing one, wounding and blinding the other. He had parked some distance away, near a fire hydrant. His car had been ticketed.

A woman out walking her dog had seen both the ticketing and, later, a man running to the car and driving away. When the latest Sam murders hit the press, she called the police. There had been only a few tickets given in the area at that time of night, and only one for parking at a hydrant. The police were able to read the car's license number off the carbon of the ticket. Sam was caught.

The maddog was reading in bed. He dropped the book on his chest and stared at the ceiling. He had known this story, but had forgotten it. He thought about his last note, the one dropped on Wheatcroft. *Isolate yourself from random discovery,* it said. He thought about his car. All it would take was a ticket. Now that he thought about it, it was a certainty that police were checking tickets issued near the killings.

He tossed the book on the bed and padded out to the kitchen, heated water in a teakettle, and made a cup of instant cocoa. Cocoa was one of his favorites. As soon as the hot bittersweet chocolate hit his tongue, he was back at the ranch, standing in the kitchen with . . . Whom? He shook it off and went back to the bedroom.

He had done it right with Wheatcroft. He had driven so that he wouldn't be seen leaving his house on foot. He had parked and walked in to the killing so that his car wouldn't be spotted at the crime scene.

Walk in to the killing. Keep the car out of the way. Make sure, make doubly sure, that the car was legally parked. And get it close enough to the house that he could reach it in a minute or so, at a run, but far enough away that it would not be immediately remembered as being a strange car near the site of a killing.

Five blocks? What would five blocks be? He got out a sheet of paper and drew streets and blocks. All right, if he parked five blocks away, the cops would have to check some fifty blocks before they got as far out as his car.

If he parked six blocks out from McGowan's house, they'd have to check seventy-two blocks. It would be double that if it weren't for that damned creek across the street.

He looked at his map and figured. If he parked north of her house, he could get six blocks out along the end blocks, which were narrow. He would also have access to alleys that came out of the end blocks, good places to hide, if hiding became critical.

The plat books had indicated that the lots were seventy feet deep, with a fifteen-foot alley. The streets were thirty feet. He figured on his piece of paper. A little over two hundred yards. He should be able to run that in less than a minute. He got up, went back into the kitchen, found a city map in a drawer, and counted up six blocks.

Not six blocks, he thought. Five blocks would be better. If he parked five blocks up, he'd be on a street that had access to Interstate 35. Once in the car, he could be on the highway in less than a minute, even driving at the speed limit.

He closed his eyes and visualized it. At a dead run, panic situation, it was two minutes from her house to the highway. Once on the highway, eight minutes to his garage. He would have to think.


The maddog got McGowan's phone number from a city cross-reference directory. Called her at home, spoke to her: "Phyllis? . . . Sorry, I must have misdialed," he said. Called back. Called back again. An answering machine, but never a strange voice.

The maddog did one reconnaissance. He did it in his midnight-blue Thunderbird.

Sunday afternoon. Annie McGowan was visiting her parents in Brookings, South Dakota. She was due back to work on Monday. There were still cops watching her house, one in front, from the architect's, one in back, from the retired couple's house. The cops out on the wings, in cars, had been temporarily withdrawn while McGowan was out of town.

With McGowan gone, it was hard to take the surveillance seriously. The cop at the post in back was reading through a stack of 1950's comic books he'd found in the attic, wondering about the possibility of stealing them. God only knew what they were worth, and the old couple certainly didn't seem to care about them or even remember they were there. Every two or three minutes the cop would glance out the window at the back of McGowan's house. But everyone knew the maddog never attacked on a weekend. He wasn't paying much attention.

He was reading a *Superman* when the maddog rolled past in front. If the maddog had driven down the alley behind the house, the cop would have seen him for sure—would have heard the car going by—and might have caught him or identified him right there. But a garbage can had fallen over at the far end of the alley. When the maddog started to turn in, he saw it, considered it, and backed out. No point in being seen outside the car, in daylight, fooling around with somebody else's garbage can.

The cop in the architect's house, across the street from McGowan's, should have seen him go by in front. He knew the maddog might be driving a dark-colored Thunderbird. But when the maddog went past, he was downstairs, his head in the refrigerator, deciding between a yogurt and a banana to go with the caffeine-free Diet Coke. He was in no hurry to get back to the attic. The attic was boring.

All told, he was away from the window for twenty minutes, although it seemed like only four or five. When he got back, he opened the yogurt and looked out the window. A kid up the street was washing his old man's car. A dog was watching him work. Nothing else. The maddog had come and gone.

And the maddog thought to himself: Tomorrow night.

# 21

When Lucas pulled in, Carla was sitting in the yard, wrapped in an old cardigan sweater with a drawing pad in her lap. He got out of the car, walked through the dry leaves, deep-breathing the crystalline North Woods air.

"Great day," he said. He dropped beside her and looked at the pad. She was drawing the forms of the fallen leaves with sepia chalk on blue-tinted paper. "And that's nice."

"I think—I'm not sure—but I think I'm going to get the best weavings I ever did out of this stuff," Carla said. She frowned. "One of the problems with the form is that the best of it is symbolic but the best art is antisymbolic."

"Right," Lucas said. He flopped back in the leaves and looked up at the faultless blue sky. A light south wind rippled the surface of the lake.

"Sounds like baloney, doesn't it?" she asked, smiling, her face crinkling at the corners of her eyes.

"Sounds like business," he said. He turned his head and saw a cluster of small green plants pushing up through the dead leaves. He reached out and picked a few of the shiny green leaves.

"Close your eyes," he said, holding his hand out toward her and crumbling the leaves in his fingertips. She closed her eyes and he held the crumbled leaves beneath her nose. "Now, sniff."

She sniffed and smiled and opened her eyes. "It's the candy," she said in delight. "Wintergreen?"

"Yeah. It grows all over the place." She took the crumbled leaves from him and sniffed again. "God, it smells like the outdoors."

"You still want to go back?"

"Yes," she said, a note of regret strong in her voice. "I have to work. I've got a hundred drawings and I have to start doing something with them. And I called my gallery in Minneapolis and I've sold a couple of good pieces. I've got money waiting."

"You could almost start making a living at this," Lucas said wryly.

"Almost. They tell me a man from Chicago, a gallery owner, saw some of my pieces. He wants to talk to me about a deal. So I've got to get going."

"You can come back. Anytime."

Carla stopped drawing for a minute and patted his leg. "Thanks. I'd like to come back in the spring, maybe. You've no idea what this month has done for me. God, I've got so much work, I can't even fathom it. I needed this."

"Go back Tuesday night?"

"Fine."

Lucas rolled to his feet and walked down to the dock, looked at his boat. It was a fourteen-foot fiberglass tri-hull with a twenty-five-horsepower Johnson outboard mounted on the back. A small boat, wide open, just right for fishing musky. There was a scum line around the hull. The boat had not been used enough during the fall.

He walked back up the bank. "I'm going to have to take the boat out before we leave," he said. "It hasn't been getting much use. The maddog has killed the fall."

"And I've been too busy walking in the woods to go out on the water," Carla said simply.

"Want to go fishing? Now?"

"Sure. Give me ten minutes to finish this." She looked up and across the lake. "God, what a day."


In the afternoon, after lunch, they walked back into the woods. Carla carried the pistol on her belt. At the base of the hill, firing at the cutbank from twenty yards, she put eighteen consecutive shots into an area the size of a large man's hand. They were dead center on the silhouette she'd sketched in the sand. When she fired the last round, she put the muzzle of the pistol to her lips and nonchalantly blew off the nonexistent smoke.

"That's decent," Lucas said.

"Decent? I thought it was pretty great."

"Nope. Just decent," Lucas repeated. "If you ever have to use it, you'll have to make the decision in a second or so, maybe in the dark, maybe with the guy rushing you. It'll be different."

"Jeez. What's the use?"

"Wait a minute," Lucas said hastily. "I don't mean to put you down. That's really pretty good. But don't get a big head."

"Like I said, pretty great." She grinned up at him. "What do you think of the holster? Pretty neat, huh?" She had sewn a rose into the black nylon flap.

*       *       *

Much later that night she blew in his navel and looked up and said, "This could be the best vacation I ever had. Including the next couple of days. I want to ask you a question, but I don't want to ruin it."

"It won't. I can't think of any question that would ruin it."

"Well. First we have a preamble."

"I love preambles; I hope you finish with a postscript. Even an index would be okay, or maybe—"

"Shut up. Listen. Besides being a vacation, I've gotten an enormous amount of work done up here. I think I've broken through. I think I'm going to be an artist like I've never been an artist before. But I've met men like you . . . there's a painter in St. Paul who's an awful lot like you in some ways . . . and you're going to move on to other women. I know it, that's okay. The thing is, when you do, can we still be friends? Can I still come up here?"

Lucas laughed. "Nothing like a little honesty to destroy an incipient hard-on."

"We can get it back," she said. "But I want to know—"

"Listen. I don't know what's going to happen to us. I have had . . . a number of relationships over the years and a lot of the women are still friends of mine. A couple of them come up here, in fact. Not like this, for a month at a time, but for weekends. Sometimes we sleep together. Sometimes we don't, if the relationship has changed. We just come up and hang out. So . . ."

"Good," she said. "I'm not going to fall apart when we break it off. In fact, I'm going to be so busy I don't know if I could keep a relationship together. But I would like to come back."

"Of course you would. That's why my friends call it a pussy trap—ouch, ouch, let go, goddammit. . . ."

"You got a minute?" Sloan leaned in the doorway. He was sucking on a plastic cigarette substitute.

"Sure."

Lucas had gotten back to Minneapolis so relaxed that he felt as though his spine had been removed. The feeling lasted for fifteen sour minutes at police headquarters, talking to Anderson, getting his notebook updated. He had wandered down to his office, the North Woods mood falling apart. As he put the key in his door, Sloan appeared up the hallway, saw him, and walked down.

"Remember me talking about this Oriental-art guy?" Sloan asked as he lowered himself into Lucas' spare chair.

"Yeah. Something there?"

"Something. I don't know what. I wonder if you might have a few words with him."

"If it'll help."

"I think it might," Sloan said. "I'm mostly good at sweet talk. This guy needs something a little harder."

Lucas glanced at his watch. "Now?"

"Sure. If you've got time."

Alan Nester was crouched over a tiny porcelain dish, his back to the door, when they walked in. Lucas glanced around. An Oriental carpet covered a parquet floor. A very few objects in porcelain, ceramics, and jade were displayed in blond oak cabinetry. The very sparsity of offerings hinted at a storehouse of art elsewhere. Nester pivoted at the sound of the door chimes and a frown creased his lean pale face.

"Sergeant Sloan," he said crossly. "I told you quite clearly that I have nothing to contribute."

"I thought you should talk to Lieutenant Davenport here," Sloan said. "I thought maybe he could explain things more clearly."

"You know what we're investigating, and Sergeant Sloan has the feeling that you're holding something back," Lucas said. He picked up a delicate china vase and squinted at it. "We really can't permit that . . . Ah, I'm sorry, I didn't mean to make that sound so severe. But the thing is, we need every word we can get. Everything. If you're holding back something, it must have some importance or you wouldn't hold it back. You see where we're coming from?"

"But I'm not holding back," Nester cried in exasperation. He stood up, a tall man, but thin, like a blue heron, and stepped across the rug and took the vase from Lucas' hand. "Please don't touch anything. This is delicate material."

"Yeah?" Lucas said. As Nester replaced the vase, he picked up a small ceramic bowl.

"All we want to know," he said, "is everything that happened at the Rice house. And then we'll go away. No sweat."

Nester's eyes narrowed as he watched Lucas holding the small bowl by its rim.

"Excuse me for a second." He crossed to a glass case at the end of the room, picked up a telephone, and dialed.

"Yes, this is Alan Nester. Let me speak to Paul, please. Quickly." He looked across the room at Lucas as he waited. "Paul? This is Alan. The police officers came back, and one of them is holding a S'ung Dynasty bowl worth seventeen thousand dollars by its very rim, obviously threatening to drop it. I have nothing to tell them, but they won't believe me. Could you come down? . . . Oh? That would be fine. You have the number."

Nester put the receiver back on the hook. "That was my attorney," he said. "If you wait here a moment, you can expect a phone call either from your chief or from the deputy mayor."

"Hmph," Lucas said. He smiled, showing his eyeteeth. "I guess we're really not welcome, are we?" He carefully set the bowl back on its shelf and turned to Sloan. "Let's go," he said.

Outside, Sloan glanced sideways at him. "That wasn't much."

"We'll be back," Lucas said contentedly. "You're absolutely right. The motherfucker is hiding something. That's good news. Somebody has something to hide in the maddog case, and we know it."

They called Mary Rice from a street phone. She agreed to talk to them. Sloan led the way up to the house and knocked.

"Mrs. Rice?"

"You're the policemen."

"Yes. How are you feeling?" Mary Rice's face had gotten old, her skin a ruddy yellow and brown, tight and hard, like an orange left too long in a refrigerator.

"Come in, don't let the cold in," she said. It wasn't quite a moan. The house was intolerably hot, but Mary Rice was wrapped in a heavy Orlon cardigan and wore wool slacks. Her nose was red and swollen.

"We talked to the man who bought the ivory carvings from your husband," Sloan said as they settled around the kitchen table. "And we're wondering about him. Did your—"

"You think he's the killer?" she asked, her eyes round.

"No, no, we're just trying to get a better reading on him," Sloan said. "Did your husband say anything about him that you thought was unusual or interesting?"

Her forehead wrinkled in concentration. "No . . . no, just that he bought them little carvings and asked if Larry had any other things. You know, old swords and stuff. Larry didn't."

"Did they talk about anything else?"

"No, I don't know . . . Larry said this man was kind of in a hurry and didn't want any coffee or anything. Just gave him the money and left."

Sloan looked at Lucas. Lucas thought a minute and asked, "What did these carvings look like, anyway?"

"I still got one," she offered. "It's the last one. Larry gave it to me as a keepsake when we were married. You could look at that."

"If you could."

Rice tottered off to the back of the house. She returned a few minutes later and held her hand out to Lucas. Nestled in her palm was a tiny ivory mouse. Lucas picked it up, looked at it, and caught his breath.

"Okay," he said after a minute. "Can we borrow this, Mrs. Rice? We can give you a receipt."

"Sure. But I don't need no receipt. You're cops."

"Okay. We'll get it back to you."

Outside, Sloan said, "What?"

"I think we've got our friend Alan Nester by the short and curlies, but I also think I know what he's lying about. And it isn't the maddog," Lucas said gloomily. He opened his hand to look at the mouse. "Everything I know about art you could write on the back of a postage stamp. But look at this thing. Nester bought fifteen of them for five hundred bucks. I bet this thing is worth five hundred bucks by itself. I've never seen anything like it. Look at the expression on the mouse's face. If this isn't worth five hundred bucks, I'll kiss your ass on the courthouse lawn."

They were both peering into Lucas' hand. The mouse was exquisite, its tiny front and back legs clenching a straw, so that a hole ran between the legs from front to back. "They must have used it for something, a button or something," Lucas said.

Sloan looked up and Lucas turned to follow his gaze. A patrol car was in the street, almost at a stop, the two cops peering out the driver's-side window at them.

"They think we're doing a dope deal," Sloan laughed. He pulled his badge and walked toward the car. The cops rolled down the window and Lucas called, "Want to see a great-lookin' mouse?"


The Institute of Art was closed by the time they left Rice's house, and Lucas took the mouse home overnight. It sat on a stack of books in his workroom, watching him as he finished the last of the hit tables on the Everwhen game.

"God damn, I'd like to have you," Lucas said just before he went to bed. Early the next morning he got up and looked at it first thing. He thought it might have moved in the night.

It took a while to find out about it. Lucas picked up Sloan at his house. Sloan's wife came out with him and said, "I've heard so much about you I feel like I know you."

"It's all good, I expect."

She laughed and Lucas liked her. She said, "Take care of Sloan," and went back inside.

"Even my wife calls me Sloan," Sloan said as they drove away.

A curator at the art institute took one look at the mouse, whistled, and said, "That's a good one. Let's get the books."

"How do you know it's a good one?" Lucas asked as he tagged along behind.

"Because it looks like it might walk around at night," the curator said.

The search took time. Sloan was wandering through the photo gallery when Lucas returned.

"What?" he said, looking up.

"Eight thousand," Lucas said to him.

"For what? For the mouse or for all fifteen?"

"For the mouse. That's his low estimate. He said it could be twice as much at an auction. So if it's eight thousand and the others are as good, Nester paid a man dying of cancer five hundred dollars for netsukes worth something between a hundred and twenty thousand dollars and a quarter-million." He said "net-skis."

"Whoa." Sloan was nonplussed. The amounts were too big. "That's what they are? Net-skis?"

"I guess. That's what the curator was saying."

"I didn't know."

"I bet Alan Nester does."

They stopped at Rice's house.

"Eight thousand dollars?" she said in wonderment. A tear trickled down one cheek. "But he bought fifteen of them . . ."

"Mrs. Rice, I expect that when your husband asked Mr. Nester to come over here, all he really wanted was an evaluation so he could sell them later, isn't that what you told us?" Lucas asked.

"Well, I don't really remember . . ."

"I remember your saying that in the first interview," Sloan said insistently.

"Well, maybe," she said doubtfully.

"Because if he did, then he cheated you," Lucas said insistently. "He committed a fraud, and you could recover them."

"Well, that's what he come over for, to valuate them," Mary Rice said, nodding her head vigorously, her memory suddenly clearing up. She picked up the mouse, handling it tenderly. "Eight thousand dollars."

"Now what? Get a warrant?" Sloan asked. They were on the walk outside Rice's house again.

"Not yet," Lucas said. "I don't know if we have enough. Let's hit Nester first. Tell him what we've got, ask him to cooperate on the gun thing. Tell him if he cooperates, we'll let it go as a civil matter between his attorney and Rice's attorney. If he doesn't, we get a warrant, bust him, and put it in the press. How he ripped off a man who was dying of cancer and was trying to leave something for his wife."

"Oooh, that's ugly." Sloan smiled. "I like it."

"Where's Nester?"

The man behind the counter was small, dark, and much younger than Nester.

"He's not here," the man said. There was a chill in the air; Lucas and Sloan didn't look like customers. "Might I ask who is inquiring?"

"Police. We need to talk to him."

"I'm afraid you can't," the young man said, raising his eyebrows. "He left for Chicago at noon. He'll already be there and I have no idea where he's staying."

"Shit," Sloan said.

"When's he due back?" Lucas asked.

"Tuesday morning. He should be in by noon."

"Do you have any netsukes?" Sloan asked.

The young man's eyebrows went up again. "I believe we do, but you'd have to ask Alan. He handles all the more expensive items."

# 22

Lucas took off his coat and tossed it on the mattress. The two surveillance cops, one tall, one short, were sitting on folding chairs, facing each other, with another chair between them. They were playing gin, the cards laid out on the seat of the middle chair. One of the cops watched the window while the other surveyed his hand. They were good at it. Their shift covered the prime time.

"Nothing?" asked Lucas.

"Nothing," said the tall cop.

"Anything from the cars?"

"Not a thing."

"Who's in them?"

"Davey Johnson and York, up north, behind McGowan's. Sally Johnson and Sickles, out east. Blaney is over on the west side with a new guy, Cochrane. I don't know him."

"Cochrane's that tall blond kid, plays basketball in the league," the short cop chipped in. He fanned his cards, dropped them on the seat of the chair between them, and said, "Gin."

A radio against one wall played golden-oldie rock. A police radio sat silently next to it.

"He's about due," Lucas said, peering out into the street.

"This week," the short one agreed. "Which is odd, when you think about it."

"What's odd?"

"Well, one of the notes he left said something about 'Don't set a pattern.' So what does he do? He kills somebody every two weeks. That's a pattern if I ever saw one."

"He kills when he needs to," Lucas said. "The need builds up, and eventually he can't stand it."

"Takes two weeks to build up?"

"Looks like it."

The police radio burped and all three of them turned to look at it. "Car," it said. And a moment later, "This is Cochrane. It's a red Pontiac Bonneville."

The tall cop leaned back, picked up a microphone, and said, "Watch it. It's the right size, even if it's the wrong color."

"Coming your way," Cochrane said. "We got the tag, we'll run it."

Lucas and the surveillance cop watched the car roll down the street and ease to the curb two houses down. It sat with its lights on for one minute, two, and Lucas said, "I'm going down there."

He was at the stairs when the tall cop said, "Hold it."

"What?"

"It's the girl."

"High-school girl down the street," said the short cop. "She's going up to the house now. Must be a date."

Lucas walked back in time to see her going through the porch door. The car left.


"Could be something going on with her phones," the short cop said a while later. The phone-monitoring station was at the other surveillance post, behind McGowan's house.

"What? You mean McGowan's?" asked Lucas.

"There were a bunch of calls last week and over the weekend. There'd be a whole group, a half-hour apart, more or less. But whoever it is doesn't leave a message on the answering machine. The machine answers and they hang up."

"Everybody does that—hangs up on machines," Lucas said.

"Yeah, but this is a little different. It's the first time it's happened, for one thing, a bunch of calls. And she has an unlisted number. If it was a friend, you'd think he'd leave a message instead of calling over and over."

"It's like somebody's checking on her," said the tall cop.

"Can't trace them?"

"It's two rings and click, he's gone."

"Maybe we ought to change the machine," said Lucas.

"Maybe. She's due home in, what, an hour and a half?"

"Something like that."

"We could do it then. Set it for five rings."

Lucas went back to the mattress and the two cops started the gin game again.

"What do I owe you?" asked the tall cop.

"Hundred and fifty thousand," said the short one.

"One game, double or nothing?"

Lucas grinned, closed his eyes, and tried to think about Alan Nester. Something there. Probably the fear that the netsuke purchase would be discovered and questioned. The purchase bordered on fraud. That was almost certainly it. Damn. What else was there?

Half an hour later, the cop radio burped again.

"This is Davey," a voice said, carrying an edge of excitement. "It's showtime, folks."

Lucas rolled to his feet and the tall cop reached back and grabbed the microphone.

"What do you got, Davey?"

"We got a single white male dressed in dark slacks, dark jacket, dark gloves, watch cap, dark shoes, on foot," Davey Johnson said. Johnson had been on the street for years. He didn't get excited without reason, and his voice was crackling with intensity. "He's heading your way, coming right down the street toward you guys. If he's heading for McGowan's, he'll be in sight of the side of the back-lot house in one minute. This dude's up to something, man, he ain't out for no country stroll."

"York with you?"

"He's gone on foot, behind this guy, staying out of sight. I'm staying with the unit. God damn, he's walking right along, he's crossing the street, you other guys out on the wings, start moving up, goddam—"

"We see him out the side windows of our house," said a new voice.

"That's Kennedy at the other post," the tall cop said to Lucas.

Lucas turned and headed for the stairs. "I'm going."

"He's going in the alley," he heard Kennedy call as he ran down the first few steps. "He's in her yard. You guys move . . ."

Lucas ran down the three flights of steps to the front door and brushed past the white-haired architect who stood in the hallway with a newspaper and a pipe, and ran out into the yard.


The maddog parked five blocks from McGowan's house, facing the Interstate. Checked the street signs. Parking was okay. Lots of cars on the same side of the street.

The weather had turned bad early in the morning. A cold rain fell for a while in the afternoon, died away, started again, stopped. Now it felt like snow. The maddog left the car door unlocked. Not much of a risk in this neighborhood.

The sidewalk was still damp, and he walked along briskly, one arm swinging, the other holding a short, wide pry bar next to his side. Just the thing for a back door.

Down one block, another, three, four, onto McGowan's block. A car started somewhere and the maddog turned his head in that direction, slowed. Nothing more. He glanced quickly around, just once, knowing that furtiveness attracts attention all by itself. His groin began to tingle with the preentry excitement. This would be a masterpiece. This would set the town on its ear. This would make him more famous than Sam, more famous than Manson.

Maybe not Manson, he thought.

He turned into the alley. Another car engine. Two cars? He walked down the alley, reached McGowan's yard, glanced around again, took a half-dozen steps into the yard. A car's wheel squealed in deceleration a block away, the other end of the alley.

Cops.

In that instant, when the turning wheels squealed against the blacktop, he knew he had been suckered.

Knew it. Cops.

He ran back the way he had come.

Another car, down the block. A tremendous clatter behind him; one of the cars had hit something. More cops. A door slammed. Across the street. Another one, behind McGowan's.

He turned out of the alley, the pry bar slipping from beneath his jacket and falling to the grass, and he ran across the yard one house down from McGowan's, through bridal wreath, running in the night, hit a lilac bush, fell, people shouting, "Hold it hold it hold it . . ."

The maddog ran.


The rookie Cochrane was at the wheel, and tires squealed as he slowed and cranked left into the alley, an unintended squeal, and his partner blurted "Jesus!" and quick as a turning rat, they saw the maddog run into the alley ahead of them. Cochrane wrenched the car straight in the alley, smashed through two empty garbage cans, and went after him.

The maddog was running between houses when the other wing car burst into the alley toward them and Cochrane almost hit it. The other car's doors flew open and the two cops inside leapt out and went after the maddog. Cochrane's partner, Blaney, yelled, "Go round, go round into the street . . ." and Cochrane swung the car past the other unit toward the street at the end of the alley.


Sally Johnson jumped out of her car and saw Lucas coming from across the street, running in a white shirt, and she turned and ran after her partner, Sickles, between houses as Cochrane's car cranked around her car and went out toward the street.

The maddog had already crossed the next street, and Sally Johnson snatched her radio from her belt carrier and tried to transmit, but couldn't find words as she ran fifteen feet behind Sickles, Sickles with his gun out. Another cop, York, came in from the side and behind her, gun out, and Sally Johnson tried to get her gun out and saw the maddog go over a board fence across the street and dead ahead.

The maddog, fear and adrenaline blinding him to anything but the tunnel of space in front of him, space with no cops, sprinted across the street, as fast as he had ever run, hit the board fence, and vaulted it in a single motion. He could never have done it if he'd thought about it, the fence four feet high, as high as his chest, but he took it like an Olympian and landed in a yard with an empty swimming pool, a small boat wrapped in canvas, and a dog kennel.

The dog kennel had two separate compartments with rugs for doors and inside each compartment was a black-and-tan Doberman pinscher, one named July and the other named August.

August heard the commotion and pricked up his ears and poked his head out and just then the maddog came sailing over the fence, staggered, sprinted across the yard, and went over the back fence. Either dog could have taken him, if they'd had the slightest idea he was coming. As it was, July, exploding from her kennel, got his leg for an instant, raked it, and then the man was gone. But there was more business coming. July had no more than lost the one over the back fence than another came over the front.

The maddog never saw the Doberman until it was closing in from the side. And a good thing, because he might have hesitated. He saw it just as he hit the fence, a dark shadow at his feet, and felt the ripping pain in his calf as he went over the back fence.

Carl Werschel and his wife, Lois, were almost ready for bed when the dogs went crazy in the backyard.

"What's that?" Lois asked. She was a nervous woman. She worried about being raped on a remote North Woods highway by gangs of black biker rapists, though neither she nor anyone else had seen a black biker gang in the North Woods. Nevertheless, it was clear in her dreams, the bikers hunched over her, ravens circling overhead, as they did the foul deed on what seemed to be the hood of a '47 Cadillac. "It sounds like . . ."

"Wait here," Carl said. He was a very fat man who worried about black biker gangs himself and had stockpiled both ammo and plenty of camouflage clothing against the day. He got the Remington twelve-gauge pump from beneath the headboard and hustled for the back door, jacking a shell into the chamber as he went.

Just for an instant, Sickles, who was forty-five, felt a little kick of joy as he cleared the board fence. He was forty feet and one fence behind the maddog and he was in good shape, and with any luck, with the other guys coming in from the side . . .

The dogs hit him like a hurricane and he went down, clenching his gun but losing the flashlight he'd had in the other hand. The dogs were at his shoulders, his back, going crazy, barking, snarling, ripping his hands, the back of his neck . . .

Sally Johnson cleared the fence and almost landed in the tight ball of fury around Sickles, and one of the dogs turned toward her, slavering, coming, and Sally Johnson shot the dog twice and then the other one was coming and she turned and aimed the pistol, aware of Sickles on his hands and knees off to the left, enough clearance, and she pulled the trigger once, twice . . .

Carl Werschel ran out his side door with the twelve-gauge and saw the young punk in jeans and black jacket shooting his dogs, shooting them down. He yelled "Stop!" but he didn't really mean "Stop," he meant "Die," and with an atavistic Prussian-warrior joy he fired the shotgun at a thirty-foot range into Sally Johnson's young head. The last thing Sally Johnson saw was the long muzzle of the gun coming up, and she wished she could say something on the radio to stop it from happening. . . .

Sickles felt the dogs go, and he started to roll out, when the long finger of fire reached out and knocked back the partner who had just saved him from the dogs. He knew that much, that he'd been saved. The finger of fire flashed again and Sally went down. Sickles had been around long enough to think, "Shotgun," and the cops' tone poem muttered somewhere in his unconscious as he rolled half-blind with blood: "Two in the belly, one in the head, knocks a man down and kills him dead." He fired three times, one shot piercing Werschel's belly, wiping out his liver, knocking him backward, the second shot ruining his heart. Werschel was dead before he hit the ground, though his mind ticked over for a few more seconds. Sickles' third shot went through the wall of the house, into the dining room, through a china cabinet and a stack of plates inside it, through the opposite wall, and, as far as cops investigating later could prove, into outer space. The slug was never found.

*     *     *

When Werschel opened up with the shotgun, the maddog had crossed the street and had fallen into a trench being dug to replace a storm sewer. It was full of wet, yellow clay. He clambered out the far side, a mud ball, not understanding why he had not yet been caught.

And he would have been, except that the north car, with Davey Johnson on board, had closed onto the block when the shotgun blast lit up the neighborhood. Johnson dumped the unit and headed into the fight. His partner, York, on foot, had been caught in mid-block when the maddog changed direction, hadn't seen it happen, and wound up running behind Sickles and Sally Johnson and just ahead of Lucas, who had cut across McGowan's yard.

Cochrane and Blaney had driven out of the alley intending to turn north, in the direction the maddog was running, when the firefight started. The firefight took all priority. They assumed Sickles and Sally Johnson had cornered the maddog, found him armed, and shot it out. And when the bad guy's shooting a shotgun . . . Like Davey Johnson, they dumped their car and went in on foot.

Lucas had just crossed the fence, gun in hand, screaming for someone to call for ambulances and backup, when the maddog got out of the ditch and ran through another blacked-out yard, across an alley, another yard, and on. In forty seconds he reached his car. In another minute he was nearing the Interstate. No lights behind him. Something had happened, but what?

In the Werschels' yard, Lucas was packing his shirt into a gaping hole in Sally Johnson's neck, knowing it was pointless, and Sickles was chanting *Oh my God, oh my God* and Cochrane came over the fence with his gun in his fist and shouted *What happened, what happened* and pointed at the dead Werschel and shouted *Is that him?*

Lois Werschel came out the side door of her house and called, "Carl?"

Blaney called for backup within a few seconds of the firefight. The radio tape later released to the media showed that it was six minutes later when Lucas called in with Cochrane's handset to request that all dark late-model Thunderbirds in South Minneapolis be frozen and the occupants checked.

The dispatcher momentarily lost it when she heard that a cop was down, and started calling for identity and condition and routing the ambulances and the backup into the neighborhood. She did not rebroadcast the request that all Thunderbirds be frozen for another two minutes, assuming that it was a lower priority than the other traffic. By that time, the maddog was passing downtown Minneapolis. Two minutes later he was at his exit, and less than a minute after that, waiting in the driveway as the automatic opener rolled up his garage door.

\*      \*      \*

The paramedics got to the Werschels' house before the maddog got home, but it was too late for Sally Johnson and Carl Werschel. The paramedics took one look at Werschel and wrote him off, but Sally still had a thin thready heartbeat and they started saline and tried to compress the neck wound and there was nothing to do about the head wound and they got her in the ambulance, where they lost the heartbeat, injected a stimulant, and started toward Hennepin Medical Center, but her pupils were fixed and dilated and they kept trying but they knew she was gone. . . .

Lucas knew she was gone. When they took her out, he stood on the boulevard outside the Werschel house and watched the flashers until they disappeared. Then he headed back to the fenced yard, where two more paramedics were working with Lois Werschel and Sickles, who were both descending into shock. Carl Werschel, looking like a beached whale, lay belly-up in a bed of brown, frost-killed marigolds.

"Who was that in the car, squealed the tires?" Lucas asked quietly. Blaney glanced at Cochrane and Lucas caught the glance and Cochrane opened his mouth to explain and Lucas hit him squarely in the nose. Cochrane went down and then the light hit them and Lucas grabbed Cochrane by the shirt and lifted him halfway to his feet and hit him again in the mouth with his other hand and York wrapped Lucas up from behind and wrestled him away.

"You motherfucker, you killed Sally, you ignorant shithead," Lucas screamed and the light blinded him and York was hollering "Hold it hold it" and Cochrane was covering his broken nose and teeth with one hand and trying to push up off the ground with the other, his face cranked toward Lucas, his eyes wide with fear. Lucas struggled against York for a few seconds and finally slumped, relaxed, and York pushed him away and Lucas turned and saw the TV camera and lights over the fence, focused on the group in the yard. The figures behind the lights were unrecognizable and he started toward them, intending to pull down the lights, when Annie McGowan emerged from them and said, "Lucas? Did you get him?"

Daylight was leaking in the office windows when the meeting convened. Daniel's face look stretched, almost gaunt. He had not shaved, was not wearing a tie. Lucas had never seen him in the office without a tie. The two deputy chiefs looked stunned and fidgeted nervously in their chairs.

". . . don't understand why we didn't have automatic stop on all Thunderbirds the instant something started happening," Daniel was saying.

"We should have, but nobody decided who was going to call. When it went down and the fight started and Blaney started hollering for backup and then for the ambulances, we just lost it," said the surveillance crew's supervisor. "Lucas was on the air pretty quick, six minutes—"

"Six minutes, Jesus," said Daniel, leaning back in his chair, his eyes closed. He was talking calmly, but his voice was shaky. "If one of the surveillance crews had called the instant it started going down, it would have been rebroadcast and we'd have had cars on the way before Blaney got on the air. That would have eliminated the foul-up by the dispatcher. We'd have been eight minutes or nine minutes faster. If Lucas is right and he was parked up near the entrance to the Interstate, he was downtown having a drink by the time we started looking for his car."

There was a long silence.

"What about this Werschel guy?" asked one of the deputy chiefs.

Daniel opened an eye and looked at an assistant city attorney who sat at the back of the room, a briefcase between his feet.

"We haven't figured it out yet," the attorney said. "There's going to be some kind of lawsuit, but we were clearly within our rights to go into his yard in pursuit of the killer. Technically, his dogs should have been restrained, no matter how high the fence was. And when he came out and opened fire, Sickles was clearly within his rights to defend himself and his partner. He did right."

"So we got no problem there," said one of the deputy chiefs.

"A jury might give the wife a few bucks, but I wouldn't worry about it," the attorney said.

"Our problem," Daniel said in his remote voice, "is that this killer is still running around loose, and we look like a bunch of clowns running around killing civilians and each other. To say nothing of beating each other up afterward."

There was another silence. "Let's get back to work," Daniel said finally. "Lucas? I want to talk to you."


"What else you got?" he asked when they were alone.

"Not a thing. I had . . . a feeling about the McGowan thing—"

"Bullshit, Lucas, you set her up and you know it and I know it, and God help me, if we could do it again I'd say go ahead. It should have worked. Motherfucker. Motherfucker." Daniel pounded the top of his desk. "We had him in the palm of our hand. We had the fucker."

"I blew it," Lucas said moodily. "That gunfight went up and I came across the fence and saw Werschel lying there and I knew he wasn't the maddog because the maddog was all dressed in black. And Sally was down and still pumping some blood and Sickles was there to help her, and the other guys, and I should have kept going. I should have gone over the back fence after the maddog and left Sally to the other guys. I thought that. I had this impulse to keep going, but Sally was pumping blood and nobody else was moving . . ."

"You did all right," Daniel said, stopping the litany. "Hey, a cop got blown up right in front of you. It's only human to stop."

"I fucked up," Lucas said. "And now I don't have a thing to go on."

"Nails," Daniel said.

"What?"

"I can hear the media getting out the nails. We're going to be crucified."

"It's pretty hard to give a shit anymore," Lucas said.

"Wait for a couple days. You'll start giving a shit." He hesitated. "You say Channel Eight got some film of you and Cochrane?"

"Yeah. God damn, I'm sorry about that. He's a rookie. I just lost it."

"From what I hear, it's going to be pretty hard to take back what you said. Most of the cops out there think you're right. And Sally had some years in. If Cochrane had just taken it easy, he'd have been right down that alley before the maddog knew you were coming. You'd have squeezed him between you and nobody would ever have gone into the yard with those fuckin' dogs."

"Doesn't make it better to know how close we came," Lucas said.

"Get some sleep and get back here in the afternoon," Daniel said. "This thing should start shaking out by then. We'll know what to expect from the media. And we can start figuring out what to do next."

"I can't tell you what to do," Lucas said. "I'm running on empty."

# 23

They didn't come for him.

Somewhere, in the back of his head, he couldn't believe it, that they didn't come for him.

He staggered through the connecting door from the garage into his apartment, took a step into the front room, realized that he was tracking sticky yellow clay onto the carpet, and stopped. He stood for a minute, breathing, reorganizing, then carefully stepped back onto the kitchen's tile floor and stripped. He took off everything, including his underwear, and left it in a pile on the floor.

His leg was bleeding and he sat on the edge of the bathtub and looked at it. The bites were not too deep, but they were ragged. In other circumstances, he would go to an emergency room and get stitches. He couldn't now. He washed the wounds carefully, with soap and hot water, ignoring the pain. When he had cleaned them as well as he could, he pulled the shower curtain around the tub and did the rest of his body. He washed carefully, his hands, his hair, his face. He paid special attention to his fingernails, where some of the clay might have lodged.

Halfway through the shower, he broke down and began to gag. He leaned against the wall, choking with adrenaline and fear. But he couldn't let himself go. He didn't have the luxury of it. Nor did he have the luxury of contemplating his situation. He must act.

The maddog fought to control himself. He finished washing, dried with a rough towel, and bandaged the leg wounds with gauze and adhesive tape. Then he went into the bedroom, dressed in clean clothes, and returned to the kitchen.

All of the clothing he'd worn that night was commonly available: Levi's, an ordinary turtleneck shirt, a black ski jacket purchased from an outdoor store. Jockey underwear. An unmarked synthetic watch cap. Running shoes. He emptied the pockets of the jacket. The Kotex pad, the gloves, the tape, the sock and potato, the pack of rubbers, all went into a pile on the floor. He'd lost the pry bar when he was running, but it should be clean; the cops wouldn't get anything from it. He carried the pile of clothing and shoes to the laundry room and dumped it in the washing machine.

With the clothes washing, he got a small vacuum cleaner, went out to the garage, and cleaned the car. Some of the clay was still damp and stuck tenaciously to the carpet. He went back in the house, got a bottle of dishwashing liquid and a pan, went back out, and carefully shampooed each area that showed a sign of the clay. If the cops sent the car to a crime laboratory, they might still find some particles of the stuff. He would have to think about it. And he would, for sure, vacuum it again after the damp carpet had dried.

When he was finished with the car, the maddog went back inside and checked the washing machine—the wash cycle was done—and transferred the clothing and shoes to the dryer. Then he found the box of surgeon's gloves he used in his attacks and pulled on a pair. From under the kitchen sink he got a roll of black plastic garbage bags, opened one, took the dust bag out of the vacuum, and threw it inside. Next he threw in the equipment he'd taken from his clothing, along with the box of remaining Kotex pads that he'd kept in a back closet.

Anything else? The potatoes. But that was ridiculous. Everyone had potatoes in the house. On the other hand, maybe there was some kind of genetic examination that could show they came from the same place. The potatoes went in the garbage bag.

The clothes were still in the dryer, and the maddog went back to the bedroom and pulled out the file of newspaper clippings. SERIAL KILLER STALKS TWIN CITIES WOMEN said the first. He slipped it out and read through it quickly, one last time, as he carried the file to the bathroom. Removing the clips one by one, he tore them into confetti and flushed them down the toilet.

The clothes, when they were dry, went in another bag. By eleven o'clock he had finished collecting all of his equipment and the clothing he'd worn to McGowan's. He phoned a car-rental agency at the airport and was told that it would be open for another hour. He reserved a car on his Visa card, called for a cab, rode out to the airport, signed for a car, and brought it back. It would be best, he thought, to keep his car off the streets for a while. There had been so much commotion back at McGowan's, the gunfire, the whole neighborhood must have waked up. If somebody had noticed his car leaving . . . And the cops just might be desperate enough to stop any Thunderbird they found on the highway, taking names and running checks.

Back at the apartment, he loaded the garbage bags of clothing and equipment into the rental car. A few minutes after midnight he drove onto Interstate 94, driving east, through St. Paul and into Wisconsin. He stopped at each rest area between St. Paul and Eau Claire, disposing of different pieces of equipment and clothing in separate trashcans.

He'd paid a hundred and sixty dollars for the ski jacket and hated to see it go. But it must go. It could have microscopic particles of the yellow clay inextricably impressed in the fabric. He couldn't throw it in a trashcan. It was too expensive. Somebody might wonder why it had been discarded, and publicity about the attempt on McGowan by a black-clad maddog would be intense. He finally left the jacket hanging on a hook in a rest room at an all-night truck stop, as though it had been forgotten. With any luck, it would wind up in Boise.

He had the same problem with the shoes. They were new Reeboks, a fashionable mat black. He liked them. He pitched them separately out the car window into the roadside ditch, a mile or so apart. He would have to buy a new pair, to replace his aging Nike Airs. He'd better stick with the Airs, he thought, just in case the cops found prints in that muddy ditch and matched them to Reeboks.

At Eau Claire the maddog checked into an out-of-the-way motel and paid with his Visa card. The receipt had no time stamp. Should the police someday come after him, the sleepy clerk almost certainly wouldn't remember him, much less what time he had arrived. And he would have a receipt to prove that he was in Eau Claire the night of the McGowan attack.

In his room, he stripped, showered again, and put a new dressing on the dog bites. By three in the morning it was all done and he was in bed, the lights out, the blankets pulled up under his chin.

Time to think. He lay awake in the dark and mentally retraced his steps from the car to McGowan's house. Down the dark side streets. The car starting. Where was he? The maddog had not yet turned into the alley. Then the second car starting.

They'd had McGowan's house under surveillance, he realized. They had ambushed him, and the ambush should have worked. Davenport? Almost certainly. He had been manipulated into an attack, probably with the woman's cooperation.

The maddog knew that he might someday be caught. He had no illusions about that. But he had supposed that if he were caught, it would be through a combination of uncontrollable and unforeseeable circumstances. He had imagined, in waking nightmares, the struggle with a woman, perhaps like the struggle with Carla Ruiz. And the intervention of another man, or maybe even a crowd; a lynch mob. Somehow, in these visions, the mob seemed to pursue him through a department store, with women's clothing racks flying helterskelter and shoppers screaming and glass cases breaking. It was ludicrous, but felt real, the endless aisles of clothing through which he fled, with the crowd only a rack or two behind and closing on the flanks.

He had not imagined being manipulated, being tricked, being suckered. He had not imagined *losing the game through inferior play.*

But he nearly had.

In the back of his head he still couldn't believe that they hadn't come for him. That they didn't now know who he was.

He reviewed in his mind the destruction of the evidence at his apartment. He had done a good job, he concluded, but was there a telling trace of mud somewhere? Was it possible that somebody had seen his car license?

The videotape. Damn. He had forgotten the videotape with the news broadcasts on it. But wait: he had never known when the news broadcasts would carry stories about the maddog, so he'd carefully taped whole broadcasts. Some carried nothing at all about the maddog . . . not that there had been many of those these last few weeks. So the tape should be okay. It wasn't as specific to the maddog as individual newspaper clips.

He felt a twinge of regret about the destruction of the clips. Maybe he could have kept them, maybe he should have carried them out to the car, and in Eau Claire tomorrow he could have rented a safe-deposit box. Too late. And probably foolish. When he was done with the women, when he was leaving the Twin Cities—maybe it was time—he could get copies from the library.

With the evening's events rattling through his mind like a pachinko ball, the maddog pulled the blankets a little higher, his calf now burning like fire, and waited for dawn.

# 24

Before he went home, Lucas returned to McGowan's. There were a half-dozen squad cars, three city cars, and a technician's van at the Werschel house. Two more squads were parked in the street at McGowan's. A Channel Eight truck with a microwave remote dish mounted on top had backed into her yard and a half-dozen black cables snaked out of the back of the truck to the house and disappeared inside.

A patrol lieutenant saw Lucas coming down the sidewalk and got out of his car.

"Lucas. Thought you'd gone home," the lieutenant said.

"On my way. How's it look?"

"We're covering everything. We got some footprints out of that ditch, looks like he fell right in it. Could have hurt himself."

"Any blood?"

"No. But we put out a general alert to the hospitals with the description on the fliers and added some stuff about the clay. They should have an eye out for him."

"Good. Have you found anybody who saw him after he got out of the ditch? Further north?"

"Nobody so far. We're going to knock on doors six or seven blocks up—"

"Concentrate on the street that leads out to the expressway. I'd bet my left nut that's where he parked."

The lieutenant nodded. "We've already done that. Started while it was still dark, getting people out of bed. Nothing."

"How about the footprints? Anything clear?"

"Yeah. They're pretty good. He was wearing—"

"Nike Airs," Lucas interjected.

"No," the lieutenant said, his forehead wrinkling. "They were Reeboks. When we called in, we told the tech we had some prints and he brought along a reference book. They're making molds, so they can look at them back at the lab, but there's no doubt. They were brand-new Reeboks. No sign of wear on the soles."

Lucas scratched his head. "Reeboks?"


Annie McGowan was sparkling. Seven o'clock in the morning and she looked as though she'd been up for hours.

"Lucas," she called when she caught sight of him by the door. "Come on in."

"Big show tonight?"

"Noon, afternoon, and night is more like it. Right now we're setting up for a remote for the *Good-Morning Show*." She glanced at her watch. "Fifteen minutes."

A producer came out of the living room, saw Lucas, and hurried over. "Lieutenant, what's the chance of getting a few minutes of tape with you?"

"On what?"

"On the whole setup. How it worked, what went wrong."

Lucas shrugged. "We fucked up. You want to put that on the air?"

"With this case, if you want to say it, I think we could get it on," the producer said.

"You going to use your tape of the fight?"

The producer's eyes narrowed. "It's an incredible piece of action," he said.

"I won't comment if you're going to use it," Lucas said. "Hold it back and I'll talk."

"I can't promise you that," the producer said. "But I can talk to the news director about it."

"Okay," Lucas said wearily. "I'll do a couple of minutes. But I want to know what questions are coming and I don't want any tricky stuff."

"Great."

"And you'll see about holding the fight tape?"

"Yeah, sure."


The taping took almost an hour, with a break for McGowan's remote. When he got home, Lucas unplugged the telephones and fell facedown on the bed, not bothering to undress. He woke to a pounding noise, sat up, looked at the clock. It was a little before one in the afternoon.

The pounding stopped and he put his feet on the floor, rubbed the back of his neck, and stood up. A sharp rapping sound came from the bedroom window and he frowned and pulled back the venetian blind. Jennifer Carey, out on the lawn.

"Open the door," she shouted. He nodded and dropped the blind and went out to the door.

"I figured it out," she said angrily. "I don't know why I didn't see it, but as soon as we heard about the attack, I figured it out." She didn't take off her coat, and instead of walking through to the kitchen as she usually did, she stood in the hallway.

"Figured what out?" Lucas asked sleepily.

"You set McGowan up. Deliberately. You were feeding her those weird tips to make the maddog angry and attract him to McGowan."

"Ah, Jesus, Jennifer."

"I'm right, aren't I?"

He waved her off and started back to the living room.

"Well, she sure as hell paid you back," Jennifer said.

Lucas turned. "What do you mean?"

"That awful tape of you confessing. You know, saying it was all your fault. And then the tape of the fight, with you beating up that poor kid."

"They weren't going to show that," Lucas said hollowly. "We had a deal."

"What?"

"I gave them the interview and the producer said he'd call the news director about not using the tape of the fight."

Jennifer shook her head. "My God, Lucas, sometimes you are so *naive*. You're supposed to know all about this media stuff, right? But there was no way they wouldn't use that tape. Man, that's terrific action. Big gunfight and two people dead and a police lieutenant beating the crap out of his brother cop who caused it? That tape will probably make the network news tonight."

"Ah, fuck." He slumped on the couch and ran his fingers through his hair.

Jennifer softened and touched him on the crown of the head.

"So I came over here to see if we could use you one more time. And I do mean *use*."

"What?"

"We'd like to get a joint interview with you and Carla Ruiz. You talking about what you know about the killer, with Ruiz chipping in about the attack. Ellie Carlson will do the interview. I'm producing."

"Why now?"

"The truth? Because if we don't have something heavy to promo for tonight, McGowan and Channel Eight are going to kick us so bad that we'll hurt for weeks. They'll do it anyway, but with a joint interview we might keep a respectable piece of the audience, for at least one of the news shows. Especially if we promo it right."

"Is this sweeps week?"

"You got it."

"I'll have to talk to the chief."


Daniel was gloomy, withdrawn. He gestured Lucas to a chair and turned his own chair, staring out his office window at the street.

"I saw the interview tape on Channel Eight. Taking the blame. Nice try."

"I thought it might help."

"Fat chance. I gave Cochrane two weeks' administrative leave with pay, told him to stay away from the media, get his face fixed up. You really clobbered him."

"I'll try to find him, talk to him," Lucas said.

"I don't know," Daniel said. "Maybe it'd be better if you just stayed away for a while."

Lucas shifted uncomfortably. "This is a bad time to talk about it, but Jennifer Carey wants a joint interview with me and Carla Ruiz. She's up-front about it. It's because of the sweeps this week. But she thinks if they can get some tape, promo it, it might cut down on Channel Eight's impact. At least we'd get something positive out there."

"Go ahead, if you want," Daniel said. He didn't seem to care much, and continued staring out at the street.

"Did the guys out at the scene get anything we can use?"

"Not that they told me about," Daniel said. They sat in silence for a moment, then Daniel sighed and swung his chair around.

"Homicide isn't going to catch the guy, unless it's by accident," he said. "With this close call, we might scare him off for a week, or two weeks, but he'll be back. Or maybe he'll leave town and start somewhere else. You know something? I don't want him to do that. I want to nail him here. And you're going to have to do it. The McGowan thing was a disaster, all right, but I keep thinking, not a total disaster. I keep thinking that Davenport figured the guy out. And if he did it once, maybe he can do it again. Maybe . . . I don't know."

"I don't have an idea in my fuckin' head," Lucas said.

"You're messed up," Daniel said. "But it'll go away. Your head will start working again."

"You're wrong about the way we'll break it," Lucas said. "It won't happen because I figured him out, because I haven't. When we get him, we'll get him on a piece of luck."

"I hate to depend on luck; I'd hoped we could come up with something a little more reliable."

"There isn't anything reliable, not in this world," Lucas said. "The maddog's had a fantastic game. Ruiz should have been able to tell us more than she did—I mean, she actually had her hands on him. If she'd pulled away his mask . . . We should have gotten a better description out of the attack on Brown. I keep thinking: If only Sparks had been on the other side of the street. He might have seen him full-face. I keep thinking: If only Lewis had written the guy's name on her calendar. Or if she had written *anything* about him. We should have nailed him at McGowan's; when he got away, we should have been able to freeze his car, if it really is a Thunderbird. He's been incredibly lucky. But there's one certainty in the world of game-playing: luck will turn. It always does. When we get him, we'll get him on a piece of luck."

"Christ knows it's our turn for some," Daniel said.


Jennifer had already talked to Carla about an interview, and when Lucas called to agree, she told him that Carla was ready. They would shoot it at three o'clock and run an early, tight version at six o'clock. A longer version would be promoed for the ten-o'clock news, which the station had decided to expand to accommodate the interview.

Wear a suit, she said, and a blue shirt.

Shave again.

The interview lasted an hour, Lucas cool and distracted, Carla warm and insistent. With a proper cut, it would look good. Jennifer watched the inter-viewer talking with them, and halfway through, realized that Lucas and Carla were sleeping together. Or had slept together.

When the interview was over, she left with Lucas, trailing behind the cameraman and sound technician, who were carrying gear down to the van. Alone in the elevator she said, "I thought you might have been sleeping with Mc-Gowan. I see I was wrong. It was Carla Ruiz."

"Ah, man, Jennifer, I can't deal with this today," Lucas said, staring at the elevator floor.

"I don't mind so much," she said sadly. "I knew it was going to happen. I was hoping it wouldn't be this soon."

"I think it's done with," Lucas said dispiritedly.

"Just slam-bam-thank-you-ma'am?"

Lucas shook his head. "She gave me a little talk a few days ago. She likes me okay, but she's ready to cut me off when I conflict with her work."

"Oh, my, that hasn't happened before, has it?" Jennifer asked. Her tone was light, even sarcastic, but a tear rolled down her cheek. Lucas reached out and thumbed it away. "Don't do that, for Christ's sake."

"Why not? You can't tolerate real emotion?"

He looked at the floor between his feet, then cocked his head at her. "Sometimes people don't know each other as well as they think they do. You're giving me shit and I'm supposed to take it like a man, right? You know what I feel like? I feel like going home and sticking my forty-five in my mouth and blowing my brains out. I've been beat up by a madman. I might recover. I might not. But I'll never forget it. Not in this life."

The elevator door opened and he walked away and never looked back.


Elle watched him across the expansive game board. The bookie and attorney had gone together, the two students followed a few minutes later. The grocer was still staring at the map, figuring.

Meade was no dummy. After a day's fighting, in which the South controlled most of the heights south of Gettysburg, he cautiously withdrew to the south, toward Washington. There were prepared positions waiting. Now the ball was in Lee's court. Lee—Elle, with advice from Lucas, as Longstreet—could continue his invasion of the North. That looked increasingly untenable. Or he could go after Meade's army to the south. That army would have to be destroyed in any case. But if Lee went after Meade, it would mean the kind of Napoleonic attack that failed at the real Gettysburg. Once he got down to close-quarters fighting around Washington, with the mountains to his west and a flooding Potomac to his south, it would be kill or be killed. Lucas' game could end the Civil War two years early . . .

"You can't keep thinking about it," Elle said.

"What?" Lucas had been balancing on the back two legs of his chair, staring at the ceiling.

"You can't keep brooding about the tragedy out at the reporter's house. It's pointless. And you almost had him. You drew him in. If you'd stop feeling sorry for yourself, you'd come up with something new."

Lucas dropped the chair to the floor and stood up.

"My problem is, I can't think of anything. My head is frozen. I think he's gone."

"No. Something is going to happen," Elle said. "You know how there's a rhythm to these games? When we all know something is about to happen, even when it doesn't have to? I feel the same kind of rhythm here. The rhythm says this whole thing is about to resolve itself."

"The problem is, how?" the grocer interjected.

"That is the problem," Lucas said, snapping a finger at the grocer. "Exactly. Suppose the guy resolves it by leaving? He could start all over somewhere else, and we wouldn't even know it. And we've really got nothing to go on. Not a real clue in the bunch. If he wants to leave, he can walk."

"He won't," Elle said positively. "This thing is rushing to a conclusion. I can feel the wheels."

"I hope so," Lucas said. "I don't think I can take much more of it."

"We're praying for you," Elle said, and Lucas realized the second nun was also watching him. She nodded. "Every night. God will answer. You've got to get him."

# 25

The maddog called in sick from Eau Claire. He lay in bed watching cable television from the Cities and finally left the motel just before the noon check-out time. He got back to his apartment in the early afternoon, cleaned up, drove down to his office, and said he was feeling better. He tried to work. He failed.

The fiasco at the McGowan house was the big news. The entire office was talking about it. The maddog took no pleasure in the talk, felt no power flowing from it. He had been mousetrapped. Davenport had done it, had lured him to McGowan. Davenport understood him that well. Had stalked him. Had failed only through a set of circumstances so bizarre that they could never be repeated.

The maddog knew he had been lucky. So lucky. It was time to reconsider the game. Perhaps he should stop. He was far ahead. He had the points. But could he stop? He wasn't sure. If he couldn't, perhaps he could move somewhere else. Back to Texas. Get away from the cold. Rethink the game.

It took him until well after five to clear his desk, finish the routine real-estate and probate work. When he left, a television was flickering in one of the associates' offices, an indulgence not permitted during the regular workday. Lucas Davenport's face was on the screen, the camera tight on his features. There were dark marks under his eyes, but he was well-controlled. The picture froze momentarily and then the cameras switched to the anchorwoman.

He stepped closer to listen. ". . . the complete interview with the survivor Carla Ruiz and Lieutenant Lucas Davenport tonight on an expanded edition of TV3's Ten-O'Clock Report."

He was torn between Channel Eight and TV3. Channel Eight had been break-ing all the most interesting news during the game, but the interview on TV3 might tell him more about the man who mousetrapped him. He finally decided, after consulting his video recorder's instruction book, that he could tape TV3 while he watched Channel Eight. He tried it with a network comedy. It worked.

McGowan, so beautiful, led the evening news, dominated it. She recounted the surveillance, showed off the alert beeper she'd worn on her belt. Told of sitting in her bedroom alone at night, listening to every sound, wondering if the maddog was coming. She was taped as she made a single woman's portion of stir-fry. Unused copper skillets hung from the walls. An old-fashioned pendu-lum clock ticked in the background.

With the scene set, she recounted the attack, running through the night with a camera bouncing behind her, ending with a camera-activated reenactment of the shootings, McGowan playing all parts. Then across the final fence to the sewer ditch, where she pointed out the maddog's footprints in the yellow clay.

It was brilliant theater, and like all brilliant theater, ended with a punch: the fight in the harsh light, Davenport destroying the rookie cop, his hands moving so fast they could barely be seen. Then Davenport starting toward the cameras, murder in his eye, until stopped by McGowan's voice.

Brutal. Davenport was not just a player. He was an animal.

When the show ended, the maddog stared at the television for a few mo-ments, then punched up the tape of the TV3 interview.

Davenport again, but a different one. Cooler. Calculating. A hunter, not a fighter. The maddog recognized the quality instinctively, had seen it in the ranchers around his father's place, the men who talked about *my deer* and *my antelope*.

Ruiz still drew him, her face, her dark eyes. The connection was not essen-tial, was not the connection he felt with a Chosen—she had passed beyond that privilege. But there was an undeniable residue of their previous relationship, and the maddog felt it and thought about it.

Was he being manipulated again? Was this another Davenport trick? He thought not.

The maddog had never had a two-sided relationship with a woman, but he was acutely sensitive to the relationships between others. Halfway through the interview, he realized that Davenport and Carla Ruiz were somehow involved with each other. Sexually? Yes. The more he watched, the more he was convinced that he was right.

Interesting.

# 26

"Come on. Let's do it." Sloan was leaning in the doorway.

"No fuckin' point, man," Lucas said. He felt lethargic, emotionally frozen. "We know what he's hiding. He's worried about his reputation. He ripped off the Rices and he's afraid somebody will find out."

"How do you feel?"

"What?"

"How do you feel? Since the Fuckup?"

Lucas grinned in spite of himself. The disaster at McGowan's had been dubbed the Fuckup. Everybody from the mayor to the janitors was using it. Lucas suspected everybody in town was. "I feel like shit."

"So come on," Sloan urged. "We'll go over and jack that mother *up*. That ought to clear out your glands."

It was better than sitting in the office. Lucas lurched to his feet. "All right. But I'll drive. Afterward we can go out and get something decent to eat."

"You buying?"

The shop assistant went into the back room to get Nester, who was not happy to see them.

"I thought you understood my position," he said, heading for the telephone. "This has now become harassment. I'm going to call my attorney first thing, rather than listen to you at all."

"That's up to you, Nester," Lucas said, baring his teeth. "It might not be a bad idea, in fact. We're trying to decide whether to bust you on felony fraud or to let Mrs. Rice's attorney handle it as a civil matter. You want to be stubborn, we'll put the cuffs on and drag you downtown and book you right now."

The shop assistant's head was swinging back and forth like a spectator's at a tennis match. Nester glanced at him, his hand on the telephone, and said, "I have no idea what you're speaking of."

"Sure you do," Lucas said. "We're talking about netsukes that might be worth a quarter-million dollars, that you were asked to valuate for insurance purposes. You told the owner that they were virtually worthless and bought them for a song."

"I never," Nester sputtered. "I was never asked to valuate those netsukes. They were offered for sale and I paid the asking price. That is all."

"That's not what Mrs. Rice says. She's willing to take it to court."

"Do you think a jury would believe some . . . some *washerwoman* instead of me? It is my word against hers—"

"You wouldn't have a chance," Sloan said in his soapiest voice. "Not a chance. Here's a guy who fought for his country and brought home some souvenirs, not knowing what he had. Then he goes through life, a good guy, pushing a broom, and finally dies of cancer that slowly eats its way up his body, killing him inch by inch. He wants to sell whatever personal possessions he can, to help his wife after he's dead. She's aging herself and they're living hand to mouth. Probably eating dog food—I can guarantee they will be, by the time their lawyer gets done with it."

"Maybe cat food. Tuna parts," Lucas chipped in.

"And they've got this treasure trove, without knowing it," Sloan continued. "Could be a happy ending, just like in a TV movie. But what happens? Along comes this slick-greaser dealer in objets d'art who gives them five hundred dollars for a quarter-million bucks' worth of art. Do you really think a jury would side with you?"

"If you do, you're living in a dream world," Lucas said. "I've got some friends in the press, you know? When I feed them this story, you'll be more famous than the maddog killer."

"That's not a bad idea, you know?" Sloan said, looking sideways at Lucas as he picked up the hint. "We haul him in, book him for fraud, and put out the story. It could take some of the heat off—"

"You better come back to my office," said Nester, now deathly pale.

They followed him through a narrow doorway into the back. A storeroom protected with a steel-mesh fence took up most of the space, with a small but elegantly appointed office tucked away to one side. Nester lowered himself behind the desk, fussed with calendar pages for a moment, then said, "What can we do about this?"

"We could arrest you for fraud, but we don't really want to. We're worried about other things," Lucas said, lowering himself into an antique chair. "If you just tell us what we want to know, we'll suggest that Mrs. Rice get a lawyer and work this out in civil court. Or perhaps you could negotiate a settlement."

"I *talked* to this person," Nester protested, nodding at Sloan. "I told him everything that happened between Mr. Rice and myself."

"I had a very strong feeling that you were holding back," Sloan said. "I'm not usually wrong."

"Well. Frankly, I thought if you learned about the price paid for the net-sukes, which was the price Mr. Rice asked—let the seller beware—that you might feel it was . . . inappropriate. I was not hiding it, I was merely being discreet."

Lucas grimaced. "If you had told us that, or even suggested it, we wouldn't have hassled you," he said. "We're trying to trace the gun Rice had. We're running down everybody who talked to him while he had it."

"I never saw a gun and he never mentioned a gun or offered to sell one," Nester said. "I didn't see anyone else while I was there, not even Mrs. Rice. We didn't talk. I went in and said I would be interested in looking at the netsukes. He backed his wheelchair up, got them from a box and gave them to me, and went back to his reading. I asked how much, he said five hundred dollars. I gave him a check and left. We didn't exchange more than fifty words."

"That doesn't sound like Rice," Sloan said. "He was supposed to be quite a talker."

"Not with me," Nester said.

Lucas looked at Sloan and shook his head.

"I think because he was so involved with his will," Nester continued. "He had to read it and sign it before his attorney picked it up."

"His attorney?" Lucas asked. He turned to Sloan. "His attorney?"

Sloan started paging through his workbook.

"He said his attorney was on his way," Nester said, looking from one to the other. "Does that help?"

"We don't show any attorney," Sloan said.

Lucas felt his throat tighten. "Did he say what his attorney's name was?"

"No, nothing like that. Or I don't remember," Nester said.

"We may want to talk to you some more," Lucas said, standing up. "Come on, Sloan."

Sloan pumped a quarter into the pay phone. Mary Rice picked it up on the first ring.

"Your husband's will, Mrs. Rice, do you have a copy of it there? Could you get it? I'll wait."

Lucas stood beside him, looking up and down the street, bouncing on the balls of his feet, calculating. A lawyer. It would fit. But this was ridiculous. This would be too easy. Sloan shifted from foot to foot, waiting.

"Did you look in the top drawer of your dresser?" Sloan said finally. "Remember you told me once you'd put stuff there . . . Yeah, I can wait."

"What is she doing?" Lucas blurted. He wanted to rip the phone away from Sloan and shout the woman into abject obedience.

"Can't find it," Sloan said.

"Let's run down there and shake down the house or—"

Sloan put up a hand and went back to the phone. "You did? Good. Look at the last page. Is the lawyer's name there? No, not the firm, the lawyer. There should be a signed name with the same name typed underneath. . . . Okay, spell it for me. L-o-u-i-s V-u-l-l-i-o-n. Thank you. Thank you."

He wrote the name in his book, Lucas looking over his shoulder. "Never heard of him," Lucas said, shaking his head.

"Another call," Sloan said. He took a small black book from his shirt pocket, opened it, found a number, and dug in his pocket for a quarter. He came up empty.

"Got a quarter?" he asked Lucas.

Lucas groped in his pockets. "No."

"Shit, we gotta get change . . ."

"Wait, wait, we can use my calling card, just dial zero. Here, give me the phone. Who is this, anyway?"

"Chick I know up at the state Public Safety."

Lucas dialed the number and passed the receiver to Sloan when it started to ring. Sloan asked for Shirley.

"This is Sloan," he said, "over at Minneapolis PD. How are you? . . . Yeah. Yeah. Great. Listen, I got a hot one, could you run it for me? . . . Right now? . . . Thanks. It's Louis Vullion." He spelled it for her. He waited a moment, then said, "Yeah, give me the whole thing."

He listened, said, "Aw, shit," and, "Whoa," and, "Hey, thanks, honey." He hung up the phone and turned to Lucas.

"Yeah?"

"Louis Vullion. White male. Twenty-seven. Five ten, one ninety, blue eyes. And some good news and some bad news. What do you want first?"

"The bad news," Lucas said quickly.

"Sparks is positive he had dark hair. He doesn't. He's a fuckin' redhead."

Lucas stared at Sloan for a moment, licked his lips. "Red hair?"

"That's what his license says."

"That's fuckin' wonderful," Lucas whispered, his face like stone.

"What?" Sloan was puzzled.

"Carla was sure he was light-complexioned. She was positive. You don't get anybody lighter than a redhead. Sparky was sure he had dark hair. I couldn't figure it out. But you put a redhead under those mercury-vapor lights down on Hennepin at night . . ." He pointed a finger at Sloan's chest, prompting him.

"Son of a bitch. It might look dark," Sloan said, suddenly excited.

"Fuck *might*," Lucas said. "It *would* look dark. Especially from a distance. It fits; it's like a poem." He licked his lips again. "If that was the bad news, what's the good news?"

Sloan put up a finger. "Registered owner," he said, "of a midnight-blue Ford Thunderbird. He bought it three months ago."

Daniel's door was closed. His secretary, Linda, was typing letters.

"Who's in there?" Lucas asked, pointing at the door. Sloan was standing on his heels.

"Pettinger from accounting," Linda said. "Lucas, wait, you can't go in there . . ."

Lucas pushed into the office, with Sloan trailing self-consciously behind. Daniel, startled, looked up in surprise, saw their faces, and turned to the accountant.

"I'm going to have to throw you out, Dan," he said. "I'll get back this afternoon."

"Uh, sure." The accountant picked up a stack of computer printouts, looked curiously at Lucas and Sloan, and walked out.

Daniel pushed the door shut. "Who is he?" he rasped.

"A lawyer," said Lucas. "A lawyer named Louis Vullion."

# 27

"Where is he?" Lucas spoke into a handset as he pulled to the curb a block from the maddog's apartment. The five-year-old Ford Escort fit seamlessly into the neighborhood.

"Crossing the bridge, headed south. Looks like he might be on his way to the Burnsville Mall. We're just north of there now."

There was a six-unit net around the maddog, twelve cops, seven women, five men. They followed him from his apartment to a parking garage not far from his office. They watched him into the office, through a solitary lunch at a downtown deli. He was limping a bit, they said, and was favoring one leg. From the fall into the ditch? They watched him back to the office, through a trip to the courthouse, up to the clerk's office, back to his office.

While he worked through the afternoon, an electronics technician fastened a small but powerful radio transmitter under the bumper of his car. When the maddog left the office at night, the watchers followed him back to his car. He returned to his apartment, apparently ate dinner, and then left again. Heading south.

"He's gone into the mall parking lot."

Lucas glanced at his watch. If the maddog turned around and drove back to his apartment as quickly as he could, it would still take twenty minutes. That was almost enough time.

"Out of his car, going inside," the radio burped. The net would be on the ground now, moving around him.

Lucas turned the radio off and stuck it in his jacket pocket. He did not want police calls burping out of his pocket at an inopportune moment. The power lockpick and a disposable flashlight were under the seat. He retrieved them, shoved the flashlight in another pocket, and slipped the pick beneath his coat, under his arm.

He got out of the car, turned his collar up, and hurried along the sidewalk, his back to the wind, the last dry leaves of fall scurrying along by his ankles.

The maddog lived in a fourplex, each unit two stories with an attic, each occupying one vertical corner of what otherwise looked like a Victorian mansion. Each of the four apartments had a small one-car attached garage and a tiny front porch with a short railing for the display of petunias and geraniums. The flowerpots stood empty and cold.

Lucas walked directly to the maddog's apartment, turned in at his entry walk, and hurried up the steps. He pressed the doorbell, once, twice, listened for the phone. It was still ringing. He glanced around, took out the power pick, and pushed it into the lock. The pick made an ungodly loud clatter, but it was efficient. The door popped open, then stopped as it hit the end of a safety chain. The maddog had gone out through the garage, and that door would be automatically locked.

Lucas swore, groped in his pocket, and pulled out a board full of thumbtacks and a couple of rubber bands. Glancing around again, he saw nothing but empty street, and he pushed the door open until it hit the end of the chain. Reaching in as far as he could, he pushed a thumbtack into the wood on the back of the door, with the rubber band beneath it. Then he stretched the rubber band until he could loop it over the knob on the door chain. When he eased the door shut, the rubber band contracted and pulled the chain-knob to the end of its channel. With a couple of shakes, it fell out.

"Hey, Louis, what's happening?" Lucas called as he pushed the door open. There was no response. He whistled for a dog. Nothing. He pushed the door shut, turned on the hall light, and pried the thumbtack out of the door. The hole was imperceptible. He took out the handset, turned it on, and called the surveillance crew.

"Where is he?"

"Just went into a sporting-goods store. He's looking at jackets."

Lucas thumbed the set to the monitor position and quickly checked the apartment for any obvious indications that Vullion was the maddog. As he passed the ringing telephone, he lifted it off the hook and then dropped it back on, silencing it.

In a quick survey of the first floor he found a utility room with the water heater, washer and dryer, and a small built-in workbench with a drawer half-full of inexpensive tools. A door in the utility room led out to the garage. He opened it, turned on the light, and looked around. A small snow-blower, a couple of snow shovels, and a stack of newspapers packaged for disposal in brown shopping bags. If he had time, he would stop back and go through the papers. With luck, he might find one that had been cut to make the messages left on the maddog's victims' bodies. There was nothing else of interest.

He shut the garage door, walked through the tiny kitchen, opening and closing cabinet doors as he passed through, poked his head into the living room, checked a small half-bath and a slightly larger office space with an IBM computer and a few lawbooks.

The second floor was divided between two bedrooms and a large bathroom. One of the bedrooms was furnished; the other was used as storage space. In the storage room he found the maddog's luggage, empty, an electronic keyboard which looked practically unused, and an inexpensive weight bench with a set of amateur weights. He checked the edges of the weights. Like the keyboard, they appeared practically untouched. Vullion was a man with unconsummated interests . . .

A battered couch sat in one corner, along with three boxes full of magazines, a *Playboy* collection that appeared to go back a dozen years or more. He left the storeroom and walked to the other bedroom.

In the ceiling of the hallway between the two bedrooms was an entry panel for the attic, with a steel handle attached to it. Lucas pulled down on the handle, and a lightweight ladder folded down into the hallway. He walked up a few steps, stuck his head into the attic, and flashed the light around. The attic was divided among the four apartments with thin sheets of plywood. Vullion's space was empty. He backed out, pushed the ladder with its attached door back into place, and took out the handset.

"Where is he?"

"Still in the store."

Time to work.

Lucas put the radio back in his pocket, took a miniature tape recorder from the other, thumbed it on, and went into the bedroom.

"Bedroom," he said. "Closet. Sport coat, forty-two regular. Suit, forty-two regular. Pants, waist thirty-six. Shoes. Nike Airs, blue, bubble along outer sole. No Reeboks. . . .

"Bedroom dresser . . . lubricated Trojan prophylactics, box of twelve, seven missing. . . .

"Office," he said. "Bill from University of Minnesota Law Alumni Association. Federal tax returns, eight years. Minnesota, Minnesota, Minnesota, Minnesota, Minnesota, Texas, Texas, Texas. Shows address in Houston, Texas, under name Louis Vullion.

"Computer files, all law stuff and correspondence, opening correspondence, all business. . . .

"Kitchen. Under sink. Bag of onions, no potatoes . . ."

Lucas went methodically through the apartment looking for anything that would directly associate Vullion with the killings. Except for the Nike Airs, there was nothing. But the indirect evidence piled up: the life in Texas before the year at the University of Minnesota law school, the clothes that said his size was right, the prophylactics . . .

"Where is he?"

"Looking at shoes."

The lack of direct evidence was infuriating. If Vullion had kept souvenirs of the kills, if Lucas had found a box of surgeon's gloves in association with a box of Kotex, with a roll of tape next to them . . . or if the kitchen table had been littered with the shreds of a newspaper that one of his messages had been cut from . . .

If he had kept those things, they could find a way to get a warrant and take him. But there was none of it. Standing arms akimbo, Lucas looked around the unnaturally neat living room, and then realized: it was unnaturally neat.

"We scared the cocksucker and he cleaned the place out," Lucas said aloud. If they had talked to Nester the previous week, before the incident at McGowan's . . . No point in thinking about it. He started to turn out of the living room, when the videocassette recorder caught his eye. There were no tapes in evidence, but an empty tape carton sat beside the television. He reached down, turned the machine on, and punched the eject button. After a minute's churning, the VCR produced a tape.

"Where is he?"

"Leaving the shoe store."

Lucas turned on the television and started the tape. It was blank. He stopped it, backed it up, ran it again, and was startled when his own face popped up on the screen.

"God damn, the interview," Lucas muttered to himself. The camera cut to Carla. He watched the interview through to the end, waited until the screen went blank, and turned off the recorder and the television.

What little doubt he had had disappeared with the video recording. He walked back to the bedroom, lifted the bedspread, and pushed his arm between the mattress and box springs. Nothing.

He dipped back in his jacket pocket and took out an envelope and shook out the pictures. Lewis, Brown, Wheatcroft, the others. Handling the photos by their edges, he pushed them under the mattress as far as he could reach. A thorough search would find them.

When it was done, he straightened the bedspread and began moving out of the apartment, working as methodically on his way out as he had on the way in. Everything in place. Everything checked. All lights out. He peered out at the sidewalk. Nobody there. He put the chain back on the front door and went into the garage. He took ten minutes to check the newspapers. None were shredded. He restacked the bundles as he'd found them, and let himself out through the garage door.

Back on the sidewalk, he walked briskly away. He had almost reached the Ford Escort when the monitor beeped.

"He's out of the mall, headed toward his car. Three and five stay on the ground, lead cars saddle up now. . . ."

\*　　\*　　\*

Lucas and Daniel sat alone in Daniel's dimly lit office, looking at each other through a yellow pool of light cast by a desk lamp. "So even if we got in, we wouldn't find anything," Daniel concluded.

"I couldn't swear to that, but it looks to me like he cleaned the place out. He may have hidden something—I didn't have enough time to really tear the place apart," Lucas said. "But I didn't find anything conclusive. The Nikes are right, the rubbers are right, his size is right, the car is right. But you know and I know that we could find that combination in fifty people out there."

"Fifty people who are also lawyers and hang around the courthouse and have a Texas accent and would get a gun from Rice?"

"But we've got no direct evidence that he got the gun from Rice. And all the other stuff is real thin. You've got to believe that he'd get the best attorney around, and a good attorney would cut us to pieces."

"How about voice analysis on the tapes?"

"You know what the courts think of that."

"But it's another thing."

"Yeah. I know. It's tempting . . ."

"But?"

"But if we keep watching him, we should get him. He didn't get his kill. He's scared now, but if he's compelled to kill, he'll be going back out. Sooner or later. I'd bet in the next week. This time, we won't lose him. We'll get him entering some place and he'll have all that shit with him, the Kotex and the potato and the gloves. We'll have him cold."

"I'll talk to the county attorney. I'll tell him what we have now and what we might get. See what he says. But basically, I think you're right. It's too thin to risk."


Surveillance posts were set up in an apartment across the street from the maddog's and one house down; and behind and two houses down.

"It was the best we could do, and it ain't bad," the surveillance chief said. "We can see both doors and all windows. With the freeway on the south, he can only get out of the neighborhood to the north, and we're north of him. And he ain't going to see us anyway."

"What's that glow? Is he reading in bed?"

"Night-light, we think," the surveillance chief said.

Lucas nodded. He recalled seeing one in the bedroom but couldn't say so. "He's trying to keep away the nightmares," he said instead.

"He'd have them if anybody did," said the surveillance chief. "Are you going to work a regular schedule with us?"

"I'll be here every night," Lucas said. "If he breaks off his regular work pattern during the day, I want you to beep me. I'll come running. He hasn't ever hit anybody in the early morning, so I'll head home after he goes to bed. Get some sleep. I'll check with the surveillance team first thing in the morning."

"Stay close. When it goes down, it could go fast."

"Yeah. I was at the Fuckup, remember?"

Lucas looked out the window at the maddog's apartment, at the steady dim glow from the second floor. This time there wouldn't be a fuckup.

# 28

The maddog should never have spotted the surveillance. It was purely an accident.

He left a late-afternoon real-estate closing at a bank in the Mississippi River town of Hastings, twenty-odd miles south of the Twin Cities. It was dark. He crossed the Mississippi at the Hastings bridge and drove north on Highway 61, through the suburban towns of Cottage Grove, St. Paul Park, and Newport. As he passed through St. Paul Park he found himself behind an uncovered gravel truck. Pieces of gravel bounced out of the back of the truck and along the highway. A big one could star a windshield.

The maddog, thinking of the shiny finish on his new Thunderbird, moved into the left lane and accelerated around the truck. The close-surveillance car behind him caught the truck a moment later. Since the maddog appeared to be in no particular hurry, intent only on staying ahead of the truck, the surveillance car fell in behind it.

Gravel bounced around the surveillance car, but the cops inside didn't care. The car was mechanically sound, but, like most surveillance cars, was not much to look at, just a plain vanilla Dodge. A few dings more or less wouldn't make any difference. And the gravel truck made excellent cover.

None of it would have mattered if one particularly large rock hadn't bounced off the highway and knocked half the plastic lens off the amber left-turn light. The cops inside heard the thump, but couldn't see the broken lens.

"We oughta give this asshole a ticket," one of the surveillance cops said as the rock bounced off.

"Right," the driver answered. "Go ahead and stick the light on the roof."

"Could you see Daniel's face? We say, 'Well, we was following him when we ran into this incredible asshole with a truck full of rocks . . .'"

"He'd put us in prison," the first cop said. "He'd find a way."

The maddog decided to stop at a fast-food restaurant off the Interstate loop highway, I-494. The loop intersected with Highway 61 just north of the town of Newport. When the maddog pulled onto the circular entrance ramp for I-494, he glanced into the rearview mirror and noted, with no particular interest, the unusual turn signal on a car a hundred yards back. The signal flashed a peculiar combination of amber and unshielded white.

The close-surveillance car was tighter on the maddog's tail than it normally would have been. The lead car had continued up Highway 61 through the I-494 interchange and would now have to find a place to turn around and catch up from behind. In the meantime, until one of the trailing surveillance cars could move up into the lead position, the cops in the close-surveillance car couldn't take chances. They stuck close.

They were still close when the maddog turned off on the Robert Street exit, heading for one of the restaurants just north of the interchange. As he came down the ramp and slowed to a stop at the bottom, the maddog again noticed the car with the odd turn light. Something was wrong with it, he thought. A broken lens or something. The car was slow in coming down the ramp behind him.

When the traffic signal turned green, the maddog forgot about it and took a left, went up the hill, and pulled into a restaurant parking lot. Outside the entrance, he got a copy of *USA Today* and carried it inside.

While the maddog ate and read his newspaper, the surveillance cops took turns stocking up on burgers and Cokes at a McDonald's a half-mile away. Two teams always stayed on the maddog.

When he left the restaurant, the maddog decided to drive into St. Paul on Robert Street. It was a crowded, tricky street, but there were two movie theaters not far ahead. A movie would go down well.

He saw the shattered turn light halfway up Robert Street. It was three cars back. At first he wasn't certain, but then he saw it again, more clearly. And again.

They were on him.

He knew it.

He sat halfway through a green light, staring blindly at the street ahead, until the cars behind him started to honk. Should he run for it?

No. If he was being watched, it would tip them off that he knew. He needed time to think. Besides, maybe he was wrong. He wasn't certain about the light. It could be a coincidence.

But it didn't feel like a coincidence.

He passed a shopping center, took a right turn, and drove down to the high-speed Highway 3, which went north to intersect with Interstate 94. Coming off the exit ramp, he watched the mirror. A car followed him down the ramp, but far enough away that he couldn't see the turn light.

He thought about pulling over, feigning car trouble; but that could precipi-
tate something, force their hands. He was not sure that he wanted to do that.
He did a mental catalog. There was nothing at the apartment. Nothing. Nothing
in the car. There was nothing to hang him with. If they were really watching,
they must be waiting for an attack.

Approaching the I-94 interchange across the LaFayette Bridge, the maddog
let his speed drop sharply. The cars behind began to close up, and he picked
up the surveillance car in an adjacent lane. He still couldn't see it clearly, but
there was something definitely wrong with its turn signal.

Two cops in a trailing surveillance car had moved up and finally passed the
maddog as they all drove north on Highway 3. As they approached I-94, the
two women cops in the new lead car made the logical decision that the maddog was heading back to Minneapolis on the Interstate. They committed to the
ramp. Behind them, the maddog drove through the interchange and into the
dark warren of streets in St. Paul's Lowertown. The net spread out around him
on parallel streets, staying in touch. Again, with the lead car out of it, the
close-surveillance car moved in a bit tighter. Tight enough that when they
turned a corner and found the maddog at a dead stop, backing into a parking
place, they had to drive by.

And the maddog, who was watching for them, clearly caught the broken
lens on the turn signal.

He was being watched. Coincidence was one thing. To believe all these
sightings were coincidences was to believe in fairy tales.

The maddog locked his car and walked briskly into a downtown shopping
mall and went up two floors. The net was thinner, but still in place. The drivers
of the trailing units had been alerted by the close-surveillance car that the
maddog was parking. The passenger-cops were on the street before the maddog had fully gotten into his parking place.

They followed him into the theater. The theater was a place to think. How
had they gotten onto him? Perhaps, as part of their surveillance of McGowan's
house, they had routinely noted the license plates of all cars in the neighborhood. Perhaps somebody had heard the shots, seen him drive away, and noted
the tag number. Maybe they had nothing at all but a number that didn't quite
fit in the neighborhood. Perhaps he should start preparing an alibi for being
there. He couldn't think of any offhand, but something might occur to him if he
considered the problem.

If they were following him, there was little he could do about it. He didn't
dare try to dodge the surveillance. That would confirm that he was guilty. He
had disposed of all evidence that would put him at the crime scene. As far as
he knew, there was no conclusive evidence against him anywhere.

When the movie ended, the maddog walked down to his car, resisting the
almost overwhelming temptation to look around, to search the doorways for

watchers. He wouldn't see them, of course. They would be too good for that. He stayed on city streets out to I-94, then turned east toward his own exit. He didn't see the broken turn signal on the way out to the Interstate. That meant nothing, he knew, but he couldn't suppress a tiny surge of hope. Maybe it *had* been coincidence.

The Interstate was crowded, and though he watched, he didn't see any cars with broken turn signals. He sighed, felt the tension seeping out. When he reached his exit, he ran the car up the ramp to the traffic signal and waited. Another car came off behind. Coasted up the ramp, slowly. Too slowly.

The traffic light changed to green. The maddog waited. The other car eased up. The left-front turn signal was broken, the white light shining brightly past the amber. The maddog looked up, saw the green, and took a right.

"Jeez, you don't look so good. You sick?" His secretary seemed concerned.

"No, no. Just had a little insomnia the last few nights. Could you get the papers for the Parker-Olson closing?"

The maddog sat at his desk, the office door closed, a blank yellow pad in front of him. Think.

The news stories of the surveillance on McGowan's house mentioned that the cops set up observation posts both in front and in back. Would they have done the same at his place? Probably. There were empty apartments on the block; he'd seen the signs, but not paid much attention. Nor did he know his neighbors, other than to nod at the others in his fourplex. Could he spot the other surveillance posts?

The maddog stood and stepped over to the window, hands in his jacket pockets, staring sightlessly out at the street.

Maybe. Maybe he could spot them, maybe he could deduce where they were. Where would that get him? If they came for him, he would not resist. That would be pointless. And had he not imagined himself in court, defending himself against his accusers? Had he not dreamed of capturing the jury with his eloquence?

He had. But now the vision of a magnificent defense did not come so easily. Deep in his heart, he knew they were right. He was not a good attorney; not in court, anyway. He'd never taken the fact out and looked at it, but the fact was there, like a stone.

He paced two steps one way, two steps back, tugging at his lip. They were watching. No matter how long he suppressed the urge to take another woman, they would eventually come. They wouldn't wait forever.

He sat down, looked at the yellow pad, and summarized:

They were not sure enough to arrest him yet.

They could not wait forever.

What would they do?

He thought of Davenport, the gamer. What would the gamer do?

A gamer would frame him.

It took him a half-minute on his knees in the garage to find the radio transmitter on the car. It took another hour to find the photographs under the mattress. The beeper he left in place. The photos he stared at, frightened. If the police should come through the door at this instant, he would go to jail for eighteen years, a life sentence in Minnesota.

He took the photographs into the kitchen and, one by one, burned them, the pictures curling and charring in the flames from the stove burner. When they were gone, reduced to charcoal, he crushed the blackened remains to powder and washed them down the kitchen sink.

That night he forced himself to lie in bed for fifteen minutes, then crept to the window and looked down the street. There was a patchwork of lighted windows, and many more that were dark. He watched, and after a while crawled back to his bed, got both pillows and put one on the floor and the other upright against the wall, where he could lean on it. It would be a long night.

After three hours, the maddog dozed, his head falling forward. He jerked it back upright and peered groggily through the window. Everything was about the same, but he couldn't watch much longer. There were only two lights still on, he had noted them, and he was simply too tired to continue.

He got up, carrying the pillows, and flopped facedown on the bed. Paradoxically, as soon as he was willing to allow himself to sleep, he felt more alert. The thoughts ran through his brain like a night train, hard and quick and hardly discernible as independent ideas. A mishmash of images—his women, their eyes, Lucas Davenport, the fight outside McGowan's, the broken turn signal.

From the mishmash there came an idea. The maddog resisted it at first, because it had the quality of a nightmare, requiring a broad-scope action under the most intense stress. Finally he considered it and paraded the objections, one by one. The longer he turned it in his mind, the more substantial it became.

It was a winning stroke. And the surveillance? What better alibi could he find? Would he have the courage to attempt the stroke? Or would he sit there like a frightened rabbit, waiting to have his neck wrung by the hunter?

He bit his lip. He bit so hard that he found blood on the pillow the next morning. But he had decided. He would try.

# 29

Lucas sat on a tall three-legged stool, hunched over his workbench, manipulating pieces of white two-inch polyvinylchloride pipe, wing nuts, bolts, aluminum tubes, and lengths of the Thinsulate batting normally used as insulation in winter coats.

He had hoped to settle the maddog himself. Instead, the investigation was moving into a tedious rook-pawn endgame. The outcome would probably be determined by laborious maneuver rather than a *coup de maître*.

Nevertheless, he would prepare for the *coup*, should one unexpectedly present itself.

His first attempt at building a silencer cost him blood.

"I don't know," he said aloud. It should work, but it looked awful. A foot-long length of PVC pipe split lengthwise, screwed back together with wing nuts but with gaps down the split. Through the gaps, the tightly wound batting protruded in soft puffs. Deep inside, the aluminum pipe was pierced with dozens of hand-drilled holes.

He attached the assembly to the barrel of one of his cold street weapons, a Smith & Wesson Model 39 in nine-millimeter parabellum. He turned on a miniature tape recorder, jacked a round into the chamber, pointed the weapon at a stack of St. Paul Yellow Pages, and pulled the trigger. There was very little noise from the shot, but there was a mechanical clank as the telephone books jumped and simultaneously the silencer twisted in his hands and came half apart. A sharp edge on the PVC pipe sliced into the side of his middle finger.

"Son of a bitch," he said. He turned off the tape recorder and went upstairs, looked at the cut, which was superficial, washed it, bandaged it, and went back down the stairs.

The tape recorder had picked up the sound of the shot, along with the clank when the silencer pulled apart, but he would not have identified either of the noises as a shot.

The silencer was a mess. The internal tube had been knocked out of alignment with the gun's barrel, either by the blast of gases ahead of the slug or by the slug itself. It hadn't changed the slug's trajectory much. He made some mental notes on alterations to the silencer. The main requirement was that it had to be easily detached from the gun and just as easily disassembled. Accuracy counted not at all.

When he had finished examining the silencer and decided on the alterations he would make, he dug the slug out of the telephone books and looked at it. It was a handgun hunter's hollow-point and was so deformed that it would take an expert to identify its exact caliber.

Lucas nodded. He had the right ammunition, but he needed time to work on the silencer.

He had yet to make the blank.


Midmorning. Gray light filtered in through the kitchen window as he tried to wake up with coffee and an aging bagel. The Smith, with silencer modified and reattached, was in a disreputable-looking gym bag he'd found in a back closet. The gun/silencer combination was grossly illegal. If, somehow, it was found in his car, he would claim that he'd taken it off the street.

A car door slammed close by and he picked up the cup of coffee and stepped into the hallway and peered out the front windows. Carla Ruiz coming up the driveway, a taxi pulling away. He stuffed the gym bag under the kitchen sink, walked back to the bedroom, and pulled on a pair of sweatpants. The doorbell rang and he pulled a sweatshirt over his head, went out to the door, and let her in.

"Hi," she said softly, her face down, looking at him only in brief lateral glances.

"What's wrong?"

"I thought we should have some coffee."

"Sure," he said curiously. "I've got some hot water." He led her into the kitchen, dumped a heaping teaspoon of instant coffee into an oversize ceramic cup, and handed it to her.

"Jennifer Carey came over last night," she said as she sat down. She unbuttoned her coat but left it on.

"Oh." Lucas sat down across the table.

"We had a talk."

Lucas looked away from her into the front room. "And did you decide my future? Between the two of you?"

Carla smiled a very small smile. "Yeah," she said. She took a sip of coffee.

"Good of you to let me know," Lucas said sourly.

"We thought it was the polite thing to do," Carla said, and Lucas had to laugh in spite of himself.

"What did you decide?"

"She gets custody," Carla said.

"You don't mind?"

"I mind, kind of. It makes me angry that you were sleeping with us alternately, one down here, one up in the North Woods. But I figured our relationship wasn't long for the world. We live in different places. I weave, you shoot people. And it seemed like she had a better prior claim, with the baby and all."

"What about what I want?"

"We decided that didn't matter too much. Jennifer said you'd wiggle and squirm, but eventually you'd come around."

"Now, *that* pisses me off," Lucas said, no longer smiling.

"Tough," Carla said.

They stared at each other across the table. Lucas flinched first. "I may tell Jennifer to take a hike," he said.

"Not with her being pregnant," Carla said, shaking her head. "No chance. That's Jennifer's judgment, and I agree. I asked her what she'd do if you went with somebody else. She said she'd go over and have another talk with the somebody else."

"Jesus," Lucas said. He closed his eyes and tilted his head back and massaged the back of his neck. "What'd I do to deserve this?"

"Slept with one too many women," Carla said. "It's actually pretty flattering, when you think about it. She's good-looking and smart. And in her own screwed-up way, she's in love with you. In my own screwed-up way, I'm not—though I'd still like to use the cabin a couple of times a year. Until I can afford my own."

"Anytime," Lucas said wistfully. He wanted to say more, but couldn't think of anything.

Carla took a last sip of coffee, pushed the cup, still half-full, into the middle of the table, and stood up.

"I better get going," she said. "The cab should be back."

Lucas sat where he was. "Well, it was real."

"What's that supposed to mean?" she asked as she retrieved her purse.

"That's what you say when you can't think of anything to say."

"Okay." She buttoned her coat. "See you."

"How come Jennifer didn't deliver the message?"

"We talked about that and decided I should do it. That'd make a clean break between us. Besides, she said you'd spend about a half-hour on some kind of Catholic guilt trip, then you'd go into a rage and kick stuff, then you'd try to call her on the telephone so you could yell at her. Then in about two hours you'd start laughing about it. She said she'd rather skip the preliminaries." Carla glanced at her watch. "She'll be over in two hours."

"Motherfucker," Lucas said in disbelief.

"You got that right," Carla said as she went out the door. A yellow cab was waiting. She stopped with the screen door still open. "Call you next spring. About the cabin."

It was more like three hours. When Jennifer arrived, she wasn't embarrassed in the slightest.

"Hi," she said when he opened the door. She walked past him, took off her coat, and tossed it on the couch. "Carla called, said the talk went okay."

"I'm pretty unhappy—" Lucas started, but she waved him off.

"Spare me. McGowan's going to network, by the way. It's all over town."

"Fuck McGowan."

"Better hurry," Jennifer said. "She'll be gone in a month. But I still think what you did was awful. McGowan's just too dumb to recognize it."

"Goddammit, Jennifer . . ."

"If you're going to yell, we could have this talk some other time."

"I'm not going to yell," he said grimly. He thought he might strangle.

"Okay. So I thought I might give you my position. That is, if you'd like to hear it."

"Sure. I mean, why not? You're running the rest of my life."

"My position is, I'm pregnant and the daddy shouldn't screw anybody else until the baby is born, and maybe"—she paused, as though considering the fairness of her proposition—"maybe a year old. Maybe two years old. That way, I can kind of pretend like I'm married and talk to you about the baby and what we did during the day and his first words and how he's walking and I won't have to worry about you fooling around. And then, when you can't stand it and start fooling around again, I can just pretend like I'm divorced."

She smiled brightly. Lucas was appalled.

"That's the coldest goddamn thing I ever heard," he said.

"It's not exactly an extemporaneous speech," she said. "I rewrote it about twelve times. I thought it was rather cogently expressed, but with enough emotion to make it convincing."

Lucas laughed, then stopped laughing and sat down. He looked haggard, she thought. Or harried. "All right. I give up," he said.

"All right to all of it?"

"Yeah. All of it."

"Scout's honor?"

"Sure." He held up the three fingers. "Scout's honor."

Late in the evening, Lucas lay on the surveillance team's mattress and thought about it. He could live with it, he thought. For two years? Maybe.

"That's weird. You see that?" said the first surveillance cop.

"I didn't see anything," said his partner.

"What?" asked Lucas.

"I don't know. It's like there's some movement over there. Just a little bit, at the edge of the window."

Lucas crawled over and looked out. The maddog's apartment was dark except for the faint glow from the night-light.

"I don't see anything," he said. "You think he's doing something?"

"I don't know. Probably nothing. It's just every once in a while . . . it's like he's watching *us.*"

# 30

It was the winning stroke. If he had the nerve, he could pull it off. He imagined Davenport's face. Davenport would *know*, but he wouldn't know how, and there wouldn't be a damn thing he could do about it.

In some ways, of course, it would be his most intellectual mission. He didn't *need* this particular woman, but he would take her anyway. To the police—not Davenport, but the others—there would be a logic to it. A logic they could understand.

In the meantime, the *other* pressure had begun to build. There was a woman who lived in the town of Richfield, a schoolteacher with almond eyes and rich sable hair, wide teeth like a Russian girl's. He had seen her with a troop of her children in the basement level of the Government Center, installing an elementary-school art show . . .

No. He put her out of his mind. The need would grow, but he could control it. It was a matter of will. And his mind had to be clear to deal with the *stroke*.

He first had to break free, if only for two hours. He didn't see them, but they were there, he was sure, a web of watchers escorting him through the city's streets and skyways. His night watches and his explorations in the attic had been fruitful. He knew, he thought, where two of their surveillance posts were. The lighting patterns were wrong for families or individuals, and he saw car lights coming and going at odd hours of the night, always from the same two houses. One of the houses, he was sure, had been empty until recently.

They were waiting for him to move. Before he could, he had to break free. Just for two hours. He thought he had a way.

The law firm of Woodley, Gage & Whole occupied three floors of an office building two blocks from his own. He had twice encountered one of their attorneys in real-estate closings, a man named Kenneth Hart. After each of the closings, they'd had lunch. If someone had ever asked the maddog who his friends were, he would have mentioned Hart. Now he hoped that Hart remembered him.

At Woodley, Gage, status was signified by floor assignment. The main reception area was on the third floor, the floor shared by the partners. The lesser lights were on the fourth. The smallest lights of all were on the fifth. With a less-affluent firm, a client arriving at the third-floor reception area in search of a fourth- or fifth-floor attorney would be routed back down the hall to the elevators. With this firm, no such side trip was necessary. There was an internal elevator and an internal stairway.

Best of all, there were exits to the parking garage on all of the first eight floors. If he could go into Woodley, Gage on the third floor, and the cops didn't know about the internal elevator, he could slip out on five.

Before he could use Woodley, Gage, a preliminary excursion would be necessary, and it would have to take place under the noses of his watchers.

The maddog left the office early, drove his bugged Thunderbird south to Lake Street, found a place to park, got out, and walked along the row of dilapidated shops. He passed a dealer in antiques, peered through the dark glass, and breathed a sigh of relief. The fishing lures were still in the window.

He walked on another half-block to a computer-supply store, where he bought a carton of computer paper and headed slowly back to the car, still window-shopping. He paused at the antiques dealer's again, pretending to debate whether or not to enter. He should not overplay it, he thought; the watchers would be professionals and might sense something. He went inside.

"Can I help you?"

A woman emerged from the back of the shop. She had iron-colored hair tied back in a bun, her hands clasped in front of her. If she'd been wearing a shawl, she'd have looked like a phony grandmother on a package of chocolate-chip cookies. As it happened, she was wearing a cheap blue suit with a red tie and had the strained rheumy look of a longtime alcoholic.

"Those fishing lures in the window; are they expensive?" asked the maddog.

"Some are, some aren't," the woman said. She maneuvered around him toward the display, keeping her feet wide apart for balance. She's drunk, the maddog thought.

"How about the bluegill one?" he asked.

"That's hand-carved, hand-painted up at Winnibigoshish. There are a lot of fakes around, you know, but this is the real thing. I bought the whole bunch from an old resort owner last summer, he was cleaning out his cellar."

"So how much?"

She looked him over speculatively. "Twenty?"

"Sold."

She looked like she wished she'd asked for more. "Plus tax," she said. He left the store with the lure in a brown paper bag and went to the bank, where he wrote a check for two thousand dollars.


The bluegill was carved from a solid piece of pine and had three rusty treble hooks dangling from it. An early pike lure, the woman said, probably carved back in the thirties. The maddog knew nothing about fishing lures, but this one had the rustic rightness of real folk art. If he collected anything, he thought, he might collect this stuff, like Hart did. He would call Kenneth Hart tomorrow, just after lunch.

*    *    *

He rethought the entire project during the night and decided to call it off. At dawn, groggy, he staggered to the bathroom and took half a pill. Just before it carried him away, he changed his mind again, and decided to go ahead.

"Hello, Ken?"

"This is Ken Hart . . ." A little wary.

"This is Louis Vullion, down at Felsen . . ."

"Sure. What's up?" Friendly now.

"You going to be in for a few minutes?"

"I've got a meeting at two . . ."

"Just want to see you for a minute. Got something for you, actually."

"Come on over."


The invisible net, he supposed, spread around him as he moved through the skyways. He tried not to look, but couldn't help himself. A lot of the watchers would be women, he knew. They were the best tails. At least, the books said so.

The maddog left his regular wool overcoat in his office and went to Hart's office wearing a suit coat and carrying a briefcase. An inexpensive tan trench coat was rolled and stuffed inside the briefcase, along with a crushable tweed hat.

The maddog went directly to the third-floor reception area of Hart's firm.

"I'm here to see Ken Hart," he told the receptionist.

"Do you have an appointment, Mr. . . . ?"

"Vullion. I'm an attorney from Felsen-Gore. I called Ken a few minutes ago to tell him I was running over."

"Okay." She smiled at him. "Go down the hall . . ."

He smiled back as pleasantly as he could. "I know the way."

He went down the hall and punched the private elevator for the fifth floor. The net, he hoped, was fixed on the third-floor reception area.

"Ken?" The other attorney was paging through a brief, and looked up at the maddog.

"Hey. Louis. Come on in, sit down."

"Uh, I really can't, I'm in a rush," the maddog said, glancing at his wristwatch. "I wanted to drop something off. Remember when we ate lunch, you mentioned you collected old fishing lures? I was up north a couple weeks ago . . ." He dumped the lure out of the paper bag onto Hart's desk.

"Whoa. That's a good one," Hart said, looking pleased. "Thanks, man. How much do I owe you?"

"I virtually stole the thing," the maddog said, shaking his head. "I'd be embarrassed to tell you. Of course, if you want to buy the cheeseburgers after the next closing . . ."

"You got a deal," Hart said enthusiastically. "Damn, this is really a good one."

"I've got to get out of here. Can I get out on this floor, or do I have to run back down . . . ?"

"No, no, just down the hall," Hart said. He came with him to his office door and pointed. "And jeez, Louis, thanks a lot."

Thank *you*, the maddog thought as he left. The whole charade had been an excuse to walk through the door on the fifth floor. He hesitated before he pushed through. This was critical. If there were people outside in the hallway, and if one of them happened to wander along behind as he went out through the parking ramp, he would have to call it off. He took a breath and pushed through the door. The hallway was empty.

The maddog walked the width of the building to the parking ramp, stopped before the steel fire door, took out the coat and hat, put them on, and stepped outside. The ramp had its own elevator, but the maddog took the stairs, looking down each flight before he took it. At the ground floor he kept his head down and strode out onto the sidewalk a full block from the entrance to Hart's building. He crossed the street, jaywalking, walked into another office building, up one floor, and into one of the remotest skyways in the system. He walked for two minutes and glanced back. There was nobody behind him.

He was alone.


The maddog called for a cab and took it directly to a used-car lot on University Avenue, a mile from his apartment.

He looked over the row of cars and picked out a brown Chevrolet Cavalier. "$1,695" was written on the windshield in poster paint. He peered through the driver's-side window. The odometer said 94651. A salesman approached him crablike through the lot, rubbing his hands as though they were pincers.

"How do you like this weather, really something, huh?" the salesman said.

The maddog ignored the gambit. The car was right. "I'm looking for something cheap for my wife. Something to get through the winter," he said.

"This'll do 'er, you betcha," the salesman said. "Good little car. Uses a little oil, but not—"

"I'll give you fourteen hundred for it and you pick up the tax," the maddog said.

The salesman looked him over. "Fifteen hundred and *you* pick up the tax."

"Fifteen hundred flat," said the maddog.

"Fifteen and we split the tax."

"Have you got the title here?" the maddog asked.

"Sure do."

"Get somebody to clean the paint off the windshield and take the consumer notice off the side window," the maddog said. He showed the salesman a sheaf of fifties. "I'll take it with me."

He told them his name was Harry Barber. With the stack of fifties sitting there, nobody asked for identification. He signed a statement that said he had insurance.

On the way back to his apartment, the maddog stopped at a salvage store and bought a two-foot length of automobile heating hose, a bag of cat litter, a roll of silver duct tape, and a pair of work gloves. As he was going past the cash register he saw a display of tear-gas canisters like the one Carla Ruiz had used on him.

"Those things work?" he asked the clerk.

"Sure. Works great."

"Give me one."

In the car, he wrapped the open end of the heating tube with the duct tape until it was sealed, then poured the tube full of cat litter and sealed the other end. When he was done, he had a slightly flexible two-foot-long weighted rubber club. He put the club under the seat and the tape in the bag with the cat litter.

Then, if he remembered right from his university days . . .

The motel vending machines were all gathered in a separate alcove. He dropped in the coins and got the single-pack Kotex and stuffed it in his pocket. A few more coins bought two slim roles of medical adhesive tape.

He dumped the sack of kitty litter and the duct tape in a motel garbage can, locked everything else in the trunk of the car, and drove quickly but carefully back to his own neighborhood. He parked on a side street three blocks from his apartment, carefully checking to make sure he was in a legal space. The car should be fine for a few days. With any luck, and if his nerve held, it wouldn't have to wait for more than a few hours.

He glanced at his watch. He'd been out of Hart's office for an hour and a half. If he wanted to attempt the pinnacle of gaming elegance, he would go back to Hart's office on the fifth floor, walk down the stairs, and exit past the receptionist. There was a chance—even a good chance—that the cops would never have made inquiries about where he was.

But if they had, and knew he had left Hart's office, then a faked return would tip them off. They would know that he *knew*. They would move on him, if they could, and he didn't want to spring any traps prematurely.

On the other hand, if he innocently walked back past the third-floor law office in the well-used main skyway, right past the watchers, wearing only his suit, without a coat or hat . . .

They'd almost certainly assume that however he'd gotten out, he had been on an innocent trip of some kind. Lunch.

He hoped they'd think that.

The *stroke* depended on it.

The maddog walked over to a university dormitory to call a cab.

# 31

"You lost him?" Lucas' eyes were black with rage.

"For at least two hours," the surveillance chief admitted, hangdog. He was remembering Cochrane and the fight after the Fuckup. "We don't know whether he suckered us or just wandered away."

"What happened?" They were in the front seat of Lucas' car on the street outside Vullion's office. The maddog was inside, at work.

"He started out just like he always does, carrying his briefcase, except he wasn't wearing a coat or hat or anything."

"No coat?"

"No coat, and it's cold out. Anyway, he walks over two blocks to another law office. It's a big one. It's got a glassed-in reception area on the third floor of the Hops Exchange."

"Yeah, I know it. Woodley and something-something."

"That's it. So we set up to watch the door and the rest of the third floor, in case he came out the back. We had guys on the skyway level and on the first floor, watching the exits there. After an hour and a half or so, when he didn't come out, we started to get worried. We had Carol call—"

"I hope she had a good excuse."

"It was semihorseshit but it held up okay. She called and said she had an important message for Mr. Vullion and could the receptionist get him. The receptionist called somebody—we're watching this through the glass—and then she comes back on and tells Carol that he'd left a long time ago. Just stopped in to see some guy named Hart for five minutes."

"So where'd he go?"

"I'm getting to that," the surveillance man said defensively. "So Carol says this message is important, and asks, like girl-to-girl, did she see him leave? He's so absentminded, she says, you know how lawyers are. The receptionist says no, she didn't see him leave, but she assumed he left through the fifth-floor exits. See, you can only get in through the reception area, but there are three floors, and you can get out on any of them. They've got an internal elevator, and we didn't know."

"He could have known that," Lucas said. "He probably did. Was it deliberate? Do you think he spotted you?"

"I don't think so. I talked to the people, they all think we're clean."

"Christ, what a mess," said Lucas.

"You think we ought to take him?"

"I don't know. How'd you get him back?"

"Well, we were freaking out and I was talking to everybody to see if there was *anything,* any trace. And then here he comes, bigger'n shit, right through the skyway. He's got his briefcase and a rolled-up *Wall Street Journal* and he goes motoring past the skyway man like he's in a hurry."

"He went right back to his office?"

"Straight back."

"So what do you think?"

The surveillance man nibbled his lip and considered the problem. "I don't know," he said finally. "The thing is, if he was deliberately trying to lose us, he could have gone out through the parking ramp from the fifth floor. But the other thing . . ."

"Yeah?" Lucas prompted.

"I hate to admit it, but he might have gotten by the skyway guy. Completely innocently. We had a lot of spots to block, in case he got by us, somehow. We had a guy in the skyway, watching both the elevators and the stairs. If the elevators opened at just the right minute, and our guy looked over at them, and Vullion popped out of the stairway just at that minute and turned the other way . . ."

"He could have gotten past?"

"He could have. Without ever knowing we were there."

"Jesus. So we don't know," Lucas said. He peered up at Vullion's office window, which was screened by venetian blinds. The lights were still on.

"I kind of think . . ."

"What?" Lucas prompted.

"There's a bunch of fern-type restaurants down from where he was coming when we picked him up again. And he was carrying that paper all rolled up, like he already looked at it. I wouldn't swear to it in a court, but I think he just might've gone down to have lunch. He hadn't eaten lunch yet."

"Hmph."

"So? What do we do?"

Lucas raked his hair with his fingertips and thought about the Fuckup. It shouldn't influence him, he knew, but it did.

"Leave him," Lucas said. "I just hope no dead bodies show up under a counter in a skyway shop."

"Good," the surveillance chief said in relief. If they'd had to grab Vullion because the surveillance had screwed up, somebody could wind up working the tow-truck detail in February.

The game was done; the final night had been one of discussion, not play. It was deemed a great success. A few touches might be desirable . . .

Lee had been mauled by Meade's well-protected troops dug in along Pipe Creek. Meade himself had taken severe casualties. The three days of fighting were as confusing and bloody as the Wilderness or Shiloh. The worst of it had fallen on Pickett: as the first into Gettysburg, his division had held the high ground just south of town. In the pursuit of the Union forces as they retreated on Washington, Pickett's division had been last in the route of march. On the final day at Pipe Creek, Lee had thrown Pickett's relatively fresh division into the center of the line. It died there. The Union held the ground and the Confederates reeled toward a hasty recrossing of the Potomac. The southern tide was going out.

"Something's changed," Elle said to Lucas. They were standing near the exit, away from the others. Elle spoke in a low voice.

Lucas nodded, his voice dropping to match hers. "We think we know who he is. Maybe it was your prayers: a gift from God. An accident. Fate. Whatever."

"Why haven't you arrested him?"

Lucas shrugged. "We know who he is, but we can't prove it. Not quite. We're waiting for him to make a move."

"Is he a man of intelligence?"

"I really don't know." He glanced around the room, dropped his voice another notch. "A lawyer."

"Be careful," Elle said. "This is galloping to a conclusion. He's been playing a game, and if he's a real player, I'm sure he feels it too. He may go for a *coup de maître.*"

"I don't see that one's available to him. We'll just grind him down."

"Perhaps," she said, touching his coat sleeve. "But remember, his idea of a win may not be a matter of avoiding capture. He's a lawyer: perhaps he sees himself winning in court. Walking off the board with impunity after an acquittal. This is a very tricky position all the way around."


Lucas left St. Anne's at eight o'clock, drove restlessly home, punched up his word processor, sat in a pool of light, and tried to put the finishing touches on the Everwhen scenario. The opening prose must be lush, must hint of bare-breasted maidens with great asses, sword fights in dark tunnels, long trips, and hale-and-hearty good friends—everything a fifteen-year-old suburban computer freak doesn't have and yearns for. And it had to do all that while scrupulously avoiding pornography or anything else that would offend the kid's mother.

Lucas didn't have it in him. He sighed and shut down the computer, tossed the word-processing disk into his software file, and walked down to the library and sat in the dark to think.

The missing two hours worried him. It *could* have been an accident. And if the maddog had slipped away deliberately, why had he done it? Where had he gone? How and when did he spot the watchers? He hadn't gone out to kill—he wouldn't have his equipment, unless he carried it around in his briefcase, and he wasn't that stupid.

The trip to the antiques shop on the previous day was also worrisome. True, the maddog had stopped first at the computer store and picked up a case of paper. But Lucas remembered a half-case of paper sitting under the printer. He really didn't need any more. Not badly enough to make a special trip for it. Then he'd gone into the antiques shop, and one of the watchers, who had been passing on the opposite side of the street, saw the shop owner take the fishing lure out of the window. That had been confirmed after the maddog left, when Sloan had been sent in to pump the woman.

An antique fishing lure. Why? The maddog's apartment was virtually bare of ornament, so Lucas couldn't believe he'd bought it for himself.

A gift? But for whom? As far as they could tell, he had no friends. He made no phone calls, except on business, and got none at home. His mail consisted of bills and advertisements.

What was the lure for?

Sitting in the dark, his eyes closed, he turned the problem in his mind, manipulated it like a Rubik's Cube, and always came up with mismatched sides.

No point in sitting here, he thought. He looked at his watch. Nine o'clock. He got up, put on a jacket, and went out to the car. The nights were getting very cold now, and the wind on his face triggered a memory of skiing. Time to get his downhill skis tuned and the cross-country skis scraped and hot-waxed. He was always tired of winter by the time it ended, but he kind of liked the beginning.

The maddog's apartment was five miles from Lucas' house. Lucas stopped at a newsstand to buy copies of *Powder* and *Skiing*.

"Nothing," the surveillance cop said when he came up the stairs. "He's watching television."

Lucas peered out the window at the maddog's apartment. He could see nothing but the blue glow of a television through the living-room curtains. "Move, you motherfucker," he said.

# 32

The maddog forced himself to eat dinner, to clean up. Everything as usual. At seven o'clock he turned on the television. All drapes pulled. He glanced around. Now or never.

The maddog had never had a use for many tools, but this would not be a sophisticated job. He got a long-handled screwdriver, a clawhammer, a pair of pliers, and an electric lantern from the workroom and carried them upstairs. In his bedroom he put on two pairs of athletic socks to muffle his footsteps. When he was ready, he pulled down the attic stairs.

The attic was little better than a crawl space under the eaves of the apartment house, partitioned among the four apartments with quarter-inch plywood. Since the apartment's insulation was laid in the attic floor and the attic itself was unheated, it was cold, and suitable only for the storage of items that wouldn't be damaged by Minnesota's winter cold. The maddog had been in it only twice before: once when he rented the apartment, and again on the day when he conceived the *stroke*, to examine the plywood partitions.

Padding silently across the attic floor, the maddog crossed to the partition for the apartment that was beside his, facing the street. The plywood paneling between his part of the attic and the opposite side had been nailed in place from his side. The work was sloppy and he was able to slip the end of the screwdriver under the edge of the panel and carefully pry it up. It took twenty minutes to loosen the panel enough that he could draw the nails out with the clawhammer and the pliers. Again, the work had been sloppy: no more than a dozen nails held the plywood panel in place.

When the panel was loose, he pulled it back enough that he could slip into the opposite side of the attic. The other side was almost as empty as his, with only a few jigsaw puzzles stacked near the folded stairs. Silence was now critical, and he took his time with the next job. He had plenty of time, he thought. He wouldn't move until the police spies thought he was in bed. Working quietly and doggedly in the light of the electric lantern, he loosened the plywood panels between his neighbor's attic and the attic of the woman who lived in the apartment diagonally opposite his.

That was his goal. The owner was a surgical nurse, recently divorced, who, ever since moving into the apartment, had worked the overnight shift in the trauma-care unit of St. Paul Ramsey Medical Center. He had called the hospital from his office, asked for her, and been told that she would be on at eleven o'clock.

It took a cold half-hour to get into her side of the attic. When the access was clear, he quietly propped the panels back in place so a casual inspection wouldn't reveal the missing nails. He stole back down the stairs to his bedroom, leaving the flashlight, tools, and nails at the top of the steps. When he got back, he would push the nails as best he could into their holes. Tomorrow morning, when the people opposite had gone to work, and before the maddog's last victim was found, he would go back and hammer them in place.

Downstairs again, he considered a quick trip to a neighborhood convenience store. A walking trip. It might be an undue provocation, but he thought not. He turned off the television, put on his jacket, checked his wallet, and went out the front door. He tried to goof along, two blocks, obviously not in a hurry. He crossed the blacktopped parking area of the convenience store, went inside, bought some bakery goods, some instant hot cereal, a jug of milk, and a copy of *Penthouse*. Back outside, he bit into a bismarck, savored the cherry filling that squirted into his mouth, and sauntered back home.

That should do it. That should prepare them psychologically for the idea that he would be in for the rest of the evening. He crossed his porch, pushed inside, locked the door behind him, put the cereal and milk away, and turned on the football game.

It was just starting. The Cowboys and the Giants. He watched the first half, staring blankly at the screen, not much caring what happened; caring less when the Giants started to roll. At halftime he slipped the tape of Davenport into the videocassette recorder and watched the interview. Davenport, the player. Carla Ruiz, the once-and-never Chosen. He ran it a second time and turned it off and deliberately walked around the apartment. Out to the kitchen. Look in the silverware drawer. Open refrigerator, drink milk, put glass on cupboard. Ten-forty-five. Pick up phone, call nurse. Twenty rings. Thirty rings. Forty. Fifty. He was tempted to call the hospital and ask for her, but better not. The phone could be tapped. A risk, but he would have to live with it.

He turned out the lights and went upstairs, where he undressed, dropped his clothes in a heap, and began to dress again. Dark turtleneck. Jeans. Nike Airs, with laces tied together and looped around his neck. New ski jacket, navy blue with a dark turquoise flash on the breast. Gloves. Watch cap. He turned out the bedroom light.

He went down the hallway and up the attic stairs on stocking feet, guiding himself through the dark with a hand on the wall. At the top of the steps he found the light, switched it on, and eased into the opposite quadrant of the attic, then into the nurse's quadrant. He pushed down on the release for the stairs, opening the hallway hatch just an inch, and listened. Not a sound. No lights.

Her apartment was laid out like a left-handed version of his own. He checked the bedroom first, flashing the light through the open door. The bed was neatly made and empty. He went down through the kitchen, saw the phone, paused, and thought: Why not? He checked the phone book, called the hospital, and asked for her.

"This is Sylvia." He hung up, clicking the hook rapidly, as though there had been line trouble. She was there, at the hospital.

He went through the kitchen, into the utility room, and cracked the door to the garage. Empty. Given the landscaping—the hedge across the back of the lot—he should be able to open the garage door a foot or more without being seen. He checked to make sure the garage wasn't locked, and lifted it, slowly, slowly. When it was up a foot, he slid out on his back.

It was a dark night, cloudy, and he lay for a moment in the door inset, invisible from the street, gathering his courage. When he had controlled himself, he eased the door most of the way down, leaving a gap of an inch or so. When he returned, it would be easier to lift.

Now for the bad part, he thought. On his hands and knees, he crossed to the base of the hedge and followed it out to the sidewalk. He looked both ways. The houses around him were all occupied by families. The two surveillance houses, which would cover the sides of his own apartment, were behind him now. His only problem would come if there were wing cars out on the street, out of sight of his apartment. That wouldn't make much sense, from the police point of view, stationing men where they couldn't see the target's apartment, but who knew what they might be doing?

Steeling himself, he made his move. Stepped out on the sidewalk and walked along, his head bobbing, straight away from the house. He tried not to be obvious about it, but he checked parked cars. Nobody. If there were surveillance cars, they should be out on the wings. It was unlikely that they would be parked back by the Interstate: there was no way out that way.

It was three blocks down to the car. He unlocked it, slipped inside, and took stock. He was loose, he was sure of it. It all *felt* right. He sat for a moment, *feeling* the environment around him, extending himself into the night. He was free. He turned on the light, cranked the engine, and headed out. He had thought about this, and hadn't made up his mind. Now he did. Davenport drove a Porsche, the papers said. Would it be parked at one of the surveillance houses? If they were surveillance houses? He took the street one back from his own, cruising by the house he suspected. Two cars, nondescript Ford sedans. Like cops might drive. How about the other house? He took a left, two blocks, his headlights raking an oncoming car. A Porsche, in fact. He caught a quick glimpse of Davenport's face as he rounded the corner. The maddog slowed, did a U-turn, and went back. Davenport's car had stopped outside the second surveillance house. He was getting out with a white rectangular box of some kind . . . A pizza.

A pizza.

It answered the next question for him. He had not decided how to get into Ruiz' apartment. He had thought of pulling the fire alarm. He would hit her when she stepped into the hallway. But when the janitor learned that it was a false alarm, he might check the building's occupants to see if anybody had a problem. And there was the possibility that somebody else would come into the hallway before Ruiz. He had thought of imitating Lucas' voice—but what if the door was on a chain and she peeked out and a stranger was there? She would *know*.

But a pizza . . .

He stopped and got a pizza, waiting impatiently as the slow-moving pizza-maker kneaded the dough, tossed it around, pounded it out, and pushed it into the oven. Cooking took another ten minutes. The maddog glanced at his watch. Eleven-thirty-five. He'd have to hurry. The janitor usually locked Ruiz' building at midnight.

It was another ten minutes to the squat old St. Paul warehouse; he could see it from the Interstate as he started into the exit ramp. He parked near the building's main door and got his equipment out of the trunk: the hose full of cat litter, the can of Mace, the roll of tape, the work gloves. Everything but the hose went in his pockets.

He went in the door and up the stairs; the janitor, who doubled as the elevator operator, usually hung out by the elevator door where he could listen to his boombox. The first two floors were silent. Somebody on the third floor was playing a radio, and a faint laugh trickled down the concrete hallways. The fourth floor was quiet, as was the fifth.

Down four doors. Light under her door. He breathed a sigh of relief. She was in. He had been prepared to abort, to do it over again if he had to. Now he wouldn't. The *stroke* would happen.

He pulled on the yellow cotton gloves, took a breath, let it out, rapped on the door, and called, "Pizza." She had never seen his face.

He heard her footsteps crossing the floor. "I didn't order a pizza," she said from the other side of the door.

"Well, I got a pizza for this studio for Lucas Davenport. I'm supposed to say the wine is on the way, if it isn't already here."

There was a moment of silence, then a soft, "Oh, no."

What? What was wrong? The maddog tensed, ready to flee, but the door was opening. There was a chain. Ruiz seemed to be alone. She peeked out, saw the box.

"Just a minute," she said with a note of resignation in her voice. There was something going on that he didn't understand. She pushed the door shut and he heard the chain come off. He had the pizza balanced on the hand that held the hose. The Mace was in the other. Ruiz opened the door, nobody behind her. The maddog thrust the pizza at her and stepped forward. She stepped back, looking up at him as the pizza came at her so unexpectedly hard, she saw the gloves, and then, in an instant, she *knew,* but the can was up and he hit her in the mouth and eyes with the spray and she dropped the pizza and tried to cover her face and choked and staggered backward. The maddog pressed into the apartment and swung the hose. She had one arm up and it glanced off. Gagging, she half-turned and stumbled toward a bookshelf with her hands outstretched, and the maddog stopped just for an instant and kicked the door shut and went after her. She was pawing the bookshelf, still blind, looking for something, looking, and the maddog was on her and she had one hand on a small chrome-steel pistol and he hit her with the hose and she went down and still had the weapon and with a vision as acute and clear and sharp as water crystal he saw that she had it by the butt only, that her fingers were not fitted through the trigger guard and he took just an extra fragment of a second to get the right backswing and he hit her again on the back of the head and then again, bouncing off her shoulder, and again, straight into her face . . . she stopped moving, curled into a fetal position . . .

The maddog, breathing hard, dropped the hose and fell on her like a tiger on a staked goat. Pulling her head back, he thrust the Kotex into her mouth, wrapped her head with tape. She was dazed and unresisting. He worried for a moment that he had killed her and thought, absurdly: This is not a Chosen, this is a raid, it makes no difference when she dies . . .

The pistol was lying on the floor and he pushed it away, stood up, grabbed her by the shirt collar, and dragged her into the bedroom and used the tape to bind her to the bed. She was wearing a man's flannel shirt and he ripped it open, a button popping off and clicking against the wall, the maddog's hearing now supernaturally keen, the sensory high coming with a rush. He snatched the side of her bra and wrenched the back strap, breaking it, and the shoulder straps. Unfastened her jeans, pulled them halfway down her legs. Ripped the crotch out of her underpants and pulled them up her belly.

Stood back, surveyed the prisoner. Just right. She wasn't a Chosen, but she could be fun. He reached out, rubbed her patch of pubic hair.

"Don't go away," he said in sweet sarcasm. "I'll need something sharp for the rest of this."

# 33

"Has he gone to bed?" Lucas asked.

"Yeah," said the first watcher, the tall one.

"Shit." Lucas looked at the ceiling, brooding. Maybe he'd spotted them. "He's got to move soon. He's *got* to."

"My stomach's moving now," said the second surveillance cop. "I need something to eat."

"Three more hours," said the first one.

"Christ." The second cop looked at Lucas. "So. What're you doing?"

Lucas had been lying on the surveillance mattress, reading the copy of *Powder*.

"Uh . . ."

"I don't suppose you'd be interested in a pizza?"

"Sure. I guess." Lucas rolled to his feet.

"There's a place over by the university. Pretty good," said the hungry cop. "I'll call, they'll have it ready when you get there."

"You got your handset?" asked the first cop.

"Yeah."

"I'll holler if anything happens."

\*    \*    \*

The pizza wasn't ready when he got there, but it was ready five minutes later. He took it out to the car and headed back, letting the Porsche run a bit, cutting dangerously close to an oncoming car as he turned into the street that led to the surveillance house. Can't do this, he thought as the other car's lights raked over him. The last thing he needed was a fistfight with some outstate redneck who didn't like being cut off.

He hustled the hot pizza up three flights of steps to the surveillance post on the top floor.

"Nothing," said the first cop.

"Quiet as a fuckin' bunny rabbit," said the hungry one. He pried the top off the pizza box. "If this thing has anchovies on it, you're a dead man."

Lucas took a piece of the pizza and went back to the magazine.

"Night-light must have burned out," the first cop said after a while.

"Hmmph?"

"No night-light tonight."

Lucas crawled to the window and looked out. The maddog's bedroom window was a flat black rectangle. Not a glimmer of light. That was odd, Lucas thought. If a guy slept with a night-light, he usually needed it . . .

"Dammit," he said, pivoting and sitting with his back against the wall, his knees bent in front of him.

"What?"

"I don't know." He turned his head and stared over the windowsill. "That freaks me out. That's not right."

"Just a fuckin' night-light," the hungry cop said as he finished the last of the pizza and licked his fingers.

"It's not right," Lucas said. He smelled the wrongness. Watching him now for almost two weeks, a night-light every night. But there was no other way out of the house. Not unless he poked a hole in the walls.

The attic, he thought. That fuckin' attic.

Lucas crawled to the telephone. "What's his number?" he asked the first surveillance cop, snapping his fingers.

"Jesus, are you gonna—?"

"Give me the goddamn number," Lucas said, his voice cold.

The first cop glanced at his no-longer-hungry companion, who shrugged and took a small notebook from his pocket and read the number. Lucas punched it in.

"If he answers, it's just a wrong number," he said, glancing at the others. "I'll ask for Louise." The maddog's phone rang. Fifteen times. Thirty. Fifty. No light in the window. Nothing.

"Son of a gun," said the first cop.

"Give me the number again. Maybe I misdialed," Lucas said. The cop read him the number and he punched it in again. "You sure it's the right number?"

"It's right," said the cop. The phone rang. And rang. No answer.

"Let it ring," Lucas said, running for the door. "I'm going over there."

"Jesus . . ."

Lucas banged out the front door of the surveillance house, ran across the street to the maddog's porch. He could hear the phone ringing and he pushed the doorbell and kept it down. Five seconds, ten. No light. He wrenched open the storm door and tried the interior door. Locked. No time for subtlety. He backed off a step and kicked the door at the lock with all of his strength, smashing it open.

Inside, he ran to the base of the stairs.

"Vullion?" He was carrying the Heckler & Koch P7, and had it in his fist as he went up the stairs. "Vullion?"

A light went on in the living room, and Lucas' head snapped back and he saw the first surveillance cop following him with his pistol drawn. Lucas went the rest of the way up the stairs and saw the steps from the attic. They had been pulled down into the hallway.

"Motherfucker's gone," he yelled at the cop behind him. "Kill that phone, will you?" Lucas checked the bedroom, then climbed the steps into the attic. The partitions separating the attic quadrants were loose. The phone stopped ringing as Lucas backed down the steps.

"He went through the attic into one of the other apartments and out that way," he shouted to the cop. "Get everybody on the street, look for a guy on foot. Bust him. We got him for housebreaking, if nothing else."

The surveillance cop ran out the front door. Lucas moved through the front room, turned once, and looked at it. Nothing. Not a thing. His eyes narrowed and he went back up to the bedroom, slid his hand under the mattress. Then swept it around. The pictures were gone.

He went back down and headed for the telephone. Call Daniel, he thought. Get some help out here. As he picked up the phone, his eye caught the tiny rectangular red light on the VCR. Vullion had been watching a tape. Lucas dropped the phone, turned on the television, ran the tape back a few numbers, and punched the On button. Carla. Lucas looked up, his eyes gone blank. The interview. Carla.

He ran, his mind sifting the possibilities, his body already doing what his mind would eventually decide. Vullion was going after Carla. He wouldn't take a bus, so he must, somehow, have gotten wheels. Lucas had a handset. He could call the St. Paul cops and have somebody at Carla's apartment in three or four minutes. That's what it would take for the cops to understand what he was saying, to get together, and get over to Carla's warehouse.

But he was only six miles away. All of it Interstate. The Porsche could be there in five minutes, six at the outside. Would the extra minutes kill her? If they would not, he might make the *coup*.

Lucas dove into the Porsche, cranked it, and hammered the accelerator, slid through the first turn, hit the second at forty-five, braked to fifty to get onto the Interstate ramp. A Honda Civic was ahead of him on the ramp and Lucas put two wheels on the grass and blew past the Honda at seventy, the other driver's frightened face a half-moon on the periphery of his vision. He was doing eighty-five coming off the ramp, and floored it, the speedometer climbing without hesitation through the hundred mark, one ten, one twenty. He left it there, sweeping past the cars on the highway, the exits clicking past like heartbeats.

Two minutes. Lexington Avenue. Three minutes. Dale. Three minutes, twenty seconds, sweeping into the Tenth Street exit, downshifting, the machine clawing through the first intersection, the warehouse looming in front of him. He wrenched the car to the side of the street, took the gym bag with the silenced pistol from behind the seat, and ran toward the building's side door.

As he approached, the janitor appeared with keys in his hands.

"No," Lucas shouted, and the janitor paused. Lucas groped in his shirt pocket, found his identification, and flashed it as he pushed through the door.

"You stay right here," he told the janitor, who stood with his mouth hanging open. "Some St. Paul cops are going to come here, and you take them up in the elevator. You wait right here, you got it?"

The janitor nodded. "Wait right here," he said.

"Right." Lucas patted him on the shoulder and dashed up the stairs.

Carla's door had better locks, he thought breathlessly as he came up the last few steps, but it was still a crappy door. No time to think about it really. Christ, if the maddog wasn't here, this was going to be embarrassing. He hurried down to the doorway, saw the light coming from beneath it. He dropped the gym bag, took a step back, and kicked the door in. Lucas exploded into the room, his pistol in a two-handed grip.

The studio was empty.

# 34

There was a quiet sound from the left, like a cat dropping from a bookcase. But it was no cat. Lucas pivoted and extended the gun. There was a small room, dark, cavelike. A groan. He stepped forward. Couldn't see. Stepped forward, still couldn't see. Another step, three feet from the door. A white shape, trussed, arched, on the bed, another groan, nothing else. . . .

Another step, and suddenly Vullion was there, his eyes wide and hard like boiled eggs, his hands covered with fuzzy yellow gloves, a pipe of some kind in one hand, the pipe sweeping down, and Lucas twisted the last three inches he needed to fire and the pipe smashed into the back of his hand and the gun went down on the floor. Lucas felt the bones in his right hand go and he pushed the pipe sideways with his left and Vullion's other hand was coming up in a long sweeping thrust and in it the knife was glittering like a short-sword toward Lucas' bowels. Lucas pivoted and caught the thrust with his broken hand and felt the hand flex and he screamed but the blade passed clear, under his arm, and he caught Vullion's knife hand with his left hand and smashed his right elbow into Vullion's eye socket. The impact lifted Vullion back, and they staggered together back into the tiny bedroom and Vullion's legs folded beneath him as he hit the bed and they fell together on top of Carla and Lucas pounded Vullion's face with his forearm once, twice, three times, the pain from his broken hand like lightning in his brain.

And then Vullion stopped. Then Lucas twisted the knife arm, and the knife fell to the floor. Vullion was stunned, not out. Lucas hit him twice with his left hand, pounding Vullion's ear, then rolled him off Carla into the narrow space between the bed and the wall and knelt on his head and shoulders.

"Motherfucker," Lucas groaned. His own breath was harsh and ragged in his ears. He reached awkwardly into his pocket with his good hand and took out his key ring. A miniature Tekna knife dangled from the ring. He pulled the knife out of its plastic sheath and gently slipped the blade under the tape that circled Carla's head, holding the gag in place. When he pulled the Kotex from her mouth, she gasped and then whimpered, an animal cry, like a rabbit's. She was alive.

"Hurt me," Vullion moaned from beneath Lucas' knees. "I'm hurt."

"Shut up, motherfucker," Lucas said. He hit him on the head with his closed left fist and Vullion twitched and moaned again.

Lucas reached forward and cut the tape that bound Carla's arms to the bed, then freed her legs.

"It's me, Lucas," he said next to her ear. "You're going to be okay. The ambulance is coming, just stay here."

He levered himself up off the bed, grabbed Vullion by the back of his shirt and physically lifted him from the floor and half-dragged, half-led him into the studio. Lucas' pistol was lying against the wall. With a sweeping kick he knocked Vullion's legs out from beneath him, and guided his upper body down to the floor, protecting his head. He didn't want him unconscious. Vullion went down like a rag man.

While he was down, Lucas picked up the pistol and walked quickly backward to the hallway, got the gym bag, and brought it inside. He pushed the door closed with his foot.

Vullion, on his stomach, brought his hands to his ears.

"Get up," Lucas said to Vullion. Vullion made no response, and Lucas kicked him in the hip. "Get up. Come on, get up."

Vullion struggled up, fell back to his stomach, then pushed up to one knee. Blood was running from his nose into his mouth. The pupil of one eye was dilated. The other eye was closed, the lid and flesh around the socket bloody and swollen.

"On your feet, asshole, or I swear to Christ I'll kick you to death."

Vullion was watching him as best he could, still dazed. With an exhausted heave he got to his feet and swayed.

"Now, back up. Five steps." Lucas thrust the pistol at Vullion's chest. Vullion stepped back carefully, but looked as though he might be recovering.

"Now, you just stand there," Lucas said as he stepped toward the telephone.

"I knew about the surveillance," Vullion said through broken teeth.

"I figured that out about ten minutes ago," Lucas said. He gestured with his left hand.

"Is your hand broken?"

"Shut up," said Lucas. He lifted the receiver from the phone.

"Did you deliberately lure me here? With your friend? Like you did with McGowan?"

"Not this time. McGowan was bait, though," Lucas said.

"You're worse than I am in some ways," Vullion said. Blood dribbled down his chin. He swayed again, and he reached out to Carla's sink to brace himself. "I was taking people who were . . . chips. You set up a friend. If I had a friend, I would never do that."

"Like I told the papers, you're not that much of a player," Lucas said quietly in a voice just above a whisper.

"We'll see about that," the maddog said. He was growing stronger, and Lucas was impressed in spite of himself. "I have defenses. You won't be able to prove any of the murders. After all, I did not kill Miss Ruiz. And you'll notice that my method is different this time. You won't find a note. I was going to make it here, afterward. If it comes to negotiations, I'll get an insanity plea. A few years at the state hospital and I'm out. And even if worse comes to worst, and I get a first-degree, well, it's eighteen years at Stillwater. I can do it."

Lucas nodded. "I thought of that. It would be like losing, seeing you get away alive. I really couldn't stand that. Not with an inferior player."

"What?"

Lucas ignored him. He groped in his pants pocket and took a single nine-millimeter shell from his pocket. Watching Vullion carefully, he braced the pistol against his armpit and punched the magazine out of the pistol butt. This was when Vullion would act, if he was going to, but he did not; he stood still, puzzled, as Lucas pushed the blank into the top slot, slammed the magazine back into the butt, and jacked the shell into the chamber.

"What are you doing?" Vullion asked. Something was happening. Something not right.

"First, I'm going to call the cops," Lucas said. He stepped to Carla's wall phone and dialed 911. When he got the dispatcher, he identified himself and asked for an ambulance and backup. The operator asked that he leave the line open and Lucas said he would. That was standard operating procedure. Lucas let the phone dangle and stepped away from it.

Vullion was still watching him, frowning. When Lucas stepped away from the phone, the maddog stepped back from the sink. Lucas pointed his pistol at the ceiling, fired once, his eyes tracking the ejected shell, the maddog's eyes involuntarily widening at the sharp explosion. He was still reacting when Lucas fired two more shots. One hit Vullion in the right lung, one in the left.

The three shots were in a quick musical rhythm, a bang; bang-bang.

Vullion was swatted back a step, two, and then he fell, going straight down as though his bones had melted. His mouth worked a few times and he rolled onto his back. The shots were killing shots, but not too good; not too aimed. It was supposed to have been a gunfight. Lucas stepped over to look down at the dying man.

"What happened?"

The voice might have come from an animal. Lucas turned, and Carla stood in the doorway to the bedroom. She was no longer bleeding, but had been battered, her nose broken, her face cut. She tottered over to Lucas.

"You've got to go back and lie down," Lucas said.

A witness could kill him.

"Wait," Carla said as he gripped her arm. She looked down at Vullion. "Is he dead?"

"Yeah. He's gone."

But Vullion was not quite gone. His eyes moved fractionally toward the dark-haired woman who stood over him, and a tiny spate of blood trickled out of the corner of his mouth as his lips spasmed and opened.

"Mom?" he asked.

"What?" said Carla. Vullion's legs spasmed.

"Forget it," Lucas said. He moved her physically back toward the bedroom, pushed her onto the bed. "Stay here. You're hurt." She nodded dumbly and let her body fall back.

There was almost no time now. The St. Paul cops would be here in seconds. He stepped quickly back out of the room, over to Vullion. Vullion was dead. Lucas nodded, retrieved the gym bag, and lifted out the silenced pistol. He fitted it to Vullion's gloved hand, pointed it at Carla's shelf of art books, and pulled the trigger. There was a *phut* and *pop!* as the slug hit a three-inch-thick copy of *The Great Book of French Impressionism*. Lucas pulled the silencer off the muzzle and laid the weapon on the floor a few feet from Vullion's outstretched hand. He looked around on the floor, found the shell casing from the blank he'd fired, and pocketed it.

The elevators started up and Lucas pulled the silencer apart as he reviewed the scene.

There would be powder residue, nitrites, on Vullion's glove, on his bare wrist, on the sleeve of his coat and his face. The slug in the bookshelf, if it could be salvaged at all, would match test shots from the Smith found on the floor next to Vullion's body. Both the Smith and Lucas' P7 were nine-millimeters, so that would account for the fact that the shots would sound the same on the 911 tape. And the shots were sequenced so closely that no one would doubt that Lucas had fired in self-defense.

It would hold up, he thought with satisfaction. He would have to work on his story a bit. He and Vullion fought in the bedroom. He dragged Vullion out, not wanting to endanger Carla, and outside the room, Vullion had pulled the pistol, which had been tucked into his waistband. That would do it. Nobody would want to know too much, anyway.

He walked to a window, pulled it open, and threw out the two big plastic pieces of the silencer. Just more street junk. The Thinsulate wrapping and the internal tube he tossed among Carla's stock of weaving materials. He would retrieve it later, get rid of it.

He slipped his own pistol into its holster and walked back to Carla's bedroom. She lay unmoving on the bed, but her chest was rising and falling regularly.

"It's Lucas again," he told her, gripping her leg with his good hand. "Everything's going to be okay. It's Lucas."

He heard the first St. Paul cop enter the room, and yelled, "Back here, Minneapolis police, Lucas Davenport, we need an ambulance quick . . ."

As he called out, Vullion's stunned and dying face flashed through the back of Lucas' mind.

He thought, "That's six."

# 35

Two days after Christmas, his hand still in a cast six weeks after the surgery, Lucas walked across an empty campus, through a driving snowstorm, to Elle Kruger's office in Fat Albert Hall. Her office was on the third floor. He took the worn concrete steps, unzipping his parka and brushing snow from his shoulders as he climbed. The third-floor hallway was dark. At the far end, one office showed a lighted pane of frosted glass. His footsteps echoed as he walked down and knocked.

"Come in, Lucas."

He pushed open the door. Elle was reading in an armchair that sat to one side of the desk, facing a small couch. An inexpensive stereo played "The Great Gate of Kiev" from *Pictures at an Exhibition.* Lucas handed her a package he'd carried in his coat pocket.

"A gift." She smiled happily, her face lighted, weighing the package in her hand. "I hope it wasn't expensive."

Lucas hung his parka on a coatrack and dropped onto the couch. "Tell you the truth, it cost an arm and a leg."

Her smile diminished slightly. "You know we seek poverty."

"This won't make you any richer," Lucas said. "If you ever sell it, I'll come over and strangle you."

"Ah. Then I suppose . . ." She shook her head and began to unwrap the box. "My biggest problem, the cause of my most grievous sin, is curiosity."

"I'll never understand the Church," Lucas said.

The nun opened the small red box and fished out a medallion of yellow gold on a long gold chain. "Lucas," she said.

"Read it," he said.

She turned it in her hands and read, " '*Agnus Dei: qui tollis peccata mundi, miserere nobis*' . . . it's from the Missal. 'O Lamb of God, who takest away the sins of the world, have mercy on us.' "

"That's certainly pious enough."

She sighed. "It's still gold."

"So wear it with disdain. When you start to like it, send it to Mother Teresa."

She laughed. "Mother Teresa," she said. She looked at the medallion again, then looked closer and said, "What's this? On the other side."

"A minor inscription."

"The letters are so small." She held it eight inches from her nose, peering at it.

*Necessity has no law*
*As Augustine descries her,*
*So the maddog's brought to earth*
*With the help of Nun the Wiser.*

She gasped, then started to laugh, throwing her head back and letting it roll out. "This is *terrible*," she said at last. "Augustine is whirling in his grave."

"It's not *that* bad," Lucas said with a bit of frost. "In fact . . ."

"Lucas, it's *awful*." She started laughing again, and finally Lucas began laughing with her. When she stopped, she brushed tears from her eyes and said, "I'll treasure it forever. I don't know what my sisters will think when they find it on my body . . ."

"*They* can send it to Mother Teresa," Lucas suggested.


They talked as old friends: of phony fainting spells during the rosary after school, of the boy who admitted in fourth grade that he didn't believe in God. His name was Gene, that's all they could remember.

"Are you okay?" she asked after a while.

"I think so."

"And your relationship . . ."

"Is doing well, thank you. I want to marry her, but she won't."

"Officially, I'm appalled. Unofficially, I suspect she must be quite an intelligent woman. You are definitely a high-risk proposition. . . . What about Carla Ruiz?"

"Gone to Chicago. She has a new friend."

"The nightmares?"

"Getting worse."

"Oh, no."

"She's seeing a counselor."


And later still.

"You feel no qualms about Louis Vullion's death?"

"None. Should I?"

"I had wondered at the circumstances," she said.

Lucas pondered for a moment. "Elle. If you want to know everything, I'll tell you everything."

It was her turn to ponder. She turned to the big window, a black silhouette against the snow that drove against the glass.

Finally she shook her head, and he noticed she was clutching the medallion. "No. I don't want to know everything. I'm not a confessor. And I will pray for you and for Louis Vullion. But as for knowing . . ."

She turned back, a tiny, grim smile on her face. ". . . I'm content to be Nun the Wiser."

# SHADOW PREY

# In the Beginning...

*They were in a service alley, tucked between two dumpsters. Carl Reed, a beer can in his hand, kept watch. Larry Clay peeled the drunk Indian girl, tossing her clothes on the floor of the backseat, wedging himself between her legs.*

*The Indian started to howl. "Christ, she sounds like a fuckin' coon-dog," said Reed, a Kentucky boy.*

*"She's tight," Clay grunted. Reed laughed and said, "Hurry up," and lobbed his empty beer can toward one of the dumpsters. It clattered off the side and fell into the alley.*

*Clay was in full gallop when the girl's howl pitched up, reaching toward a scream. He put one big hand over her face and said, "Shut up, bitch," but he liked it. A minute later he finished and crawled off.*

*Reed slipped off his gunbelt and dumped it on top of the car behind the light bar. Clay was in the alley, staring down at himself. "Look at the fuckin' blood," he said.*

*"God damn," Reed said, "you got yourself a virgin." He ducked into the backseat and said, "Here comes Daddy. . . ."*

*The squad car's only radios were police-band, so Clay and Reed carried a transistor job that Reed had bought in a PX in Vietnam. Clay took it out, turned it on and hunted for something decent. An all-news station was babbling about Robert Kennedy's challenging Lyndon Johnson. Clay kept turning and finally found a country station playing "Ode to Billy Joe."*

*"You about done?" he asked, as the Bobbie Gentry song trickled out into the alley.*

*"Just . . . fuckin' . . . hold on . . ." Reed said.*

*The Indian girl wasn't saying anything.*

*When Reed finished, Clay was back in uniform. They took a few seconds to get some clothes on the girl.*

*"Take her, or leave her?" Reed asked.*

*The girl was sitting in the alley, dazed, surrounded by discarded advertising leaflets that had blown out of the dumpster.*

*"Fuck it," Clay said. "Leave her."*


*They were nothing but drunk Indian chicks. That's what everybody said. It wasn't like you were wearing it out. It's not like they had less than they started with. Hell, they liked it.*

*And that's why, when a call went out, squad cars responded from all over Phoenix. Drunk Indian chick. Needs a ride home. Anybody?*

*Say "drunk Indian," meaning a male, and you'd think every squad in town had driven off a cliff. Not a peep. But a drunk Indian chick? There was a traffic jam. A lot of them were fat, a lot of them were old. But some of them weren't.*


*Lawrence Duberville Clay was the last son of a rich man. The other Clay boys went into the family business: chemicals, plastics, aluminum. Larry came out of college and joined the Phoenix police force. His family, except for the old man, who made all the money, was shocked. The old man said, "Let him go. Let's see what he does."*

*Larry Clay started by growing his hair out, down on his shoulders, and dragging around town in a '56 Ford. In two months, he had friends all over the hippie community. Fifty long-haired flower children went down on drugs, before the word got out about the fresh-faced narc.*

*After that it was patrol, working the bars, the nightclubs, the after-hours joints; picking up the drunk Indian chicks. You could have a good time as a cop. Larry Clay did.*

*Until he got hurt.*

*He was beaten so badly that the first cops on the scene thought he was dead. They got him to a trauma center and the docs bailed him out. Who did it? Dope dealers, he said. Hippies. Revenge. Larry Clay was a hero, and they made him a sergeant.*

*When he got out of the hospital, Clay stayed on the force long enough to prove that he wasn't chicken, and then he quit. Working summers, he finished law school in two years. He spent two more years in the prosecutor's office, then went into private practice. In 1972, he ran for the state senate and won.*

*His career really took off when a gambler got in trouble with the IRS. In exchange for a little sympathy, the gambler gave the tax men a list of senior cops he'd paid off over the years. The stink wouldn't go away. The city fathers, getting nervous, looked around and found a boy with a head on his shoulders. A boy from a good family. A former cop, a lawyer, a politician.*

*Clean up the force, they told Lawrence Duberville Clay. But don't try too hard. . . .*

*He did precisely what they wanted. They were properly grateful.*

*In 1976, Lawrence Duberville Clay became the youngest chief in the department's history. He quit five years later to take an appointment as an assistant U.S. attorney general in Washington.*

*A step backward, his brothers said. Just watch him, said the old man. And the old man was there to help: the right people, the right clubs. Money, when it was needed.*

*When the scandal hit the FBI—kickbacks in an insider-trading investigation—the administration knew where to go. The boy from Phoenix had a rep. He'd cleaned up the Phoenix force, and he'd clean up the FBI. But he wouldn't try too hard.*

*At forty-two, Lawrence Duberville Clay was named the youngest FBI director since J. Edgar Hoover. He became the administration's point man for the war on crime. He took the FBI to the people, and to the press. During a dope raid in Chicago, an AP photographer shot a portrait of a weary Lawrence Duberville Clay, his sleeves rolled above his elbows, a hollow look on his face. A huge Desert Eagle semiautomatic pistol rode in a shoulder rig under his arm. The picture made him a celebrity.*

*Not many people remembered his early days in Phoenix, the nights spent hunting drunk Indian chicks.*

*During those Phoenix nights, Larry Clay developed a taste for the young ones. Very young ones. And some of them maybe weren't so drunk. And some of them weren't so interested in backseat tag team. But who was going to believe an Indian chick, in Phoenix, in the mid-sixties? Civil rights were for blacks in the South, not for Indians or chicanos in the Southwest. Date-rape wasn't even a concept, and feminism had barely come over the horizon.*

*But the girl in the alley . . . she was twelve and she was a little drunk, but not so drunk that she couldn't say no, or remember who put her in the car. She told her mother. Her mother stewed about it for a couple of days, then told two men she'd met at the res.*

*The two men caught Larry Clay outside his apartment and beat the shit out of him with a genuine Louisville Slugger. Broke one of his legs and both arms and a whole bunch of ribs. Broke his nose and some teeth.*

*It wasn't dope dealers who beat Larry Clay. It was a couple of Indians, on a comeback from a rape.*

*Lawrence Duberville Clay never knew who they were, but he never forgot what they did to him. He had a lot of shots at Indians over the years, as a prosecutor, a state senator, a police chief, an assistant U.S. attorney general.*

*He took them all.*

*And he didn't forget them when he became director of the FBI, the iron fist on every Indian reservation in the nation.*

*But there were Indians with long memories too.*

*Like the men who took him in Phoenix.*

*The Crows.*

# 1

Ray Cuervo sat in his office and counted his money. He counted his money every Friday afternoon between five and six o'clock. He made no secret of it.

Cuervo owned six apartment buildings scattered around Indian Country south of the Minneapolis Loop. The cheapest apartment rented for thirty-nine dollars a week. The most expensive was seventy-five. When he collected his rent, Cuervo took neither checks nor excuses. If you didn't have the cash by two o'clock Friday, you slept on the sidewalk. Bidness, as Ray Cuervo told any number of broken-ass indigents, was bidness.

Dangerous business, sometimes. Cuervo carried a chrome-plated Charter Arms .38 Special tucked in his pants while he collected his money. The gun was old. The barrel was pitted and the butt was unfashionably small. But it worked and the shells were always fresh. You could see the shiny brass winking out at the edge of the cylinder. Not a flash gun, his renters said. It was a shooter. When Cuervo counted the week's take, he kept the pistol on the desktop near his right hand.

Cuervo's office was a cubicle at the top of three flights of stairs. The furnishings were sparse and cheap: a black dial telephone, a metal desk, a wooden file cabinet and an oak swivel chair on casters. A four-year-old *Sports Illustrated* swimsuit calendar hung on the left-hand wall. Cuervo never changed it past April, the month where you could see the broad's brown nipples through the wet T-shirt. Opposite the calendar was a corkboard. A dozen business cards were tacked to the corkboard along with two fading bumper stickers. One said SHIT HAPPENS and the other said HOW'S MY DRIVING? DIAL 1-800-EAT-SHIT. Cuervo's wife, a Kentucky sharecropper girl with a mouth like barbed wire, called the office a shithole. Ray Cuervo paid no attention. He *was* a slumlord, after all.

Cuervo counted the cash out in neat piles, ones, fives and tens. The odd twenty he put in his pocket. Coins he counted, noted and dumped into a Maxwell House coffee can. Cuervo was a fat man with small black eyes. When he lifted his heavy chin, three rolls of suet popped out on the back of his red neck. When he leaned forward, three more rolls popped out on his side, under his armpits. And when he farted, which was often, he unconsciously eased one obese cheek off the chair to reduce the compression. He didn't think the movement either impolite or impolitic. If a woman was in the room, he said "Oops." If the company was all male, he said nothing. Farting was something men did.

A few minutes after five o'clock on October 5, an unseasonably warm day, the door slammed at the bottom of the stairs and a man started up. Cuervo put his fingertips on the Charter Arms .38 and half stood so he could see the visitor. The man on the stairs turned his face up and Cuervo relaxed.

Leo Clark. An old customer. Like most of the Indians who rented Cuervo's apartments, Leo was always back and forth from the reservations. He was a hard man, Leo was, with a face like a cinder block, but Cuervo never had trouble with him.

Leo paused at the second landing, catching his breath, then came up the last flight. He was a Sioux, in his forties, a loner, dark from the summer sun. Long black braids trailed down his back and a piece of Navaho silver flashed from his belt. He came from the West somewhere: Rosebud, Standing Rock, someplace like that.

"Leo, how are you?" Cuervo said without looking up. He had money in both hands, counting. "Need a place?"

"Put your hands in your lap, Ray," Leo said. Cuervo looked up. Leo was pointing a pistol at him.

"Aw, man, don't do this," Cuervo groaned, straightening up. He didn't look at his pistol, but he was thinking about it. "If you need a few bucks, I'll loan it to you."

"Sure you will," Leo said. "Two for one." Cuervo did a little loansharking on the side. Bidness was bidness.

"Come on, Leo." Cuervo casually dropped the stack of bills on the desktop, freeing his gun hand. "You wanna spend your old age in the joint?"

"If you move again, I'll shoot holes in your head. I mean it, Ray," Leo said. Cuervo checked the other man's face. It was as cold and dark as a Mayan statue's. Cuervo stopped moving.

Leo edged around the desk. No more than three feet separated them, but the hole at the end of Leo's pistol pointed unwaveringly at Ray Cuervo's nose.

"Just sit still. Take it easy," Leo said. When he was behind the chair, he said, "I'm going to put a pair of handcuffs on you, Ray. I want you to put your hands behind the chair."

Cuervo followed instructions, turning his head to see what Leo was doing.

"Look straight ahead," Leo said, tapping him behind the ear with the gun barrel. Cuervo looked straight ahead. Leo stepped back, pushed the pistol into the waistband of his slacks and took an obsidian knife from his front pants pocket. The knife was seven inches of beautifully crafted black volcanic glass, taken from a cliff at Yellowstone National Park. Its edge was fluted and it was as sharp as a surgeon's scalpel.

"Hey, Ray?" Leo said, stepping up closer to the slumlord. Cuervo farted, in either fear or exasperation, and the fetid smell filled the room. He didn't bother to say "Oops."

"Yeah?" Cuervo looked straight ahead. Calculating. His legs were in the kneehole under the desk: it'd be hard to move in a hurry. Let it ride, he thought, just a couple more minutes. When Leo was putting on the cuffs, maybe the right move . . . The gun glittered on the desk a foot and a half from his eyes.

"I lied about the handcuffs, Ray," Leo said. He grabbed Cuervo by the hair above his forehead and jerked his head back. With a single powerful slash, Leo cut Ray Cuervo's throat from ear to ear.

Cuervo half stood and twisted free and groped helplessly at his neck with one hand while the other crawled frantically across his desk toward the Charter Arms .38. He knew even as he tried that he wouldn't make it. Blood spurted from his severed carotid artery as though from a garden hose, spraying the leaves of green dollars on the desk, the *Sports Illustrated* broad with the tits, the brown linoleum floor.

Ray Cuervo twisted and turned and fell, batting the Maxwell House coffee can off the desk. Coins pitched and clattered and rolled around the office and a few bounced down the stairs. Cuervo lay faceup on the floor, his vision narrowing to a dim and closing hole that finally settled around Leo Clark, whose face remained impassively centered in the growing darkness. And then Ray Cuervo was dead.

Leo turned away as Cuervo's bladder and sphincter control went. There was $2,035 on the desktop. Leo paid it no attention. He wiped the obsidian knife on his pants, put it back in his pocket and pulled his shirt out to cover the gun. Then he walked down the stairs and six blocks back to his apartment. He was splattered with Cuervo's blood, but nobody seemed to notice. The cops got only a very slender description. An Indian male with braids. There were five thousand Indian males with braids in Minneapolis.

A large number of them were delighted to hear the news about Ray Cuervo.


Fuckin' Indians.

John Lee Benton hated them. They were worse than the niggers. You tell a nigger to show up, and if he didn't, he had an excuse. A reason. Even if it was bullshit.

Indians were different. You tell a guy to come in at two o'clock and he doesn't show. Then he comes in at two the next day and thinks that's good enough. He doesn't *pretend* to think so. He *really* thinks so.

The shrinks at the joint called it a cultural anomaly. John Lee Benton called it a pain in the ass. The shrinks said the only answer was education. John Lee Benton had developed another approach, all on his own.

Benton had seven Indians on his case load. If they didn't report on schedule, he'd spend the time normally used for an interview to write the papers that would start them back to Stillwater. In two years, he'd sent back nine men. Now he had a reputation. The fuckin' Indians walked wide around him. If you're going out on parole, they told each other, you didn't want to be on John Lee Benton's case load. That was a sure ride back inside.

Benton enjoyed the rep.

John Lee Benton was a small man with a strong nose and mousy hair combed forward over watery blue eyes. He wore a straw-colored mustache, cut square. When he looked at himself in the bathroom mirror in the morning, he thought he looked like somebody, but he couldn't think who. Somebody famous. He'd think of it sooner or later.

John Lee Benton hated blacks, Indians, Mexicans, Jews and Asians, more or less in that order. His hate for blacks and Jews was a family heritage, passed down from his daddy as Benton grew up in a sprawling blue-collar slum in St. Louis. He'd developed his animus for Indians, Mexicans and Asians on his own.

Every Monday afternoon Benton sat in a stifling office in the back of the Indian Center off Franklin Avenue and talked to his assholes. He was supposed to call them clients, but fuck that. They were criminals and assholes, every single one.

"Mr. Benton?"

Benton looked up. Betty Sails stood in the doorway. A tentative, gray-faced Indian woman with a beehive hairdo, she was the office's shared receptionist.

"Is he here?" John Lee spoke sharply, impatiently. He was a man who sweated hate.

"No, he's not," Betty Sails said. "But there's another man to see you. Another Indian man."

Benton frowned. "I didn't have any more appointments today."

"He said it was about Mr. Cloud."

Glory be, an actual excuse. "All right. Give me a couple of minutes, then send him in," Benton said. Betty Sails went away and Benton looked through Cloud's file again. He didn't need to review it but liked the idea of keeping the Indian waiting. Two minutes later, Tony Bluebird appeared at the door. Benton had never seen him before.

"Mr. Benton?" Bluebird was a stocky man with close-set eyes and short-cropped hair. He wore a gingham shirt over a rawhide thong. A black obsidian knife dangled from the thong and Bluebird could feel it ticking against the skin below his breastbone.

"Yes?" Benton let his anger leak into his tone.

Bluebird showed him a gun. "Put your hands on your lap, Mr. Benton."


Three people saw Bluebird. Betty Sails saw him both coming and going. A kid coming out of the gym dropped a basketball, and Bluebird stopped it with a foot, picked it up and tossed it back, just as Betty Sails started screaming. On the street, Dick Yellow Hand, who was seventeen years old and desperately seeking a taste of crack, saw him walk out the door and called, "Hey, Blue-bird."

Bluebird stopped. Yellow Hand sidled over, scratching his thin beard. "You look bad, man," Bluebird said.

Yellow Hand nodded. He was wearing a dirty T-shirt with a fading picture of Mick Jagger on the front. His jeans, three sizes too large, were cinched at the waist with a length of clothesline. His elbow joints and arms looked like cornstalks. He was missing two front teeth. "I feel bad, man. I could use a few bucks, you know?"

"Sorry, man, I got no money," Bluebird said. He stuck his hands in his pockets and pulled them out empty.

"That's okay, then," Yellow Hand said, disappointed.

"I seen your mama last week," Bluebird said. "Out at the res."

"How's she?"

"She's fine. She was fishing. Walleyes."

Sails' hysterical screams became audible as somebody opened an outside door to the Indian Center.

"That's real good about Mama," said Yellow Hand.

"Well, I guess I gotta go," Bluebird said, easing away.

"Okay, man," said Yellow Hand. "See you."


Bluebird walked, taking his time, his mind in another place. What was her name? It had been years ago. Anna? She was a pretty woman, with deep breasts and warm hazel eyes. She'd liked him, he thought, though they were both married, and nothing ever happened; nothing but a chemistry felt across back-yard hedges, deep down in Minneapolis' Indian Country.

Anna's husband, a Chippewa from Nett Lake, had been put in the Hennepin County Jail. Drunk, late at night, he'd seen a Coke machine glowing red-and-white through the window of a gas station. He'd heaved a chunk of concrete through the window, crawled in after it and used the concrete to crack the machine. About a thousand quarters had run out onto the floor, somebody told

Bluebird. Anna's husband had still been picking them up, laboriously, one at a time, when the cops arrived. He'd been on parole and the break-in was a violation. He'd gotten six months on top of the remaining time from the previous conviction.

Anna and her husband had never had money. He drank up most of it and she probably helped. Food was short. Nobody had clothes. But they did have a son. He was twelve, a stocky, withdrawn child who spent his evenings watching television. One Saturday afternoon, a few weeks after his daddy was taken to jail, the boy walked down to the Lake Street bridge and jumped into the Mississippi. A lot of people saw him go and the cops had him out of the river in fifteen minutes. Dead.

Bluebird had heard, and he went down to the river. Anna was there, her arms wrapped around the body of her son, and she looked up at him with those deep pain-filled eyes, and . . . what?

It was all part of being Indian, Bluebird thought. The dying. It was something they did better than the whites. Or more frequently, anyway.

When Bluebird walked out of the room after slashing Benton's throat, he'd looked down at the man's face and thought he seemed familiar. Like a famous person. Now, on the sidewalk, as he left Yellow Hand behind, as he thought about Anna, Benton's face floated up in his mind's eye.

Hitler, he thought. John Lee Benton looked exactly like a young Adolf Hitler. A young *dead* Adolf Hitler.

# 2

Lucas Davenport lounged on a brocaded couch in the back of a used-book store, eating a roast beef sandwich. In his lap was a battered paperback copy of T. Harry Williams' biography of Huey Long.

T. Harry had gotten it right, Lucas reflected. The man in the white suit flashing among the Longites as they stood outside the governor's office. The shot. The Kingfish hit, the screaming, the running. The cops going berserk.

"Roden and Coleman fired at almost the same time, with Coleman's bullet probably reaching the man first," T. Harry wrote. "Several other guards had unholstered their guns and were blazing away. The man crumpled and fell facedownward near the wall of the corridor from which he had come. He lay there with his face resting on one arm and did not move and was obviously dead. But this did not satisfy some of the guards. Crazed with rage or grief, they stood over the body and emptied their guns into it. It was later discovered to have thirty bullet holes in the back and twenty-nine in the front (many of these were caused by the same bullet making an entry and exit) and two in the head. The face was partially shot away, and the white suit was cut to ribbons and drenched with blood."

Murder was never as neat as it was on television. No matter how brutal it was on the screen, in real life it was worse. In real life, there was always an empty husk lying there, the spirit departed, the flesh slack, the eyes like ball bearings. And it had to be dealt with. Somebody had to pick up the body, somebody had to mop up the blood. Somebody had to catch the killer.

Lucas rubbed his eyebrow where the scar crossed it. The scar was the product of a fishing accident. A wire leader had snapped back from a snag and buried itself in his face. The scar was not a disfigurement: the women he knew said it made him look friendlier. The scar was fine; it was his smile that was scary.

He rubbed his eyebrow and went back to the book. He did not look like a natural reader, sitting on the couch, squinting in the dim light. He had the air of the street about him. His hands, which were covered with a dark fuzz for three inches below his wrists, seemed too large and blocky as he handled the paperback. His nose had been broken, more than once, and a strong neck was rooted in heavy shoulders. His hair was black, just touched with gray.

He turned the page of the book with one hand and reached under his jacket and adjusted his holster with the other.

" 'Kingfish, what's the matter?'

" 'Jimmie, my boy, I've been shot,' Huey moaned. . . ."

Lucas' handset beeped. He picked it up and thumbed the volume control. A woman's voice said, "Lieutenant Davenport?"

"Go ahead."

"Lucas, Jim Wentz needs you down at the Indian Center on that guy that got cut. He's got a witness he wants you to look at."

"All right," Lucas said. "Ten minutes."

It was a beautiful day, one of the best of a good autumn. A murder would damage it. Murders were usually the result of aggressive stupidity mixed with alcohol and anger. Not always. But almost always. Lucas, given the choice, stayed away from them.

Outside the bookstore, he stood on the sidewalk for a moment, letting his eyes adjust to the sun and finishing the last bite of the sandwich. When he was done, he threw the sandwich bag into a trash barrel and crossed the street to his car. A panhandler was working the sidewalk, saw Lucas and said, "Watched yer car for ya?" and held out his hand. The panhandler was a regular, a schizophrenic pushed out of the state hospital. He couldn't function without his meds but wouldn't take the mind-numbing drugs on his own. Lucas passed him a dollar and dropped into the Porsche.

Downtown Minneapolis is a workbox of modernist architecture, blocks of glass and chrome and white marble. The aging red wart of City Hall hunkers in the middle of it. Lucas shook his head as he rolled past it, took a left and a right and crossed the interstate. The glitter fell behind, giving way to a ramshackle district of old clapboard houses cut into apartments, junker cars and failing businesses. Indian Country. There were a half-dozen squad cars outside the Indian Center and Lucas dumped the 911 at the curb.

"Three witnesses," the Homicide detective told him. Wentz had a flat, pallid Scandinavian face. His lower front teeth had been broken off in a fight, and he wore crowns; their silvery bases glittered when he talked. He counted the three witnesses on his fingers, as if he didn't trust Lucas' arithmetic.

"There's the receptionist," he said. "She saw him twice and says she can identify him. There's a neighborhood kid. He was playing basketball and says this guy had blood all over his pants. I believe it. The office looks like a fuckin' swimming pool."

"Can the kid identify him?" Lucas asked.

"He says he can. He says he looked the guy right in the face. He's seen him around the neighborhood."

"Who's number three?"

"Another kid. A junkie. He saw the killer outside the place, talked to him. We think they know each other, but he's not talking."

"Where is he?" Lucas asked.

"Out in a squad."

"How'd you find him?"

Wentz shrugged. "No problem. The receptionist—the one who found the body—called nine-one-one, then she went over to the window for some fresh air. She was feeling queasy. Anyway, she saw this kid and the killer talking on the sidewalk. When we got here, the kid was up the block. Standing there. Fucked up, maybe. We just put him in the car."

Lucas nodded, walked down the hallway and stepped inside the counseling office. Benton lay faceup on the tile floor in a pool of purplish blood. His hands extended straight out from his sides as though he had been crucified. His legs were spread wide, his blood-flecked wingtips pointing away from each other at forty-five-degree angles. His shirt and sport coat were saturated with blood. There were footprints and kneeholes in the puddle of blood, where the paramedics had tracked through, but no medical debris. Usually the packaging from the syringes, sponges, tape and compresses was all over the place. With Benton, they hadn't bothered.

Lucas sniffed at the coppery smell of the blood as the detective came in behind him.

"Looks like the same guy who did Ray Cuervo," Lucas said.

"Maybe," Wentz said.

"You better get him or the papers'll start peeing on you," Lucas said mildly.

"Could be worse than that," the Homicide cop said. "We got a rough description of the guy who did Cuervo. He had braids. Everybody says this guy had short hair."

"Could have cut it," Lucas suggested. "Got scared . . ."

"I hope, but it don't feel right."

"If it's two guys, that'd be big trouble. . . ." Lucas was getting interested.

"I know, fuck, I know." Wentz took off his glasses and rubbed a heavy hand up and down the side of his face. "Christ, I'm tired. My daughter piled up the car last Saturday. Right downtown by the IDS building. Her fault, she ran a light. I'm trying to deal with the insurance and the body shop and this shit happens. Two hours later and I'd be off. . . ."

"She okay?"

"Yeah, yeah." He settled his glasses back on his nose. "That's the first thing I asked. I say, 'You okay?' She says, 'Yeah.' I say, 'I'm coming down and I'm gonna kill you.' "

"As long as she was okay," Lucas said. The toe of his right loafer was in the blood puddle and he stepped back a few inches. He was looking at Benton's face upside down. It occurred to him that Benton resembled someone famous, but with the face upside down, he couldn't tell who.

". . . the apple of my eye," Wentz was saying. "If anything happened to her . . . You got a kid now, right?"

"Yeah. A daughter."

"Poor fuck. Wait a few years. She'll wreck that Porsche of yours and the insurance company will own your ass." Wentz shook his head. Goddamned daughters. It was nearly impossible to live with them and clearly impossible to live without them. "Look, you might know this kid we got in the car. He said we weren't to mess with him 'cause Davenport was his friend. We think he's one of your snitches."

"I'll go see," Lucas said.

"Any help . . ." The Homicide cop shrugged.

"Sure."

Outside, Lucas asked a patrolman about the junkie and was directed to the last car in line. Another patrolman sat behind the wheel and a small dark figure sat behind him, the two separated by a steel screen. Lucas bent over the open front window on the passenger side, nodded to the patrolman and looked into the backseat. The kid was bouncing nervously, one thin hand tangled in his dark hair. Yellow Hand.

"Hey, Dick," Lucas said. "How's things at K Mart?"

"Oh, man, Davenport, get me outta here." Yellow Hand's eyes were wide and frightened. He kept bouncing, faster now. "I didn't do nothing, man. Not a fuckin' thing."

"The people at K Mart would like to talk to you about that. They say you were runnin' for the door with a disc player. . . ."

"Shit, man, it wasn't me. . . ."

"Right. But I'll tell you what: You give me a name, and I'll put you on the street again," Lucas said.

"I don't know who it was, man," Yellow Hand squealed.

"Bullshit," grunted the uniform officer in the driver's seat. He shifted a toothpick and looked at Lucas. He had a wide Irish face and a peaches-and-cream complexion. "You know what he said to me, Lieutenant? He said, 'You ain't getting it out of me, dickhead.' That's what he said. He knows who it was."

"That right?" Lucas asked, turning back to Yellow Hand.

"Fuck, man, I didn't know him," Yellow Hand whined. "He was just this fuckin' guy. . . ."

"Indian guy?"

"Yeah, Indian guy, but I didn't know him. . . ."

"Bullshit," said the uniform.

Lucas turned his head and looked at the uniform. "You hold him here, okay? If anybody wants to transport him, you tell them I said to hold him here."

"Okay. Sure. Whatever." The uniform didn't care. He was sitting in the sunshine and had a pocket full of peppermint toothpicks.

"I'll be back in twenty minutes," Lucas said.


Elwood Stone set up a hundred feet from the halfway house. It was a good spot; the inmates could get their cocaine on the way home. Some of them, the inmates, were running on tight schedules: they were clocked out of their jobs and allowed a set amount of time to get home. They didn't have the leisure to run all over the place, looking for toot.

Lucas spotted Stone at the same time Stone spotted Lucas' Porsche. The dealer started running south down the street, but it was all two- and three-story apartments and townhouses with no spaces between them to run into. Lucas cruised alongside until Stone gave up, breathing hard, and sat on the stoop of one of the apartments. As he sat down, it occurred to Stone that he should have tossed the tube of crack into the weeds. Now it was too late.

"Stone, how are you?" Lucas said amiably, as he walked around the nose of the 911. "Sounds like you're a little out of shape."

"Fuck you, Davenport. I want a lawyer." Stone knew him well.

Lucas sat on the stoop beside the dealer and leaned back, tilted his head up to the sun, taking in the rays. "You ran the four-forty in high school, didn't you?"

"Fuck you, Davenport."

"I remember that track meet against Sibley, they had that white boy, what's his name? Turner? Now that boy could motor. Christ, you don't see that many white boys . . ."

"Fuck you, I want a lawyer."

"So Turner's old man is rich, right?" Lucas said conversationally. "And he gives the kid a Corvette. Turner takes it up north and piles it into a bridge abutment, you know? They had to stick him together with strapping tape to have a funeral."

"Fuck you, I got a right to an attorney." Stone was beginning to sweat. Davenport was a stone killer.

Lucas shook his head with a stage sigh. "I don't know, Elwood. Can I call you Elwood?"

"Fuck you. . . ."

"Sometimes life ain't fair. You know where I'm coming from? Like the Turner kid. And take your case, Elwood. They've got all bureaucrats on the sentencing commission. You know what they did? They cranked up the guidelines on possession with intent. Guess what the guidelines are for a three-time loser going down on possession with intent?"

"I ain't no fucking lawyer. . . ."

"Six years, my friend. Minimum. Cute guy like you, your asshole will look like the I-94 tunnel when you come out. Shit, if this had been two months ago, you'd of got off with two years."

"Fuck you, man, I want an attorney."

Lucas leaned close to him and bared his teeth. "And I need a few rocks. Now. You lay a few rocks on me, now, and I walk away."

Stone looked at him in wild surmise. "You? Need rock?"

"Yeah. I need to squeeze a guy."

The light in Stone's eyes went out. Blackmail. That made sense. Davenport actually smoking the stuff, that didn't make sense. "I walk?"

"You walk."

Stone thought about it for a few seconds, then nodded, stood up and fished in his shirt pocket. He pulled out a glass tube stoppered with black plastic. There were five chunks of crack stacked inside.

"How much you need?" he asked.

"All of it," Lucas said. He took the tube away from Stone. "And stay the fuck away from that halfway house. If I catch you here again, I'll bust your ass."


The medical examiner's assistants were hauling Benton's body out of the Indian Center when Lucas got back. A TV cameraman walked backward in front of the gurney as it rolled down the sidewalk carrying the sheet-shrouded body, then did a neat two-step-and-swivel to pan across the faces of a small crowd of onlookers. Lucas walked around the crowd and down the line of squad cars.

Yellow Hand was waiting impatiently. Lucas got the patrolman to open the back door and climbed in beside the kid.

"Why don't you hike over to that 7-Eleven and get yourself a doughnut," Lucas suggested to the cop.

"Nah. Too many calories," the cop said. He settled back in the front seat.

"Look, take a fuckin' hike, will you?" Lucas asked in exasperation.

"Oh. Sure. Yeah. I'll go get a doughnut," the uniform said, finally picking up the hint. There were rumors about Davenport. . . .

Lucas watched the cop walk away and then turned to Yellow Hand.

"Who was this guy?"

"Aw, Davenport, I don't know this guy. . . ." Yellow Hand's Adam's apple bobbed earnestly.

Lucas took the glass tube out of his pocket, turned it in his fingers so the kid could see the dirty-white chunks of crack. Yellow Hand's tongue flicked across his lips as Lucas slowly worked the plastic stopper out of the tube and tipped the five rocks into his palm.

"This is good shit," Lucas said casually. "I took it off Elwood Stone up at the halfway house. You know Elwood? His mama cooks it up. They get it from the Cubans over on the West Side of St. Paul. Really good shit."

"Man. Oh, man. Don't do this."

Lucas held one of the small rocks between a thumb and index finger. "Who was it?"

"Man, I can't . . ." Yellow Hand was in agony, twisting his thin hands. Lucas crushed the rock, pushed the door open with his elbow, and let it trickle to the ground like sand running through an hourglass.

"Please, don't do that." Yellow Hand was appalled.

"Four more," Lucas said. "All I need is a name and you can take off."

"Oh, man . . ."

Lucas picked up another rock and held it close to Yellow Hand's face and just started to squeeze when Yellow Hand blurted, "Wait."

"Who?"

Yellow Hand looked out the window. It was warm now, but you could feel the chill in the night air. Winter was coming. A bad time to be an Indian on the streets.

"Bluebird," he muttered. They came from the same reservation and he'd sold the man for four pieces of crack.

"Who?"

"Tony Bluebird. He's got a house off Franklin."

"What house?"

"Shit, I don't know the number. . . ." he whined. His eyes shifted. A traitor's eyes.

Lucas held the rock to Yellow Hand's face again. "Going, going . . ."

"You know that house where the old guy painted the porch pillars with polka dots?" Yellow Hand spoke in haste now, eager to get it over.

"Yeah."

"It's two up from that. Up towards the TV store."

"Has this guy ever been in trouble? Bluebird?"

"Oh, yeah. He did a year in Stillwater. Burglary."

"What else?"

Yellow Hand shrugged. "He's from Fort Thompson. He goes there in the summer and works here in the winter. I don't know him real good, he was just back on the res, you know? Got a woman, I think. I don't know, man. He mostly knows my family. He's older than I am."

"Has he got a gun?"

"I don't know. It's not like he's a friend. I never heard of him getting in fights or nothing."

"All right," Lucas said. "Where are you staying?"

"In the Point. The top floor, with some other guys."

"Wasn't that one of Ray Cuervo's places? Before he got cut?"

"Yeah." Yellow Hand was staring at the crack on Lucas' palm.

"Okay." Lucas tipped the four remaining rocks back into the test tube and handed it to Yellow Hand. "Stick this in your sock and get your ass back to the Point. If I come looking, you better be there."

"I will," Yellow Hand said eagerly.

Lucas nodded. The back door of the squad had no handles and he had carefully avoided closing it. Now he pushed it open and stepped out, and Yellow Hand slid across and got out beside him. "This better be right. This Bluebird," Lucas said, jabbing a finger into Yellow Hand's thin chest.

Yellow Hand nodded. "It was him. I talked to him."

"Okay. Beat it."

Yellow Hand hurried away. Lucas watched him for a moment, then walked across the street to the Indian Center. He found Wentz in the director's office.

"So how's our witness?" the cop asked.

"On his way home."

"Say what?"

"He'll be around," Lucas said. "He says the guy we want is named Tony Bluebird. Lives down on Franklin. I know the house, and he's got a sheet. We should be able to get a photo."

"God damn," Wentz said. He reached for a telephone. "Let me get that downtown."


Lucas had nothing more to do. Homicide was for Homicide cops. Lucas was Intelligence. He ran networks of street people, waitresses, bartenders, barbers, gamblers, hookers, pimps, bookies, dealers in cars and cocaine, mail carriers, a couple of burglars. The crooks were small-timers, but they had eyes and memories. Lucas was always ready with a dollar or a threat, whatever was needed to make a snitch feel wanted.

He had nothing to do with it, but after Yellow Hand produced the name, Lucas hung around to watch the cop machine work. Sometimes it was purely a pleasure. Like now: when the Homicide cop called downtown, several things happened at once.

A check with the identification division confirmed Yellow Hand's basic information and got a photograph of Tony Bluebird started out to the Indian Center.

At the same time, the Minneapolis Emergency Response Unit began staging in a liquor store parking lot a mile from Bluebird's suspected residence.

While the ERU got together, a further check with utility companies suggested that Bluebird lived in the house where Yellow Hand had put him. Forty minutes after Yellow Hand spoke Bluebird's name, a tall black man in an army fatigue jacket and blue jeans ambled down the street past Bluebird's to the house next door, went up on the porch, knocked, flashed his badge and asked himself inside. The residents didn't know any Bluebird, but people came and went, didn't they?

Another detective, a white guy who looked as if he'd been whipped through hell with a soot bag, stopped at the house before Bluebird's and went through the same routine.

"Yeah, Tony Bluebird, that's the guy's name, all right," said the elderly man who met him at the door. "What's he done?"

"We're not sure he did anything," said the detective. "Have you seen this guy lately? I mean, today?"

"Hell, yes. Not a half an hour ago, he came up the walk and went inside." The old man nervously gummed his lower lip. "Still in there, I guess."

The white detective called in and confirmed Bluebird's presence. Then he and the black detective did a careful scan of Bluebird's house from the windows of the adjoining homes and called their information back to the ERU leader. Normally, when they had a man pinned, they'd try to make contact, usually by phone. But Bluebird, they thought, might be some kind of maniac. Maybe a danger to hostages or himself. They decided to take him. The ERUs, riding in nondescript vans, moved up to a second stage three blocks from Bluebird's.

While all that was going on, Betty Sails picked Bluebird out of a photo spread. The basketball player confirmed the identification.

"That's a good snitch you got there, Lucas," Wentz said approvingly. "You coming along?"

"Might as well."

*    *    *

The ERU found a blind spot around the back door of Bluebird's house. The door had no window, and the only other window near it had the shade pulled. They could move up to the door, take it out and be inside before Bluebird had even a hint of their presence.

And it would have worked if Bluebird's landlord hadn't been so greedy. The landlord had illegally subdivided the house into a duplex. The division had been practical, rather than aesthetic: the doorway connecting the front of the house to the back had been covered with a sheet of three-quarter-inch plywood.

When the tac commander said "Go," one of the ERUs tossed a flash-bang grenade through Bluebird's side window. The terrific explosion and brilliant flash would freeze anyone inside for several seconds, long enough for the ERU team to get on top of him. When the flash-bang went off, another ERU blew the back door open with an AVON round fired from his shotgun, and the team leader went through the door, followed by three of his men.

A young Mexican woman was lying half asleep on the sofa, a baby on her stomach. An older kid, a toddler, was sitting in a dilapidated playpen. The Mexican woman had been nursing the baby and her shirt was open, her breasts exposed. She struggled to sit up, reacting to the flash-bang and the AVONs, her mouth and eyes wide with fear.

The team leader blocked a hallway, and the biggest man on the squad hit the plywood barrier, kicked it twice and gave up.

"We're blocked out, we're blocked out," he shouted.

"Is there any way to the front?" the team leader yelled at the Mexican woman. The woman, still dazed, didn't understand, and the team leader took his men out and rotated them down the side of the house.

They were ten seconds into the attack, still hoping to do it clean, when a woman screamed from the front of the house. Then there were a couple of shots, a window shattered, and the leader figured Bluebird had a hostage. He called the team off.

Sex was strange, the team leader thought.

He stood with his back against the crumbling white siding of the house, the shotgun still in his hand, sweat pouring down his face. The attack had been chaotic, the response—the shooting—had been the kind of thing he feared, a close-up firefight with a nut, where you might have a pistol right up your nose. With all that, the image of the Mexican woman's thin breast stayed in his mind's eye and in his throat, and he could barely concentrate on the life-and-death confrontation he was supposed to be directing. . . .

When Lucas arrived, two marked squads were posted in front of Bluebird's house, across the street, and ERUs waited on the porches of the houses on either side of Bluebird's. A blocking team was out back. Drum music leaked from the house.

"Are we talking to him?" Lucas asked the tac commander.

"We called him on the phone, but we lost the phone," the tac commander said. "Phone company says it's out of order. We think he pulled the line."

"How many people are in there?"

The tac commander shrugged. "The neighbors say he's got a wife and a couple of kids, preschool kids. Don't know about anybody else."

A television truck rolled up to the end of the street, where a patrolman stopped it. A *StarTribune* reporter appeared at the other end of the block, a photographer humping along behind. One of the TV crew stopped arguing with the patrolman long enough to point at Lucas and yell. When Lucas turned, she waved, and Lucas ambled down the block. Neighbors were being herded along the sidewalk. There'd been a birthday party going on at one house and a half-dozen kids floated helium balloons over the gathering crowd. It looked like a carnival, Lucas thought.

"What's happening, Davenport?" the TV reporter yelled past the patrolman. The reporter was a Swede of the athletic variety, with high cheekbones, narrow hips and blood-red lipstick. A cameraman stood next to her, his camera focused on the Bluebird house.

"That killing down at the Indian Center today? We think we got the guy trapped inside."

"He got hostages?" the reporter asked. She didn't have a notebook.

"We don't know."

"Can we get any closer? Any way? We need a better angle. . . ."

Lucas glanced around the blocked-off area.

"How about if we try to get you in that alley over there, between those houses? You'll be further away, but you'll have a direct shot at the front. . . ."

"Something's going down," the cameraman said. He was looking at the Bluebird house through his camera's telephoto setting.

"Ah, shit," said the reporter. She tried to ease past the patrolman to stand next to Lucas, but the patrolman blocked her with a hip.

"Catch you later," Lucas said over his shoulder as he turned and started back.

"C'mon, Davenport . . ."

Lucas shook his head and kept going. The ERU team leader on the porch of the left-hand house was yelling at Bluebird's. He got a response, stepped back a bit and took out a handset.

"What?" asked Lucas, when he got back to the command unit.

"He said he's sending his people out," said a cop on a radio.

"I'm backing everybody off," said the tac commander. As Lucas leaned on the roof to watch, the tac commander sent a patrolman scrambling along the row of cars, to warn the ERUs and the uniformed officers that people were coming out of the house. A moment later, a white towel waved at the door and a woman stepped out, holding a baby. She was dragging another kid, maybe three years old, by one arm.

"Come on, come on, you're okay," the detective called out. She looked back once, then walked quickly, head down, on the sidewalk through the line of cars.

Lucas and the tac commander moved over to intercept her.

"Who are you?" the tac commander asked.

"Lila Bluebird."

"Is that your husband in there?"

"Yes."

"Has he got anybody with him?"

"He's all alone," the woman said. Tears streamed down her face. She was wearing a man's cowboy shirt and shorts made of stretchy black material spotted with lint fuzzies. The baby clung to her shirt, as though he knew what was going on; the other kid hung on her hand. "He said to tell you he'll be out in a minute."

"He drunk? Crack? Crank? Anything like that?"

"No. No alcohol or drugs in our house. But he's not right."

"What's that? You mean he's crazy? What . . ."

The question was never finished. The door of the Bluebird house burst open and Tony Bluebird hurdled onto the lawn, running hard. He was bare-chested, the long obsidian blade dangling from his neck on a rawhide thong. Two eagle feathers were pinned to his headdress and he had pistols in both hands. Ten feet off the porch, he brought them up and opened fire on the nearest squad, closing on the cops behind it. The cops shot him to pieces. The gunfire stood him up and knocked him down.

After a second of stunned silence, Lila Bluebird began to wail and the older kid, confused, clutched at her leg and began screaming. The radio man called for paramedics. Three cops moved up to Bluebird, their pistols still pointed at his body, and nudged his weapons out of reach.

The tac commander looked at Lucas, his mouth working for a moment before the words came out. "Jesus Christ," he blurted. "What the fuck was that all about?"

# 3

Wild grapes covered the willow trees, dangling forty and fifty feet down to the waterline. In the weak light from the Mendota Bridge, the island looked like a three-masted schooner with black sails, cruising through the mouth of the Minnesota River into the Mississippi.

Two men walked onto a sand spit at the tip of the island. They'd had a fire earlier in the evening, roasting wieners on sharp sticks and heating cans of SpaghettiOs. The fire had guttered down to coals, but the smell of the burning pine still hung in the cool air. A hundred feet back from the water's edge, a sweat lodge squatted under the willows.

"We ought to go up north. It'd be nice now, out on the lakes," said the taller one.

"It's been too warm. Too many mosquitoes."

The tall man laughed. "Bullshit, mosquitoes. We're Indians, dickhead."

"Them fuckin' Chippewa would take our hair," the short one objected, the humor floating through his voice.

"Not us. Kill their men, screw their women. Drink their beer."

"I ain't drinkin' no Grain Belt," said the short one. There was a moment's comfortable silence between them. The short one took a breath, let it out in an audible sigh and said, "Too much to do. Can't fuck around up north."

The short man's face had sobered. The tall man couldn't see it, but sensed it. "I wish I could go pray over Bluebird," the tall man said. After a moment, he added, "I hoped he would go longer."

"He wasn't smart."

"He was spiritual."

"Yep."

The men were Mdewakanton Sioux, cousins, born the same day on the banks of the Minnesota River. One had been named Aaron Sunders and the other Samuel Close, but only the bureaucrats called them that. To everyone else they touched, they were the Crows, named for their mothers' father, Dick Crow.

Later in life, a medicine man gave them Dakota first names. The names were impossible to translate. Some Dakota argued for Light Crow and Dark Crow. Others said Sun Crow and Moon Crow. Still others claimed the only reasonable translation was Spiritual Crow and Practical Crow. But the cousins called themselves Aaron and Sam. If some Dakota and white-wannabees thought the names were not impressive enough, that was their lookout.

The tall Crow was Aaron, the spiritual man. The short Crow was Sam, the practical one. In the back of their pickup, Aaron carried an army footlocker full of herbs and barks. In the cab, Sam carried two .45s, a Louisville Slugger and a money belt. They considered themselves one person in two bodies, each body containing a single aspect. It had been that way since 1932, when the daughters of Dick Crow and their two small sons had huddled together in a canvas lean-to for four months, near starving, near freezing, fighting to stay alive. From December through March, the cousins had lived in a cardboard box full of ripped-up woolen army blankets. The four months had welded their two personalities into one. They had been inseparable for nearly sixty years, except for a time that Aaron had spent in federal prison.

"I wish we would hear from Billy," said Sam Crow.

"We know he's there," Aaron Crow said quietly.

"But what's he doing? Three days now, and nothing."

"You worry that he's gone back to drinking. You shouldn't, 'cause he hasn't."

"How do you know?"

"I know."

Sam nodded. When his cousin said he knew, he knew. "I'm worried about what'll happen when he goes for the hit. The New York cops are good on a thing like this."

"Trust Billy," said Aaron. Aaron was thin, but not frail: wiry, hard, like beef jerky. He had a hundred hard planes in his face, surrounding a high-ridged nose. His eyes were like black marbles. "He's a smart one. He'll do right."

"I hope so. If he's caught right away, the television coverage will come and go too fast." Sam had a broad face, with smile lines around a wide, soft chin. His hair was salt-and-pepper, his eyes deep and thoughtful. He had a belly, which bore down on a wide belt with a turquoise buckle.

"Not if Leo moves. He should be in Oklahoma City tomorrow, if his car holds out," said Aaron. "If the two . . . attacks . . . come right on top of each other, the TV'll go nuts. And the letters are ready."

Sam paced down to the water's edge, watched it for a moment, then turned and spoke back up the sand spit.

"I still think the first two were a mistake. We wasted Bluebird, doing that second one. Those killings won't have the impact we need. . . ."

"We needed some low-risk attacks to start. . . ."

"Wasn't low-risk for Bluebird . . ."

"We knew he might have a problem . . . but we had to set a tone. We had to make it a war. We can't just have a couple of assassinations. We have to make the media think . . . War. We have to pump this motherfucker up. It has to be big, if we want to get . . ."

"The Great Satan," Sam snorted. "It'll be for nothing if we can't get him out here."

"It wouldn't be for nothing—the ones we've already taken are bad enough. But he'll come," Aaron said confidently. "We know he comes out here. We know why. We know where. And we can get at him."

"No," said Sam. "We know he *used* to come here. But maybe no more. He's got the media watching. He wants to be president. . . . He's careful. . . ."

"But once he's here, he won't stay away. Not with the monkey he's got on his back."

"Maybe," said Sam. He thrust his hands into his pockets. "I still think the first two were bullshit killings."

"You're wrong," Aaron said flatly.

Sam stared out at the water. "I don't want to waste anybody, that's all." He bent, picked up a flat rock and tried to skip it across the river. Instead of skipping, it cut into the surface like a knife and was gone. "Shit," he said.

"You never were any good at that," Aaron said. "You need more of a sidearm."

"How many times have you told me that?" Sam asked, hunting up another rock.

"About a million."

Sam flipped the second rock out at the water. It hit and sank. He shook his head, thrust his hands back into his jean pockets, stood quietly for a moment, then turned to his cousin. "Have you talked to Shadow Love?" he asked.

"No."

"Are you still planning to send him to Bear Butte?"

"Yeah. I want him out of here," Aaron said.

"Shadow Love is a weapon," Sam Crow said.

"He's our kid."

"Every man comes to earth with a purpose. I'm quoting the famous Aaron Crow himself. Shadow Love is a weapon."

"I won't use him," said Aaron, walking down to the water's edge to stand by his cousin.

"Because he's our kid," Sam said. "Don't let that fuck you up."

"It's not that. The fact is, Shadow scares the shit out of me. That's the real problem." Aaron kicked off his battered sneakers and took a half-step so his toes were in the water. It felt cool and healing. "I fear for what we did to that boy, when we left him with Rosie. We had work to do, but . . . She wasn't quite right, you know. She was a lovely woman, but she had some wrong things in her mind. You say we made a weapon. I think we made a crazy man."

"Remember, once, a Crazy Horse . . . ?"

"Not the same. Crazy Horse loved a kind of life. A warrior life. Shadow's not a warrior. He's a killer. You've seen him; he hungers for pain and the power to create it."

The two men fell silent for a moment, listening to the water ripple past the sandbar. Then Aaron said, in a lighter tone, "How long before we fuck up, do you think?"

Sam threw back his head and laughed. "Three weeks. Maybe a month."

"We'll be dead, then," Aaron said. He made it sound funny.

"Maybe not. We could make it up to Canada. Sioux Valley. Hide out."

"Mmmm."

"What? You think we don't have a chance? We're just a couple of dead flatheads?" asked Sam.

"People who do this kind of thing . . . don't get away. They just don't." Aaron shrugged. "And there's always the question, *Should we try?*"

Sam ran a hand through his hair. "Jesus," he muttered.

"Exactly," Aaron said, with a quick, barking laugh. "If we go down . . . it'd make the point. Everybody knows Sitting Bull, because he died. Everybody knows Crazy Horse, because he died. Who knows about Inkpaduta? He was maybe the greatest of them all, but he went to Canada and got old and died. Not many remember him now. We're going to . . . *war* . . . to wake up the people. If we just sneak off, I don't think that'll be the same."

Sam shook his head but said nothing. He found another flat rock and sidearmed it at the water. It sank instantly. "Asshole," he called after the rock.

Aaron looked down at the sandbar at his cousin, sighed and said, "I'm going back to town with you. I hear too many voices tonight. I can't handle it."

"You shouldn't come here so often. Even I can feel them, groaning under the sand." He made a brushing motion that took in the sandbar, the river and the hillside. The land around the island had once been a concentration camp. Hundreds of Sioux died in it, most of them women and children.

"Come on," Aaron said. "Let's load the truck and get our ass out of here."

Billy Hood lay on the Jersey motel bed and stared at the ceiling. He'd made a preliminary reconnaissance, across the river into Manhattan, and concluded that he could do it. He could kill the man. The stone knife weighed on his chest.

To cut a man's throat . . . Hood's own throat tightened. Last year, hunting out of Mille Lacs in central Minnesota, he'd taken a deer. He'd spotted it walking through a grove of birches, a tan wraith floating through the white-on-white of trees and snow. It had been a doe, but a big one. The .30-.30 had knocked it down and it hadn't gotten up again. It hadn't died, either. It had lain there on its side in the shallow snow, its feet making feeble running motions, its visible eye blinking up at him and his brother-in-law Roger.

"Better cut her throat, brother," Roger had said. Roger was smiling. Turned on? Feeling the power? "Put her out of her misery."

Hood had taken his hunting knife from its sheath, a knife he'd honed to a razor sharpness. He'd grabbed the doe by an ear and lifted its head and cut its throat with a quick, heavy slash. Blood had spurted out on the snow and the doe had kicked a few times, its eye still blinking up at him. Then the death film crossed it and the doe went.

"It's the only place you ever see red blood, you know?" Roger had said. "In the snow. You see blood out in the woods in the fall, or in the summer, it always looks black. Boy, in this snow, it sure does look red, don't it?"

Andretti's blood would look black on the beige carpet of his office. That's how far Hood had gotten on his recon run. Andretti was famous for his long hours. The hall all around his office was closing down, but his "team" stayed on the job. Andretti called it a team. A photograph on an employee bulletin board outside his office showed Andretti and his staff gathered around a cake, wearing basketball jerseys. Andretti, of course, wore number 1.

"Mother," Hood said, closing his eyes to dream and maybe to pray. The stone pressed on his chest. Andretti's blood would be black on the carpet. He would do it tomorrow, just after the hall closed.

The night was dark and filled with visions, even in the suffocating motel room. Hood woke at one o'clock, and three, four and five. At six, he got up, weary but unable to sleep. He shaved, cleaned up, put on his best suit, feeling the stone weight around his neck, the small pistol in his pocket.

He walked to the train station, caught a ride across the river, walked to Central Park. Checked the zoo and the Metropolitan Museum. Cruised the van Goghs and the Degas, lingered with the Renoirs and Monets. He liked the outdoor lushness of the Impressionists. His own country, out along the Missouri in South Dakota, was all brown and tan for most of the year. But there were times, in the spring, when you'd find small mudflats overflowing with wildflowers, where side creeks ran down to the river. He could peer at the Monets and smell the hot prairie spice of the black-eyed Susans. . . .

It took forever for the time to come. When it did, he rode downtown on the subway, pinching out his emotions, one by one. Thinking back to his hours on Bear Butte, the arid, stoic beauty of the countryside. The distant scream of the Black Hills, raped by the whites who promoted each natural mystery with a chrome-yellow billboard.

By the time he reached the hall, he felt as close to stone as he ever had. A few minutes before five, he walked into the hall and took the stairs to the fifth floor.

Andretti's welfare department took up twelve floors of the hall, but his personal office consisted of a suite of four rooms. Hood had calculated that six to eight people regularly worked in those rooms: Andretti and his secretary; a receptionist; three aides, one male and two female; and a couple of clerks on an irregular basis. The clerks and receptionist fled at five o'clock on the dot. He shouldn't have more than five people to deal with.

On the fifth floor, Hood checked the hallway, then walked quickly down to the public rest room. He entered one of the stalls, sat down and opened his shirt. The obsidian knife hung from his neck on a deerhide thong, taken from the doe killed the year before. He pulled the thong over his neck and slipped the knife into his left jacket pocket. The gun was in his right.

Hood looked at his watch. Three minutes after five. He decided to wait a few more minutes and sat on the toilet, watching the second hand go 'round. The watch had cost twelve dollars, new. A Timex; his wife had bought it when it looked as if he might get a job with a state road crew. But the job had fallen through and all he had left was the Timex.

When the Timex said 5:07, Hood stood up, his soul now as hard as the knife. The hallway was empty. He walked quickly down to Andretti's office, looking to his right as he passed the main hall. A woman was waiting for the elevator. She glanced at him, then away. Hood continued to Andretti's office, paused with his hand on the knob, then pushed it open. The receptionist had gone, but he heard laughter from the other side of the panel behind her desk.

Putting his hand in his jacket pocket, on the gun, he stepped around the panel. Two of the aides, a man and a woman, were leaning on desks, talking. Through an open door, he could see Andretti, working in shirtsleeves behind a green goosenecked lamp. There was at least one more person in his office with him.

When he came around the panel, the woman didn't notice him for a moment, but the man saw him and frowned slightly. Then the woman turned her head and said, "I'm sorry, we're closed."

Hood took his hand from his pocket, with the gun in it, and said, "Don't say a word or make a sound. Just walk into Mr. Andretti's office."

"Oh, no," said the woman. The man clenched his fists and slipped off the desk.

Hood pointed the gun at his head and said, "I don't want to kill you, but I will. Now walk." He had now moved out of Andretti's line of sight. "Move," he said.

They moved reluctantly, toward Andretti's office. "If you do anything, if you touch a door, if you say anything, I will shoot you," Hood said quietly as they approached Andretti's office.

The man stepped inside, followed by the woman. Hood said, "Off to the side." The man said, "Boss, we've got a problem." Andretti looked up and said, "Oh, shit."

A woman was slumped in a chair in front of Andretti's desk, her face caught in a smile which seeped away when she saw Hood; Hood thought the word *seeped,* because of the slowness with which it left. As though she didn't want to disturb him. As though she wanted to think it was a joke.

"Where's the secretary?" Hood asked Andretti.

"She went home early," Andretti said. "Listen, my friend . . ."

"Be quiet. We've got some business to do, but I have to arrange these people first. I don't want them rushing me while we talk."

"If you've got a problem . . ."

"I've got a problem, all right," Hood interrupted. "It's how to keep from shooting one of these people if they don't do what I say. I want you to all lay down, facedown, on the rug against that wall."

"How do we know you won't shoot us?"

"Because I promise not to. I don't want to hurt you. But I promise I *will* shoot you if you don't get down on the floor."

"Do it," Andretti ordered.

The three backed away toward the wall, then sat down.

"Roll over, facedown," Hood said. They flattened themselves out, one of the women craning her neck to see him. "Look at the rug, lady, okay?"

When they were staring at the rug, Hood moved slowly around Andretti's desk. Andretti was a big man, and young; early thirties. No more than thirty-five.

"Let me explain what I'm about to do, Mr. Andretti," Hood said as he moved. He and Bluebird and the others had thought this out, and decided that lying would be best. "I'm going to put some cuffs on you and then I'm going to make some phone calls downtown on behalf of my people. I'm going to put the cuffs on because I don't want you causing trouble. If everybody cooperates, nobody gets hurt. Do you understand?"

"I understand what you're saying, but I don't understand what you want."

"We'll talk that out," Hood said reassuringly. He was behind Andretti, and he reached out and touched him on the temple with the barrel of the pistol. "Put your hands behind your back, clasp them."

When Andretti had done that, Hood said, "Now, look straight back. No, arch your back and tilt your head back. I want to show you this before I do it."

"What?" Andretti asked, dropping his head straight back.

"This," Hood said. He'd changed the gun for the knife, caught Andretti's hair in his left hand and slashed him with the stone, cutting deeper, much deeper, much fiercer, than he had with the doe.

"Ahh," he grunted as the blood spurted from Andretti's neck. Andretti's hands pounded on his desk and he began coughing, choking, looking for Hood. One of the women half sat, saw Andretti and screamed. Hood fired a single shot at her white face and she dropped down. He didn't know whether he had hit her or not, but the man now rolled and the other woman began scrambling across the rug. Hood hollered "Stop" and fired a shot into the man's back. The man arched and Hood was out the door, down the hallway and in the stairwell, running, the screams fading as doors closed.

Gun in pocket, knife in pocket, first landing down. He looked at his hands. Clean. Looked at his pants. Clean. Blood on his shirt, a spot on his jacket. He pulled the jacket shut, third landing down. Ground floor. Into the lobby. Guard at the desk, looking up. Past the guard, into the street. Down a block. Into the subway. The token. Wait. Wait. Wait for running feet, shouts, cops, but nothing but the damp smell of the subway and the clatter of an approaching train.

It took him an hour to get back to Jersey. A half-hour after that, he was in his car, heading west into the setting sun.


In Oklahoma City, Leo Clark stood outside the federal courthouse and looked up. Scouting. The stone blade hung heavy around his neck.

# 4

Jennifer came out of the bathroom, still naked. She was tall, slender, small-breasted and blonde; she had dark eyebrows under her champagne bangs and blue eyes that sometimes, when she was angry, went the color of river ice. Lucas hooked her with his arm as she passed the bed, and pulled her stomach into his face.

"That was nice," he said. "We should do it more often."

"I'm here," she said.

Lucas nuzzled her stomach and she pushed his head away.

"You're messing with my flab."

"It's all gone."

"No, it's not." Jennifer flipped on the room light, pushed the door shut and pirouetted in the full-length mirror mounted on the back. "I've got tummy-stretch and butt-hang. I can handle the butt. The tummy is tough."

"You goddamn yuppie women have the weirdest enthusiasms," Lucas said lazily, lying back on the bed, watching her. "You look perfect."

She skipped past him, eluding his arm, and took a cotton nightgown off the dresser. "I can't decide whether you're just naturally full of shit or unnaturally horny," she said as she slipped it over her head.

Lucas shrugged, grinned and leaned back on the oversize pillow. "Whichever it is, it works. I get laid a lot."

"I should kick you out of here, Davenport," Jennifer said. "I . . . Is that the baby?"

He listened and heard the baby's low crying from the next room. "Yup."

"Time to eat," Jennifer said.

They had never married, but Lucas and Jennifer Carey had an infant daughter. Lucas pressed for a wedding. Jennifer said maybe—sometime. Not now. She lived with the baby in a suburban townhouse south of Minneapolis, fifteen minutes from Lucas' house in St. Paul.

Lucas rolled off the bed and followed Jennifer into the baby's room. The moment the door opened, Sarah stopped crying and began to gurgle.

"She's wet," Jennifer said when she picked her up. She handed Sarah to Lucas. "You change her. I'll go heat up the glop."

Lucas carried Sarah to the changing table, pulled the tape-tabs loose from the diaper and tossed the diaper in a disposal can. He whistled while he worked, and the baby peered at him in fascination, once or twice pursing her lips as though she were about to start whistling herself. Lucas cleaned her bottom with wet-wipes, tossed the wipes after the diaper, powdered her and put a new diaper on her. By the time he finished, Sarah was bubbling with delight.

"Jesus Christ, you are positively dangerous around *anything* female," Jennifer said from the doorway.

Lucas laughed, picked up Sarah and bounced her on the palm of one hand. The baby chortled and grabbed his nose with surprising power.

"Whoa, whoa, wet go ub Daddy's nose. . . ." Jennifer said he sounded like Elmer Fudd when he spoke in baby talk. Sarah whacked him in the eye with her other hand.

"Jesus, I'm getting mugged," Lucas said. "What do you think you're doing, kid, whopping on your old man . . . ?"

The phone rang. Lucas glanced at his wrist, but he'd taken his watch off. It was late, though, after midnight. Jennifer stepped down the hall to the phone. A second later, she was back.

"It's for you."

"Nobody knew I was here," Lucas said, puzzled.

"It's the shift commander, what's-his-name . . . Meany. Daniel told him to try here."

"I wonder what's going on?" Lucas padded down the hall to the phone, picked it up and said, "Davenport."

"This is Harry Meany," said an old man's voice. "The chief said to track you down and get your ass in here. He'll see you in his office in half an hour."

"What happened?"

"I don't know. Lester and Anderson are already here and Sloan's on his way."

"You've got nothing going?" Lucas asked.

"Not a thing," Meany said. "A 7-Eleven got knocked off over on University, but that's nothing new. Nobody hurt."

"Hmph." Lucas scratched his chin, considering. "All right, I'll be down."

Lucas hung up and stood with his hand on the phone, staring blankly at the picture hung above it, a hand-colored print of an English cottage. Jennifer said, "What?"

"I don't know. There's a meeting. Daniel, Lester, Anderson, Sloan. Me."

"Huh." She posed with her hands on her hips. "What are you working?"

"Not much," Lucas said. "We're still getting rumors about guns going out of here, but nothing we can pin down. There's been a lot of crack action. That's about it."

Jennifer nodded. She had been TV3's top street reporter for ten years. After Sarah had arrived, she'd taken a partial leave of absence and begun working as a producer. But the years on the street were still with her: she had both an eye and a taste for breaking news.

"You know what it sounds like?" she asked, a calculating look on her face. "It sounds like the team Daniel set up last year. The Maddog group."

"But there's nothing going on," Lucas said. He shook his head again and walked to the bathroom.

"You'll let me know?" she called after him.

"If I can."

Lucas suspected that early city fathers had built the Minneapolis City Hall as an elaborate practical joke on their progeny. A liverish pile of granite, it managed to be both hot in the summer and cold in winter. In the spring and fall, in the basement, where his office was, the walls sweated a substance that looked like tree sap. Another detective, a lapsed Catholic like Lucas, had suggested that they wait for a good bout of sweating, carefully crack his office wall in a likeness of Jesus and claim a holy stigmata.

"We could make a buck," he said enthusiastically.

"I'm not real big in the Church anymore," Lucas said dryly. "But I'd just as soon not be excommunicated."

"Chickenshit."

Lucas circled the building, dumped the Porsche in a cops-only space. The chief's corner office was lit. As he walked around the nose of the car and stepped onto the curb, a Chevy station wagon pulled up behind the Porsche and the driver tapped the horn. A moment later, Harrison Sloan climbed out of the wagon.

"What's happening?" Lucas asked.

Sloan shrugged. He was a thin man with soft brown puppy eyes and a thin mustache. He might have played an RAF fighter pilot in a World War II movie, a pilot named Dicky. He was wearing a sweatsuit and tennis shoes. "I don't know. I was asleep. Meany called and told me to get my ass down here."

"Same with me," Lucas said. "Big mystery."

As they pushed through the outer doors, Sloan asked, "How's the hand?"

Lucas looked down at the back of his hand and flexed it. The Maddog had broken several of the bones between his wrist and knuckles. When he squeezed hard, it still hurt. The doctors said it might always hurt. "Pretty good. The strength is back. I've been squeezing a rubber ball."

"Ten years ago, if you'd been hurt like that, you'd have been a cripple," Sloan said.

"Ten years ago I might have been quick enough to shoot the sonofabitch before he got to me," Lucas said.

City Hall was quiet, smelling of janitor's wax and disinfectant. The soles of their shoes made a rubbery flap-flap-flap as they walked down the dim hallways, and their voices rattled off the marble as they speculated about Daniel's call. Sloan thought the hurried meeting involved a political problem.

"That's why the rush in the middle of the night. They're trying to sort it out before the newspapers get it," he said.

"So why Lester and Anderson? Why bring Robbery–Homicide into it?"

"Huh." Sloan nibbled at his mustache. "I don't know."

"It's something else," said Lucas. "Somebody's dead."

The outer door of the chief's office was open. Lucas and Sloan stepped inside and found Quentin Daniel in the dark outer office, poking at his secretary's desk. Daniel was a broad man with the open, affable face of a neighborhood butcher. Only his eyes, small, quick, probing, betrayed the brain behind the friendly face.

"Stealing paper clips?" Sloan asked.

"You can never find any goddamn matches when you need them, and nobody smokes anymore," Daniel grumbled. He was an early-to-bed, early-to-rise type, but he looked alert and almost happy. "Come on in."

Frank Lester, the deputy chief for investigations, and slat-thin Harmon Anderson, a computer savant and Lester's assistant, were perched on side chairs opposite Daniel's desk. Lucas and Sloan took empty chairs and Daniel settled behind the desk.

"I've been on the phone all evening. Frank and Harmon have been here for most of it," Daniel told Lucas and Sloan. "There's been a killing in New York City. A commissioner of welfare. A little after five o'clock this evening, their time. He was a prize Italian named John Andretti. Either of you guys hear of him?"

Lucas and Sloan both shook their heads. "Nope," said Sloan. "Should we?"

"He's been in the *Times* quite a bit," said Daniel, with a shrug. "He was a businessman who was getting into politics. Had some different ideas about welfare . . . Anyway, he's got big family money. Construction, banking, all that. Went to Choate. Went to Harvard. Went to Yale Law. He had these great teeth and this great-looking old lady with great-looking tits and four great-looking kids and nobody in the family pushes dope or drinks too much or fucks anybody else's husband or wife, and they all go to church on Sunday. His old man had him set to run for Congress this fall and then maybe the Senate in four years. You know, the New York media were starting to call him the Italian John Kennedy. . . ."

"So what happened?" Lucas asked.

"He got himself killed. In his office. There were three witnesses. This guy comes in, he's got a pistol. He backs everybody off, then steps around behind Andretti. Before anybody can say 'Boo,' this guy—he's an Indian, by the way—he grabs Andretti, pulls his head back and slits his throat with a weird-looking stone knife."

"Oh, fuck," said Lucas. Sloan was sitting in his chair with his mouth open. Anderson watched them in amusement, while Lester looked worried.

"That's exactly right," said Daniel. He leaned forward, took a cigar from a brand-new humidor, held it under his nose, sniffed, then put the cigar back in the humidor. " 'Oh, fuck.' The Indian also shot one of Andretti's aides, but he'll be okay."

Anderson picked up the story. "The Andretti family went berserk and started calling in debts. The governor, the mayor, everybody is getting in on the act." Anderson was wearing plaid pants, a striped shirt and shiny yellow-brown vinyl shoes. "The New York cops are running around like chickens with their heads cut off."

"Andretti was one of the best-connected guys in New York City," Daniel added. "He's got twenty brothers and sisters and cousins and his old man and his old lady. They got an ocean of money and two oceans of political clout. They want blood."

"And they think whoever killed Andretti was working with this Bluebird guy?" asked Lucas.

"Look at the killings," Daniel said, spreading his arms. "It's obvious. And there's more to it. Andretti's office building had a videotape monitor on a continuous loop. The witnesses picked out the killer. It's a horseshit picture and they've only got him for about ten seconds, walking through the lobby, but they released it to the television stations an hour ago. A few minutes after they put it on TV, a motel owner from Jersey called up and said the guy might have been at his motel. The Jersey cops checked and they think he's right. They've got no license-plate number—it wasn't that kind of motel—but the owner remembers the guy had Minnesota plates. He remembers that when the guy was checking out, he said he was heading back home. The motel owner said there was no question about him being an Indian. And then there was the other thing."

"What's that?" Sloan asked.

"The New York cops held back the part about the stone knife," Daniel said. "They told the media that Andretti had been stabbed, but nothing about the knife. So this motel owner asked the Jersey cops, 'Did he stab him with that big fucking stone knife?' The cops say, 'What?' And this motel owner, he says his Indian wore a stone knife around his neck, on a leather thong. He saw him at the Coke machine, wearing an undershirt with the knife hanging down."

"So we know for sure," Sloan said.

"Yeah. And he seems to be coming this way." Daniel leaned back in his chair, put his hands on his stomach and twiddled his thumbs.

Lucas pulled his lip, thinking about it. After a moment of silence, he looked up at the chief. "This guy have braids?"

"The killer? Didn't say anything about braids . . ." He hunted around his desktop for a moment, picked up a piece of computer printout, read it and said, "Nope. Hair down over the tops of his ears and just over his shirt collar. Longish, but not long enough for braids."

"Shit."

"Why?"

"Because the guy who did Cuervo had braids."

The others glanced at each other and Daniel said, "He could have cut it."

"I said the same thing about Bluebird, when we took him down," Lucas said.

"Oh, boy," Lester rasped, rubbing the back of his neck. He was the department's front man on cases that drew media attention. "That'd make three. If there are two, the media's gonna go nuts. If there's three . . . I've been burned before, I don't need this shit."

Sloan grinned at him. "It's gonna be bad, Frank," he said, teasing. "This guy sounds like big headlines. When the networks and the big papers get a whiff of conspiracy, they'll be on you like white on rice. Especially with the part about the stone knives. They'll love the stone knives."

"The local papers already figured it out. Five minutes after the news came across on the Indian angle, we were getting calls on Bluebird. *StarTribune, Pioneer Press,* all the stations. AP's got it on the wire," said Anderson.

"Like flies on a dead cat," Sloan said to Lester.

"So we're setting up a team, just like we did with the Maddog. I'll announce it at a press conference tomorrow morning," said Daniel. "Frank will run the out-front investigation and handle the press on a daily basis. Harmon will get the database going again. Just like with the Maddog. Every goddamn scrap of information, okay? Notebooks for everybody."

"I'll set it up tonight," Anderson said. "I'll get somebody to duplicate copies of the Bluebird mug shot."

"Good. Get me a bunch for the press conference." Daniel turned to Sloan. "I want you to backtrack everybody connected with Bluebird. He's our hold on this thing. If we get an ID on the New York killer, I want you to track down everybody who knew him. You'll be pretty much independent, but you report to Anderson every day, every move. Everything you get goes into the database."

"Sure," Sloan nodded.

"Lucas, you're on your own, just like with the Maddog," Daniel said. "Our contacts with the Indian community are fuckin' terrible. You're the only guy who has any."

"Not many," said Lucas.

"They're all we got," said Daniel.

"What about bringing in Larry Hart? We've used him before. . . ."

"Good." Daniel snapped his fingers and pointed at Lester. "Call Welfare tomorrow and ask them if we can detach Hart as a resource guy. We'll pick up his salary."

"What is he?" asked Sloan. "Chippewa?"

"Sioux," said Lucas.

"He's strange, is what he is," said Anderson. "He's got some genealogical stuff stored away in the city computers. The systems guys would shit if they knew about it."

Lucas shrugged. "He's an okay guy."

"So let's get him," said Daniel. He stood up and paced slowly away from his desk, his hands in his pants pockets. "What else?"

Bluebird's funeral would be monitored. Intelligence would attempt to identify everyone who attended and run histories on them. Sloan would build a list of friends and relatives who might have known about Bluebird's activities. They would be interviewed by selected Narcotics and Intelligence detectives. Anderson would press the Jersey cops for any available details on the killer's appearance and his car and run them against known Indian felons from Minnesota, Wisconsin, Nebraska and the Dakotas.

"It'll be a fuckin' circus, starting bright and early tomorrow morning," said Daniel. "And I'll tell you what: When this New York guy gets here, I want us on top of this thing. I want us to look good, not like a bunch of rube assholes."

Anderson cleared his throat. "I don't think it's a guy, chief. I think it's a woman," he said.

Sloan and Lucas glanced at each other. "What are you talking about?" asked Sloan.

"We told you, didn't we? No? The goddamn Andretti family is putting the screws on the New York cops. They want to send somebody out here to *observe* our investigation," said Daniel. He turned to Anderson. "You say it's a woman?"

"Yeah. That's what I understood. Unless they got male cops named Lillian. She's a lieutenant."

"Huh," said Daniel. He stroked his chin, as though grooming a goatee. "Whoever it is, I can guarantee she's heavy-duty."

"Where'll we put her?" asked Lester.

"Let her work with Sloan," Daniel said. "That'll give her some time on the street. Give her the feeling she's doing something."

He looked around the room. "Anything else? No? Let's do it."

# 5

The barbershop had one chair, a turn-of-the-century model with cracked black leather seats. A mirror was mounted on the wall behind the chair. Below the mirror, on a shelf, stood a line of bottles with luminescent yellow lotions and ruby-red toilet waters. Sunlight played through them like a visual pipe organ.

When Lucas walked in, William Dooley was pushing a flat broom around the floor, herding snips of black hair into a pile on the flaking brown linoleum.

"Officer Davenport," Dooley said gravely. Dooley was old and very thin. His temples looked papery, like eggshells.

"Mr. Dooley." Lucas nodded, matching the old man's gravity. He climbed into the chair. Dooley moved behind him, tucked a slippery nylon bib into his collar and stood back.

"Just a little around the ears?" he asked. Lucas didn't need a haircut.

"Around the ears and the back of the neck, Mr. Dooley," Lucas said. The slanting October sunlight dappled the linoleum below his feet. A sugar wasp bounced against the dusty window.

"Bad business about that Bluebird," Lucas said after a bit.

Dooley's snipping scissors had been going chip-chip-chip. They paused just above Lucas' ear, then resumed. "Bad business," he agreed.

He snipped for another few seconds before Lucas asked, "Did you know him?"

"Nope," Dooley said promptly. After another few snips, he added, "Knew his daddy, though. Back in the war. We was in the Pacific together. Not the same unit, but I seen him from time to time."

"Did Bluebird have any people besides his wife and kids?"

"Huh." Dooley stopped to think. He was halfbreed Sioux, with an Indian father and a Swedish mother. "He might have an aunt or an uncle or two out at Rosebud. That's where they'd be, if there are any left. His ma died in the early fifties and his old man went four or five years back, must have been."

Dooley stared sightlessly through the sunny window. "No, by God," he said in a creaking voice after a minute. "His old man died in the summer of 'seventy-eight, right between those two bad winters. Twelve years ago. Time passes, don't it?"

"It does," Lucas said.

"You want to know something about being an Indian, Officer Davenport?" Dooley asked. He'd stopped cutting Lucas' hair.

"Everything helps."

"Well, when Bluebird died—the old man—I went off to his funeral, out to the res. He was a Catholic, you know? They buried him in a Catholic cemetery. So I went up to the cemetery with the crowd from the funeral and they put him in the ground, and everybody was standing around. Now most of the graves were all together, but I noticed that there was another bunch off in a corner by themselves. I asked a fellow there, I said, 'What's them graves over there?' You know what they were?"

"No," said Lucas.

"They were the Catholic suicides. The Catholics don't allow no suicides to be buried in the regular part of the cemetery, but there got to be so many suicides that they just kind of cut off a special corner for them. . . . You ever hear of anything like that?"

"No, I never did. And I'm a Catholic," Lucas said.

"You think about that. Enough Catholic suicides on one dinky little res to have their own corner of the cemetery."

Dooley stood looking through the window for another few seconds, then caught himself and went back to work. "Not many Bluebirds left," he said. "Mostly married off, went away east or west. New York and Los Angeles. Lost their names. Good people, though."

"Crazy thing he did."

"Why?" The question was so unexpected that Lucas half turned his head and caught the sharp point of the scissors in the scalp.

"Whoa, did that hurt?" Dooley asked, concern in his voice.

"Nah. What'd you . . . ?"

"Almost stuck a hole in you," Dooley interrupted. He rubbed at Lucas' scalp with a thumb. "Don't see no blood."

"What do you mean, 'Why?' " Lucas persisted. "He cut a guy's throat. Maybe two guys."

There was a long moment of silence, then, "They needed them cut," Dooley said. "There weren't no worse men for the Indian community. I read the Bible, just like anybody. What Bluebird did was wrong. But he's paid, hasn't he? An eye for an eye. They're dead and he's dead. And I'll tell you this, the Indian people got two big weights off their backs."

"Okay," said Lucas. "I can buy it. Ray Cuervo was an asshole. Excuse the language."

"I heard the word before," Dooley said. "I wouldn't say you was wrong. And not about this Benton fella, either. He was bad as Cuervo."

"So I'm told," Lucas said.

Dooley finished the trim above Lucas' ear, pushed his head forward until his chin rested on his chest, and did the back of his neck.

"There's been another killing, in New York," Lucas said. "Same way as Cuervo and Benton. Throat cut with a stone knife."

"Saw it on TV," Dooley acknowledged. He pointed at the black-and-white television mounted in the corner of the shop. "*Today* show. Thought it sounded pretty much the same."

"Too much," Lucas said. "I've been wondering . . ."

"If I might of heard anything? Just talk. You know Bluebird was a sun-dancer?"

"No, I didn't know," Lucas said.

"Check his body, if you still got it. You'll find scars all over his chest where he pulled the pegs through." Lucas winced. As part of the Sioux ceremony, dancers pushed pegs through the skin of their chests. Cords were attached to the pegs, and the dancers dangled from poles until the pegs ripped out. "There's another thing. Bluebird was a sun-dancer for sure, but there's folks around saying that a couple years ago, he got involved in this ghost-dance business."

"Ghost dance? I didn't think that was being done," Lucas said.

"Some guys came down from Canada, tried to start it up. They had a drum, went around to all the reservations, collecting money, dancing. Scared the heck out of a lot of people, but I haven't heard anything about them lately. Most Indian people think it was a con game."

"But Bluebird was dancing?"

"That's what I heard. . . ." Dooley's voice trailed off and Lucas turned and found the old man staring out the window again. There was a park across the street, with grass worn brown by kids' feet and the fall frosts. An Indian kid was working on an upturned bike in the middle of the park and an old lady tottered down the sidewalk toward a concrete drinking fountain. "I don't think it means much," Dooley said. He turned back to Lucas. "Except that Bluebird was a man looking for religion."

"Religion?"

"He was looking to be saved. Maybe he found it," Dooley said. He sighed and moved close behind Lucas and finished the trim with a few final snips. He put the scissors down, brushed cut hair off Lucas' neck, unpinned the bib and shook it out. "Sit tight for a minute," he said.

Lucas sat and Dooley found his electric trimmers and shaved the back of Lucas' neck, then slapped on a stinging palmful of aromatic yellow oil.

"All done," he said.

Lucas slid out of the chair, asked, "How much?" Dooley said, "The regular." Lucas handed him three dollars.

"I haven't heard anything," Dooley said soberly. He looked Lucas in the eyes. "If I had, I'd tell you—but I don't know if I'd tell you what it was. Bluebird was the Indian people, getting back some of their own."

Lucas shook his head, sensing the defiance in the old man. "It's hard to believe you said that, Mr. Dooley. It makes me sad," he said.

Indian Country was full of Dooleys.

Lucas quartered through it, touching the few Indians he knew: a seamstress at an awnings shop, a seafood broker, a heating contractor, clerks at two gas stations and a convenience store, an out-of-business antique dealer, a keymaker, a cleaning lady, a car salesman. An hour before Bluebird's funeral was scheduled to begin, he left his car in an alley and walked across the street to Dakota Hardware.

A bell over the door jingled, and Lucas stopped for a moment, waiting for his eyes to adjust to the gloom. Earl May came out of the back room wearing a leather apron and flashed a smile. Lucas walked back and watched the smile fade.

"I was about to say, 'Good to see you,' but I guess you're here to ask questions about Bluebird and that killing in New York," May said. He turned his head and yelled into the back, "Hey, Betty, it's Lucas Davenport."

Betty May stuck her head through the curtain between the back room and the store. "Lucas, it's been a while," she said. She had a round face, touched by old acne scars, and a husky voice that might have sung the blues.

"There's not much around about Bluebird," said Earl. He looked at his wife. "He's asking about the killings."

"That's what everybody tells me," Lucas said. Earl was standing with his arms crossed. It was a defensive position, a push-off stance, one that Lucas had not seen before with the Mays. Behind her husband, Betty unconsciously took the same position.

"You'll have trouble dealing with the community on this one," she said. "Benton was bad, Cuervo was worse. Cuervo was so bad that when his wife got down to his office, after the police called her, she was smiling."

"But what about this guy in New York, Andretti?" Lucas asked. "What the hell did he do?"

"Andretti. The liberal with good accountants," Earl snorted. "He called himself a realist. He said there were people that you have to write off. He said that it made no difference whether you threw money at the underclass or just let it get along. He said the underclass was a perpetual drag on the people who work."

"Yeah?" said Lucas.

"A lot of people want to hear that," Earl continued. "And he might even be right about some people—winos and junkies. But there's one big question he doesn't answer. What about the kids? That's the question. You're seeing a genocide. The victims aren't the welfare queens. The victims are the kids."

"You can't think this is right, these people being killed," Lucas argued.

Earl shook his head. "People die all the time. Now some folks are dying who were hurting the Indian people. That's too bad for them and it's a crime, but I can't get too upset about it."

"How about you, Betty?" Lucas asked. He turned to the woman, disturbed. "Do you feel the same way?"

"Yeah, I do, Lucas," she said.

Lucas peered at them for a moment, studying Earl's face, then Betty's. They were the best people he knew. What they thought, a lot of people would think. Lucas shook his head, rapped the counter with his knuckles and said, "Shit."

\*        \*        \*

Bluebird's funeral was . . . Lucas had to search for the right word. He finally settled on *peculiar*. Too many of the gathered Indians were shaking hands, with quick grins that just as quickly turned somber.

And there were too many Indians for one guy who wasn't that well known. After the coffin had been lowered into the ground, and the last prayers said, they gathered in groups and clusters, twos and threes, talking. An air of suppressed celebration, Lucas thought. Somebody had lashed out. Bluebird had paid, but there were others still at it, taking down the assholes. Lucas watched the crowd, searching for faces he knew, people he might tap later.

Riverwood Cemetery was a working-class graveyard in a working-class neighborhood. Bluebird was buried on a south-facing slope under an ash tree. His grave would look up at the sun, even in winter. Lucas stood on a small rise, next to one of the city's increasingly rare elms, thirty yards from the gravesite. Directly opposite him, across the street from the cemetery and a hundred feet from the grave, were more watchers. The catsup-colored Chevy van fit into the neighborhood like a perfect puzzle piece. In the back, two cops made movies through the dark windows.

Identifying everyone would be impossible, Lucas thought. The funeral had been too big and too many people were simply spectators. He noticed a white woman drifting along the edges of the crowd. She was taller than most women and a little heavy, he thought. She glanced his way, and from a distance, she was a sulky, dark-haired madonna, with an oval face and long heavy eyebrows.

He was still following her progress through the fringe of the crowd when Sloan ambled up and said, "Hello, there." Lucas turned to say hello. When he turned back to the funeral crowd a moment later, the dark-haired woman was gone.

"You talk to Bluebird's old lady?" Lucas asked.

"I tried," Sloan said. "I couldn't get her alone. She had all these people around, saying, 'Don't talk to the cops, honey. Your man is a hero.' They're shutting her down."

"Maybe later, huh?"

"Maybe, but I don't think we'll get much," Sloan said. "Where're you parked?"

"Around the corner."

"So am I." They picked their way between graves, down the shallow slope toward the street. Some of the graves were well tended, others were weedy. One limestone gravemarker was so old that the name had eroded away, leaving only the fading word FATHER. "I was talking to one of the people at her house. The guy said Bluebird hadn't been around that much. In fact, he and his old lady were probably on the edge of breaking up," Sloan said.

"Not too promising," Lucas agreed.

"So what're you doing?"

"Running around picking up bullshit," Lucas said. He looked one last time for the dark-haired woman but didn't see her. "I'm headed over to the Point. Yellow Hand's up there. Maybe he's heard something more."

"It's worth a try," Sloan said, discouraged.

"He's my last shot. Nobody wants to talk."

"That's what I get," Sloan said. "They're rootin' for the other side."


The Point was a row of red-brick townhouses that had been converted to single-floor apartments. Lucas stepped inside the door, pushed it shut and sniffed. Boiled cabbage, a few days old. Canned corn. Oatmeal. Fish. He reached back to his hip, slipped the Heckler and Koch P7 out of its holster and put it in his sport coat pocket.

Yellow Hand's room was five floors up, in what had once been a common-storage attic. Lucas stopped on the landing at the fourth floor, caught his breath and finished the climb with his hand on the P7. The door at the top of the stairs was closed. He tried the knob without knocking, turned it and pushed the door open.

A man was sitting on a mattress reading a copy of *People* magazine. An Indian, wearing a blue work shirt with the sleeves rolled above his elbows, and jeans and white socks. An army field jacket lay next to the mattress, along with a pair of cowboy boots, a green ginger-ale can, another copy of *People* and a battered volume of *Reader's Digest Condensed Books*. Lucas stepped inside.

"Who are you?" the man asked. His forearms were tattooed—a rose inside a heart on the arm nearer to Lucas, an eagle's wing on the other. Another mattress lay across the room with two people on it, asleep, a man and a woman. The man wore jockey shorts, the woman a rose-colored rayon slip. Her dress lay neatly folded by the mattress and next to that were two chipped cups with a coil heater inside one of them. The floor was littered with scraps of paper, old magazines, empty food packages and cans. The room stank of marijuana and soup.

"Cop," said Lucas. He stepped fully into the room and looked off to his left. A third mattress. Yellow Hand, asleep. "Looking for Yellow Hand."

"He's passed out," said the tattooed man.

"Drinking?"

"Yeah." The man rolled off the mattress and picked up his jacket. Lucas pointed a finger at him.

"Stick around for a minute, okay?"

"Sure, no problem. You got a cigarette?"

"No."

The woman on the second mattress stirred, rolled onto her back and propped herself up on her elbows. She was white, and older than Lucas thought when he first saw her. Forties, he thought. "What's going on?" she asked.

"Cop to see Yellow Hand," said the tattooed man.

"Oh, shit." She squinted at Lucas and he saw she was missing her front teeth. "You got a cigarette?"

"No."

"God damn, nobody ever got no smokes around here," she whined. She looked at the man beside her, poked him. "Get up, Bob. The cops are here." Bob moaned, twitched and snored.

"Leave him," said Lucas. He moved over to Yellow Hand and pushed him with his toe.

"Don't fuck w' me," Yellow Hand said sleepily, batting at the foot.

"Need to talk to you."

"Don't fuck w' me," Yellow Hand said again.

Lucas prodded him a little harder. "Get up, Yellow Hand. This is Davenport."

Yellow Hand's eyes flickered and Lucas thought he looked too old for a teenager. He looked as old as the woman, who was now sitting slouched on the mattress, smacking her lips. The tattooed man stood bouncing on his toes for a second, then reached for a cowboy boot.

"Leave the boots," Lucas said, pointing at him again. "Wake up, Yellow Hand."

Yellow Hand rolled to a sitting position. "What is it?"

"I want to talk." Lucas turned to the tattooed man. "Why'n't you come over here and sit on the mattress?"

"I ain't done a fuckin' thing," the man snarled, suddenly defiant. He was rake thin and had one shoulder turned toward Lucas in an unconscious boxing stance.

"I'm not here to fuck with anybody," Lucas said. "I'm not asking for ID, I'm not calling in for warrants. I just want to talk."

"I don't talk to the fuckin' cops," the tattooed man said. He looked around for support. The woman was staring at the floor, shaking her head; then she spat between her feet. Lucas put his hand in his pocket. The attic space was crowded. Ordinarily, he wouldn't worry about a couple of derelicts and a drifter, but the tattooed man exuded an air of toughness. If there were a fight, he wouldn't have much room to maneuver.

"We can do it the easy way or we can do it the hard way," he said softly. "Now get your ass over here or I'll kick it up between the ears."

"What you gonna do, cop, you gonna fuckin' shoot me? I ain't got no knife, I ain't got no gun, I'm in my own fuckin' apartment, I ain't seen no warrant, you gonna shoot me?"

The man stepped closer and Lucas took his hand back out of his pocket.

"No, but I might beat the snot out of you," Lucas said. Both the older man and the woman were looking away. If the tattooed man jumped, he would have no support from them. Yellow Hand wasn't likely to help the stranger, so it would be one on one. He braced himself.

"Take it easy, Shadow, you don't want to fight no cop," Yellow said from the mattress. "You know what'd happen then."

Lucas looked from Yellow Hand to the tattooed man and guessed that the tattooed man was on parole.

"You know Benton?" he snapped. "He your PO?"

"No, man. I never met him," the tattooed man said, suddenly closing his eyes and half turning away. The tension ebbed.

"All I want to do is talk," Lucas said mildly.

"You want to talk with a gun in your pocket," said the tattooed man, turning back to him. "Like all whites."

He looked straight at Lucas, and Lucas saw that his eyes were light gray, so light they looked as though cataracts were floating across his irises. The man's body trembled once, again, and then settled into a low vibration, like a guitar string.

"Take it easy," Yellow Hand said again, rubbing his face. "Come on over and sit down. Davenport won't fuck with you."

There was another moment of stress; then, as suddenly as he'd become angry, the tattooed man relaxed and smiled. His teeth were a startling white against his dark face. "Sure. Jeez, I'm sorry, but you come on sudden," he said. He bobbed his head in apology.

Lucas backed up a few steps, wary of the sudden change, uneasy about the eyes. Witch eyes. The tattooed man moved over to Yellow Hand's mattress and sat down on a corner. Lucas watched him for a second, then stepped closer to Yellow Hand, until he was looming over him. He spoke at the top of the teenager's head.

"What do you hear, Yellow Hand? I need everything about Ray Cuervo getting his throat cut. Anything about this guy Benton. Anybody who was friends with Bluebird."

"I don't know about that shit," Yellow Hand said. "I knew Bluebird from out on the res."

"At Fort Thompson?"

"Yeah, man. His sister and my mom used to walk down below the dam and go fishing."

"What do you hear about him lately?" Lucas reached down and grabbed Yellow Hand's hair, just above his ear, and pulled his head back. "Gimme something, Yellow Hand. Talk to me."

"I don't know shit, man, I'm telling the truth," Yellow Hand said sullenly, jerking his hair free. Lucas squatted so he could look Yellow Hand straight in the face. The tattooed man watched Lucas' face over Yellow Hand's shoulder.

"Look. When Benton got killed, you got picked up as a witness," Lucas said, putting a friendly note in his voice. "That's on the record. There are some cops putting together a list. Your name is on it. That means some hardasses from Robbery–Homicide will be checking you out. They aren't going to be friendly, like me. They aren't gonna be no fuckin' pussycats. They aren't going to take care of you, Yellow Hand. If you give me something, I can deal them off. But I got to have something. If I don't get something, they'll figure I didn't squeeze hard enough."

"I could go back to the res," Yellow Hand said.

Lucas shook his head. "What are you going to smoke on the res? Sagebrush? What are you gonna do, sneak down to the tribal store and shoplift boom-boxes? Gimme a break, Yellow Hand. You got all these nice K Marts you can work in the Cities. You got the candy man coming around every night. Shit, you got guys peddling crack at Fort Thompson?"

A tear trickled down Yellow Hand's face and he sniffed. Lucas looked at him. "What have you got, man?" Lucas asked again.

"I heard one thing," Yellow Hand admitted. He glanced at the tattooed man, then quickly looked away. "That's all. It probably don't mean shit."

"Let me hear it. I'll decide."

"You know that hassle last summer? Like two, three months ago, between the bikers and the Indian people out in the Black Hills?"

"Yeah, I saw something about it in the papers."

"What it was, was these bikers come in from all over. They have this big rally up in Sturgis and they have like a truce. There's Angels and Outlaws and Banditos and Satan's Slaves and every fuckin' thing. A whole bunch of them stay in this campground out at a place called Bear Butte. They call it the Bare Butt campground, which already makes some Indian people angry."

"What's this got to do with Bluebird?"

"Let me finish, man," Yellow Hand said angrily.

"Okay."

"Some of these bikers, they get drunk at night and they like to run up the side of the butte on their bikes. The butte's a holy place and there were some medicine people up there, with some guys looking for visions. They came down and they had guns. That's what started the trouble."

"And Bluebird was there?" asked Lucas.

"That's what I heard. He was with this group, searching for visions. And they came down with guns. Yesterday, when this guy in New York gets killed, I was in Dork's Pool Hall down on Lyndale?"

"Yeah?"

"Some guy had a picture cut out of the *StarTribune* from the biker thing. He was showing it around. There was a bunch of cops and a bunch of bikers and the Indian medicine people. One of the guys with a rifle was Bluebird."

"Okay, that's something," Lucas said, patting Yellow Hand on the knee.

"Jesus," said the tattooed man, looking at Yellow Hand.

"What about you?" Lucas asked him. "Where were you during this shit?"

"I got back from Los Angeles yesterday. I still got the bus ticket over by my bed. And I ain't heard nothing, except bullshit."

"What bullshit?"

"You know, that Bluebird went crazy and decided to kill a few of the white people sitting on his back. And how that's a good thing. Everybody says it's a good thing."

"What do you know about Bluebird?"

The tattooed man shrugged. "Never met him. I know the family name, but I'm from Standing Rock. I never went over to Fort Thompson except once, for a powwow. The place is out of the way of everything."

Lucas looked at him and nodded. "What were you doing in Los Angeles?"

"Just went there to look around, you know. Look at movie stars." He shrugged.

"All right," Lucas said after a moment. He looked down at Yellow Hand. There wouldn't be much more. "You two just sit here for a minute, okay?"

Lucas stepped over to the tattooed man's bed. On the floor on the far side, out of sight from the door, was a willow stick with a small red rag tied around the tip in a bundle, what looked like a crumpled bus ticket, and a money clip. Inside the clip were a South Dakota driver's license and a photograph pressed between two pieces of plastic. Lucas bent over and scooped it up.

"What you doin' with my stuff, man?" the tattooed man said. He was on his feet again, vibrating.

"Nothing. Just looking," Lucas said. "Is this what I think it is?"

"It's a prayer stick, from an old ceremony down on the river. I carry it for luck."

"Okay." Lucas had seen one once before. He carefully laid it on the mattress. The bus ticket was out of Los Angeles, dated three days earlier. It might have been an arranged alibi, but didn't feel that way. The SoDak license carried a fuzzy photo of the tattooed man in a white T-shirt. The white eyes glistened like ball bearings, like the eyes of Jesse James in nineteenth-century photographs. Lucas checked the name. "Shadow Love?" he said. "That's a beautiful name."

"Thank you," said the tattooed man. His smile clicked on like a flashlight beam.

Lucas looked at the fading color snapshot. A middle-aged woman in a shapeless dress stood by a rope clothesline. The line was strung between a tree and the corner of a white clapboard house. There was a board fence in the background, and in the distance, a factory chimney. A city, maybe Minneapolis. The woman was laughing, holding up a pair of jeans that had frozen board-stiff. The trees in the background were bare, but the woman was standing on green grass. Early spring or late fall, Lucas thought.

"This your mom?" he asked.

"Yeah. So what?"

"So nothing," Lucas said. "A guy who carries a picture of his mom, he can't be all bad."

After the Point, Lucas gave up and headed back toward City Hall, stopping once at a public telephone outside the *StarTribune*.

"Library," she said. She was small and wistful, falling into her forties. Nobody at the paper paid her any attention.

"You alone?" he asked.

"Yes." He could feel her catch her breath.

"Could you call something up for me?"

"Go ahead," she said.

"Last week of July, first week of August. There was a confrontation between bikers and Indians out in South Dakota."

"Do you have a key word?" she asked.

"Try 'Bear Butte.' " Lucas spelled it for her. There was a moment's silence. "Three hits," she said.

"Did you use any art?" There was another moment of silence.

"Yes," she said. "August first. Three columns, page three."

"Yours or AP?"

"Ours." She named the photographer.

"What are the chances of getting a print?"

"I'd have to lift it from the files," she said, in a hushed voice.

"Could you?"

Another few seconds passed. "Where are you?"

"Right down at the corner, in my car."

"It'll be a minute."

Sloan was leaving City Hall when Lucas arrived.

"Winter coming," he said as they stopped on the sidewalk.

"Still warm," said Lucas.

"Yeah, but it's already getting dark," Sloan said, looking up the street. Cars were creeping out toward the interstate, their lights on.

"Did you get anything today? After I left you?"

"Naw." Then the other man brightened. "I did get a look at that woman cop from New York."

Lucas grinned. "She's worth looking at?"

"Oh, yeah. She's got a lip, you know? She's got this little overbite and she's got this kind of soft look about her like, I don't know, like she'd *moan* or something. . . ."

"Jesus, Sloan . . ."

"Wait'll you take a look at her," Sloan said.

"Is she still here?"

"Yeah. Inside. She went out with Shearson this morning," Sloan laughed. "The lover boy. The good suits."

"He made a move on her?" Lucas asked.

"I'd bet on it," Sloan said. "When he came back, he spent two hours studying his files awful hard. She was sitting around looking cool."

"Hmph." But Lucas grinned. "How'd she get with Shearson? I thought she was going out with you."

"Naw. Shearson gave Lester a blow job and got her assigned to him. Squire her around."

"He's so suave," Lucas said. He said "swave."

"Good title. You ought to write a song," Sloan said, and went on his way.

Lucas saw her in the hallway outside the Robbery–Homicide office. The madonna from the cemetery. She was walking toward him on high heels and he noticed her legs first, then her dark eyes, like pools. He thought about the tattooed man, the shiny pale eyes like flint, eyes you bounced off. With the woman, you fell in. She was wearing a tweed jacket and skirt with a ruffled-front blouse and black tie. She had a paper coffee cup in her hand and Lucas held the door for her.

"Thanks." She smiled and went through, headed for Anderson's cubbyhole. Her voice was low and buttery.

"Um," said Lucas, tagging behind. Her hair was done up in a slightly lop-sided bun and a few loose strands fell across her neck.

"I'm leaving," she told Anderson, leaning into his cubbyhole. "If anything comes overnight, you've got the number."

Anderson was sitting behind an IBM terminal, chewing on the end of a chopstick. The remains of a Chinese dinner were congealing in a white foam carton on his desk and the office stank of overcooked water chestnuts and rum-soaked cigars. "Okay. We'll see if we can find something better for you tomorrow."

"Thanks, Harmon."

She turned and almost bumped into Lucas. He caught a faint scent that was neither water chestnut nor cigar, something expensive from Paris. Anderson said to her, "Do you know Lucas? Davenport?"

"Nice to meet you," she said, stepping back and offering her hand. Lucas took it and shook once, smiling politely. She was larger than he'd thought at first. Deep-breasted, a little pudgy. "You're the guy who blew up the maddog."

"He's the one," Anderson said from behind her. "You get anything, Lucas?"

"Maybe," Lucas said, still looking at the woman. "Harmon didn't mention your name."

"Lily Rothenburg," she said. "Lieutenant, NYPD."

"Homicide?"

"No. I work out of the . . . out of a precinct in Greenwich Village."

Anderson's head was swiveling between them like a spectator at a tennis match.

"How come you're on this one?" Lucas asked. Inside his head, he was doing an inventory. He was wearing a $400 Brooks Brothers tweed sport coat with a pale rose stripe, a dark-blue shirt, tan slacks and loafers. He should look pretty good, he thought.

"Long story," she said. She nodded at the manila envelope in his hand. "What did you get? If you don't mind my asking?"

"A photograph of Bluebird taken on the first of August," he said. He took the photo out of the envelope and handed it to her. "He's the guy with the rifle over his shoulder."

"Who are these people?" A small frown line appeared on her forehead, connecting her bushy dark eyebrows.

"A group of Sioux vision-seekers and a couple of medicine men. I don't know who's who, but they had guns and Bluebird was with them a month ago."

She looked at him over the top of the photograph and their eyes clicked together like two pennies in a pocket. "This could be something," she said. "Where did you get it?"

"Friend," Lucas said.

She broke her eyes away and turned the photo over. The remnants of routing slips were pasted on the back. "A newspaper," she said. "Can we get the other shots on the roll?"

"Think it'd be worth the trouble?"

"Yes," she said. She put her index finger on the head of one of the figures in the photo. "See this guy?"

Lucas looked at the photo again. The tip of her finger was touching the head of a stocky Indian man, but only the outer rim of his face and one eye were visible. The rest was eclipsed behind the head of another figure in the foreground.

"What about him?" He took the photograph and looked more closely at it.

"That could be our man," she said. "The guy who lit up Andretti. It looks a lot like him, but I need a better shot to be sure."

"Whoa." Anderson eased out of his chair to take a look. The lumpy mound of Bear Butte was in the background, gray and brooding, a lonely northern outpost of the Black Hills. In the foreground, a group of Indians, wearing calico shirts and jeans, were gathered behind one of the elderly medicine men. Most of the men were looking to the left of the camera, toward a group of sheriff's deputies. Bluebird was there with his gun, one of the few who were looking more or less at the camera.

"So how do we get back to your friend and see what else is on the negatives?" Lily asked.

"I'll talk to the chief tonight," Lucas said. "We'll have to meet with some of the people at the paper tomorrow morning. First thing."

"Tomorrow?" she snapped, incredulous. "Christ, the guy's on his way here right now. We've got to get going tonight."

"That would be . . . difficult," Lucas said hesitantly.

"What's difficult? We get the negs, print them and find somebody who knows my guy's name."

"Look, I know the papers here. They'll need three meetings and eight consultations before they'll make the pictures," Lucas said. "That won't get done tonight. There's no way that we'll see the negatives."

"If we put on enough heat . . ."

"We're talking bureaucracy here, okay? We can't move it faster than it's willing to move. And if we go tonight, there's a good chance I'll burn my friend. The first thing they'll do is look at their files, and they'll find their record photo's gone. I don't want to do that. I want to get it back in the file."

"Jesus Christ, you fuckin' . . .'" She snapped her mouth shut.

"Shitkickers?"

"I wasn't going to say that," she lied.

"Bullshit. I'll tell you what. I'll get as much done tonight as can get done. All the newspaper people will get called, it'll all be explained, they can have all their meetings, and we'll be over there at eight tomorrow morning, looking at prints."

Her eyes searched his face for a moment. "I don't know," she said finally.

"Look," said Lucas, trying to win her over. "Your killer is driving a junker. If he pushed it as hard as he could, he wouldn't get here until tomorrow night anyway. Not unless he's got a relief driver and they really hammered it out the whole way."

"He was alone in the motel. . . ."

"So we don't lose anything," Lucas said. "And I save my friend's ass, which is a pretty high priority."

"Okay," Lily said. She nodded, her eyes on his face, then stepped past him toward the door. "I'll see you tomorrow, Harmon."

"Yeah." Anderson looked after her as she went through the door. When she was gone, he turned to Lucas, a small smile playing on his face.

"You got the look," he said.

"What's that?"

"Like a bunch of people look after they talk to her. Like you been hit on the forehead with a ball-peen hammer," Anderson said.

*     *     *

Daniel was eating dinner.

"What happened?" he asked when Lucas identified himself.

"We came up with a photo from the *StarTribune*," Lucas said. He explained the rest of it.

"And Lillian thinks he might be the killer?" Daniel asked.

"Yeah."

"Damn, that's good. We can get some mileage out of this. I'll talk to the people at the *Trib*," Daniel said. "What do you think about the approach?"

"Tell them we need the rest of the negatives on that roll and any other rolls they have. Argue that the photos were taken at a public news event, that there is no secret film involved—nothing involving sources, nothing confidential. Tell them if they help catch Andretti's killer, we'll give them the story. And they'll already have the exclusive pictures that solved the assassination."

"You don't think they'll pull the confidentiality shit?" Daniel asked.

"I don't see why they should," Lucas said. "The pictures weren't confidential. And we're talking about serial assassination of major political figures, not some kind of horseshit inciting-to-riot thing."

"Okay. I'll call now."

"We need them as early as we can get them."

"Nine o'clock. We'll get them by nine," Daniel said.

Lucas hung up and dialed the *StarTribune* library. He gave his friend a summary of what had happened and arranged to meet her near the paper's offices.

"It's kind of exciting," she whispered as she leaned over his car. He handed her the manila envelope. "It's like being a mole, in John le Carré."


He left her in a glow and headed home.

Lucas lived in St. Paul. From his front-room window, he could see a line of trees along the Mississippi River gorge and the lights of Minneapolis on the other side. He lived alone, in a house he once thought might be too big. Over ten years, he'd spread out. The double garage took an aging Ford four-wheel-drive that he used for backcountry trips and boat-towing. The basement filled up with weights and workout pads, a heavy bag and a speed bag, shooting gear and a gun safe, tools and a workbench.

Upstairs, the den was equipped with a deep leather chair for dreaming and watching basketball on television. One bedroom was for sleeping, another for guests. He'd converted a third bedroom into a workroom, with an oak drawing table and a bookcase full of references.

Lucas invented games. War games, fantasy games, role-playing games. Games paid for the house and the Porsche and a cabin on a lake in northern Wisconsin. For three months, he had been immersed in a game he called Drorg. "Drorg" was an invented word, inspired by *cyborg*, which itself was a contraction of the words *cybernetics organism*. Cyborgs were humans with artificial parts. A drorg, in Lucas' game, was a drug organism, a human altered and enhanced by designer drugs. To see in the dark, to navigate by sonar with enhanced hearing, to have the strength of a gorilla, the reflexes of a cat. The brain of a genius.

Not all at once, of course. That's where the game came in. And the drugs had penalties. Some lingered: Call for superstrength and it hung on when you needed superintelligence. Call for superintelligence and the drug pushed you to madness and suicide if you couldn't acquire the antidote. Take the pan-effects drug and it flat killed you, period; but not before you achieved su-perabilities and eventually intolerable pleasure.

It all took work. There was the basic plot to write—Drorg was essentially a quest, like most role-playing games. There were also scoring systems to build, opponents to create, boards to design. The publisher was excited about it and was pressing. He wanted to do a computer version of it.

So five or six nights a week, for three months, Lucas had been in the workroom, sitting in a pool of light, plotting his patterns. He listened to classic rock, drank an occasional beer, but mostly laid out a story of information bureaucracies, corporate warfare, 'luded-out underclasses and drorg warriors. Where the story came from, he didn't know; but every night the words were there.

When he got home, Lucas put the car in the garage, went inside and popped a frozen chicken dinner into the microwave. In the five minutes before it was ready, he checked the house, got the paper off the front porch and washed his hands. He'd eaten all the french fries and three of the four chicken nibbles—he wasn't exactly sure what part they were, but they did have bones—when Lily Rothenburg's face popped into his mind.

She came out of nowhere: he hadn't been thinking about her, but suddenly she was there, like a photograph dropped on a table. A big woman, he thought. A little too heavy, and not his style; he liked the athletes, the small muscular gymnasts, the long sleek runners.

Not his style at all.

Lily.

# 6

———•◦•———

Leo Clark was a drunk by the time he was fifteen. At forty, he had been twenty-two years on the street, begging nickels and dimes from the rich burgh-ers of Minneapolis and St. Paul. A lifetime lost.

Then one bitterly cold night in St. Paul, he and another drunk, a white man, were turned out of the mission after an argument with a clerk. They stopped at a liquor store and bought two bottles of rye whiskey. After some argument, they walked down to the railroad tracks. An old tunnel had been boarded up, but the boards were loose. They pried them back and crawled inside.

Late that night, Leo went out, found sticks of creosote-covered scrap lumber along the tracks, dragged it back to the tunnel and started a fire. The two men finished the whiskey in the stinking smoke. Their cheeks, hands and stomachs felt like fire, but their legs and feet were blocks of ice.

The white man had an idea. Up along the bluffs on the Mississippi, he said, were storm sewers that led into the tunnel system under the city. If they could crawl back there, they could lie up on steam pipes. The tunnels would be as warm as the mission and it wouldn't cost them a dime. They could get a Coleman lantern, a few books. . . .

When Leo Clark woke the next morning, the white man was dead. He was lying facedown on the cold ground and had taken a few convulsive bites of the earth as he died: his mouth was half full of oily dirt. Leo Clark could see one of his eyes. It was open, and as flat and silvery and empty as the dime that the steam tunnels wouldn't cost him.

"He died in a fuckin' cave, man; they let him die in a fuckin' hole in the ground," Leo told the cops. The cops didn't give a shit. Nobody else did either: the body went unclaimed, and was eventually dumped in a pauper's grave. Dental X rays were filed with the medical examiner in the improbable case that somebody, someday, showed up looking for the dead man.

After the white man died in the cave, Leo Clark stopped drinking. It didn't happen all at once, but a year later he was sober. He drifted west, back to the res. Became a spiritual man, but with a twist of hate for people who would let men die in holes in the ground. He was forty-six years old, with a face and hands like oak, when he met the Crows.


Leo Clark hid in a corner of a dimly lit parking ramp, between the bumper of a Nissan Maxima and the outer wall of the ramp. He was thirty feet from the locked steel door that led into the apartment building.

A few minutes earlier, he had looped a piece of twelve-pound-test monofilament fishing line around the doorknob. He led the line to the bottom of the door, fastened it with a piece of Magic mending tape and trailed it on to the Maxima. In the low light, the line was invisible. He was waiting for somebody to walk through the door—going in, he hoped, but out would be okay, as long as it wasn't to the Maxima. That would be embarrassing.

Leo Clark lay bathed in the odors of exhaust and oil and thought about his mission. When he had killed Ray Cuervo, the overwhelming emotion had been fear—fear of failure, fear of the cops. He'd known Ray personally, had suffered from his greed, and anger and hate had been there too. But this judge? The judge had been bribed by an oil company in a lawsuit involving the illegal disposal of toxic wastes at the Lost Trees reservation. Leo Clark *knew* that, but he didn't *feel* it. All he felt was the space in his chest. A . . . sadness? Was that what it was?

He had thought his years on the street had burned all of that away: that he'd lost all but the most elemental survival emotions. Fear. Hate. Anger. He wasn't sure whether this discovery, this renewal of feeling, this *sadness,* was a gift or a curse. He would have to think about that: Leo Clark was a careful man.

As for the judge, it would make no difference. He had been weighed and he would die.

Leo Clark had been waiting for twenty minutes when a car pulled into an empty space halfway down the garage. A woman. He could hear her high heels rapping on the concrete. She had her keys in her hand. She opened the door into the building, stepped inside. The door began to swing shut and Leo pulled in the line, popping off the Magic mending tape, putting tension on the line, easing the door shut . . . but not quite enough to latch. He kept up the tension, waiting, waiting, giving the woman time for the elevator, hoping that nobody else came out. . . .

After three minutes, he slid from beneath the car. Keeping the line tight, he walked to the door and eased it open. Nobody in the elevator lobby. He stepped inside, walked past the elevator to the fire stairs, and went up.

The judge was on the sixth floor, one of three apartments. Leo listened at the fire door, heard nothing. Opened the door, looked through, stepped into the empty hallway. Six C. He found the door, rapped softly, though he was sure it was empty. No answer. After another quick look around, he took a bar from his jacket, slipped it into the crack between the door and the jamb and slowly put his weight to it. The door held, held; then there was a low ripping sound and it popped open. Leo stepped inside, into the dark room. Found a chair, sat down and let the sadness flow through him.

Judge Merrill Ball and his girlfriend, whose name was Cindy, returned a few minutes after one in the morning. The judge had his key in the lock before he noticed the damage to the door.

"Jesus, it looks like . . ." he started, but the door flew open, freezing him. Leo Clark was there, his long black braids down on his chest, his eyes wide and straining, his mouth half open, his hand driving up. And in his hand, the razor-edged stone knife . . .

An hour later, in a truck stop off I-35 north of Oklahoma City, Leo Clark sat at the wheel of his car and wept.

*       *       *

Shadow Love walked into the wind, his shoulders hunched, his running shoes crunching through the fallen maple leaves. The black spot floated out ahead of him.

The black spot.

When Shadow Love was a child, his mother had taken him to a neighbor's home. The house smelled of cooking gas and boiled greens, and he could remember the neighbor's fat white legs as she sat on a kitchen table, sobbing. Her husband had a black spot on his lungs. The size of a dime. Nothing to be done, the woman said. Make him comfortable, the doctors said. Shadow Love remembered his mother, gripping the other woman around the shoulders. . . .

And now he had a name for the thing on his mind. The black spot.

Sometimes the invisible people would talk to his mother, plucking at her arms and face and her dress and even her shoes, to get her attention, to tell her what Shadow Love had done. He couldn't remember doing all those things, but the invisible people said he had. They were never wrong, Rosie Love said. They saw everything, knew everything. His mother would beat him with a broom handle for doing those things. She would chase him and pound him on the back, the shoulders, the legs. Afterward, when the invisible people had gone, she would fall on him weeping, begging forgiveness, trying to rub off the bruises as if they were shoe polish. . . .

The black spot had come with the invisible people. When Shadow Love got angry, the black spot popped up in front of his eyes, a hole in the world. He never told his mother about the black spot: she would tell the invisible people and they would demand a punishment. And he never showed his anger, for the same reason. Defiance was the worst of all sins, and the invisible people would howl for his blood.

At some point, the invisible people stopped coming. His mother killed them with alcohol, Shadow Love thought. Her bouts of drunkenness were bad enough, but nowhere near as bad as the invisible people. Although the invisible people were gone, the black spot stayed. . . .

And now it floated in front of his eyes. The fuckin' cop. Davenport. He treated them like dirt. He came in and pointed his finger. Made them sit. Like a trained dog. *Sit,* he said. *Speak,* he said. *Arf.*

The black spot grew and Shadow Love felt dizzy with the humiliation of it. Like a *dog.* His pace picked up, until he was almost running; then he slowed again, threw his head back and groaned, aloud. *Fuckin' dog.* He balled a fist and hit himself on the cheekbone, hard. The pain cut through his anger. The black spot shrank.

*Like a fuckin' dog, you crawled like a fuckin' dog. . . .*

Shadow Love was not dumb. His fathers were running their war and would need him. He couldn't be taken by the cops, not for something as stupid as a fistfight. But it ate at him, the way Davenport had treated him. Made him be *nice . . .*

Shadow Love bought a pistol from a teenaged burglar. It wasn't much of a gun, but he didn't need much of a gun. He gave the kid twenty bucks, slipped the pistol into his waistband and headed back to the Point. He would need a new place to stay, he thought. He couldn't move in with his fathers: they were already jammed into a tiny efficiency. Besides, they didn't want him in their war.

A place to stay. The last time he was in town, he'd have gone to Ray Cuervo. . . .

Yellow Hand's day had been miserable. Davenport had started it, kicking him out of a stupor. A stupor he'd valued. The longer he was asleep, the longer he could put off his problem. Yellow Hand needed his crack. He rolled his upper lip and bit it, thinking about the rush. . . .

After Davenport had gone, Shadow Love had put on his boots and jacket and left without a word. The old white woman had fallen back on her mattress and soon was snoring away with her man, who had never woken up. Yellow Hand had made it out on the street a half-hour later. He'd cruised the local K Mart, but left with the feeling he was being watched. It was the same way at a Target store. Nothing obvious, just white guys in rayon neckties . . .

He wished Gineele and Howdy were still in town. If Gineele and Howdy hadn't gone to Florida, they'd all be rich.

Gineele was very black. When she was working, she wore her hair in corn rows and sported fluorescent pink lipstick. She had a nasty scar on her right cheek, the end product of an ill-considered fight with a man who had a beer can opener in his hand. The scar scared the shit out of everybody.

If Gineele was bad, Howdy was a nightmare. Howdy was white, so white he looked as if he'd been painted. A quick glance at his eyes suggested that this boy was snorting something awful. Ether, maybe. Or jet fuel. Toxic waste. In any case, his eyes were always cranked wide, his mouth was always open, his tongue flicking out like a snake's. To complement his insane face, Howdy wore steel rings around his neck, black leather cuffs with spikes, and knee-high leather boots. He was twenty years old—you could see the youth in his carriage—but his hair was dead-white and fine as spun silk. When Howdy and Gineele went into a K Mart, the white guys in the rayon neckties went crazy. While the two decoys caromed around the store, Yellow Hand took boomboxes out the front door by the cartload.

Jesus. Yellow Hand really needed them. . . .

An hour after he hit the street, he scored a clock-radio and three calculators at a Walgreen's drugstore. He cashed them for a chunk, smoked it, floated away to never-never land. But it was a soiled trip, because even as he went out he was anticipating the cold reality of the crash.

Early in the evening, he tried to steal a toolbox from a filling station. He almost made it. As he was turning the corner, a guy by the gas pumps spotted him and yelled. The box was too heavy to run with, so he dumped it and hauled ass through two blocks of backyards. The gas jockey called the cops and Yellow Hand spent an hour hiding under a boat trailer as a squad car cruised the neighborhood. By the time he started back to the Point, it was fully dark. He had to think. He had to plan. He had only two more days at the Point; then he'd need money for the rent. The nights were getting cold.

Shadow Love was smoking a cigarette when Yellow Hand came in.

"Loan me a couple bucks?" Yellow Hand begged.

"I don't have no money to spend on crack," Shadow Love said. He reached for the hardpack of Marlboros. "I can give you a smoke."

"Aw, man, I wouldn't buy no crack," Yellow Hand whined. "I need to eat. I ain't had nothin' to eat all day." He took the cigarette and Shadow Love held a paper match for him.

"Tell you what," Shadow Love said after a moment, fixing Yellow Hand with his pale eyes. "We can walk up to that taco joint by the river road. I'll buy you a half-dozen tacos."

"That's a long way, man," Yellow Hand complained.

"Fuck ya, then," Shadow Love said. "I'm going. Thanks for lettin' me stay." He'd paid Yellow Hand three dollars to use the mattress.

"All right, all right," Yellow Hand said. "I'm coming. I'm so fuckin' hungry. . . ."

Walking slow, they took twenty minutes to get from the Point to the Mississippi. The river was a hundred feet below them and Shadow Love sidestepped down the slope.

"Where are you going, man?" Yellow Hand asked, puzzled.

"Down to the water. Come on. It's not much further this way." Shadow Love thought about Yellow Hand and Davenport. Yellow Hand had told the cop about the newspaper clipping: that was something. The black spot popped up.

"We gotta climb back up, man," Yellow Hand complained.

"Come on," Shadow Love snapped. The black spot floated out in front of him. His heart was pounding, and the rising power flowed through his blood like gold. He wasn't arguing anymore. Yellow Hand looked back toward the lights of the street, undecided, and finally followed, still bitching under his breath.

They crossed a river access road and continued down to the water, where the riverbank was supported by a concrete wall. Shadow Love stepped onto the wall, drew in a breath of the river air and exhaled. Smelled real. He turned to Yellow Hand, who had climbed onto the wall behind him.

"Lights look great from down here, don't they?" Shadow Love asked. "Look at the reflections in the water."

"I guess," Yellow Hand said, puzzled.

"Look over there, under the bridge," Shadow Love said.

Yellow Hand turned to look. Shadow Love stepped closer, taking the pistol from his waistband. He put it behind Yellow Hand's ear, waited a delicious second, then another and a third, thrilling to the darkness of the act; when he couldn't stand it anymore, the glorious tension, he pulled the trigger.

There was a sharp *pop* and Yellow Hand went down like a puppet whose strings had been cut. Shadow Love had intended that the body fall into the river. Instead it landed on the concrete wall. It took a minute to get it off the edge, into the water.

Yellow Hand's shirt ballooned up around his body, supporting it, a white lump in the current. Then there was a bubble, and another, and Yellow Hand was gone.

A traitor to the people. The man who'd put the hunter cop onto the Bluebird picture.

While Leo Clark sat at a truck stop and wept, Shadow Love sat in the taco stand eating ravenously, hunched over his food like a wolf. His body sang with the kill.

# 7

Lucas worked on Drorg until four in the morning, and Daniel called at eight. When the phone rang, Lucas rolled onto his side, thrashing at the nightstand like a drowning swimmer. He hit the phone and the receiver bounced on the floor, and he took another moment to find it.

"Davenport? What the hell . . . ?"

"Dropped the phone," Lucas said sleepily. "What happened?"

"They did another one. A federal judge in Oklahoma City."

"Shit." Lucas yawned and sat up. "The way you're talking, the killer got away."

"Yeah. He had braids, like . . ."

". . . the guy who did Cuervo. So there had to be at least three of them, counting Bluebird."

"Yeah. Anderson's getting everything he can out of the Oklahoma cops. And those pictures—we're getting them at nine. We'll meet in Wink's office."

"No problems?"

"Aw, we gotta go through the usual bullshit, but we'll get them," Daniel said.

"Somebody ought to call Lily," Lucas said.

"My secretary'll take care of it. There's one more thing. . . ."

"What?"

"The feds are in it."

Lucas groaned. "Aw, no, please . . ."

"Yeah. With both feet. Made the announcement an hour ago. I talked to the Minneapolis agent-in-charge and he says Lawrence Duberville Clay himself is taking a personal interest."

"Sonofabitch. Can we keep them off the street? Those guys could screw up a wet dream."

"I'll suggest that they focus on intelligence, but it won't work," Daniel said. "Clay thinks he can ride the crime business into the attorney general's job, and maybe the presidency. The papers are calling these killings 'domestic terrorism.' That'll get him out here for sure, just like when he went out to Chicago on that dope deal, and L.A. for the Green Army bust. When he gets here, he'll want some action."

"Fuck him. Let him find his own action."

"Try to be nice, all right? And in the meantime, let's get these pictures from the *Trib* and start hammering the street. If we nail these cocksuckers, Lawrence Duberville won't have any reason to come out."

They met with *StarTribune* executives in the office of Louis Wink, the paper's bald-as-a-cueball editor. Harold Probst, the publisher, and Kelly Lawrence, the city editor, sat in. Lily arrived on Daniel's arm; his elbow, Lucas noticed, was pressing Lily's breast. Daniel wore a gray suit that was virtually a mirror image of Wink's, and a self-satisfied smile. The meeting lasted ten minutes.

"The reason I object is that it brings up the question of whether we're an arm of the police. It damages our credibility," said the round-faced Lawrence.

"With who?" Lily asked heatedly. She was dressed in a rough silk blouse and another tweed skirt. She either had the world's best complexion or did the world's best makeup, Lucas thought.

"With people on the street," said the city editor. Lawrence was wearing a rumpled cotton dress that was just the wrong color of blue for her eyes. Lily looked so much better that Lucas wished she'd waited outside.

"Oh, bullshit," Lily snapped. "You have this great big goddamned building full of yuppies in penny loafers and you're worried about damaging your reputation with street people? Jesus H. Christ on a crutch."

"Take it easy," Lucas said soothingly. "She's right. It's a sensitive question."

"We wouldn't even ask, if the crimes weren't so horrendous. They killed a federal judge last night; butchered him. They killed one of the brightest up-and-coming politicians in the country and two people here," Daniel said in a syrupy voice. He turned to Lily. "The fact is, the press is in a very delicate situation."

He turned back to Wink and Probst, where the power was. "All we want to do is look at the face of the man that Lily thinks might be the New York killer. And we want to look at the people around him, so we can question them. You might very well have run all of those pictures in the paper, for anyone to see. You promised confidentiality to nobody. In fact, they were soliciting attention by their very presence at this confrontation."

"Well, that's right," said Probst. A flash of irritation crossed Wink's face. Probst had come up on the advertising side.

"And you'll get a tremendous story out of it," Lucas put in. "You'll stick it right up the *Pioneer Press*'s ass."

Lawrence, the city editor, brightened, but Lily continued to stew. "And if you don't we'll go to court and drag it out of you anyway," she snarled.

"Hey . . ." Wink sat up.

Daniel broke in before he could go any further. He pointed a finger at Lily's face and said, "No, we won't, Lieutenant. If they decide against us in this room, we'll look for other pictures, but we won't go to court. And if you keep this up, I'll ship your ass back to New York faster than you can say 'Avenue of the Americas.' "

Lily opened her mouth and just as suddenly snapped it shut. "Okay," she said. She glanced at Wink. "Sorry."

Daniel smiled his most charming smile at Wink and said, *"Please?"*

"I think . . . we should get some prints in here," Wink said. He nodded at Lawrence. "Get them."

They all sat silently until the city editor came back with three manila envelopes and handed them to Wink. Wink opened one, took out a set of eight-by-ten prints, looked at them, then passed them to Daniel. Daniel dealt them out across the table to Lily, who stood up, spread them out and began studying them.

"It's him," she said after a moment. She tapped one of the faces. "That's my man."

They got two sets of photos and stopped on the street corner before Daniel walked back to City Hall.

"Larry Hart is coming over this afternoon. He had to get his case load closed out," Daniel said to Lucas. "I'll get him a set of photographs. He may know somebody."

"All right. And I'll show my set around."

Daniel nodded and looked at Lily. "You should watch your temper. You almost lost it for us."

"Newsies piss me off," she said. "You were getting pushed around."

"I wasn't getting pushed. Everybody knew what would happen. We had to go through the ritual," Daniel said mildly.

"Okay. It's your turf. I apologize," she said.

"You should apologize. Being a hell of guy, I accept," Daniel said, and started off across the street.

Lily looked after him. "He's a piece of work," she said after a moment.

"He's okay. He can be an asshole, but he isn't stupid," Lucas said.

"So who's this Larry Hart?" Lily asked.

"He's a Welfare guy, a Sioux. Good guy, knows the streets, probably knows a thousand Indians. He's fairly large in Indian politics. He's written some articles, goes out to all the powwows and so on."

"We need him. I spent six hours on the street yesterday and didn't learn a thing. The guy I was with—"

"Shearson?"

"Yeah. He wouldn't know an Indian from a fire hydrant. Christ, it was almost embarrassing," she said, shaking her head.

"You're not going back out with him?"

"No." She looked at him without a sign of a smile. "Besides his woefully inadequate IQ, we had a little problem yesterday."

"Well . . ."

"I thought I might ride along with you. You're showing the pictures around, right?"

"Yeah." Lucas scratched his head. He didn't like working with a partner: he sometimes made deals that were best kept private. But Lily was from New York and shouldn't be a problem that way. "All right, I guess. I'm parked down this way."

"Everybody says you've got the best contacts in the Indian community," Lily said as they walked along. Lucas kept looking at her and tripped on an uneven sidewalk slab. She grinned, still looking straight ahead.

"I know about eight guys. Maybe ten. And not well," Lucas said when he recovered.

"You came up with the picture from the paper," she pointed out.

"I had a guy I could squeeze." Lucas stepped off the curb and walked around the nose of his Porsche. Lily walked behind him.

"Uh, around there," he said, pointing back to the passenger-side door.

She looked down at the 911, surprised. "Is this your car?"

"Yeah."

"I thought we were crossing the street," Lily said as she stepped back to the curb.

Lucas got in and popped open her door; she climbed inside and fastened the seat belt. "Not many New York cops would have the guts to drive around in a Porsche. Everybody would figure he was in the bag," she said.

"I've got some money of my own," Lucas said.

"Even so, you wouldn't have to buy a Porsche with it," Lily said primly. "You could buy a perfectly good car for ten or fifteen thousand and give the other twenty or thirty thousand to charity. You could give it to the Little Sisters of the Poor."

"I thought about that," Lucas said. He gunned the Porsche through an illegal U-turn and punched it up to forty in the twenty-five-mile-per-hour business zone. "And I decided, fuck 'em."

Lily threw back her head and laughed. Lucas grinned at her and thought that maybe she was carrying a few too many pounds, but maybe that wasn't all bad.


They took the photographs to the Indian Center, showed them around. Two of the men in the photos were known by face but not by name. Nobody knew where they lived. Lucas called Anderson, told him about the tentative IDs, and Anderson promised to get more photos on the street.

After leaving the Indian Center, they stopped at an Indian-dominated public housing project, where Lucas knew two old men who worked as caretakers. They got no new IDs. The hostility was palpable.

"They don't like cops," Lily said as they left.

"Nobody around here likes cops," Lucas said, looking back at the decrepit buildings. "When they see us, we're mostly getting their cars towed away in the winter. They don't like us, but at least they're not against us. But this is something else. This time, they're against us."

"Maybe they got reasons," Lily said. She was looking out the window at a group of Indian children sitting on the porch of a decaying clapboard house. "Those kids ought to be in school. What you've got here, Davenport, is a clean slum. The people are fucked up, but the street gets cleaned twice a week."

They spent the rest of the morning running the photos down Lucas' Indian acquaintances. Lily trailed behind, not saying much, studying the faces of the Indians, listening to them, the Indians looking curiously back.

"They think you might be an Indian, or part Indian, but they're not sure until they hear your voice," Lucas said between stops. "You look a little Indian."

"I don't sound Indian."

"You sound Lawn Guyland."

"There's an Indian reservation on Long Island," she said.

"No shit? Jesus, I'd like to hear those people talk. . . ."

Late in the morning, Lucas drove to Yellow Hand's apartment at the Point, describing him to Lily as they went. Outside, on the stoop, he reached back and freed the P7 in its holster.

"Is this trouble?" she asked.

"I doubt it," he said. "But you know."

"Okay." When they were inside the door, she slipped her hand into a mufflike opening in her shoulder bag, took out a short Colt Officer's Model .45 and jacked a shell into the chamber.

"A forty-five?" Lucas said as she put it back in the purse.

"I'm not strong enough to wrestle with assholes," she said bluntly. "If I shoot somebody, I want him to go down. Not that the P7 isn't a nice little gun. But it's a bit light for serious work."

"Not if you can shoot," Lucas said through his teeth as he headed up the stairs.

"I can shoot the eyes out of a moving pigeon," she said. "And not hit the feathers."

The door on the top floor was open. Nobody home. Lucas eased inside, looked around, then tramped across a litter of paper, orange peels and empty personal-size catsup packs from McDonald's. "This is where he was," Lucas said, kicking Yellow Hand's mattress.

"Place feels vacant," Lily said. She touched one of the empty catsup packs with the toe of her shoe. Street people stole them from fast-food joints and used the catsup to make tomato soup. "They're really hurting for money."

"Crackheads," Lucas said.

Lily nodded. She took the Colt out of the purse, pulled the magazine, stuck it between the little and ring fingers of her gun hand, cupped the ejection port with her free hand and jacked the slide. The chambered round ejected into her palm. She snapped it back into the magazine and pushed the magazine back into the butt of the pistol. She'd done it smoothly, without thinking, Lucas thought. She'd spent some time with the gun.

"The trouble with single-action weapons," Lucas said, "is that shit happens and you're caught with an empty chamber."

"Not if you've got half a brain," she said. She was looking around at the litter. "I've learned to anticipate."

Lucas stopped and picked up an object that had been almost hidden by Yellow Hand's mattress where it had pressed against the wall.

Lily asked, "What?" and he tossed it to her. She turned it over in her hands. "Crack pipe. You said he was a crackhead."

"Yeah. But I wonder why he left it here? I wouldn't think the boy would be without it. All of his other shit is gone."

"I don't know. Nothing wrong with it. Yet," Lily said. She dropped the glass pipe on the floor and stepped on it, crushing it.


On the street again, Lucas suggested a check at Cuervo's rental office. If there was anyone running the place, he told Lily, there might be some word of where Yellow Hand had gone. She nodded. "I'm following you," she said.

"I hope the dipshit hasn't gone back to the res," Lucas said as they climbed back in the car. "Yellow Hand would be hell to find out there, if he didn't want to be found."

Lucas had been in Cuervo's office a dozen times over the years. Nothing had changed in the shabby stairway that went up to it. The building had permanent bad breath, compounded of stale urine, wet plaster and catshit. As Lucas reached the top of the stairs, Cuervo's office door opened on a chain and a woman looked out through the crack.

"Who're you?" Lucas asked.

"Harriet Cuervo," the woman snapped. All Lucas could see were her eyes, which were the color of acid-washed jeans, and a pale crescent of face. "Who in the hell are you to be asking?"

"Police," Lucas said. Lucas fished his badge case out of his jacket pocket and flashed the badge at her. Lily waited behind him, down a step. "We didn't know you'd taken over Ray's operation."

"Know now," the woman grunted. The chain rattled off and she let the door swing open. Her husband's murder had left a faint stain on the wooden floor and Harriet Cuervo was standing in the middle of it. She was wearing a print dress that fell straight from her neck to her knees. "I told the other cops everything I knew," she said bluntly.

"We're looking for a different kind of information," Lucas said. The woman went back around Cuervo's old desk. Lucas stepped inside the office and glanced around. Something had changed, something was wrong, but he couldn't put his finger on it. "We're asking about one of his tenants."

"So what do you want to know?" she asked. She was five feet, nine inches tall and weighed perhaps a hundred pounds, all of it rawboned knobs. There were short vertical lines above and below her lips, as though they'd once been stitched shut.

"You've got a renter named Yellow Hand, down at the Point?"

"Sure. Yellow Hand." She opened a ledger and ran a finger down an open column. "Paid up 'til tomorrow."

"You didn't see him yesterday or today?"

"Shit, I don't do no surveys. I just rent the fuckin' apartments," she said. "If he don't have the money tomorrow, out he goes. Today, I don't care what he does."

"So you haven't seen him?"

"Nope." She peered around Lucas at Lily. "She a cop too?"

"Yeah."

Cuervo looked Lily up and down. "Dresses pretty good for a cop," she sniffed.

"If Yellow Hand doesn't pay, do you go down and evict him yourself?" Lily asked curiously.

"I got an associate," Cuervo said.

"Who's that?" Lucas asked.

"Bald Peterson."

"Yeah? I thought he'd left town."

"He's come back. You know him?"

"Yeah. We go back."

"Say . . ." Harriet Cuervo's eyes narrowed and she made a gun of her index finger and thumb and pointed it at Lucas' heart. "You ain't the cop that pounded him, are you? Years ago? Like fuckin' crippled him?"

"We've had some disagreements," Lucas said. "Tell him hello for me." He took a step toward the door. "How about a guy named Shadow Love? You seen him around?"

"Shadow Love? Never even heard of him."

"He was living up at the Point. . . ."

She shrugged. "Didn't rent from me," she said. "Must've been one of those other flatheads let him in. You know how it goes."

"Yeah," Lucas said as he turned away again. "Sorry about Ray."

"It's nice somebody is, 'cause I ain't," Cuervo said flatly. Her face showed some animation for the first time. "I was trying to think what I remembered best about Ray. One thing, you know? And you know what come to mind? He had a bunch of porno videotapes. He had one called *Airtight Brunette*. You know what an airtight brunette is? That's one who is filled up everyplace, if you know what I mean. Three guys. Anyway, his favorite part was when this guy 'jaculates on the brunette's chest. He was running that back and forth, back and forth. Every time he stopped the VCR and rewound the tape, the regular TV show come on. You know what that was?"

"Uh, no, I wouldn't," Lucas said. He glanced quickly at Lily, who was staring at Cuervo, fascinated.

"*Sesame Street*. Big Bird was finding out how doctors take your blood pressure. So this guy 'jaculates on the brunette's chest and we get Big Bird. And he 'jaculates again and we get Big Bird. It was like that for fifteen minutes. 'Jaculate, Big Bird, 'jaculate, Big Bird."

She stopped to take a breath. "That," she said, "is how I remember Ray."

"Okay. Well, jeez, we gotta get going," Lucas said desperately. He pushed Lily out the door toward the stairs. They were ten steps down when Harriet Cuervo came to the landing.

"I wanted to have kids," she shouted down at them.


Lily grinned at him as they walked back to the car. "Nice girl," she said. "We wouldn't do much better in New York."

"Fuckin' gerbil," Lucas grumbled.

"Did you see the calendar on the wall? Big Boys' Buns?"

Lucas snapped his fingers. "I knew there was something different about the place," he said. "Ray used to have this old *Sports Illustrated* swimsuit calendar. A wet–T-shirt shot. These great . . . ah . . . ."

"Tits?"

"Right. Anyway, it was always the same picture. He found one he liked and stopped right there."

"So what we got is a change in management, but no change in style," Lily said.

"You got it."

In the car, Lucas checked the time. They had been on the street for three hours. "We ought to think about lunch."

"Is there a deli in town?" Lily asked.

Lucas grinned at her. "Can't stand to be away?"

"It's not that," she said. "I've been eating hotel food for too long. Everything tastes like oatmeal."

"All right, a deli," Lucas agreed. "There's one a couple blocks from my place, over in St. Paul. Got a restaurant in the back."

They headed east on Lake, across the Mississippi, then south down along the river through a forest of maples, elms and oaks, past a couple of colleges.

"All religious colleges. Highest density of virgins in the Twin Cities, right here," Lucas said.

"Your neighborhood too. What a shame; what a workload," she said.

"What's that mean?" Lucas asked.

"When I told people I was planning to go out with you, they all gave me the look. Like, Uh-oh, into the hands of Lothario."

"Bullshit," said Lucas.

The deli was in a yellow cinder-block building with a parking lot in back. When they got out of the car, an old woman was watching them through a restaurant window while she gnawed on the end of a whole pickle. Lily's face lit up when she saw it.

"That pickle . . . There's a marginal chance that this place could be all right," she said. Inside, she scanned the sandwich menu, then ordered a corned beef and cheese combo with coleslaw, a side order of french fries, a seven-layer salad and a raspberry-flavored Perrier.

"A thousand calories," she said five minutes later, looking ruefully at the brown plastic tray the counterman had just delivered. The counterman snorted as he turned away. "What, you think more than a thousand?" she called after him.

"Honey, the sandwich is six, seven hundred and that's only half of it," the counterman said.

"I don't want to hear it," Lily said, turning back to the food.

Lucas got a sausage on rye, a bag of potato chips and a Diet Coke and led the way to the back.

"I'm an eater," Lily said as they slid into the booth. "I'll weigh two hundred pounds when they bury me."

"You look all right," Lucas said.

Her eyes came up. "I'd look great with ten less pounds."

"I'll stand by my original statement."

Lily got busy with her food, keeping her eyes away from his. "So," she said a moment later. "I understand you've got a new kid but aren't married."

"Yup."

"Doesn't that embarrass you a little?" She licked a fleck of slaw off her upper lip.

"Nope. I wanted to get married, but the woman wouldn't do it. We're still together, more or less. We don't live together."

"When did you last ask her to marry you?" Lily asked.

"Well, I used to ask her once a week. Then I just made a general open offer."

"Do you love her?"

"Sure," Lucas said, nodding.

"Does she love you?"

"She says so."

"So why doesn't she marry you?" Lily asked.

"She says I'd be a great father but a fuckin' terrible husband."

"Hmph." Lily took a big bite of her sandwich and chewed thoughtfully, watching him. "Well," she said after she swallowed, "it sounds like you might fool around a little."

"Not since she got pregnant," Lucas said. "Before that . . ."

"A little?"

"Yeah." He grinned. "Now and then."

"How about you?" Lucas asked. "You're wearing a ring."

"Yup." She snapped off a french fry. "My husband's a sociology professor at NYU. He did position papers for Andretti. That's one of the reasons I'm out here. I knew the family."

"Good guy?"

"Yeah, for a politician, I guess."

"I meant your husband."

"David? David's great," Lily said positively. "He is the gentlest man I've ever known. I met him when I was going to school. He was a graduate assistant, I took a class. It was about the time everything was going to hell up at Columbia, people were in the streets, McCarthy was running for president. . . . Good times. Interesting times."

"So, what, you got married right after college?"

"Before graduation. Then I got my degree, applied to the department under a special program to bring in women, and here I am."

"Huh. How about that." Lucas watched her for a few seconds, finished a last chip and slid out of the booth. "I'll be right back."

*They've got problems, Lily and David,* he thought as he walked to the counter. He ordered another bag of chips and another Diet Coke. *She likes him okay, but there's no heat.* When he looked back, she was watching people in the street, a shaft of sunlight cutting across the table and her hands. She's beautiful, he thought.

When he got back to the table, she was licking her fingertips. "Done," she said. "Where to next?"

"Gotta go see a nun."

"Say what?"


A seven-foot-tall alabaster statue of the Virgin Mary hung over the driveway. Lily looked doubtfully up at it.

"I've never been to a nunnery," she muttered.

"It's not a nunnery," Lucas said. "It's a college."

"You said nuns lived here."

"There's a residence on the other side of the campus," Lucas said.

"How come her eyes are rolled back like that?" Lily asked, still looking up at the Virgin.

"The ecstasy of perfect grace," Lucas suggested.

"What's she doing to that snake?" The tail of a snake was visible beneath the Virgin's sandals. The snake's body curled up one of her robed legs, its head poised to strike at knee level.

"Crushing it. That's the devil."

"Huh. Looks like one of the investigators on my squad. The snake, I mean."

Lucas had been to grade school with Elle Kruger. They'd tracked each other over the years, Lucas on the Minneapolis police force, Elle Kruger as a psychologist and a Sister of Mercy. Her office was on the third floor of Albertus Magnus Hall. Lucas led Lily down a long, cool hallway that echoed with their footsteps. At Elle's office, he knocked once, opened the door and stuck his head inside.

"About time," Elle Kruger snapped. She was a traditionalist, and wore the black habit with a band of beads hanging down beside her hand.

"Traffic," said Lucas in way of apology. He stepped inside, Lily close behind. "Elle, this is Lieutenant Lily Rothenburg of the New York Police Department, out here investigating the death of John Andretti. Lily, this is my friend Sister Mary Joseph. She's the chief shrink around here."

"Pleased to meet you, Lily," Elle said, and reached out a bony hand.

Lily took it and smiled. "Lucas tells me you've helped on some of his cases."

"Where I can. But we mostly play games," Elle said.

Lily looked at Lucas, and Lucas explained, "We have a gaming group that meets once a week."

"That's interesting," Lily said, looking from one of them to the other. "Like Dungeons and Dragons?"

"No, no role playing," Elle said. "Historical reconstruction. Get Lucas to tell you about his Gettysburg. We played it three times last year and it always comes out wildly different. Last time, Bobby Lee almost got himself into Phila-delphia."

"I've still got to do something about that damn Stuart," Lucas said to the nun. "When he gets loose too early, he fouls up all the calculations. I'm thinking of . . ."

"No game talk," Elle said. "Let's get some ice cream."

"Ice cream?" Lily said. She put her fingers over her mouth to cover a tiny burp. "Sounds good."

As they walked down the hall, Lily turned to Elle and asked, "What did you mean when you said, 'his Gettysburg'? Did Lucas make the game or some-thing?"

Elle raised an eyebrow. "Our boy is a famous games inventor. Didn't you know that?"

"No, I didn't," Lily said, looking at Lucas.

"He surely is," Elle said. "That's how he got rich."

"Are you rich?" Lily asked Lucas.

"No," Lucas said. He shook his head.

"He is, take my word for it," Elle said to Lily with a phony confidentiality. "He bought me a gold chain last year that has scandalized my entire wing of the residence."

"For a good German Catholic girl, I think the influence of the Irish is begin-ning to seep in," Lucas said.

"The Irish?"

"The blarney." Lucas turned to Lily and said in a stage whisper, "I'd never use a word like 'bullshit' around a nun."

They sat in a booth in the ice cream shop, Lucas and Lily side by side, Elle across the table. Elle ate a hot-fudge sundae while Lily worked on a banana split. Lucas blew into a cup of coffee and thought about Lily's warm thigh next to his.

"So you're working on Andretti," Elle prompted them.

"There's some kind of conspiracy," Lily said.

"The Indian man who killed the people in Minneapolis, and the Indian man who killed Andretti?"

"Yeah," said Lucas. "Except we think that two different guys killed the people in Minneapolis. And now the judge in Oklahoma City . . ."

"I haven't heard . . ."

"Last night . . . I was wondering . . . what kind of group would we be dealing with? If there is a group."

"Religious," Elle said promptly.

"Religious?"

"There are few things in the world that can hold together a murder conspiracy. Hate by itself is not enough, because it's too unfocused and not intellectual enough. There has to be some positive energy, as it were. That usually comes from religion. It's difficult to be intellectual and murderous at the same time, without some complicated rationale."

"How about these groups that develop in prison?" asked Lily. "You know, a group of guys gets together and they start holding up armored cars . . ."

". . . raising money for a cause. Which usually has some kind of quasi-religious doctrine behind it. Save the white race from mongrelization by blacks, Arabs, Jews, whatever. You see the same thing in the leftist radical groups and even the groups or pairs of psychotic killers you get from time to time. There's a religious aspect, there's a group feeling of oppression. Usually there's a messiah figure who tells the others that it's all right to kill. That it's necessary."

"One of my people in the Indian community said that Bluebird—"

"That was the man killed in Minneapolis?" Elle interrupted.

"Yeah. He said Bluebird was a man looking for religion."

"I'd say he found it," Elle said. She had been saving the maraschino cherry for last, and finally she ate it, savoring the sweetness.

"You know how they make maraschino cherries?" Lucas asked, covering his eyes with his hand as it disappeared.

"I don't want to hear," Elle said. She pointed her long spoon at Lucas' nose. "If there's a group doing these killings, there probably aren't more than a dozen people in it and that would be an extreme. More likely it's five or six. At the most."

"Six? Jesus," Lily blurted. "Excuse me, my language. But six?"

"What are the chances that it's three?" Lucas asked. "Bluebird and this guy in New York and the guy in Oklahoma?"

Elle tipped her head back and peered at the ceiling, calculating. "No. I don't think so, but then, who knows? But I have the sense . . . these men in New York and Oklahoma, they traveled some way to do the killings, if they came from here. If they know Bluebird. I have a sense that they were sent out . . . that they are on missions. Bluebird was apparently ready to die. That would be more typical of people who saw themselves as part of a process, rather than as a last chance to strike back."

"So there'll be more?"

"Yes. But there is a limit on size. There really is no such thing as a grand criminal conspiracy. Or at least no such thing as a secret one. I suppose Adolf Hitler and his henchmen were a grand criminal conspiracy, but they needed the collaboration of a nation to pull it off."

"So there'd probably be at least two or three more, and maybe six or eight," Lucas said. "Probably held together by some sort of religious mania."

"That's right," Elle said. "If you want to stop it, look for the preacher."

In the car going back to Lucas' office, Lily looked him over.

"I have the feeling I'm being looked over," Lucas said.

"You have interesting friends," Lily said.

He shrugged. "I'm a cop."

"You invent games and play them with nuns?"

"Hey, I'm a wild kind of guy." He looked at her over the top of his sunglasses, winked and turned back to the traffic.

"Oooh, Mr. Cool," she said. "It makes my thighs hot."

Lucas thought, Mine too. He glanced quickly at her and she turned away, a blush creeping up her neck. She knew what he was thinking, and she had been aware of him in the booth. . . .

At home, Larry Hart wore cowboy boots, blue jeans and work shirts with string ties. The string ties always had a chunk of turquoise buried in a silver slide. He could have worn that outfit to work, with a jacket to complete it, but he never did. He wore brown suits, with neckties in shades of brown and gold, and brown wingtip shoes. In the dead of summer, with the temperatures climbing into the nineties, Hart would sweat through the tiny tinderbox apartments of his welfare clientele, always in a brown suit.

Lucas had once asked him why. Hart shrugged and said, "I like it." What he meant was, *I have to.*

Hart jammed himself into the cookie-cutter frame of a municipal executive. It never worked, as hard as he tried. There was no way a brown suit could disguise his heritage. He was broad-shouldered and powerfully built, with black eyes and gray-shot hair. He was Sioux. Hart had the biggest case load in Welfare. Some of his clients refused to talk to anyone else.

"Lucas, what's happenin', babe?" Hart asked. Lucas lounged in his office chair with his feet on the rim of a wastebasket, while Lily rolled back and forth, a few inches one way and then a few inches the other, in an office chair on casters. Hart stepped inside the tiny office and dropped his bulk on a corner of Lucas' desk.

"Larry Hart, Lily Rothenburg, NYPD," Lucas said, gesturing between them.

"Nice to meet you," Lily said, taking Hart in. "You've been out?"

"Yup. Down on Franklin . . ."

Hart had been working through Indian Country with the photos. He knew two of the men himself.

"Bear is down at Rosebud and so is Elk Walking," Hart said. "They're pretty tough, but they ain't crazy. I can't see them getting involved in anything like this."

"You didn't know anybody else in the pictures?" Lily asked.

"Not names, but I know some of the faces. There are a couple of guys I see down at the Indian Center. You were asking Anderson about one of them. I played basketball against him last year."

"Could we get the team rosters?"

"They're mostly pickup games," Hart said. "But if I ask around enough, I could probably find out who he is. There are a couple more faces I've seen at powwows, at Upper Sioux and Flandreau, Sisseton, Rosebud, all over the landscape."

"All Sioux?" asked Lucas.

"I think all but one. Give me the pictures again, let's see. . . ." Hart thumbed through the stack of photographs until he found the one he wanted. He poked a finger at a man's face. "This guy's Chippewa. I don't know his name, it's Jack something, maybe like Jack Bordeaux. I think he's from White Earth, but I'm not sure."

"So how do we find out about Lily's man?" Lucas asked.

"There're a couple of guys out in SoDak who'd probably know him. Deputies. I gave Daniel the names, he called them and they're driving down to Rapid City tonight. I'm catching a plane out at six o'clock. I should be in Rapid City by seven-thirty. I'll take the pictures along."

"You think they'll know all these guys?" Lily asked.

"Most of them. They try to keep track of who has guns," Hart said.

"Why don't we just wire the pictures out . . . ?"

"The technical guys said we'd lose too much resolution. We decided it'd just be best all around if I went. I could spend some time talking to them."

"That sounds right," Lily said.

"What about this computer tree you're building?" Lucas asked. "I understand you got all kinds of family stuff in there from Minnesota Sioux. Anything on Bluebird or Yellow Hand?"

"I looked up Bluebird. He's just about the last of the family. A lot of Bluebirds went East and married into the Mohawks and that bunch. There are still quite a few Yellow Hands out at Crow Creek and Niobrara. Those used to be Minnesota Indians before they got run out. But I know this Yellow Hand you talked to. He doesn't have much to do with the other Yellow Hands. This one is a loser."

"Nothing else?"

" 'Fraid not." Hart checked his watch. "I've got a plane to catch."

"When will you know? About the pictures?" asked Lily.

"About five minutes after I get off the plane. Do you want me to call tonight?"

"Could you? I'll come back here and wait for the call," Lucas said.

"So will I," Lily added.

" 'Bout seven-thirty, we should know," Hart said.

"So now what?" Lily asked. They were standing on the sidewalk. Hart was on his way to the airport, riding in a squad.

Lucas glanced at his watch. "I've got to see my kid, get something to eat," he said. "Why don't we meet back here at seven o'clock? We can wait for Larry to call and figure out what we're going to do tomorrow."

"Depending on what he finds out," Lily said.

"Yeah," Lucas said, flipping his key ring around his finger. "Need a ride down to your hotel?"

"No, thanks." She smiled, starting away. "It's a nice walk."

Sarah was crawling around on the living room rug when Lucas arrived. He got down on his hands and knees, his tie dragging on the carpet, and played backup with her. First he backed up and she crawled toward him, gurgling; then, with her eyes wide, she backed away and he prowled forward.

"That'd be a lot more charming if you didn't have that big bump on your ass," Jennifer said from the kitchen. Lucas reached back, pulled out the P7 and put it on a lamp table.

"Jesus, not there," Jennifer said with asperity. "She could pull herself up and grab it."

"She can't pull herself up yet," Lucas objected.

"She will soon. It's a bad habit."

"Okay." Lucas stood up, slipped the pistol back in its holster and scooped up his daughter, who had been quivering in anticipation of the flight. He bounced her in his hands as he wandered toward the kitchen and propped himself in the doorway. "Have we got some kind of problem?"

Jennifer was making a salad. She turned her head. "No. Not unless you have."

"I just got here and I'm fine," Lucas said. "You sound a little tight."

"Not at all. I just don't want guns lying around the house."

"Sure," he said. "Come on, Sarah, time for bed. Besides, your mom's being a grouch."

Lucas waited for it during dinner, watching Jennifer's face. Something was going on.

"Any lines on the guy from New York?" Jennifer asked finally. Rumors about the meeting at the *StarTribune* were circulating through all the media. Daniel had already fended off a half-dozen inquiries, but leaks were inevitable. Jennifer, called by her former partner at TV3, had spent the afternoon talking to old sources by phone. By the time Lucas had arrived, she had most of the story.

"Maybe. I've got a call coming in at seven-thirty."

"You're going back?"

"Yeah. Around seven."

"If Kennedy called you from the station, could you give him something for the ten-o'clock broadcast?"

"He'd have to talk to Daniel," Lucas said.

"Is he going to be there tonight?"

"No, I don't think so."

"How about this New York cop lady?"

Lucas thought, Ah, and said, "She'll be there."

"I hear she's terrific-looking," Jennifer said. She looked up from her dinner plate, straight into Lucas' eyes.

"She's pretty good," Lucas said. "A little chubby, maybe . . . Is this going to be a problem? Who I work with?"

"No, no." Jennifer looked down at her plate again. "There's something else too," she said.

"Okay," Lucas said, putting his fork down. "Let's have it."

"A guy at the station asked me out."

"Who?"

"Mark Seeton."

"What'd you say?"

"I said . . . I'd get back to him."

"So you want to go?"

Jennifer stood up, picked up her plate and carried it to the sink. "Yes, I think so," she said. "No big heavy deal. Mark's a nice guy. He wants somebody to go to the symphony with."

Lucas shrugged. "So go."

She looked sideways at him. "You wouldn't mind?"

"I'd mind. I just wouldn't try to stop you."

"Jesus, that's worse than trying to stop me," she said, one fist planted against her hip. "You're trying to mind-fuck me, Davenport."

"Look, if you want to go, go," Lucas said. "You know I'm not going to take you to the symphony. Not on any regular basis."

"It's just that you have your friends and the things you do, the games, the fishing, the police work . . . me and Sarah. You see somebody almost every day, one way or another. I hardly see anybody at all, outside of work. And you know what I'm like about music. . . ."

"So go," Lucas said shortly. Then he grinned. "I can take Mark Seeton, I'm not worried," he said. He pointed a finger at her. "But I don't want to hear any shit about this New York cop. She *is* good-looking, but she's also happily married to a big-shot professor at NYU. Shearson made some kind of move on her yesterday and he's now carrying his nuts around in his lunch box."

"You're protesting too much," Jennifer said.

"No, I'm not. But you're looking for an excuse. . . ."

"Let's not fight, okay?"

"Are we still in bed?" Lucas asked.

"You might get lucky," Jennifer said. "A little romance wouldn't hurt, though."

\*       \*       \*

Lily had a short white line on her upper lip when she got back to Lucas' office. They were alone in the tiny office, the door open on the darkened hallway.

"Did you have a glass of milk?"

She cocked her head. "You're also psychic, right? In addition to the game-making and the money."

He grinned and reached out and wiped his thumb across her lip. "No. Just a little rim of milk, here. Like my daughter."

"What's her name? Your daughter?"

"Sarah."

"We've got a Marc and a Sam," Lily said. "Marc's fifteen now, God, I can't believe it. He's started high school and he plays football. Sam's thirteen."

"You've got a kid who's fifteen?" Lucas asked. "How old are you, anyway?"

"Thirty-nine."

"I thought maybe thirty-four."

"Oh, la, such a gentleman," Lily laughed. "How about you?"

"Forty-one."

"Poor guy. Your daughter will be hanging out with all the metal-heads at the high school and you'll be too old and feeble to do anything about it."

"I'm looking forward to my feebletude," Lucas said. "Sit around in a good leather chair, read poetry. Go up to the cabin, sit on the dock, watch the sun go down . . ."

"With your fly down and your dick hanging out because you're senile and can't remember how to dress yourself . . ."

"Jesus, I can barely stand the flattery," Lucas said, laughing despite himself.

"You were getting a little carried away with the retirement bullshit," Lily said wryly.

Hart called at quarter to eight from the Rapid City airport. "They knew him right away," he said. "His name's Bill Hood. He's a Sioux from Rosebud, but he married a Chippewa woman a few years ago. He lives in Minnesota. Some-where up around Red Lake, they think."

"What?" Lily said. There was no extension in the office and she was watching Lucas' face.

Lucas nodded at her and said into the phone, "How about the other people. You got any more names?"

"Yeah, they know quite a few of them. During the trouble with the bikers, they did a bunch of IDs. I'll give them to Anderson, get him to crank them through the computer."

"What?" Lily asked again, when Lucas got off the phone.

"Your man's name is Bill Hood. He supposedly lives somewhere up by Red Lake. . . ."

"Where's Red Lake?" she asked.

"It's a reservation up north."

"Let's get going. We'll have to stop at my—"

"Whoa. We've got things to do. We'll start with our identification people tonight, see if we can figure out exactly where he lives. The Indians are always back and forth from here to the res. For all we know, he may be down here, with Bluebird. If he's not, we'll arrange some contacts up north, then go. If we head up there tonight, we'd spend most of our time thrashing around."

Lily stood and put her hands on her hips and leaned toward him. "Why do guys always have to wait another day? Jesus, in New York . . ."

"You're not in New York. In New York, you want to go somewhere, you take a taxi. You know how far Red Lake is from here?"

"No. I don't know."

"About the same distance as it is from New York to Washington, D.C. It ain't just a taxi ride. I'll get some calls going tonight, and tomorrow . . ."

"We go."

# 8

"You heard?" She called.

Lily strode down the hall toward him, a sheaf of papers clutched in one hand. Before, she'd always worn soft pinkish lipstick, and just a touch. This morning, her lipstick was hard and heart-red, the color of street violence and rough sex. She had changed her hair as well; black bangs curled down over her brow, and she looked out from under them, like the wicked queen in *Snow White*.

"What?" Lucas was carrying a paper cup of microwaved coffee and had a *Trib* pinched under his arm.

"We found Hood. Right here in town. Anderson got on the computers early this morning," she said. The papers were computer printouts with notes scrawled in the margins in blue ink. She looked down at the top one. "Hood used to live at a place called Bemidji. It's not on a reservation, but it's close."

"Yeah. It's right next to Red Lake," Lucas said. He opened the metal door of his office and led the way in.

"But we got a problem," Lily said as she settled into the second chair in the office. Lucas put the coffee on his desk, pulled off his sport coat, hung it on a hook and sat down. "What happened is . . ."

Lucas rubbed his face and she frowned. "What's wrong?"

"My face hurts," Lucas said.

"Your face hurts?"

"It's sensitive to morning light. I think my grandfather was a vampire."

She looked at him for a moment and shook her head. "Jesus . . ."

"So what's the problem?" Lucas prompted, smothering a yawn.

She got back on track. "Hood's not driving his own car. He's the listed owner of a 1988 Ford Tempo four-wheel-drive. Red. That car's still at his former home up in Bemidji, along with his wife and kid. The Bemidji cops have some kind of source in his neighborhood—some cop's sister-in-law—and the red car's been there all along. We're not sure what Hood was driving out of that Jersey motel, but it was big and old. Like a 'seventy-nine Buick or Oldsmobile. It had bad rust."

"So we've got no way to spot him on the highway."

"Unfortunately. But . . ." She thumbed through the printouts. "Anderson did a computer run on him and talked to the state people. He's got a Minnesota driver's license but no second-car registration. So Anderson went through everything else in the computers and *bingo*. Found him listed as a defendant in a small-claims-court filing. He bought a TV on time and couldn't make the payments."

"And his address was on the filing."

"Nope. Anderson had to call Sears. They looked up the address on their accounts computer. It's an apartment on Lyndale Street."

"Lyndale Avenue," Lucas said. He sat forward now, intent.

"Whatever. The thing is, the apartment's rented to a guy named Tomas Peck. Sloan and a couple of Narcotics guys are over in the neighborhood now, trying to figure it out."

"Maybe he moved."

"Yeah, but Peck has been listed as the occupant for two years. So maybe Hood's living with him."

"Huh." Lucas thought it over as she sat leaning forward, waiting for a comment. "Are you sure you've got the right Bill Hood? There have got to be a lot of them. . . ."

"Yeah, we're sure. The Sears account had a change of address."

"Then I'd bet he's still living at that apartment," Lucas said. "We're on a roll, and when you get on a roll . . ."

". . . it all works," Lily said.

Lily had not gone down to look for Hood, she said, because Daniel wanted to keep the police presence in the neighborhood to a minimum. "The FBI's all over the streets. They must have half a dozen agents going through the community," she said.

"Isn't he going to tell them about identifying Hood?"

"Yeah. He's already talked to a guy." She glanced at her watch. "There's a meeting in half an hour. We're supposed to be there. Sloan should be back and Larry Hart's coming in sometime this morning," Lily said. She was quivering with energy. "God damn, I was afraid I'd be here for a month. I could be out of here tomorrow, if we get him."

"Did Daniel say who the FBI guy is?" Lucas asked.

"Uh, yeah. A guy named . . ." She looked at her notes. "Kieffer."

"Uh-oh."

"Not good?" She looked up at him and he shook his head, frowning.

"He doesn't like me and I don't like him. Gary Kieffer is a most righteous man. Most righteous."

"Well, get your phony smile in place, then, because we're meeting with him in twenty-seven minutes." She looked at her watch again, then at his nearly empty coffee cup. "Where can we get more coffee and a decent Danish?"

They walked through the tunnel from City Hall to the Hennepin County Government Center, took a couple of escalators to the Skyway level, walked along the Skyway to the Pillsbury building. Standing on the escalator a step above him, she could look straight into his eyes; she asked if he had had a long night.

"No, not particularly." He glanced at her. "Why?"

"You look a little beat."

"I don't get up early. I usually don't get going until about noon." He yawned again to prove it.

"What about your girlfriend? Is she a night person too?"

"Yeah. She spent half her life reporting for the ten-o'clock news, which meant she got off work about eleven. That's how we met. We'd bump into each other at late-night restaurants."

Going across the Skyway, Lily looked through the windows at the glossy downtown skyscrapers, monuments to the colored-glass industry. "I've never been in this part of the country," she said. "I made a couple of cross-country trips when I was doing the hippie thing, back in college, but we always went south of here. Through Iowa or Missouri, on the way out to California."

"It's out of the way, Minnesota is," Lucas conceded. "Lake Michigan hangs down there and cuts us off, with Wisconsin and the Dakotas. You've got to want to come here. And I suppose you don't often get out of the Center of the Universe."

"I do, once in a while," she said mildly, refusing to rise to the bait. "But it's usually on vacation, down to the Bahamas or the Keys or out to Bermuda. We went to Hawaii once. We just don't get into the middle part of the country."

"It's the last refuge of American civilization, you know—out here, between the mountains," Lucas said, looking out the windows. "Most of the population is literate, most people still trust their governments, and most of the governments are reasonably good. The citizens control the streets. We've got poverty, but it's manageable. We've got dope, but we've still got a handle on it. It's okay."

"You mean like Detroit?"

"There are a couple of spots out of control . . ."

"And South Chicago and Gary and East St. Louis . . ."

". . . but basically, it ain't bad. You get the feeling that nobody even knows what goes on in New York or Los Angeles and that nobody really cares. The politicians have to lie and steal just to get elected."

"I think my brain would shrivel up and die if I was living here. It's so fuckin' peaceful I don't know what I'd do," Lily said. She looked down at a street-cleaning machine. "The night I came in, I got here late, after midnight. I caught a cab at the airport and went downtown, and I started seeing these women walking around alone or waiting for buses by themselves. Everywhere. Jesus. That's such . . . an odd sight."

"Hmph," Lucas said.

They left the Skyway and got on an escalator to the main floor of the Pillsbury building. "You have a little hickey on your neck," she said lightly. "I thought maybe that's why you looked so tired."

They sat in the dining area of a bakery, Lily eating a Danish with a glass of milk, Lucas staring out the window over a cup of coffee.

"Wish I was out there with Sloan," she said finally.

"Why? He can handle it." Lucas sipped at the scalding coffee.

"I just wish I was. I've handled a lot of pretty serious situations."

"So have we. We ain't New York, but we ain't exactly Dogpatch, either," Lucas said.

"Yeah, I know. . . ."

"Sloan's good at talking to people. He'll dig it out."

"All right, all right," she said, suddenly irritable. "But this means a lot to me."

"It means a lot to us too. We're up to our assholes in media; Jesus, the street outside the office this morning looked like the press parking lot at a political convention."

"Not the same," she insisted. "Andretti was a major figure. . . ."

"We're handling it," Lucas said sharply.

"*You're* not handling much. You didn't even get here until ten o'clock, for Christ's sake. I'd been standing around for two hours."

"I didn't ask you to wait for me; and I told you, I work nights."

"I just don't have the right feeling from this. You guys—"

"And if I read the newspapers right, you guys in New York have screwed more than your share of cases to the wall," Lucas interrupted, talking over her. "If you guys aren't deliberately blowing up some black kid, you're taking money from some fuckin' crack dealer. We're not only pretty good, we're clean. . . ."

"I never took a fuckin' nickel from anybody," Lily said, her voice harsh. She was leaning over the table, her jaw tight.

"I didn't say you did, I said . . ."

"Hey, fuck you, Davenport, I just want to nail this sonofabitch, and the next thing I hear is that New York cops are taking payoff money. . . ." She threw a paper napkin on the table, picked up the Danish and the carton of milk, and stood and stalked away.

"Hey, Lily," Lucas said. "God damn it."

Gary Kieffer didn't like Lucas and made no effort to hide it. He was waiting in Daniel's office when Lily arrived, with Lucas just behind her. He and Lucas nodded at each other.

"Where's Daniel?" Lily asked.

"Off somewhere," Kieffer said coldly. He was wearing a navy-blue business suit, a tie knotted in a full Windsor, and well-polished black wingtips.

"I'll go check," Lucas grumped. He backed out of the office, looking at Lily. She dropped her purse beside the chair next to Kieffer's and sat down.

"You'd be the New York lady officer," Kieffer said, looking her over.

"Yes. Lily Rothenburg. Lieutenant."

"Gary Kieffer." They shook hands, he with an exaggerated gentleness. Kieffer wore thick glasses and his large red nose was pitted with old acne scars. He crossed his hands over his stomach.

"What's the problem with you and Davenport?" Lily asked. "There's a certain chill. . . ."

Kieffer's blue eyes were distorted by the heavy glasses and looked almost liquid, like ice cubes in a glass of gin and tonic. He was in his early fifties, his face lined by weather and stress. He was silent for a moment, then asked, "Are you friends?"

"No. We're not friends. I just met him a couple of days ago," she said.

"I don't like to talk out of turn," Kieffer said.

"Look, I've got to work with him," Lily prompted.

"He's a cowboy," Kieffer continued. His voice dropped a notch and he looked around the office, as though checking for recording devices. "That's my estimation. He's gunned down six people. Killed them. I don't believe there's another officer in Minnesota, including SWAT guys, who has killed more than two. No FBI man has. Maybe nobody in the country has. And you know why? Because in most places, if a guy kills two people, he goes on a desk. They won't let him out anymore. They worry about what they've got on their hands. But not with Davenport. He does what he pleases. Sometimes that's killing people."

"Well, I understand that in his area . . ."

"Yeah, yeah, that's what everybody says. That's what the news people say. He's got the media people in his pocket, the reporters. They say he does dope, he does vice, he does intelligence work on violent criminals. I say he's a gunman, and I don't hold with that. Except for Davenport, we don't have the death penalty in Minnesota. He's a gunman, plain and simple."

Lily thought it over. A gunman. She could see it in him. She'd have to be careful. But gunmen had their uses. . . . Kieffer was staring straight ahead, at the photos on Daniel's wall, caught in his own thoughts of Davenport.

Lucas came back a moment later, Daniel trailing behind him with a cup of coffee. Sloan and another cop, the second one unshaven and dressed like a parking-lot attendant, were a step behind Daniel. Everybody called the second cop Del, but nobody introduced him to Lily. She assumed he was undercover Narcotics or Intelligence.

"So what do we got?" Daniel asked as he settled behind his desk. He looked into his humidor, then snapped it shut.

"We've got a map. Let me explain the situation," Sloan said. He moved up to Daniel's desk and unrolled a copy of a plat map from the City Planner's Office.

Billy Hood had apparently left Bemidji a year before, drifted down to the Twin Cities and moved into an apartment with two friends. The apartment was on the first-floor corner of the building, just to the right of the entrance. A careful, secretive questioning of the elderly couple who worked as building superintendents suggested that Hood's roommates were in residence. Hood had been gone for more than a week, perhaps ten days, but his clothes were still in the apartment.

"What are the chances of getting a search warrant?" Lucas asked.

"If Lily will swear that she has probable cause to think Hood's the man who killed Andretti, there'd be no problem," Daniel said.

"The problem is, we've got those two guys who live with him," said Sloan. "We've got nothing against them, so we can't kick the door and bust them. But if we go talk nice to them, what happens if they're part of the whole deal? Maybe Hood's calling them every night to find out what's happening. They could have a voice code to warn him off. . . ."

"So what are you suggesting?" Daniel asked.

The cop named Del pointed at the map. "See this building across the street? We can get a ground-floor apartment and set up there. There's only two ways out of Hood's building—the other way's on the side—and we can see both of them from the apartment across the street. We think the ideal thing would be to set up a surveillance. Then, depending on how he arrives, grab him just before he goes in, or when he comes back out."

"What do you mean, 'how he arrives'?" Daniel asked, looking up from the map.

"There're not many cars on the street. He could pull up right to the front door, hop out and go inside. If he's nuts, we want to be in a position where we can tackle him. You know, a couple guys walk down the street, talking, and when they get to him, wham! Take him down, put on the cuffs."

"We could put somebody inside . . ." Daniel suggested, but Del was already shaking his head.

"We've got those goddamned roommates to worry about. Or, as far as we know, somebody else in the building. If he's warned off somehow, we'd never know it. We could be there watching the building and he's laying on a beach in San Juan."

They talked for another five minutes before Daniel nodded.

"All right," he conceded, standing up. "It looks like you've got it figured. When do you think he'll get back?"

"No sooner than tonight, even if he drove like crazy," Sloan said. "He'd have to do six, seven hundred miles a day to get here tonight. New York says he's driving an old car."

"That's what we got from his motel," Lily said.

Lucas looked at Daniel. "If there was some way to make sure the other two guys were out of there, it might not be a bad idea to go in and take a look," he said. "We could check for weapons and anything that might tell us where he is right now."

"Are we talking about an illegal entry?" Kieffer blurted suddenly. They were the first words he had spoken since the meeting began, and everybody turned to look at him.

"No. We're not, Gary," Daniel said promptly. "Everything will be on the up-and-up. But instead of kicking in the door, Lieutenant Davenport, I take it, is proposing to go in without disturbing the place."

"That is very close, very close to an illegal search. You know that searches are supposed to be announced. . . ."

"Hey, take it easy, everything will be okayed by a judge, all right?" Daniel said, staring Kieffer down. "And if it wasn't, it's still better'n getting one of my people shot."

Kieffer grunted in disgust. "I've got nothing to do with this. In my judgment, it's a bad move. And I think we ought to grab him the minute we see him. Put some guys in cars, take him. Or if he gets in that apartment, kick the door. We could put an entry team in there, take the door off, and we're inside before they can move. . . ."

"But what if he's willing to die? Like Bluebird?" Lucas asked. "You can get the drop on somebody, but if he's willing to die, and if he goes for a gun, what're you gonna do? You're gonna shoot him. I don't give a shit if you kill him, but I'd like to talk to him first."

Kieffer shook his head. "It's a bad plan," he said. "He'll slip away. I'm telling you that on the record."

"Lemme know when the record's released," Lucas said.

Lily grinned without thinking, but killed the smile when Lucas looked at her. She was still mad.

Daniel turned to Del. "These two guys, the roommates. What do we know about them?"

"One of them works at a bakery. One of them's unemployed. He spends most of his time at a health club, lifting. He supposedly does some modeling for art classes, big scandal in the building. You know, nude stuff. Anyway, that's what we get from the super."

"Can you locate them, put a guy on each one of them?"

"I think so."

"Do it. Lily, we're going to need you for the warrant." Daniel looked at Lucas. "And you better figure out how you'll get in. We'll want you to do the search."

Kieffer got up and walked to the door. "I don't know anything about this," he said, and left.


Lucas stopped Del in the hallway.

"How are we going to do this?" he asked.

"I could get a key. . . ."

"That'd be quicker'n a power pick. The fuckin' pick sounds like you dropped a tray full of silverware."

"I'll talk to the super. . . ."

"You got a little weight on them?" Lucas asked.

"A little," Del said. "They push some toot out the back door, supplement the old man's Social Security."

"Okay. As long as they're fixed. Are you going down there now?"

"Yeah."

"I've got to stop in my office, pick up a tape recorder and a Polaroid. I'll be right behind you."


The building across from Hood's had an alleyway access. Lucas dumped the Porsche a block away and walked in. Del was waiting with the key.

"The baker's halfway through his shift. He gets off at four. The other guy's at the club. He's doing bench presses and he told Dave that he always sits in the whirlpool after a heavy workout, so he'll be a while." Del handed Lucas a

Yale key. "The warrant's on the way. Daniel said to stick it into one of Hood's coat sleeves before you leave. Like in a parka or something. Someplace he won't look right away."

Lily arrived five minutes later, with Sloan.

"We've got a warrant," she told Lucas. She made no move to hand it to him. "I'm coming along."

"Fuck that."

"I'm coming," she insisted. "He's my man and two of us can go through the place faster than one."

"Not a bad idea," said Del. "No offense, man, but you kinda smell like a cop. If somebody sees you in the hallway, before you get in . . . Lily'd be a little camouflage."

Lucas looked from Lily to Del and back. "All right," he said. "Let's go."

"Hope there's nobody crashing in here. You know, a guest," Lily said as they crossed the street. Hood's building was made of old red sandstone; the wooden windows showed dry rot.

"Don't worry, I'll cover you," Lucas said. He tried to make it light, a joke, but it came out macho.

She stared back at him. "You can be a pain in the ass, you know?"

"That was supposed to be a joke."

"Yeah. Well." Her eyes broke away.

Lucas shook his head. He wasn't doing anything right. He followed her up the stoop into the building. First door on the right. He knocked once. No answer. And again. No answer. He put the key in the lock, cracked the door. Lily looked down the hall, checking the other doorways for watchers.

"Hello?" Lucas made it loud, but not too loud. Then he whistled. "Here, boy. Here, pup."

After a few seconds of silence, Lily said, "Nobody home."

"Probably a fuckin' Rottweiler under the bed with its tongue cut out to make it mean," Lucas said. He pushed open the door and they stepped inside.

"That's a heck of a door," Lucas said as he eased it shut.

"What?"

"It's an old building. They still have the original doors—solid oak or walnut or something," Lucas said, rapping on the door with his knuckles. "By the time apartments get this old, one landlord or another has usually stripped out all the original doors and sold them. They're probably worth as much as the apartment building."

They were in the living room. Two rickety occasional chairs, a recliner with a stained fabric cover, the brown metal cube of an aging color television. Two red vinyl beanbag chairs lay on the floor in front of the TV, leaking tiny white Styrofoam beads on the wooden floor. The apartment smelled of some kind of stew or soup—lentils, maybe. White beans.

Lucas led the way through a quick check of the apartment, glancing into two bedrooms, a tiny kitchen with its peeling linoleum and thirties gas stove with a fold-down top.

"How do we know which is Hood's room?" Lily asked.

"You look at the stuff on the chests," Lucas said. "There's always some shit."

"You sound like you do this quite a bit," she said.

"I mostly talk to a lot of burglars," Lucas said, suppressing a grin. He headed toward a bedroom.

"What do you want me to do?" Lily asked.

"Look in the kitchen, around the telephone," Lucas said. He took the miniature tape recorder out of his pocket. "Push the red button to record. Dictate any phone numbers you find written around. Any times or place names. Anyplace Hood might have been."

The first bedroom had one bed and a ramshackle chest. The bed was unmade, the bedclothes twisted in a pile. Lucas stooped and looked under it. There were several boxes, but a patina of dust suggested that they hadn't been moved recently. He stood and went over to the six-drawer chest. Notes, gas-station charge slips, cash-register receipts, ballpoint pens, paper clips and pennies were scattered across the top. He checked the charge slips: Tomas Peck. Wrong guy. Lucas quickly looked through the drawers and the closet for weapons. Nothing.

The second bedroom had two beds and no chests. All the clothing was stacked inside boxes, some plastic and made for storage, some cardboard and made for moving. Personal papers were scattered across a windowsill next to one of the beds. He picked up a letter, glanced at the address: Billy Hood. The return address was in Bemidji and the handwriting was feminine. His wife, probably. Lucas looked through the letter, but it was mostly a litany of complaints followed by a request for money for the wife and a daughter.

He quickly went through the boxes stacked beside the bed. One was half full of underwear and socks, a second was stacked with several pairs of worn jeans and a couple of belts. A third held winter-weight shirts and sweaters, with a couple sets of thermal underwear.

The bedroom had one closet. The door was standing open and Lucas patted down the shirts and jackets hanging inside. Nothing. He dropped to his knees and pushed the clothing out of the way and checked the bottom. A lever-action Sears .30-.30. He cranked the lever down. Unloaded. A box of shells sat on the floor beside the butt. He got up, looked around, found a torn pair of underpants.

"What're you doing?" Lily was in the doorway.

"Found a gun. I'm going to jam it. What'd you get in the kitchen?" He ripped a square of material out of the underpants.

"There were some phone numbers on papers around the phone. I got them."

"Look in all the drawers."

"I did. Paged through the calendar, looked through a kind of general catch-all basket and drawer full of junk. Went through the phone book. There was a number written in the back with a red pen and there was a red pen right next to the book, so it might be recent. . . ." She glanced at a piece of paper in her hand. "It has a six-one-four area code. That's the Twin Cities, right? Maybe . . ."

"No, we're six-one-two," Lucas said. "I don't know where six-one-four is. Sure it was six-one-four?"

"Yeah . . ." She disappeared and Lucas made a tight little ball of the under-pants material and pushed it down the muzzle with a ballpoint. The material was tightly packed, and after two or three inches, he couldn't force it down any farther. Satisfied, he put the rifle back in the closet and closed the door.

"That six-one-four code is southwestern Ohio," Lily said from the doorway. She was looking at a phone book.

"He could be coming back that way," Lucas said.

"I'll get somebody to run down the number," Lily said. She closed the phone book. "What else?"

"Check the front-room closets. I gotta finish here."

There was a box under Hood's bed. Lucas pulled it out. A photo album, apparently some years old, covered with dust. He glanced through it, then pushed it back under the bed. A moment later, Lily called, "Shotgun." Lucas stepped into the living room just as she cracked open an old single-shot twelve-gauge.

"Shit," Lucas said. "No point in trying to jam that. He'll be looking right through the barrel when he puts a shell in."

"Don't see any shells," Lily said. "Should we take it?"

"Better not. If his roommates are involved, we don't want anything missing. . . ."

Lucas went back to the bedroom and looked through the other man's boxes. There was nothing of interest, no letters or notes that might tie the others more intimately to Hood. He went back into the living room. "Lily?"

"I'm in the bathroom," she called. "Find anything else?"

"No. How about you?" He poked his head into the bathroom and found her carefully going through the medicine cabinet.

"Nothing serious." She took a prescription-drug bottle out of the cabinet and looked at it, her forehead wrinkling. "There's a prescription here for Hood. Strong stuff, but I don't see how you could abuse it."

"What is it?"

"An antihistamine. The label says it's for bee stings. My father used it. He was allergic to bees and fire ants. If he got stung, his whole body would swell up. It used to scare the shit out of him; he'd think he was smothering. And he might have too, if he didn't have his medicine around. The swelling can pinch off your windpipe. . . ."

Lucas shrugged. "No use to us."

Lily put the plastic bottle of pills back in the cabinet, closed it and followed him into the living room. "Anything else?"

"I guess not," Lucas said. "We fucked up a gun; I hope there aren't any shells for the shotgun."

"Didn't see any. Are you going to do any pictures?"

"Yeah. Just a few views." Lucas took a half-dozen Polaroid photos of the rooms and paced off the main room's dimensions, which he dictated into the tape recorder.

"You know, we really could spend more time going through the place," Lily suggested.

"Better not. What you get quick is probably all you're going to get," Lucas said. "Never push when you're inside somebody else's house. All kinds of shit can happen. Friends stop by unexpectedly. Relatives. Get in and get out."

"You sound more and more experienced. . . ."

Lucas shrugged. "You got the warrant?"

"Oh, yeah." Lily took it out of her purse and stuck it in the sleeve of a winter coat in the living room closet. "We'll tell the court we put it one place he'd find it for sure. Of course, he's got to put on the coat."

"Which he probably wouldn't do until winter . . ."

"Which is not that far away," Lily said.

"So all right," Lucas said. "Did we change anything?"

"Nothing I can see," Lily said.

"Let me take a last look in the bedroom." He stepped into the bedroom, looked around and finally opened the closet door an inch. "I'm slipping," he said. "The damn door was open when I came in and I closed it."

Lily was looking at him curiously. Lucas said, "What?"

"I'm really kind of impressed," she conceded. "You're pretty good at this."

"That's the nicest thing you ever said to me."

She grinned and shrugged. "So I'm a little competitive."

"I'm sorry about ragging you this morning," Lucas said, the words tumbling out. "I'm not a responsible human being before noon. I don't daylight; I really don't."

"I shouldn't have picked on you," she said. "I just want to get this job done."

"Are we making up?"

She turned away toward the door, her back to him.

"It's all right with me," she said. "Let's get out of here." She opened the door and peered down the hallway.

"Clear," she said.

Lucas was just behind her. "If we're going to make up, we ought to do it right," he said.

She turned and looked at him. "What?"

He leaned forward and kissed her on the mouth, and the kiss came back for just the barest fraction of a second, a returned pressure with a hint of heat. Then she pulled away and stepped out into the hall, flustered.

"Enough of that shit," she said.

It was a five-minute walk down the block, around the corner, up the alley and into the surveillance apartment. Lily kept her head turned, apparently interested in watching the apartment buildings go by. Once or twice, Lucas felt her glance at him, and then quickly away. He could still feel the pressure of her lips on his.

"How'd we do?" Del asked when they got back to the apartment. Sloan stood up and wandered over. A third detective had arrived and was sitting on an aluminum lawn chair, reading a book and watching the street. A man in a gray suit sat on a folding canvas camp stool next to the window. He was reading a hardcover book and smoking a pipe.

"Found a couple of guns, fucked one of them up," Lucas said. Under his breath he asked, "Feeb?"

Del nodded, and they glanced at the FBI man in the gray suit. "Observing," Del muttered. In a louder voice he said, "Get anything else?"

"A phone number," Lily said. "I'll call Anderson and see how quick he can run down that Ohio phone."

Anderson called Kieffer and Kieffer called Washington. Washington made three calls. Ten minutes after Lily talked to Anderson, Kieffer got a call from the agent-in-charge in Columbus, Ohio. The number was for a motel off Interstate 70 near Columbus. An hour later, an FBI agent showed a motel desk clerk a wire photograph of Hood. The clerk nodded, remembering the face, and said Hood had stayed at the motel the night before. The clerk found the registration, signed as Bill Harris. There was a license-plate number, but a check showed that the number had never been issued in Minnesota.

"He's careful," Anderson said. They were gathered in Daniel's office.

"But he's moving right along," said Kieffer.

"He ought to be here. Or close," Lily said, looking from Lucas to Anderson to Daniel to Kieffer.

Kieffer nodded. "Very late tonight or sometime tomorrow, if he keeps push-ing it. He's got Chicago in the way. He either has to go through it, or go way around it. . . . He'd have to push like a sonofabitch to make it here tonight. It's more likely that he'd make it to Madison tonight and get into the Cities tomor-row."

"How far is Madison?" Lily asked.

"Five hours."

"He is pushing it," she said. "So it could be tonight. . . ."

"We'll keep a watch," Daniel said. He looked around. "Anything else?"

"I can't think of anything," Lucas said. "Lily?"

"I guess we wait," Lily said.

# 9

Lily went back to the surveillance post with Del, the undercover cop, while Lucas filled out the return on the search warrant. As he was finishing, Larry Hart walked in, carrying an overnight bag.

"Anything more?" Lucas asked.

"Nothing but a bunch of rumors," Hart said, dumping the bag against the wall. "There was something weird going on, just about the time of the bikers. There was a sun dance up at Standing Rock, but that was on the up-and-up. But there was maybe a ceremony of some kind at Bear Butte. A midnight deal. That's the rumor."

"Any names?"

"No. But the guys out there are asking around."

"We need names. In this business, names are the game."

Hart checked in with Anderson, then went home to clean up. Lucas filed the return on the search warrant, walked across the street to a newsstand and bought half a dozen magazines, then headed down to Indian Country.

Del was asleep on an inflatable mattress, his mouth half open. He looked exactly like a bum, Lucas decided. Two Narcotics cops were perched on match-ing aluminum lawn chairs, watching the street. A cooler sat next to the cop on the left and a boombox was playing "Brown Sugar." The FBI man was gone, although his stool was still there: the seat read L. L. BEAN. Lily was sitting on a stack of newspapers, leaning back against a wall.

"You guys are such a bunch of cutups," Lucas said as he walked in.

"Fuck you, Davenport," the two surveillance cops said in unison.

"I second that," Lily said.

"Anytime, anyplace," Lucas said. The cops laughed, and Lily said, "You talking to me or them?"

"Them," said Lucas. "Duane's got such a nice ass."

"Takes a load off my mind," said Lily.

"*Puts* a load on mine," said Duane, the fat surveillance cop.

"Nothing happening?" asked Lucas.

"Lot of fuckin' dope," Duane said. "I was kinda surprised. We don't hear too much about it from this area."

"We don't know too many Indians," Lucas said. He looked around the bare apartment. "Where's the feeb?"

"He went out. Said he was coming back. He seems kinda touchy about his chair, if that's what you were thinking," said the thin cop.

"Yeah?"

"Stacks of newspaper down the hall," Lily said.


One of the magazines had a debate on ten-millimeter automatic pistols. A gun writer suggested that it was the perfect defensive cartridge, producing twice the muzzle energy of typical nine-millimeter and .45 ACP rounds and almost half again as much as the .357 Magnum. The writer's opponent, a Los Angeles cop, worried that the ten-millimeter was a little *too* hot, tending to punch holes not only through the target but also through the crowd at the bus stop two blocks away. Lucas couldn't follow the details of the argument. His mind kept straying to the shape of Lily's neck, the edge of her cheek from the side and slightly behind, the curve of her wrist. Her lip. He remembered Sloan saying something about her overbite, and he smiled just a bit and nibbled at his own lip.

"What're you smiling about?" Lily asked.

"Nothing," Lucas said. "Magazine."

She heaved herself to her feet, stretched, yawned and wandered over. "Hot-hot-hot," she said. "It's a ten-MM?"

Lucas closed the magazine. "Dumb fucks," he said.

Anderson called on the portable a few minutes after one o'clock: The killer in Oklahoma City had vanished. Kieffer had talked to FBI agents in South Dakota about the rumors Hart had heard of a midnight ceremony, Anderson added, but nobody had much.

"There's some question about whether there ever was such a thing," he said.

"What do you mean?"

"Kieffer talked to the lead investigator out there and this guy thinks the rumors came out of the confrontation with the bikers. One night the Indians surrounded Bear Butte, wouldn't let the bikers down the road around it. The bikers supposedly saw fires and so on, and heard drum music—and that eventually got turned into this secret-ceremony business."

"So it could be another dead end," Lily said.

"That's what Kieffer says."

"I could be watching *The Young and the Restless,*" Lily said twenty minutes later.

"Go for a walk?" Lucas suggested.

"All right. Take a portable."

They went out the alley, two blocks to a 7-Eleven, bought Diet Cokes and started back.

"So fuckin' boring," Lily complained.

"You don't have to sit there. He probably won't be in until this evening," Lucas said.

"I feel like I oughta be there," Lily said. "He's my man."

On the way back, Lucas took a small gun-cleaning kit out of the Porsche. Inside the apartment, he spread newspapers on the floor, sat cross-legged, broke down his P7 and began cleaning it. Lily went back to her stack of newspapers for a few minutes, then moved over across from him.

"Mind if I use it?" she asked after watching for a moment.

"Go ahead."

"Thanks." She took her .45 out of her purse, popped the magazine, checked the chamber to make sure it was empty and began stripping it. "I break a fingernail about once a week on this damn barrel bushing," she said. She stuck her tongue out in concentration, rotated the bushing over the recoil spring plug and eased the spring out.

"Pass the nitro," she said.

Lucas handed her the cleaning solvent.

"This stuff smells better than gasoline," she said. "It could turn me into a sniffer."

"Gives me headaches," Lucas said. "It smells good but I can't handle it." He noticed that her .45 was spotless before she began cleaning it. His P7 didn't need the work either, but it was something to do.

"Ever shot a P7?" he asked idly.

"The other one. The eight-shot. The big one, like yours, has a lot of fire-power, but I can't get my hand around the butt. I don't like the way it carries either. Too fat."

"That's not exactly a Tinker Toy you've got there," he said, nodding at her Colt.

"No, but the shape of the butt is different. It's skinnier. That's what I need. It's easier to handle."

"I really don't like that single-action for street work," Lucas said conversationally. "It's fine if you're target-shooting, but if you're only worried about hitting a torso . . . I like the double-action."

"You could try one of the forty-five Smiths."

"They're supposed to be good guns," Lucas agreed. "I probably would have, if the P7 hadn't come out first. . . . How come you never went to a Smith?"

"Well, this thing just feels right to me. When I was shooting in competition I used a 1911 from Springfield Armory in thirty-eight Super. I want the forty-five for the street, but all that competition . . . the gun feels friendly."

"You shot competition?" Lucas asked. The cops at the window, who had been listening in an abstract way, suddenly perked up at an undertone in Lucas' voice.

"I was New York women's champ in practical shooting for a couple of years," Lily said. "I had to quit competition because it was taking too much time. But I still shoot a little."

"You must be pretty good," Lucas offered. The cops by the window glanced at each other. A bet.

"Better than anybody you're likely to know," she said offhandedly.

Lucas snorted and she squinted at him.

"What? You think you can shoot with me?"

"With you?" Lucas said. His lip might have curled.

Lily sat up, interested now. "You ever compete?"

He shrugged. "Some."

"You ever win?"

"Some. Used a 1911, in fact."

"Practical or bull's-eye?"

"A little of both," he said.

"And you think you can shoot with me?"

"I can shoot with most people," Lucas said.

She looked at him, studied his face, and a small smile started at the corners of her lips. "You want to put your money where your mouth is?"

It was Lucas' turn to stare, weighing the challenge. "Yeah," he said finally. "Anytime, anyplace."

Lily noticed the cops by the window watching them.

"He's sandbagging me, right?" she said. "He's the North American big-bore champ or some fuckin' thing."

"I don't know, I never seen him shoot," one of the cops said.

Lily stared at him with narrowed eyes, gauging the likelihood that he was lying, then turned back to Lucas. "All right," she said. "Where do we shoot?"


They shot at a police pistol range in the basement of a precinct house, using Outers twenty-five-foot slow-fire pistol targets. There were seven concentric rings on each target face. The three outer rings were marked but not colored, while the inner four rings—the 7, 8, 9 and 10—were black. The center ring, the 10 ring, was a bit smaller than a dime.

"Nice range," Lily said when Lucas turned on the lights. A Hennepin County deputy had been leaving just when they arrived. When he heard what they were doing, he insisted on judging the match.

Lily put her handset on the ledge of a shooting booth, took the .45 from her purse, held it in both hands and looked downrange over the sights. "Let's get the targets up."

"This P7 ain't exactly a target pistol," Lucas said. He squinted downrange. "I never did like the light in here either."

"Cold feet?" Lily asked.

"Making conversation," he said. "I just wish I had my Gold Cup. It'd make me feel better. It'd also punch a bigger hole in the paper. The same size as yours. If you're as good as you say, that could make the difference."

"You could always chicken out if the extra seven-hundredths of an inch makes you nervous," Lily said. She pushed a magazine into the Colt and jacked a shell into the chamber. "And I don't have my match guns either."

"Fuck it. We'll flip to shoot," Lucas said. He dug in his pocket for a quarter.

"How much?" Lily asked.

"It's got to be enough to feel it," Lucas said. "We ought to give it a little bite of reality. You say."

"Best two out of three rounds . . . One hundred dollars."

"That's not enough," Lucas said, aiming the P7 downrange again. "I was thinking a thousand."

"That's ridiculous," Lily said, tossing her head. The deputy was now watching them with real interest. The story would be all over the sheriff's department and the city cops, and probably St. Paul, before the night was done. "You're trying to psych me, Davenport. A hundred is all I can afford. I'm not a rich game-inventor."

"Hey, Dick," Lucas said to the deputy. "Lily's not gonna let me put the targets up, you want to . . ."

"Sure . . ."

The deputy began running the target sheets out to twenty-five feet. Lucas stepped closer to Lily, his voice low. "I'll tell you what. If you win, you take down a hundred. If I win, I get another kiss. Time and place of my choosing."

She put her hands on her hips. "That's the most goddamned juvenile thing I ever heard. You're too fuckin' old for that, Davenport. You've got lines in your face. Your hair is turning gray."

Lucas reddened but grinned through the embarrassment. Dick was walking back toward them. "It might be juvenile, but that's what I want," he said. "Unless you're chicken."

"You really do a number on a person's head, don't you?"

"Puk-puk-puk," he said, doing an imitation of a chicken's cackle.

"Fuck-you, Davenport," she said.

"So maybe we just have a pleasant afternoon shooting guns. We don't have to compete. I mean, if you've got cold feet."

"Fuck you."

"Anytime, anyplace."

"What an asshole," she muttered under her breath.

"What does that mean?" Lucas asked.

"It means you're on," she said.

Lucas tossed the quarter and won. They shot a round of five shots for familiarization. Neither showed the other the practice target.

"You ready?" Lucas asked.

"Ready."

Lucas fired first, five shots. He used both hands, his right shooting hand cupped in his left, the left side of his body slightly forward of the right. He kept both eyes open. Lily could tell he was hitting the black, but she couldn't tell how close he was to the center 10 ring. When Lucas finished, she stepped to the line and took a position identical to the one Lucas had used. She fired her first shot, said, "Shit," and fired four more.

"Problem?" Lucas said when she took down the gun after the last shot.

"First shot was a flier, I think," she said. The deputy rolled the targets back to the shooting line. Two of Lucas' five shots had clipped the 10 ring. The third and fourth counted 9, a fifth was in the 8 ring. Forty-six.

Three shots from Lily's .45 had obliterated the center of the target, a fourth was in the nine, but the flier was out in the four. Forty-three.

"Without the flier, I'd of won," Lily said. She sounded angry with herself.

"If pigs had wings they could fly," said Lucas.

"That's the worst round I've shot in a year."

"It's the less than ideal conditions, shooting targets with a gun you don't use on the range," Lucas said. "It gets you range shooters every time."

"I'm not a range shooter," she said, now angry at Lucas. "Let's get the new targets up, huh?"

"Jesus, what'd you guys bet? Must be something, huh?" asked the deputy, looking from one of them to the other.

"Yeah," said Lily. "A hundred bucks and Davenport's honor. He loses either way."

"Huh?"

"Never mind."

Lucas grinned as he finished reloading. "Bitch, bitch, bitch," he said, just barely audibly.

"Keep it up, buster," she said through her teeth.

"Sorry. Wasn't trying to psych you," he said, trying to psych her. "You shoot first this time."

She fired five shots and all five felt good. She smiled at him this time and said, "I just a fifty or close to it. Stick that in your nose, asshole."

"Temper, temper . . ."

Lucas fired his five. After the last shot he looked at her and said, "If that doesn't beat you, I'll kiss your ass in Saks' front window."

"Side bet?" she asked before the deputy reeled in the targets. "I got fifty bucks that says I win this round. And don't give me any shit about anything else."

"All right," he said. "Fifty."

Dick pulled in the targets and whistled. "I'll have to count these careful," he said.

All ten shots were deep in the black. Dick spread the targets on a workbench and started counting, Lily and Lucas looking over his shoulder.

"Wait a minute," Lucas started, when the deputy wrote down an eight.

"Not a fuckin' word," Lily said, pointing her finger at Lucas' nose.

The deputy added up the totals, turned to Lucas and said, "You owe the lady fifty bucks. I count it forty-seven to forty-six."

"Bullshit. Let me see those. . . ."

Lucas counted them forty-eight to forty-seven. He took two twenties and a ten out of his wallet and handed them to her.

"This pisses me off," he said, his voice tight.

"I hope being pissed off doesn't make your hand shake," she said sweetly.

"It won't," he promised.

Lucas shot first on the third round. All five shots felt good, and he turned to her and nodded. "If you beat me this time, you deserve it. This time, I got the fifty."

"We'll see," she said.

She fired her five and they followed Dick down to the targets. He shook his head. "Jesus. You guys . . ."

He took five minutes to count, then glanced at Lily. "I think he's got you, Lily, Lieutenant. Either one point or two . . ."

"Let me see that. . . ."

Lily went over the targets, counting, her lips moving as she totaled them up. "I don't believe it," she grunted. "I shoot two of the worst rounds of my fuckin' career and you take me out by a point."

Lucas was grinning. "I'll collect tonight," he said.

She peered at him for a second, then said, "Double or nothing. One round, five shots."

Lucas thought about it. "I'm happy where I'm at."

"Yeah, maybe, but the question is, Are you greedy enough to go for more? And do you have the balls for it?" Lily said.

"I'm happy," he repeated.

"Think how happy you'll be if you win."

Lucas looked at her for a moment, then said, "One shot. Just one. Double or nothing."

"You're on," she said. "You shoot first."

Dick sent down a new target sheet. When he was out of the way, Lucas lined up in a one-handed bull's-eye–shooter's stance, brought the P7 up once, lowered it, scratched his forehead, brought the gun up again, let out half a breath and fired.

"That's a good one," he said to her.

"I thought you shot practical."

"Most of the time," he said. Then he added, innocently, "But I was really better at bull's-eye."

She took her two-handed stance and squeezed off the shot. "A hair to the left."

"I win, then."

"We ought to look." They looked. Lucas' shot wiped out the 10 ring. Lily's shot counted nine. "God damn it," she said.

Outside the precinct station, it was already getting dark. They turned a corner into the parking lot and were alone for a moment.

"Well," she said.

He took in her big dark eyes and the heavy breasts beneath her tweed jacket, looked down at her and shook his head. "Later."

"God damn it, Davenport . . ." But Lucas was already popping open the door to the car. They were back at the surveillance post in fifteen minutes, Lily stewing.

"Anything?" Lucas asked, as they stepped into the surveillance room. The FBI man's camp stool had disappeared.

"Quiet as death," said one of the cops. Del was still asleep. "Who won?"

"He did," Lily said grimly. "Two points out of a hundred and fifty."

"All right," said the heavier of the two cops. He held out his hand and the other cop gave him a dollar.

"A whole fuckin' dollar?" Lucas said. "I'm impressed."

The street was absolutely empty. At times it seemed as though an hour passed between cars. Sloan stopped by, watched an hour and finally said, "Why don't you get a portable and come down to King's Place. My wife is gonna meet me there. It's about two minutes away."

"What is it?" Lily asked.

"Tex-Mex cowboy-lumberjack bar down on Hennepin. They don't allow fights, they've got a band and terrific tacos, three for a dollar," Sloan said.

"Food," said Lily.

Lily expected Lucas to collect at the car, in the dark, but he walked around her again.

"Jesus, you're an asshole sometimes," she said.

"You're so impatient," he said. "Why can't you relax?"

"I want to pay off and be done."

"We got plenty of time," he said. "We got all night."

"In a pig's eye we got all night," she said.


The bar had thirty-pound muskies and deer heads on the wall, a stuffed black bear in the entrance and a wooden cactus in the middle of a room full of picnic tables. A three-piece Mexican rock band banged away in a corner, and pitchers of Schmidt beer went for two dollars.

Sloan got things rolling by ordering a round of pitchers, which only Lily thought was excessive. The band came on with a south-of-the-border version of "Little Deuce Coupe."

"Let's dance," Lucas said, pulling Lily away from her tacos and pitcher. "Come on, they're playing rock 'n' roll." Lucas danced with Lily and then with the wife of a local cowboy while the cowboy danced with Lily. Then Lily danced with Sloan, and Lucas with a tall single woman whose beehive hairdo had just begun to topple, while Sloan's wife danced with the cowboy. Then they did it again. Lily was giggling when she finally got back to the table. Lucas waved at the waitress and pointed at Lily's pitcher.

" 'Nother round, all the way," Lucas called.

"You're trying to get me drunk, Davenport," Lily said. Her voice was clear, but her eyes were moving too much. "It'll probably work."

Sloan laughed immoderately and started on the second round.

At midnight, they checked the surveillance room. Nothing. Both of Hood's roommates were home. The lights were out. At one o'clock, they checked again. Nothing.

"So what do you want to do?" Lucas asked when King's closed.

"I dunno. I guess you better take me back to the hotel. I doubt he'd be driving this late."

Lucas pulled the Porsche into the hotel parking lot and hopped out.

"Time to collect?" Lily asked.

"Yeah."

A half-dozen people were walking through the lot, and more were going in and out.

"This is not an invitation, so I don't want you to read anything into it. . . . ."

"Yeah?"

"You can come up for just long enough to collect."

They rode up in the elevator without speaking and walked down the hall to her room, Lucas feeling increasingly awkward. Inside, when she closed the door, it was dark. Lucas fumbled for the light switch but she caught his hand and said, "Don't. Just collect and then you can leave."

"All of a sudden, I feel like a fuckin' idiot," Lucas said, abashed.

"Let's get it over with," she said, a little drunkenly.

He found her in the dark, pulled her in and kissed her. She hung in his arms for just a fraction of a moment, then returned the kiss, powerfully, pushing him against the door, her face and pelvis pressed to his, her hands clenching his rib cage. They clung together for a long moment; then she broke her lips away and squeezed him tighter and groaned, "Oh, Jesus."

Lucas held her for a moment and then whispered in her ear, "Double or nothing," and found her lips again and they walked in a tight little circle and Lucas felt the bed hit the back of his knees and he dropped on it, pulling her with him. He expected her to resist, but she did not. She rolled to one side and held him, kissing him again on the lips, then on the edge of the jaw, and Lucas rolled over half on top of her and pulled at her shirt, getting it out of her trousers, slipping his hand inside, fighting the brassiere, finally reaching around her, unsnapping the bra and then catching one of her breasts in his hand. . . .

"Oh, God," she said, arching against him. "God, Davenport . . ."

He found her belt, pulled it open, slipped his hand inside her trousers, under the edge of her underpants, down, to the hot liquid center. . . .

"Ah, Jesus," she said, and she rolled away from him, pushing his hand away, off the side of the bed onto the floor.

"What?" It was pitch black in the room, and Lucas was groggy from the sudden struggle. "Lily . . ."

"God, Lucas, we can't. . . . I'm sorry, I don't mean to tease. Jesus, I'm sorry."

"Lily . . ."

"Lucas, you're going to make me cry, go away. . . ."

"Jesus, don't do that." Lucas stood up, pushed his shirt back in his pants, discovered he was missing a shoe. He groped in the dark for a second, found the light. Lily was sitting on the floor on the far side of the bed, clutching her shirt around her.

"I'm sorry," she said. Her eyes were black with remorse. "I just can't."

"That's okay," Lucas said, trying to catch his breath. He half laughed. "My fuckin' shoe is missing. . . ."

Lily, her face drawn, looked around the edge of the bed and said, "Under the curtain. Behind you."

"Okay. Got it."

"I'm sorry."

"Look, Lily, whatever is right, okay? I mean, I'm going back home to blow my brains out, to relieve the pressure, but don't worry about it."

She smiled a tentative smile. "You're a nice guy. See you tomorrow."

"Sure. If I survive."

When he was gone, Lily stripped off her clothes and stood in the shower, letting the water pour down her breasts and then her back. After a few minutes, she began reducing the temperature until finally she stood in what felt like a torrent of ice water.

Sober, she went to bed. And just before she went to sleep, she remembered that last shot. Had she flinched? Or had she deliberately thrown the shot?

Lily Rothenburg, faithful wife, went to sleep with lust in her heart.

# 10

The knock came a few minutes after ten o'clock. Sam Crow was washing a coffee cup in the kitchen sink. He stopped at the knock and looked up. Aaron Crow was sitting in front of a battered Royal typewriter, pecking at a press release on the Oklahoma killing. Shadow Love was in the bathroom. When the knock came, Aaron went to the door and spoke through it.

"Who is that?"

"Billy."

Billy. Aaron fumbled at the lock, pulled the door open. Billy Hood stood in the hallway, bowlegged in his cowboy boots, a battered, water-stained Stetson perched on his head. His square face was drawn and pale. He took a step forward and Aaron wrapped his arms around him and picked him up off his feet.

"God damn, Billy," he said. He could feel the stone knife dangling beneath Billy's shirt.

"I feel bad, man," Billy said when Aaron released him. "Man, I've been fucked up all the way back. I can't stop thinking about it."

"Because you're a spiritual man."

"I don't feel so fuckin' spiritual. I cut that dude," Billy said as he walked farther into the room. Aaron glanced once into the hallway and pushed the door shut.

"A white man," said Aaron.

"A man," Shadow Love said from the bathroom. He stood squarely in the doorway, arms slightly away from his sides, like a gunslinger. His cheeks were hollow. His white eyes hooked up at the corners, like a starving wolf's. "Don't make it sound small."

"I don't mean that it's small," said Aaron. "I mean that it's different. Billy killed the enemy in a war."

"A man is a man," Shadow Love insisted. "It's all the same."

"And an Indian man is an Indian man, and that's different, to be one of the people," Sam retorted. "One reason Aaron won't use you is that you don't understand the difference between war and murder."

The two Crows were squared off against their son. Hood broke it.

"Everybody's looking for me," he said. Billy looked scared, like a rabbit that's been chased until there's no more room to run. "Me and Leo. Christ, I heard about Leo and the judge. He took him off, man. Have you heard from him?"

"No. We're getting worried. They haven't got him, but we haven't heard a thing."

"Unless they've got him but they aren't saying, so they can squeeze him," said Shadow Love.

"I don't think so. This is too big to hide something like that," Sam Crow said.

Billy took off his hat, tossed it on a chair and wiped his hair back with his hand. "We've been on the radio every hour. In all the newspapers all the way from New York. Every town I come to."

"They don't know your names," Sam said.

"They connected us with Tony Bluebird. They'll be looking for us here in the Cities."

"That won't help them if they don't know who you are, Billy," said Aaron, trying to reassure him. "There are twenty thousand Indians in the Cities. How will they know which one? And we knew they'd connect you to Bluebird; that was the whole point."

"They'll find out who you are," Shadow Love said. His voice was gravelly, cold. He looked at the Crows. "It's time for you guys to go to the safe house, get out of this place. If you want to live."

"Too early," said Sam. "When we feel some pressure, we go to the safe house. Not before. If we go in too early and there's nothing happening, we'll get careless. We'll fuck around and somebody will see us."

"And they still don't have any names, nothing that will identify Billy or Leo," Aaron said again.

Shadow Love stepped out into the room and put a hand on Billy Hood's shoulder, ignoring his fathers. "I'll tell you now: They'll find your name. And they'll find Leo's. Eventually, they'll get the rest of us. They've got some movies from a camera in the building where you killed Andretti, so they've got your face. The cops'll take the pictures and go around and squeeze and squeeze, and somebody will tell them. And there was a witness who saw Leo. They'll have her looking at mug shots right now."

"You're a big authority?" Aaron asked sarcastically. "You know all the rules?"

"I know enough," Shadow Love said. His eyes were white and opaque, like marble chips from a tombstone. "I've been on the street since I was seven. I know how the cops work. They pick-pick-pick, talk-talk-talk. They'll find out."

"You don't know that. . . ."

"Don't be an old woman, Father," Shadow Love snapped. "It's dangerous." He held the older man's eyes for a moment, then turned back to Billy. "Somebody will tell. Somebody will tell on us all, sooner or later. I met one of the cops doing the investigation. He's a hunter, you can smell it on him. He'll be after us, and he's not some South Dakota sheriff's cousin, some retreaded shitkicker calling himself a cop. He's a hard man. And even if he doesn't get us, somebody will. Sooner or later. Everyone in this room is a dead man walking."

Billy Hood looked into Shadow Love's face for a moment, then nodded and seemed to grow taller. "You're right," he said, his voice suddenly calm. "I should do another while I can. Before they get me."

Sam clapped him on the back. "Good. We have a target."

"Where's John? Is he out?"

"Yeah. Out in Brookings."

"Ah, Jesus, he's going after Linstad?"

"Yup."

"That's a big one," Billy said. He ran his hand through his hair. "I gotta get home, get some sleep. Maybe I'll go up north and see Ginnie and the girl, you know? Tomorrow or the day after."

"Come on down to the river with us," Sam suggested. "We're doing a sweat. You'll feel a hundred percent better afterwards. We got some bags too, and a couple of tents. You can sleep out on the island."

"All right," Billy nodded. "My ass is whipped, man. . . ."

"And we've got to talk about a man in Milwaukee," said Sam. "The guy who's figuring the strategy for attacking the land rights up north. Smart guy . . ."

"I don't know if I can do the knife again, man. This Andretti guy, the blood was coming out of his neck like a hose." Billy sounded shaky again and Sam stopped him with a wave of his hand.

"The knife is good because it means something to the people and something to the media," he said, "But it's not the main thing. In Milwaukee, use a pistol. Use a rifle. The important thing is to kill the guy."

Aaron nodded. "Wear the knife around your neck. If you're taken, that'll be good enough."

"I won't be taken," Billy said. His voice was trembling and low, but he held it together. "If I can't get away, I'll go like Bluebird."

They talked for another fifteen minutes while Aaron gathered up the dried sage and red willow he used in the sweats. Sam couldn't sleep without a pillow, so he got one off the bed. They were walking out the door when the phone rang.

Aaron picked it up, said hello, listened a second, smiled and said, "Leo, God damn. We were worried. . . ."

Leo Clark was calling from Wichita. Oklahoma City was a war zone, he said. The police and the FBI were crawling through the Indian community. He'd gotten out of town immediately after the killing, hidden at a friend's house the next day, gotten a haircut and then driven to Wichita.

"What's happening there?" Leo asked.

"Not much. But there are FBI agents all over the place. So it's just a matter of time. . . ."

"I wish we'd hear . . ."

"The media's talking about *war*, so we got that across."

"Gotta keep pumping . . ."

"Yeah. Tell me what the judge said just before you took him," Aaron said. He listened intently and finally said, "Okay. I'm going to put some of that in the press release, so they'll know it's for real . . . and I'll put in a quote from you, like we agreed."

They talked for another minute and then Aaron hung up. "He's on his way in," he said. "He cut his hair. No more braids."

"Too bad," said Sam. "That boy had a good hair on him."

"No more. He's got sidewalls and a flattop," Aaron Crow said, chuckling. "He says he looks like a fuckin' Marine."

The sweat lodge was on the island below Fort Snelling, at the junction of the Minnesota and Mississippi, on the ground that held Sioux bones from the death camp. Aaron Crow could feel them there, still crying, tearing his flesh like fishhooks. Sam Crow held him, fearing that his other half would die of a burst heart. Billy Hood prayed and sweated, prayed and sweated, until the fear and anguish of the Andretti kill ran out of him into the ground. Shadow Love glowered in the heat, watching the others. He felt the bones in the ground, but he never prayed a word.

Long after midnight, they sat on the edge of the river, watching the water roll by. Billy lit a cigarette with a Zippo lighter, took a drag.

"Killing a man is a lot harder than I thought. It's not *doing it* that's so hard. It's afterwards. Doing it, it's like cutting the head off a chicken with a hatchet. You just do it. Later, thinking about it, I got the sweats."

"You think too much," said Shadow Love. "I've killed three. The feeling isn't bad; it's pretty good, really. You win. You send another one of them assholes straight to hell."

"You killed three?" Aaron said sharply. "I know two. One in South Dakota, one in Los Angeles: the drug man and the Nazi."

"There's another one now," Shadow Love said. "I put his body into the river below the Lake Street bridge." He gestured at the river. "He may be floating past right now, while we smoke."

The Crows looked at each other, and a tear ran down Aaron's face. Sam reached out and thumbed it away.

"Why?" Aaron asked his son.

"Because he was a traitor."

"You mean he was one of the people?" Aaron's voice rose in fear and anguish.

"A traitor," Shadow Love said. "He put the police on Bluebird."

Aaron was on his feet, his hands at the sides of his head, pressing together. "No, no no no no . . ."

"Yellow Hand he was, from Fort Thompson," Shadow Love said.

"I can hear the bones," Aaron groaned. "Yellow Hand's people were free warriors. They died for us and now we have killed one of theirs. They are screaming at us. . . ."

Shadow Love stood and spit into the river. "A man is a fuckin' man and that's all," he said. "Just a fuckin' piece of meat. I'm trying to keep you free and you won't even give me that."


Billy Hood never could get his head quite right in the borrowed sleeping bag. After a difficult night, he woke well before dawn with a crick in his neck. While the Crows and Shadow Love slept, he crawled out of the tent and lit the Coleman lantern, moved quietly into the woods, dug a cathole and used it. When he finished, he kicked dirt in the hole and started collecting wood.

A jungle of dead trees stood along the waterline. Hood gathered a dozen limbs as long and thick as his forearm and hauled them back to the campsite. Using twigs and finger-thick sticks, he built a foot-high tepee-shaped starter fire, fanned it, waited until it was going good, then stacked on the heavier wood and topped the structure with a steel grate. The Crows kept a blue enameled-steel coffeepot in their truck, with a jar of instant coffee inside. He got it, filled the pot with water from a jug, dumped in what looked like enough coffee and put it on the grate.

"God damn." Aaron Crow, moving. "Nothing smells as good as cookout coffee."

"Got a couple of quarts of it out here," Billy said.

Aaron crawled out of the tent, wearing a V-necked T-shirt and green boxer shorts. "Cups in the cooler, in the back of the truck," he said.

Billy nodded and went to get them. Aaron looked toward the east, but there was no sign of the sun. He sniffed and the air smelled like morning, redolent of dew and river mud and boiling coffee. When Billy returned, Sam and Shadow Love were stirring.

"John ought to be in Brookings by now," Billy said.

"Yeah." Aaron handled the coffeepot off the fire with a hot pad and poured two cups. "So what are you going to do?"

"Go home, get cleaned up, maybe catch a few more hours of sleep, then go on up to Bemidji and see Ginnie and the kid. I'll give you a call," Billy said.

"Did you think about Milwaukee?" Aaron asked.

"All night." Billy took a sip of the scalding coffee, looking at Aaron over the rim of the cup. "I think I can handle it. The sweat helped."

Aaron looked back at the sweat lodge. "Sweats always help. Sweats'd cure cancer, if they'd give them a chance."

Billy nodded, but after a moment he said, "Don't seem to help Shadow. No offense, Aaron, but that boy is one crazy motherfucker."

# 11

The phone woke Lucas a few minutes before six.

"Davenport," he groaned.

"This is Del. Billy Hood just walked into his building."

Lucas sat up: "You made him for sure?"

"No question, man. It's him. He pulled up, hopped out and went inside before we could move. You better get your ass over here."

"Did you call Lily?" Lucas put a finger behind his bedroom curtain and looked out. Still dark.

"She's next on the list."

"I'll call her. You call Daniel. . . ."

"Already did. He said go with the plan, like we talked," Del said.

"How about the feebs?"

"The guy here called his AIC."


Lily answered on the third ring, her voice croaking like a rusty gate.

"You awake?" Lucas asked.

"What do you want, Davenport?"

"I thought I'd call and see if you were lying there naked."

"Jesus Christ, are you nuts? What time . . . ?"

"Billy Hood just rolled into his apartment."

"What?"

"I'll pick you up outside your hotel in ten minutes. Ten to fifteen. Brush your teeth, take a shower, run downstairs. . . ."

"Ten minutes," she said.

\*      \*      \*

Lucas showered, brushed, pulled on jeans, a sweatshirt and a cotton jacket, and was outside five minutes after he talked to Lily. Rush hour was beginning: he punched the Porsche down Cretin Avenue, driving mostly on the wrong side of the street, jumping one red light and stretching a couple of greens. He put the car on I-94 and made it to Lily's hotel twelve minutes after he had hung up the phone. She was walking out of the lobby doors when he pulled in.

"No question about the ID?" she snapped.

"No." He looked at her. "You're a little pale."

"Too early. And I'm a little queasy. I thought about stopping in the coffee shop for a roll, but I thought I better not," she said. Her voice was all business. She wouldn't meet his eye.

"You had a few last night."

"A few too many. I appreciate . . . you know."

"You were hot," Lucas said bluntly, but with a smile.

She blushed, furious. "Christ, Davenport, give me a break?"

"No."

"I shouldn't be riding with you," she said, looking out the window.

"You wanted to roll, last night. You backed out. I can live with it. The big question is . . ."

"What?"

"Can you?"

She looked at him and her voice carried an edge of disdain. "Ah, the Great Lover speaks. . . ."

"Great Lover, bullshit," Lucas said. "You were hungry. That didn't develop since you met me."

"I happen to be . . ." she started.

". . . very happily married," they said in unison.

"I want you pretty bad," Lucas said after a moment. "I feel like I'm smothering."

"Jesus, I don't know about this," she said, looking away.

Lucas touched her on the forearm. "If you really . . . rule it out completely . . . we probably ought to hang out with different people. . . ."

She didn't say she ruled anything out. She did change the subject.

"So why didn't they take Hood when he pulled in? Was it like they thought . . ."

A half-dozen detectives and the FBI agent were waiting in the surveillance apartment when Lucas and Lily arrived. Del took them aside. He was wide-awake.

"Okay. Talked to Daniel, we all agreed. We wait until the baker leaves for his job. He leaves at seven-thirty, twenty minutes of eight, something like that."

Lucas glanced at his watch. Six-twenty.

"The other guy, the lifter, we can't tell when he leaves," Del continued. "The super says that some days he's out of there by nine, other days he sleeps 'til noon. We can't wait that long. We figure that if Hood comes in at six, he's probably pretty beat. Maybe driving all night. Anyway, there's a good chance he's asleep. So we call it this way: We go in and cut their phone, just in case somebody else in the building is with them. Then we put an entry team in the hall, four guys, and stick a microphone on the door. Listen awhile. See who's up. Then, when the baker opens the door to come out, we grab him and boom—we're in."

"Jesus, if Hood's awake and has the gun handy . . ."

"He'd hardly have time to get at it," Del said confidently. "You know that Jack Dionosopoulos guy, that big Greek with the ERU? Used to play ball at St. Thomas?"

"Yeah." Lucas nodded.

"He's going in first, bare hands. If Hood's there with a gun in his hand, we got no choice. Jack goes down and the second man takes Hood with the shotgun. If there's no gun showing, Jack takes him down. If he can't see him, he hits the bedroom. Just fucking jumps him, pins him. Hood's not that big a guy. . . ."

"Fuckin' Jack, he's taking a chance. . . ."

"He's all armored up. He thinks he's back at St. Thomas."

"I don't know," Lucas said. "It's your call, but it sounds like Jack might have played too long without a helmet."

"He did it before. Same deal. Gang guy, needed him to talk. He had a gun in his belt when Jack went in. He never had a chance to pull it. Jack was on him like holy on the pope."

"So we sit some more," Lily said, peering through the venetian blinds at the apartment across the street.

"Not here," Del said. "We sent your drawing of the apartment down to the ERU—they're staging in the garage of that Amoco station three blocks up. We need you to go down there and talk to them about the apartment."

"All right," said Lucas. "If anything happens, call."

"Del's pretty sharp for this time in the morning," Lily said on the way down to the ERU meeting.

"Uh." Lucas glanced at her.

"He's maybe got his nose in the evidence? He was sleeping so hard yesterday it kinda looked like a chemical crash."

Lucas shook his head. "No coke," he muttered.

"Something?"

Lucas shrugged. "There're some stories," his voice still low. "He maybe does a black beauty from time to time."

"Like once a fuckin' hour," she said under her breath.

The ERU felt like a ball team. They were psyched, already on their toes, talking with the distracted air of a team already focusing on the game. The apartment diagram had been laid out on plastic board with a black marker. The Polaroid photos Lucas had shot in the apartment were Scotch-taped to one side. He spent a few minutes spotting chairs, sofas, tables, rugs.

"What kind of rug is that? Is that loose?" Dionosopoulos asked. "I don't want to run in there and fall on my ass."

"That's what you did at St. Thomas," one of the other ERU men said.

"Fuck you and all pagan Lutherans," Dionosopoulos said casually. "What about the rug, Lucas?"

"It's small, that's all I can tell you. I don't know, I'd say be careful, you could slide. . . ."

"It's one of those old fake Persian carpets, you know, you can see the threads," said Lily. "I think it'd slide."

"Okay."

"Lucas?" One of the other team members moved up. "Del just called. He sounds weird, man, but he says to get your ass back to the surveillance post. Like instantly."

"What do you mean, 'weird'?" Lucas asked.

"He was whispering, man. On the radio . . ."

Del met them in the hallway outside the apartment. His eyes looked like white plastic poker chips.

"What?" asked Lucas.

"The feds are here. They've got an entry team on the way in."

"What?" Lucas brushed past him into the apartment. The Minneapolis agent-in-charge was standing by the window, next to the FBI surveillance man. Both were wearing radio headsets and looking across the street.

"What the fuck is going on?" Lucas asked.

"Who are you?" the AIC asked, his voice cold.

"Davenport, lieutenant, Minneapolis Police. We've got this scene wrapped. . . ."

"It's not your scene anymore, Lieutenant. If you doubt that, I suggest you call your chief—"

"We got guys on the street," a Minneapolis surveillance man suddenly blurted. "We got guys on the street."

"Motherfucker," Del said, "motherfucker . . ."

Lucas looked through the slats of the venetian blind. Lily was at his shoulder. There were six men on the street, two in long coats, four in body armor. Three of the men in armor and one man in a coat were climbing the stoop into the apartment building; the other man in a coat waited at the base of the steps, while the last man in armor posted himself at the corner of the building. One of the men on the steps showed a shotgun just before going inside. The man in the coat turned and looked at the surveillance post. Kieffer.

"Oh, no, no," Lily said, "He's got an AVON, they're gonna hit the door with AVONs."

"It'll never fall, man," Lucas said urgently to the AIC. "The door's a solid chunk of oak. Call them down, man, it'll never fall."

"What?" The AIC couldn't sort it out, and Lily said, "The door won't fall to AVONs."

Lucas turned and ran out of the apartment and down the hall to the front door of the building. He could hear Del chanting, *"Motherfuckers, motherfuckers . . ."*

Lucas crashed through the front door, startling the FBI man on the street. The agent made a move toward his hip and Lucas swerved, screaming "No, no . . ."

There was a boom, then a second and a third, not sharp reports, but a hollow, echoing *boom-boom-boom,* as though someone in the distance were pounding a timpani. Lucas stopped, waiting, one second, two, three; then another *boom, boom* . . . And then a pistol, a sharper sound, nastier, with an edge, six, seven rounds, then a pause, then an odd cracking explosion . . .

"Minneapolis cops," Lucas shouted to the FBI man at the base of the stairs. Lily was with him now and they crossed the street. The FBI man had one hand out at them, but with the series of pistol shots he turned and looked at the building.

"Get out of the fuckin' street, dummy," Lucas screamed. "That's fuckin' Hood with the pistol. If he comes to the window, you're a dead sonofabitch."

Lucas and Lily crossed the sidewalk to the building until they were standing behind the stoop. The FBI man came over and stood with them, his pistol out now. There was shouting in the hallway.

"They got him," the agent said, looking at them. He sounded unsure.

"Bullshit," said Lily. "They never got inside. If you got a radio, you better call the paramedics, because it sounds like Hood sprayed the place. . . ."

The building door popped open and Kieffer, in a crouch, his gun drawn, stepped down onto the stoop.

"What's happening, what's happening?" shouted the armored agent on the corner.

"Back it off, back it off," Kieffer shouted. "He's got hostages."

"You dumb sonofabitch, Kieffer . . ." Lucas shouted.

"Get out of here, Davenport, this is a federal crime scene."

"Fuck you, asshole. . . ."

"I'll arrest your ass, Davenport."

"Come down here and you can arrest me for kicking a federal agent's ass, 'cause I will," Lucas shouted back. "You dumb cocksucker . . ."


The federal entry team and the Minneapolis teams stabilized the area and hustled the other tenants out of the apartment building and adjacent buildings. The city's hostage negotiator set up a mobile phone to call Hood.

When Lucas and Lily returned to the surveillance apartment, Daniel was talking with the AIC and Sloan was leaning against the apartment wall, listening.

". . . go on television and explain exactly what happened," Daniel was droning piously. "We've had substantial experience with this type of situation, we had the scene cleared and stable, we had an excellent action plan prepared by our best officers. Suddenly, with no coordination and without proper intelligence—intelligence that we had: we knew that door wouldn't fall to AVONs, which is one reason we didn't try them—suddenly, an FBI team takes jurisdiction and promptly launches what I can only describe as a rash action, which not only endangered the lives of many police officers and innocent people in adjoining apartments, but also jeopardizes the chances of capturing Bill Hood alive, and cracking this terrible conspiracy which has taken the lives of so many people. . . ."

"It should have worked," the AIC said bitterly.

Daniel discarded his pious-preacher voice and turned hard. "Bullshit. You know, I never would have believed you'd have tried this. I thought you were too smart. If you'd come in with your team, taken some time, talked it over, we could have done a joint operation and you would have gotten the credit. The way it happened . . . I ain't taking the rap."

"Could I get everybody out of here? Just for a minute," the AIC asked loudly. "Everybody?"

"Lucas, you stay," Daniel said.

When the other cops were gone, the AIC looked briefly at Lucas, then turned to Daniel.

"You need a witness?"

"Never hurts," Daniel said.

"So what do you want?"

"I don't know. I'll probably want your seal of approval and some active lobbying on a half-dozen federal law-enforcement-assistance grant applications . . ."

"No problem . . ."

". . . and a line into your files. When I call you on something, I want what you got and no bullshit."

"Jesus Christ, Daniel."

"You can write me a letter to that effect."

"Nothing on paper . . ."

"If there's nothing on paper, there's no deal."

The AIC was sweating. He could have had a coup. He was now in charge of a disaster. "All right," he said finally. "I gotta trust you."

"Hey, we've always been friends," Daniel offered, slapping the FBI man on the back.

"Fuck that," said the AIC, wrenching away. "That fuckin' Clay. He's calling me every fifteen minutes, screaming for action. He's coming here, you know. He'll have that fuckin' gun in his armpit, the asshole."

"I feel for you," Daniel said.

"I don't give a shit about that," the AIC said. "Just find something that'll get me off the hook."

"I think we can do that," Daniel said. He glanced at Lucas. "We'll say that Minneapolis made the call and we decided to use FBI experts to attempt an entry. When that couldn't be accomplished, we went to an alternate plan that used city officers to negotiate a surrender."

"The fuckin' TV'll never buy it," the agent said unhappily.

"If we both agree, what choice have they got?"

Del, Lily and Sloan were standing together in the hallway when Lucas and Daniel left the surveillance apartment.

"What'd we do?" Del asked.

"A deal," Daniel said.

"I hope you got a lot," Del said.

"We did all right, as long as we can pull Hood out of there," Daniel said.

"Maybe this wasn't a time to deal," Sloan suggested. "Maybe this was a time to tell it like it is."

Daniel shook his head. "You always deal," he said.

"Always," said Lucas.

Lily and Del nodded and Sloan shrugged.

Hood had fired seven shots with a big-bore pistol through the oak door after the molded-compound AVON rounds had failed to blow it open. When they saw that the door wasn't going to fall, the agents had cleared away from it and nobody was hurt. The firing stopped, there was the odd explosion, and then silence.

Twenty minutes after the attempted entry, with Daniel still meeting with the agent-in-charge, the police hostage negotiator called Hood. Hood answered, said he wasn't coming out, but that his friends in the apartment had nothing to do with any of it.

"You know me?" he asked.

"Yeah, we've had a line on you, Billy," the negotiator said. "But that wasn't us at the door, that was another *agency*."

"The FBI . . ."

"We're just trying to get everybody out, including you, without anybody getting hurt. . . ."

"These guys in here, they didn't have anything to do with it."

"Could you send them out?"

"Yeah, but I don't want any of those white guys to snipe them. You know? The fuckin' FBIs, man, they shoot us down like dirty dogs."

"You send them out, I guarantee no harm will come to them."

"I'll ask them," Hood said. "They're scared. They're sleeping, and all of a sudden somebody tries to blow up the fuckin' apartment, you know?"

"I guarantee . . ."

"I'll ask them. You call back in two minutes." He hung up.

"What's going on?" Lucas asked. He and Lily had cut around the building to come up on the negotiator's car.

"I think he's gonna let the other two guys out."

"Just like that?"

"Just like that. He's not thinking like they're hostages."

"They're not. They're his friends."

"What happened with Daniel?" the negotiator asked.

"The feebs are out," Lucas said.

*"All right."*

The negotiator called back after a little more than two minutes.

"They're coming out, but they gotta come out the window. The goddamn door is all fucked up, we can't get it open," Hood said.

"All right. That's fine. Break the window, whatever you have to do."

"Tell those white boys, so they don't get sniped."

"We'll pass the word right now. Give us a minute, then send them out. And you ought to think about it too, Billy; we really don't want to do you any harm."

"Save the bullshit and pass the word not to snipe these guys," Hood said, and hung up.

"The two guys are coming out," the negotiator told the radio man next to him. "Pass the word."

\*    \*    \*

As they watched, with Lucas and Lily standing beside the car, a chair sailed through the front window and broken glass was knocked out of the window frame with a broom. Then a blanket was thrown over the window ledge. The first man stood in the window, jumped the five feet to the ground and hurried down the street toward the blocking police cars. A patrolman met him as he crossed the line of cars.

Lily looked at him and shook her head. "Don't know him. Wasn't in any of the photos."

The second man followed a half-minute later, sitting on the window ledge with his legs dangling, talking back into the apartment. After a few seconds, he shrugged, hopped down and walked to the police line. The negotiator got back on the phone.

"Billy? Billy? Talk to me, man. Talk to me. . . . Come on, Billy, you know that's not right. That was the FBI, we cleared those fuckers out of here. . . . I know, I know. . . . No, bullshit, I don't do that and the men here don't do that. You tell me one time . . . Billy? Billy?" He shook his head and dropped the receiver to his lap. "Fuck it, he hung up."

"What's he say?" Lily asked.

"He says us white boys are going to snipe him," the negotiator said. The negotiator, who was burly and black, smiled and picked up the phone and started dialing again. "He's probably right, fuckin' white boys with guns."

The line was busy.

"Where's that file Anderson made?" the negotiator asked his radio man. The radio man passed a notebook. "Call the phone company, tell them what's happening and ask them to check the number, see where the call's going."

"Check his family," Lucas suggested. "There oughta be a phone number."

The negotiator found the Bemidji number in Anderson's notebook, dialed it, found it busy. "That's it," he said. "We ought to have somebody get onto the sheriff's office up there, get them to go see his wife. We might want to talk to her. We can get her to call here, and then switch her in, so we can hear what they're saying."

A plainclothes cop hurried up. "One of the roommates says that Hood tried to fire a rifle and it blew up on him. He's hurt. He's got a cut on his face, he's bleeding. The roommate doesn't think it's too bad."

Lucas looked at Lily, and Lily grinned and nodded.

Five minutes later, the negotiator got through again.

"You can't get out, Billy. All that's gonna happen is that somebody's gonna get hurt. We'll get you a lawyer, free, we'll get you . . . Fuck."

"Try his wife?" Lucas suggested.

"How about those two guys who came out?" asked Lily. "Maybe they'd help. . . ."

Kieffer drifted up to the car. "I thought you were out of here," Lucas said, standing to confront him.

"We're observing," Kieffer said bitterly.

"Observe my ass." Lucas stood directly in front of Kieffer, their chests almost touching.

"Fuckin' touch me, Davenport," Kieffer said. "I'll have your ass in jail. . . ."

"I'll touch you," Lily said, pushing between them. Lucas reluctantly gave a step. "You gonna put me in jail for assault? I'm not so polite as these Minneapolis assholes, Kieffer, and I don't have to honor any of Daniel's deals. I can go talk to the TV on my own."

"Fuck it," Kieffer said, stepping back. "I'm observing."


The negotiator tried again, spoke longer this time. "You can trust us. . . . Wait a minute, let me talk to a guy. . . ."

He finally turned to Lucas, covered the mouthpiece on the phone and said, "You know any Indians?"

"A few."

"You want to try him? He's scared. Mention these people you know. . . ."

Lucas took the phone. "Billy Hood. This is Lucas Davenport from the Minneapolis cops. Listen, you know Dick Yellow Hand, a friend of Bluebird's? Or Chief Dooley, the barber? Do you know Earl and Betty May? They're friends of mine, man. They'd be worried about you. I'm worried about you. There's nothing you can do in there. You'll just get hurt. If you come out, you'll be okay. I swear."

There was another moment of silence. Then Hood said, "You know Earl and Betty?"

"Yeah, man. You could call them. They'd tell you I'm okay."

"You white?"

"Yeah, yeah, but I don't want to hurt anybody. Come on out, Billy. I swear to God nobody wants to shoot at you. Walk on out and we can all go home."

"Let me think, man. Let me think, okay?"

"Okay, Billy." The line went dead.


"What?" Lucas asked the negotiator, who had been listening on a headset.

"He may be calling these people. Earl and Betty, was that their names?"

"Yeah. Just about everybody knows them."

"We'll give him two minutes and try again."

Two minutes later, the line was busy. After three, they got through. The negotiator said a few words, then handed the phone to Lucas.

"Is this the guy who knows Earl and Betty?" Hood asked.

"Yeah. Davenport," Lucas said.

"I'll come out, but I want you to come up here and get me. If I just come outside, one of those white boys is gonna snipe me."

"No, they won't, Billy. . . . Listen . . ." Lucas hunched over the phone.

"Bullshit, man, don't bullshit me. Those guys been against me for a long time. Ever since I was born, man. They're just waiting. I got nothing against you, so you'd be safe. You want me out, you come up here."

Lucas looked at the negotiator. "What do you think?"

"He killed the guy in New York," the negotiator said. "He tried to kill the FBI team."

"He had a reason. Maybe he really wants the protection."

"He's scared," the negotiator agreed.

"What are you going to do?" Hood asked.

"Hold on a minute, we're talking," Lucas said. He looked at Lily. "There might not be any other way to take him alive."

"You'd be nuts to go in there," Lily objected. "We've got him. Sooner or later he's got to come out and nobody has to get hurt. Nobody out here . . ."

"We need to talk to him."

"I don't need to talk to him," she said. "I just need him any way we can get him. Dead or alive."

"You don't care if we get the rest of the group?" Lucas asked.

"Sure. Theoretically. But Hood's my man. After he's taken care of, the rest is up to you and the feebs."

Kieffer had been standing back from the car, looking down the street at the apartment. "It'd take some balls to go in there," he said.

His tone was ambiguous, as if he weren't sure that Lucas would do it.

"Hey, we aren't talking balls here," the negotiator said, anger in his voice.

"Yeah, what the fuck did that crack mean, Kieffer?" Lily asked, turning to Kieffer with her hands on her hips.

"Take it easy," Lucas said, waving them off. He didn't look at Kieffer but stared past the negotiator at the apartment window. With the glass broken out, it was a black square in the red stone. "I'll give it a try."

"God damn it, Davenport, you're crazy," Lily said. But then she said, "Talk to him through the window. Don't go inside, just talk over the ledge."

Lucas got back on the phone. "Billy? I'm ready, man."

"Well, come on."

"You're not bullshitting me?"

"I'm not, I just don't want one of them white boys to snipe me, man."

"They see him from across the street. They got a gun on him. He's halfway up into the room," the radio man said quietly, as he listened on his headset. "Del says that when you get up there, if he tries anything, you drop below the window; we'll hose him down."

"Okay." Lucas glanced at Lily, nodded and said into the phone, "I'm stepping out, Billy. I'm down the street, way to your right as you look out the
window."

"Come on, man. This is getting old."

Lucas stepped out from behind the car, his hands held wide and open at
shoulder height.

"Okay, man," he yelled at the window.

He walked slowly down the street, his hands wide, conscious of two dozen
sets of eyes following him. The day was cool, but he could feel sweat starting
on his back. A line of blue-and-white pigeons watched from a red-tiled roof
down the street. On another roof, beside a chimney and out of Hood's line of
sight, an ERU officer was lined up on the window with an M-16. A police radio
poked unintelligible sentences into the morning air. Lucas was thirty feet out.

"Come on, man, you're okay," Hood called from the window. Lucas moved
closer, his hands still away from his side. When he was five feet from the
window, Hood called again. "Come straight on in. I'll be off to the left. I don't
want to see no gun pointing at me, man. I'm really tight, you know?"

Lucas reached out, touched the outer wall of the building and eased up to
the window. Looking in at a sharp angle, he could see nothing but a broken-
down chair. He moved a little farther into the window opening. There was
nobody in his line of sight. The red beanbag was squashed in the middle of the
floor, with a dent in it, as though somebody had been thrown on top of it.

"I'm giving up, man," Hood said. His voice came from off to the right, but
Lucas still couldn't see him. He took another step.

"I want you inside," Hood said.

"I can't do that, Billy," Lucas said.

"You're just setting me up, man. You're just making me a target. If I come
to that window, I'm a dead man, aren't I?"

"I swear to God, Billy. . . ."

"You don't have to swear to God. Just get up in that window. I'll be there.
I want you to go out right in front of me, man, so those white boys don't snipe
me."

Lucas looked around once, muttered "Fuck it" under his breath, put his
hands on the window ledge and boosted himself up. As he crawled onto the
ledge, Hood was suddenly there, his back to the outer wall. He was looking at
Lucas over the shotgun.

"Step in further," he said. The muzzle of the shotgun followed Lucas' head
like a steel eye.

"Come on, man," Lucas said. There hadn't been any shells in the closet with
the shotgun. Since Hood was using it, he either had found the shells or was
bluffing with an empty weapon. Why would he bluff? He'd used a pistol of
some kind, anyone would be willing to believe that the pistol was loaded.
. . . "This can't do any good."

"Shut up," Hood said. He was wound tight as a spring, frightened. "Get in here."

Lucas hopped down from the window ledge.

"Did one of you wiseass cops fuck up my rifle? You did, didn't you?"

"I don't know about a rifle," Lucas said. Hood's face was bleeding from a long cut over one eye. On the floor near his foot was a .45, the slide locked open. Out of ammo, Lucas decided.

"Pulled the trigger on that cocksucker rifle and almost blew my face off. There was a rag in it," Hood said.

"I don't know anything about that," Lucas said. He could feel the P7 pushing into his back.

"Bullshit," Hood snapped. "But I *know* you didn't know about these. . . ."

He kept the shotgun muzzle on Lucas' head but opened the hand under the shotgun's fore-end. He had two shells in his hand.

"Buckshot, for deer," Hood said. "I had them stuck in with the thirty-thirty shells. Somebody missed them, huh?"

"Bill . . ." Lucas started. Inside, he was cursing himself for not taking the .30-.30 shells, or at least checking the box. "You won't get out of here this way. . . ."

"Buckshot's no good when those fuckers out there got M-16s, but this buckshot is going to get me out of here, because I got you, white boy," he said. He gestured with the muzzle. "Lay down. On the floor."

"Billy, I trusted you, man. This is no good." Lucas felt the sweat start at his temples, felt the heat in his armpits.

"So I lied, motherfucker," Hood said. "Get the fuck down." He dipped the barrel of the shotgun an inch, to indicate *down.*

Lucas got down on his knees, thought about going for the P7, but the shotgun muzzle never wavered.

"Keep your hands away from your body. . . ."

From outside, the ERU team leader called on a loudspeaker. "You coming out? Everything okay?"

"Everything fine," Hood yelled back. "We're talking. Let us talk."

"Nothing you can do is going to help . . ." Lucas started.

"On your fuckin' belly," Hood snapped.

Lucas let himself down on the floor. It smelled of city grime. Grit cut into his chin.

"I'll tell you what we're doing, so you don't fuck me up," Hood said. Sweat was pouring down his face, and Lucas could smell the fear on him. "I'm going to march you out of here with this gun. We're going to take a car and we're going down the Mississippi to the res. Someplace along the way I'll get out and get off in the woods. Once I'm in the woods, I'm gone, man."

"They'll come through with dogs. . . ."

"Let them. There'll be Indians all over the place, running them fuckin' dogs to death, man. They'll never get me out of them swamps down there." Lucas felt Hood easing up close to him; then the shotgun muzzle touched the back of his head. "Just to let you know I'm here. I want your face straight down, until I tell you different."

Lucas lay facedown, still thinking about the gun on his hip. Hood was doing something behind him, but he couldn't see what it was. There was a ripping sound and he tried tipping his face, but Hood said, "Hey," and Lucas tipped it back. "I gotta breathe," Lucas said.

"You can breathe, don't bullshit me. . . . Now you're going to feel the gun on your head. I 'spect you've got a gun and maybe you're one of them karate experts, but if you so much as jiggle, I'm going to blow your fucking brains out. . . . I got my finger on the trigger and the safety is off, you got it?"

"I got it," Lucas said.

He felt the cold touch of the muzzle on the skin behind his ear. "Now push your head back until you're looking off the floor. Look out into the kitchen, but don't move anything else but your head," Hood said. Lucas lifted his head, and a second later Hood took a quick turn of tape around his forehead, then another. Lucas gritted his teeth.

"The muzzle of the gun is taped to your head," Hood said when he had finished. His voice was a notch less tense. "If one of them white boys snipes me, you're dead. If anything happens, you're dead. A couple of pounds of pull on the trigger and you're gone, man. You know what I'm saying? Lights out." A third and fourth loop of tape overlapped the first two. The last loop partially covered Lucas' left eye. He could feel the buttons on his shirt pressing into his chest and suddenly found it hard to breathe.

"Jesus Christ, man, be careful," he said, struggling to keep a whine out of his voice.

"You just be cool, man. . . . Now get up."

Lucas got to his hands and knees and shakily stood up. The muzzle of the gun stayed with him, behind his right ear.

"Everything all right?" the ERU team leader called.

"Everything is great, motherfucker," Hood yelled back. "We're coming out in a minute." He turned back to Lucas. "My car's about fucked up. I want a cop car and I need some time. We're going out there and get it."

"Tell them what you're doing," Lucas said. The weight of the gun pulled his head to the side. The tape over his left eye was sticking to his eyelid, and he struggled with a sudden feeling of claustrophobia. "If they see me with my hands up and you behind me, maybe somebody who can't see what's going on will take a shot at you."

"You tell them," Hood said. "They'll believe you. Over to the window."

Lucas stepped over to the window. Hood held on to his shirt collar with his left hand. The shotgun was in his right and he used the end of the barrel to push Lucas to the windowsill.

"Everybody hold it," Lucas screamed as he stepped into the opening. He put his arms up over his head, his fingers spread. "Everybody fuckin' hold it. He's got a shotgun taped to my head. Everybody fuckin' hold it."

There was movement inside the apartment across the street, just a flicker at the window. Hood pulled him closer, the shotgun cutting into the flesh behind his ear.

"Billy . . ." said the loudspeaker.

"I want a car, man," Hood shouted. He prodded Lucas forward until he was sitting on the windowsill. Carefully, carefully, he climbed up beside him. "You get down first," he said.

"Jesus," said Lucas. "Don't jar anything."

"Get down."

Lucas dropped the five feet, flexing his knees, his eyes closed as he landed. The world was still there. Hood landed next to him. Lucas took another breath. "I want a cop car and I want everybody out of my way," Hood screamed.

"Billy, this isn't going to help, man, everything was fine," the team leader called. The loudspeaker echoed in Lucas' ears. He looked at the street, the cars blocking it, the people half visible behind them, and he wondered if they would suddenly wink out and Lucas Davenport would be a shell on the cold ground, with a crowd looking down at him. . . .

"Just give me the car, man, bring a car down here." Hood was tensing up again, his voice screeching toward blind panic.

"Give him the fuckin' car," Lucas yelled. The scent of pines came through. There were no pines there; no vegetation at all, but the scent of pines was there, just as though he were at his Wisconsin cabin. A refrain started running through the back of Lucas' mind, *Not yet, please not yet,* but the cold circle of the shotgun muzzle pressed into the flesh behind his ear. . . .

"Okay, okay, okay, we're calling for a car, take it easy, Billy, we don't want anybody else hurt. . . ."

"Where's the car?" Hood screamed. "Where's the car?" He jerked on the shotgun and Lucas' head snapped back.

"Take it easy, take it easy, man," Lucas said, his heart in his throat. His neck hurt, his head hurt, and Hood pressed against him like an unwanted partner in a three-legged race. "If you fire this thing accidentally, you're a dead motherfucker just like me."

"Shut up," Hood snapped.

"You can have a car, Christ, take it easy," the ERU team leader called. He was directly across the street. "Take the car down to your right, down to your right. See the cop getting out? The keys are in that car."

Hood turned to look at it and Lucas looked with him. The car was next to the negotiator's car. He could see Lily behind it.

"Okay, we're walking to the car," Hood yelled toward the ERU leader. They edged sideways, like crabs, slowly, the shotgun pressing. . . . Twenty feet out from the car.

"Billy? Billy? I'm the guy on the telephone. We've got a doctor here," the negotiator called. The negotiator took a step away from his car and Lucas noticed that he'd taken off his sidearm. "We got a doctor, a registered psychologist, we want you to talk with her. . . ."

Lily stepped out from behind the car and stood beside the negotiator, clutching her purse in both hands. She looked like a very scared public-health nurse.

"We brought her in to see if you were okay. She says she'll ride with the two of you, in case there's any trouble, she wants to talk. . . ."

"I don't want any talk, man, I just want the car." Hood prodded Lucas and Lucas sidestepped toward the car, his head twisted by the angle of the shotgun.

"I can help you," Lily called. She was fifteen feet away.

"I don't want you, man," Hood said. He was sweating, and the odor of the fear sweat filled the air around him. "Just get the fuck out of my way."

"Listen, you've got to listen to me, Billy. Please? I've worked with a lot of Indian people and this is not the Indian way." She took a step closer, and another, and with their movement toward the car, she was now less than ten feet away.

"Just get away from me, will you?" Hood said in exasperation. "I don't need no fuckin' shrink, okay?"

"Billy, please . . ." Lily said, a pleading note in her voice. Six feet. She let the purse drop to her side on its shoulder strap, one hand gesturing while the other plucked at her jacket. "Let me . . ." Her voice suddenly changed from persuasion to urgency. "Billy, you've got a problem. Okay? Let me tell you about this, okay? You've got a problem that you don't know about. I mean it. Billy, there's a wasp on your hair. Above your right ear. If it stings, don't pull the trigger, it's just a wasp. . . . We don't want a tragedy."

"A wasp, man . . . where is it?" Hood stopped, his voice suddenly tight. Lucas' mind flashed to the box of antihistamine tablets in Hood's medicine cabinet.

"On your hair just above your right ear, right there, it's crawling down toward your ear. . . ."

Hood had his left hand around Lucas' neck and Lucas felt the stock of the gun come up as Hood tried to brush the nonexistent wasp away with his gun hand. With his finger through the trigger guard, he couldn't quite reach his ear; for just the barest part of a second, not thinking, he pulled his trigger finger out of the guard, reaching toward his head. As his finger came out of the guard, Lily went into her belly with her right hand, the hand that had been nervously plucking at her jacket button, and came out with the full-cocked .45. She thrust it at Hood's head almost as if she were throwing a dart, and he saw it just soon enough to flinch. Lucas closed his eyes and started to turn away; the .45 went off and Lucas felt a hot stinging on his face, as though he'd been hit by a handful of beach sand. Hood kicked back onto the ground as Lucas fell to his knees and screamed:

"Get it off get it off get it off get it off."

The negotiator knelt beside him and said, "You're okay, you're okay." A hand grasped the shotgun barrel, held it, and Lucas, his breath ragged, groaned, "Get it off, get it off," and there was a flat cutting sound and the muzzle was gone.

Again, everything was sharp, the blacktop beneath his knees, the smell of tar and city garbage, the sound of the radios, an ERU officer running, Lily saying "Jesus, Jesus," the team leader's knee next to his face, Billy Hood's gym shoe twisted in the dirt. Then Lucas' breakfast came up, and he knelt outside Billy Hood's apartment and vomited and vomited; and when he couldn't vomit anymore, dry heaves shook his shoulders and racked his stomach. Members of the ERU team were gathering around the body, and from somewhere he could hear a woman's wail over the shouting and the chatter. The team leader's hand was on the back of his neck, warm against his cold skin. He heard somebody crack the shotgun and a green-cased shotgun shell flipped out.

When the stomach spasms stopped, when he had controlled them, Lucas turned his head and saw Billy Hood's face. The front of it was caved in, as though somebody had hit him with a claw hammer.

"One shot in the ten ring," Lily said. She was standing above him, her face pale as winter, looking down at Hood. "Right on the bridge of his nose." And although her voice was brave, she sounded ineffably sad. Lucas got to his hands and knees, then to his feet, wobbling.

The team leader helped him strip the tape off his head, and turned to look at Lily. "You okay?" he asked.

"I'm okay," Lily said.

"How about you?" the negotiator asked Lucas.

"Fuck, no." Lucas took a couple wobbly steps and Lily slipped an arm around his waist. "It could take a couple of minutes. I was a dead man."

"Maybe he would have let you go," Lily said, looking back at Hood's body.

"Maybe, but I don't think so. Billy Hood was an angry man," Lucas said. "He was ready to die and he wasn't going alone."

He stopped and turned and, like Lily, looked back at the body. Hood's face wasn't peaceful in death. It was simply dead, and empty, like a beer can crushed on the side of a road. A red-hot anger washed through Lucas.

"God damn, we needed him. We needed the motherfucker to talk, the stupid shit. The stupid shit, why'd he do this?" He was shouting and the ERU team was looking at him.

Lily tightened her grip around his waist and gave him a gentle push toward the house across the street.

"Did I say 'Thank you'?" Lucas asked, looking down at Lily.

"Not yet."

"You could have blown my fuckin' brains out, Rothenburg. And I've got all kinds of shit buried in my face."

"I'm too good a shot to have hit you. And the shit in your face is better than shotgun pellets behind your ear," she said.

"So, thanks. You saved my ass."

"I accept your abject gratitude, and while it's not enough . . ."

"I'll give you all the gratitude you can handle. You know that," he said. The hair on the top of her head brushed against his cheek.

"Fuckin' men," she muttered.

# 12

Lucas sat on a stack of newspapers.

"Are you all right?" Daniel asked, squatting beside him. Lily realized that he was trying to be gentle but didn't know how.

"In a bit," Lucas said.

Larry Hart came in, saw them and stopped. "The whole area is surrounded by media," he said. "Channel Eight had a camera on a roof down the street. They had the whole thing on the air, live. Everybody'll be looking for you and Lily."

"Fuck that," said Lucas, his elbows on his legs, his head hung down to his knees. "Has anybody talked to Jennifer?"

"I gave her a call right after Lily took Hood out," Daniel said. "She was watching. She sounded pretty calm. She even tried to screw some details out of me, for their newscast."

"Sounds like Jennifer," Lucas said. He thought about the shotgun behind his ear and gripped his knees. "If you can get somebody to take the Porsche back to my place, maybe I could sneak out in a squad. . . ."

"Sloan'll take it," Daniel said. Lucas nodded and dug the keys out of his pocket. "We've got more problems. I hate to bother you with them. . . ."

"Jesus, what?"

"The St. Paul water patrol took a body off the Ford dam this morning. It got hung up on an abutment. It's an Indian. He was carrying an ID that said 'Richard Yellow Hand.' "

"Aw, fuck," said Lucas.

"We'd like you to take a look. We're not sure yet . . . well, we're pretty sure, but he was your snitch. . . ."

"All right, all right, all right . . ."

"I'll go with you if you want," Lily offered.

"Uh, you better not," Daniel said, looking up at her. "We'll have some shooting reports to make out. You'll have to talk to our attorney, you not being a certified police officer in Minnesota. . . ."

"What . . . ?"

"No, no, there won't be any problems," Daniel said hastily. "But there's some bureaucratic rigmarole to go through. Jesus, I wish I had a cigar."

"So I look at this body . . ." said Lucas.

"There's something else," Daniel said, almost reluctantly. "They did another one."

"Another one?" asked Lily. "Where?"

"Brookings, South Dakota. It's just coming in now. The fuckin' state attorney general. They were having some kind of harvest-festival thing and they had these polka dancers. This guy, the attorney general, always went to the polka dances because he knew he'd make the local TV. A gunman was waiting for him."

"Our friend with the braids?" asked Hart.

"No. And they got this guy. They shot him, anyway. He's in a trauma room right now. Some cowboy saw the shooting, pulled a rifle out of his pickup and nailed him."

"Okay. Well, fuck. Better go see Yellow Hand, first thing. If it is Yellow Hand. I can't worry about this SoDak thing, not yet." Lucas stood up and wandered in a circle, stopped by the door. Lily, Daniel and Hart watched him, worried, and he tried to smile. "You guys look like Dorothy, the Lion and the Tin Man. Cheer up."

"So what, that makes you the Wizard of Oz?" asked Lily, still worried.

"I feel more like the Wicked Witch when the house fell on her," Lucas said. He lifted a hand. "See you."


Yellow Hand's body was at the Ramsey County Medical Examiner's Office, lying faceup on a stainless-steel tray. Lucas hated floaters. They no longer looked human. They looked . . . melted.

"Yellow Hand?" asked a deputy medical examiner.

Lucas looked the melted thing in face. Yellow Hand's eyes were open and bloated and had no pupils; they resembled milk-jug plastic. His features were twisted, some enlarged, some not. But the thing was still recognizable. He turned away. "Yeah. Yellow Hand. He's got people out in Fort Thompson, that's in South Dakota. His mother, I think."

"We'll call . . ."

"Do you have a cause of death yet?" Lucas asked.

"We took a quick look. He's got a hole at the base of his skull. Like one of those Chinese executions, one bullet. That's not official yet: the wound might not have killed him, he might have drowned or something. . . ."

"But he was shot?"

"Looks like it . . ."


Sloan arrived with the Porsche as Lucas was getting out of the squad car at his house.

"What a fuckin' car," Sloan said enthusiastically. "A hundred and fifty-five on the interstate, I couldn't believe it. . . ." He checked Lucas' face. "Just joking," he said. "Jesus, you okay? You look like shit."

"It's been a bad day. And not even noon yet," Lucas said, trying to put some humor in his voice. It came out flat.

"Was it . . . ?"

"Yeah. It was Yellow Hand."

Sloan gave him the keys and said that Lily would be up to her neck in paperwork. A couple of local stations, and one from New York, were already asking why she had been carrying a pistol in Minneapolis. Daniel was handling it, Sloan said.

"Well, I gotta go, if I want a ride back in the squad," Sloan said.

"Yeah. Thanks for bringing the car."

"Take it easy. . . ." Sloan seemed reluctant to leave him, but Lucas turned his back and walked to the house. As he unlocked the front door, he could hear the phone ringing. The answering machine kicked in before he could reach it. Jennifer Carey's voice said, "It's ten twenty-eight. We've been on the air about the Hood thing. Call me . . ."

Lucas picked up the phone. "Whoa. You still there?"

"Lucas? When did you get in?"

"Just this minute. Hang on a second, I've got to shut the front door."

When he got back to the phone, Jennifer pounced: "Damn you, Davenport, I've been going crazy. I talked to Daniel and he said he didn't know where you were, but that you were okay."

"I'm fine. Well, I'm not fine, I'm feeling a little fucked up. Where are you?"

"At the station. When I found out what was happening—thanks for not calling, by the way, we got our asses kicked by Eight, and since everybody knows that we go together, they're looking at me like I'm an alien toad. . . ."

"Yeah, yeah. Where's the baby?" Lucas asked.

"I called Ellen, the college girl. She has her. She can stay as late as I need. She can stay over if she has to."

"Can you come over later?"

"You're okay?" she asked.

"Yeah. But I could use some heavy-duty succor."

"Things are going crazy here. You heard about Elmer Linstad, out in South Dakota?"

"Yeah. The attorney general."

"Dead as a mackerel. The guy they shot, this Liss guy—"

"Whoa, whoa, you're ahead of me now. Who is he?"

"He's an Indian guy named John Liss. He's from right here in the Cities. He's in the operating room, but the word is, he's going to make it. They're talking about putting me on a plane later this afternoon. I'll be running the crew out there . . ."

"Okay." Lucas tried to keep the disappointment out of his voice.

". . . but I could sneak away around lunchtime."

"I'd like to see you," Lucas said. "I'm feeling kind of weird."

"If we sent a crew over there, could you talk . . . ?"

"No, I can't, Jen. Really. Tell them I'm not here. I'm going to turn off the phone. I've got to lie down."

"All right . . . Love you."

Lucas crawled into bed, but sleep wouldn't come. His brain was turning over, hot, he could feel the touch of muzzle behind his ear, the grotesquely bloated face of Yellow Hand floated up in front of his eyes. . . .

He was lying flat on his back, sweating. He turned his head and looked at the clock. He'd been in bed for more than an hour; he must have been asleep, he must have been somewhere, it felt like five minutes. . . .

Lucas sat up and winced as the headache hit him. He went out to the kitchen, got a bottle of lime-flavored mineral water from the refrigerator and walked unsteadily back to his workroom. The answering machine was blinking at him: eight messages. He punched the replay button. Six calls were from TV stations and the two papers. One was from Daniel, the last from Lily. He called her back.

"I'm up to my ass in paperwork," she said.

"I heard."

"And I've got a deposition tomorrow morning. . . ."

"Lunch, maybe?"

"I'll call you."

"I'll be on the street. I'll have a handset. . . ."

Daniel had called to see how he was. "We've got the feebs by the nuts," he said. "We've got one team working the people in Hood's apartment house and his roommates; Sloan and Anderson are digging for stuff on this guy in South Dakota. You heard he was from here?"

"Yeah. Jen told me."

"Okay. Listen, I've got to go. You take it easy. We got it covered."

When he got off the phone with Daniel, Lucas poured the mineral water into a tumbler and followed with three fingers of Tanqueray gin. The combination made a bad gin and tonic. He sat in the kitchen and drank it down. Fuckin' Yellow Hand. Hood and the shotgun. He reached back and rubbed the spot where the shotgun had been, then walked unsteadily back to the bathroom and got in the shower. The liquor was working on him and the hot water beat on his face, but the images of Hood and Yellow Hand would not go away.

He was out of the shower, toweling off, when the doorbell rang. He wrapped the towel around his waist, padded through the kitchen and peeked out a window at his porch.

Jennifer.

"Hi," she said, taking him in. "You still okay?"

"Kind of drunk," he said.

A worry line appeared between her eyebrows, and she leaned forward and kissed him. "Gin," she said. "I never would have believed it."

"I'm fucked up," he said, trying on a grin.

"Follow me," she said, tugging at his towel. "We'll try to unfuck you."

The afternoon sun dropped below the eaves and lit up the curtain in Lucas' bedroom. Jennifer pushed him off and swung her legs over the side of the bed, and looked back and said, "That was . . . frantic."

"I'm not sure I'm still alive," Lucas said. "Christ, I could use a cigarette."

"Were you scared?"

"Almost paralyzed. I wanted to plead, but . . . it just . . . I don't know, it wouldn't have done any good. . . . I just wanted to get it off me. . . ."

"This policewoman from New York . . ."

"Lily . . ."

"Yeah. There was a press conference, a short one, with Daniel and her and Larry Hart. She looked tough," Jennifer said, watching his face. "She looked like your type."

"I could give a shit about that," Lucas grunted. "The best thing about her is that she used to shoot in combat competition. She had that forty-five in Billy Hood's face in maybe a tenth of a second. Boom. *Adiós,* motherfucker."

"She looked pretty nice," Jennifer said.

"Jesus, yeah. She looks pretty nice. She's a little chubby, but nice-looking."

"She looked a little chubby," Jennifer agreed. Jennifer worked out every morning at a hard-core muscle gym.

"She eats everything in sight," Lucas said. "Jesus, I wish I still smoked."

"So you're all right. . . ."

"Nothing like this has ever happened," he said, bewildered. "I've come close before, shit, with the Maddog I almost got my ass killed. But this got to me . . . I don't know."

She rubbed his still-damp hair and he asked, "Did you go on the date? To the symphony?"

"Yeah."

"How was it?"

"It was okay," she said. "I'll go with him again if he asks, but I won't be sleeping with him."

"Ah. Decent of you to tell me."

"He's just too fuckin' nice," Jennifer said. "No edges. Everything I said, he agreed with."

"He's probably hung like a Tennessee stud horse."

Jennifer's forehead wrinkled. "Men worry about the goddamnedest things," she said.

"I wasn't worried."

"Sure. That's why you mentioned it," she said. "Anyway, even if I did plan to sleep with him, I'd put it off for a while. I keep looking at the baby, and I keep thinking I want to do it again. With the same daddy."

Lucas turned on his side and kissed her on the forehead.

"I'd like to help, whenever you want to. Soon?"

"I think so. In a couple, three months. This time, I'll tell you when I go off the Pill."

He kissed her again and his hand crept over her breast, circling and pressing her nipple with the palm of his hand.

"I'd like a boy," she said.

"Whatever," said Lucas. "Another daughter would be fine with me."

"Maybe we could move it up. Next month, maybe."

"I'll be on the job," he said.

She laughed, shook her head and looked at her watch. "Think you could stand some more succor? I've got barely enough time."

"Christ, I don't know, I'm getting old. . . ."

They made love again, more sedately, and later, when Jennifer was getting dressed, Lucas said, hoarsely, "I didn't want the world to go away. I would never have known, but I kept thinking . . . I don't even know if I was thinking it, but I was feeling it . . . I wanted more. More life. Jesus, I was afraid I'd just wink out, like a soap bubble. . . ."

After Jennifer left for the airport, Lucas tried again to nap. Failing, he turned on the television and caught the cable news from Sioux Falls. John Liss was out of surgery; he'd live, but he'd never walk again. The cowboy's shot had taken out a piece of spinal cord just above the hips. They ran the tape of the shooting again, then another time, in slow motion, and then cut to a picture of Lawrence Duberville Clay. It was a well-known shot, the director in shirtsleeves on the Chicago waterfront, working a cocaine bust. He had a huge Desert Eagle automatic pistol packed under his arm in an elaborate shoulder holster.

"In a related development, FBI director Lawrence Duberville Clay has announced that he will go personally to Brookings to take charge of the investigation, and said he expects to set up a temporary national FBI headquarters in

Minneapolis until the conspirators are captured," the anchorwoman said. "Clay said the move should be accomplished in the next two or three days. This is the third time that the FBI director has involved himself with a specific investigation. His action is seen as an administration effort to emphasize the importance given to its war on crime. . . ."

Lucas poked the remote control and Clay's face went away. Three o'clock. He stood, thought a moment, then went back in the kitchen for the rest of the Tanqueray.

# 13

Shadow Love saw Billy Hood's death on a television set in the corner of a Lake Street grill. The camera was a full block from the scene, but up high, and it was all as clear as a running play on *Monday Night Football.*

Billy and the hunter cop. The woman with the purse. Billy moving. Why did he do that? Why did he take his finger off the trigger? The woman's hand coming up with the pistol. The shot, Billy going down like a rag doll, and Davenport kneeling on the pavement, vomiting . . .

Shadow Love watched it once, watched it again, watched it a third time as the station endlessly ran the tape loop. *"The following news broadcast contains scenes of violence and death and may not be appropriate for children. If there are any children in the viewing area . . ."*

And then a running press conference at the shooting scene. Larry Hart: *". . . have developed evidence that these people are not just killing whites, but have killed one of our own, a Dakota man from Fort Thompson, Yellow Hand . . ."*

Larry Hart on the TV. Sweating. Pleading. Twisting his hands like Judas Iscariot.

The black spot popped up, twitching, growing, blurring his vision. Shadow Love tried to blink it away, but the anger was stirring through his chest.

Judas. Sweating, pleading . . .

Hart's face vanished in an electronic instant, to be replaced by that of a woman newscaster. "We've just gotten word that there has been another assassination attempt in Brookings, South Dakota, apparently related to the killings done by the Indian extremist group responsible for the assassinations of the New York commissioner of welfare and a federal judge in Oklahoma. The target of the South Dakota attempt was Elmer Linstad, the state's attorney general. . . ."

The woman paused, looked at her desk, then up again. "CBS news is reporting that Elmer Linstad, attorney general of South Dakota, is dead in an assassination in Brookings, South Dakota. His assailant was shot by a bystander and has been taken to a Brookings hospital. . . ."

"Billy's dead and John's been shot." Shadow Love, carrying a long cardboard box, pushed into the apartment. He kicked the door shut and tossed the box on the couch. A printed label on the side of the box said CURTAIN RODS.

"What?" The Crows, startled, stared at him.

"You deaf?" Shadow Love asked. "I said Billy's dead. John's been shot. It's on the TV."

The Crows' apartment had come with a television, but they rarely turned it on during the day. Now they did, and the loops were running.

William Two Horses Hood, the anchorman said, had been positively identified as the slayer of John Andretti, the New York City welfare commissioner. He had been shot to death by a New York police officer after Hood had taken a Minneapolis officer hostage. The Minneapolis officer was not hurt. John Liss, a Sioux Indian from Minneapolis, was in guarded condition in a Brookings hospital. . . .

"That's the hunter cop," Shadow Love said, tapping the screen over the film sequence of Lucas. "He found him."

"Motherfucker," Sam whispered as they watched the tape. Aaron began to weep and Sam patted him on the shoulder. They watched the tape again, then the one of the killing of Linstad, and then a rerun of the on-street press conference, with Larry Hart.

Sam looked at his cousin. "Remember him? He's one of the Wapeton Harts, Carl and Mary's boy?"

"Yeah. Good people," said Aaron. He turned to Shadow Love. "He's working with this cop?"

"Yes. And everybody likes him, Larry Hart. I went to school with him. Everybody liked him in school. Everybody likes him now. The hunter and Hart and this bitch from New York, they'll find us. There are people who know the Crows, who've probably seen you on the streets. And they'll talk. . . ."

"You don't know that," said Aaron.

"Yes, I do. Just like I knew they'd find Billy. If they don't find us by accident, somebody will turn us in. And it could be one of you, or Leo, or John. Or maybe one of their wives."

"Nobody would do that . . ." Aaron objected.

"Sure they would, if this hunter pushes the right buttons," Shadow Love said.

"And of all of us, you'd be the only one who wouldn't break?"

"That's right," said Shadow Love. "Because you know what gets people? Love. That's what it is. Cops use it. They say, *Help your friend; betray him.* They catch Sam and they want Aaron. So they say on the news that Sam is dying, he wants his cousin to pray him into death. . . . Could you stay away?"

Aaron didn't answer.

"I'd never betray us, because I don't have anyone I love enough," Shadow Love said with a subdued sadness. "Sometimes . . . I wish I could. I never had a laugh, you know. Never got to play catch-me-fuck-me with some chick. The only one, ever, they could use against me was Mama. With her dead, there's no pressure they could put on me."

After a moment, Aaron said, "That's the most awful thing I ever fuckin' heard." Behind him, Sam nodded, and Shadow Love turned away.

"That's the way it is," he said.

Aaron, tears running down his face, said, "They're all going. There's only Leo now."

"And us," said Sam.

Aaron nodded. "If Clay doesn't come in after South Dakota, one of us may have to go to Milwaukee."

Sam glanced at Shadow Love, involuntarily, just a peek, but Aaron caught it. "No," he said.

"Why not?" Shadow Love asked, his words like an ax-edge. "I'm part of the group; I have a stone knife."

"This action is not for you. If you want to help, go out to Rosebud and talk to the old men. Learn something."

"You don't want me here," Shadow Love said.

"That's right," Aaron said.

"You assholes," Shadow shouted. "You fuckin' assholes."

"Wait, wait, wait . . ." Sam said, pointing at the television.

Clay and his gun: ". . . to Brookings and will establish a temporary national headquarters in Minneapolis. This is the third time . . ."

The mood changed in an instant:

"The sonofabitch is coming," Sam whooped. "The cocksucker's on his way."

They had a quiet lunch, the three of them sitting around a rickety table eating cold-cut sandwiches with mustard and Campbell's chicken noodle soup.

"So what now?" Shadow asked. "There are cops all over the place, and the FBI. In a few more days, we won't be able to go on the streets."

Aaron glanced at Sam. "I'll call Barbara. Tell her we may be coming. I don't want to go in too soon; we'd fuck up, go outside, somebody'd see us."

"If you're not going out to Bear Butte, you ought to come over to Barbara's," Sam told Shadow Love. "She talks like you were her kid."

Shadow Love nodded. "Yeah. I saw her before I went to L.A. I don't know . . . we'll be a danger to her."

"She knows that," Aaron said. "We've been on the run before. She says we'll be welcome, no matter what."

"She didn't know exactly what you were planning to do. . . ."

"She'll take us," said Sam.

"Not a bad piece of ass either," Aaron said with a grin.

Sam snorted and even blushed. He and Barbara had been lovers. Nothing had been said when he talked to her on the telephone a month before, but he knew it would start again. He looked forward to it. "Jealousy. It's an ugly sight," he said into his soup.

Shadow Love stepped to the couch, picked up the cardboard box and opened it. Inside was a flat black assault rifle. He took it out of the box. "M-15," he said. He pointed it out the window at a streetlight.

"Where'd you get it? What's it for?" asked Sam.

"I got it on the street. It's for the cop, maybe. Or Hart."

Aaron had stepped toward the stove, reaching for the teapot. He stopped in mid-stride and whirled toward his son. "No. Not Hart. You don't kill the people," he said furiously.

Shadow Love looked at him with a cold glint in his eye. "I do what I think best. You and Sam disagree all the time, but you still act."

"We always agree before we do anything," said Aaron.

"That's a luxury you won't have much longer. You can argue. You can sit and think. You can fuck up. I'll try to buy you some time."

"We don't want that," Aaron said furiously.

Shadow Love shook his head, aimed out the window again and squeezed the trigger. The *click* hung in the air between them.

# 14

Hart worked through an Indian-dominated housing project while Sloan did background on John Liss. Lucas, fighting a blinding hangover, made the rounds of barbershops, bars, fast-food joints and rooming houses.

A little after noon, Lucas called the dispatcher to check on Lily and was told that she was still meeting with the county attorney. He stopped at an Arby's, ordered a roast beef sandwich and carried it outside. He was leaning on his car when his handset squawked and the shotgun touched him behind the ear again. He almost dropped the sandwich. He stood paralyzed, and the cold metal pressed against his head and Hood's apartment rose up in front of his eyes, the circle of squad cars, the radios squawking . . . A few seconds later, it all faded and Lucas staggered from the car and half fell onto a mushroom-shaped concrete stool. He sat sweating for a few moments, then got up and walked shakily to the car and started off again.

A half-hour later, the dispatcher gave him a number to call. Lily's hotel. Lucas called from a street booth across from a leather shop, staring at a Day-Glo–green sign advertising hand-tooled belts.

"Lunch?" Lucas asked, when Lily said hello.

"I can't," she said. There was a second's silence, and then she said, "I'm going home."

Lucas considered it, staring at the Day-Glo sign, then down at the telephone receiver in his hand. After a few seconds he said, "I thought you might stay over, see what happens."

"I thought about it, but then . . . I finished with the county attorney and called to see when I could get a flight out. I was thinking tonight, but they said they could get me on a flight at one-thirty. I've got a cab coming downstairs. . . ."

"I could come . . ."

"No, don't," she said quickly. "I'd really prefer that you didn't."

"Jesus, Lily . . ."

"I'm sorry . . ." she said. There was a moment's silence before she finished the sentence. "I hope you're okay. And I'll see you. Maybe. You know, someday."

"Okay," he said.

"So. Bye."

"Bye."

She hung up and Lucas stood leaning against the booth. "God damn it," he said aloud.

Two young girls were passing, carrying schoolbooks. They heard him, glanced his way and hurried on. Lucas walked slowly back to his car, confused, unsure whether he was feeling disappointment or relief. He spent another hour touring Lake Street bars, apartment buildings and stores, looking for a toehold, an edge, a whisper, anything. He came up dry; and although he was given more names, more people to check, his heart wasn't in it. He looked at his watch. Ten after two. She'd be off the ground, on her way to New York. Lily.


Daniel was in his office. He had turned the overhead fluorescent lights off and sat in a pool of yellow light cast by an old-fashioned gooseenecked desk lamp. Larry Hart was sitting in the chair in front of his desk, Sloan, Lester and Anderson off to the side. Lucas took the last chair.

"Nothing?" asked Daniel.

"Not a thing," Hart said. Lucas shook his head as he sat down.

"We've been getting some stuff about Liss. He worked for a metal fabrication plant out in Golden Valley. They said he was all right, but weird, you know, about Indian stuff."

"Big help," Anderson said.

Sloan shrugged. "I got some names of his friends, I can feed them to you, maybe the computer'll have something."

"Family?" asked Lucas.

"Wife and kid. Wife works a couple of jobs. She's a checkout at Target and works at a Holiday store at night, part-time. And they got a kid. Harold Richard, aka Harry Dick, seventeen. He's trouble, a doper. He's been downtown a half-dozen times, minor theft, possession of pot, possession of crack. Small stuff."

"That's it?" asked Daniel.

"Sorry," Sloan apologized. "We're hitting it as hard as we can."

"What about Liss himself? Are they getting anything out of him?"

Anderson shook his head. "Nope. About fifteen minutes after Liss went down, Len Meadows flew in from Chicago in his private jet. The first thing he did was bar any cops from talking to his client."

"Fifteen minutes? Did Meadows know in advance?" Lucas asked.

"It wasn't really fifteen minutes—" Sloan started.

Hart interrupted. "The Fire Creek Reservation office is in Brookings. When they heard about the shooting, they got scared about what might happen. They called Meadows' office. He'd done some pro bono criminal work for them. So then Meadows had his people call around, working with the information they were getting off the TV. They found out who Liss' old lady was. Meadows called her—Louise, that's her name—and offered his services. She said yes, so he flew out to Brookings. When Liss woke up after the docs got finished with him, Meadows went in and talked to him. That was it. No more cops."

"Damn it," Lucas said, chewing his lip. "Meadows is pretty good."

"He's a grandstanding asshole," said Lester.

"Frank, *you're* an asshole, but nobody ever said you weren't pretty good," said Daniel.

"I did once," Sloan said. "He made me go out and investigate supermarket thefts."

Lester grinned. "And I'd do it again," he said.

"The problem with Meadows is, he won't deal," Lucas said. "He's an ideologue. He prefers the crucifix to the plea bargain."

They all chewed it over for a minute, then Daniel said, "Our Indian friends are putting out press releases now."

"Say what?" asked Hart.

"We got a press release. Or rather, the media got press releases. All of them—newspapers, TV stations, WCCO radio. We got copies. They're supposedly from the killers," Daniel said.

Lucas sat up. "When did this happen?"

"They started arriving in the morning mail." Daniel passed out photocopies of the press releases. "Channel Eight was out on the street for the noon news, asking Indians to read the press releases and then asking them if they agreed."

Lucas nodded absently as he read. The authors took responsibility for all four killings, the two in the Cities, and those in New York and Oklahoma City. Nothing about the Brookings killing, so they were mailed before that. The killings were done as the beginning of a new uprising against white tyranny. There were unconvincing quotes from the Oklahoma assassin, but there were also details from Oklahoma that Lucas hadn't seen.

"This Oklahoma stuff . . ." he said, looking up at Daniel.

The chief nodded. "They got it right."

"Huh." He finished the release, glanced at the second sheet Daniel had given him, a copy of the envelope the release had arrived in, and said "Huh" again.

"Interesting envelope," Sloan remarked.

"Yeah."

"What's that?" asked Hart. He had been looking at the press release and now turned to the envelope.

"Look at the cancellation," Lucas said. "Minneapolis."

Anderson looked up. "We thought they were working out of here."

"Now everybody will know," Daniel said. "That'll crank up the pressure."

"That TV stuff we put out about Yellow Hand last night, blaming this group, I think it backfired," Hart said. "A lot of people knew Yellow Hand. They know he was a crackhead. They figure he was killed by a dealer or another crack-head. Some kind of ripoff. They think the TV stuff is just more white-cop bullshit."

"Shit," Daniel said. He pulled at his lip, then looked at Lucas. "Any ideas? We gotta break something loose."

Lucas shrugged. "We could try money. There're a lot of poor people out there. A little cash might loosen things up."

"That's ugly," Hart objected.

"We're about to get lynched by the media," Daniel snapped. He looked at Lucas. "How much?"

"I don't know. We'd be on a blind trip, just fishing. But I don't know what else to do. I've got no net with the Indians. You show me a problem with the black community, I can call two hundred guys. With the Indians . . ."

"You won't make any friends by spreading money around," Hart insisted. "That's too . . . white. That's what the people will say. That it's just like the white men. They get in trouble, and they go out and buy an Indian."

"So it's not the best way. The question is, Will it work?" Daniel said. "We can worry about rebuilding community relations later. Especially since we don't have any in the first place."

Hart shrugged. "There's always some people who'll talk for money. Indians are no different than anybody else, that way."

Daniel nodded. "And we have a source of money," he said. "We don't even have to tap the snitch fund."

"What's that?" Lucas asked.

"The Andretti family. When the word got out that we'd nailed Billy Hood, I got a call from old man Andretti himself, thanking us for our help. . . ." He frowned, remembering, and looked at Lucas. "Where's Lily? I haven't seen her."

"She headed back to New York," Lucas said. "She was done here."

"God damn it, why didn't she check out with me?" Daniel asked irritably. "Well, she'll just have to come back."

"What?"

"The Andrettis were happier'n hell about Hood, but apparently they're no longer satisfied with getting what the old man calls 'small fry.' He's convinced the NYPD that Lily should stay out here and observe until this whole crazy bunch is busted."

"So she's coming back?" Lucas asked, his breath suddenly coming harder.

"I expect she'll be back tomorrow, as hot as the Andrettis are," Daniel said. "But that's neither here nor there. Anderson has started putting together some interview files. . . ."

Daniel kept talking, but Lucas lost track of what he was saying. A slow fire of anticipation spread though his chest and stomach. Lillian Rothenburg, NYPD. Lucas bit his lip and stared into a dark corner of Daniel's office, as the chief rambled on.

Lily.

A moment later he realized Daniel had stopped talking and was staring at him.

"What?" asked Daniel.

"I got an idea," Lucas said. "But I don't want to talk about it."


An hour after dark, Lucas found Elwood Stone standing under a streetlight on Lyndale Avenue. This time, Stone didn't bother to run.

"What the fuck you want, Davenport?" Stone was wearing sunglasses and a brown leather bomber jacket. He looked like an advertisement for rent-a-thug. "I ain't holding."

Lucas handed him a deck of photographs. "You know this kid?"

Stone looked them over. "Maybe I seen him around," he said.

"They call him Harry Dick?"

"Yeah. Maybe I seen him around," Stone repeated. "What you want?"

"I don't want anything, Elwood," Lucas said. "I just want you to give the boy some credit on a couple of eight-balls."

"Shit, man . . ." Stone turned away and looked up the street, doing a comic double-take in disbelief. "Man, I don't give no credit, man. To a crackhead? You fuckin' crazy?"

"Well, it's like this, Elwood. Either you give Harry a little credit—and it's got to be tomorrow—or I'll talk to Narcotics and we'll run your little round ass right off the street. We'll have somebody in your back pocket every day."

"Shit . . ."

"Or, I can have a talk with Narcotics and tell them you're temporarily on my snitch list. I'll give you some status for say . . . two months? How about that?"

"Why me?"

" 'Cause I know you."

Stone considered. If he went on the snitch list, he'd have virtual immunity from prosecution. It was an opportunity not to be missed, as long as nobody else found out.

"Okay," Stone said after a moment. "But keep it between you and me. You don't tell Narcotics, but if I get hassled, you jump in."

Lucas nodded. "You got it."

"So where do I find this motherfucker, Harry Dick? It's not like I know where he lives."

"We'll spot him for you. You give me your beeper number and I'll call you. Tomorrow. Probably early afternoon."

Stone looked at him for another long minute, then nodded. "Right."

# 15

Lucas put a thousand dollars on the street between ten o'clock and noon, then headed out to the airport in a city car. Sloan called him on the way.

"He's there," Sloan said. "I talked to the next-door lady. She said he's usually out of there in the early afternoon. Sleeps late, usually leaves between one and two. His mother's gone out to South Dakota to see the old man."

"All right. Keep an eye on the place," Lucas said. "You got our friend's number?"

"Yeah."

"Lily's plane's on time, so I ought to hook up with you before one. If our boy goes for a walk before then, take him. No fuckin' around."

"Gotcha. Uh, our little Indian helper . . ."

"I'll pick him up. Don't worry about Larry."

"He could be a problem, the way he's talking," Sloan warned.

"I'll take care of it," Lucas said.

\*     \*     \*

Hart bitterly fought the idea of putting money on the street, and threatened to quit. Daniel went to the director of Welfare and Hart got a call.

When Lucas talked to him that morning, Hart seemed more sad than angry, but the anger was there too.

"This could fuck me forever, man," Hart said. "With the Indian people."

"They're killing guys, Larry," Lucas said. "We gotta stop it."

"This is not right," Hart said.

And when Lucas outlined the proposal to pick up Harold Richard Liss, Hart laughed in disbelief.

"Don't fuck with me, Lucas," he said. "You're setting that boy up. You're going to plant the stuff on him."

"No, no, this is a legitimate tip," Lucas lied.

"Bullshit, man . . ."

They'd left it like that, Hart heading down to Indian Country with a pocket full of cash and a growing anger. He could be handled, Lucas thought. He loved his job too much to risk it. He could be cooled out. . . .

Lily's plane was early. He found her in the luggage pick-up area, watching the carousel with the suppressed embarrassment of somebody who suspects she has been stood up.

"Jesus, I missed you at the gate," Lucas said, hurrying over. She was wearing a beige silk blouse with a tweed skirt and jacket and dark leather high heels. She was beautiful and he had trouble saying the words.

"God damn it, Davenport," she said.

"What?"

"Nothing. That was just a general 'God damn it.' About everything." She rose on her tiptoes and pecked him on the cheek. "I didn't want to come back."

"Mmm."

"There's a bag," she said. She stopped a suitcase and Lucas lifted it off the carousel. "And there's the other, coming through now."

Lily's second bag came around, and Lucas grabbed the two of them and led the way to the parking ramp. On the way, he looked down at her and said, "How've you been?"

"About the same as I was yesterday," she said with mild sarcasm, squinting as the outdoor light hit her face. "I was out of here. Finished. Job done. I got to our apartment, opened the door, and the phone was ringing. David was in the shower, so I picked it up. It was a deputy commissioner. He said, 'What the fuck are you doing here?' "

"Nice guy," Lucas said.

"If there were honorary degrees for assholes, he'd be a doctor of every-thing," Lily said.

"How's David?" Lucas asked, as though he knew her husband.

"Not so good the first time, 'cause he was a little overexcited. After that, he was great," she said. She looked up at him and suddenly blushed.

"Women are no good at that kind of talk," Lucas remarked. "But it wasn't a bad try."

They stopped at the gray Ford and Lily lifted an eyebrow.

"We got something going," Lucas said. "In fact, we're in kind of a hurry. I'll tell you about it as we go along."

Hart was worse. He'd tried to talk money with some of his acquaintances, and everything, he said, had changed. He'd be a pariah. The Indian man who bought people. And he worried about Harold Richard Liss.

"Man, I don't like this, I don't like this." He sat in the backseat, twisting his hands. Tears ran down his face. He wiped them away with the sleeve of his tweed jacket.

"He's a fuckin' criminal, Larry," said Lucas, annoyed. "Jesus Christ, quit whining."

"I'm not whining, man, I'm . . ."

Lucas let the Ford idle along. A hundred yards ahead, Harold Richard Liss ambled down Lake Street looking in the store windows. "He was making money selling chloroform to little kids. And glue," Lucas said, interrupting.

"This still isn't right, man. He's a fuckin' teenager." Hart shivered.

"It's only for a couple of days," Lucas said.

"It still isn't right."

"Larry . . ." Lucas started in exasperation. Lily touched his shoulder to stop him and turned and looked over the seat.

"There's a big difference between welfare work and police work," she said to Hart, keeping her face and voice soft and sympathetic. "In a lot of ways, we're on different sides. I think you'd be more comfortable if we just dropped you off."

"We might need his help," Lucas objected, glancing sideways at Lily.

"I won't be much help, man," Hart said. There was a new note in his voice, the sound of a trapped man who sensed an opening. "I mean, I spotted him for you. I don't know shit about surveillance. It's not like you need to interrogate him."

Lucas thought about it, sighed and picked up the radio. "Hey, Sloan, this is Davenport. You still got him?"

Sloan came back: "Yeah, no sweat. What's happening?"

"I'm dropping Larry. Don't worry when you see us stop."

"Sure. I'll hang with Harry."

Lucas pulled over to the side and Hart scrambled to get out. "Thanks, man," he said, leaning over the driver's-side window. "I mean, I'm sorry. . . ."

"That's okay, Larry. We'll see you back downtown," Lucas said.

"Sure, man. And thanks, Lily."

They pulled away from the curb and Lucas turned to Lily. "I hope we don't need him to talk to the guy."

"We won't. Like he said, you're not planning to interrogate him."

"Hmph."

Lucas watched Hart in his rearview mirror. Hart was peering after them as they continued down the street after Harry. Then Hart turned and walked away, around a corner. Up ahead, Harry stopped on the street corner to talk to a fat white man in a black parka. The parka was a full season too big, the kind you wore in January when the temperature went down to minus thirty. Harry and the white man exchanged a few words, the white man shook his head and Harry started pleading. The white man shook his head again and stepped away. Harry said something else and then turned, despondent, and started down the street again.

"Dealer," said Lily.

"Yeah. Donny Ellis. He wears that parka 'til June, puts it back on in September. He pisses in it, never washes. You don't want to get downwind of him."

"This is going to be stupid, Lucas. . . . Nobody ever sold anybody that much crack on credit. Especially not . . ."

"Hey, we don't have to convince anybody. It's just . . . Okay, there's Stone. . . ." Lucas picked up the radio and said, "Stone just came around the corner."

"I got him," Sloan said.

Lucas looked at Lily. "You know what? We should have gotten rid of Larry sooner than we did. He's the kind of guy who might go to the Human Rights Commission."

"Maybe, but I don't think so. That's why he was sweating," she said. She was watching as Elwood Stone walked toward Harry Dick, who was still shambling along the sidewalk. "It's not like we're going to do anything with the Liss kid. Hold him a couple of days and then kick him out of the system. My sense of Larry Hart is that his career means everything to him. He's a success. He makes some money. People like him. They depend on him. If he went outside with this, he'd be on the city's shit list. End of career. Back to the res. I don't think he'd risk that. Not if we kick the kid back out on the street after a couple of days."

"Okay."

"But it *will* make him feel like a small piece of shit," Lily added. "We whipsawed him between his job and his people and he's smart enough to see that. He'll never trust you again."

"I know," Lucas said uncomfortably. "God damn, I hate to burn people."

"Professionally, or personally?"

"What?" Lucas asked, puzzled by the question.

"I mean, you hate to burn a guy because it loses a contact, or because it loses a friend?"

He thought about it and after a minute said, "I don't know." Up the street, Harry spotted Elwood Stone and quickened his step. Stone was one of the tightest dealers on the street, but it never hurt to ask. All he needed was a taste. Just a taste to tide him over.

"They're talking," Sloan said on the radio. "That goddamn Stone is shuckin' like he's on Broadway."

"I told him not to overdo it," Lucas muttered to Lily. Lucas had pulled into a parking place and couldn't see well from the driver's side. He crowded against Lily, who had her face pressed against the passenger-side window, and let his hand drop on her thigh.

"Watch it."

"What?"

"The hand, Davenport . . ."

"God damn it, Lily."

"It's going down," she said.

"It's going down," Sloan said. "He's got it."

"Let's take him," Lucas said.


Sloan came in from the west, Lucas from the east. Sloan pulled into the curb ahead of Harry, Lucas did a U-turn into a fire-hydrant zone behind him. Harry was still grinning, still had his hand in his jacket pocket, when Sloan hopped out of his car. He was inside fifteen feet before Harry figured out something was happening. He turned to run and almost bumped into Lucas, who was closing in from behind. Lily stayed in the street, blocking a dash to the side. Lucas grabbed Harry by the coat collar and said, "Whoa." A second later, Sloan had him by the arm.

"Hey, man," Harry started, but he knew he had been bagged.

"Come on, on the wall," Lucas said, "on the wall." They pushed him onto the wall. Sloan frisked him and found the baggies in his pocket.

"Holy shit," Sloan said. "We got us a dealer."

He opened his palm to Lucas, showed him the two eight-balls.

"I'm no fuckin' dealer, man. . . ."

"A quarter-ounce of dog-white cocaine," Lucas said to Harry. "That's a dealer load, kid. That's presumptive prison term."

"I'm a juvenile, man, look at my ID." Harry was old enough to be worried.

"You don't get no juvenile break on a presumptive-dealer rap," Lucas said. "Not unless you're ten years old. You look older than that."

"Oh, man," Harry moaned. "I just got it, a guy give it to me. . . ."

"Right," Sloan said skeptically. "He gave it to you all right. He gave it to you right in the ass." He cranked down one arm while Lucas hung on to the other, and Sloan put on his handcuffs. "You got the right to remain silent . . ."

Daniel wanted to push as hard as they could. If they waited, he thought, Len Meadows would get Liss' family organized and protected.

"You can fly out to Sioux Falls and rent a car . . ." Daniel started.

"Fuck fly," Lucas said. "I'm driving. We'll be there in four hours. We wouldn't get there any faster if we waited for an airplane and then drove up from Sioux Falls."

"Are you going?" Daniel raised an eyebrow and looked at Lily.

"Yeah. We'll be dealing with this Louise Liss. Maybe a woman would do it better."

"Okay. But take it easy with the Liss woman, will you? This whole thing is a little shaky. Larry Hart is shitting bricks. He's scared," Daniel said. "Worse than that, he's pissed off."

"Can you talk to him?"

"I already did and I'll go back with him again. I'll tell him if we squeeze anything out of Liss, we can probably send him back to work at Welfare. . . ."

They took overnight bags to Brookings. If they didn't get the information the first night, there wouldn't be much point in staying a second.

"Your friend . . . Jennifer. She's in Brookings, right?"

"Yeah. They sent out a crew. She's producing." They were crossing the Minnesota River at Shakopee. A flock of Canada geese were standing on the riverbank, watching the water go by. Lucas said, "Geese."

"Mmm. Will you stay with her?"

"What?"

"Jennifer. Will you stay with her?"

Lucas downshifted as they came into town and rolled up to a stoplight. He glanced at her, then turned right on the red light. "No. I'd rather that she not know I was there. She has a way of reading my mind. If she sees me, she'll know something is up."

"Do you know where she's staying?"

"Sure. It's out by the interstate that comes up from Sioux Falls. The Brookings cops told me that Louise Liss is staying in a place downtown. I thought we'd check in there."

They were going through the town of Sleepy Eye on Highway 14 when they passed a man on bicycle, dressed in cycling clothes: a green-striped polo shirt, black cycling shorts, white helmet. It was cool, but his bare legs were exposed and pumped like machine pistons. Lucas estimated that he was breaking the speed limit through the downtown.

"He looks like David," Lily said. "My husband."

"David's a cyclist?"

"Yeah. He was pretty serious about it, once." She turned her head to watch the cyclist as they went by. "He'd go out every Saturday with a group of people and they'd ride centuries. Sometimes two. A century's a hundred miles."

"Jesus. He must be in great shape."

"Yeah." She was watching the storefronts in the tiny town. "Bicycles bore the shit out of me, to tell you the truth. They always break down, then you've got to fix them. Or they're not broken, then you've got to fiddle with them to get them tuned up exactly right. The tires go flat all the time."

"That's why I bought a Porsche," Lucas said.

"A Porsche's probably cheaper too," Lily said. "Those goddamned racing bikes cost a fortune. And you can't have just one."

A few minutes later, back in the countryside, they passed a herd of black-and-white dairy cows.

"Neat cows," she said. "What kind are they?"

"Beats the hell out me," Lucas said.

"What?" she said in amusement. "You're from Minnesota. You ought to know about cows."

"That's the cheeseheads over in Wisconsin who know about cows. I'm a city kid," he said. "If I had to guess, I'd say they're Holsteins."

"Why's that?"

" 'Cause that's the only cow name I know. Wait a minute. There's also Guernseys and Jerseys. But I don't think they're the spotted ones."

"Brown Swiss," Lily said.

"What?"

"That's a kind of cow."

"I thought that was a kind of cheese," Lucas said.

"I don't think so. . . . There's another bunch." She watched a herd of cows ambling down the pasture toward the barn, walking in ones and twos, like tourists coming back to a bus, shadows trailing behind them. "David knows the names of everything. You drive up toward the mountains and you say, 'What's that tree?' And he says, 'That's a white oak,' or, 'That's a Douglas fir.' I used to think he was bullshitting me, so I started checking. He was always right."

"I don't think I could stand it," Lucas said.

"He's really smart," she said. "He might be the smartest man I ever knew well."

"Sounds like fuckin' Mahatma Gandhi."

"What?"

"You once told me he was the gentlest man you ever knew. Now you say he's the smartest."

"He's really quite the guy."

"Yeah, I doubt Gandhi rode a racing bike, so he's one up . . ."

"I don't think I want to talk about this anymore."

"All right."

But a few minutes later she said, "Sometimes, I don't know . . ."

"What?"

"He's so centered. David is. Peaceful. Sometimes . . ."

"It bores the shit out of you," Lucas suggested.

"No, no . . . I just feel like I'm so taken care of, I can't hardly stand the weight of it. He's such a good guy. And I hang out at the refrigerator and eat too much and I walk around with a gun and I've shot people. . . . He was freaked out when I went back home. I mean, he wanted to know all about it. He had this friend come over, a shrink, Shirley Anstein, to make sure I was all right. He was wild when he heard I was coming back. He said I was damaging myself."

"You think he's screwing this Anstein broad?"

"Shirley?" She laughed. "I don't think so. She's about sixty-eight. She's like an adoptive mother."

"He's faithful, then."

"Oh, yeah. He's so faithful it's almost like it's part of the weight on me. I can't even get away from that."

"Walnut Grove," Lily said, looking at a highway sign as they rolled through the edge of another small town. The sun was dipping toward the horizon. It'd be dark before they got to Brookings. "When I was a kid, I used to read the Laura Ingalls Wilder books. I loved them. Then they put the TV show on, you know, *Little House on the Prairie.* I was grown-up and the show was pretty bad, but I watched anyway, because of Laura. . . . The show was set in a place called Walnut Grove."

"This is it," Lucas said.

"What?" Lily looked at the sign again. "Same place?"

"Sure."

"Jesus . . ." She looked out the windows as they went through and saw a small prairie town, a little shabby, very quiet, with side streets that Huckleberry Finn would have been comfortable on. When they were out of the town, she still looked back, and said, "Walnut Grove . . . Damn. You know, given the change in time, it looks right."

They found Louise Liss through the Brookings Police Department and went to her motel. She was in the coffee shop, sitting by herself, staring into a glass of Coke. She was overweight, worn, with tired eyes now rimmed with red. She'd been crying, Lucas thought.

"This'll be bad," Lily muttered.

"Let's get her down to her room," Lucas said.

"I'll talk," Lily said.

They closed in the last few steps to the table and Lily took her ID case from her purse. "Mrs. Liss?"

Louise Liss looked up. Her eyes were flat, dazed. "Who are you?"

"We're police, Mrs. Liss. I'm Lily Rothenburg and this is Lucas Davenport from Minneapolis. . . ."

"I'm not supposed to talk to police," Louise said defensively. "Mr. Meadows said I wasn't supposed . . ."

"Mrs. Liss, we don't want to talk about your husband. We want to talk about your son, Harold." Lily sounded like somebody's mother, Lucas thought, then remembered that she was.

"Harold?" Louise reached out and gripped the Coke, her knuckles turning white. "What happened to Harold? Harold's okay, I talked to him before I left. . . ."

"I think we should talk in your room. . . ." Lily took several steps away from the table and Louise slipped out of the booth, following.

"Your purse," Lucas said.

She reached back to get her purse, saying, "What happened, what happened?" And she started to cry. The cashier was watching them. Lucas handed him three dollars, flashed his badge and said, "Police."

Outside the coffee shop, they turned toward the room. Louise grabbed Lily's coat and said, "Please . . ."

"He was arrested on cocaine charges, Mrs. Liss."

"Cocaine . . ." She suddenly pulled herself together and looked at Lucas; her voice rose to a screech. "You did this, didn't you? You framed my boy to get at John."

"No, no," Lucas said as he tried to keep her walking toward her room. "He'll tell you himself. The Narcotics people saw him touch a dealer. They stopped him and found two eight-balls in his pockets. . . ."

"Eight-balls?"

"Eighth-ounce packets. That's a lot of cocaine, Mrs. Liss." They got to her room and she opened the door with the key. Lily followed her inside and Lucas stepped in and closed the door. Louise sat on the bed. "It's what they call a presumptive amount. With that big an amount of cocaine, the law presumes he's dealing and it's a felony."

"He's just seventeen," Louise said. She seemed barely able to hold up her head.

Lucas put a sad expression on his face. "With that much cocaine, the county attorney will put him on trial as an adult. If he's convicted, it'd be a minimum of three years in prison."

The blood drained out of Louise's face. "What do you want?" she whispered.

"We're not Narcotics people," Lily said. She sat on the bed beside Louise and touched her on the shoulder. "We're investigating these murders with the Indians, like the one with your husband. So anyway, one of the Narcotics guys, his name is Sloan, came in this afternoon and said, 'Guess what? You know that guy they got out in South Dakota? The guy who killed the attorney general? We just busted his kid.' And then he said, 'I guess the whole family is rotten.'"

"We're not rotten," Louise protested. "I work hard. . . ."

"Well, we've got some room to maneuver with Harold, your son," Lily said in a quiet voice. "The court could treat him as a juvenile. But we have to give something to the Narcotics people. Some reason. We said, 'Well, his father is refusing to talk, and that thing is a lot more important than another dope charge.' We said, 'If we can get him to tell us just a few things, could we promise that we'd treat Harold as a juvenile?' The Narcotics officers thought it over, and we talked to the chief, and they said, 'Yes.' That's why we're here, frankly. To see if we can make a deal."

"You want John to sell out his friends," Louise said bitterly. "Sell out the people."

"We don't want any more murders," Lucas said. "That's all we want to do. We want to stop them."

Louise Liss had been pressing her hands to her cheeks as she listened to the pitch; now she dropped them into her lap. It was a gesture of either despair or surrender. Lily leaned closer to her. "Hasn't your family paid enough? Your husband is going to prison. He'll never walk again. You don't see the people who are behind this thing, you don't see those people in prison. They're still out walking around. *Walking* around, Louise."

"I don't know anything myself . . ." she said tentatively.

"Could you talk to John?" Lily asked gently.

"It would really be good if he could just give us a few names. We don't need a lot of details, just a few names. Nobody would have to know, even," Lucas said.

There was a moment of silence, and then Louise said, "Nobody would have to know?"

"Nobody," Lily said flatly. "And it would save your family a lot of grief. I hate to bring this up, but I noticed that Harold was a very good-looking youth. I mean, if they put him in the prison up in St. Cloud, with some men who have not had sexual relationships in a long time . . . Well."

"Oh, no, not Harold."

"It's not like they really have a choice," Lucas said. "Some of those guys up there are bigger than football players. . . ."

\*    \*    \*

When Louise had gone, Lily asked, "How bad do you feel?"

Lucas cocked his head and rolled his eyes up, as though thinking about it, and said, "Actually, not that bad."

"I don't feel that bad myself. And I think we should. It makes me a little sad that we don't feel worse," Lily said. "We're missing some parts, Davenport."

Lucas shrugged. "They got worn off. And . . ."

"What?"

"It's a game, you know," he said, testing her. "You can't back off in a game and win. You either go balls to the wall, or somebody takes you out and you're no good anymore."

Louise Liss was back from the hospital an hour later.

"I had trouble getting in," she apologized.

"Did you talk to John?"

"Yes . . . you'll help Harold?"

"If you help us, Mrs. Liss, I'll do everything I can to see that Harold is released," Lucas promised.

"It's some people named Crow," she said in a low voice. "They may be brothers or cousins. They're big Dakota medicine men."

"Dakota?" asked Lily.

"That's Minnesota Sioux," Lucas said. "Where are they at?"

"I wrote it down," Louise said, fumbling a piece of paper out of her purse. It was the corner of an envelope, with a street address. "He thinks this is right. . . ."

"Are there any more killings planned?" Lily pressed.

"All he would give me are the names and that address," Louise said. "I think it might kill him, just doing that."

"Okay, that's fine," Lily said. "We'll see about Harold tonight. We'll call on the telephone."

"Please," Louise Liss said, snatching at Lily's coat sleeve, "help him. Please?"

"The Crows? He said the Crows?" Larry Hart was astonished.

"You know them?" asked Daniel. Lucas was in a phone booth. Daniel, Anderson, Sloan and Hart were in Daniel's office, using a speaker phone.

"I know about them." There was a long pause, as Hart thought it over. "God damn. I might even have seen them once. They're famous. Two old men, they travel around the country and up in Canada, organizing the Indian nations. They've been on the road all their lives. Aaron is powerful medicine. Sam is supposed to be brilliant. . . . Jesus, you know, it all fits. They'd be right."

"What was that on their names? Aaron?" Anderson asked.

"Aaron and Sam. They supposedly come through the Cities a lot. It's like their home base. They have a son here, you see him from time to time. I went to school with him, years ago. Shit, you might even see the Crows from time to time, but I wouldn't know them. . . ."

"What about the son?" asked Sloan.

"The son is a freak. He has visions. He doesn't know which one of the Crows is his father. They were both sleeping with his mother that winter. . . . That's how he got his name, Shadow Love, love-in-the-shadows . . . it's like an Indian joke, based on his mother's last name. He's supposed to have some of the power of Aaron. . . ."

"Wait a minute, wait a minute," Lucas said. "Shadow Love?"

"Yeah. Skinny guy . . ."

"With tattoos. God damn." Lucas slapped his forehead. He took the phone away from his mouth and spoke to Lily. "We got them. These are the right motherfuckers." He went back to the phone. "Shadow Love's the guy I saw with Yellow Hand, before Yellow Hand was killed. Sonofabitch. Shadow Love. And two guys named Crow?"

"Yeah." Hart sounded distant, almost pensive.

"All right, listen," Lucas said. He hesitated a moment, trying to remember each step of his brief encounter with Shadow Love. "All right: Shadow Love's got a South Dakota driver's license and it's in his own name. I looked at it and that's how I remember the name, because it was so strange. And I don't know why, I can't remember, but something he said made me think he'd done time in prison. Harmon, can you run that down? Check with the NCIC or whatever?"

"I got it," said Anderson.

"We'll get some guys on the way to that address, check it out," Daniel said. "We ought to know something in an hour."

"Call us," Lucas said. He gave them his room number. "We'll get something to eat, then I'll be in my room."

"Soon as we know," Daniel promised. "This is fuckin' great, you two. This is what we needed. We got those motherfuckers."

# 16

Anderson got the location of the Crows' apartment and a bonus—a phone number—from the 911 center, and ran them down to Daniel's office.

"I'll start pulling guys," Anderson said. "I can get Del and a couple of his Narcotics people down there in ten minutes. They can check the place out while we get the entry team together. We'll stage at the Mobil station on Thirty-sixth."

"Don't tell anyone but Del what we're doing. Not until the last minute, when we have the place nailed down," Daniel said. "I don't want the feebs moving in."

"All the local feebs are out in Brookings," Sloan said with an edge of sarcasm. "That fuckin' Clay came in like the President of the Universe. Eight hundred guys running around with microphones in their ears . . ."

"Okay, but still keep it under your hat," Daniel said.

Anderson hurried away to his office. "You guys stick around," Daniel said to Hart and Sloan. "If this works out, you'll want to be in on the kill."

Sloan nodded and glanced at Larry. "Want to walk down to the machines and get a bite? Could be our last chance for a while . . ."

"I'll catch you down there," Larry said. "I gotta take a leak."


The Crows had mailed the press release on the Linstad killing earlier in the day, and Sam was rereading it as he tried to get comfortable on the battered couch. "I hope John sticks to it, the Indian Nation stuff," he said. "Hope he doesn't fall apart."

"He's got Meadows covering him," Aaron said. "Meadows is pretty good. . . ."

"Fuckin' wannabee," Sam grunted.

"John's got his reasons to hold out. He ever tell you his hot-dog story?"

Aaron was sitting at the kitchen table and Sam had to crank his head around to see him. " 'Hot dog'?"


John Liss had been twelve, a weedy kid in an army shirt and jeans. His father had been gone for weeks, his mother for two days with a man he didn't know. Her car was still out front, with maybe two gallons of gas. Neither John nor his nine-year-old sister had eaten since noon the day before—a can of Campbell's cream of mushroom soup.

"I'm so hungry," Donna cried. "I'm so hungry."

John made up his mind. "Get in the car," he said.

"You can't drive."

"Sure I can. Get in the car. We'll find something to eat."

"Where? We don't got no money," she said skeptically. But she was pulling on her jacket. She wore flip-flops for shoes.

"In town."

Friday night. The lights at the football field on the edge of town were the brightest things for miles.

"Must be about done," John Liss said. He could barely see over the steering wheel on the old Ford Fairlane. They bumped off the road and across a dirt parking lot. The temperature was in the forties. As long as the car was running, the heater would work, but he worried about running out of gas. If they were careful, they could make it back home.

"Watch the hot-dog stand," John told his sister. The year before, he had gone to a game and afterward had watched the woman who ran the concession stand peel a half-dozen wieners off the spits of an automatic broiler and toss them into a garbage can. A partial bag of buns had gone with them. The stand was in the same place, and a garbage can still stood next to it. Even the woman was the same.

The game ended twenty minutes later. The hometown fans spilled out of the stands, pushing and shoving in celebration of the victory. A tall blond kid stopped at the hot-dog stand, bought a dog and a Coke, and started walking away with friends. After a few steps, he spotted a girl in the crowd and yelled, "Hey, Carol."

"What do *you* want, Jimmy?" she asked teasingly. They were both wearing red wool letter jackets with white leather sleeves and yellow letters. John and his sister watched as they sidled toward each other, grinning, friends backing up each of them.

"This remind you of anything?" Jimmy asked, sliding the wiener out of his bun.

Her friends feigned shock while his slapped themselves on their foreheads, but Carol was ready: "Well," she said, "I suppose it might look a teensy bit like your dick, only the weenie's a lot bigger."

"Oh, *right*," he said, and flipped the wiener at her. She ducked and laughed and charged him, and they wrestled through the parking lot. Two minutes later, they were all gone.

"Go get it," Donna whispered.

"Did you see where it went?"

"Right under the stands . . ."

John slipped out of the car and found the wiener in the dirt. He wiped it on his shirt, brought it back and offered it to his sister. "It's still hot," she said. "God, it's perfect."

Her eyes were shining. John looked at her and the anger that washed over him almost snapped his spine. This was his *sister*, his fuckin' *little sister*. He wanted to kill someone, but he didn't know whom, or how. Not then. Later, when he met the Crows, he learned whom and how.


"Everybody's got a story," Sam said somberly. "Every fuckin' one of us. If it's not about us, it's about somebody in the family. Jesus Christ."

The phone rang.

"Shadow Love?" Sam asked.

Aaron shrugged and picked up the phone. " 'Lo?"

*"The cops are coming,"* a man said. *"They'll be there in ten minutes."*

"What?"

*"The cops are coming. Get out now."*

Sam Crow was on his feet. "What?"

Aaron stood with the receiver in his hand, confused. "Somebody, I don't know. Said the cops are on their way. In ten minutes."

"Let's go. . . ."

"I gotta get . . ."

"Fuck it, let's go!" Sam yelled. He grabbed Aaron's jacket, threw it at him, picked up his own.

"The typewriter . . ." Aaron seemed dazed.

"Fuck the typewriter!" Sam had the door open.

"I got to get my letters. I don't know what's in them. Maybe something about Barbara or something . . ."

"Ah, shit . . ." Sam grabbed a brown supermarket bag and sailed it at Aaron. "Get as much as you can in there," he said. He jerked open a closet door, pulled a green army duffel bag out and started pushing in their clothing. "Don't look at that shit, just stuff it in the bag," he shouted at Aaron, who seemed to be moving in slow motion, thumbing through his personal papers.

It took them four minutes to fill the duffel and collect Aaron's papers. The rest of their possessions would be left behind.

"Whoever it was, maybe they were wrong," Aaron panted as they started down the stairs.

"They weren't wrong. You think somebody'd just call . . . ?"

"No. And it was an Indian guy. He had the accent. . . ."

Sam stopped at the first-floor landing and peered out at the street.

"Through the back," he said after a second. "There's a guy walking down the street."

"What about the truck?" Aaron asked as he trailed behind his cousin.

"If they know us, if they've got our names, they'll know about the truck. And our fingerprints are all over that room. . . ."

They went down another flight into the basement, then out past the furnace and a storage room, and up a short flight of concrete steps into an alley. The darkness was broken by lights from back windows of the apartments and of houses on the other side of the alley.

"Right through the yard," Sam said in a whisper.

"They'll think we're window peepers," Aaron said.

"Shhh."

They crossed the yard, crouching, staying close to the garage and then to a hedge.

"Watch the clothesline," Sam muttered a second too late. The wire line snapped Aaron across the bridge of the nose.

"Ah, boy, that hurt," he said, holding his nose.

"Quiet . . ."

They stopped behind a bridal-wreath bush by the corner of the house. A car was moving along the street; it slowed and stopped at the corner. A few seconds later, two men got out. One leaned against the fender of the car and lit a cigarette. The other wandered down the sidewalk toward the back of the Crows' apartment house. They looked like street people but walked with a hard confidence.

"Cops," Sam whispered.

"We got to get across the street before everything is blocked," Aaron said.

"C'mon." Sam led the way again, dragging the duffel bag. They went down the length of the block, crossing yards behind the houses. Most windows were still lit. They heard music from several, or television dialogue muffled by the closed windows.

Aaron suddenly laughed, a delighted sound that stopped Sam in his tracks.

"What?"

"Remember back in Rapid City, when we was hitting those houses? Shit, we wasn't hardly teenagers. . . . It feels kind of good."

"Asshole," Sam grunted, but a moment later he chuckled. "I remember that broad with the yellow towel. . . ."

"Oh yeah . . ."

At the last house, they moved into a hedge and looked into the street.

"Nobody," said Sam. "Unless they're sitting in one of those cars."

"Right straight across and into the alley," Aaron said. "Go."

They crossed the street as quickly as they could, the duffel banging against Sam's legs. They hurried down the length of the alley.

"I can't carry this motherfucker much farther," Sam panted.

"There's a phone up by the SuperAmerica store. One more block," Aaron said.

They humped down another alley, Aaron helping with the duffel bag. At the end of the alley they stopped, and Aaron sat down behind between a bush and a chain-link fence. The SuperAmerica was straight across the street, the phone mounted on an outside wall.

"I'll call Barbara," Sam said, fumbling for change. "You wait here. Stay out of sight. I'll have her pull right into the alley."

"What about Shadow Love? If this is right, if there are cops, he'll walk right into them."

"There's nothing we can do about that," Sam said bleakly. "We gotta hope that he spots them, or calls Barb."

"Maybe it's nothing," Aaron said.

"Bullshit," said Sam. "Those were cops. They figured us out, cousin. They're on our ass."

# 17

Two pickups and a car with a Sioux Falls television logo were angle-parked outside the all-night coffee shop. A single man in a cowboy hat sat in a window booth, hunched over a cup of coffee and a grilled-cheese sandwich. Lucas hesitated outside the window, looking in, then followed Lily through the door.

"Checking for Jennifer?" she asked with a small smile.

Lucas blushed. "Well, it'd be better if she weren't . . ."

"Sure." He followed her down the row of booths, watching her hips. She'd changed from slacks to a dress and low heels. She still carried the shoulder bag with the .45.

The waitress, a tired young woman with vagrant strands of black hair dangling in her face, took their order of cheeseburgers and coffee and slouched away.

"What do you think about this Crows business?" Lily asked while they waited for the food.

"I don't know. Larry sounded weird. And shit, I was talking to this other guy, this Shadow Love. I knew at the time there was something not right about him. He . . . vibrated, you know?"

"Fruitcake?"

"There was something wrong. I don't know." The coffee came, scalding hot, oily.

There was nothing like the Minneapolis Indian community in New York, Lily said. Indians were there, all right, but weren't as visible. "They look kind of . . . mysterious," she said. "You see them on the street, on the corners. They're not threatening, not hostile. They just seem to watch. . . ."

Lucas nodded. "Sometimes they're like the biggest up-country Scandinavian redneck shitkickers in the world. They bang around in old pickups and work in the lumber business or ranching. Then other times you'll be out fuckin' around somewhere and you'll come across a bunch of Indians doing a ceremony. It looks like a tourist thing, but it's not. It's real. . . ."

They talked for an hour. Lucas at one point decided he was babbling. On the way back to the motel, in the car, they spoke almost not at all. Lucas parked behind the motel and locked the car.

"Think they'll know anything?" she asked as they walked down the hall toward their rooms.

"Maybe. We can call."

"Come on in. We can call from my room." She pushed the door open and Lucas followed her inside. She gestured at the phone, and he sat on the bed, picked up the receiver and dialed. Daniel answered on the first ring.

"Chief: Lucas. What happened?"

"We went in, but we missed them," Daniel said. "They're the right guys, though. There were a couple of press releases balled up and tossed in a garbage bag under the sink and the typewriter's right . . ."

"They left the typewriter?"

"Yeah. Sloan's down there, with Del, and they say it's kind of odd. They left a lot of junk behind, but the personal stuff is gone. Sloan thinks they blew out of the place in a hurry—maybe when they heard that Liss wasn't dead. Figured he might talk."

"Are you talking to the neighbors?"

"Yeah. Nobody saw them much. They are two old Indians, though. And they left prints all over the place, the FBI's running them now. And somebody said they drove a truck, and that's still parked out front. . . ."

"Jesus. Maybe you ought to shut down the scene and watch it, maybe they'll be back. . . ."

"We're doing that, but Del doesn't think it'll work. He says word'll be up and down the street in an hour, about the raid."

"That's probably right," Lucas said. "Damn."

"We'll talk to you tomorrow—we ought to have everything figured out by then. We'll meet at one o'clock, if you can make it."

"We'll be there," Lucas said. He hung up and turned to Lily, shaking his head. "Missed them."

"But they're the right guys?"

"Yeah, they left some stuff behind. They got a definite ID."

"God damn it," Lily said irritably. She dropped her head and reached back with one hand and rubbed her neck. She was less than a foot away and Lucas could smell the elusive scent she'd worn the first day he'd met her.

"How much longer are we going to fool around?" he asked quietly.

"I'm all done," she said.

"Say what? You're all done?"

"Yeah." She stood and stepped across the room. Lucas started after her, but she reached the lights, snapped them off and then stepped back into the dark, her arms crossed in front of her breasts.

"I'm really scared," she said.

"Jesus." He wrapped her tightly with his left arm, caught the back of her neck in his right hand and pulled her face to his. The kiss locked them together, swaying, for ten seconds; then she pulled her chin back, gasping, and they stumbled sideways together and fell on the bed.

"Lucas, dammit, give me a minute in the shower. . . ."

"Fuck the shower," he said. His voice was coarse, fevered. He kissed her again, his body pressing her into the bed, one hand tugging at the buttons that held the top of her dress together.

"Jesus, let me . . ."

"I got it." A button popped and his hand was on her warm skin, her stomach, then around behind, unlatching her brassiere. Lily began to moan, trying to catch his lips. They rolled across the bed, she fumbling with his belt, he with his hand now beneath her dress, pulling at her underpants.

"My God, a garter belt, what's it made out of, steel mesh? I can't . . ."

"Slow down, slow down. . . ."

"No."

He got the garter belt off one leg, though it was still twisted around her ankle, and then her underpants were off one leg, and his hands were on her. Finally he entered her and she nearly screamed with the intensity of the feeling . . . and sometime later, she thought, she did scream.

"Christ, I wish I still smoked," he said. He'd turned on a bedside lamp and was sitting up, still mostly dressed. She was gasping for air. Like a carp, she thought. She'd never seen one, but had read in good books about carp gasping for air on riverbanks. He looked down at her. "Are you okay?"

"Yeah. My God . . ."

"Can I . . . let me take some of this stuff . . ."

After the violence of the first episode, he was suddenly tender, moving her body, lifting her, stripping off her remaining clothing. She felt almost like a child, until he kissed her on the front of her thigh, just where it joined her hip, and the fire ran through her belly again and she gasped. Lucas was on her again and the bedside lamp seemed to grow dimmer. Then again, after a while, she thought, she may have screamed again.

"Did I scream?" she blurted. She stood facing the showerhead, the water beating off her breasts. Lucas stood behind her. She could feel him pressing against her buttocks, his soapy hand on her stomach.

"I don't know. I thought it was me," he said.

She giggled. "What are you doing?"

"Just washing."

"I think you already washed there."

"A little more couldn't hurt."

She closed her eyes and leaned back against him, his soapy hand moving, and it started once again. . . .

# 18

Barbara Gow's house had gray siding, once white, and a red asbestos-shingle roof. A single box elder stood in the front yard and a swayback garage hunkered hopelessly in back. A waist-high chain-link fence surrounded her holdings.

"It looks pretty bad," she said sadly. They were ten minutes off the expressway, in a neighborhood of tired yards. The postwar frame houses were crumbling from age, poor quality and neglect: roofs were missing shingles, eaves showed patches of dry rot. In the dim illumination of the streetlights, they could see kids' bikes dumped unceremoniously on the weedy lawns. The cars parked in the streets were exhausted hulks. Oil stains marked the driveways like Rorschachs of failure.

"When I bought it, I called it a cottage," she said as they rolled into the driveway. "God damn, it makes me sad. To think you can live in a place for thirty years, and in the end, not care about it."

Sam Crow closed one eye and stared at her with the other, gauging the level of her unhappiness. In the end, he grunted, got out of the car and lifted the garage door.

"I hope Shadow Love's okay," she said anxiously as she pulled into the garage.

She had picked them up ten minutes after Sam called her. As they headed back to her house, they crossed the street that the apartment was on. There were cars in the street. Cops. The raid was under way.

"He was due back," Sam said as they got out of the car. "With all those cops in the street . . ."

"If he wasn't there when they arrived . . ."

"If they didn't get him, we should be hearing from him," said Aaron.

Barbara's house was musty. She was never a housekeeper, and she smoked: the interior, once bright, was overlaid with a yellowing patina of tobacco tar. Sam Crow dragged the duffel bag up the stairs. Aaron headed for a sitting room that had a foldout couch.

"You guys got any money?" Barbara asked when Sam came back down.

"A couple of hundred," he said, shrugging.

"I'll need help with the groceries if you stay here long."

"Shouldn't be too long. A week, maybe."

Twenty minutes later, Shadow Love called. Barbara said, "Yes, they're here. They're okay," and handed the phone to Sam.

"We were afraid they got you," Sam said.

"I almost walked right into them," Shadow Love said. He was in a bar six blocks from the Crows' apartment. "I was thinking about something else, I was almost on the block when I realized something was wrong, with all those cars. I watched for a while, I was worried I'd see them taking you out."

"You coming here?" Sam asked.

"I better. I don't know where they got their information, but if they're tracking me . . . I'll see you in a half-hour."

When Shadow Love arrived, Barbara stood on her tiptoes to kiss him on the cheek and took him straight into the kitchen for a sandwich.

"Somebody betrayed us," Shadow Love said. "That fuckin' Hart was in the street outside the apartment. He's passing out money now. The hunter cop too."

"We're not doing as well as I hoped," Sam confessed. "I'd hoped Billy would get at least one more and that John would make it out of Brookings. . . ."

"Leo's still out and I'm available," Shadow Love said. "And you can't complain about the media. Christ, they're all over the goddamned Midwest. I saw a thing on television from Arizona, people out on the reservations there, talking. . . ."

"So it's working," Aaron said, looking at his cousin.

"For now, anyway," Sam said.

Later that night, Sam watched Barbara move around the bedroom and thought, She's old.

Sixty, anyway. Two years younger than he was. He remembered her from the early fifties, the Ojibway bohemian student of French existentialists, her dark hair pulled back in a bun, her fresh heart-shaped face without makeup, her books in a green cloth sack carried over her shoulder. Her beret. She wore a crimson beret, pulled down over one eye, smoked Gauloises and Gitanes and sometimes Players, and talked about Camus.

Barbara Gow had grown up on the Iron Range, the product of an Ojibway father and a Serbian mother. Her father worked in the open-pit mines during the day and for the union at night. Her mother's Bible sat in a small bookcase in the living room. Next to it was her father's *Das Kapital*.

As a teenager, she had done clerical work for the union. After her mother died, leaving a small insurance policy, she'd moved to Minneapolis and started at the university. She liked the university and the talk, the theory. She liked it better when she heard the news from existential France.

Sam could still see all of that in her, behind the wrinkled face and slumping shoulders. She shivered nude in the cold air and pulled on a housecoat, then turned and smiled at him, the smile lighting his heart.

"I'm surprised that thing still works, much as you abuse it," she said. Sam's penis curled comfortably on his pelvis. It *felt* happy, he thought.

"It'll always work for you," Sam said. He lay on top of the blankets, on top of the handmade quilt, impervious to the cold.

She laughed and left the room, and a moment later he heard the water start in the bathroom. Sam lay on the bed, wishing he could stay for a year or two years or five, wrapped in the quilt. Scared. That's what it was, he thought. He put the thought out of his mind, rolled off the bed and walked to the bathroom. Barbara was sitting on the toilet. He stepped in front of the vanity and turned on the water to wash himself.

"Shadow Love's still watching that movie," Barbara said. The sounds of TV gunfire drifted up the stairs.

*"Zulu,"* said Sam. "Big fight in Africa, a hundred years ago. He says it was better than the Custer fight."

Barbara stood up and flushed the toilet as Sam dried himself with a towel. "Is this the end?" she asked quietly as they walked back into the bedroom.

He knew what she meant, but pretended he did not. "The end?"

"Don't give me any bullshit. Are you going to die?"

He shrugged. "Shadow Love says so."

"Then you will," Barbara said. "Unless you go away. Now."

Sam shook his head. "Can't do that."

"Why not?"

"The thing is, these other people have died. If it comes my turn and I don't fight, it'll be like I turned my back on them."

"You've got a gun?"

"Yeah."

"And this is all necessary?"

"Yes. And it's almost necessary that we . . . die. The people need this story. You know, when we were kids, I knew people who rode with Crazy Horse. Who's alive now to talk to the kids? The only legends they have are dope dealers. . . ."

"So you're ready."

"No, of course not," Sam admitted. "When I think about dying . . . I can't think about dying. I'm not ready."

"Nobody ever is," Barbara said. "I look at myself in the mirror, on the door . . ." She pushed the bedroom door shut, and the full-length mirror mounted on the back reflected the two of them, naked, looking into it. ". . . and I see this old woman, shriveled up like last year's potato. A clerk at the historical society, all gray and bent over. But I feel like I'm eighteen. I want to go out and run in the park with the wind in my hair, and I want to roll around on the grass with you and Aaron and hear Aaron putting the bullshit on me, trying to get into my pants . . . and I can't do any of that because I'm old. And I'm going to die. I don't want to be old and I don't want to die, but I will. . . . I'm not ready, but I'm going."

"I'm glad we had this talk," Sam said wryly. "It really cheered me up."

She sighed. "Yeah. Well, the way you talk, I think when the time comes, you'll use the gun."

*　　*　　*

Shadow Love paced.

Sam lay at Barbara's right hand, asleep, his breathing deep and easy, but all during the night Barbara could hear Shadow Love pacing the length of the downstairs hallway. The television came on, was turned off, came on again. More pacing. He'd always been like that.

Almost forty years earlier, Barbara had lived a half block from Rosie Love, and had met the Crows at her house. They had been radical hard-cases even then, smoking cigarettes all night, drinking, talking about the BIA cops and the FBI and what they were doing on the reservations.

When Shadow was born, Barbara was the godmother. In her mind's eye, she could still see Shadow Love walking the city sidewalks in his cheap shorts and undersize striped polo shirt, his pale eyes calculating the world around him. Even as a child, he had had the fire. He was never the biggest kid on the block, but none of the other kids fooled with him. Shadow Love was electric. Shadow Love was crazy. Barbara loved him as she would her own child, and she lay in her bed and listened to him pace. She looked at the clock at 3:35, and then she drifted off to sleep.

In the morning, she found him sitting, asleep, in the big chair in the living room, the chair she once called her man-trap. She tiptoed past the doorway toward the kitchen, and his voice called to her as she passed: "Don't sneak."

"I thought you were asleep," she said. She stepped back to the doorway. He was on his feet. Light was coming in the window behind him and he loomed in it, a dark figure with a halo.

"I was, for a while." He yawned and stretched. "Is this house wired for cable?"

"Yeah, I got it for a while. But when there was nothing on, I had them turn it off."

"How about if I give you the money and you have them turn it back on? HBO or Cinemax or Showtime. Maybe all of them. When the heat gets heavy, we'll really be cooped up."

"I'll call them this morning," she said.


At midmorning, after breakfast, Barbara got a stool, a towel and a pair of scissors and cut Sam's and Shadow Love's hair. Aaron sat and watched in amusement as the hair fell in black wisps around their shoulders and onto the floor. He told Sam that when old men get their hair cut, they lose their potency.

"Nothin' wrong with my dick," Sam said. "Ask Barb." He tried to slap her on the butt. She dodged his hand and Shadow Love flinched. "Watch it, God damn it, you're going to stick the scissors in my ear."

When she finished, Shadow Love put on a long-sleeved cowboy shirt, sunglasses and a baseball cap.

"I still look pretty fuckin' Indian, don't I?"

"Get rid of the sunglasses," Barbara said. "Your eyes could pass for blue. You could be a tanned white man."

"I could use some ID," Shadow Love said, tossing the sunglasses on the kitchen table.

"Just a minute," Barbara said. She went upstairs and came back a few minutes later with a man's billfold, all flat and tired and shaped to another butt. "It was my brother's," she said. "He died two years ago."

The driver's license was impossible. Her brother had been four years older than she, and bald and heavy. Even with the bad picture, there was no way Shadow Love could claim to be the man in the photo.

"All this other stuff is good," he said, thumbing through it. Harold Gow had credit cards from Amoco, Visa and a local department store. He had a membership card from an HMO, a Honeywell employee's ID without a photo, a Social Security card, a Minnesota watercraft license, a credit-union card, a Prudential claim card, two old fishing licenses, and other odd bits and pieces of paper. "If they shake me down, I'll tell them I lost my license on a DWI. When an Indian tells them that, they believe you."

"What about you guys?" Barbara asked the Crows.

Sam shrugged. "We got driver's licenses and Social Security cards under our born names. I don't know if the cops have those figured out yet, but they will."

"Then you shouldn't go out on the street. At least not during the day," Barbara said.

"I've got to talk to people, find out what's going on," Shadow Love said.

"You be careful," Barbara said.


Shadow Love was in a bar on Lake Street when an Indian man came in and ordered a beer. The man glanced sideways at Shadow Love and then ignored him.

"That Welfare guy's down at Bell's Apartments handing out money again," the Indian man told the bartender.

"Christ, half the town is drinking on him," the bartender said. "I wonder where they're getting all the loot?"

"I bet it's the CIA."

"Boy, if it's the CIA, somebody's in trouble," the bartender said wisely. "I met some of those boys in 'Nam. You don't want to fuck with them."

"Bad medicine," the Indian man said.

A man at the back of the bar yelled, "Nine-ball?" and the Indian man called,

"Yeah, I'm coming," took the beer and wandered back. The bartender wiped the spot he'd been leaning on with a wet rag and shook his head.

"The CIA. Man, that's bad business," he said to Shadow Love.

"That's bullshit, is what it is," Shadow Love said.

He finished his beer, slid off the stool and walked outside. The sun was shining and he stopped, squinting against the bright light. He thought for a moment, then turned west and ambled down Lake Street toward the apartments.

Bell's Apartments were an ugly remnant of a sixties housing program. The architect had tried to disguise an underlying prison-camp barrenness by giving each apartment a different-colored door. Now, years later, the colored doors together looked like a set of teeth with a few punched out.

Behind the building, an abandoned playground squatted in a rectangle of dead weeds. The hand-push merry-go-round had broken off its hub years before and had rusted into place, like a bad minimalist sculpture. The basketball court offered pitted blacktop and bare hoops. The swing sets had lost all but two swings.

Shadow Love sat in one of the swings and watched Larry Hart working his way down to the first floor of the building. Hart would look at a piece of paper in his hand, knock on a door, talk to whoever answered, then move on. Sometimes he talked for ten seconds, sometimes for five minutes. Several times he laughed, and once he went inside and came back out a few minutes later, chewing something. Frybread.

The problem, Shadow Love thought, was that there were too many people in on the Crows' secret. Leo and John and Barbara, and a bunch of wives who might know or have guessed something.

The Crows had been proselytizing for years. Though they had stayed resolutely in the background, their names were known, as was the extreme nature of their gospel. Once those names popped up on a police computer as suspects, they'd go right to the top of the hunters' list. That normally wouldn't be too much of a problem. The cops' resources in the Indian community were minimal.

Hart was something else. Shadow Love had known him in high school, but only from a distance, in the days when the boys in one grade didn't mix with the boys in the grades above. Hart had been popular then, with both Indians and whites. He still was. He was one of the people and he had friends and he had money.

Shadow Love watched him working down through the building, heard him laughing, and before Hart reached the bottom level, Shadow Love knew that something would have to be done.

\*     \*     \*

Hart saw Shadow Love sitting in the swing as he walked toward the steps that would take him to the bottom floor, but he didn't recognize him. He watched the man swinging, then dropped into a blind section of the stairwell. Five seconds later, when he came out of the stairwell, the man was gone.

Hart shivered. The man must have simply gotten off the swing, walked around the bush at the edge of the playground and gone down the street. But that was not the effect Hart felt. The man was there when he went into the stairwell and gone a few seconds later. He had vanished, leaving behind a swing that still rocked back and forth from his energy.

It was as though he had disappeared, as Mexican wizards were said to do, changing into crows and hawks and jumping straight up in the air.

Indian demons.

Hart shivered again.


A block away, Shadow Love was on the phone.

"Barb? Could you pick me up?"

# 19

Lucas woke in the dark, listening, and finally identified the sound that had woken him. He reached across the bed and touched her.

"Crying?"

"I can't help it," she squeaked.

"A little guilt, maybe."

She choked, unable to answer for a moment. Then came a muffled "Maybe." She rolled over to face him, her knees pulled up in fetal position. "I've never done this before."

"You told me that," he said into the dark. He groped around for a moment, found the switch on the bedside lamp and turned it on. Her head was down, her face concealed.

"The thing is, I knew I would be. Unfaithful. That one night, in my room, I almost didn't stop you. I shouldn't have. But it was . . . too quick. I couldn't handle it," she said. "Then when Hood went down and I was freaked out and you were freaked out and I got out of town. . . . On the way to New York, on the plane, I cried. I thought I wouldn't see you again, wouldn't get to sleep with you. But I was relieved, you know. When they told me I had to come back, I was crying again. David thought I was crying because I didn't want to come back. But I was crying because I knew what would happen. I was so . . . hungry."

"Hey, look. I've been through this," Lucas said. "I feel bad about it some-times, but I can't stay away from women. A shrink would probably find some-thing weird is wrong with me. But I just . . . want women. It's like you said, I get hungry. I can't stop it. It's a drug, you crave it."

"Just the sex?" She rolled over a bit, her head cocked toward him, watching his eyes.

"No. The woman. The back-and-forth. Hanging around. The sex. Every-thing."

"You're a relationship junkie. Always need something new."

"No, that's not quite right. There's a woman in Minneapolis, I think I've gotten in bed with her once or twice a year since I was a rookie. Sixteen, eighteen years. I see her and I want her. I call her up, she calls me up, I want her. It's not newness. It's something else."

"Is she married?"

"Yeah. For fifteen years, must be. Has a couple of kids."

"That is strange." There was a moment of silence, then she said, "Part of the guilt is that I don't feel worse than I do. You know what I mean? I liked it. I haven't had sex that good since . . . I don't know. Ever, I think. It was like a blackout. With David, it's soft and gentle and the orgasms come, most of the time anyway, but nothing feels . . . driven. Everything is always under control. David is thin and doesn't have much hair. You're hard, and you've got all this body hair. It's like . . . it's so different."

"Too much analysis," Lucas said after a moment. She reached out and touched his face. "I just wanna fuck," he said in a gravelly parody of lust.

"That's ridiculous," she said. She pulled herself closer to him, snuggled on his arm. "Do you think the guilt will go away?"

"I'm pretty sure of it," he said.

"That's what I think too," she said.


They left early, Lucas grumpy in the morning sunlight, but touching her often, on the elbow, the cheek, the neck, brushing hair out of her face. "Let's go for a while. We can stop on the road for breakfast. I can't eat when I'm up this early," he grumbled.

"Your internal clock is screwed up," Lily said as they settled into the Porsche. "You need to get reoriented."

"Nothing happens in the morning, so why get up?" Lucas said. "All the bad people are out at night. And most of the good ones, as far as that goes."

"Let's just try to make it back to the Cities in one piece," she said as he spun the drive wheels and left the motel parking lot. "If you want me to drive . . ."

"No, no."

They drove straight into the morning sun. Lily was feeling chatty and craned her neck at the oddities of the prairie.

"I'm going back a different way, a little further south," Lucas said. "I like to see as many roads as I can. I don't get out here very often."

"That's fine."

"It won't add much time," he said.

The day started cold but rapidly warmed up. A few minutes after they crossed the Minnesota line, Lucas pulled into a roadside diner. They were the only customers. A fat woman worked in the kitchen behind a chest-high stainless-steel counter. They saw only her head. The counterman was a thin, big-eyed man wearing a dirty apron. He had two days of beard and rolled a Lucky Strike, half smoked and now unlit, between his thin lips. Lucas ordered two hard-fried eggs and bacon.

"I'd recommend that," he said to Lily.

"I'll have the eggs, anyway," she said. The waiter yelled back to the cook and then stumped off to a chair and picked up the local weekly.

"Have you been here before?" Lily asked quietly when the waiter's back was turned.

"No."

"So how can you recommend the bacon and eggs?"

Lucas looked around the diner. Paint was peeling off the ceiling and a black mold was attacking the seams of the aging wallpaper. "Because they've got to fry it and that ought to sterilize it," he said under his breath.

She glanced around and suddenly giggled, and Lucas thought he might be in love.


After breakfast, when they were back in the car, the talk slowed and Lily moved her seat to a reclined position. Her eyes fell shut.

"A nap?" asked Lucas.

"Relaxing," she said. Her breathing grew steady, and Lucas drove on. Lily dozed but didn't sleep, opening her eyes and sitting forward at turns and stops. After a while, she found the steady soft vibration of the car had become arousing. She opened her eyes just a crack. Lucas had put on sunglasses and was driving with a steady, relaxed watchfulness. Now and then he turned his head to look at passing attractions that she couldn't see from her low position. She reached out and put a hand on his leg.

"Uh-oh," he said. He glanced at her and grinned. "The animal is alive."

"Just thinking," she said. She stroked his thigh, her eyes closed again, letting herself feel the coarse weave of his jeans.

"Dammit," Lucas said after a few more minutes. "My dick is going to break off." He pushed himself up in the seat, reached down the front of his pants and changed things around. She laughed, and when he sat down, she put her hand back in his lap. He was erect, his penis reaching up beneath his fly to his belt.

"Ooo, too bad we're in a car," she said.

He looked over at her, grinned and said, "You've played this game before?"

"What game?" She stroked and he pushed her hand away.

"You're done," he said. "It's my turn. Take off your panty hose."

"Lucas . . ." she said. She sounded shocked, but she sat upright and looked out the car windows. They were alone on the rural highway.

"Come on, chicken. Off with the pants."

She looked at the speedometer. A steady sixty miles per hour. "You could kill us."

"Nope. I've played before."

"Mr. Experience, huh?"

"Come on, come on, you're bullshitting now. Off with the pants. Or live with the consequences."

"What consequences?"

"Deep in your heart, you'll know that I know you're chicken."

"All right, Davenport." She pushed herself off the seat, and with some difficulty pulled off her panty hose.

"Now the pants."

She pushed herself up again and took off her underpants.

"Here, I'll take them," Lucas said. Without thinking, she handed him the pants; he quickly dropped his window and threw them out.

"Davenport, for Christ's sakes . . ." She was looking back down the highway where the underpants had disappeared into a roadside ditch.

"I'll buy you new ones."

"Goddamn right," she said.

"So now you lean back and close your eyes." She looked at him and felt a blush crawling up her face. "Come on," he said.

She leaned back and his hand touched her thighs, the fingers just trailing along, from the joint of her hip to her knee, and back again. It was warm in the car and she felt the blood moving to her groin. Her mouth dropped open and the warmth continued to build.

"Oh, boy," she said after a few minutes. "Boy . . ."

"Moan for me," he said.

"What?"

"Moan for me. One good moan and Davenport stops the car."

She reached over and touched him. He felt huge under the jeans and she giggled. "I've got to stop giggling," she said lazily. She reached out again; then Lucas hit the brake and she rocked forward.

"What?" She looked wildly out the window.

"Jeffers petroglyphs," he said. "I've heard about them, but I've never seen them."

"What?" Lily was gasping, like a fish out of water. The car rocked as Lucas pulled into a grass-covered parking area. She pulled her skirt down.

"Indian carvings on some exposed rock," Lucas said. There were two other cars in the parking area, although a sign said the petroglyph monument was closed for the season. Lucas hopped out of the car and Lily got out on her side. In the distance, across a fence, they could see a half-dozen people looking down at a slab of reddish rock.

"Must have climbed the fence," Lucas said. "Come on."

Lucas vaulted the gate, then helped Lily clamber over.

"Christ, this is the last time I wear a dress on the road. And I feel so bare . . . you and your fucking games," she said. "From now on, it's tennis shoes and pants."

"You look good in a dress," he said as they walked up a graveled path. "You look terrific. And you look great without the underpants."

The petroglyphs were scratched into the flat surfaces of exposed red rock. There were outlines of hands, drawings of animals and birds, unknown symbols.

"Look how small their hands were," Lily said. She stooped and placed her own hand over one of the glyphs. Her hand was larger.

"Maybe it was a kid or a woman," Lucas said.

"Maybe." She stood straight and looked around at the rolling prairie and the adjoining cornfield. "I wonder what in the hell they would have been doing out here. There's nothing here."

"I don't know." Lucas looked around. The sky seemed huge, and he felt as though he were standing on the point of the planet. "You've got this rise, you can see forever. But I suppose it was really the rock. Further out west, there's an Indian quarry. It's old. The Indians would take out a soft red rock called pipestone. They made pipes and other stuff out of it."

The petroglyphs were carved on a gently sloping hillside and Lucas wandered with Lily down the slope, passing the other visitors. The others were on their hands and knees, tracing out the glyphs with their fingers. One woman was doing a charcoal rubbing on brown paper, transferring the designs. Two of them said hello. Lucas and Lily nodded.

"We've got to get going pretty soon if we want to make that meeting," Lucas said finally, glancing at his watch.

"Okay."

They walked slowly back to the car, the prairie wind blowing Lily's hair around her face. At the fence, she put one foot on the wire, and Lucas caught her from behind and squeezed.

"One small kiss," he said.

She turned and tipped up her face. The kiss started small and turned warmer, until they were dancing around slowly in the tall grass. She pushed him away after a moment and, breathing hard, looked down.

"These shoes . . . these heels, I'm going to twist my ankle."

"All right. Let's go." He helped her over the fence, then followed. As they walked to the car, he slipped his arm around her waist.

"I'm still turned on from fooling around in the car," he said.

"Hey. It's only three hours back to the Cities," she said playfully.

"And about two meetings after that."

"Tough luck, Davenport . . ."

He led her around the car, opened the passenger-side door, caught her by the arm, sat in the car and pulled her on top of him. "Come on."

"What?" She struggled for a moment, but he pulled her in.

"They can't see us from the road, and those other people are looking at the rocks," he said. "Face me."

"Lucas . . ." But she turned to face him.

"C'mon."

"I don't know how . . ."

"Just bend your knees up and sit, that's good, that's good."

"The car's too small, Lucas. . . ."

"That's fine, you're fine. Jeez, has anybody ever told you that you've got one of the great asses in Western history?"

"Lucas, we can't . . ."

"Ah . . ."

She sat astride him, facing him, her knees apart, just enough room to move a half-dozen inches, and he began to rock, and she felt the morning's play coalescing around her. She closed her eyes, and rocked, and rocked, and the orgasm gathered and flowed and washed over her. She came back only when she heard Lucas say, "Oh, man, man . . ."

"Lucas," she said, and she giggled again and caught herself. She never giggled and now she was giggling every fifteen minutes.

"I needed that," he said. He was sweating and his eyes looked distant and sated. The door was partway open, and Lily looked out the window, then pushed it open with a foot and eased out onto the grass and pulled her skirt down. Lucas followed awkwardly, zipped up, then leaned forward and kissed her. She wrapped her arms around him and pushed against his chest. They swayed together for a moment, then Lucas released her, looking dazed, and half staggered around the car.

"We better get going," he said.

"Right . . . okay." She got into the car, and Lucas started it and found the reverse gear. He slowly eased out onto the roadway, watching for traffic. The road was empty, but Lucas was preoccupied, so Lily saw them first.

"What are they doing?" she asked.

"What?" He looked in the same direction she was. The people who had been looking at the petroglyphs were lined up along the fence, facing them, repeatedly slapping their hands together.

Lucas stared for a moment, perplexed, then caught it and threw back his head and laughed.

"What?" asked Lily, still puzzled, looking at the line of people across the fence. "What are they doing?"

"They're applauding," Lucas laughed.

"Oh, no," Lily said, her face flaming as they accelerated away. She looked back and after a moment added, "They certainly got their money's worth. . . ."

# 20

In the car, Barbara looked him over.

"Why am I doing this? Driving you?"

"I'm looking for a guy," Shadow Love said. "I want you to talk to him on the telephone."

"You're not going to do anything, are you?"

"No. Just want to talk," Shadow Love said. He turned away and watched the street roll by. It took an hour of cruising and a half-dozen stops, with Barbara growing increasingly anxious, but Shadow Love finally spotted Larry Hart as he went into the Nub Inn.

"Let's find a phone," Shadow Love said. "You know what to say."

"What're you going to do?" Barbara asked.

"I want to talk to him. See what he's getting. If there's any possibility that we'll be seen, I'll call it off. You can wait out of sight down the road. If anything goes wrong and they grab me, I just won't show up and you can drive away."

"All right. Be careful, Shadow."

Shadow Love glanced at her. Her knuckles were white on the steering wheel. *She knows what's coming.* The pistol he'd used to kill Yellow Hand pressed into his side. His fingers touched the cold stone knife in his pocket.

Hart took the bait. Barbara called him at the Nub Inn, explained that she'd seen him go inside, and said that she had some information. But she was scared, she said. Scared of the assassins, scared of the cops. She was an old client of his, she said, and knew him by sight. She said she'd meet him by the green dumpster outside the sheet-rock warehouse by the river.

"You've got to come alone, Larry, please. The cops scare me, they'll beat me up. I trust you, Larry, but the cops scare me."

"Okay. I'll see you in ten minutes," Hart said. "And don't be scared. There's nothing to be scared of."

She looked through the glass of the phone booth toward her car. Shadow Love was slumped in the passenger seat, and she could just see the top of his head. "Okay," she said.

It took Hart fifteen minutes to get out of the inn, into his car and down to the warehouse. "There he is," Shadow Love said as Hart pulled over to the curb near the warehouse. They watched as he got out of the car, locked it, looked around and began walking cautiously toward the dumpster at the corner of the building.

"Drive around the block, like I told you. I'll look for cops," Shadow Love said.

Nothing moving on the street, nobody sitting in parked cars. Shadow Love took a breath. "Okay," he said. "Up behind the warehouse. And then you go on down where I showed you, and wait."

When they finished circling the block, they were on the back side of the warehouse. Shadow Love got out of the car. "Take care," Barbara said. "And be quick."

As she drove away, Shadow Love walked across a vacant lot littered with construction debris to the warehouse. He slipped carefully around the corner and was then directly behind the dumpster. Through a narrow space between the warehouse wall and the dumpster, he saw, for just a second, the dark sleeve of a man's coat on the other side. Hart was wearing a black jacket. Shadow Love touched the pistol under his shirt and stepped around the dumpster.

"Larry," he said. Hart jumped and spun around.

"Jesus," he said, his face stricken. "Shadow."

"It's been a long time," Shadow Love said. "I think I saw you a time or two out on Lake Street, after you graduated."

"Yeah, long time," Hart said. He tried to smile. "Are you still living around here?"

Shadow Love ignored the question. "I heard in the bars that you've been looking for me," he said, stepping closer. Hart was bigger than he was, but Shadow Love knew that Hart would be no contest in a fight. Hart knew it too.

"Yeah, yeah. The cops have. They want to talk to you about your fathers."

"My fathers? The Crows?"

"Yeah. Some people think they might, you know . . ." Hart bobbed his head uncomfortably.

". . . have a connection with these killings?"

"Yeah."

"Well, I don't know about that," Shadow Love said. He was standing on the sides of his feet, the fingers of both his hands in his jeans pockets. "Are you a cop now, Larry?"

"No, no, I still work for the Welfare."

"You're sure talking like a cop, out on the street," Shadow Love said, pressing.

"Well, I know," Hart said. "I don't like it either. I got my clients, but the cops won't leave me alone, you know? They don't have anybody else who knows the people."

"Mmmm." Shadow Love looked down at the toes of his cowboy boots, then up at the sky. It had been slate-gray for a day and a half, but now there was a big blue hole in the clouds right over the river. "Come on, Larry. I want to talk some more. Let's go on down where we can see the river. Nice day."

"It's cold," Hart said. He shivered but walked along. Shadow Love stayed just a few inches behind him, his fingers still in his pockets.

"That's a big old hole, there," Shadow Love said, looking at the sky.

"They call it a sucker hole, pilots do," Hart said, looking up at it. "I took a couple of flying lessons once. That's what they called those things. Sucker holes."

"What do you think, that the Crows are behind all this?" Shadow Love asked.

Hart had to half turn to talk to him, and he lost his footing for a moment and stumbled. Shadow Love caught his elbow and helped him regain his balance. "Thanks," Hart said.

"The Crows?" Shadow Love prompted. They continued walking.

"Well, old man Andretti shipped a lot of money out here —that's the money the cops have been spreading around town—and those were the names that came up," Hart said. "The Crows."

"How about me?"

"Well, the cops know you're their son. They thought maybe you'd know . . ."

". . . where they are? Well, yeah. I do," Shadow Love said.

"You do?"

"Mmm." They got off the blacktopped street and walked along the grassy top of the hill that ran down to the Mississippi. Shadow Love stopped and looked down the river. The black spot floated out in front of his eyes, a funnel of darkness in the day. Fuckin' Hart, probing to find his fathers. "Love the river," he said.

"It's a hell of a river," Hart agreed. A harbor tow was pushing a single empty barge downstream toward the Ford lock and dam. The light from the sucker hole poured down on it, and from the height of the hillside, the boat and barge looked like kids' toys, every detail standing out in high relief.

"Look up there," Shadow Love said. "There's an eagle."

Hart looked up and saw the bird, but he thought maybe it was a hawk. He didn't say so but stood looking at it, aware of Shadow Love beside and slightly behind him. Shadow Love slipped his hand in his pocket and felt the knife. He'd never used it before, never thought of it as a real weapon.

"Breathe it in, Larry, the cold air. God, it feels good on your skin. Breathe it in. See the eagle circling? Look at the hillside over there, Larry. Look at the trees, you can pick them all out. . . . Breathe it in, Larry. . . ."

Hart stood with his back to Shadow Love, his eyes half closed, taking great gulping breaths of the cold air, feeling the tingle on his skin, on the back of his neck. He turned his head up again and said, "You know, I talked . . ."

He was going to tell Shadow Love that he'd called the Crows from the police station, to tell them about the coming raid. But he couldn't do that. It would sound as though he were trying to ingratiate himself, as if he were crawling. Tears started down his cheeks. The cold, he thought. Just the cold.

He was taking it all in, breathing it, feeling the eagle soar, when Shadow Love put a hand on his shoulder. Hart turned his head, but the other man had stepped behind him.

"What—" Hart began to say, and then he felt the fire in his throat, a stinging, and looked stupidly at the blood on his coat, pouring like a stream onto his hands. Hart sank to his knees in wonder, then fell on his face, rolled a few feet and stopped, the eagle gone forever.

Shadow Love watched his body for a moment, then put the knife back in his jacket and looked around. Nobody.

*That's two, he thought.* He turned and climbed the embankment, and as he did, the TV tape of the killing of Billy Hood unrolled before his eyes, the woman cop with her pistol, blasting young Billy in the face. Lillian Rothenburg, the TV said.

He crossed the top of the hill, walked down the street, turned the corner and got in the car with Barbara.

"You okay?" Barbara asked fearfully. She looked quickly around. "See anybody around? Where's Hart?"

"Hart's gone," Shadow Love said, slumping in the passenger seat, his eyes half closed. "Saw an eagle. Great big fuckin' bald eagle, floating out over the river."

He looked away from her fear, out the window. In the reflections on the glass, he saw Lily's face, and nodded to it.

# 21

Daniel was in a dark mood. He prowled his office, peering at the political photographs that lined his walls.

"I thought we were doing good," Sloan ventured.

"So did I," said Lester. He had his loafers off and his feet hung over the side of his chair. He was wearing white sweatsocks with his blue suit.

"I can't complain," Daniel admitted. He was nose to nose with a black-and-white photo of Eugene McCarthy that dated back to the Children's Crusade of '68. McCarthy looked pleased with himself. Daniel scowled at him and counted the coups.

"One: We took out Bluebird and cleared the only killings on our turf. Two: We got Hood with Lily's help. Three: We broke the names out of Liss and damn near nailed the Crows at their apartment. That's all good."

"But?" Lily asked.

"Something's going to happen," Daniel said, turning back toward the group around his desk. "And it'll happen here. I feel it in my bones."

"Maybe the Crows'll call it off for a while, cool out," Lucas suggested. "Maybe they'll figure that if they lie low, the heat'll die down, give them a break."

Daniel shook his head. "No. The tempo's wrong," he said. "This has been a planned progression. They kill two people to establish a philosophical basis, then Andretti to grab major headlines, then the judge and the attorney general, major federal and state law officials. The next act is going to be something big. It won't get smaller."

Anderson arrived as Daniel was talking. He took a chair and nodded to Lucas and Lily.

"Got something?" Daniel asked.

Anderson cleared his throat. "It ain't good," he said.

South Dakota authorities had located Shadow Love's driver's license. The license showed an address at Standing Rock. Standing Rock cops said he hadn't lived there for years. They had no idea where he was. The news from the National Crime Information Center was both bad and good: there was plenty of information on Shadow Love, and it was all frightening. Most of it came from California, where he'd served two years on an assault charge.

"Two years? Must have been a hell of an assault," Lily said.

"Yeah. There was a race fight outside a bar. Shadow Love took some guy down and put the boot to him. Damn near kicked him to death."

"How about here in Minnesota?" Daniel asked. "He grew up here?"

"Yeah. Went to Central. We've got Dick Danfrey over at the school board now, looking through their records. He should be getting back anytime. We're looking for addresses, friends, attorneys, anything that might make a connection."

"Is he a psycho? Shadow Love?" asked Lucas.

"The California people did a pretty thorough psychiatric evaluation on him," Anderson said, shuffling through his papers. "They're going to fax the records to us. There were indications of schizophrenia. They say he talked to invisible friends and sometimes invisible animals. And the prison shrink said the other inmates were scared of him. Even the guards. And this was in a hard-core California prison."

"Jesus," Lucas said.

"We'll have a whole file on him later this afternoon," Anderson said. "Pictures, prints, everything. Pretty recent too. Last five years, anyway."

There was nothing on the Crows. "Zilch," Anderson said.

"Nothing?"

"Well, Larry's heard of them and he knows some stuff. Mostly rumors, or legend. Nothing that would track them."

"Where is Larry?" asked Daniel, looking around.

Sloan shrugged. "He's been pretty down in the mouth since that business with the Liss kid, and us putting the money on the street."

"What the fuck, he think we're playing tic-tac-toe or something?" Daniel asked angrily.

Sloan shrugged again and Lucas asked Anderson, "What about the feebs and the fingerprints? What about the truck?"

"The FBI's still running the prints, but they say if they're old . . . it could take a while. The truck has different plates front and back. When we checked, the plates were supposedly lost off trucks out in South Dakota. There was no theft report, because the owners thought they'd just bounced off. So we got more prints, but no IDs."

"What you're telling us is, we've probably got them in the system, pictures and all, but we don't have any way to figure out which ones they are?" Daniel asked.

"That's about it," said Anderson. "The feebs are giving top priority to picking out the prints. . . ."

"Maybe you could check with State Vital Records. Look for a birth certificate on Shadow Love, see who the father is, if one is listed," Lucas suggested.

"I'll do that," Anderson said. He made a note on a file cover.

"What else?" asked Daniel. The question met with silence. "Okay. Now. Something's going to happen. It's given me the creeps. We gotta get these motherfuckers. Today. Tomorrow. God damn it. And when you see Larry, tell him I want his ass in here for these meetings."


Two kids found Hart's body. They were playing on the hillside in the late-afternoon shadows when they saw him, crumpled in the weeds. For a few seconds, the older of the two thought it was a bum; but the lump was so unmoving, so awkwardly piled on itself without regard to tendon or muscle strain that even the younger one quickly realized that it must be death.

They looked at the body for a moment, then the older boy said, "We better go get your mom to call the cops."

The younger boy stuck his thumb in his mouth; it was something he hadn't done for two years. When he realized what he was doing, he pulled his thumb out and thrust his hands in his pants pockets. The older one grabbed him by the shirt and tugged him up the hillside.

The first cop on the scene was a patrolman riding single in his squad. He stepped close enough to see the blood, leaned forward to feel the cold neck and backed away. If there was evidence around the body, he didn't want to destroy it.

Two Homicide cops arrived fifteen minutes later, but nobody had yet recognized Hart.

"Throat cut," one cop said. "Could be a Crow hit. That'd be bad. Look at his clothes—decent clothes, the guy's got some bread."

The second cop, the same bespectacled investigator who'd caught the Benton murderer, eased Hart's billfold out of his hip pocket, stood up, opened it and looked at the driver's license behind the plastic window.

"Sweet bleedin' Jesus," he said aloud, his face suddenly ashen.

His partner, who was on his knees, looking at the side of Hart's head, looked up when he heard the tone of his voice. "What?"

"This is Larry Hart, the guy working with the special squad on the Indian killings."

His partner stood up and said, "Gimme the license." His voice was tight, choked. He took the license and carefully pinched a lock of Hart's hair and tugged on it, rolling the dead man's face just slightly. He compared it to the photo on the license.

"Aw, fuck," he said. "It's him."


Lily picked up the bedside phone and said hello. It was Daniel: "Lily, is Lucas there?"

"Lucas?" she said.

"Lily, don't dog me around, okay? We got big fuckin' trouble."

"Just a minute."

Lucas was in the shower. She pulled him out, and wet as a duck dog, he took the phone. "Daniel," Lily told him quietly.

"Yeah?" Lucas said.

"Larry Hart's been hit," Daniel said, his voice shaky. "He's dead. Throat cut."

"Sonofabitch," Lucas groaned.

"What?" Lily stood up. She was wearing a slip and nylons, and she watched Lucas while she groped for her dress.

"When did it happen?" he asked. As an aside to Lily he said, "Hart's been killed."

"We don't know shit," Daniel said. "A couple of kids found him on the hill above the river by the Franklin Avenue bridge, about an hour ago. He'd been dead for a while. The last time anybody talked to him was about noon. Sloan saw him down on Lake. Sloan's down there now, trying to backtrack him."

"All right, I'll get down there," Lucas said.

"Lucas, this isn't what I thought was coming. This is something else. I still think we're going to get hit big. Hart's personal and it makes me feel like shit, but something else is coming." Daniel had started quietly, but by the time he finished, his voice was rising and the words were tumbling out in anger.

"I hear you," Lucas said.

"Find it, God damn it. Stop it," Daniel roared.

In the car on the way down, Lily said, "Why did they call my room, looking for you?"

Lucas accelerated through a red light, then turned and looked at her in the dark. "Daniel knows. He probably knew five minutes after we got in bed. I told you he was smart; but he'll keep his mouth shut."

Sloan was standing at the edge of the hill, his hands in his coat pockets. A half-block away, three television trucks sat at the side of the street, their engines running, their microwave dishes pointed at the sky. A reporter and photographer from the *StarTribune* were sitting on the hood of their car, talking to a TV cameraman.

"Ain't this the shits?" Sloan asked when Lucas and Lily came up.

"Yeah." Lucas nodded at the reporters. "Have we put anything out yet? To the newsies?"

"Nothing, yet," Sloan said. "Daniel's calling a press conference. He's decided to release the names, by the way—the Crows and Shadow Love. He's going to ask for help and come down hard on the idea that the Crows are killing other Indians."

"People liked Hart," Lucas said.

"That's what they say," Sloan agreed.

Down the hill, under portable lights, the assistant medical examiners were lifting Hart's body onto a stretcher. "Did anybody see anything at all?" Lucas asked.

"Yeah. A woman back up the hill," Sloan said. "She's on her way downtown now, to look at Shadow Love's pictures. She saw a couple of guys walk over the hill, and then later she saw one of them getting in a car. Younger guy, skinny, wearing a fatigue jacket."

"Shadow Love," said Lucas.

"Could be. A woman was driving the car. She was real short. She could barely see over the steering wheel. She had dark hair pulled back in a bun."

"What about the car?"

"Older. No make or model. The witness never looked at the license number. She said one of the back corner windows—you know, one of those little triangle things?—had been knocked out and there was a piece of box cardboard in it. That's about it. It was green. Pale green."

"You saw Larry earlier, right?"

"Yeah. Just before noon. He said he was heading back down Lake. He was planning to hit the bars up at the top of the street. I backtracked him as far as the Nub Inn. The bartender who was on duty earlier in the day had already gone home, but I talked to him on the phone and he said Hart got a call there. He said he seemed surprised, like he couldn't figure out how anybody would know he was there. Anyway, he took the call and a couple of minutes later went running out of the place."

"Setup," said Lily.

"That's what I figure," Sloan said. "We've got a guy over, talking to the bartender, but I don't think he'll have much more to say."

"Christ, what a mess," Lucas said, running his fingers through his hair.

"My wife is going to be excreting bricks when she finds out one of our people got hit," Sloan said.

"I never heard of it before, not around here," Lucas said, shaking his head. He glanced at Lily. "You get this kind of stuff?"

"Every once in a while. Some dealers hit a cop a couple years ago, just to show they could do it."

"What happened?"

"The guys that did it . . . they're not with us anymore."

"Ah." Lucas nodded.

The bespectacled Homicide cop made his way up the hill, pushing his knees down with his hands as he climbed the last few feet. He was breathing heavily when he got to the top.

"How's it going, Jim?" Lucas asked.

"Not so good. Not a goddamned thing down there."

"No shell?"

"Nope. Not so far. We've worked it over pretty good. I think it was all the knife. Hell of a way to go."

"Tracks?"

"Can't find any," the Homicide cop said. "Too grassy. That long stuff is like walking on sponges. They must have come off the street, right onto it. . . . You know, Hart had his back to the guy, the cutter. No struggle. Nothing. I wonder if it was somebody he trusted?"

"Probably held him at gunpoint, like Hood did with Andretti," Lily said.

"Yeah, there's that," the cop said. He looked down the steep embankment. "But you'd think that he'd have tried to run or jump. One big jump down that hill, he'd be ten or fifteen feet from the shooter . . . but there was no sign of a jump. No place where his feet dug in. No grass stains on his pants. Nothing."

"He gave up," Lily said, looking at Lucas.

*      *      *

A crowd had gathered behind the reporters. Several of the onlookers were Indian, and Lily decided to mingle, hoping that someone else had seen something. While she worked the crowd, Lucas went down the block to a pay phone and called TV3. A receptionist hunted down Jennifer. "A tip," Lucas said when she came on the line.

"Is there a price?"

"Yeah. We'll get to that later."

"So what's the tip?"

"You've got some guys out by the river, working a homicide?"

"Yes. Jensen and . . ."

"It's Larry Hart. The Indian expert from Welfare that we brought in to help track these assassins."

"Holy shit," she said. Her voice was hushed. "Who else knows?"

"Nobody, at the moment. Daniel's calling a press conference, probably in a half-hour or so. . . ."

"He already did, we've got people on the way."

"If you go on the air ahead of time, you've got to cover me. Don't give it to that fuckin' Kennedy, because everybody knows you guys lay off stories on each other."

"Okay, okay," she said, a touch of intensity in her voice. "What else? Cut?"

"Yeah. Just like the others. Throat cut, bled to death."

"When?"

"We don't know. This afternoon. Early afternoon, probably. He was found by a couple of kids who were playing along the hill."

"Okay. What else? Was he breaking the case? Was he close?"

"He wasn't this morning, but maybe he ran into something. We don't know. Now: Here's the price."

"Yeah?"

"We think the guy who did it is named Shadow Love. Thirties, Sioux, skinny, tattoos on his arms. Daniel's going to release the name. Don't use it until he does, but when he does, pound it. I want Shadow Love's name on the air every ten seconds. I want you to pound on the idea that he's killing other Indians. Push Daniel for some photos—they've got good photos of him from California, and don't let them bullshit you on that. Demand the fuckin' photos. Give them as much airtime as you can. Tell the boss that if you cooperate, I feed you more exclusive stuff."

"Hammer Shadow Love," she said.

"Hard as you can," Lucas said.

*      *      *

Lily got nothing from the crowd. When she was done, she asked Lucas to drop her at her room: "I need some sleep, and I need to think. Alone."

Lucas nodded. "I could use some time myself."

At her door, Lily turned to him. "What the fuck are we going to do, Davenport?" she blurted, her voice low and gravelly.

"I don't know," Lucas said. He reached out and brushed a lock of dark hair away from her cheek, back over her ear. "I just can't stop with you."

"I'm having a little trouble myself," Lily said. "But I've got too much with David to make a break. I don't think I'd want to break . . . ."

"And I don't want to lose Jen," Lucas said. "But I just can't stop with you. I'd like to take you right now. . . ." He pushed her back into the room, and she had her arms around his neck, and they rocked together for a minute, the heat growing until she pushed him back.

"Get out of here, God damn it," she said. "I need some rest."

"All right. See you tomorrow?"

"Mmm. Not too early."


After dropping Lily off, Lucas drove back through town. Four trucks equipped with microwave dishes were clustered around the door to City Hall, black electronics cables snaking across the sidewalk into the building. On impulse, he pulled into a vacant cops-only parking spot and went inside.

The press conference was almost over. Lucas watched from the back as Daniel went through his routine. The television reporters were looking at their watches, ready to break away, while they listened to the newspaper people ask a few final questions.

As he turned to leave, Jennifer stepped into the room and bumped him with an elbow.

"Thanks again. We were on the air an hour ago," she said quietly. "Look at Shelly. . . ."

Shelly Breedlove, a reporter for Channel 8, was staring spitefully at them from across the room. She'd made the connection on TV3's exclusive break on Larry Hart's murder.

Jennifer smiled pleasantly back and said, "Fuck you, bitch," under her breath. To Lucas she said, "Are you on your way home?"

"Yeah."

"I've got a baby-sitter. . . ."


Lucas slept poorly, his legs twitching, curling, uncurling. Jennifer curled against his bare back, her forehead against the nape of his neck, tears trickling down her cheeks. She could smell the perfume on him. It wasn't hers and it wasn't

something he'd picked up sitting next to another woman. There'd been contact. A lot of contact. She lay awake, with the tears, and Lucas dreamed of a
cold round circle of a shotgun pressed against his head, and of Larry Hart
tumbling down the hillside above the Mississippi, the barges curling away,
rolling down the river, their pilots unaware of the light going out on the hill
above them. . . .

# 22

Sam Crow raged through the house while Aaron sat silently in the La-Z-Boy,
bathed in flickering light from the television set. Shadow Love's picture was
everywhere, views from the front and both sides, close-ups of his tattooed
arms.

"That fuckin' kid is ruinin' us," Sam shouted. He crowded against Barbara,
who, frightened by his anger, wrapped and rewrapped her hands with a damp
dish towel and pretended to do dishes between bouts of weeping. "How could
you fuckin' go along?"

"I didn't want to," she cried, "I didn't know . . ."

"You knew." Sam spat. "For Christ's sakes, did you think he was delivering
a fuckin' Christmas card?"

"I didn't know . . ."

"Where'd you leave him?"

"He got out by Loring Park. . . ."

"Where was he going?"

"I don't know. . . . He said you wouldn't want him here. He said he had to
work alone. . . ."

"Fuck meee," Sam called out. "Fuck meee. . . ."

Aaron appeared in the doorway. "C'mere, look at this."

Sam followed him back to the living room. For the past half-hour, they'd
seen report after report from Minneapolis: from the hillside where Hart's body
had been found, from the chief's office, from Indian Country. Man-in-the-street
interviews. Lily, working the crowd, an NYPD badge pinned to her coat. People talking to her, thrusting their faces in front of the camera.

Now that had changed. A room with light blue walls. An American flag. A
podium with a circular American-eagle seal under a battery of microphones,
and a man in a gray double-breasted suit with a handkerchief in his breast
pocket.

"It's Clay," Aaron said.

". . . terrorist group has now begun striking at its own people. That doesn't make them any less dangerous but will, I hope, make it obvious to the Indian people that these killers don't care any more about Indians than they do about whites. . . ."

And later:

". . . worked with Indian people during my entire career, and I'm asking my old friends of all Indian nations to call us at the FBI with any information about this group . . ."

And more:

". . . I will be accompanied by a task force of forty specialists, men and women from around the nation who will be brought in to break this ring. We are prepared to stay in Minnesota until we are successful in this endeavor. We will remain in full and immediate contact with the Washington center. . . ."

"Lawrence Duberville Clay," Sam said, almost reverently, as he stared at the man on the TV screen. "Hurry up, motherfucker. . . ."

"There's somebody here," Barbara called from the kitchen, fear thick in her voice. "Somebody on the porch."

The doorbell rang as Aaron hurried into the back bedroom, where he had been sleeping, and returned with an old blue .45. The bell rang again and then the front door pushed open. A dark figure, short hair, black eyes; Aaron, flattened against the hallway wall, at first thought it might be Shadow Love, but the man was too big. . . .

"Leo," Aaron called in delight. A smile lit the old man's face and he dropped the pistol to his side. "Sam, it's Leo. Leo's home."

# 23

———◦—◦———

"You're sleeping with that New York cop. Lily." Jennifer looked at him over the breakfast bar. Lucas was holding a glass of orange juice and looked down at it, as if hoping it held an answer. The newspaper sat next to his hand. The headline read: CROWS KILL COP.

*He wasn't a cop,* Lucas thought. After a moment he glanced away from the table and then back at the newspaper and nodded. "Yes," he said.

"Are you going to again?" Her face was pale, tired, her voice low and whispery.

"I can't help it," he said. He wouldn't look at her. He turned the glass in his hand, swirling the juice.

"Is this . . . a long-term thing?" Jennifer asked.

"I don't know."

"Look at me," she said.

"No." He kept his eyes down.

"You can come back and see the baby, but call first. Once a week for now. I won't continue our sexual relationship and I don't want to see you. You can see the baby on Saturday nights, when I have a sitter. After Lily goes back to New York, we'll talk. We'll make some kind of arrangement so you can visit the baby on a regular basis."

Now he looked up. "I love you," he said.

Tears started in her eyes. "We've been through this before. You know what I feel like? I feel pathetic. I don't like feeling pathetic. I won't put up with it."

"You're not pathetic. When I look at you . . ."

"I don't care what you see. Or anybody else. I'm pathetic in my own mind. So fuck you, Davenport."

When Jennifer left, Lucas wandered around the house for a few moments, then drifted into the bedroom, undressed, and stood under a scalding shower. Daniel wanted every man on the street, but after Lucas had toweled off, he stood in front of an open closet, looking at the array of slacks and shirts, and then crawled back into bed and lapsed into unconsciousness. The Crows, Lily, Jennifer, the baby and game monsters from Drorg all crawled through his head. Every once in a while he felt the pull of the street scene outside Hood's apartment: he'd see the bricks, the negotiating cop, a slice of Lily's face, her .45 coming up. Each time he fought it down and stepped into a new dream fragment.

At one o'clock, Lily called. He didn't answer the phone, but listened as her voice came in through his answering machine.

"This is Lily," she said. "I was hoping we could get some lunch, but you haven't called and I don't know where you are and I'm starving so I'm going out now. If you get in, give me a call and we can go out to dinner. See you."

He thought about picking up the phone, but didn't, and went back to the bed. The phone rang again a half-hour later. This time it was Elle: "This is Elle, just calling to see how you are. You can call me at the residence."

Lucas picked up the receiver. "Elle, I'm here," he croaked.

"Hello. How are you?"

"A down day," he said.

"Still the shotgun dream?"

"It's still there. And sometimes during the day. The sensation of the steel."

"It's a classic flashback. We see it all the time with burn victims and shooting victims and people who've gone through other trauma. It'll go away, believe me. Hold on."

"I'm holding on, but it's scary. Nothing's ever gotten to me like this."

"Are you going to play Thursday night?" Elle asked.

"I don't know."

"Why don't you come a half-hour early? We can talk."

"I'll try to make it."

The bed was like a drug. He didn't want it, but he fell back on the sheets and in a minute was gone again. At two o'clock, suddenly touched with fear, he sat up, sweating, staring at the clock.

What? Nothing. Then the cold ring of the shotgun muzzle rapped him behind the ear. Lucas clapped a hand over the spot and let his head fall forward on his chest.

"Stop," he said to himself. He could feel the sweat literally pop out on his forehead. "Stop this shit."

Lily called again at five o'clock and he let it go. At seven, the phone rang a fourth time. "This is Anderson," a voice said to the answering machine. "I've got something. . . ."

Lucas picked up the phone. "I'm here," he said. "What is it?"

"Okay. Lucas. God damn." There was the sound of computer printouts rustling. Anderson was excited; Lucas could picture him going through his notes. Anderson looked, talked and sometimes acted like an aging hillbilly. A few months earlier he had incorporated his private computer business and was, Lucas suspected, on his way to becoming rich with customized police software. "I went into Larry's genealogical files for the Minnesota Sioux—you know how he had them stored in the city database?"

"Yeah, I remember."

"I looked up all the Crows. They were all too old—not many Crows in Minnesota. So I got a typist and had her put all the names from Larry's file into my machine in a sort routine. . . ."

"What?"

"Never mind. She put them in my machine in a list. Then I went over to State Vital Records and found all the women named Love who had babies between 1945 and 1965. You said this Shadow Love dude looked like he was in his thirties. . . ."

"Yeah."

"So I pulled all of those. There were a hell of a lot of them, more than four hundred. But I could eliminate all the girl babies. That got rid of all but a hundred and ninety-seven. Then I put the names of the fathers into my machine—"

"So you could run them against the genealogy—"

"Right. I got about halfway through and found a Rose E. Love. Mother of Baby Boy Love. No name for the kid, but that wasn't uncommon. Get this. I don't know how she did it, but she got them to list two names in the space for the father."

"Interesting . . ."

"Aaron Sunders and Samuel Close."

"Shit, Aaron and Sam, it's gotta be . . ."

"Their race is listed as 'other.' This was back in the fifties, so it's probably Indian. And they turn up on Larry's genealogy. They are the grandsons of a guy named Richard Crow. Richard Crow had two daughters, and when they married, the Crow name ended. We got Sunders and Close—but I'd bet my left nut those are the real names for Aaron and Sam Crow."

"God damn, Harmon, that's fuckin' terrific. Have you run—"

"They both had Minnesota driver's licenses, but only way back, before the picture IDs. The last one for Sunders was in 1964. I called South Dakota, but they were shut down for the day. I asked for a special run and the duty guy told me to go shit in my hat. So then I rousted the feebs and they got on the line to the SoDak people. They got to the duty guy and now *he's* shitting in *his* hat. Anyway, we got the special run. They're checking the records now. I figure with everything that's happened, that's the most likely place. . . ."

"How about NCIC?"

"We're running that now."

"We ought to check prison records for Minnesota and the Dakotas and the federal system. Be sure you check the feds. The federal system gets the bad-asses off the reservations. . . ."

"Yeah, I've got that going. If the Crows were inside in the last ten or fifteen years, it'll show at the NCIC. The feebs said they'll check with the Bureau of Prisons to see about their records before that."

"How about vehicles? Besides the truck?" Lucas asked.

"We're looking for registrations. I doubt they'd leave a car on the street, but who knows?"

"Any chance that Rose Love is still alive?"

"No. Since I was over there anyway, I went through the death certificates. She died in 'seventy-eight in a fire. It was listed as an accident. It was a house in Uptown."

"Shit." Lucas pulled at his lip and tried to think of other data-run possibilities.

"I went through old city directories and followed her all the way back to the fifties," Anderson continued. "She was in the 'fifty-one book, in an apartment. Then she missed a couple of years and was in 'fifty-four, in an apartment. Then in 'fifty-five she was in the Uptown house. She stayed there until she died."

"All right. This is great," Lucas said. "Have you talked to Daniel?"

"Nobody's at his house, that's why I called you. I had to tell *somebody*. It freaked me out, the way it all came out of the machines, boom-boom-boom. It was like a TV show."

"Get us some fuckin' photos, Harmon. We'll paper the streets with them."

Anderson's discoveries brought a flush of energy. Lucas paced through the house, still naked, excited. If they could put the Crows' faces on the street, they'd have them. They couldn't hide out forever. Names were almost nothing. Pictures . . .

Half an hour later Lucas was back in bed, falling into unconsciousness again. Just before he went out, he thought, *So this is what it's like to be nuts.* . . .


"Lucas?" It was Lily.

"Yup."

He looked down at the bed. He could see the outline of where his body had been from the sweat stains. The dreams had stayed with him until he woke, a little after seven in the morning. He reached out, popped up the window shade, and light cut into the gloom. A moment later, the phone rang.

"Jesus, where were you yesterday?" Lily asked.

"In and out," he lied. "Tell you the truth, I went back to my old net, to see if any of my regulars had heard anything. They're not Indians, but they're on the street. . . ."

"Get anything?" she asked.

"Naw."

"Daniel's pissed. You missed the afternoon meet."

"I'll talk to him," Lucas said. He yawned. "Have you had any breakfast yet?"

"I just got up."

"Wait there. I'll get cleaned up and come get you."

"Turn on a TV before you do that. Channel Eight. But hurry."

"What's on?"

"Go look," she said, and hung up.

Lucas punched up the TV and found an airport press conference with Lawrence Duberville Clay.

". . . in cooperation with local enforcement officials . . . expect to have some action soon . . ."

"Bullshit, local officials," Lucas muttered at the television. The camera pulled back and Lucas noticed the screen of bodyguards. There were a half-dozen of them around Clay, professionals, light suits, identical lapel pins, backs to their man, watching the crowd. "Thinks he's the fuckin' president . . ."


Lucas' heart jumped when Lily came out of the hotel elevator. The angles of her face. Her stride. The way she brushed at her bangs and grinned when she saw him . . .


Anderson had a stack of files for the morning meeting. South Dakota, he said, had files on Sunders and Close. There were photos in the driver's-license files, bad but recent. And when the white names were run through the NCIC files, a list of hits came back, along with fingerprints. With a direct comparison available, fingerprint specialists confirmed that Sunders and Close were the men the Minneapolis cops had just missed in the apartment raid. An FBI computer specialist said later that the wide-base search of the fingerprint files would have identified them in "another four to six hours, max."

The South Dakota files had been faxed to Minneapolis, and the best possible reproductions of the driver's-license photos arrived on an early-morning plane. Copies were being made for distribution to all the local police agencies, the FBI and the media.

"Press conference at eleven o'clock," Daniel said. "I'll hand out the photographs of the Crows."

"We got some more coming from the feds," Anderson announced. "Sunders spent time in federal prison, fifteen years ago. He shot a guy out at Rosebud, wounded him. He spent a year inside."

"Old man Andretti has agreed to put up an unofficial reward for information leading to the Crows. They don't have to be arrested or anything. He'll pay just to find out where they are," Daniel said. He looked at Lucas. "I'd like to get that out to the media through the back door. . . . I'll confirm it, but I don't want to come right out and say there's a price on their heads. I want to keep some distance from it. I don't want it to sound like we're turning a bunch of vigilantes loose on the Indians. We've got to live with these people later."

Lucas nodded. "All right. I can set that up. I'll get the guy from TV3 to ask a question at the press conference."

Daniel flipped through his Xerox copies of the rap sheets. "It doesn't seem like they've done much. A couple of small-time crooks. Then this."

"But look at the pattern," Lily said. "They weren't small-time crooks like most small-time crooks. They weren't breaking into Coke machines or running a pigeon-drop. They were organizing, just like Larry said."

The files on Sunders and Close showed a sporadic history of small crime, except for the shooting that sent Sunders to prison. Most of it was trespassing on ranches, unlawful discharge of firearms, unlawful threats.

The latest charge was six years old, on Sunders, who had been arrested for trespassing. According to the complaint file, he had entered private property and allegedly damaged a bulldozer. He denied damaging the bulldozer, but he did tell police that the rancher was putting a service trail through a Dakota burial ground.

Close's file was thinner than Sunders'. Most of the charges against him were misdemeanors, for loitering or vagrancy, back when those were legal charges. There was a notation by a Rapid City officer that Close was believed to have been responsible for a series of burglaries in the homes of government officials, but he had never been caught.

On a separate slip of paper was a report from an FBI intelligence unit that both Sunders and Close had been seen at the siege of Wounded Knee, but when the siege ended, they were not among the Indians in the town.

"I'd say they've got a deep organization, going all the way back to the sixties, and maybe back to the forties," Lily said, looking at the file over Lucas' shoulder. A lock of her hair touched his ear, and tickled. He moved closer and let her scent settle over him. He had not yet told her about Jennifer. The thought of it made him uncomfortable.

"The *StarTribune* this morning called them our first experience with dedicated domestic terrorists," Lucas said.

"They picked that up from the *Times*," Lily said. "The *Times* had an editorial Friday, said the same thing."

Daniel nodded gloomily. "It'll get worse when they do whatever it is they're planning to do. Something big."

"You don't think . . . like the airport?" Anderson asked.

"What?" asked Sloan.

"You know, like the Palestinians? I mean, if you were going to do something big, shooting up the airport or blowing up a plane would do it. . . ."

"Oh, Christ," Daniel said. He gnawed on his lower lip, then got up and took a turn around his desk. "If we go out there and suggest tighter controls and the word gets out, the airlines'll take it right in the ass. And I'll be right there with them, gettin' it in the same place."

"If we don't tell them, and something happens . . ."

"How about just a light touch . . . just talk to the security, a hint to the FBI, maybe put some people out there undercover?" suggested Sloan.

"Maybe," said Daniel, sitting down again. He looked at Anderson. "Do you really think . . . ?"

"Not really," Anderson said.

"I don't think so either. All the people they've hit so far have been symbols of something. Shooting up an airport full of innocent people wouldn't prove anything."

"How about the Bureau of Indian Affairs?" Lucas asked. "A lot of old-line Indians hate the BIA."

"Now that's something," Daniel said, his eyes narrowing. "An institution instead of an individual . . . It'd be a logical step, to go after the people they see as their oppressors. I better talk to the feebs. Maybe they could put a couple of people in the BIA office."

"Wait a minute," Lucas said. He stood up and walked around his chair, thinking. Then he looked at Daniel and said, "Jesus—it could be Clay."

They all thought about it for a moment, and Daniel shook his head. "Everything they've done has been pretty well planned. Nobody knew that Clay was coming in until the last couple of days."

"No, no, think about it," said Lucas, jabbing a finger at Daniel. "If you look at this whole . . . progression . . . in the right way, you could see it as a lure to pull Clay in. The terrorist angle, the publicity. . . . That's exactly the kind of thing Clay'd bite on."

"That's an awful big jump," Daniel argued. "They couldn't be sure he'd come. You could wind up killing a half-dozen people and getting all of your own people killed, and Clay might sit on his ass in Washington."

"And why Clay?" Sloan asked.

"Because he's a big target and he's got a bad rep among Indians," Lily said. "You remember that hassle out in Arizona with the two factions on that reservation? I can't remember what the deal was. . . ."

"Yeah, he sent in all those agents to kick ass . . ." Anderson said.

"If I remember right, there was an article in *Time* that said Clay has had a bunch of run-ins with Indians over the years. Doesn't like them . . ." Lucas said.

"The Crows can't get at him," said Sloan. "He's got an unbelievable screen of bodyguards—you should have seen them this morning. If the Crows tried to shoot their way through them . . . I mean, these guys got Uzis in their armpits."

"All it takes is a guy on a rooftop with a deer rifle," said Lucas.

"Ah, shit," said Daniel. He whacked the desktop with an open palm. "We can't take a chance. We'll talk to Clay's security people. And let's put some people around his hotel. Up on the rooftops, in the parking garage. Just put some uniforms in street clothes. . . . Christ, the guy is a pain in the ass."

"We oughta take a look at the hotel too," Lucas said. He was still moving around the office, thinking about it. The idea fit: but how could the Crows get at Clay? "Look for a hole in the security. . . ."

"I still don't think it's Clay. It's gotta be something they could plan for," Daniel said. "Keep thinking about it. Let's get some more ideas going."


The meeting broke up, but ten minutes before the press conference, Daniel called them back together.

"I'm going to tell you this quick and I don't want any argument. I've been talking to Clay and his people, and the mayor. Clay will come here and will make the announcement about the identification of the Crows. He'll pass out the photos."

"God damn it," said Anderson, white-faced. "That's our work. . . ."

"Take it easy, Harmon. There's a lot going on here. . . ."

"They bought the information from us, is that right?" Anderson demanded. "What'd we get?"

"You won't believe it." Daniel smiled a self-satisfied smile, spread his arms and peered at the ceiling, as though receiving manna from heaven. "You're looking at the new Midwest on-line information-processing center. . . ."

"Holy shit," Anderson whispered. "I thought Kansas City had that wrapped."

"They just came unwrapped. We're doing the deal right now."

"Our own Cray II," Anderson said. "The fastest fucking machine ever built . . ."

"What a crock of shit," said Lily.

"Let's try to keep that opinion to ourselves," Daniel said. "After the press conference, Clay wants to talk to the *team*. I think he wants to give us a pep talk."

"What a crock of shit," Lily repeated.

"Did you suggest that he might be the target?" asked Lucas.

"Yeah," Daniel nodded. "He agreed with me that it was unlikely, but he also went along with the idea of a screen of cops on the buildings around the hotel. And his guys are looking for holes in the security."

Four advance men arrived ahead of Clay. One waited outside City Hall, where Clay's car would unload. The other three, guided by a cop, walked the hallway to the room where the press conference would be held. Lucas and Lily, lounging outside the door of the conference room, watched them coming. Two of the men stopped, a pace away.

"Police officers?" he asked.

"Yeah," said Lucas.

"Got an ID?"

Lucas shrugged. "Sure."

"I'd like to see it," the advance man said. His tone was courteous, but his eyes were not.

Lucas looked at Lily, who nodded and flashed her NYPD case. Lucas handed over his ID. "Okay," said the advance man, still courteous. "Could you point out the other plainclothes people inside . . . ?"

It was quick and professional. In five minutes, the room was secure. When Clay arrived, he got out of his car alone, but two more advance men blocked either end of the car. The mayor came out and met Clay at the car, and they walked, chatting as casual friends, into City Hall. If any of the newsies noticed that the two men were walking through an invisible corridor of professional security, none of them said anything.

Clay and Daniel did the press conference together, the mayor beaming from the wings. Anderson and an FBI functionary passed out photos of the Crows.

"An hour from now, the Crows won't be able to go on the streets," Lucas said as the conference ended.

"We've had Shadow Love's face out there, and that hasn't gotten anywhere . . ." Lily said, when he got in the car beside her.

"We're tightening down. It'll work, with a little time."

"Maybe. I just hope they don't pull some shit first. We better get down to Daniel's office for this meeting with Clay."

                                *    *    *

Sloan, Lucas, Lily, Anderson, Del and a half-dozen other cops had been waiting ten minutes when Daniel and Clay arrived, trailed by the mayor, two of Clay's bodyguards and a half-dozen FBI agents.

"Your show, Larry," Daniel said.

Clay nodded, stepped behind Daniel's desk and gazed around the crowded office. He looked like an athlete gone to fat, Lucas thought. You wouldn't call him porky, but you could get away with "heavyset."

"I always like to talk to local police officers, especially in serious situations like this where everything depends on cooperation. I spent several years on the streets as a patrolman—got to the rank of sergeant, in fact . . ." Clay began, and he nodded at a uniform sergeant standing in the corner of the room. He was a solid speaker, picking out each local cop in turn, fixing him with his eyes, soliciting agreement and cooperation. Lily glanced up at Lucas after Clay had given them the treatment, and cracked a smile.

"Good technique," she whispered.

Lucas shrugged.

". . . wide experience with Indians, and I will tell you this. Indian rules are not our rules, are not the rules of a rational, progressive society. That state-ment—I'd prefer to keep it in this room—is not a matter of prejudice, although it can be twisted to sound that way. But it's a solid fact; and most Indians themselves recognize it. But we don't have two sets of rules in America. We have law, and it applies to everybody. . . ."

*"Heil Hitler,"* Lucas muttered.


When they finished, Clay whipped out of the building in his cloud of body-guards.

"Let's go look at his hotel," Lucas suggested.

"All right," Lily said. "Though I'm starting to have my doubts. His guys are pretty good."


Clay's chief of security was a nondescript, pale-eyed man who looked like a desk clerk until he moved. Then he looked like a viper.

"We've got it nailed down," he said after Lucas and Lily identified them-selves. "But if you think you might see something, I'd be happy to walk you through."

"Why?" asked Lucas.

"Why what?"

"Why are you happy to walk us through, if it's all nailed down?"

"I never figured myself to be the smartest guy in the world," the security man said. "I can always learn something."

Lucas looked at him for a minute, then turned to Lily. "You're right. They're good," he said.

They took the tour anyway. Clay was on the fourteenth floor. There were higher buildings around, but none closer than a half-mile.

"Couldn't take him through a window," the security man said.

"How about something set up in advance? Clay's stayed at this hotel before, right?"

"Like what?"

Lucas shrugged. "A bomb in an elevator?"

"We sniffed the place out. Routine," the security man said.

"How about a suicide run? The Crows are crazy. . . ."

"We've checked the staff, of course. No Indians at all, nobody with the kind of background that we'd worry about. Most of them are career people, been here a while. A few new people on the desk and kitchen staff, but we screen them out when the boss comes and goes. . . . And when he does come and go, we check the lobby and the street first. He's in and out in a hurry, with no warning. So it wouldn't be anybody on the street."

"Hmmph," said Lucas.

They were headed back down in the elevator and Lucas asked, "Is there any way to get up on top of the elevator from the basement or the roof, ride up that way?"

The security man allowed himself a small grin. "I'm not going to talk about that," he said, glancing at Lucas. "But in a word, no."

"You've got the elevators wired," said Lily.

The security man shrugged as the elevator stopped at the third floor. An elderly woman wearing a fur wrap got on, peered nearsightedly at the lighted buttons and finally pushed the button for the second floor. A room-service waiter pushed a dinner cart past the elevators just as the doors were closing.

"How about a disguise?" Lucas asked after the old lady had gotten off. "What if somebody came in disguised as an old lady . . ."

"Metal detectors would pick up the gun."

". . . and had a gun stashed on the third floor. Rode up to the third floor, picked it up and then went up to fourteen . . ."

The security man shrugged again. "That's a fantasy. And when they got up there, they'd have to shoot their way past three trained agents. And the boss is armed, and he knows how to use it."

Lucas nodded. "All right. But I got a bad feeling," he said.

He and Lily left the security man in the lobby and headed for the doors. Just as they were about to go out, Lucas said, "Wait a minute," and turned back.

"Hey," he called to the security man. "How did that room-service food get up on three?"

The security man looked at Lucas, then at Lily, then at the elevators.

"Let's go ask," he said.


"In a dumbwaiter," a cook told them. He pointed to an alcove, where they could see the opening for the chain-driven lift.

The security man looked from the dumbwaiter to the cook to Lucas. "Could a man ride up in that?" he asked the cook.

"Well . . . I guess a couple guys have. Sometimes," the cook said, his eyes shifting nervously.

"What do you mean, 'sometimes'?"

"Well, when it's busy, you know, the boss doesn't want a lot of waiters riding up in the elevators with the customers. The waiters are supposed to take the stairs. But sometimes, I mean, if it's on the tenth floor . . . ."

"How often do guys ride up?" the security man asked.

"Look, I don't want to get anybody in trouble. . . ."

"Nobody'll hear a word from us," Lily promised.

The cook wiped his hands on his apron, then lowered his voice and said, "Every day."

"Shit," said the security man.


The security man laid it out: "A suicide run. Four guys. They come down the alley to the service dock. They push the bell. One of the staff opens the door to see who it is. The Crows stick a gun in his stomach. One guy stays in the kitchen while the other three ride up in the dumbwaiter, one at a time. They come out in the service area on fourteen. They've got automatic weapons or shotguns. They check the hall, somehow . . . maybe just peek, or they use a dental mirror . . . they come out and take the two agents in the hall. That leaves one guy with the chief. They knock the door out with a shotgun, and then it's three on two, maybe three machine guns or shotguns against two pistols. . . ."

"It's a possibility," said Lily.

Now it was Lucas' turn to shake his head. "You know, when you lay it out like that, it sounds pretty unlikely. . . ."

"The Crows are pretty unlikely," the security man said. "I'll tell you what we're going to do. We'll freeze the kitchen. Stick a monitor somewhere. If they come in, we'll snap them up."

"A trap," said Lily.

"Right. Well—excuse me, I gotta go talk to the chief. And listen: Thanks."

* * *

On the sidewalk in front of the hotel, Lucas shook his head again.

"It was a hole, but that's not what the Crows are up to," he said.

"Then what?"

"I don't know."

In the car, Lily looked at her watch. "Why don't we talk about it over lunch?"

"Sure. Want to go to my place?" Lucas asked.

Lily looked at him curiously. "This is a new attitude," she said. "What happened?"

"Jennifer . . ."

". . . figured us out," she finished, sitting up straight in her seat. "Oh, shit. Did she throw you out?"

"That's about it," Lucas conceded. He cranked the car and pulled away from the curb.

"You don't think she'd call David, do you?" Lily asked anxiously.

"No. No, I don't. She's spent some time in bed with married men—I know some of them—and she'd never have thought of talking to their wives. She wouldn't break up a marriage."

"It makes me nervous," Lily said. "And that must be why you're so bummed out. You sat in Daniel's office looking like your dog had died."

"Yeah. It's Jen and it's this fuckin' case. Larry killed, executed. And I've been useless. That feels weird, you know? When something important is happening—drugs, gambling, credit-card scams, burglary rings—I've got these contacts. Daniel comes to me and says, 'Talk to your net. We got thirty-six burglaries on the southeast side last week, all small shit, stereos and TVs.' So I go out and talk to the net. A good part of the time, I'll find out what's happening. I'll squeeze a gambler and get sent to a fence and squeeze the fence and find a junkie, and squeeze the junkie and get the whole ring. But this thing . . . I got nobody. If they were regular crooks, I could find them. Dopers need dope or need to sell it, so they're out and about. Burglars and credit-card hustlers need fences. But who do these guys need? An old friend. Maybe a former university professor. Maybe an old sixties radical. Maybe some kind of right-wing lunatic. Maybe Indian, maybe white. Who the fuck knows? I spent my whole goddamn life in this town, and most of the time I lived right around where the Indians live and I never saw them. I know a few, but it's because they're in drugs or burglary, or because they're straight and I go to their stores. Other than that, I just don't have a net out there. I've got a black net. I've got a white net. I've even got an Irish net. I don't have an Indian net."

"Stop feeling sorry for yourself," Lily said. "You got the tip on the trouble out at Bear Butte and found the photograph that I picked Hood out of."

"I got tied up like a fuckin' pig by Hood and almost got my brains blown out. . . ."

"You figured out how to squeeze the Liss woman and got the names of the Crows out of her. You're doing all right, Davenport."

"It's been luck, and that ain't going to hack it from here on out," Lucas said, glancing at her. "So stop trying to cheer me up."

"I'm not," she said cheerfully. "We don't have a lot to be cheerful about. As a matter of fact, unless we get real lucky, we're completely fucked."

"Not completely," Lucas said. He downshifted, let the car wind down to a red light and touched her thigh. "But in an hour, who knows?"


Lily prowled through the house like a potential buyer, checking each of the rooms. Once, Lucas thought, he caught her sniffing the air. He grinned, said nothing and got two beers.

"Pretty good," she said finally, as she came up the stairs from the basement. "Where'd you get that old safe?"

"I use it as a gun safe," Lucas said, handing her a beer. "I picked it up cheap when they were tearing out a railroad ticket office here in St. Paul. It took six guys to get it in the house and down the stairs. I was afraid the stairs were going to break under the weight."

She took a sip of beer and said, "When you invited me for lunch . . ."

"Yeah?"

". . . am I supposed to make it?"

"Oh, fuck no," he said. "You got your choice. Pasta salad or chicken-breast salad with slices of avocado and light ranch dressing."

"Really?"


"It's a zoo over on Franklin and down on Lake," Lily said as she worked down into her salad. "With Clay in town, the feebs are crawling all over the place."

"Assholes," Lucas grunted. "They've got no contacts, the people hate them, they spend twenty-four hours a day stepping on their dicks. . . ."

"They're doing that now, in major numbers," Lily agreed. She looked up from her chicken-breast salad and said, "That was delicious. That pasta looks pretty good too. . . ."

"Want a bite?"

"Maybe just a bite?"


After lunch, they went to the study and Lily pulled out one of Anderson's notebooks for review. They both drank another beer, and Lucas put his feet up on a hassock and dozed.

"Warm in here," Lily said after a while.

"Yeah. The furnace kicked in. I looked at the thermometer. It's thirty-six degrees outside."

"It felt cold," she said, "but it's so pretty, you don't notice it. With the sun and everything."

"Yeah." He yawned and dozed some more, then cracked his eyes open as Lily peeled off her cotton sweater. She had a marvelously soft profile, he thought. He watched her read, nibbling at her lower lip.

"Nothing in the notebooks," he said. "I've been through them."

"There must be something, somewhere."

"Mmm."

"Why did the Crows kill Larry? They must have known that it would be counterproductive, in the political sense. And they didn't *have* to kill him—he wasn't helping us that much."

"They didn't know that. He was on TV after the raid on the Crows' apartment. . . . Maybe they thought . . ."

"Ah. I didn't think of that," she said. Then she frowned. "I was on TV the other night. After Larry was cut."

"Might be a good idea to lie low for a while," Lucas said. "These guys are fruitcakes."

"I still can't figure Larry," she said. "Or this other guy, Yellow Hand. Why kill Yellow Hand? Revenge? But revenge doesn't make any sense in this kind of situation, against one of your own people. It just muddies things up. And they never mention those shootings in their press releases. . . ."

"I got no ideas," Lucas said. After a moment he added, "Well, that's not *quite* right. I do have one idea. . . ."

"What's that?"

"Why don't we sneak back to the bedroom?"

She sighed, smiled a sad smile and said, "Lucas . . ."


When they talked about it later, Lucas and Lily agreed that there wasn't anything notable about the time they spent in bed that afternoon. The love was soft and slow, and they both laughed a lot, and between times they talked about their careers and salaries and told cop stories. It was absolutely terrific; the best of their lives.

"I've decided what I'm going to do about David," Lily said later in the day, rolling out to the edge of the bed and putting her feet on the floor.

"What are you going to do?" Lucas asked. He had been putting on his jockey shorts, and he stopped with one foot through a leg hole.

"I'm going to lie to him," she said.

"Lie to him?"

"Yeah. What we've got going, David and I, is pretty good. He's a good guy.

He's attractive, he's got a nice sense of humor, he worries about me and the kids. It's just . . ."

"Keep talking."

"There's not the same kind of heat as there is with you. I can look at him sometimes and I get a lump in my throat, I can't even talk. I just feel so . . . *warm* toward him. I love him. But I don't get that kind of driving hot feeling. You know what I mean?"

"Yeah. I know."

"I was thinking about it the other night. I was thinking, Here's Davenport. He's large and he's rough and he makes himself happy first. He's not always asking me if I'm okay, have I come. So what is this, Lily? Is this some kind of safe rape fantasy?"

"What'd you decide?"

"I don't know. I didn't decide anything, really. Except to lie to David."

Lucas got fresh underwear from his chest of drawers and said, "Come on. I'll give you a shower."

She followed him into the bathroom. In the shower she said, "David wouldn't do this either. I mean, you just kind of . . . work me over. Your hands are . . . in everything, and I . . . kind of like it."

Lucas shrugged. "You're hurting yourself. Stop talking about David, for Christ's sake."

She nodded. "Yeah. I better."

When they got out of the shower, he dried her, starting the rough towel around her head and slowly working down her legs. When he finished, he was sitting on the side of the bathtub; he reached around her and pulled her pelvis against his head. She ruffled his hair.

"God, you smell good," he said.

She giggled. "We've got to stop, Davenport. I can't handle much more of this."

They dressed slowly. Lucas finished first and lay on the bed, watching her.

"The hardest part of lying to him will be the first ten or fifteen minutes," he said suddenly. "If you can get through the first few minutes, you'll be okay."

She looked up, a guilty expression on her face. "I hadn't thought of that. The first . . . encounter."

"You know when you bust a kid for something, a teenager, and you're not sure that they did it? And they get that look on their face when you tell them you're a cop? And then you *know*? If you're not careful, you'll look like that."

"Ah, Jesus," she said.

"But if you can get through the first ten minutes, just keep bullshitting along, you'll stop feeling guilty and it'll go away."

"The voice of experience," she said, with the tiniest stain of bitterness in her voice.

"I'm afraid so," he said, a little despondently. "I don't know. I love women. But I look at Sloan. You know, Sloan's *wife* calls him Sloan? And they're always laughing and talking. It makes me jealous."

Lily dropped onto the foot of the bed. "Let's not talk about this," she said. "It'll put me in an early grave. Like Larry."

"Poor old Larry," Lucas said. "I feel for the sonofabitch."


The next day was sunny. Lucas had on his best blue suit with a black wool dress coat. Lily wore a dark suit with a blue blouse and a tweed overcoat. Just before they left Lily's hotel room, TV3 had begun live coverage of Larry Hart's funeral. The coverage opened with a shot of Lawrence Duberville Clay arriving at the funeral. Clay spoke a few clichés into a microphone and went inside.

"He thinks he's the fuckin' president," Lucas said.

"He might be, in six more years," Lily said.

The Episcopalian church was crowded with welfare workers and clients, cops and Indian friends and family. Daniel spoke a few words, and Hart's oldest friend, whom he'd called brother, spoke a few more. The casket was closed.

The cortege to the cemetery shut down traffic in central Minneapolis for five minutes. The line of funeral cars ran bumper to bumper through the Loop, escorted by cops on motorcycles.

"It's better out here," Lily said as they walked into the cemetery. "Churches make me nervous."

"This is the first place I ever saw you," Lucas said. "Bluebird's buried here."

"Yup. Weird."

Gravestones were scattered over twelve acres of slightly shaggy grounds, beneath burr oaks. Lucas supposed it would be a spooky place on moonlit nights, the oaks looming like shadows cast by the Headless Horseman. Anderson, stiff in a black suit, looking more like an undertaker than the undertaker, wandered over to stand beside them.

"This is where Rose E. Love is buried," he said after a while.

"Oh, yeah? Where'd you find that out?" Lucas said.

"I found it in some notes with the old coroner's files. There weren't any relatives handy when she died, so they made a note on the death certificate about the funeral home and cemetery, in case somebody came looking for her."

"Hmph."

"Bluebird too," Lily said.

"Mmm."

After a while, Anderson wandered away, edging around the accumulation of funeralgoers. Film crews from all the local television stations and several foreign and national news services stood as close as seemed circumspect, as the cops rolled out their most martial ceremony. When it was over, they passed a folded flag to Hart's mother and fired a military salute.

When the service ended, Anderson strolled up again.

"She's right along here," he said.

"Who?"

"Rose E. Love. I had them look up the gravesite in the cemetery office."

Lucas and Lily, pulled along by Anderson's interest, followed him a hundred yards to a gravesite under the boughs of an aging oak, a dozen feet from the wrought-iron fence surrounding the cemetery.

"Nice spot," Anderson said, looking up into the spreading oak tree with its hand-size leaves still clinging to the branches.

"Yeah." The grave had been kept up spotlessly; on the oblong pink granite stone was inscribed ROSE E. LOVE, in large letters, and below that MOTHER, in smaller script. Lucas looked around. "The grave looks a lot better than the other ones around here. You don't think maybe Shadow Love stops by and works on it?"

Anderson shook his head. "Naw. The cemeteries don't allow that. They'd get all kinds of shit going on. Me and my old lady bought our plots, you know, a couple of years back. They had all these care plans you could sign up for. Give them two thousand bucks now and they'll take care of your grave in perpetuity. It's called Plan Perpetual. You can put it right in your will."

"That's a little steep, isn't it?" Lily asked. "Two thousand bucks?"

"Well, I mean, it's *forever*," Anderson said. "When the next ice age comes through, they'll have a guy out here with a heater. . . ."

"Still a little steep."

"If you can't afford it all at once, you can pay by the year. You know, like seventy-five, a hundred bucks."

"Gives me the creeps thinking about it," Lucas said.

"He doesn't plan to die," Lily confided to Anderson.

"I hate to tell you this," Anderson said as they wandered away from Rose Love's grave, "but there comes a time in every man's life . . ."

Lucas thought of a question for Anderson. As he opened his mouth to speak, the cold steel of a gun barrel touched him behind the ear. He jerked to a halt, staggered, closed his eyes, slapped his neck and let out a deep breath.

"Lucas?" asked Lily. She had stopped and was looking up at him. "What's wrong?"

"Nothing," he said after a moment. "I was just daydreaming."

"Jesus, I thought you had a heart attack or something." Anderson was looking at him curiously, but Lucas shook his head and took Lily's arm. Anderson broke off just before they got to the fence, and headed across the slope toward the cemetery road. Lily and Lucas strolled out of the cemetery through a side exit, away from the remnants of the somber crowd.

The question was lost.

*　　*　　*

"What do you want to do?" Lily asked.

"I think I might go back out on my regular net," Lucas said. He had been thinking about his lie of the day before, and decided that talking to his regulars might be a good idea.

"Okay. You can drop me at the hotel," Lily said. "I'm going to sit around and read Anderson's notebooks for a while. Maybe go for a run before dinner."

"I told you. There's nothing in it—Anderson's stuff," Lucas said. "We won't find them on paper. If the Crows are lying low, we need somebody to talk to us."

"Yeah. But somewhere, there's something. A name. Something. Maybe somebody from their prison days . . ."

The day was chilly, but the bright sunlight felt fine on Lily's face. She walked with her head tilted back as they crossed the street, taking in the rays, and Lucas' heart thumped as he walked behind her, marveling.

Shadow Love was parked a block away, watching them.

# 24

Shadow Love stole a Volvo station wagon from the reserved floor of an all-day parking ramp. He drove it to the cemetery and waited a half-block from the hillside where they'd bury Hart.

The wait was a short one: Hart's funeral moved like clockwork. The funeral cortege came in from the other side of the graveyard, but Davenport and the New York woman came in from his side. They all gathered on the hillside and prayed, and Shadow Love watched, slipping back to the warm moment when he slashed Hart, feeling the power of the knife. . . . The knife was in his pocket, and he touched it, tingling. No gun had ever affected him the same way, nor had the knife, before the Hart killing.

*Blood made the stone holy. . . .*

When the funeral ended, Davenport and the New York cop walked away from the crowd with another man, down the hill toward his mother's grave. When they stopped, Shadow Love's forehead wrinkled: They were *at* his mother's grave. What for? What did they want?

Then they split up. The other man wandered away, and Davenport and the woman continued on until they crossed through the wrought-iron fence onto the sidewalk. The woman tilted her head back, smiling, the sunlight playing across her face. Davenport caught her arm as they got to the car and bumped his hip against hers. *Lovers.*

He would have trouble staying with the Porsche, Shadow Love thought, if Davenport stayed on city streets. He couldn't get too close. But Davenport went straight to I-35W and headed north. Shadow stayed several cars back as Davenport drove into the Loop, made one left and dropped the woman in front of her hotel.

As Shadow Love waited at the curb, Davenport pulled out of the hotel's circular driveway, crossed two lanes of traffic and headed straight back toward him. Shadow Love turned in his seat and looked out the passenger window until Davenport was past. Following him would be impossible. Davenport would see the U-turn close behind him, and the tomato-red Volvo was not inconspicuous. The woman, on the other hand . . .

Lily.

Shadow Love touched the stone knife, felt it yearning for drink. . . .


Shadow Love had worked intermittently as a cabdriver, and he knew the Minneapolis hotels. This was a tough one: it was small, mostly suites, and played to a wealthy clientele. Security would be good.

Shadow Love left the car at the curb, walked to the hotel entrance, and carefully stepped into the lobby and looked around. No sign of the woman. She had already gone up. Three bellhops were leaning on the registration desk, talking to the woman behind it. If he went farther inside, he'd be noticed. . . .

A flower shop caught his eye. It had an exterior entrance, but it also had a doorway that led directly into the hotel lobby. He thought for a moment, then checked his billfold. Forty-eight dollars and change. He went back outside and walked to the flower shop.


"One red rose? How romantic," the woman said, her eyebrows arching, a skeptical note in her voice. The hotel was expensive. Shadow Love was not the kind of man who would have a lover inside.

"Not my romance," Shadow grunted, picking up her skepticism. "I just dropped her off in the cab. Her old man give me ten extra bucks for the rose."

"Ah." The woman's face broke into a smile. Everything was right in the world. "For ten dollars you could buy two roses. . . ."

"He said one and keep the change," Shadow Love said grumpily. He had forty-eight dollars between himself and the street, and this flower shop was selling roses at five dollars a pop. "Her name is Rothenburg. I don't know how you spell it. Her old man said you could get the room."

"Sure." The woman wrapped a single red rose in green tissue paper and said, "Is the card to be signed?"

"Yeah. 'Love, Lucas.' "

"That's nice." The woman picked up the phone, rapped in four numbers and said, "This is Helen. You got a Rothenburg? Don't know the spelling. Yeah . . . Four-oh-eight? Thanks."

"We'll send it right up," the woman said as she gave Shadow Love his change.

Room 408. "Thanks," he said.

He left the shop and went outside. It was late afternoon, getting cooler. He looked both ways, then walked away from the car toward Loring Park and took a long turn around the pond, thinking. The woman was good with a gun. He couldn't fuck up. If he waited awhile, then went straight in to the elevators, as though he belonged there, he might get up. Then again, maybe not—but if they stopped him, they wouldn't do more than throw him out. He dug in a pocket, took out a Slim Jim sausage and chewed on it.

If he got up, what then? If he knocked on her door and she opened it, bang. But what if the chain was on? He had no faith in the idea of shooting through the door. The pistol was a .380, good enough for close work, but it wouldn't punch through a steel fire-liner. Not for sure. She'd recognize him. And she was a killer. If he missed, she'd be all over him. It'd be hell just getting out of the hotel. . . .

*Have to think.*

He was still working it out when he got back to the car. A Federal Express truck stopped across the street and the driver hopped out. Shadow Love, his mind far away, automatically tracked him as he went into the lobby of an office building and began emptying the local package box. A moment later, when the driver came out with his load of packages, Shadow Love skipped out of the car and walked into the lobby.

The Federal Express box had an open rack of packaging envelopes and address slips, with ballpoint pens on chains.

*Lily Rothenburg, Police Officer,* he wrote. *Room 408 . . .*

He still didn't know how he'd get in her door. Sometimes you had to pray for luck. When he got back on the sidewalk, it was dark. . . .

The rose was totally unexpected: the last thing she would have expected, but it thrilled her. David sent flowers; Davenport did not. That he should . . .

Lily put it in a water glass and set it on top of the television set, looked at it, adjusted it and sat down with Anderson's computer printouts. In two minutes, she knew she couldn't read.

*Davenport, God damn it. What's this rose shit?* She took a turn around the room, caught her image in a mirror. *That's the silliest smile I've seen on you since you were a teenager.*

She couldn't work. She glanced at a copy of *People,* put it aside and walked around the room again, stopping to sniff at the rose.

She was in a *feeling* mood, she decided. *A hot bath . . .*


Shadow Love went straight through the lobby with the Federal Express package in his hand, slightly in front of his body, so the bellhops could see the colors. He stopped at the elevators, poked 4 and resolutely *did not* look at the desk and the bellhops. The elevator chimed, the doors opened . . . he was in, and alone.

He gripped the knife, feeling its holy weight, then touched his belly, feeling the gun there. But the knife was the thing.

The doors opened on the fourth floor and he stepped out, still holding the package in front of him. Room 408. He turned right and heard a vacuum cleaner behind him. He stopped. Luck.

He turned back, went around the corner and found a maid with a vacuum cleaner. There was nobody else in the hallway.

"Got a package," he grunted. "Where's four-oh-eight?"

"Down there," the maid said, flipping a thumb down the hall behind her. She was a short woman, slender, early twenties; already worn out.

"Okay," Shadow said. He slipped a hand under his jacket, looked around once to make sure they were alone, pulled the gun and pointed it at the woman's head.

"Oh, no . . ." she said, backing away, her hands out toward him.

"Down to the room. And get your keys out. . . ." The woman continued backing away, Shadow matching her pace for pace, the muzzle of the gun never leaving her face. "The keys," he said.

She groped in her apron pocket and produced a ring with a dozen keys.

"Open four-oh-eight . . . but let me knock first." He thrust the package at her, his voice rising, an edge of madness to it. "If she answers, tell her you've got a package. Let her see it. If you try to warn her, if you do anything to spook her, bitch cunt, I'll blow your motherfuckin' brains out. . . ."

The thought that the maid might betray him gripped Shadow Love's stomach, and the black spot popped into his line of vision, obscuring her face. He forced it down, down, concentrating: *Not this one; not yet.*

The maid was terrified. She clutched at the package, holding it to her chest.

"Here," she squeaked.

The black spot was still there, smaller, floating like a mote in God's eye, but he could read the number on the door: 408. Shadow reached out and knocked, quietly. No answer. The killing rush was coming now, like cocaine, even better. . . . He knocked again. No answer.

"Open it," he said. He pressed the gun against the woman's forehead. "If there's a noise, I'll fuckin' kill you, bitch. I'll blow your fuckin' brains all over the hall."

The woman slipped the key into the lock. There was a tiny metallic click and she flinched, and Shadow Love tapped her with the barrel. "No more," he whispered. "Open it."

She turned the key. There was another click and the door eased open.


Lily got out of the bathtub, steam rolling off her body; she felt languid and soft from the bath oils. She heard the knock and stopped toweling. It wasn't a maid's knock. It was too soft, too . . . furtive. She frowned, took a step toward the bathroom door, looked through the bedroom to the outer sitting room; it was dark. A lamp was on in the bedroom, as were the lights in the bathroom. There was another knock, a pause, then a click. Somebody coming in.

Lily looked around for her purse, with the gun in the concealed holster: outer room. *Shit*. She reached back, hit the bathroom light switch and started for the lamp.


Shadow Love pushed the maid forward. The door opened and the woman went through. There was little light, apparently coming from a bathroom. . . . *No. There's another room. Fuckin' rich bitch has a suite.* . . . The light suddenly went out, and they were in darkness, Shadow Love and the maid silhouetted against the light from the hallway.


Lily killed the lamp as the door opened. She felt a tiny surge of relief when she saw the small woman and the familiar colors on the package. She reached again for the wall switch, then saw the man behind the woman and what looked like a gun.

"Freeze, motherfucker," she screamed at the dark figures, dropping automatically into her Weaver stance, her hands empty. But the movement, in the dark, might be convincing. . . .


The scream startled him. Shadow Love sensed the cop woman dropping into a shooter's stance, and swept the maid's feet from under her and went down on top of her. He could feel the woman moving sideways in the minimal light in the room, and he pivoted and kicked the outer door shut. The dark was complete.

"Got a woman, here, a maid," Shadow Love called. He pointed the gun toward where he thought the other door was, although he was disoriented and felt he might be off. But if she fired at him, he'd get her in the muzzle blast. "Come out and talk; I just want to talk about the Indians, about the Crows. I've worked with the police."

*Bullshit. Shadow Love. Must be.*

"Bullshit. You move, motherfucker, and I'll spread you around like spaghetti sauce."

Lily, nude, crawled across the bedroom floor in the dark, her hands sweeping from side to side, looking for a weapon. Anything. *Nothing. Nothing.* Back toward the bathroom, creeping in silence, waiting for the killing light . . . Into the bathroom. Groping. Up the walls. A towel rack. She tugged on it. It held. She put her full weight on it, bouncing frantically, and suddenly, explosively, it came free. She went flat again, frozen, waiting for the light, but nothing came. She went back to the floor and, with the towel bar in her hand, crawled out the bathroom door toward the front room.

There was a sudden, terrific clatter. Shadow Love started, put his face next to the maid's and whispered, "Move, bitch, and I'll slit your fuckin' throat." He could feel the woman trembling in her thin maid's uniform. "And I got the gun; if you go for the door, I'll shoot you."

He left her then, and crawled toward the spot where he thought the inner door was, feeling his way across the carpet in the dark.

*What was the noise? What was she doing? Why hadn't she risked a light? She wouldn't be any worse off. . . .*

The problem was, the first one to turn on a light would be most exposed. . . .

"I'm not here to hurt anybody," he called.

His voice was a shock: he was so close. Two feet away, three. And now she could smell him: his breath. He'd been eating something spicy, sausage maybe, and his warm breath trickled toward her over the carpet. Could he smell the bath oils on her? She thought she might be a yard from the door, and he was coming through. She rolled to one side, a slow, inching, agonizing movement, holding the towel bar between her breasts.

*Where was she? Why wasn't she answering?* She could be standing over him, pointing a .45 at his skull, tightening on the trigger. The injustice of his death gripped him, and for a full beat, two beats, he waited for the crashing blow that would kill him. There was nothing. He reached ahead in the dark, feeling the baseboard on the wall ahead, sliding his hand to the right, finding the corner and the doorway. *The bathroom . . . that noise she made, that sounded like it came out of a bathroom, the hollow-sharp sound you get from tile walls . . . What was she doing in there?* Moving a few inches at a time, he crossed through the doorway, low-crawling toward the bathroom. *Nothing from her. Nothing. Maybe she's not armed. . . .*

"Don't got no gun, bitch. That's it. Well, I'm putting my gun away, you know? You know why? 'Cause I'm getting my knife out. Cut open Larry Hart with it, you know? You know what I did then? After I cut him? You know?"

*Where is she? Where is the bitch?* He strained into the darkness. Got to scare her, got to make her move.

"I sucked the blood, that's what I did," Shadow Love called. "All hot. Better'n deer's blood. Sweeter . . . Bet yours'll be sweeter yet . . ."

*Where the fuck is she?*


There was a change in the darkness next to her, a movement through it. Shadow Love, on the floor next to her, not more than two feet away, low-crawling toward the bathroom. She couldn't see him, but she could sense him there, moving in the dark. Moving as slowly as he was, she pulled her feet under her and quietly stood up, her hand sliding up the woodwork along the edge of the door. She could no longer sense him—standing, she was quite literally too far away—but she figured he had to be through the door.


"You don't have a gun, do you, bitch?" Shadow Love screamed. The cry was as hard and sharp as a sliver of glass and Lily gasped involuntarily. He heard the gasp and froze. She was close by. He could feel it. *Very close. Where?* He swung an arm out to the right, then his gun hand to the left. And he touched her, raked the back of her calf with his gun hand as she went through the door, into the outer room, and he pivoted and fired the pistol once through the door. . . .


*No,* she thought. *He must have heard . . .*

She took a fast step through the door, high, over him, in case his legs were still in the doorway, and was pushing off with her back leg when his hand struck her calf. Shit. She dodged sideways; there was a flash and a deafening crack, and she twisted sideways toward the television set, crawling. . . .

"Noooo . . ." The scream clutched at Lily as she hit a body in the dark. *Soft . . . woman . . .* She had just registered the thought as the other woman, sobbing frantically, clubbed at her and she went down, twisting, back on her hands and knees, crawling toward the television, reaching out, sweeping the carpet for the purse. . . .

*    *    *

The muzzle blast blinded him for a second, but now he knew for sure: She had no gun and was heading for the door. The maid's scream froze him, then Shadow Love struggled to his feet, groping for the wall and a light switch. He found the wall and ran his hand toward the switch, watching the doorway in case the cop tried for the door.

And then, in the instant before he would turn on the light . . .

He heard the slide.

There was no other sound like it. A .45, at full cock.

And then Lily, her voice like a gravedigger's: "I'm out here, motherfucker. Go ahead—turn on the light."

Shadow Love, poised in the doorway, felt the voice coming from his left. One chance: he took it. With the gun in his hand he launched himself straight through the dark toward the other door, where he could hear the maid sobbing. Two steps, three, and then he hit her. She was standing and she screamed, and he held her for an instant as he found the door, gripped the knob and then thrust the woman toward the place Lily's voice had come from. He felt the maid go, stumbling, and he wrenched open the door. As he went through, he fired once, toward the two women, and then ran toward the stairs, waiting for the bite from the .45. . . .

Light from the hallway flooded the room, and Lily saw movement toward her and realized it was too small to be Shadow Love: *maid.*

She pivoted to a shooting line past the falling woman and saw Shadow Love in the doorway, his gun arm out toward her. She was still turning past the woman, and then he was gone, his arm trailing behind, like a bat in a drag bunt. Lily was still following with the .45 when Shadow Love pulled the trigger.

The bullet hit her in the chest.

Lillian Rothenburg went down like a tenpin.

# 25

Lucas was chatting with a gambler outside a riverfront bar when his handset beeped. He stepped off the curb, reached through the open window of the Porsche and thumbed the transmit switch.

"Yeah. Davenport." The sun had set and a chill wind was blowing off the river. He stuck his free hand in his pants pocket and hunched his back against the cold.

"Lucas, Sloan says to meet him at Hennepin Medical Center just as fast as you can get there," the dispatcher said. "He says it's heavy-duty. Front entrance."

"Okay. Did he say what it's about?"

After a second's hesitation, the dispatcher said, "No. But he said lights and sirens and get your ass over there."

"Five minutes," Lucas said.

Lucas left the gambler standing on the sidewalk and pushed the Porsche across the bridge, south through the warehouse district to the medical center, wondering all the time. A break? Somebody nailed a Crow? There were three squad cars and a remote television truck at emergency receiving. Lucas wheeled around front, dumped the car in a no-parking space, flipped down the sunshade with the police ID and walked up the steps. Sloan stood waiting behind the glass doors, and Lucas saw a patrol captain and a woman sergeant standing in the lobby. They seemed to be staring at him. Sloan pushed the glass door open, and when Lucas stepped inside he linked his arm through Lucas'.

"Got your shit together?" Sloan asked. His face was white, drawn, deadly serious.

"What the fuck you talking about?" Lucas said, trying to pull away. Sloan hung on.

"Lily's been shot," Sloan said.

For just a second, the world stopped, like a freeze frame in a movie. A guy being wheeled across the lobby in a wheelchair: frozen. A woman behind an information desk: caught with her mouth half open, staring carplike at Lucas and Sloan. All stopped. Then the world jerked forward again and Lucas heard himself saying, "My fuckin' Christ." Then bleakly, "How bad?"

"She's on the table," Sloan said. "They don't know what they got. She's breathing."

"What happened?" Lucas said.

"You okay?" asked Sloan.

"Ah, man . . ."

"A guy—Shadow Love—forced a maid to open her hotel room. Lily was taking a bath, but she got to her gun, and there was some kind of fight and he shot her. He got away."

"Motherfucker," Lucas said bitterly. "We were over looking at Clay's hotel security, we never thought about hers."

"The maid's all shook up, but she's looked at a picture and she thinks it was Shadow. . . ."

"I don't give a fuck about that, what about Lily? What are the docs saying? Is she bad? Come on, man."

Sloan turned away, shrugged, then turned back and gestured helplessly. "You know the fuckin' docs, they ain't gonna say shit because of the malpractice insurance. They don't want to say she's gonna make it, then have her croak. But one of the hotel guys was in combat in Vietnam. He says she was hit hard. He said if she'd of been in Vietnam, it would of depended on how fast they got her back to a hospital whether she made it. . . . He thinks the slug took a piece of lung, and he rolled her up on her side to keep her from drowning in blood. . . . The paramedics were there in two or three minutes, so . . . I don't know, Lucas. I think she'll make it, but I don't know."

Sloan led the way through the hospital to the surgical suite. Daniel was already there with a Homicide cop.

"You okay?" Daniel asked.

"What about Lily?"

"We haven't heard anything yet," Daniel said, shaking his head. "I just ran over from the office."

"It's Shadow Love, you know. Doing security work for the Crows."

"But why?" Daniel's forehead wrinkled. "We're not that close to them. And there's no percentage in killing Lily, not for political reasons. I'm a politician and they're politicians, and I can see what they're doing. It makes sense, in a bizarre way. They were so careful to explain the others—Andretti, the judge in Oklahoma, the guy in South Dakota. This doesn't fit. Neither did Larry. Or your snitch."

"We don't know exactly what's going on," Lucas said, his voice on the edge of desperation. "If I could just find something . . . some little hangnail of information, just a fuckin' scrap . . . anything."

They thought about it in silence for a moment, then Daniel, in a lower voice, said, "I called her husband."


Two hours later, long done with conversation, they were staring bleakly at the opposite wall of the corridor when the doors from the operating suite banged open. A redheaded surgeon came through, still wrapped in a blue surgical gown dappled with blood. She snapped the mask off her face and tossed it into a bin already half full of discarded masks and gowns, and began peeling off the gown. Daniel and Lucas pushed off the wall and stepped toward her.

"I'm good," she said. She tossed the used gown in the discard bin and wiggled her fingers in front of her face. "Seriously gifted."

"She's okay?" Lucas asked.

"You the family?" the surgeon asked, looking from one of them to the other.

"The family's not here," Lucas said. "They're on their way from New York. I'm her partner and this is the chief."

"I've seen you on TV," she said to Daniel, then looked back at Lucas. "She'll be okay unless something weird happens. We took the slug out—it looks like a light thirty-eight, if you're interested. It entered through her breast, broke a rib, pulped up a piece of her lung and stuck in the muscle wall along the rib cage in back. Cracked the rib in back too. She's gonna hurt like hell."

"But she'll make it?" Daniel said.

"Unless something weird happens," the surgeon nodded. "We'll keep her in intensive care overnight. If there aren't any problems, we'll have her sitting up and maybe walking around her bed in a couple of days. It'll take longer before she's feeling right, though. She's messed up."

"Aw, Jesus, that's good," said Lucas, turning to Daniel. "That's decent."

"Bad scars?" asked Daniel.

"There'll be some. With that kind of wound, we can't fool around. We had to get in to see what was going on. We'll have the entry wound from the slug, and then the surgical scars where I went in. In a couple or three years, the entry wound will be a white mark about the size and shape of a cashew on the lower curve of her breast. In five years, the surgical scars will be white lines maybe an eighth-inch across. She's olive-complected, so they'll show more than they would on a blonde, but she can live with them. They won't be disfiguring."

"When can we see her?"

The surgeon shook her head. "Not tonight. She won't be doing anything but sleeping. Tomorrow, maybe, if it's necessary."

"No sooner?"

"She's been *shot*," the surgeon said with asperity. "She doesn't need to talk. She needs to heal."


David Rothenburg came in at two o'clock in the morning on a cattle-car flight out of Newark, the only one he could get. Lucas met him at the airport. Daniel wanted to send Sloan, or go himself, but Lucas insisted. Rothenburg was wearing a rumpled blue seersucker suit and a wine-colored bow tie with a white shirt; his hair was messed up and he wore half-moon reading glasses down on his nose. Lucas had talked to the airline about the shooting, and Rothenburg was the first person out of the tunnel into the gate area. He had a black nylon carry-on bag in his left hand.

"David Rothenburg?" Lucas asked, stepping toward him.

"Yes. Are you . . ." They moved in a circle around each other.

"Lucas Davenport, Minneapolis Police."

"How is she?"

"Hurt, but she'll make it, if there aren't any complications."

"My God, I thought she was dying," Rothenburg said, sagging in relief. "They were so vague on the phone. . . ."

"Nobody knew for a while. She's had an operation. They didn't know until they got inside how bad it was."

"But she'll be okay?"

"That's what they say. I've got a car. . . ."

Rothenburg was two inches taller than Lucas but slender as a rope. He looked strong, like an ironman runner, long muscles without bulk. They walked stride for stride across the terminal and out to the parking ramp to the Porsche.

"You're the guy she bailed out of trouble. The hostage, when she shot that man," Rothenburg said.

"Yeah. We did some work together."

"Where were you tonight?" There was an edge to the question, and Lucas glanced at him.

"We split up. She went back to her hotel to read some stuff while I was out working my regular informant net. This guy we're looking for, Shadow Love, tracked her there."

"You know who did it?"

"Yes, we think so."

"Jesus Christ, in New York the guy'd be in jail."

Lucas looked directly across at Rothenburg and held the stare for a moment, then grunted, "Bullshit."

"What?" Rothenburg's anger was beginning to show.

"I said 'bullshit.' He fired one shot and got lost. He's got a safe house somewhere and he knows what he's doing. The New York cops wouldn't do any better than we're doing. Wouldn't do as good. We're better than they are."

"I don't see how you can say that, people are being shot down here."

"We have about one killing a week in Minneapolis and we catch all the killers. You have between five and eleven a night in New York and your cops hardly catch any of them. So don't give me any shit about New York. I'm too tired and too pissed to listen to it."

"It's my wife who's shot . . ." Rothenburg barked.

"And she was working with me and I liked her a lot, and I feel guilty about it, so stay off my fuckin' back," Lucas snarled.

There was a moment of silence; then Rothenburg sighed and settled further into his seat. "Sorry," he said after a moment. "I'm scared."

"No sweat," said Lucas. "I'll tell you something, if it makes you feel better. As of tonight, Shadow Love is a dead motherfucker."


Lucas left Rothenburg at the hospital and went back on the street. There were few places open; he found a bar in a yuppie shopping center, drank a scotch, then another, and left. The night was cold and he wondered where Shadow Love was. He had no way to find out, not without a break.

# 26

Leo came in at three in the morning. "No sign of Clay, but his man's at home."

"Drake? You saw him?"

"Yeah. And he's got a girl with him."

"Blonde?" asked Sam.

"Yeah. Real small."

"Far out . . . real young?"

"Probably eight or ten years old. Took Drake's hand when they walked up to the door."

"Clay'll be coming," Aaron said with certainty. "When you got his kind of twist, you don't get away from it." When he said 'twist,' he made a twisting motion with his fist.

Sam nodded. "Another night," he said. "Tomorrow night."

"Did you hear about the cop?" asked Aaron.

Leo took off his jacket and tossed it at the couch. "The woman? Yeah. It's Shadow."

"God damn, the fool will ruin us," Aaron said bitterly.

"One more night," said Leo. "One or two."

"Killing cops is bad medicine," Aaron said. He looked at his cousin. "If it's gonna happen with Clay, it's gotta be soon. We might start thinking about taking him at the hotel or on the street."

Sam shook his head. "The plan is right. Don't fuck with the plan. Clay's got a platoon of bodyguards with machine guns. They'd flat kill us on the street and Clay'd be a hero. If we can get him at Drake's, he'll be alone. And he won't be no hero."

"Tomorrow night," said Leo. "I'd bet on it."

Shadow Love hid in a condemned building six blocks out from the Loop. The building, once a small hotel, became a flophouse and finally was condemned for its lack of maintenance and the size of its rats. Norway rats: the fuckin' Scandinavians ran everything in the state, Shadow Love thought.

There were a few other men living in the building, but Shadow Love never really saw them. Just shambling figures darting between rooms, or moving furtively up and down the stairs. When you took a room, you closed the door and blocked it with a four-by-four from a pile of lumber on the first floor. You braced one end of the timber against the door, one end against the opposite wall. It wasn't foolproof, but it was pretty good.

The three-story structure had been built around a central atrium with a skylight at the top. When the men had to move their bowels—a rare event, most of them were winos—they simply hung over the atrium railing and let go. That kept the upper rooms reasonably tidy. Nobody stayed long on the bottom floors.

When Shadow Love moved in, he brought a heavy coat, a plastic air mattress, a cheap radio with earphones, and his gun. Groceries were slim: boxes of crackers, cookies, a can of Cheez Whiz, and a twelve-pack of Pepsi.

After the shooting, Shadow Love had run down the stairs, tried to *stroll* through the lobby, then hurried on to the Volvo. He drove it until he was sure he couldn't have been followed, and dumped it. He stopped once at a convenience store to buy food and then settled into the hideout.

There was nothing on the radio for almost two hours. Then a report that Detective Lillian Rothenburg had been shot. Not killed but shot. More than he'd hoped for. Maybe he got her. . . .

Then, a half-hour later, word that she was on the operating table. And two hours after that, a prognosis: The doctors said she'd live.

Shadow Love cursed and pulled the coat around him. The nights were getting very cold. Despite the coat, he shivered.

The bitch was still alive.

# 27

Lucas spent the next day working his net, staying in touch with the hospital by telephone. In the early afternoon, Lily woke up and spoke to David, who was sitting at her bedside, and later to Sloan. She could add little to what they knew.

Shadow Love, she said. She had never seen his face, but it felt right. He was middle-height, wiry. Dark. Ate sausage.

That said, she went back to sleep.

At nine, Lucas called a friend at the intensive care unit: he had been calling her hourly.

"He just left, said he was going to get some sleep," the friend told Lucas.

"Is she awake?"

"She comes and goes. . . ."

"I'll be right there," he said.

Lily was wrapped in sheets and blankets, propped half upright on the bed. Her face was pale, the color of notebook paper. A breathing tube went to her nose. Two saline bags hung beside her bed, and a drip tube was patched into her arm below the elbow.

Lucas' friend, a nurse, said, "She woke up a while ago, and I told her you were coming, so she knows. Don't stay long, and be as quiet as you can."

Lucas nodded and tiptoed to Lily's bedside.

"Lily?"

After a moment, she turned her head, as if the sound of his voice had taken a few seconds to penetrate. Her eyes, when she opened them, were clear and calm.

"Water?" she croaked. There was a bottle of water on the bedstand with a plastic straw. He held it to her mouth and she sucked once. "Damn breathing tube dries out my throat."

"You feel pretty bad?"

"Doesn't . . . hurt much. I feel like I'm . . . really sick. Like I had a terrible flu."

"You look okay," Lucas lied. Except for her eyes, she looked terrible.

"Don't bullshit me, Davenport," she said with a small grin. "I know what I look like. Good for the diet, though."

"Jesus, it freaked me out." He couldn't think of anything else to say.

"Thanks for the rose."

"What?"

"The rose . . ." She turned her head away, then back and forth, as though trying to loosen up her neck muscle. "Very . . . romantic."

Lucas had no idea what she was talking about, and then she said, "I got through the first fifteen minutes . . . with David. I hurt so bad I wasn't thinking of you or anything, I was just happy to be here. And we were talking and when I thought of you, the first fifteen minutes were gone . . . and it was okay."

"Jesus, Lily, I feel so bad."

"Nothing you could do: but you be careful," she said in her rusty voice. Her eyelids drooped. "Are you getting anywhere?"

Lucas shook his head. "We've got a screen of people around Clay—I still think it's him. I just haven't figured out how. We're watching the dumbwaiter, but that's not it."

"I don't know," she said. Her eyes closed and she took two deep breaths. "I'm so damn sleepy all the time. . . . Can't think . . ."

And she was gone, sleeping, her face going slack. Lucas sat by her bed for five minutes, watching her face and the slow rise and fall of her chest. He was lucky, he thought, that he wasn't walking beside her coffin across another cemetery, just as with Larry. . . .

Larry.

It came back in a flash, as real as the shotgun behind his ear. He'd been walking across the cemetery grass with Lily and Anderson, after leaving Rose Love's well-tended grave. Anderson was talking about the cost of grave maintenance and the perpetual-care contract he and his wife had bought. . . .

And the question popped into his head: Who paid to take care of Rose

Love's grave? Neither Shadow Love nor the Crows had enough money to endow a perpetual-care fund, so they must pay it annually or semiannually. But if they were on the road all the time, where would the bill be sent? Lucas stood, looked down at Lily's sleeping face, paced out of the ICU, past a patient who looked as though he were dying, and then back in, until he was standing by her bed again.

The Crows or Shadow Love, whoever paid for maintenance, might simply remember to write a check once or twice a year and mail it, without ever getting a bill. But that didn't feel right; there must be a bill. Maybe they had a postal box; but if they had their mail sent to a box, and didn't get back into town for a while, important messages might sit there for weeks. Lucas didn't know what the Crows had done, but he knew what he would do in their circumstances. He'd have a mail drop. He'd have the cemetery bill and other important stuff sent to an old, trustworthy friend. Somebody he could rely on to send the mail on to him. He half ran from the ICU to the nurses' station.

"I gotta have a phone," Lucas snapped at his friend. She stepped back and pointed at a desk phone. He picked it up and called Homicide. Anderson was just getting ready to leave.

"Harmon? I'm heading out to Riverwood Cemetery in a hurry. You get on the line, find out where Riverwood does its paperwork and call me. I've got a handset. If the office is closed, run down somebody who can open it up, somebody who does the bills. I'll be there in ten minutes."

"What have you got?" Anderson asked.

"Probably nothing," Lucas said. "But I've got just the smallest fuckin' hang-nail of an idea. . . ."


Clay and a security man stood in the parking garage and argued.

"It's a fuckin' terrible idea," the security man said intently.

"No, it's not. When you get a little higher in management, you'll recognize that," Lawrence Duberville Clay replied. An undertone in his voice hinted that it was unlikely the security man would ever rise higher in management.

"Look: one car. Just one. You wouldn't even see it."

"Absolutely not. You put a car on me and you better warn the people inside that I'll fire their asses. And you with them. No. The only way for me to do this is to go out on my own. And I'll probably be safer than if I was here. Nobody'll expect me to be out on the street."

"Jesus, boss . . ."

"Look, we've been through this before," Clay said. "The fact is, when you're surrounded by a screen of security, you don't have any *feel* for anything. I *need* to get away, to be effective."

They had a car for him, a nondescript rental that one of the agents had picked up at the airport. Clay took the wheel, slammed the door and looked out at the unhappy security man.

"Don't worry, Dan. I'll be back in a couple, three hours, no worse for the wear."


Lucas had to wait ten minutes at the cemetery office, watching the moon ghost across the sky behind dead oak leaves. He shivered and paced impatiently, and finally a Buick rolled up and a woman got out.

"Are you Davenport?" she asked in a sour voice, jingling her keys.

"Yes."

"I was at a dinner," she said. She was a hard woman in her early thirties, with a beehive hairdo from the late fifties.

"Sorry."

"We really should have some kind of papers," she said frostily as she unlocked the door.

"No time," Lucas said.

"It's not right. I should call our chairman."

"Look, I'm trying to be fuckin' nice," Lucas said, his voice rising as he spoke. "I'm trying as hard as I can to be a nice guy because you seem like an okay woman. But if you drag your feet on this, I'll call downtown for a warrant. It'll be here in five minutes and we'll seize your whole goddamn billing system. If you get lucky, you'll get it back sometime next year. You can explain that to your chairman."

The woman stepped away from him and a spark of fear touched her eyes. "Please wait," she said. She went into a back room, and soon Lucas could hear her typing on a computer keyboard.

It was all bullshit, Lucas told himself. Not a chance in a fucking million. A moment later a printer started, and then the woman came out of the back room.

"The bills have always been sent to the same place, every six months, forty-five dollars and sixty-five cents. Sometimes they're slow-pay, but they always pay."

"Who?" asked Lucas. "Where'd you send the bill?"

The woman handed Lucas a sheet of computer paper, with one short line pinched between her thumb and forefinger. "It's right here," she said. "A Miss Barbara Gow. That's her address under her name. Does that help?"


Corky Drake had been born with a silver spoon in his mouth, only to have it rudely snatched away in his teens. His father had for some years neglected to report his full income to the Internal Revenue Service. When the heathens had learned of Corky Senior's oversight . . . well, the capital barely covered what was owed, much less the fines.

His father had removed himself from the scene with a garden hose that led from the tailpipe of a friend's Mercedes into the sealed car. The friend had refused to forgive him, even in death, for what he had done to the upholstery.

Corky, who was seventeen, was already a person of refined taste. A life of poverty and struggle simply was not on the menu. He did the only thing he was qualified to do: he became a pimp.

Certain friends of his father's had exceptional interests in women. Corky could satisfy those, for a price. Not only were the women very beautiful, they were very young. They were, in fact, girls. The youngest in his current stable was six. The oldest was eleven, although, Corky assured the wits among his clientele, she still had the body of an eight-year-old. . . .

Corky Drake met Lawrence Duberville Clay at a club in Washington. If they hadn't become friends, they had at least become friendly. Clay appreciated the services offered by Drake.

"My little perversion," Clay called it, with a charming grin.

"No. It's not a perversion, it's perfectly natural," Drake said, swirling two ounces of Courvoisier in a crystal snifter. "You're a connoisseur, is what you are. In many countries of the world . . ."

Drake would serve his clients in Washington or New York, if they required it, but his home base was in Minneapolis, and his resources were strongest there. Clay, in town on business, visited Corky's home. After that, the visits became a regular part of his life. . . .

Drake was talking to the current queen of his stable when he heard the car in the driveway.

"Here he is now," he said to the girl. "Remember, this could be the most important night of your life, so I want you to be good."

Leo Clark sat in a clump of brush thirty yards from Drake's elaborate Kenwood townhouse. He was worried about the cops. Barbara Gow's car was parked up the street. It didn't fit in the neighborhood. If they checked it and had it towed, he'd be fucked.

He sat in the leaves and waited, looking at his watch every few minutes and studying the face of the Old Man in the Moon. It was a clear night for the Cities, and you could see him staring back at you, but it was nothing like the nights on the prairie, when the Old Man was so close you could almost touch his face. . . .

At ten minutes after nine, a gray Dodge entered Corky's circular driveway. Leo put up a pair of cheap binoculars and hoped there'd be more light when Corky opened the door. There was, and just enough: the elegant gray hair of Lawrence Duberville Clay was unmistakable. Leo waited until Clay was inside the house, then picked his way through the wood to Barbara's car, quickly started it and headed back to her house. He stopped only once, at a pay phone.

The message was simple: "Clay's at the house."


Anderson was waiting in his office when Lucas hurried in.

"What you got?"

"A name," Lucas said. "Let's run it through the machine."

They put Barbara Gow's name into the computer and got back three quick hits.

"She's Indian, and she's a rad, or used to be," Anderson said, scanning down the monitor. "Look at this. Organizing for the union, busted in a march . . . Christ, this was way back in the fifties, she was ahead of her time. . . . Civil rights and then antiwar stuff there in the sixties . . ."

"She'd of known the Crows," Lucas said. "There weren't that many activist Indians back in the fifties, not in Minneapolis. . . ."

Anderson was scanning through one of his notebooks; he found a page and held it up to the screen. "Look at this," he said. He tapped an address in the notebook and touched an address on the screen. "She lived just a couple blocks from Rose E. Love, and at the same time."

"All right, I'm going down there," Lucas said. "Get onto Del and some of his narcs, tell them I might need surveillance help. I'll look the place over now. It's too much to hope that they'll be there."

"You want me to start some squads that way, just in case?"

"Yeah, you could start a couple, but keep them off the block unless I holler."


Leo pulled into Barbara Gow's driveway and Aaron lifted the garage door. Leo rolled the car inside but left the engine running. Sam stepped out of the house carrying a chopped-down shotgun. Leo had cut the gun down himself. What had been a conventional Winchester Super-X, a four-shot semiauto, wound up as an ugly illegal killing machine that looked as much like a war club as a shotgun. Sam opened the car door and slipped the shotgun under the passenger seat, and then helped Aaron load a six-foot chunk of railroad tie into the cargo space. They'd sharpened one end with an ax and screwed handles to the top. When it was in, Aaron slammed the tailgate and he and Sam got in.

"You want to leave the garage door up?" Leo asked.

"Yeah. If we gotta get off the street in a hurry when we come back, it'll get us an extra minute."


Lucas cruised by the side of the Gow house, moving as slowly as he could without being conspicuous. There were lights on in both front and back, probably the living room and the kitchen or a bedroom. The upper floor was dark. He turned the corner to pass in front of the house and saw that the garage door was up, the garage empty. As he passed, a shadow crossed the living room blind. Someone inside. Since the car was gone, that meant more than one person was living in the house. . . .

He picked up the handset and put in a call to Anderson.

"Get me the description of the woman who was seen with Shadow Love," he said.

"Just a second," Anderson said. "I've got the notebook right here. Can't get Del, he's on the street, but one of his guys has gone after him. There are a couple of squads waiting out on Chicago."

"Okay."

There was a moment of silence. Lucas took another corner and went around the block. "Uh, there's not much. Very small, barely see over the steering wheel. Indian. Maybe an older woman. She didn't seem young. Green car, older, a wagon, with white sidewall tires."

"Thanks. I'll get back to you."

He took another corner, then another, and came back up along the side of Gow's house. As he did, a man walked out of the house across the street from Gow's, leading a dog. Lucas stopped at the curb as the man strolled out to the sidewalk, looked both ways, then headed around the side of his house, the dog straining at the leash. Lucas thought about it, let the man get a full lot down the opposite block, then called Anderson.

"I need Del or a couple of narcs in plain cars."

"I got a guy looking for Del; we should have him in a minute."

"Soon as you can. I want them up the block from Gow's place, watching the front."

"I'll pass the word."

"And keep those squads on Chicago."

The dog was peeing on a telephone pole when Lucas pulled up next to the night walker. He got out of the car, his badge case in hand.

"Excuse me. I'm Lucas Davenport, a lieutenant with the Minneapolis Police Department. I need a little help."

"What d'you want?" the man asked curiously.

"Your neighbor across the street. Mrs. Gow. Does she live alone?"

"What'd she do?" the man asked.

"Maybe nothing at all . . ."

The man shrugged. "She usually does, but the last few days, there's been other people around. I never seen them, really. But people are coming and going."

"What kind of car does she drive?"

"Old Dodge wagon. Must be fifteen years old."

"What color?"

"Apple green. Ugly color. Never seen anything like it, except in those Dodges."

"Huh." Lucas could feel his heart pounding harder. "White sidewalls?"

"Yep. You don't see them like that anymore. Bet she don't drive a couple thousand miles a year. The tires are probably originals. What's she done?"

"Maybe nothing," Lucas said. "Thanks for your help. I'd appreciate it if you'd keep this to yourself."

As Lucas started back to the car, the man said, "Those other people . . . they left about five minutes ago. Somebody drove up in her car and somebody else opened the garage door, and one minute later, they left."

Lucas called Anderson: "I got something," he said. "I'm not sure what, but the Crows may be on the street."

"Sonofabitch. You think they're hitting somebody?"

"I don't know. Don't let those squads get away, though. I don't care what happens. And get me Del's man."

"I got Del. He was maybe a mile away, he oughta be there anytime."

"All right. Tell him I'll wait at Twenty-fourth and Bloomington, right by Deaconess Hospital."

Del was waiting when Lucas arrived. The street was empty, and Lucas crossed into the left lane until their cars were door to door. Both men rolled their windows down.

"Got something?"

"Could be heavy," Lucas said. "I think I got the Crows' hideout, but they're on the street."

"What do you want from me?"

"I was gonna ask for some surveillance help, but if the Crows are on the street . . . I'm going in. I need some backup."

Del nodded. "Let's do it."

"Let me introduce you to Lucy," Drake said. He turned toward the back and called, "Lucy? Darling?"

They were standing in front of the fireplace, glasses in their hands. A moment after he called, Lucy appeared from the back. She was tiny, blonde, shy, and wore a pink kimono.

"Come over here, darling, and meet a friend of mine," Drake said.

"Cop," Leo said.

"Shit. He's going in," Sam said.

Drake's house was on a long loop road, to the left. The cop had just turned into the loop, then stayed to the right. If he continued along the loop, he'd pass Drake's house on the way back out.

"We gotta wait," Sam said. He pointed at a supermarket parking lot. "Pull in there. We can watch for him to come out."

"What if Clay leaves?"

Aaron looked at his watch. "He's only been there a half-hour. He usually stays two or three. This is not something you do quick. Not if you can help it."

Lucas and Del left their cars just down the block, and Lucas led the way to the porch. Del took a short black automatic out of a hip holster and stood to one side of the door as Lucas knocked.

He knocked once, then again.

A woman's voice: "Who is it?"

Before Lucas could answer, Del piped up, in a childish falsetto, *"Star-Tribune."*

There was a moment's hesitation and then the door started to open. As it opened, Lucas realized that it was on a chain. A woman's eye appeared in the crack. Lucas said, "Police," and the woman screamed, "No," and tried to push the door shut. She was small and dark and not young, and Lucas knew for sure. As she tried to push the door shut he rocked back and kicked it; the chain ripped off and they were inside, the woman running awkwardly toward the back. Lucas was on her, punching her between the shoulder blades, and she went down on her face in the hallway. Del was braced in the entrance to the living room, his gun in front of him, scanning.

"You don't fuckin' move," Lucas snarled at the woman. "You don't fuckin' move, you hear?"

Lucas and Del went through the house in thirty seconds, rotating down the hallway, clearing out the two bedrooms, then taking the stairs, cautiously, ready . . . Nothing.

At the top, Lucas heard the woman on her feet, and as Del held the stairs, Lucas shouted, "Wait here," and ran back down. Gow was headed for the front door when Lucas hit her again. She yelped and went down, and he dragged her to a radiator and cuffed her to it. Del was still waiting at the top of the stairs; Lucas came and they cleaned out the second floor. Nobody.

Downstairs they checked the bedrooms again, this time for any sign of the Crows. It was all there: a stack of unmailed press releases, letters, two different sets of men's clothing.

"I'm gonna talk to this woman," Lucas told Del. "You shut the front door and call Anderson, tell him what we've got. Get a warrant down here, maybe we can finesse things later. And tell him we may want an ERU team for when the Crows come back."

While Del went to call, Lucas walked back to Barbara Gow, who was lying on her side with her knees up to her face, weeping. Lucas uncuffed her and prodded her back with his foot.

"Sit up," he said.

"Don't hurt me," she wailed.

"Sit the fuck up," Lucas said. "You're under arrest. Seven counts of first-degree murder. You have the right to remain silent . . ."

"I didn't do anything."

"You're an accomplice . . ." Lucas said, squatting next to her, his face two inches from hers. He was not quite shouting, and he deliberately let spittle rain on her face.

"I didn't do anything."

"Where are the Crows . . . ?"

"I don't know any Crows. . . ."

"Bullshit. All their stuff is in back." He grabbed her by the blouse and shook her.

"I don't know," she said. "I don't know where they went. They took my car."

"She's lying," Del said. Lucas looked up and found Del standing over them. His eyes were dilated and he hadn't shaved for several days. "Stay with her for just a second. I wanna run down to the bathroom."

Lucas waited, watching the woman's face. A few seconds later, they heard the bath water running.

"What're you going to do?" Lucas asked when Del returned. He tried to sound interested—curious—but not worried.

"She's got nice hot water," Del said. "So I thought maybe I'd give the bitch a bath."

"Shit, I wish I'd thought of that," Lucas said happily.

Gow tried to roll away from him but Del caught the old woman by the hair. "You know how many old women drown in the bathtub? Suck in that scalding hot water and can't get out?"

"It's a tragedy," Lucas said.

"Let me go," Gow screamed, struggling now. Del dragged her toward the hallway by the hair. She flailed at him, but he ignored it.

"There's some coffee in the kitchen," Del called. "Why don't you go heat up some water, we can have a cup. This'll only take a minute. She don't look too strong."

"They went to kill Clay," Gow blurted.

"Jesus Christ." Del let her go and the two men crouched over her.

"They can't get to him. He's got round-the-clock bodyguards," Lucas argued.

"He sneaks out," Gow said. "He has sex with little girls, so he sneaks out."

Lucas looked at Del: "Motherfucker. They don't crack the security. They get

Clay to come out. Call Anderson and have him get onto the feebs. Find out where Clay is. And get Daniel."

Del dashed down the hall toward the telephone and Lucas gripped the old woman's hair.

"Tell me the rest. I'll testify in court for you. I'll tell them you helped; it might get you off. Where'd they go?"

Tears ran down her face and she sobbed, unable to talk.

"Talk to me," Lucas screamed, shaking the old woman's head.

"There's a man named Christopher Drake. Corky Drake. He lives up in Kenwood somewhere," Barbara Gow sobbed. "Clay goes to his house for the girls."

Lucas let her go and ran into the kitchen, where Del was on the phone. "I gotta go," he shouted. "Stay with her. Tell Anderson I'll call in ten seconds, tell him I'll need those squads."

Lucas sprinted to the Porsche, cranked it, picked up the handset and called Dispatch.

"A Christopher Drake," he told the dispatcher. "In Kenwood. I need the address now."

Twenty seconds later, as he turned onto Franklin Avenue, he had it.

"I need everything you've got. No sirens, but make it fast," he told Dispatch.

Anderson came on: "I'm talking to Del, we're going out to the FBI now. How long before you make this Drake's place?"

Lucas ran a red light and calculated. "If I don't hit anything, about two minutes," he said. He crossed the center line into the left lane and blew past two cars, the speedometer nudging sixty.

The squad car came out of the loop road, turned away from them and kept going. Aaron grunted, checked his watch again and said, "Let's go."

Drake's house was a quarter-mile down the lane. They did a U-turn in front of the house, so the car would be pointed out, and left it on the street. The yards were wooded, and the brush would screen them as they approached the house.

"Let's get the tie," Sam said as they climbed out of the car.

Aaron looked up at the sky as Sam popped the tailgate. "Good moon for a killing," Aaron said.

In the soundproofed privacy of the bedroom, the girl dropped the kimono around her feet and slipped onto the bed. Lawrence Duberville Clay peeled off his underwear and slipped in beside her, and she put her arm over his chest.

"Smell so good," she said. He looked over her shoulder at the video camera and the monitor screen. The light was just right. It would be an evening to remember.


Leo held the cut-down shotgun by his side as they pulled the railroad tie out of the car and held it by the handles. A battering ram. Nearly a hundred pounds, swung hard, focused on a point no bigger than a hammerhead. Better than any sledgehammer made.

Swinging the tie, they moved swiftly through the dark into Drake's yard.

"Go through it one more time," Leo said.

Sam recited in a monotone. "Aaron and I swing it. When the door goes down, we drop it and you run right over it, freeze anyone inside. Aaron takes the ground floor, blocking anyone out, and you and I go up the stairs. There are four bedrooms up the stairs, and they'll be in one of them."

"Drop the tie, go in, freeze anyone, then Aaron takes over and we go up the stairs."

"Clay carries a gun; you've seen the pictures," Aaron said. He looked up at the moon. "So be careful."

They stayed in a screen of trees as they came up the drive, then broke across an open space to a lilac bush, paused to adjust their holds on the railroad tie.

"You got it?" Aaron asked.

"Let's go," said Sam.

Running awkwardly, they rushed at the door, then stopped at the last second and swung the tie as hard as they could. It hit the door two inches from the knob and blew it open as effectively as a stick of dynamite. They let go as the door flew open; the tie fell half inside, and Leo was in the living room. Drake was there, coming off the couch, a pearl-gray suit and pink open-necked shirt, his mouth open. Leo, his face twisted into a mask of hate, shoved the shotgun at him and said in a coarse whisper:

"Where is he?"

Integrity had never been one of Drake's burdens. "Up the stairs," he blurted. "First door on the left."

"If he's not there, motherfucker, you gonna be sucking on this shotgun," Leo snarled.

"He's there. . . ."

Aaron held Drake as Leo and Sam took the stairs, struggling with the railroad tie as they went, their footfalls muffled by the thick carpet. At the top, they looked at each other, and Leo held the shotgun over his head. They went at the bedroom door with the tie. The bedroom door was no more match for the ram than the front door had been. It blew open and Leo went through.

Music was playing from a stereo; the lights were low enough for comfort, bright enough for spectating. A video camera was mounted on a steel tripod, with a television flickering beside it. Clay was there, his flesh obscenely white, sluglike, on the red satin sheet. The girl was beside him, nearly as pale as he was, except for a streak of scarlet lipstick.

"Get away," Leo said to the girl, gesturing with the shotgun.

"Wait," said Clay. The girl rolled away from him and off the bed.

"Wait, for Christ's sakes," Clay said.

"On your feet," Leo said. "This is a citizen's arrest."

"What?"

"On your feet and turn around, Mr. Clay," Leo said. "If you don't, I swear to God I'll blow you to pieces."

Clay, frightened, crawled off the bed and turned. Sam slipped his pistol into his pocket, took out his obsidian knife and stepped behind him.

"We're going to handcuff you, Mr. Clay," Sam said. "Put your hands behind your back. . . ."

"You're the Crows. . . ."

"Yeah. We're the Crows."

"Do I know you? I've seen you? Your faces . . ."

Clay was facing curtains that covered windows overlooking the driveway. A set of headlights swept into the drive, then a set of red flashers.

"Cops," said Leo.

"We met a long time ago," Sam said. "In Phoenix."

Clay started to turn his head, recognition lighting his eyes, and Sam reached up from the other side, grabbed his hair and dragged the knife across his throat. Clay twisted away screaming, and the girl broke for the door. Blood pumped through Clay's hands and he fell faceup on the bed, trying to hold himself together. Sam shouted, "Let's go."

Leo shouted, "Run," and as Sam went, he stepped close to the supine Clay and fired the shotgun into his chest.

Lucas turned into the loop road fifty yards in front of the first cruiser. He had to slow to find the address, then saw Barbara Gow's wagon in the street and the open door of the white Colonial house. He slid into the circular drive, stood on the brake and piled out, the P7 in his hand. The cruiser was just behind him, and then there were more lights on the lane, more cops coming in. He waited just a second for the first cruiser and heard the shotgun roar. . . .

"Cops," Sam screamed from the top of the stairs, his scream punctuated by the shotgun blast. Both he and Aaron favored old-model .45s, and had them in their hands. The girl, nude, ran down the stairs, saw Aaron waiting and stopped. Sam pushed past her, with Leo just behind.

Drake had his hands on his head and began to back away. "Fucker," Aaron said, and shot him in the chest. Drake flipped back over a sofa and disappeared.

"Try the back?" Leo shouted.

"Fuck it," said Aaron. "Clean the driveway out with the shotgun, then get out of the way."

Leo ran to the door. The car's headlights were focused on it but he could see figures behind the lights. He fired three quick shots, emptying the gun, and ducked back inside as a hail of bullets tore through the doorway into the living room.

"Go out the back," Aaron said to him. He kissed Leo on the cheek, looked at his cousin.

"Time to die, you flatheaded motherfucker," Sam shouted.

The return fire from outside had stopped. There were shouts, and Sam lifted his head, smelling the perfume of the house. Then Aaron was out the door at a dead run, Sam a step behind, the .45s jumping in their hands.


Lucas looked at the cop and said, "Get somebody around back. They're in there, I just heard . . ."

He never finished the sentence. There was a shot inside the house, a pause, and then a shotgun opened from the doorway. The muzzle blast flickered like lightning in the dark and the cop who'd started for the back went down. More squads were roaring into the driveway, one sliding sideways as another cop went down.

Lucas fired a quick three shots at the doorway and started toward it as the gunner ducked inside. Then the Crows were there, coming out the door at a run, their pistols firing wildly. Lucas fired twice at the first one as the other cops opened up. The Crows were down a half-second later, bullets kicking up dirt around them, plucking at their shirts, their jeans, enough lead to kill a half-dozen men.


And then there was silence.

Then a few words, like morning birds outside a bedroom window. *"Jesus God,"* somebody was saying. *"Jesus God."*

Sirens. Static from the radios. More sirens. Lots of them. Lucas crouched behind the car.

"Where's the shotgun?" he screamed. "Anybody see the shotgun?"

A cop was crying for help, the pain on him. Another was a lump in the dirt.

"Who's around back?" somebody called.

"Nobody. Get somebody around back."

A uniform dashed into the headlights, stopped next to the cop who was lying still in the dirt, and began tugging him out of the light. Lucas stood, aiming his pistol through the doorway, and squeezed off two suppression shots.

"He's gone," the uniform screamed, holding the dead cop in his arms. "Jesus, where are the paramedics?"

More lights in the lane, then Sloan coming up the driveway.

"Heard you on the radio," he grunted. "What have we got?"

"Maybe a shotgun inside."

There was a figure at the door, and two or three separate voices screamed warnings.

"Hold it, hold it," somebody shouted.

The girl appeared in the doorway, her eyes as wide as a deer's, shambling out of the wreckage.

"Who's in there?" Lucas called as she came across the driveway.

"Nobody," she wailed. She half turned to the house as though she couldn't believe it. "Everybody's dead."

# 28

"I don't know what else we could have done," Lucas said. In his own ears, the words sounded like excuses, quick and chattery as if tumbling out of a teletype, harsh with guilt. "If we hadn't gone straight in, we'd have lost Clay for sure. We knew they weren't far in front of us."

"You did okay," Daniel said grimly. "It was that fuckin' Clay, sneaking out like that. The Crows must have known. They set him up, slicker'n shit. Fuckin' Wilson is dead, Belloo's maybe crippled, it's that fuckin' Clay's fault."

"It must have been Shadow Love with the shotgun," Lucas said. He was leaning against the wall, his hands in his pockets and his head down. His shirt was covered with blood. He thought it might be Belloo's. He was missing the heel of one shoe. Shot off? He wasn't sure. That foot hurt, but there were no wounds. Not a scratch. A uniformed captain, his face pale as the moon, stood down the hall and watched them talk. "He did Clay and Wilson and Belloo, all three. One of the Crows must have shot Drake. But that motherfucker Shadow Love, he caught us with that shotgun. . . ."

"The whole thing lasted no more than eight seconds," Daniel said. "That's what they're getting from the tapes. . . ."

"Christ . . ."

"The main thing is Shadow Love," Daniel said. "He must have gone out the back. We've got the neighborhood blocked off. We'll get him in the morning; I just hope he didn't get out before we set up the line."

"What if he's in somebody's house? What if he went in somewhere and he's got somebody's family on the wall?"

"We'll be going door to door."

"Motherfucker's a fruitcake and he's carrying a shotgun and we just killed his fathers. . . ."

They were standing in the antiseptic hallways of Hennepin Medical Center, outside the surgical suite, one set of doors closer to the operating rooms than was usually permitted. Two dozen family members, friends and cops were corralled one set of doors farther out, waiting for news.

And beyond the next set, a hundred newsmen, maybe more. Doctors and nurses shuttled in and out of the operating suite, half of them with no business there, but officiously correct in demeanor. They wanted to see what was going on.

Clay had been taken in, but he was gone; so was Drake, shot in the heart. The first cop shot was brain dead, but they had him on a respirator; the hospital was talking to his family about organ donations. The second cop was still on the table. A nurse had pointed out the doc working on Belloo, the same redheaded surgeon who'd done Lily. Two more surgeons joined her, and an hour after Belloo went on the table, she came through the doors into the waiting area.

"You guys are giving me more business than I need," she said grimly.

"What's the story?"

"It'll be a while before we know. We've got a neurosurgeon looking at some crap around his spinal cord. There's some bone splinters in there but he's still got function. . . ."

"He can walk?"

The surgeon shrugged. "He's going to lose something but not all of it. And we had to get a urologist down. A couple pellets went through a testicle."

Lucas and Daniel both winced. "Is he going to lose . . . ?"

"We're evaluating that. I don't know. He'd still be functional, even with one, but there's some plumbing in there. . . . Do you know if he has kids?"

"Yeah, three or four," said Daniel.

"Good," said the surgeon. She looked tired as she dumped her mask and gloves in the discard bin. "I better go talk to the family."

She was headed toward the family waiting area when the automatic doors swung open. The mayor and one of his aides came through, followed by the FBI's agent in charge.

"We gotta do something for the TV," the mayor snapped.

"I think we need more investigation . . ." the AIC said urgently.

"Bullshit, we got Davenport and a half-dozen cops saw the girl and we've got her statement and his body. There's no question. . . ."

"There's always a question," said the AIC.

"There's a videotape," said Daniel.

"Aw, Jesus," said the AIC. He turned to a hospital wall and leaned his head against it.

"We could deal," the mayor said to Daniel. "He was one of the administration's point men on crime. I don't know what we could get, but it'd be a lot. More urban renewal; new sewage treatment; our own air force; you name it."

Daniel shook his head. "No."

"Why not?" the AIC asked heatedly. "Why the fuck not? We stood down in that surveillance post after the fuckup with Bill Hood and we cut a deal. Remember what you said? You said, 'You always deal. Always.' "

"There's a corollary to that rule," Daniel said.

"What's that?"

"You always deal, except sometimes," Daniel said. He looked at the mayor. "This is one of those times."

The mayor nodded. "First, it just wouldn't be right."

"And second, we'd get caught," said Daniel. "You want to tell the TV, or you want me to?"

"You do it; I'm going to call somebody in the White House," the mayor said. "It's going to be bad, but there are levels of badness. Maybe I can cut a deal to make it less bad. . . ."

The AIC argued that the mayor should talk to the president before any announcement; the aide suggested that they had nothing to lose. Daniel pointed out that the discussion they were having could already bring big political trouble: they were talking about a conspiracy to cover up a crime. The politicians began backing away. The AIC still wanted to talk. As tempers got hotter, the night seemed to close in on Lucas, until he felt he might suffocate.

"I'm going," he told Daniel. "You don't need me and I need to sit down somewhere."

"All right." Daniel nodded. "But if you can't help thinking about it, think about Shadow Love."

Sloan was coming in as Lucas left.

"You okay?" Sloan asked.

"Yeah," Lucas said wearily. "Considering."

"How's Wilson?"

"Dead. They're selling off his heart and lungs and liver and kidneys and probably his dick. . . ."

"Jesus fuckin' Christ," Sloan blurted, appalled.

"Belloo's gonna make it. Might lose one of his balls."

"Jesus . . ." Sloan ran a hand through his hair. "You stop to see Lily?"

"No . . ."

"Look, man . . ." Sloan started.

He hesitated, and Lucas said, "What?"

"Do you feel bad about her now? With her husband here and all?"

Lucas thought about it for a second before he shook his head. "No," he said.

"Good," said Sloan. " 'Cause you shouldn't."

"Got my goddamn car shot up," Lucas said. "My fuckin' insurance agent is gonna jump out a window when he hears about it."

"I got no sympathy for you," Sloan said. "You're the luckiest motherfucker on the face of the earth. Cothron said you walked right into the Crows' guns, like Jesus walking across the water, and never anything happened."

"I can't remember too well," Lucas said. "It's just all fucked up in my head."

"Yeah. Well, take it easy."

"Sure." Lucas nodded and limped away down the hall.


The Porsche had three bullet holes in it, each in a separate piece of sheet metal. Lucas shook his head and climbed in.

The night was not quite cold. He ran down through the Loop, in sync with traffic lights, and made it out to the interstate without stopping. He was flying on automatic: east across the river, off at the Cretin Avenue exit, south down Cretin, right to Mississippi River Boulevard, south to home.

Jennifer was waiting.

Her car was in the driveway, a light was on in a window of the house. He pulled into the drive and jabbed the transmitter for the garage door opener. As he waited for the door to open, she came to the window and looked out. She had the baby on her arm.

"I freaked out," she said simply.

"I'm all right," he said. He was limping from the lost heel.

"How about the other guys?"

"One dead. One pretty busted up. The Crows are dead."

"So it's over."

"Not quite. Shadow Love got away."

They were staring at each other across the narrow space of the kitchen, Jennifer unconsciously bouncing the baby on her arm.

"We've got to talk. I can't just walk away from you. I thought I could, but I can't," she said.

"Man, Jen, I'm fuckin' crazy right now. I don't know what's going on. . . ." He looked around wildly, the peaceful neighborhood hovering around them like a joke. "Come on," he said. "Come on and talk. . . ."


Shadow Love had heard about the shoot-out on his radio, and now he waited in a thicket just over the lip of the slope that went down to the river. He'd planned to take Davenport when he got out of the car, but he hadn't counted on the automatic garage door opener. The door rolled up with Davenport still in the car, waiting. Shadow Love crouched, considered a dash across the street, but Davenport's house was set too far back from the road. He'd never make it.

When the door went down, Shadow Love walked fifty feet down the street, into the shadow of a spreading oak, and hurried across the street, through a corner of another yard and into the dark space beside Davenport's garage. Front doors were usually stout. Back doors, on garages, usually were not, since they didn't lead directly into the house. Shadow Love slipped around the garage to the back door and tested the knob. Locked.

The door had two panes of inset glass. Shadow Love peeled off his jacket, wrapped a sleeve around the middle joints of his fingers and pressed on the glass, hard, harder, until it cracked. There was almost no noise, but he paused, counted to three, then put more pressure along the crack. Another crack radiated out from the pressure point, then another. Two small pieces of glass fell almost noiselessly into the garage. Shadow Love stopped and checked the night around him: nothing moving, no *sense* of anything. Still using the jacket as padding, he pushed his little finger through the hole and carefully pulled two of the larger shards of glass from the door. In another minute, he had a hole large enough to reach through. He turned the lock knob and eased the door open.

The garage was not quite pitch dark: some light filtered in from the neighbor's house in back, enough that he could see large shapes, such as the car. With his left hand on the Porsche's warm hood, he moved carefully toward the door that led into the house. His right hand was wrapped around the pistol grip of the M-15. Once he was lined up on it, he would blow the knob off the door, and he'd be inside in a matter of a second or two. . . .

He never saw the shovel hanging from a nail on the garage wall. His sleeve hooked the blade and the shovel came down like a thunderclap, hammering into a garbage can, rattling off the car and onto the floor.


"What?" said Jennifer, starting at the noise.

Lucas knew. "Shadow Love," he whispered.


# 29

"The basement," Lucas snapped.

He grabbed Jennifer by the shoulder and threw her toward the stairs as he drew his gun. She wrapped her arms around Sarah and went down, taking three steps at a time and leaping the last four, staggering as she hit the bottom.


\*       \*       \*

In the garage, Shadow Love, stunned by the thunderclap of the falling shovel, brought the M-15 to his hip and fired three shots at the door's knob plate. One shot missed and blew through the door, into the kitchen cabinets and stove. The other two hit the knob plate, battering the door open. Half blinded by the flash from the weapon, his brain unconsciously registering the stink of the gunpowder, Shadow Love took two steps toward the door, then dropped to his face as three answering shots punched through the opening into the garage.

Lucas took the stairs a half-second behind Jennifer, but stopped three steps from the bottom. Jennifer was flattened against the wall, her arms wrapped around the baby, holding its head to her shoulder. Her face was distorted, as though she wanted to cry out but couldn't: it was a face from a macabre fun-house mirror. Lucas would remember it for the rest of his life, a split-second tableau of total terror. As the first of Shadow Love's shots smashed through the door, Sarah began to scream and Jennifer clutched her tighter, shrinking against the wall.

"Workroom," Lucas shouted, flattening himself against the stairwell wall, his gun hand extended up the stairs. "Get under the workbench."

Shadow Love's next two shots blew open the door from the garage, the slugs ricocheting through the kitchen. The door was at an angle to the stairway. Lucas fired three shots through the opening, hoping to catch Shadow Love coming in. There was a clatter in the garage, then a whip-quick series of flashes with the crack of the rifle. Lucas slid to the bottom of the stairs as the vinyl flooring came apart at the top of the stairs, the slugs slamming into the slanting headwall over the steps. Shooting from the garage, with the rifle, Shadow Love had the advantage: he could fire down with a good idea of where his shots were going, but Lucas couldn't see to shoot up. Shadow Love knew that. The garbage can rattled and Lucas risked a quick step up and put two more shots through the wall where the can was. Shadow Love opened up again. This time, the shots were angled down into the stairwell. Though they were still overhead, Lucas was forced out of the stairwell and into the workroom, with the door left open.

Shadow Love controlled the stairs.

The garage stank of burnt gunpowder, auto exhaust and gasoline from the lawn mower. Shadow Love, panting, squatted by the step into the house and tried to figure the shots he'd taken. Eight or nine, total: better count it as nine. The gun was loaded with a thirty-shot banana clip, and he had one more clip in his jacket. He might need everything he had—they might not be enough—if Davenport barricaded himself in the basement.

The black spot was there, and he could feel the anger cooking in his heart.

There was a very good chance that Davenport would kill him. The cop was on his home ground; he was well trained; and Shadow Love felt his luck had broken when he'd failed with the New York woman.

Still he had to try. The black spot grew, calling him in, and the anger rode into his veins like fire.


Jennifer was huddled under the workbench, wrapped protectively around Sarah, who was screaming beyond comfort.

"What are we doing?" she cried. "What are we doing?"

"The St. Paul cops should be coming in. We've only got to hold out a few minutes," Lucas said. "He'll have to make a move or get out. You stay put."

Lucas scrambled crabwise across the basement to his gun safe and spun the combination dial. He missed the second number, cursed and started over.


Upstairs, Shadow Love was torn between attack and retreat. He wouldn't stay free on the streets for long. He had no place to hide, his picture was everywhere. If he was careful, very careful, he might grab a car somewhere and make it out into the countryside. But with Clay's killing, the hunt would be remorseless. He would never have another chance at Davenport. Never have another chance to avenge his fathers. On the other hand, the hunter cop was armed and waiting in a house he knew intimately. An attack straight down the stairs would be suicide.

He held his breath, listening. No sirens. With the cool nights of October, windows were closed and furnaces were running; the firefight would not be particularly audible. On the other hand, Mississippi River Boulevard was a favorite jogging route. He'd be lucky if a passerby hadn't already heard the gunfire. Somehow, he had to pry Davenport out of the basement, and quickly. . . .

Squatting just outside the garage door, the M-15 pointed diagonally through the door at the stairwell, he noticed a telephone on the wall.

*Shit. An extension in the basement?*

Shadow Love crouched in a sprinter's position, listened for a second, then sprang through the open door into the kitchen, rolling when he hit the floor, coming up with the gun pointed at the stairwell. Nothing. He was inside.

With the gun leveled at the stairway door, he took a step backward, picked up the phone with his free hand. Just a dial tone. *Okay.* He let the phone dangle off the hook and eased back to the doorway, silent in his sneakers.

He needed a way to blow them out. Chancing a look down the stairwell, he stepped forward, feeling the vinyl kitchen floor creak below his weight. The floor. The floor would never stop a slug from an M-15. . . .

Moving in a gunman's crouch, he crossed quickly in front of the open stairway door into the living room, listened again, then took a half-dozen strides farther into the house. A picture window looked out toward the street. Nobody. Shadow Love pointed the rifle at the floor and pulled the trigger a half-dozen times.

Lucas pulled open the safe door as Shadow Love opened fire. The barrage came as a shock. Splinters exploded through the basement and shrapnel from the .223 slugs filled the air like hundreds of tiny bees. Jennifer screamed once and rolled, one arm wrapped over her head, her body covering the crying baby.

"The baby," she screamed. "The baby," and she plucked at the baby's back.

"Over here," Lucas shouted as the firing stopped. Changing magazines? "Jen, Jen, over here . . ."

Jennifer was partially sheltered by the workbench and sat sobbing, plucking at the baby. Lucas crawled across the floor and pulled her out and she flailed at him, resisting, not understanding.

"Into the safe, into the safe . . ."

Lucas dragged her and the screaming Sarah to the turn-of-the-century safe, threw the guns out on the floor and unceremoniously shoved them both inside.

"The baby," Jennifer screamed at him. She turned Sarah, and Lucas saw the splinters protruding from the baby's back.

"Don't touch them," he shouted. He and Jennifer were inches from each other, shouting, and Sarah was beyond tears: she'd reached the stage where she could barely breathe, her eyes wide with terror.

"Hold the door open an inch. An inch. An inch. You understand? You'll be okay," Lucas shouted. "Do you understand me?"

"Yes, yes . . ." Jennifer nodded, still wrapped around Sarah.

Lucas left them.

He owned twelve guns; he carried four away from the safe, along with three boxes of ammunition. He crawled into the space under the workbench where Jennifer had been. It would give him some protection from direct hits coming through the floor, and he could see the stairs. He first loaded the Browning Citori over and under; he used the twenty-gauge shotgun for hunting. His only shells were number-six shot, but that was fine. At a short distance, they would punch a convincing hole through a man's head.

Next he loaded the two Gold Cup .45s that he'd used in competition, seven rounds per magazine, one round in each chamber, both weapons cocked and locked. Then the P7, loaded with nine-millimeter rounds, waiting. As he finished loading the P7, he began to wonder if Shadow Love had fled: the firing had been stopped for nearly a minute. . . .

\*　　\*　　\*

Shadow Love could hear the woman screaming, could hear Davenport's voice, but not what he said. Damn walls, it was hard to tell where they were, but he thought to the right, and they sounded somehow distant, toward the far end of the basement. He watched the stairs for a few seconds, then took a fast dozen strides through the house, almost to the end, and once again began to pour gunfire through the floor. This time, though, he fired as he ran back to the basement door, blowing a trail of bullet holes through the carpet. . . .

In the basement, the metal fragments and splinters filled the air, plucking at Lucas' back and sleeve. He was hit and it hurt, but it felt superficial. He rubbed at his back and left a trail of pain where the slivers stuck through his shirt. If he stayed in the basement, he could be blinded. Shadow Love's last run had gone the whole length of the basement. Lucas got the Gold Cups ready. If he tried it again . . .

Shadow Love had been counting on the bullets to ricochet rather than fragment. He imagined the basement as a blizzard of wildly careening slugs. Pleased with the idea of making a trail the length of the house, he waited near the top of the stairs for a rush, waited, waited . . . Nothing. He refigured his ammunition supply. He'd fired at least twenty shots, he decided. He pulled the clip, slapped in the new one and checked the first. Six rounds left. Still plenty for a fight.

He waited another few seconds, then hurried again through the house, picked out a new pattern and raced back toward the stairwell, firing as he went. He was almost at the stairs when the rug suddenly popped up once, then again, not six feet away, and he realized that Davenport was shooting back through the floor, something big, something coming up through the carpet and into the ceiling, close, and Shadow Love dove into the garage. . . .

Lucas watched the firing pattern develop, tried to anticipate where Shadow Love would move and fired back with one of the .45s. He had little hope of hitting him, but he thought it might force Shadow Love to stop firing through the floor.

As the firing run ended at the back of the house, Lucas stood and walked quickly across the width of the basement to the safe.

"Jen, Jen?"

"What?"

"The next time he fires through the floor, I'm going to pull the circuit breaker and try the stairs. The lights will be out. Stay cool."

"Okay." The baby was gasping. Jennifer now sounded remote and cold; she had it under control.

One of the .45s was almost empty. Lucas laid it on the floor, stuck the other in his pants pocket with the butt sticking out, and crossed the basement floor and waited, the shotgun pointing at the base of the stairs, the switch box open.

Shooting through the floor wasn't good enough: Shadow Love wouldn't know when or if Davenport was hit, and his time must be running out. The black spot, larger, pressed against his consciousness. Attack now. He had to attack.

The door to the garage was still open, and in the shaft of light coming from the kitchen, he saw the gas can for the lawn mower.

"Motherfucker," he whispered. He glanced at the stairwell, groped for a minute, found the switch for the garage light and turned it on.

There was a rack of shelves next to the door, with a variety of bottles, mostly plastic. One, containing a tree-borer insecticide, was made of brown glass. Keeping the M-15 pointed at the stairwell, Shadow Love unscrewed the top of the insecticide bottle, turned it upside down and drained it. When it was empty, he stepped over to the gas can, picked it up, then stepped back to a position that would keep the stairwell covered. Moving as quickly as he could, he filled the quart bottle with gasoline, then looked around for a plug. Newspaper. There were bundles of newspapers along the garage wall. He ripped off a sheet of paper, soaked it in gasoline and plugged the neck of the bottle.

When he was ready, he vaulted through the door, past the open stairwell and into the living room. From there he could lob the bottle down the stairs to the tiled floor at the bottom.

"Hey, Davenport," he yelled.

No answer. He lit the newspaper with a cigarette lighter, and it flamed up.

"Hey, Davenport, suck on this," he yelled, and threw the bomb down the stairs. It hit and smashed, the gasoline igniting in a fireball. Shadow Love braced himself against the living room wall, waiting.

". . . suck on this," Shadow Love yelled, and a bottle came down the stairs. There was a *crack* and a *whoosh* and the gasoline went up in a fireball.

"Sonofabitch," Lucas said. He looked around wildly and spotted a gallon paint can. He pulled the main circuit breaker, throwing the house into darkness, except for the light from the fire. Dashing across the basement floor, he grabbed the paint can, vaulted the fire at the base of the stairs, fired one barrel of the shotgun up the stairs and went up them two at a time. Three steps from the top, he hurled the paint can through the door.

\*    \*    \*

The sudden and virtually complete darkness disoriented Shadow Love for a moment, and then Davenport was on the stairs, coming, and Shadow Love, not waiting, fired a shot through the wall from the living room, then tracked the dimly seen movement out of the stairwell and fired once, the muzzle blast blinding him, firing again, seeing the can and thinking, *No. . . .*

The first shot nearly took Lucas' head; it sprayed his face with plaster and blinded him in one eye. The second shattered the paint can. The third gave him a muzzle blast to follow. Lucas fired once with the shotgun, panning behind the blast; he dropped the long gun and pulled the .45.

Thinking, *No,* Shadow Love saw Davenport and dragged the muzzle of the M-15 around, the movement taking an eternity, then Davenport's face froze as though caught by a strobe light, but it was no strobe, it was the flash from a shotgun muzzle reaching out, and Shadow Love soaked up the impact as if he had been hit in the side with a baseball bat. He flattened back against the wall and rebounded, still desperately struggling to bring the muzzle around, still trying, his finger closing spasmodically on the trigger. . . .

Lucas saw Shadow Love in the flash of the shotgun, just the pale eyes, saw the M-15 coming around, the muzzle flash, the bullet going somewhere, and then he was firing the .45, and Shadow Love went over, falling, tumbling. The M-15 stuttered again, three shots that went through the ceiling, and Lucas fired again and again and again, and then the pain and the smell hit him, and he turned, seeing the fire on his leg, and he rolled into the kitchen, rolling it out. . . .

Shadow Love couldn't move. He didn't hurt, but he couldn't move. He couldn't sit up. He couldn't move the gun. *I'm dying; why's my mind so clear? Why's it all so clear?*

Lucas crawled across the kitchen floor in the dark and groped under the sink for the fire extinguisher, thinking that it was old and might not work. He pulled the seals and squeezed the trigger, and it worked, spraying a stinging foam on his leg, wiping out the small tongues of flame that crawled over the surface of his trousers. He took his hand off the trigger and dragged himself back to the stairs. The gasoline was still burning and the carpet had caught fire, but nothing else. He hosed the fire down, wiped it out, then crossed in the dark to the switch box and turned the lights on.

Jennifer: "Lucas?"

"We're all right," Lucas said, his voice creaking. The stench of gasoline, burnt carpet, gunpowder and fire-extinguisher fluid was almost overpowering. He had to hold on to the doorjamb to keep himself upright. "But I'm hurt."

He staggered back across the basement and pulled himself up the stairs and looked carefully around the corner. Shadow Love was lying on the rug like a pile of dirty clothing. Lucas stepped over to him, keeping the .45 centered on the man's chest, and kicked the M-15 across the room.

He felt Jennifer behind him.

"You're a mean sonofabitch," Shadow Love groaned. Nothing moved but his lips.

"Die, motherfucker," Lucas croaked.

"Is he dead?" Jennifer asked.

"In a few minutes," Lucas said.

"Lucas, we gotta call . . ."

Lucas grabbed Jennifer's coat and sank to the floor, pulling her down with him. She had the baby, who now looked almost sleepy.

"Lucas . . ."

"Give him a few minutes," Lucas said. He looked at Shadow Love. "Die, motherfucker," he said again.

"Lucas," Jennifer screamed, trying to pull away, "we got to call an ambulance."

Lucas looked at her and shook his head. "Not yet."

Jennifer tore at her coat, but Lucas wrapped her up and pinned her on the floor. "Lucas . . ." She beat at him with her free hand and the baby started to whimper again.

"Who told? Who gave us away?" Shadow Love coughed. Still no pain, only a growing cold. Davenport was a *mean* sonofabitch, Shadow Love thought.

"You did," Lucas snapped.

"I did?"

"Yeah. Your mom's grave. You had them send the bills to Barbara Gow."

"I?" Shadow Love asked again. As he exhaled, a blood bubble formed on his lips and then burst. The salty taste of the blood was his last sensation.

"Die, motherfucker," Lucas said.

He was talking to a dead man. After another moment, with no further movement from Shadow Love, Lucas released Jennifer. She was looking at him in horror.

"Call the cops," he said.

# 30

"You got him?" Daniel asked.

"He's dead," Lucas said. "I'm looking at him," he explained, and told him that Jennifer and the baby had been injured, but the injuries didn't appear serious.

"How bad are you?"

"My leg's burned. I'm full of splinters. My house is fucked up," Lucas said.

"So take the day off," Daniel said. His voice was flat, not funny.

"Pretty fuckin' funny," Lucas said coldly.

"What do you want me to say? You're so fucked up I don't know why you're talking to me on the telephone."

"I needed to tell somebody," Lucas said. He looked out of the kitchen to the open front door. After Jennifer had called 911, she'd stalked past him, out the door and into the yard to wait. When he'd called after her, she'd refused to look at him.

"Get your ass to the hospital," Daniel said. "I'll see you there in ten minutes."


Jennifer had a sliver taken from her arm. The anchor from TV3 called her at the hospital and Jennifer told him to go fuck himself.

The baby had a half-dozen splinters in her back. The docs said that by the time she was old enough to be told about the fight, the scars would be virtually invisible.

Lucas spent the night, the next day and part of the following day at Ramsey Medical Center, first receiving treatment for the burns on his leg and the plaster particles in his right eye. He wouldn't need skin grafts, but it was a near thing. The plaster was washed out: the eye would heal. When the docs had finished with the eye, a physician's assistant went to work on the splinters. They weren't in deep, but there were dozens of them, from his thigh across his butt and up his back and his left arm.

He got out early the second afternoon, still wearing a massive gauze bandage that covered his eye, and went to look at his house. The insurance man, he decided, would jump out of his window twice when he saw it.

Late that night, after a number of calls to clear the way, he drove to Hennepin Medical Center and took a back elevator to the surgical floor. At ten minutes past midnight, he got out of the elevator and walked down a tiled corridor to a nursing station, where he found his friend.

"Lucas," she said, "I told her you were coming. She's still awake."

"Is she alone?"

"Do you mean, 'Has her husband gone?' Yeah, he's gone," the nurse said, grinning wryly.

A younger nurse, barely out of her teens, leaned on the station counter and said, "The guy is really something else. He reads to her, gets videos for her, gets snacks. He's here all the time. I've never seen anybody so . . ." She groped for the word. *". . . faithful."*

"Just like my cocker spaniel," said the older nurse.


Lily was propped up in bed, watching the Letterman show.

"Hey," she said. She touched the remote and Letterman winked out. Her face was pale, but she talked easily. "You got him. And he got you. You look like shit."

"Thanks," Lucas said. He kissed her on the lips and eased himself into the bedside chair. "I got him more."

"Mmm," she said. "The legend of Lucas Davenport grows another couple of inches."

"So how do you feel?" Lucas asked.

"Not too bad, as long as I don't laugh or sneeze," Lily said. She looked tired, but not sick. "My ribs are messed up. They had me walking around today. It hurt a lot."

"How much longer will you be here?"

Lily hesitated, then said, "I get out tomorrow. They're going to brace me up. I'm taking Andretti's plane to New York tomorrow afternoon."

Lucas frowned and sat back in the chair. "That's pretty quick."

"Yes." There was another silence, then Lily said, "I can't help it."

Lucas looked down at her. "I think we have some unfinished business. Somehow." He shrugged. There was another space of silence.

"I don't know," she said finally.

"David?" Lucas asked. "Do you love him?"

"I must," she said.

A while later she said, "Will you get back with Jennifer?"

Lucas shook his head. "I don't know. She's . . . kind of freaked out after what happened in the house. I'll see her tomorrow. Maybe."

"Don't come see me off," Lily said. "I don't know if I could handle things, if you and David were there at the same time."

"Okay," Lucas said.

"And could you . . ."

"What?"

"Could you leave?" she said, in a tiny, distant voice that squeaked toward despair. "If you stay any longer I'll cry, and crying hurts. . . ."

Lucas stood awkwardly, shuffled his feet, then leaned over and kissed her again. She caught his shirt in her hand, pulling him, and the kiss went on, fiercer, with heat, until suddenly she let go and instead of pulling him, pushed against his chest.

"Get the fuck out of here, Davenport," she said. "We can't start this again, God damn it, get the fuck out of here."

"Lily . . ."

"Lucas, please . . ."

He nodded and took a breath, let it go. "See you." He couldn't think of anything else to say. He backed out of the hospital room, looking into her eyes until the swinging door flapped shut.

At the nurses' desk, he asked his friend what time Lily would check out. Ten o'clock, he was told, with an ambulance scheduled to drive to the St. Paul municipal airport, where she would be loaded into a private jet.


Lucas drove out to the airport the next morning in his Ford four-by-four, and sat and watched as Lily was lifted from the ambulance and wheeled in a chair through the gate to the waiting jet. David bent over her, still wearing the blue seersucker suit, his hair rumpled in the wind. He looked like an academic. David.

They had to carry Lily up the steps to the jet. As they picked her up, Lucas felt her eyes on him, but she never raised a hand. She looked at him for three seconds, five, and then was gone.

The jet left and Lucas rolled out of the airport toward the Robert Street bridge.


He talked to Jennifer that afternoon. She wanted to set up a visitation schedule, she said, so Lucas could see Sarah. Lucas said he wanted to talk. She asked if Lily was gone and Lucas said yes. She wasn't sure if she wanted to talk, Jennifer said, but she would meet him. Not today, not tomorrow. Sometime soon. Next week, next month. She couldn't forget about those last minutes at the house, when Shadow Love was dying, the baby was hurt, and Lucas wouldn't let her call. . . . She was trying to forget, but she couldn't. . . .


That was Thursday. He went to the games group that night, and played. Elle asked him about the shotgun. It was gone, he said. He hadn't felt its touch since the shoot-out. He felt fine, he said, but he thought he might be lying.

Everything should have been fine, but it didn't feel quite right. He felt as though he were in the last hours of a prolonged journey on speed, in the mental territory where everything has more contrast than it does in real life, where buildings overhang in a threatening way, where cars move too fast, where people talk too loud, where sideways looks in bars can mean trouble. That lasted through the weekend, and began to fade early in the next week.

A little more than three weeks after the shoot-out, on a Saturday afternoon, Lucas sat in an easy chair and watched an Iowa–Notre Dame football game. Notre Dame was losing and no amount of prayer would help. It was a relief when the phone rang. He picked it up and heard the hiss of the long-distance satellite relay.

"Lucas?" Lily, her voice soft and husky.

"Lily? Where are you?"

"I'm at home. I'm looking out the window."

"What? Out the window?" He flashed on the first time he'd seen her in the hallway at the police station: her dark eyes, her hair slightly askew, strands of it falling across her graceful neck. . . .

"David and the boys are down in the street, loading the van. They're leaving for Fort Lauderdale, on a father-son big-game fishing trip. First time for the boys . . ."

"Lily . . ."

"Lucas, Jesus, I'm starting to cry. . . ."

"Lily . . ."

"They'll be gone for a week, Lucas—my husband and the boys," she groaned. "Ah, fuck, Davenport, this is so fuckin' miserable. . . ."

"What? What?"

"Can you come to New York?" Her voice had gone rough, sensual, dark. "Can you come in tomorrow?"

# In the End...

Leo climbed the dark side of Bear Butte, through the loose rubble, through the fine black sand, slipping at times, using his hands, moving steadily toward the peak.

The night still gripped the world when he reached the top. He eased himself down on a convenient hump, took the blanket-roll off his shoulders and wrapped the rough army wool around himself.

To the south, he could see the lights of Sturgis and I-90, and beyond that, the Stygian darkness of the Black Hills. In every other direction, the only break in the night came from yard lights on the scattered ranches.

The sunrise was spectacular when it came.

In the west, the stars were as bright and as profuse as ever; in the east, there was a growing pale light at the knife-edged horizon. Suddenly, with the unexpectedness of a shooting star, there was a flame at the horizon, a flowing golden presence as the world turned into the sun.

The sunlight touched the top of the butte long before it flooded the flatlands, so from the top he could watch the dawn racing toward him, rippling over the empty countryside below. Leo sat with the blanket around his shoulders, his eyes half closed. When the light crossed through the base of the butte, he sighed, turned and looked west, watching the day chase the night into Wyoming.

There was a lot to do.

A lot of talk about the Crows and about Shadow Love.

Legends to build.

Leo said a quick prayer and started down. The last of the stars were going and he looked up at them as he dropped over the crest.

"See you guys," he said. "Flatheaded motherfuckers."

# EYES OF PREY

# 1

Carlo Druze was a stone killer.

He sauntered down the old, gritty sidewalk with its cracked, uneven paving blocks, under the bare-branched oaks. He was acutely aware of his surroundings. Back around the corner, near his car, the odor of cigar smoke hung in the cold night air; a hundred feet farther along, he'd touched a pool of fragrance, deodorant or cheap perfume. A Mötley Crüe song beat down from a second-story bedroom: plainly audible on the sidewalk, it had to be deafening inside.

Two blocks ahead, to the right, a translucent cream-colored shade came down in a lighted window. He watched the window, but nothing else moved. A vagrant snowflake drifted past, then another.

Druze could kill without feeling, but he wasn't stupid. He took care: he would not spend his life in prison. So he strolled, hands in his pockets, a man at his leisure. Watching. Feeling. The collar of his ski jacket rose to his ears on the sides, to his nose in the front. A watch cap rode low on his forehead. If he met anyone—a dog-walker, a night jogger—they'd get nothing but eyes.

From the mouth of the alley, he could see the target house and the garage behind it. Nobody in the alley, nothing moving. A few garbage cans, like battered plastic toadstools, waited to be taken inside. Four windows were lit on the ground floor of the target house, two more up above. The garage was dark.

Druze didn't look around; he was too good an actor. It wasn't likely that a neighbor was watching, but who could know? An old man, lonely, standing at his window, a linen shawl around his narrow shoulders . . . Druze could see him in his mind's eye, and was wary: the people here had money, and Druze was a stranger in the dark. An out-of-place furtiveness, like a bad line on the stage, would be noticed. The cops were only a minute away.

With a casual step, then, rather than a sudden move, Druze turned into the darker world of the alley and walked down to the garage. It was connected to the house by a glassed-in breezeway. The door at the end of the breezeway would not be locked; it led straight into the kitchen.

"If she's not in the kitchen, she'll be in the recreation room, watching television," Bekker had said. Bekker had been aglow, his face pulsing with the heat of uncontrolled pleasure. He'd drawn the floor plan on a sheet of notebook paper and traced the hallways with the point of his pencil. The pencil had trembled on the paper, leaving a shaky worm trail in graphite. "Christ, I wish I could be there to see it."


Druze took the key out of his pocket, pulled it out by its string. He'd tied the string to a belt loop, so there'd be no chance he'd lose the key in the house. He reached out to the doorknob with his gloved left hand, tried it. Locked. The key opened it easily. He shut the door behind him and stood in the dark, listening. A scurrying? A mouse in the loft? The sound of the wind brushing over the shingles. He waited, listening.

Druze was a troll. He had been burned as a child. Some nights, bad nights, the memories ran uncontrollably through his head, and he'd doze, wretchedly, twisting in the blankets, knowing what was coming, afraid. He'd wake in his childhood bed, the fire on him. On his hands, his face, running like liquid, in his nose, his hair, his mother screaming, throwing water and milk, his father flapping his arms, shouting, ineffectual . . .

They hadn't taken him to the hospital until the next day. His mother had smeared lard on him, hoping not to pay, as Druze howled through the night. But in the morning light, when they'd seen his nose, they took him.

He was four weeks in the county hospital, shrieking with pain as the nurses put him through the baths and the peels, as the doctors did the skin transplants. They'd harvested the skin from his thighs—he remembered the word, all these years later, *harvested,* it stuck in his mind like a tick—and used it to patch his face.

When they'd finished he looked better, but not good. The features of his face seemed fused together, as though an invisible nylon stocking were pulled over his head. His skin was no better, a patchwork of leather, off-color, pebbled, like a quilted football. His nose had been fixed, as best the doctors could, but it was too short, his nostrils flaring straight out, like black headlights. His lips were stiff and thin, and dried easily. He licked them, unconsciously, his tongue flicking out every few seconds with a lizard's touch.

The doctors had given him the new face, but his eyes were his own.

His eyes were flat black and opaque, like weathered paint on the eyes of a cigar-store Indian. New acquaintances sometimes thought he was blind, but he was not. His eyes were the mirror of his soul: Druze hadn't had one since the night of the burning. . . .

\*      \*      \*

The garage was silent. Nobody called out, no telephone rang. Druze tucked the key into his pants pocket and took a black four-inch milled-aluminum penlight out of his jacket. With the light's narrow beam, he skirted the car and picked his way through the litter of the garage. Bekker had warned him of this: the woman was a gardener. The unused half of the garage was littered with shovels, rakes, hoes, garden trowels, red clay pots, both broken and whole, sacks of fertilizer and partial bales of peat moss. A power cultivator sat next to a lawn mower and a snowblower. The place smelled half of earth and half of gasoline, a pungent, yeasty mixture that pulled him back to his childhood. Druze had grown up on a farm, poor, living in a trailer with a propane tank, closer to the chicken coop than the main house. He knew about kitchen gardens, old, oil-leaking machinery and the stink of manure.

The door between the garage and the breezeway was closed but not locked. The breezeway itself was six feet wide and as cluttered as the garage. "She uses it as a spring greenhouse—watch the tomato flats on the south side, they'll be all over the place," Bekker had said. "You'll need the light, but she won't be able to see it from either the kitchen or the recreation room. Check the windows on the left. That's the study, and she could see you from there—but she won't be in the study. She never is. You'll be okay."

Bekker was a meticulous planner, delighted with his own precise work. As he led Druze through the floor plan with his pencil, he'd stopped once to laugh. His laugh was his worst feature, Druze decided. Harsh, scratching, it sounded like the squawk of a crow pursued by owls. . . .

Druze walked easily through the breezeway, stepping precisely toward the lighted window in the door at the end of the passage. He was bulky but not fat. He was, in fact, an athlete: he could juggle, he could dance, he could balance on a rope; he could jump in the air and click his heels and land lightly enough that the audience could hear the *click* alone, like a spoken word. Midway through, he heard a voice and paused.

A voice, singing. Sweet, naive, like a high-school chorister's. A woman, the words muffled. He recognized the tune but didn't know its name. Something from the sixties. A Joan Baez song maybe. The focus was getting tighter. He didn't doubt that he could do her. Killing Stephanie Bekker would be no more difficult than chopping off a chicken's head or slitting the throat of a baby pig. Just a shoat, he said to himself. It's all meat. . . .

Druze had done another murder, years earlier. He'd told Bekker about it, over a beer. It wasn't a confession, simply a story. And now, so many years later, the killing seemed more like an accident than a murder. Even less than that: like a scene from a half-forgotten drive-in movie, a movie where you couldn't remember the end. A girl in a New York flophouse. A hooker maybe, a druggie for sure. She gave him some shit. Nobody cared, so he killed her. Almost as an experiment, to see if it would rouse some feeling in him. It hadn't.

He never knew the hooker's name, doubted that he could even find the flophouse, if it still existed. At this date, he probably couldn't figure out what week of the year it had been: the summer, sometime, everything hot and stinking, the smell of spoiled milk and rotting lettuce in sidewalk dumpsters . . .

"Didn't bother me," he had told Bekker, who pressed him. "It wasn't like . . . Shit, it wasn't like anything. Shut the bitch up, that's for sure."

"Did you hit her? In the face?" Bekker had been intent, the eyes of science. It was, Druze thought, the moment they had become friends. He remembered it with perfect clarity: the bar, the scent of cigarette smoke, four college kids on the other side of the aisle, sitting around a pizza, laughing at inanities . . . Bekker had worn an apricot-colored mohair sweater, a favorite, that framed his face.

"Bounced her off a wall, swinging her," Druze had said, wanting to impress. Another new feeling. "When she went down, I got on her back, got an arm around her neck, and *jerk* . . . that was it. Neck just went pop. Sounded like when you bite into a piece of gristle. I put my pants on, walked out the door. . . ."

"Scared?"

"No. Not after I was out of the place. Something that simple . . . what're the cops going to do? You walk away. By the time you're down the block, they got no chance. And in that fuckin' place, they probably didn't even find her for two days, and only then 'cause of the heat. I wasn't *scared,* I was more like . . . hurried."

"That's something." Bekker's approval was like the rush Druze got from applause, but better, tighter, more concentrated. Only for him. He had gotten the impression that Bekker had a confession of his own but held it back. Instead the other man had asked, "You never did it again?"

"No. It's not like . . . I enjoy it."

Bekker had sat staring at him for a moment, then had smiled. "Hell of a story, Carlo."


He hadn't felt much when he'd killed the girl. He didn't feel much now, ghosting through the darkened breezeway, closing in. Tension, stage fright, but no distaste for the job.

Another door waited at the end of the passage, wooden, with an inset window at eye level. If the woman was at the table, Bekker said, she would most likely be facing away from him. If she was at the sink, the stove or the refrigerator, she wouldn't be able to see him at all. The door would open quietly enough, but she would feel the cold air if he hesitated.

*What was that song?* The woman's voice floated around him, an intriguing whisper in the night air. Moving slowly, Druze peeked through the window. She wasn't at the table: nothing there but two wooden chairs. He gripped the doorknob solidly, picked up a foot, wiped the sole of his shoe on the opposite pantleg, then repeated the move with the other foot. If the gym shoe treads had picked up any small stones, they would give him away, rattling on the tile floor. Bekker had suggested that he wipe, and Druze was a man who valued rehearsal.

His hand still on the knob, he twisted. The knob turned silently under his glove, as slowly as the second hand on a clock. The door was on a spring, and would ease itself shut. . . . And she sang: Something, Angelina, *ta-dum, Angelina.* Good-bye, Angelina? She was a true soprano, her voice like bells. . . .

The door was as quiet as Bekker had promised. Warm air pushed into his face like a feather cushion; the sound of a dishwasher, and Druze was inside and moving, the door closed behind him, his shoes silent on the quarry tile. Straight ahead was the breakfast bar, white-speckled Formica with a single short-stemmed rose in a bud vase at the far end, a cup and saucer in the center and, on the near end, a green glass bottle. A souvenir from a trip to Mexico, Bekker had said. Hand-blown, and heavy as stone, with a sturdy neck.

Druze was moving fast now, to the end of the bar, an avalanche in black, the woman suddenly there to his left, standing at the sink, singing, her back to him. Her black hair was brushed out on her shoulders, a sheer silken blue negligee falling gently over her hips. At the last instant she sensed him coming, maybe felt a rush in the air, a coldness, and she turned.

*Something's wrong:* Druze was moving on Bekker's wife, too late to change course, and he knew that something was wrong. . . .


*Man in the house. In the shower. On his way.*

*Stephanie Bekker felt warm, comfortable, still a little damp from her own shower, a bead of water tickling as it sat on her spine between her shoulder blades. . . . Her nipples were sore, but not unpleasantly. He'd shaven, but not recently enough. . . . She smiled. Silly man, must not have nursed enough as a baby . . .*

*Stephanie Bekker felt the cool air on her back and turned to smile at her lover. Her lover wasn't there; Death was. She said, "Who?" and it was all there in her mind, like a fistful of crystals: the plans for the business, the good days at the lakes, the cocker spaniel she had had as a girl, her father's face lined with pain after his heart attack, her inability to have children . . .*

*And her home: the kitchen tile, the antique flour bins, the wrought-iron pot stands, the single rose in the bud vase, red as a drop of blood . . .*
*Gone.*

Something wrong . . .

"Who?" she said, not loud, half turning, her eyes widening, a smile caught on her face. The bottle whipped around, a Louisville Slugger in green glass. Her hand started up. Too late. Too small. Too delicate.

The heavy bottle smashed into her temple with a wet crack, like a rain-soaked newspaper hitting a porch. Her head snapped back and she fell, straight down, as though her bones had vaporized. The back of her head slammed the edge of the counter, pitching her forward, turning her.

Druze was on her, smashing her flat with his weight, his hand on her chest, feeling her nipple in his palm.

Hitting her face and her face and her face . . .

The heavy bottle broke, and he paused, sucking air, his head turned up, his jaws wide, changed his grip and smashed the broken edges down through her eyes. . . .

"Do it too much," Bekker had urged. He'd been like a jock, talking about a three-four defense or a halfback option, his arm pumping as though he was about to holler *"Awright!"* . . . "Do it like a junkie would do it. Christ, I wish I could be there. And get the eyes. Be sure you get the eyes."

"I know how to do it," Druze had said.

"But you must get the eyes. . . ." Bekker had had a little white dot of drying spittle at the corner of his mouth. That happened when he got excited. "Get the eyes for me. . . ."

Something wrong.

There'd been another sound here, and it had stopped. Even as he beat her, even as he pounded the razor-edged bottle down through her eyes, Druze registered the negligee. She wouldn't be wearing this on a cold, windy night in April, alone in the house. Women were natural actors, with an instinct for the appropriate that went past simple comfort. She wouldn't be wearing this if she were alone. . . .

He hit her face and heard the thumping on the stairs, and half turned, half stood, startled, hunched like a golem, the bottle in his gloved hand. The man came around the corner at the bottom of the stairs, wrapped in a towel. Taller than average, too heavy but not actually fat. Balding, fair wet hair at his temples, uncombed. Pale skin, rarely touched by sunlight, chest hair gone gray, pink spots on his shoulders from the shower.

There was a frozen instant, then the man blurted "Jesus" and bolted. Druze took a step after him, quickly, off balance. The blood on the kitchen tile was almost invisible, red on red, and he slipped, his feet flying from beneath him. He landed back-down on the woman's head, her pulped features imprinting themselves on his black jacket. The man, Stephanie Bekker's lover, was up the stairs. It was an old house and the doors were oak. If he locked himself in a bedroom, Druze would not get through the door in a hurry. The man might already be dialing 911. . . .

Druze dropped the bottle, as planned, and turned and trotted out the door. He was halfway down the length of the breezeway when it slammed behind him, a report like a gunshot, startling him. *Door,* his mind said, but he was running now, scattering the tomato plants. His hand found the penlight as he cleared the breezeway. With the light, he was through the garage in two more seconds, into the alley, slowing himself. *Walk. WALK.*

In another ten seconds he was on the sidewalk, thick, hunched, his coat collar up. He got to his car without seeing another soul. A minute after he left Stephanie Bekker, the car was moving. . . .

*Keep your head out of it.*

Druze did not allow himself to think. Everything was rehearsed, it was all very clean. Follow the script. Stay on schedule. Around the lake, out to France Avenue to Highway 12, back toward the loop to I-94, down 94 to St. Paul.

Then he thought:

He saw my face. And who the fuck was he? So round, so pink, so startled. Druze smacked the steering wheel once in frustration. *How could this happen? Bekker so smart . . .*

There was no way for Druze to know who the lover was, but Bekker might know. He should have some ideas, at least. Druze glanced at the car clock: 10:40. Ten minutes before the first scheduled call.

He took the next exit, stopped at a SuperAmerica store and picked up the plastic baggie of quarters he'd left on the floor of the car: he hadn't wanted them to clink when he went into Bekker's house. A public phone hung on an exterior wall, and Druze, his index finger in one ear to block the street noise, dialed another public phone, in San Francisco. A recording asked for quarters and Druze dropped them in. A second later, the phone rang on the West Coast. Bekker was there.

"Yes?"

Druze was supposed to say one of two words, "Yes" or "No," and hang up. Instead he said, "There was a guy there."

"What?" He'd never heard Bekker surprised, before this night.

"She was fuckin' some guy," Druze said. "I came in and did her and the guy came right down the stairs on top of me. He was wearing a towel."

"What?" More than surprised. He was stunned.

"Wake up, for Christ's fuckin' sake. Stop saying 'What?' We got a problem."

"What about . . . the woman?" Recovering now. Mentioning no names.

"She's a big fuckin' Yes. But the guy saw me. Just for a second. I was wearing the ski jacket and the hat, but with my face . . . I don't know how much was showing. . . ."

There was a long moment of silence; then Bekker said, "We can't talk about it. I'll call you tonight or tomorrow, depending on what happens. Are you sure about . . . the woman?"

"Yeah, yeah, she's a *Yes*."

"Then we've done that much," Bekker said, with satisfaction. "Let me go think about the other."

And he was gone.

Driving away from the store, Druze hummed, harshly, the few bars of the song: *Ta-dum, Angelina, good-bye, Angelina* . . . That wasn't right, and the goddamned song would be going through his head forever until he got it. *Ta-dum, Angelina.* Maybe he could call a radio station and they'd play it or something. The melody was driving him nuts.

He put the car on I-94, took it to Highway 280, to I-35W, to I-694, and began driving west, fast, too fast, enjoying the speed, running the loop around the cities. He did it, now and then, to cool out. He liked the wind whistling through a crack in the window, the oldie-goldies on the radio. *Ta-dum* . . .

The blood-mask dried on the back of his jacket, invisible now. He never knew it was there.


Stephanie Bekker's lover heard the strange thumping as he toweled himself after his shower. The sound was unnatural, violent, arrhythmic, but it never crossed his mind that Stephanie had been attacked, was dying there on the kitchen floor. She might be moving something, one of her heavy antique chairs maybe, or perhaps she couldn't get a jar open and was rapping the lid on a kitchen counter—he really didn't know what he thought.

He wrapped a towel around his waist and went to look. He walked straight into the nightmare: A man with a beast's face, hovering over Stephanie, the broken bottle in his hand like a dagger, rimed with blood. Stephanie's face . . . What had he told her, there in bed, an hour before? You're a beautiful woman, he'd said, awkward at this, touching her lips with his fingertip, so beautiful. . . .

He'd seen her on the floor and he'd turned and run. *What else could he do?* one part of his mind asked. The lower part, the lizard part that went back to the caves, said: *Coward*.

He'd run up the stairs, flying with fear, reaching to slam the bedroom door behind him, to lock himself away from the horror, when he heard the troll slam out through the breezeway door. He snatched up the phone, punched numbers, a 9, a 1. But even as he punched the 1, his quick mind was turning. He stopped. Listened. No neighbors, no calls in the night. No sirens. Nothing. Looked at the phone, then finally set it back down. Maybe . . .

He pulled on his pants.

He cracked the door, tense, waiting for attack. Nothing. Down the stairs, moving quietly in his bare feet. Nothing. Wary, moving slowly, into the kitchen. Stephanie sprawled there, on her back, beyond help: her face pulped, her whole head misshapen from the beating. Blood pooled on the tile around her; the killer had stepped in it, and he'd left tracks, one edge of a gym shoe and a heel, back toward the door.

Stephanie Bekker's lover reached down to touch her neck, to feel for a pulse, but at the last minute, repelled, he pulled his hand back. She was dead. He stood for a moment, swept by a premonition that the cops were on the sidewalk, were coming up the sidewalk, were reaching toward the front door. . . . They would find him here, standing over the body like the inno-cent man in a Perry Mason television show, point a finger at him, accuse him of murder.

He turned his head toward the front door. Nothing. Not a sound.

He went back up the stairs, his mind working furiously. Stephanie had sworn she'd told nobody about their affair. Her close friends were with the university, in the art world or in the neighborhood: confiding details of an affair in any of those places would set off a tidal wave of gossip. They both knew that and knew it would be ruinous.

He would lose his position in a scandal. Stephanie, for her part, was deathly afraid of her husband: what he would do, she couldn't begin to predict. The affair had been stupid, but neither had been able to resist it. His marriage was dying, hers was long dead.

He choked, controlled it, choked again. He hadn't wept since childhood, couldn't weep now, but spasms of grief, anger and fear squeezed his chest. Control. He started dressing, was buttoning his shirt when his stomach re-belled, and he dashed to the bathroom and vomited. He knelt in front of the toilet for several minutes, dry heaves tearing at his stomach muscles until tears came to his eyes. Finally, the spasms subsiding, he stood up and finished dressing, except for his shoes. He must be quiet, he thought.

He did a careful inventory: billfold, keys, handkerchief, coins. Necktie, jacket. Coat and gloves. He forced himself to sit on the bed and mentally retrace his steps through the house. What had he touched? The front doorknob. The table in the kitchen, the spoon and bowl he'd used to eat her cherry cobbler. The knobs on the bedroom and bathroom doors, the water faucets, the toilet seat . . .

He got a pair of Stephanie's cotton underpants from her bureau, went down the stairs again, started with the front door and worked methodically through the house. In the kitchen, he didn't look at the body. He couldn't look at it, but he was always aware of it at the edge of his vision, a leg, an arm . . . enough to step carefully around the blood.

In the bedroom again, and the bathroom. As he was wiping the shower, he thought about the drain. Body hair. He listened again. Silence. *Take the time.* The drain was fastened down by a single brass screw. He removed it with a dime, wiped the drain as far as he could reach with toilet paper, then rinsed it with a direct flow of water. The paper he threw into the toilet, and flushed once, twice. Body hair: the bed. He went into the bedroom, another surge of despair shaking his body. He would forget something. . . . He pulled the sheets from the bed, threw them on the floor, found another set and spent five minutes putting them on the bed and rearranging the blankets and the coverlet. He wiped the nightstand and the headboard, stopped, looked around.

Enough.

He rolled the underpants in the dirty sheets, put on his shoes and went downstairs, carrying the bundle of linen. He scanned the living room, the parlor and the kitchen one last time. His eyes skipped over Stephanie. . . .

There was nothing more to do. He put on his coat and stuffed the bundle of sheets in the belly. He was already heavy, but the sheets made him gross: good. If anybody saw him . . .

He walked out the front door, down the four concrete steps to the street and around the long block to his car. They'd been discreet, and their discretion might now save him. The night was cold, spitting snow, and he met nobody.

He drove down off the hill, around the lake, out to Hennepin Avenue, and spotted a pay telephone. He stopped, pinched a quarter in the underpants and dialed 911. Feeling both furtive and foolish, he put the pants over the mouth-piece of the telephone before he spoke:

"A woman's been murdered . . ." he told the operator.

He gave Stephanie's name and address. With the operator pleading with him to stay on the line, he hung up, carefully wiped the receiver and walked back to his car. No. Sneaked back to his car, he thought. Like a rat. They would never believe, he thought. Never. He put his head on the steering wheel. Closed his eyes. Despite himself, his mind was calculating.

The killer had seen him. And the killer hadn't looked like a junkie or a small-time rip-off artist killing on impulse. He'd looked strong, well fed, pur-poseful. The killer could be coming after him. . . .

He'd have to give more information to the investigators, he decided, or they'd focus on him, her lover. He'd have to point them at the killer. They'd know that Stephanie had had intercourse, the county pathologists would be able to tell that. . . .

God, had she washed? Of course she had, but how well? Would there be enough semen for a DNA-type?

No help for that. But he could give the police information they'd need to track the killer. Print out a statement, Xerox it through several generations, with different darkness settings, to obscure any peculiarities of the printer . . .

Stephanie's face came out of nowhere.

At one moment, he was planning. The next, she was there, her eyes closed, her head turned away, asleep. He was seized with the thought that he could go back, find her standing in the doorway, find that it had all been a nightmare. . . .

He began to choke again, his chest heaving.

And Stephanie's lover thought, as he sat in the car: Bekker? Had he done this? He started the car.

Bekker.

It wasn't quite human, the thing that pulled itself across the kitchen floor. Not quite human—eyes gone, brain damaged, bleeding—but it was alive and it had a purpose: the telephone. There was no attacker, there was no lover, there was no time. There was only pain, the tile and, somewhere, the telephone.

The thing on the floor pulled itself to the wall where the telephone was, reached, reached . . . and failed. The thing was dying when the paramedics came, when the glass in the window broke and the firemen came through the door.

The thing called Stephanie Bekker heard the words "Jesus Christ," and then it was gone forever, leaving a single bloody handprint six inches below the Princess phone.

# 2

Del was a tall man, knobby, ungainly. He put his legs up on the booth seat and his jeans rode above his high-topped brown leather shoes, showing the leather laces running between the hooks. The shoes were cracked and caked with mud. Shoes you'd see on a sharecropper, Lucas thought.

Lucas drained the last of his Diet Coke and looked over his shoulder toward the door. Nothing.

"Fucker's late," Del said. His face flicked yellow, then red, with the Budweiser sign in the window.

"He's coming." Lucas caught the eye of the bartender, pointed at his Coke can. The barkeep nodded and dug into the cooler. He was a fat man, with a mustard-stained apron wrapped around his ample belly, and he waddled when he brought the Diet Coke.

"Buck," he grunted. Lucas handed him a dollar bill. The bartender looked at them carefully, thought about asking a question, decided against it and went back behind the bar.

They weren't so much out of place as oddly assorted, Lucas decided. Del was wearing jeans, a prison-gray sweatshirt with the neckband torn out, a jean jacket, a paisley headband made out of a necktie, and the sharecropper's shoes. He hadn't shaved in a week and his eyes looked like North Country peat bogs.

Lucas wore a leather bomber jacket over a cashmere sweater, and khaki slacks and cowboy boots. His dark hair was uncombed and fell forward over a square, hard face, pale with the departing winter. The pallor almost hid the white scar that slashed across his eyebrow and cheek; it became visible only when he clenched his jaw. When he did, it puckered, a groove, whiter on white.

Their booth was next to a window. The window had been covered with a silver film, so the people inside could see out but the people outside couldn't see in. Flower boxes sat under the windows, alternating with radiator cabinets. The boxes were filled with plastic petunias thrust into what looked like Kitty Litter. Del was chewing Dentyne, a new stick every few minutes. When he finished a stick, he lobbed the well-chewed wad into a window box. After an hour, a dozen tiny pink wads of gum were scattered like spring buds among the phony flowers.

"He's coming," Lucas said again. But he wasn't sure. "He'll be here."

Thursday night, an off-and-on hard spring rain, and the bar was bigger than its clientele. Three hookers, two black, one white, huddled together on barstools, drinking beer and sharing a copy of *Mirabella*. They'd all been wearing shiny vinyl raincoats in lipstick colors and had folded them down on the barstools to sit on them. Hookers were never far from their coats.

A white woman sat at the end of the bar by herself. She had frizzy blond hair, watery green eyes and a long thin mouth that was always about to tremble. Her shoulders were hunched, ready for a beating. Another hooker: she was pounding down the gin with Teutonic efficiency.

The male customers paid no attention to the hookers. Of the men, two shitkickers in camouflage hats, one with a folding-knife sheath on his belt, played shuffleboard bowling. Two more, both looking as if they might be from the neighborhood, talked to the bartender. A fifth man, older, sat by himself in front of a bowl of peanuts, nursing a lifelong rage and a glass of rye. He'd nip from the glass, eat a peanut and mutter his anger down into his overcoat. A half-dozen more men and a single woman sat in a puddle of rickety chairs, burn-scarred tables and cigarette smoke at the back of the bar, watching the NBA playoffs on satellite TV.

"Haven't seen much crack on TV lately," Lucas said, groping for conversation. Del had been leading up to something all night but hadn't spit it out yet.

"Media used it up," said Del. "They be rootin' for a new drug now. Supposed to be ice, coming in from the West Coast."

Lucas shook his head. "Fuckin' ice," he said.

He caught his own reflection in the window glass. Not too bad, he thought. You couldn't see the gray thatch in the black hair, you couldn't see the dark rings under his eyes, the lines beginning to groove his cheeks at the corners of his mouth. Maybe he ought to get a chunk of this glass and use it to shave in.

"If we wait much longer, she's gonna need a cash transfusion," Del said, eyeing the drunk hooker. Lucas had staked her with a twenty and she was down to a pile of quarters and pennies.

"He'll be here," Lucas insisted. "Motherfucker dreams about his rep."

"Randy ain't bright enough to dream," Del said.

"Gotta be soon," Lucas said. "He won't let her sit there forever."

The hooker was bait. Del had found her working a bar in South St. Paul two days earlier and had dragged her ass back to Minneapolis on an old possession warrant. Lucas had put the word on the street that she was talking about Randy to beat a cocaine charge. Randy had shredded the face of one of Lucas' snitches. The hooker had seen him do it.

"You still writing poems?" Del asked after a while.

"Kind of gave it up," Lucas said.

Del shook his head. "Shouldn't of done that."

Lucas looked at the plastic flowers in the window box and said sadly, "I'm getting too old. You gotta be young or naive to write poetry."

"You're three or four years younger'n I am," Del said, picking up the thought.

"Neither one of us is a fuckin' walk in the park," Lucas said. He tried to make it sound funny, but it didn't.

"Got that right," Del said somberly. The narc had always been gaunt. He liked speed a little too much and sometimes got his nose in the coke. That came with the job: narcs never got out clean. But Del . . . the bags under his eyes were his most prominent feature, his hair was stiff, dirty. Like a mortally ill cat, he couldn't take care of himself anymore. "Too many assholes. I'm gettin' as bad as them."

"How many times we had this conversation?" Lucas asked.

" 'Bout a hundred," Del said. He opened his mouth to go on, but they were interrupted by a sudden noisy cheer from the back and a male voice shouting, "You see that nigger fly?" One of the black hookers at the bar looked up, eyes narrowing, but she went back to her magazine without saying anything.

Del lifted a hand to the bartender. "Couple beers," he called. "Couple Leinies?"

The bartender nodded, and Lucas said, "You don't think Randy's coming?"

"Gettin' late," Del said. "And if I drink any more of this Coke, I'll need a bladder transplant."

The beers came, and Del said, "You heard about that killing last night? The woman up on the hill? Beat to death in her kitchen?"

Lucas nodded. This was what Del had been leading up to. "Yeah. Saw it on the news. And I heard some stuff around the office. . . ."

"She was my cousin," Del said, closing his eyes. He let his head fall back, as though overcome with exhaustion. "We grew up together, fooling around on the river. Hers were the first bare tits I ever saw, in real life."

"Your cousin?" Lucas studied the other man. As a matter of self-defense, cops joked about death. The more grotesque the death, the more likely the jokes; you had to watch your tongue when a friend had a family member die.

"We used to go fishing for carp, man, can you believe that?" Del turned so he could lean against the window box. *Thinking about yesterdays.* His bearded face drawn long and solemn, like an ancient photo of James Longstreet after Gettysburg, Lucas thought. "Down by the Ford dam, just a couple blocks from your place. Tree branches for fishing poles. Braided nylon line, with dough balls for bait. She fell off a rock, slipped on the moss, big splash . . ."

"Gotta be careful . . ."

"She was, like, fifteen, wearing a T-shirt, no bra," Del said. "It was plastered to her. I said, 'Well, I can see it all, you might as well take it off.' I was kidding, but she did. She had nipples the color of wild roses, man, you know? That real light pink. I had a hard-on for two months. Stephanie was her name."

Lucas didn't say anything for a moment, watching the other man's face, then, "You're not working it?"

"Nah. I'm no good at that shit, figuring stuff out," Del said. He flipped his hands palm out, a gesture of helplessness. "I spent the day with my aunt and uncle. They're all fucked up. They don't understand why I can't do something."

"What do they want you to do?" Lucas asked.

"Arrest her husband. He's a doctor over at the U, a pathologist," Del said. He took a hit of his beer. "Michael Bekker."

"Stephanie Bekker?" Lucas asked, his forehead wrinkling. "Sounds familiar."

"Yeah, she used to run around with the political crowd. You might even have met her—she was on the study group for that civilian review board a couple of years ago. But the thing is, when she was killed, her old man was in San Francisco."

"So he's out," Lucas said.

"Unless he hired it done." Del leaned forward now, his eyes open again. "That alibi is a little too convenient. I personally think he's got a loose screw."

"What're you telling me?"

"Bekker feels wrong. I'm not sure he killed her, but I think he might've," Del said. A man in a T-shirt dashed to the bar with a handful of bills, slapped them on the bar, said, "Catch us later," and ran three beers back to the TV set.

"Would he have a motive?" Lucas asked.

Del shrugged. "The usual. Money. He thinks he's better than anyone else and can't figure out why he's poor."

"Poor? He's a doctor. . . ."

"You know what I mean. He's a doctor, he oughta be rich, and here he is working at the U for seventy, eighty grand. He's a pathologist, and there ain't no big demand for pathology in the civilian world. . . ."

"Hmph."

Out on the sidewalk, on the other side of the one-way window, a couple shared an umbrella and, assuming privacy, slowed to light a joint. The woman was wearing a short white skirt and a black leather jacket. Lucas' Porsche was parked next to the curb, and as they walked by it, the man stopped to look, passing the joint to the girl. She took a hit, narrowed her eyes as she choked down the smoke and passed the joint back.

"Gotta get your vitamins," Del said, watching them. He reached forward and quickly traced a smiley face in the condensation on the window.

"I heard in the office . . . there was a guy with her? With your cousin?"

"We don't know what that is," Del admitted, his forehead wrinkling. "Somebody was there with her. They'd had intercourse, we know that from the M.E., and it wasn't rape. And a guy called in the report. . . ."

"Lover's quarrel?"

"I don't think so. The killer apparently came in through the back, killed her and ran out the same way. She was working at the sink, there were still bubbles on the dishwater when the squad got there, and she had soap on her hands. There wasn't any sign of a fight, there wasn't any sign that she had a chance to resist. She was washing dishes, and *pow*."

"Doesn't sound like a lover's quarrel . . ."

"No. And one of the crime-scene guys was wondering how the killer got so close to her, assuming it wasn't Loverboy who did it—how he could get so close without her hearing him coming. They checked the door and found out the hinges had just been oiled. Like in the past couple of weeks, probably."

"Ah. Bekker."

"Yeah, but it's not much. . . ."

Lucas thought it over again. A gust of rain brought a quick, furious drumming on the window, which just as quickly stopped. A woman with a red golf umbrella went by.

"Listen," Del said. "I'm not just sitting here bullshitting. . . . I was hoping you'd take a look at it."

"Ah, man . . . I hate murders. And I haven't been operating so good. . . ." Lucas gestured helplessly.

"That's another thing. You need an interesting case," Del said, poking an index finger at Lucas' face. "You're more fucked up than I am, and I'm a goddamned train wreck."

"Thanks . . ." Lucas opened his mouth to ask another question, but two pedestrians were drifting along the length of the window. One was a very light-skinned black woman, with a tan trench coat and a wide-brimmed cotton hat that matched the coat. The other was a tall, cadaverous white boy wearing a narrow-brimmed alpine hat with a small feather.

Lucas sat up. "Randy."

Del looked out at the street, then reached across the table and took Lucas' arm and said, "Take it easy, huh?"

"She was my best snitch, man," Lucas said, in a voice like a gravel road. "She was almost a friend."

"Bullfuck. Take it easy."

"Let him get all the way inside. . . . You go first, cover me, he knows my face. . . ."

Randy came in first, his hands in his coat pockets. He posed for a moment, but nobody noticed. With twelve seconds left in the NBA game, the Celtics were one point down with a man at the line, shooting two. Everybody but the drunk hooker and the bitter old man who was talking into his overcoat was facing the tube.

A woman came in behind Randy and pulled the door shut.

Lucas came out of the booth a step behind Del. *She's beautiful,* he thought, looking at the woman past Del's shoulder; then he put his head down. *Why would she hang with a dipshit like Randy?*

Randy Whitcomb was seventeen and a fancy man, with a gun and a knife and sometimes a blackthorn walking stick with a gold knob on the end of it. He had a long freckled face, coarse red hair and two middle teeth that pointed in slightly different directions. He shook himself like a dog, flicking water spray off his tweed coat. He was too young for a tweed coat and too thin and too crazy for the quality of it. He walked down the bar toward the drunk hooker, stopped, posed again, waiting to be seen. The hooker didn't look up until he took a hand out of his coat and slid a church key down the bar, where it knocked a couple of quarters off her stack of change.

"Marie," Randy crooned. The bartender caught the tone and looked at him. Del and Lucas were closing, but Randy paid them no attention. He was focused on Marie like fire: "Marie, baby," he warbled. "I hear you been talking to the cops. . . ."

Marie tried to climb off the stool, looking around wildly for Lucas. The stool tipped backward and she reached out to catch herself on the bar, teetering. Randy slid around the corner of the bar, going for her, but Lucas was there, behind him. He put a hand in the middle of the boy's back and pushed him, hard, into the bar.

The bartender hollered, "Hey," and Del had his badge out as Marie hit the floor, her glass shattering.

"Police. Everybody sit still," Del shouted. He slipped a short black revolver out of a hip holster and held it vertically in front of his face, where everybody in the bar could see it.

"Randy Ernest Whitcomb, dickweed," Lucas began, pushing Randy in the center of his back, looping his foot in front of the boy's ankles. "You are under . . ."

He had Randy leaning forward, his feet back, one arm held tight, the other going into his pocket for cuffs, when Randy screamed, "No," and levered himself belly-down onto the bar.

Lucas grabbed for one of his legs, but Randy kicked, thrashed. One foot caught Lucas on the side of the face, a glancing impact, but it hurt and knocked him back.

Randy fell over the bar, scrambled along the floor behind it and up over the end of it, grabbed a bottle of Absolut vodka and backhanded it at Del's head. Then he was running for the back of the bar, Lucas four steps behind him, knowing the back door was locked. Randy hit it, hit it again, then spun, his eyes wild, flashing a spike. They were all the fashion among the assholes. Clipped to a shirt pocket, they looked like Cross ballpoint pens. With the cap off, they were six-inch steel scalpels, the tip honed to a wicked point.

"Come on, motherfucker cop," Randy howled, spraying saliva at Lucas. His eyes were the size of half-dollars, his voice high and climbing. "Come on, motherfucker, get cut. . . ."

"Put the fuckin' knife down," Del screamed. His gun pointed at Randy's head. Lucas, glancing at Del, felt the world slowing down. The fat bartender was still behind the bar, his hands on his ears, as though blocking out the noise of the fight would stop it; Marie had gotten to her feet and was staring at a bleeding palm, shrieking; the two shitkickers had taken a step away from the shuffleboard bowling machine, and one of them, his Adam's apple bobbing up and down, was fumbling at the sheath on his belt. . . .

"Fuck you, cop, kill me," Randy shrieked, doing a sidestep shuffle. "I'm a fuckin' juvenile, assholes. . . ."

"Put the fuckin' blade down, Randy. . . ." Del screamed again. He glanced sideways at Lucas. "What d'ya wanna do, man?"

"Let me take him, let me take him," Lucas said, and he pointed. "The shitkicker's got a knife." As Del started to turn, Lucas was facing Randy, his eyes wide and black, and he asked, "You like to fuck, Randy?"

"Fuckin' A, man," Randy brayed. He was panting, his tongue hanging out. Nuts: "Fuck-in-A."

"Then I hope you got a good memory, 'cause I'm gonna stick that point right through your testicles, my man. You fucked up Betty with that church key. She was a friend of mine. I been looking for you. . . ."

"Well, you got me, Davenport, motherfucker, come get cut," Randy shouted. He had one hand down, as he'd been shown in reform school, the knife hand back a bit. Cop rule of thumb: An asshole gets within ten feet of you with a knife, you're gonna get cut, gun or no gun, shoot or no shoot.

"Easy, man, easy," Del shouted, looking at the shitkicker. . . .

"Where's the woman? Where's the woman?" Lucas called, still facing Randy, his arms wide in a wrestler's stance.

"By the door . . ."

"Get her. . . ."

"Man . . ."

"Get her. I'll take care of this asshole. . . ."

Lucas went straight in, faked with his right, eluded Randy's probing left hand, and when the knife hand came around, Lucas reached in and caught his right coat sleeve, half threw him and hit him in the face with a roundhouse right. Randy banged against the wall, still trying with the knife, Lucas punching him in the face.

"Lucas . . ." Del screamed at him.

But the air was going blue, slowing, slowing . . . the boy's head was bouncing off the wall, Lucas' arms pumping, his knee coming up, his elbow, then both hands pumping, a slow motion, a long, beautiful combination, a whole series of combinations, one-two-three, one-two, one-two-three, like working with a speed bag . . . the knife on the floor, skittering away . . .

Suddenly Lucas was staggering backward; he tried to turn, and couldn't. Del's arm was around his throat, dragging him away. . . .

The world sped up again. The people in the bar stared in stunned silence, all of them on their feet now, their faces like postage stamps on a long, unaddressed envelope. The basketball game was going in the background, broadcast cheers echoing tinnily through the bar.

"Jesus," Del said, gasping for breath. He said, too loudly, "I thought he got you with that knife. Everybody stay away from the knife, we need prints. Anybody touches it, goes to jail."

He still had a hand on Lucas' coat collar. Lucas said, "I'm okay, man."

"You okay?" Del looked at him and silently mouthed, *Witnesses*. Lucas nodded and Del said loudly, "You didn't get stabbed?"

"I think I'm okay. . . ."

"Close call," Del said, still too loud. "The kid was nuts. You see him go nuts with that knife? Never saw anything like that . . ."

Steering the witnesses, Lucas thought. He looked around for Randy. The boy was on the floor, faceup, unmoving, his face a mask of blood.

"Where's his girlfriend?" Lucas asked.

"Fuck her," Del said. He stepped over to Randy, keeping one eye on Lucas, then squatted next to the boy and cuffed his hands in front. "I thought you were gonna get stuck, you crazy fuck."

One of the hookers, up and wrapping a red plastic raincoat around her shoulders, ready to leave, looked down at Randy and into the general silence said, in a long, calm Kansas City drawl, "You better call an ambliance. That motherfucker is *hurt*."

# 3

Bekker was of two minds.

There was an Everyday Bekker, the man of science, the man in the white lab coat, doing his separations in the high-speed centrifuge, the man with the scalpel.

And then there was Beauty.

Beauty was up. Beauty was light. Beauty was dance. . . .

Beauty was the dextroamphetamines, the orange heart-shaped tablets and the half-black, half-clear capsules. Beauty was the white tabs of methamphetamine hydrochloride, the shiny jet-black caps of amphetamine, and the green-and-black bumblebees of phendimetrazine tartrate. All legal.

Beauty was especially the *illegals,* the anonymous white tabs of MDMA, called ecstasy, and the perforated squares of blotter, printed with the signs of the Zodiac, each with its drop of sweet acid, and the cocaine.

Beauty was anabolic steroids for the body and synthetic human growth hormone to fight the years. . . .

Everyday Bekker was down and dark.

Bekker was blood-red capsules of codeine, the Dilaudid. The minor benzodiazepines smoothed his anxieties, the Xanax and Librium and Clonopin, Tranxene and Valium, Dalmane and Paxipam, Ativan and Serax. The molindone, for a troubled mind. All legal.

And the illegals.

The white tabs of methaqualone, coming in from Europe.

Most of all, the phencyclidine, the PCP.

The power.

Bekker had once carried an elegant gold pillbox for his medicines, but eventually it no longer sufficed. At a Minneapolis antique store he bought a brass Art

Deco cigarette case, which he lined with velvet. It would hold upward of a hundred tablets. Food for them both, Beauty and Bekker . . .

Beauty stared into the cigarette case and relived the morning. As Bekker, he'd gone to the funeral home and demanded to see his wife.

"Mr. Bekker, I really think, the condition . . ." The undertaker was nervous, his face flickering from phony warmth to genuine concern, a light patina of sweat on his forehead. Mrs. Bekker was not one of their better products. He didn't want her husband sick on the carpet.

"God damn it, I want to see her," Bekker snapped.

"Sir, I have to warn you . . ." The undertaker's hands were fluttering.

Bekker fixed him with a cold stare, a ferret's stare: "I am a pathologist. I know what I will see."

"Well. I suppose . . ." The undertaker's lips made an O of distaste.

She was lying on a frilly orange satin pad, inside the bronze coffin. She was smiling, just slightly, with a rosy blush on her cheeks. The top half of her face, from the bridge of the nose up, looked like an airbrushed photograph. All wax, all moldings and makeup and paint, and none of it quite right. The eyes were definitely gone. They'd put her together the best they could, but considering the way she'd died, there wasn't much they could do. . . .

"My God," Bekker said, reaching out to the coffin. A wave of exultation rose through his body. He was rid of her.

He'd hated her for so long, watching her with her furniture and her rugs, her old paintings in the heavy carved frames, the inkwells and cruets and compotes and Quimper pots, the lopsided bottles dug from long-gone outhouses. She'd touch it, stroke it, polish it, move it, sell it. Caress it with her little piggy eyes . . . Talk about it, endlessly, with her limp-wristed antiquarian friends, all of them perched on rickety chairs with teacups, rattling on endlessly, *Mahogany with reeded legs, gilt tooled leather, but you almost couldn't tell under the horrible polish she'd absolutely poured on the piece, well, she obviously didn't know what she had, or didn't care. I was there to look at a Georgian tea table that she'd described as gorgeous, but it turned out to be really very tatty, if I do say so. . . .*

And now she was dead.

He frowned. Hard to believe that she had had a lover. One of those soft, heavy pale men who talked of teapots and wing chairs . . . unbelievable. What did they do in bed? Talk?

"Sir, I really think . . ." The undertaker's hand on his arm, steadying him, not understanding.

"I'm okay," Bekker said, accepting the comforting arm with a delicious sense of deception. He stood there for another minute, the undertaker behind him, ignored. This was not something he'd want to forget. . . .

Michael Bekker was beautiful. His head was large, his blond hair thick and carefully cut, feathering back over small, perfect ears. His forehead was broad and unlined, his eyebrows light, near-white commas over his startlingly blue deep-set eyes. The only wrinkles on his face were barely noticeable crow's-feet: they enhanced his beauty, rather than detracted from it, adding an ineffable touch of masculinity.

Below his eyes, his nose was a narrow wedge, his nostrils small, almost dainty. His chin was square, with a cleft, his complexion pale but healthy. His lips were wide and mobile over even white teeth.

If Bekker's face was nearly perfect, a cinema face, he had been born with a body no better than average. Shoulders a bit too narrow, hips a little too wide. And he was, perhaps, short in the leg.

The faults gave him something to work for. He was so close. . . .

Bekker exercised four nights a week, spending a half-hour on the Nautilus machines, another hour with the free weights. Legs and trunk one night, arms and shoulders the next. Then a rest day, then repeat, then two rest days at the end of the week.

And the pills, of course, the anabolic steroids. Bekker wasn't interested in strength; strength was a bonus. He was interested in shape. The work broadened his apparent shoulder width and deepened his chest. There wasn't anything he could do about the wide hips, but the larger shoulders had the effect of narrowing them.

His legs . . . legs can't be stretched. But in New York, just off Madison Avenue, up in the Seventies, he had found a small shop that made the most beautiful calfskin half-boots. The leather was so soft that he sometimes held the boots against his face before he put them on. . . .

Each boot was individually fitted with the most subtle of lifts, which gave him an inch and made him as near to perfect as God would come with Nordic man.

Bekker sighed and found himself looking into the bathroom mirror, the bathroom down the hall from his bedroom, the cold hexagonal tiles pressing into his feet. Staring at his beautiful face.

He'd been gone again. How long? He looked at his watch with a touch of panic. Five after one. Fifteen minutes gone. He had to control this. He'd taken a couple of methobarbitals to flatten out the nervous tension, and they'd thrown him outside himself. They shouldn't do that, but they had, and it was happening more and more often. . . .

He forced himself into the shower, turned on the cold water and gasped as it hit his chest. He kept his eyes closed, turned his back, lathered himself, rinsed and stepped out.

Did he have time? Of course: he always had time for this. He rubbed emollients into his face, dabbed after-shave along his jawline, cologne on his chest, behind his ears and under his balls, sprinkled powder across his chest, under his arms, between his buttocks.

When he was done, he looked into the mirror again. His nose seemed raw. He considered just a touch of makeup but decided against it. He really shouldn't look his best. He *was* burying Stephanie, and the police would be there. The police investigators were touchy: Stephanie's goddamned father and her cop cousin were whispering in their ears.

An investigation didn't much worry him. He'd hated Stephanie, and some of her friends would know that. But he'd been in San Francisco.

He smiled at himself in the mirror, was dissatisfied with the smile, wiped it away. Tried a half-dozen new expressions, more appropriate for the funeral. Scowl as he might, none of them detracted from his beauty.

He cocked his head at himself and let the smile return. All done? Not quite. He added a hair dressing with a light odor of spring lilacs and touched his hair with a brush. Satisfied, he went to the closet and looked at his suits. The blue one, he thought.


Quentin Daniel looked like a butcher in good clothes.

A good German butcher at a First Communion. With his lined red face and incipient jowls, the stark white collar pinching into his throat, the folds of flesh on the back of his neck, he would look fine behind a stainless-steel meat scale, one thumb on the tray, the other on your lambchops. . . .

Until you saw his eyes.

He had the eyes of an Irish Jesuit, pale blue, imperious. He was a cop, if he was one at all, with his brain: he'd stopped carrying a gun years before, when he'd bought his first tailored suits. Instead, he had spectacles. He wore simple military-style gold-rimmed bifocals for dealing with the troops, tortoise-shell single-vision glasses for reading his computer screen, and blue-tinted contact lenses for television appearances.

No gun.


Lucas pushed through the heavy oak door and slouched into Daniel's office. He was wearing the leather bomber jacket from the night before but had shaved and changed into a fresh houndstooth shirt, khaki slacks and loafers.

"You called?"

Daniel was wearing his computer glasses. He looked up, squinted as though he didn't recognize his visitor, took the computer glasses off, put on the gold-rimmed glasses and waved Lucas toward a chair. His face, Lucas thought, was redder than usual.

"Do you know Marty McKenzie?" Daniel asked quietly, his hands flat, palms down, on his green baize blotter.

"Yeah." Lucas nodded as he sat down. He crossed his legs. "He's got a practice in the Claymore Building. A sleaze."

"A sleaze," Daniel agreed. He folded his hands over his stomach and peered up at the ceiling. "The very first thing this morning, I sat here smiling for half an hour while the sleaze lectured me. Can you guess why?"

"Randy . . ."

". . . Because the sleaze had a client over in the locked ward at Hennepin General who had the shit beat out of him last night by one of my cops. After the sleaze left, I called the hospital and talked to a doc." Daniel pulled open a desk drawer and took out a notepad. "Broken ribs. Broken nose. Broken teeth. Possible cracked sternum. Monitored for blunt trauma." He slapped the pad on the desktop with a crack like a .22 short. "Jesus Christ, Davenport . . ."

"Pulled a knife on me," Lucas said. "Tried to cut me. Like this." He turned the front panel of the jacket, showed the deep slice in the leather.

"Don't bullshit me," Daniel said, ignoring the coat. "The Intelligence guys knew a week ago that you were looking for him. You and your pals. You've been looking for him ever since that hooker got cut. You found him last night and you kicked the shit out of him."

"I don't think . . ."

"Shut up," Daniel snapped. "Any explanation would be stupid. You know it, I know it, so why do it?"

Lucas shrugged. "All right . . ."

"The police department is not a fuckin' street gang," Daniel said. "You can't do this shit. We've got trouble and it could be serious. . . ."

"Like what?"

"McKenzie went to Internal Affairs before he came here, so they're in it and there's no way I can get them out. They'll want a statement. And this kid, Randy, might have been an asshole, but technically he's a juvenile—he's already got a social worker assigned and she's all pissed off about him getting beat up. She doesn't want to hear about any assault on a police officer. . . ."

"We could send her some pictures of the woman he worked over. . . ."

"Yeah, yeah, we'll do that. Maybe that'll change her around. And your jacket will help, the cut, and we're getting statements from witnesses. But I don't know. . . . If the jacket wasn't cut, I'd have to suspend your ass," Daniel said. He rubbed his forehead with the heel of his hand, as though wiping away sweat, then swiveled in his chair and looked out the window at the street, his back to Lucas. "I'm worried about you, Davenport. Your friends are worried about you. I had Sloan up here, he was lying like a goddamn sailor to cover your ass, until I told him to can it. Then we had a little talk. . . ."

"Fuckin' Sloan," Lucas said irritably. "I don't want him. . . ."

"Lucas . . ." Daniel turned back to Lucas, his tone mellowing from anger to concern. "He's your friend and you should appreciate that, 'cause you need all the friends you've got. Now. Have you been to a shrink?"

"No."

"They've got pills for what you've got. They don't cure anything, but they make it a little easier. Believe me, because I've been there. Six years ago this winter. I live in fear of the day I go back. . . ."

"I didn't know . . ."

"It's not something you talk about, if you're in politics," Daniel said. "You don't want people to think they've got a crazy man as police chief. Anyway, what you've got is called a unipolar depression."

"I've read the books," Lucas snapped. "And I ain't going to a shrink."

He pushed himself out of the chair and wandered around the office, looking into the faces of the dozens of politicians who peered from photos on Daniel's walls. The photos came mostly from newspapers, special prints made at the chief's request, and all were black-and-white. Mug shots with smiles, Lucas thought. There were only two pieces of color on the government-yellow walls. One piece was a Hmong tapestry, framed, with a brass plate that said: "Quentin Daniel, from His Hmong Friends, 1989." The second was a calendar with a painting of a vase of flowers, bright, slightly fuzzy, sophisticated and childlike at the same time. Lucas parked himself in front of the calendar and studied it.

Daniel watched him for a moment, sighed and said, "I don't necessarily think you should see a shrink—shrinks aren't the answer for everybody. But I'm telling you this as a friend: You're right on the edge. I've seen it before, I'll see it again, and I'm looking at it right now. You're fucked up. Sloan agrees. So does Del. You've got to get your shit together before you hurt yourself or somebody else."

"I could quit," Lucas ventured, turning back to the chief's desk. "Take a leave . . ."

"That wouldn't be so good," Daniel said, shaking his head. "People with a bad head need to be around friends. So let me suggest something. If I'm wrong, tell me."

"All right . . ."

"I want you to take on the Bekker murder. Keep your network alive, but focus on the murder. You need the company, Lucas. You need the teamwork. And I need somebody to bail me out on this goddamn killing. The Bekker woman's family has some clout and the papers are talking it up."

Lucas tipped his head, thinking about it. "Del mentioned it last night. I told him I might look into it. . . ."

"Do it," Daniel said. Lucas stood up, and Daniel put on his computer glasses and turned back to a screen full of amber figures.

"How long has it been since you were on the street?" Lucas asked.

Daniel looked at him, then up at the ceiling. "Twenty-one years," he said after a moment.

"Things have changed," Lucas said. "People don't believe in right and wrong anymore; if they do, we write them off as kooks. Reality is greed. People believe in money and power and feeling good and cocaine. For the bad people out there, we *are* a street gang. They understand that idea. The minute we lose the threat, they'll be on us like rats. . . ."

"Jesus Christ . . ."

"Hey, listen to me," Lucas said. "I'm not stupid. I don't even necessarily think—in theory, anyway—that I should be able to get away with what I did last night. But those things have to be done by somebody. The legal system has smart judges and tough prosecutors and it don't mean shit—it's a game that has nothing to do with justice. What I did was justice. The street understands that. I didn't do too much and I didn't do too little. I did just right."

Daniel looked at him for a long time and then said soberly, "I don't disagree with you. But don't ever repeat that to another living soul."


Sloan was propped against the metal door of Lucas' basement office, flipping through a throw-away newspaper, smoking a Camel. He was a narrow man with a foxy face and nicotine-stained teeth. A brown felt hat was cocked down over his eyes.

"You been shoveling horseshit again," Lucas said as he walked down the hall. His head felt as if it were filled with cotton, each separate thought tangled in a million fuzzy strands.

Sloan pushed himself away from the door so Lucas could unlock it. "Daniel ain't a mushroom. And it ain't horseshit. So you gonna do it? Work Bekker?"

"I'm thinking about it," Lucas said.

"The wife's funeral is this afternoon," Sloan said. "You oughta go. And I'll tell you what: I've been looking this guy up, Bekker. We got us an iceman."

"Is that right?" Lucas pushed the door open and went inside. His office had once been a janitor's closet. There were two chairs, a wooden desk, a two-drawer filing cabinet, a metal wastebasket, an old-fashioned oak coatrack, an IBM computer and a telephone. A printer sat on a metal typing table, poised to print out phone numbers coming through on a pen register. A stain on the wall marked the persistent seepage of a suspicious but unidentifiable liquid. Del had pointed out that a women's restroom was one floor above and not too much down the hall.

"Yeah, that's right," Sloan said. He dropped into the visitor's chair and put his heels up on the edge of the desk as Lucas hung his jacket on the coatrack.

"I've been reading background reports, and it turns out Bekker was assigned to the Criminal Investigation Division in Saigon during the Vietnam War. I thought he was some kind of cop, so I talked to Anderson and he called some of his computer buddies in Washington, and we got his military records. He wasn't a cop, he was a forensic pathologist. He did postmortems in criminal cases that involved GIs. I found his old commanding officer, a guy named Wilson. He remembered Bekker. I told him who I was, and he said, 'What happened, the sonofabitch kill somebody?' "

"You didn't prompt him?" Lucas asked, settling behind his desk.

"No. Those were the first words out of his mouth. Wilson said Bekker was called 'Dr. Death'—I guess he liked his work a little too much. And he liked the hookers. Wilson said he had a rep for pounding on them."

"How bad?"

Sloan shook his head. "Don't know. That was just his rep. . . . Wilson said a couple of whores got killed while Bekker was there, but nobody ever suggested he did it. The cops were looking for an Army enlisted man. They never found anybody, but they never looked too hard, either. Wilson said the place was overrun with AWOLs, deserters, guys on leave and pass, guys going in and out. He said it was an impossible case. But he remembers people around the office talking about the killings and that Bekker was . . . he was spooky. Since there were GIs involved, Bekker was in on the autopsies. He either did them himself or with a Vietnamese doc, Wilson couldn't remember. But when he came back, it was like he was satisfied. Fucked out."

"Huh." The printer burped up a number. Lucas glanced at it, then turned back to Sloan. "Did Bekker kill Stephanie? Hire it done?"

Sloan pulled the wastebasket over to his chair and carefully snubbed out his cigarette. "I think it's a major possibility," he said slowly. "If he did, he's cold: we checked on her insurance. . . ."

"Ten million bucks?" Lucas' eyebrows went up.

"No. Just the opposite. Stephanie was starting a business. She was gonna sell architectural artifacts for restoring old homes. Stained-glass windows, antique doorknobs, like that. An accountant told her she could save money by buying all the family insurance through the company. So she and Bekker canceled their old life insurance and bought new insurance through the company. It specifically won't pay off on any violent nonaccidental death—murder or suicide—in the first two years of coverage."

"So . . ."

"So she had no insurance at all," Sloan said. "Not that Bekker can collect on. A month ago she had a hundred grand, and she'd had it for a while."

Lucas' eyes narrowed. "If a defense attorney got that into court . . ."

"Yeah," Sloan said. "It'd knock a hell of a hole in a circumstantial case."

"And he's got an alibi."

"Airtight. He was in San Francisco."

"Jesus, I'd find him not guilty myself, knowing all that."

"That's why we need you. If he's behind it, he had to hire a hitter. There are only so many guys in the Cities who'd do it. You probably know most of them. Those you don't, your people would know. There must have been a big payoff. Maybe somebody came into a big hunk of unexplained cash?"

Lucas nodded. "I'll ask around. What about the guy who was in the sack with Bekker's old lady? Loverboy?"

"We're looking for him," Sloan said. "So far, no luck. I talked to Stephanie's best friend and she thought something might be going on. She didn't know who, but she was willing to mong a rumor. . . ."

Lucas grinned at the word: "So mong it to me," he said.

Sloan shrugged. "For what it's worth, she thinks Stephanie might have been screwing a neighborhood shrink. She'd seen them talking at parties, and she thought they . . . She said they quote stood in each other's space unquote."

"All right." Lucas yawned and stretched. "Most of my people won't be around yet, but I'll check."

"I'll Xerox the file for you."

"You could hold off on that. I don't know if I'll be in that deep. . . ." Sloan was standing, ready to leave, and Lucas reached back and punched the message button on his answering machine. The tape rewound, there was an electronic beep and a voice said: *"This is Dave, down at the auto parts. There're a couple of Banditos in town, I just did some work on their bikes. I think you might want to hear about it. . . . You got the number."*

"I'll Xerox it," Sloan said with a grin, "just in case."

Sloan left and Lucas sat with a yellow legal pad in his lap, feet up, listening to the voices on the answering machine, taking numbers. And watched himself.

His head wasn't working right. Hadn't been for months. But now, he thought, something was changing. There'd been just the smallest quieting of the storm. . . .

He'd lost his woman and their daughter. They'd walked: the story was as simple as that, and as complicated. He couldn't accept it and had to accept it. He pitied himself and was sick of pitying himself. He felt his friends' concern and he was tired of it.

Whenever he tried to break out, when he worked two or three days into exhaustion, the thoughts always sneaked back: If I'd done A, she'd have done B, and then we'd have both done C, and then . . . He worked through every possible combination, compulsively, over and over and over, and it all came up ashes. He told himself twenty times that he'd put it behind himself, and he never had. And still he couldn't stop. And he grew sicker and sicker of himself. . . .

And now Bekker. A flicker, here. An interest. He watched the first tickle, couldn't deny it. Bekker. He ran his hand through his hair, watching the interest bud and grow. On the legal pad he wrote:

1. Elle
2. Funeral

How can you lose with a two-item list? Even when—what was it called? a unipolar depression?—even when a unipolar depression's got you by the balls, you can handle two numbers. . . .

Lucas picked up the phone and called a nunnery.


Sister Mary Joseph was talking to a student when Lucas arrived. Her door was open a few inches, and from a chair in the outer office he could see the left side of her scarred face. Elle Kruger had been the prettiest girl in their grade school. Later, after Lucas had gone, transferred to the public schools, she'd been ravaged by acne. He recalled the shock of seeing her, for the first time in years, at a high school district hockey tournament. She had been sitting in the stands, watching him on the ice, eyes sad, seeing his shock. The beautiful blonde Elle of his prepubescent dreams, gone forever. She'd found a vocation with the Church, she had told him that night, but Lucas was never quite sure. A vocation? She'd said yes. But her face . . . Now she sat in her traditional habit, the beads swinging by her side. Still Elle, somewhere.

The college girl laughed again and stood up, her sweater a fuzzy scarlet blur behind the clouded glass of Elle's office door. Then Elle was on her feet and the girl was walking past him, looking at him with an unhidden curiosity. Lucas waited until she was gone, then went into Elle's office and sat in the visitor's chair and crossed his legs.

Elle looked him over, judging, then said, "How are you?"

"Not bad . . ." He shrugged, then grinned. "I was hoping you could give me a name at the university. A doctor, somebody who'd know a guy in the pathology department. Off the record. A guy who can keep his mouth shut."

"Webster Prentice," Elle said promptly. "He's in psychology, but he works at the hospital and hangs out with the docs. Want his phone number?"

Lucas did. As she flipped through a Rolodex, Elle asked, "How are you really?"

He shrugged. "About the same."

"Are you seeing your daughter?"

"Every other Saturday, but it's unpleasant. Jen doesn't want me there and Sarah's old enough to sense it. I may give it up for a while."

"Don't cut yourself off, Lucas," Elle said sharply. "You can't sit there in the dark every night. It'll kill you."

He nodded. "Yeah, yeah . . ."

"Are you dating anybody?"

"Not right now."

"You should start," the nun said. "Reestablish contact. How about coming back to the game?"

"I don't know . . . what're you doing?"

"Stalingrad. We can always use another Nazi."

"Maybe," Lucas said noncommittally.

"And what's this about talking to Webster Prentice? Are you working on something?"

"A woman got killed. Beaten to death. I'm taking a look," Lucas said.

"I read about it," Elle said, nodding. "I'm glad you're working it. You need it."

Lucas shrugged again. "I'll see," he said.

She scribbled a phone number on an index card and passed it to him.

"Thanks . . ." He leaned forward, about to stand.

"Sit down," she said. "You're not getting out of here that easy. Are you sleeping?"

"Yeah, some."

"But you've got to exhaust yourself first."

"Yeah."

"Alcohol?"

"Not much. A few times, scotch. When I'd get so tired I couldn't move, but I couldn't sleep. The booze would take me out. . . ."

"Feel better in the morning?"

"My body would."

"The Crows beat you up pretty bad," Elle said. The Crows were Indians, either terrorists or patriots. Lucas had helped kill them. Television had tried to make a hero out of him, but the case had cost him his relationship with his woman friend and their daughter. "You finally found out that there's a price for living the way you do. And you found out that you can die. And so can your kid."

"I always knew that," Lucas said.

"You didn't feel it. And if you don't feel it, you don't believe it," Elle rapped back.

"I don't worry about dying," he said. "But I had something going with Jennifer and Sarah."

"Maybe that'll come back. Jennifer's never said it was over forever."

"Sounds like it."

"You need time, all of you," Elle said. "I won't do therapy on you. I can't be objective. We've got too much history. But you should talk to somebody. I can give you some names, good people."

"You know what I think about shrinks," Lucas said.

"You don't think that about me."

"Like you said—we have a history. But I don't want a shrink, 'cause I can't help what I think about them. Maybe a couple of pills or something . . ."

"You can't cure what you've got with pills, Lucas. Only two things will do that. Time or therapy."

"I'll take the time," he said.

She threw up her hands in surrender, her teeth flashing white in a youthful smile. "If you really get your back against the wall, call me. I have a doctor friend who'll prescribe some medication without threatening your manhood with therapy."

She went with him to the exit and watched as he walked out to his car, down the long greening lawn, the sun flicking through the bare trees. When he stepped from the shelter of the building, the wind hit him in the face, with just a finger of warmth. Spring wind. Summer coming. Behind him, on the other side of the door, Elle Kruger kissed her crucifix and began a rosary.

# 4

Bekker dressed as carefully as he had cleaned himself: a navy suit, a blue broadcloth shirt, a dark tie with small burgundy comma figures, black loafers with lifts. He slipped a pair of sunglasses into his breast pocket. He would use them to hide his grief, he thought. And his eyes, should there be anyone of unusual perception in the crowd.

The funeral would be a waste of his time. He had to go, but it would be a waste of his time. He sighed, put on the sunglasses, and looked at himself in the mirror. Not bad. He flicked a piece of lint off the shoulder of the suit and smiled at himself.

Not bad at all.

When he was ready, he took one of the Contac capsules from the brass cigarette case, pulled it apart and dumped the powder on the glass top of the bedstand. The Contac people would pee down their pant legs if they'd known, he thought: pure medical cocaine. He snorted it, absorbed the rush, collected himself and walked out to the car.

The drive to the funeral home was short. He liked this one funeral home. He was *familiar* with it. He giggled and just as quickly smothered the giggle. He must not do that. He must not. And then he thought: *Compassionate leave,* and almost giggled again. The University had given him compassionate leave. . . . God, funny as that was, he couldn't let it show.

Phenobarbital? About right for a funeral. It'd give him the right *look*. He took the brass cigarette case from his pocket, keeping one eye on the road, opened it, popped a phenobarbital tab. Thought about it, took a second. Naughty boy. And just a lick of PCP? Of course. The thing about PCP was, it stiffened you, gave you a wooden look. He'd seen it in himself. And that would be right, too, for a grieving husband. But not too much. He popped a PCP tab, bit it in half, spit half back into the cigarette case, swallowed the other half. Ready now.

 He parked a block from the funeral home, walked briskly, if a bit wood-enly—the PCP already?—down the sidewalk. Minnesota had turned springlike with its usual fickle suddenness. It could revert to winter just as quickly, but for now it was wonderful. A warm slanting sun; red-bellied robins in the yards, bouncing around, looking for worms; fat buds on the trees, the smell of wet grass . . . The warm feeling of the phenobarbital coming on.

 He stopped outside the funeral home and took a deep breath. God, it was fine to be alive. Without Stephanie.

 The funeral home was built of tan stone, in what some funereal architect must have supposed was a British style. Inside, it was simply cold. A hundred people came to the funeral, people from the decorating world, from the univer-sity. The women, he thought, all in their dark dresses, looked at him speculatively as he walked slowly up the aisle. Women were like that. Stephanie not yet cold in the grave . . .

 He sat down, blocked out the organ music that seeped from hidden speak-ers and began toting up the assets. Hard to do with the phenobarbital in his blood, but he persisted. The house was worth better than half a million. The furnishings another two hundred thousand—not even her asshole relatives realized that. Stephanie had bought with an insider's eye, had traded up, had salvaged. Bekker didn't care for the place, but some people considered it a treasure house. For himself, Bekker wanted an apartment, up high, white walls, pale birch woodwork, a few Mayan pieces. He'd get it, and still put a half-million in the mutual funds. He'd drag down seventy-five thousand a year, if he picked his funds carefully. On top of his salary . . .

 He almost smiled, thinking about it, caught the impulse and glanced around.

 There were a number of people he didn't recognize, but most of them were sitting with people he did, in obvious groups and pairings. People from Stepha-nie's world of antiques and restoration. Stephanie's family, her father, her brothers and sisters, her cop cousin. He nodded at her father, who had fixed him with a glare, and looked farther back into the crowd.

 One man, sitting alone near the back, caught his attention. He was muscular, dark-complected, in a gray European-cut suit. Good-looking, like a boxer might be. And he seemed interested in Bekker. He'd followed his progress up the aisle, into the chair that half faced the coffin, half faced the mourners. Safe behind the sunglasses, Bekker returned the man's gaze. For one goofy minute, Bekker thought he might be Stephanie's lover. But that was crazy. A guy like this wouldn't go for Stephanie, would he? Chunky Stephanie? Stephanie No-Eyes?

Then Swanson, the cop who had interviewed him when he got back from San Francisco, walked into the church, looked around and sat next to the stranger. They leaned their heads closer and spoke a few words, the stranger still watching Bekker. The tough guy was a cop.

All right. Bekker dismissed him, and looked again through the gathering crowd. Philip George came in with his wife, Annette, and sat behind the cop. Bekker's eyes traveled across him without hesitating.

The lover. Who was the lover?

The funeral was mercilessly long. Twelve people spoke. Stephanie was good, Stephanie was kind. Stephanie worked for the community.

Stephanie was a pain in the ass.

*Yea, though I walk through the valley of the shadow of death, I will fear no evil: for thou art with me; thy rod and thy staff, they comfort me. . . .*

Bekker went away. . . .

When he came back, the mourners were on their feet, looking at him. It was over, what? Yes, he should walk out, one hand on the side rail of the coffin. . . .

Afterward, at the cemetery, Bekker walked alone to his car, aware of the eyes on him. The women, looking. He composed his face: I need a mask, a *grave* mask, he thought. He giggled at the pun. He couldn't help himself.

He turned, struggling to keep his face straight. The crowd was watching, all right. And on the hillside, in the grass, the man in the European suit, watching.

He needed something to enhance his mood. His hand strayed to the cigarette case. He had two more of the special Contacs, a half-dozen methamphetamines. They'd be fine after the barbs.

And a little ecstasy for dessert?

But of course . . .

The funeral was crowded, the coffin closed. Lucas sat next to Swanson, the lead investigator. Del sat with Stephanie Bekker's family.

"The sonofabitch looks stoned," Swanson mumbled, poking Lucas with an elbow. Lucas turned and watched Bekker go by. Astonishingly good-looking: almost too much, Lucas thought. Like a mythological beast, assembled from the best parts of several animals, Bekker's face seemed to have been assembled from the best features of several movie stars.

"Is he hurt?" Lucas whispered. Bekker was walking awkwardly, his legs like lumber.

"Not that I know of," Swanson whispered back.

Bekker walked down the aisle; one hand on the coffin, unbending, his eyes invisible behind dark sunglasses. Occasionally his lips moved, as though he were mumbling to himself, or praying. It did not seem an act: the woodenness appeared to be real.

He followed the coffin to the hearse, waited until it was loaded; then walked down the block to his car. At the car he turned and looked directly at Lucas. Lucas felt the eyes and stood still, watching, letting their gazes touch. And then Bekker was gone.

Lucas went to the cemetery, curious. What was it with Bekker? Grief? Despair? An act? What?

He watched from a hillside as Stephanie Bekker's coffin was lowered into the ground. Bekker never changed: his beautiful face was as immobile as a lump of clay.

"What do you think?" Swanson asked, when Bekker had gone.

"I think the guy's a fruitcake," Lucas said. "But I don't know what kind."

Lucas spent the rest of the afternoon and early evening putting the word out on his network, a web of hookers, bookstore owners, barbers, mailmen, burglars, gamblers, cops, a couple of genteel marijuana dealers: *Anything on a hit? Any nutso walking around with big cash?*

A few minutes after six, he took a call on his handset and drove back downtown to police headquarters in the scabrous wart of Minneapolis City Hall. Sloan met him in the hall outside the chief's office.

"You hear?" Sloan asked.

"What?"

"We got a letter from a guy who says he was there when Stephanie got killed. Loverboy."

"No ID?"

"No. But there's a lot of stuff in the letter. . . ."

Lucas followed Sloan past the vacant secretary's desk to the inner office. Daniel sat behind his desk, rolling a cigar between his fingers, listening to a Homicide detective who sat in a green leather chair in front of the desk. Daniel looked up when Sloan rapped on the open door.

"C'mon in, Sloan. Davenport, how are you? Swanson's filling me in."

Lucas and Sloan pulled up chairs on either side of the Homicide detective and Lucas asked him, "What's this letter?"

Swanson passed him a Xerox copy. "We were just talking about possibilities. Could be a doper, scared off by Loverboy. Unless Loverboy did it."

"You think it's Loverboy?"

The detective shook his head. "No. Read the letter. It more or less hangs together with the scene. And you saw Bekker."

"Nobody has a good word for the guy," Sloan said.

"Except professionally. The docs at the university say his work is top-notch," Swanson said. "I talked to some people in his department. 'Ground-breaking,' is what they say. . . ."

"You know what bothers me?" Lucas said. "In this letter, Loverboy says she was on her back in a pool of blood, dead. I saw the pictures, and she was facedown next to the wall. He doesn't mention a handprint. I think he left her there alive. . . ."

"He did," Swanson said, nodding. "She died just about the time the paramedics got there—they even gave her some kind of heart shot, trying to get it going again. Nothing happened, but she hadn't been dead very long, and the blood under her head was fresh. The blood on the floor, though, the blood by the sink, had already started to coagulate. They figure she was alive for fifteen or twenty minutes after the attack. Her brain was all fucked up—who knows what she could have told us? But if Loverboy had called nine-one-one, she might still be around."

"Fucker," Sloan said. "Does that make him an accomplice?"

Swanson shrugged. "You'd have to ask a lawyer about that."

"How about this doctor, the guy she talked with at parties . . ." Lucas asked.

"That's under way," Daniel said.

"You doing it?" Lucas asked Sloan.

"No. Andy Shearson."

"Shit, Shearson? He couldn't find his own asshole with both hands and a pair of searchlights," Lucas said in disbelief.

"He's what we've got and he's not that bad," Daniel said. He stuck the end of the cigar in his mouth, nipped it off, took the butt end from his mouth, examined it and then tossed it into a wastebasket. "We're getting a little more TV on this one—random-killer bullshit. I'd hate to see it get any bigger."

"The story'll be gone in a week. Sooner, if we get a decent dope killing," Sloan said.

"Maybe, maybe not," Daniel said. "Stephanie Bekker was white and upper middle class. Reporters identify with that kind of woman. They could keep it going for a while."

"We'll push," Swanson said. "Talk to Bekker some more. We're doing the neighborhood. Checking parking tickets in the area, talking to Stephanie Bekker's friends. The main thing is, find the boyfriend. Either he did it or he saw it."

"He says the killer looks like a goblin," Lucas said, reading through the letter. "What the hell does that mean?"

"Fuck if I know," said Swanson.

"Ugly," said Daniel. "Barrel-chested . . ."

"Do we know for sure that the goblin's not Bekker? That Bekker was actually in San Francisco?" Lucas asked.

"Yeah, we do," Swanson said. "We wired a photo out, had the San Francisco cops show it to the desk people at Bekker's hotel. He was there, no mistake."

"Hmph," Lucas grunted. He stood up, slipped his hands in his pockets and wandered over to Daniel's wall of trophy photos. Jimmy Carter's smiling face looked back at him. "We're leaning the wrong way with the media. If Bekker hired a killer, the best handle we've got is the boyfriend. The witness . . ."

"Loverboy," said Sloan.

"Loverboy," said Lucas. "He's got some kind of conscience, because he called and he wrote the letter. He could've walked out and we might never have suspected . . ."

"We would have known," Swanson said. "The M.E. found that she'd had intercourse not too long before she was killed. And he did leave her to die."

"Maybe he really thought she was dead," Lucas said. "Anyway, he's got *some* kind of conscience. We ought to make a public appeal to him. TV, the papers. That does two things: it might bring him out of the woodwork, and it might put pressure on the killer, or Bekker, to make a move."

"No other options?" asked Daniel.

"Not if you want to catch the guy," Lucas said. "We could let it go: I'd say right now that the chance of convicting Bekker is about zero. We'll only get him one way—the witness has to identify the killer and the killer has got to give us Bekker on a plea bargain."

"I hate to let it go," Daniel said. "Our fuckin' clearance rate . . ."

"So we get the TV people in here," Lucas said.

"Let's give it another twenty-four hours," Daniel said. "We can talk again tomorrow night."

Lucas shook his head. "No. You need to think about it overnight, 'cause if we're going to do it, we got to do it quick. Tomorrow'd be best, early enough for the early evening news. Before this boyfriend, whoever he is, gets his head set in concrete. You should say flatly that we don't believe the boyfriend did the killing, that we need all the help we can get. That we need him to come in, that we'll get him a lawyer. That if he didn't murder the woman, we'll offer him immunity—maybe you can get the county attorney in on this angle. And that if he still doesn't think he can come in, we need him to communicate with us somehow. Send us letters with more detail. Cut out pictures from magazines, people who most look like the killer. Do drawings, if he can. Maybe we can get the papers to print identikit drawings, have him pick the best ones, change them until they're more like the killer."

"I'll think about it."

"And we watch Bekker. If we make a heavy-duty appeal to the boyfriend and if Bekker really did buy the hit, he'll get nervous. Maybe he'll give us a break," Lucas said.

"All right. I'll think about it. See me tomorrow."

"We gotta move," Lucas urged, but Daniel waved him off.

"We'll talk again tomorrow," he said.

Lucas turned back to Jimmy Carter and inspected the former president's tweed jacket. "If it's Bekker who did it, or hired it, if he's the iceman Sloan thinks he is . . ."

"Yeah?" Daniel was fiddling with his cigar, watching him from behind the desk.

"We better find Loverboy before Bekker does," Lucas said.

# 5

The evening sky shaded from crimson to ultramarine and finally to a flat gray; Lucas lived in the middle of the metro area, and the sky never quite got dark. Across the street, joggers came and went on the river path, stylish in their phosphorescent workout suits, flashing Day-Glo green and pink. Some wore headsets, running to rock. Beyond them, on the other side of the Mississippi, the orange sodium-vapor streetlights winked on as a grid set, followed by a sprinkling of bluer house lights.

When the lights came on across the river, Lucas pulled the window shade and forced himself back to the game. He worked doggedly, without inspiration, laying out the story for the programmer. A long ribbon of computer paper flowed across the library table, in and out of the puddle of light around his hands. With a flowchart template and a number-two pencil, he blocked out the branches of Druid's Pursuit. He had once thought that he might learn to program, himself. Had, in fact, taken a community college course in Pascal and even dipped into C. But programming bored him, so he hired a kid to do it. He laid down the stories with the myriad jumps and branches, and the kid wrote the code.

The kid programmer had no obvious computer-freak personality flaws. He wore a letter jacket with a letter and told Lucas simply that he'd gotten it in wrestling. He could do chin-ups with his index fingers and sometimes brought a girlfriend along to help him.

Lucas, tongue in cheek, thought to ask him, *Help you do what?,* but he didn't. Both kids came from Catholic colleges in the neighborhood and needed a cheap, private space. Lucas tried to leave them alone.

And maybe she *was* helping him. The work got done.

Lucas wrote games. Historical simulations played on boards, to begin with. Then, for the money, he began writing role-playing quest games of the Dungeons & Dragons genre.

One of his simulations, a Gettysburg, had become so complicated that he'd bought an IBM personal computer to figure times, points and military effects.

The flexibility of the computer had impressed him—he could create effects not possible with a board, such as hidden troop movements and faulty military intelligence. With help from the kid, he'd moved the entire game to an IBM 386 clone. A computer database company in Missouri had gotten wind of the game, leased it from him, altered it and put it on line. On any given night, several dozen Civil War enthusiasts would be playing Gettysburg via modem, paying eight dollars an hour for the privilege. Lucas got two of the dollars.

Druid's Pursuit was something else, a role-playing game with a computer serving as game master. The game was becoming complex. . . .

Lucas stopped to change discs in the CD player, switching Tom Waits' *Big Time* for David Fanshawe's *African Sanctus,* then settled back into his chair. After a moment, he put the programming template down and stared at the wall behind the desk. He kept it blank on purpose, for staring at.

Bekker was interesting. Lucas had felt the interest growing, watching it like a gardener watching a new plant, almost afraid to hope. He'd seen depression in other cops, but he'd always been skeptical. No more. The depression—an unfit word for what had happened to him—was so tangible that he imagined it as a dark beast, stalking him, off in the dark.

Lucas sat in the night, staring at his patch of wall, and the sickly smell of Stephanie's funeral flowers came back, the quiet dampness of the private chapel, the drone of the minister, . . . *all who loved this woman Stephanie* . . .

"Dammit." He was supposed to be concentrating on the game, but he couldn't. He stood and took a turn around the room, the *Sanctus* chants banging around in his head. A manila folder caught his eye. The case file, copied by Sloan and left on his desk. He picked it up, flipped through it. Endless detail. Nobody knew what might or might not be useful, so they got it all. He read through it and was about to dump it back on the desk, when a line of the lab narrative caught his eye.

"Drain appeared to have been physically cleaned . . ."

The bedroom and the adjoining bath had been wiped, apparently by Loverboy, to eliminate fingerprints. That demonstrated an unusual coolness. But the drain? That was something else again. Lucas looked for returns on Stephanie Bekker's bed but found nothing in the report. The lab report was signed by Robert Kjellstrom.

Lucas dug in his desk and found the internal police directory, looked up Kjellstrom's phone number and called. Kjellstrom had to get out of bed to take the call.

"There's nothing in the report on hair in the bed. . . ."

"That's 'cause there wasn't any," Kjellstrom said.

"None?"

"Nope. The sheets were clean. They looked like they'd just been washed."

"The report said Stephanie Bekker had just had intercourse. . . ."

"Not on those sheets," Kjellstrom said.

Lucas finished with the file and looked at his watch: ten o'clock. He walked back to the bedroom, changed from tennis shirt, slacks and loafers to a flannel shirt, jeans and boots, pulled on a shoulder rig with his new Smith & Wesson double-action .45, and covered it with a fleece-lined Patagonia jacket.

The day had been good, but the nights were still nasty, cutting with the last claws of winter. Even the bad people stayed inside. He rolled the Porsche out of the garage, waited in the driveway until the garage door was firmly down, then headed north on Mississippi River Boulevard. At Summit Avenue he considered his options and finally drove out to Cretin Avenue, north to I-94 and then east, past downtown St. Paul to the eastern rim of the city. Three St. Paul cop cars were parked outside a supermarket that had a restaurant in the back. Lucas locked the Porsche and went inside.

"Jesus, look what the fuckin' cat drug in," said the oldest cop. He was in his late forties, burly, with a brush mustache going gray and gold-rimmed glasses. He sat in a booth with three other cops. Two more huddled over coffee cups in the next booth down.

"I thought you guys could use some guidance, so I drove right over," Lucas said. A circular bar sat at the center of the restaurant floor, surrounded by swivel stools, with booths along the wall. Lucas took one of the stools and turned it to face the cops in the booth.

"We appreciate your concern," said the cop with the mustache. Three of the four men in the booth were middle-aged and burly; the fourth was in his twenties, slender, and had tight blue eyes with prominent pink corners. The three older cops were drinking coffee. The younger one was eating French toast with sausage.

"This guy a cop?" the youngest one asked, a fork poised halfway to his mouth with a chunk of sausage. He was staring at Lucas' jacket. "He's carrying. . . ."

"Thank you, Sherlock," an older cop said. He tipped his head at Lucas and said, "Lucas Davenport, he's a detective lieutenant with Minneapolis."

"He drives a Porsche about sixty miles an hour down Cretin Avenue at rush hour," said another of the cops, grinning at Lucas over his coffee cup.

"Bullshit. I observe all St. Paul traffic ordinances," Lucas said.

"Pardon me while I fart in disgust," said the speed-trap cop. "It must've been somebody else's Porsche I got a picture of on my radar about five-thirty Friday."

Lucas grinned. "You must've startled me."

"Right . . . You workin' or what?"

"I'm looking for Poppy White," Lucas said.

"Poppy?" The three older cops looked at each other, and one of them said, "I saw his car outside of Broobeck's last night and a couple of nights last week. Red Olds, last year's. If he's not there, Broobeck might know where he is."

Lucas stayed to talk for a few minutes, then hopped off the stool. "Thanks for the word on Poppy," he said.

"Hey, Davenport, if you're gonna shoot the sonofabitch, could you wait until after the shift change . . . ?"

A red Olds was parked under the neon bowling pin at Broobeck's. Lucas stepped inside, looked down toward the lanes. Only two were being used, by a group of young couples. Three people sat at the bar, but none of them was Poppy. The bartender wore a paper hat and chewed a toothpick. He nodded when Lucas walked up.

"I'm looking for Poppy."

"He's here somewhere, maybe back in the can."

Lucas went to the men's restroom, stuck his head inside. He could see a pair of Wellington boots under one of the stall doors and called, "Poppy?"

"Yeah?"

"Lucas Davenport. I'll wait at the bar."

"Get a booth."

Lucas got a booth and a beer, and a minute later Poppy appeared, holding wet hands away from his chest.

"You need some towels back there," he complained to the bartender. The man pushed him a stack of napkins. Poppy dried his hands, got a beer and came over to Lucas. He was too heavy, in his middle fifties, wearing jeans and a black T-shirt under a leather jacket. His iron-gray hair was cut in a Korean War flattop. A good man with a saw and a torch, he could chop a stolen Porsche into spare parts in an hour.

"What's going on?" he asked, as he slid into the booth. "You need a starter motor?"

"No. I'm looking for somebody with new money. Somebody who might of hit a woman over in Minneapolis the other day."

Poppy shook his head. "I know what you're talkin' about and I ain't heard even a tinkle. The dopers are sweatin' it, because the papers are saying a doper done it and they figure somebody's got to fall."

"But not a thing?"

"Not a thing, man. If somebody got paid, it wasn't over on this side of town. You sure it was a white guy? I don't know about the coloreds anymore."

\*       \*       \*

He was looking for a white guy. That's the way it went: whites hired whites, blacks hired blacks. Equal-opportunity bigotry, even in murder. There were other reasons, too. In that neighborhood, a black guy would be noticed.

He left Poppy at the bowling alley and headed west to Minneapolis, touched a gay bar on Hennepin Avenue, two more joints on Lake Street and finally, having learned nothing, woke up a fence who lived in the quiet suburban town of Wayzata.

"I don't know, Davenport, maybe just a freak. He wastes the woman, splits for Utah, spends the money buyin' a ranch," the fence said. They sat on a glassed-in porch overlooking a pond with cattails. The lights from another house reflected off the surface of the water, and Lucas could make out the dark shapes of a raft of ducks as they bobbed shoulder to shoulder in the middle of the pond. The fence was uncomfortable on a couch, in his pajamas, smoking an unfiltered cigarette, his wife sitting beside him in a bathrobe. She had pink plastic curlers in her hair and looked worried. She'd offered Lucas a lime mineral water, cold, and he rolled the bottle between his hands as they talked. "If I were you," the fence said, "I'd check with Orville Proud."

"Orville? I thought he was in the joint, down in Arizona or someplace," Lucas said.

"Got out." The fence picked a piece of tobacco off his tongue and flicked it away. "Anyway, he's been around for a week or so."

"Is he setting up again?" He should have known. Proud had been in town for a week—*he should have known*.

"Yeah, I think so. Same old deal. He's hurtin' for cash. And you know the kind of contacts he's got. Fuckin' biker gangs and the muscle guys, the Nazis, everybody. So I says, 'The word's out that it might have been a hit, the husband brought somebody in.' And he says, 'That ain't a good thing to be talking about, Frank.' So I stopped talking about it."

"Huh. You know where he is?"

"I don't want none of this coming back," the fence said. "Orville's a little strange. . . ."

"Won't be coming back," Lucas assured him.

The fence looked at his watch. "Try room two twenty-one at the Loin. There's a game."

"Any guns?"

"You know Orville. . . ."

"Yeah, unfortunately. All right, Frank, I owe you."

" 'Preciate it. You still got that cabin up north?"

"Yeah . . ."

"I got some good deals coming on twenty-five-horse Evinrudes."

"Don't push your luck," Lucas said.

"Hey, Lieutenant . . ." Frank grinned, reaching for charm, and his teeth were not quite green.

\*      \*      \*

The Loin was the Richard Coeur de Lion Lounge & Motel on the strip across from Minneapolis–St. Paul International. The place started straight, lost money for a few years, then was picked up by a more creative management out of Miami Beach. After that, it was called either the Dick or the Loin, but Loin won out. As a nickname, it was felt by the people who decided such things, "Loin" had more class. The better gamblers, slicker coke peddlers, prettier whores and less discriminating Viking football players populated the bar and, most nights, the rooms in the attached motel.

The bar was done in red velvet and dark wood with oval mirrors. There were two stuffed red foxes in the foyer, mounted on chunks of driftwood, on either side of a bad reproduction of *The Blue Boy*. Upstairs, the rooms had water beds and pornographic movies on cable, no extra charge.

Lucas walked through the lobby, nodded at the woman behind the desk, who smiled, almost as though she remembered checking him in, and walked up the steps to the single hallway that ran the length of the motel. Room 221 was the last one on the left. He stood outside the door for a moment, listening, then took his .45 out of the shoulder rig and stuck it under his belt in the small of his back. He knocked on the door and stepped back across the hall, where he could be seen through the peephole. The peephole got dark for a moment; then a voice said, "Who is it?"

"Lucas Davenport wants to see Orville."

"No Orville here."

"Tell him. . . ."

The eye left the peephole and a minute passed. Then the peephole got dark again and another voice said, "You alone?"

"Yeah. No problem."

Orville Proud opened the door and looked down the hall.

"No problem?" he asked.

"I need to talk," Lucas said, looking past Orville. Room 221 was a suite without beds. Seven men sat frozen around an octagonal table, their eyes like birds' eyes, picking him up; cards on the table but no chips, ashtrays and bottles of mineral water on the table and the floor by their feet. Behind them, a short man in a hip-length leather coat sat on the heat register. He had a thin pointed beard under delicate gold-rimmed eyeglasses. He looked like Lenin, and he knew it. Ralph Nathan. Lucas put his hand on his hip, six inches from the butt of the .45.

"You're gonna get your fuckin' ass killed someday," Orville said flatly. He stepped into the hall and pulled the door shut behind him. "What do you want?"

"I need to know if there's been any talk about a hit on a woman in Minneapolis. Got herself beat to death, some people think her husband might have hired it. There's a lot of heat coming down."

Orville shook his head, frowning. He didn't need any heat. "A couple of people mentioned it, but I ain't heard a thing. I mean, I think I would've heard. I been scratching around for cash, trying to get back into business, and I been calling everybody I know. There's not a fuckin' thing, man."

"Nobody got rich, nobody bought a car . . . ?"

Proud shook his head. "Not a fuckin' thing. Terry Meller come into a whole load of Panasonic color TVs, fell off the train in St. Paul, but that's about it."

"You're sure?"

"Man, I spent the last three weeks running all over the metro, talking to everybody. That's all I've been doing. There's nothing out there."

"All right," Lucas said, discouraged. "How was Arizona?"

Proud shook his head. "New Mexico. You don't wanna do any time in New Mexico, man. That place is like . . . primitive."

"Sorry to hear it . . ."

"Yeah, sure . . ."

"You check in with me, okay? You got my number?"

Proud nodded, dug in his pocket and came up with a business card printed with a nine-digit number, broken into groups of three, two and four digits, like a Social Security number. He handed the card to Lucas. "Call the last seven numbers, backward. That's my beeper. You want to see me again, phone ahead, huh? Don't come knocking on the fucking door."

"Okay. And I'll give you some free advice, Orville," Lucas said as he stepped away. "Get rid of Ralph. Ralph's a head case and he's looking for somebody to kill. Get yourself a baseball bat or something. If you stay with Ralph, you'll go to Stillwater with him on a murder rap. I guarantee it."

"I hear you," Proud said, but he didn't.

Back in the parking lot, Lucas leaned against the car, thinking it over. They were at a dead end.

Daniel'd have to go for the TV.

# 6

Beauty danced.

A jig, to music that played only in his brain.

He hopped from one foot to another, his penis bobbing like the head of a blind waxen cave worm, his arms, crooked at the elbow, flapping like chicken wings. He laughed with the pleasure of it, the feel of Persian wool carpet under the bare soles of his feet, the sight of himself in the freestanding mirrors.

He danced and he twirled and he hopped and he laughed. . . .

He felt a wetness on his chest and looked down. A crimson rain was falling on his chest. He touched his nose. His fingers came away sticky, red. Blood. Running across his lips, dripping from his chin, trickling down across his pale, hairless chest to the thatch of hair at his crotch. The music drained from his brain.

"Blood," he moaned. "You're bleeding. . . ."

His heart pounding, Bekker got on his knees, groped under the desk and pulled out his briefcase. Knowing that the police would be in his house, he had thought it prudent to move his medications to his office. He'd not yet returned them to the medicine chest. He fumbled at the tiny combination lock on the case and got it open. Dozens of medical vials were jammed inside, amber plastic with white caps and taped-on labels, mostly prescription, a few over-the-counter dietary supplements. He pawed through them, still dripping blood.

Amobarbital. Dextroamphetamine. Loxapine. Secobarbital. Ethotoin. Chlordiazepoxide. Amiloride. No, no, no, no . . . He should have a color-coding system, he thought; but once he had them back on the shelves, it would be easier. He could put the uppers on top, the downers at the bottom, the smoothers on the second shelf, the vitamins and supplements under that. . . . Haloperidol. Diazepam. Chlorpromazine. No. Where was it? Where? He was sure . . . Ah. Here. Vitamin K. How many? No problem with vitamin K, better safe than sorry. He tossed five caps in his mouth, grimaced and swallowed.

Better. The bleeding was slowing anyway, but the extra K couldn't hurt. He pulled a wad of tissues from a Kleenex box on his desk, pressed it to his nose. He'd bled before. There was no pain, and the bleeding would soon stop. But, he thought, only two this time and I'm bleeding. He'd taken them, why had he taken them, the methamphetamines? There was a reason. . . .

He looked at the corner of his desk, at the brass cigarette case, the lid popped open, an invitation. Three black-coated methamphetamine tablets nestled in one quadrant of the box, sharing space with the phenobarbitals, the butalbitals and the criminals of the crew, all in a single, separate cell: the one remaining pale blue tab of acid, the four white innocuous-looking hits of phencyclidine and the three innocent Contac capsules.

Only three methamphetamines? But he usually kept seven in the box. Could he have taken four by mistake? He couldn't remember, but he felt up, wired, he'd danced for . . . how long? A long time, he thought. Maybe he'd better . . .

He did a phenobarbital to level himself out. And it wouldn't hurt the bleeding, either. Maybe . . . He did one more, then carried the cigarette case, the emergency kit, back to the briefcase, the mother ship, and carefully refilled it.

Still bleeding? Bekker took the Kleenex away from his face. The blood looked black against the blue tissue, but the flow had stopped. He stood and stepped carefully around the clothes he'd strewn on the floor when the amphetamines came on him. Why had he eaten them? *Must think.*

His study was neat, with wooden in boxes and out boxes on the antique desk, an IBM electric on an antique corner table, a wall of shelves filled with books, journals, magazines. On the wall next to the door was a photograph of himself, standing next to an E-type Jaguar. Not his, unfortunately, but a beautiful car. A silver frame around the photograph.

Stephanie smiled from a matching frame, on the other side of the door. She was wearing jodhpurs, why was she . . . ? *Hard to think.* Must. Stephanie? The lover. Who was the lover?

That was the critical question. He'd thought the amphetamines might help him with that. . . . If they had, he couldn't remember.

He sat down in the middle of the floor, his legs spread. Must think . . .


Bekker sighed. His tongue slipped out, tasted salt. He looked down and found himself covered with a dark crust. Crust? He touched his chest with a fingertip. Blood. Drying blood . . .

He got to his feet, stiff, climbed the stairs, hunched over, touching each riser with his hands as he went up, and then went down the hall to the bathroom. He turned the tap handles, started the water running, ducked his head toward the sink, splashed cold water on his face, stood, looked into the mirror.

His face was pink, his chest still liver-red with the blood crust. He looked like the devil, he thought. The thought came naturally. Bekker knew all about the devil. His parents, immersed in the severities of their Christian faith, had hammered the devil into him, hammered in the old, dead words of Jonathan Edwards. . . .

*There are in the souls of wicked men those hellish principles reigning, that would presently kindle and flame out into hell fire, were it not for God's restraints.*

He'd never seen God's restraints, Bekker had told the preacher one Sunday night. For that he had gotten a beating that at the time he thought would kill him. Had, in fact, not been able to go to school for a week, and had seen not a gram of pity in his parents' eyes.

Bekker, sopping up the blood, looked into the mirror and spoke the old words, still remembered: "*God holds you over the pit of hell, much as one holds a spider or some loathsome insect over the fire, abhors you, and is dreadfully provoked.* Bullshit."

But was it? Did the consciousness go somewhere after death? Was there a pit? The children he'd seen die, that change of gaze at the last instant . . . was that ecstasy? Did they see something beyond?

Bekker had studied the films taken by the Nazis at the death camps, stared into the filmed faces of dying medical experiments, films considered collectible by certain influential Germans. . . . Was there something beyond?

Bekker's rational scientist mind said no: We are no more than animated mud, a conscious piece of dirt, the consciousness no more than a chemical artifact. *Remember thou that thou art dust and to dust thou shalt return.* Isn't that what the Catholics professed? Odd candor, for a Church Political. Whatever his rational mind said, the other parts, the instinctive parts, couldn't imagine a world without Beauty. He couldn't simply *vanish* . . . could he?

He glanced at his watch. He had time. With the proper medication . . . He looked out of the bathroom at the brass box on the bureau.


Michael Bekker, very smooth, a little of the cocaine, just a lick of the phencyclidine, slipped through the halls of University Hospital.

"Dr. Bekker . . ." A nurse, passing, calling him "Doctor." The word flushed him with power; or the lick of PCP did. Sometimes it was hard to tell.

The hallway lights were dimmed, for night. Three women in white sat under the brighter lights of the nursing station, thumbing through papers, checking medication requirements. Overhead, a half-dozen monitors, flickering like the components of a rich man's stereo system, tracked the condition of the ICU patients.

Bekker checked his clipboard. Hart, Sybil. Room 565. He headed that way, taking his time, past a private room where a patient was snoring loudly. He looked around quickly: nobody watching. Stepped inside. The patient was sound asleep, her head back, her mouth hanging open. Sounded like a chainsaw, Bekker thought. He went to the bedside table, opened the drawer. Three brown vials of pills. He took them out, half turned to the dim light coming in from the hall. The first was penicillamine, used to prevent kidney stones. No need for that. He put it back. Paramethasone. More kidney stuff. The third vial said "Chlordiazepoxide hydrochloride 25mg." He opened it, looked inside at the green-and-white caps. Ah. Librium. He could always use some Librium. He took half of the tablets, screwed the top back on the vial and put the vial in the drawer. The Librium caps he dropped into his pocket.

At the door, he stopped to listen. You had to be careful in this: nurses wore running shoes, and were silent as ghosts. But if you knew what to listen for, you could pick up the almost imperceptible squawk-squawk-squawk of the shoes on polished tile. . . .

The hall was silent and he stepped out, squinting at his clipboard, ready to look confused if a nurse was in the hall. There were none, and he went on toward Sybil Hart's room.

Sybil Hart had raven hair and dark liquid eyes. She lay silently watching the screen of the television bolted into a corner of her room. An earplug was fitted in one ear, and although the inanities of late-night television sometimes made her want to scream . . . she didn't.

Couldn't.

Sybil Hart lay unmoving, propped semi-erect on her bed. She was not in the

ICU proper, but was accessible, where the nurses could check her every half-hour or so. She'd be dead in three weeks, a month, killed by amyotrophic lateral sclerosis—ALS, Lou Gehrig's disease.

The disease had started with a numbness in the legs, a tendency to stumble. She'd fought it, but it had taken her legs, her bowel control, her arms and, finally, her voice. Now, and most cruelly, it had taken her facial muscles, including her eyelids and eyebrows.

As the ALS had progressed and her voice had gone, she'd learned to communicate through an Apple computer equipped with special hardware and a custom word-processing program. When the disease had taken her voice, she'd still had some control of her fingers, and using two fingers and a special switch, she could write notes almost as effortlessly as if she were typing.

When her fingers had gone, the therapist had fitted her with a mouth switch, and still she could talk. When her mouth control had gone, another special switch had been fitted to her eyebrow. Now that was going, was almost gone. Sybil Hart began to sink into the final silence, waiting for the disease to take her diaphragm. When it did, she would smother . . . in another two or three weeks. . . .

In the meantime, there was nothing wrong with her brain and she could still move her eyes. The CNN commentator was babbling about a DEA raid on a drug laboratory at UCLA.

Bekker stepped inside her room and Sybil's eyes shifted to him.

"Sybil," he said, his voice quiet but pleasant. "How are you?"

He had visited her three times before, interested in the disease that incapacitated the body but left the brain alive. With each visit he'd seen further deterioration. The last time she had barely been able to respond with the word processor. A nurse had told him several days before that now even that was gone.

"Can we talk?" Bekker asked in the stillness. "Can you shift to your processor?"

He looked at the television in the corner of the room, but the screen stayed with CNN.

"Can you change it?" Bekker stepped closer to her bed, saw her eyes tracking him. He moved closer, peering into them. "If you can change it, make your eyes go up and down, like you're nodding. If you can't, make them go back and forth, like you're shaking your head."

Her eyes moved slowly back and forth.

"You're telling me you can't change it?"

Her eyes moved up and down.

"Excellent. We're communicating. Now . . . just a moment." Bekker stepped away from Sybil's bed and looked down the corridor. He could see just the corner of the nurses' station, a hundred feet away, and the cap on the head of a nurse, bowed over the desk, busy. Nobody else. He went back to the bed, pulled a chair up and sat where Sybil could see him. "I would like to explain my studies to you," he said. "I'm studying death, and you're going to be a wonderful participant."

Sybil's eyes were fixed on him as he began to talk.

And when he left, fifteen minutes later, she looked up at the CNN commentator and began to strain. If only . . . if only. It took twenty minutes, exhausting her, but suddenly there was a click and the word processor was up. Now. She needed a B.

When the nurse came by a half-hour later, Sybil was staring at the word processor. On the screen was a single B.

"Oh, what happened?" the nurse asked.

They all knew Sybil Hart could no longer operate the equipment. They'd left the switch attached because her husband had insisted. For morale. "You must've had a little twitch, there," the nurse said, patting Sybil's unfeeling leg. "Let me get the TV back for you."

Sybil watched in despair as the B disappeared, replaced by the tanned face and stupid shining teeth of the CNN commentator.

Four floors below, Bekker wandered through the pathology lab, whistling tunelessly, lost in not-quite-thought. The lab was cool, familiar. He thought of Sybil, dying. If only he could have a patient just a little early, just five minutes. If he could take a dying patient apart, watch the mechanism . . .

Bekker popped two MDMAs. Beauty broke into his jig.

# 7

Light.

Lucas moved his head and cracked an eye. Sunlight sliced between the slats in the blinds and cut across the bed. Daylight? He sat up, yawning, and looked at the clock. Two o'clock. Telephone ringing.

"Jesus . . ." He'd been in bed for nine hours: he hadn't slept that long for months. He'd unplugged the bedroom phone, not wanting it to ring if he did manage to sleep. Now he rolled out, yawned and stretched as he walked into the kitchen and picked up the telephone.

"Yeah. Davenport." He'd left the kitchen blinds up the night before and saw, up the block, a woman walking with an Irish setter on a leash.

"Lucas? Daniel . . ."

"Yeah."

"I've been talking to people. We're going with television."

"Terrific. What time's the press conference?" The woman was closer now, and Lucas was suddenly aware that he was standing naked in front of a window that was barely knee-high.

"Tomorrow."

"Tomorrow?" Lucas frowned at the phone. "You gotta do it today."

"Can't. No time. We didn't decide until a half-hour ago—Homicide still doesn't like it."

"They think it makes them look bad. . . ." The woman was one lot away, and Lucas squatted, getting down out of sight.

"Whatever. Anyway, it'll take the rest of the day to get a package together. I've got to meet with the county attorney about the legal angles, figure out if we're gonna try to pull full-time surveillance on Bekker, and all that. We're sorting it out now. I left some messages at your office, but when you didn't get back, I figured you were on the street."

"Uh, yeah," Lucas said. He looked around the kitchen. Unwashed dishes were stacked in the sink and microwave-dinner boxes were crushed into a plastic wastebasket. Bills were piled on the kitchen table with books, magazines, catalogues—two weeks' worth of mail, unopened. He was living like a pig. "Just walked in the door."

"Well, we're gonna do the conference early tomorrow afternoon. Probably two o'clock. We'll want you around. You know, for the PR. Wear the usual undercover rig, you know they like that, the TVs. . . ."

"All right. I'll be down a little early tomorrow, talk it over. But today would be better."

"Can't do it," Daniel said. "Too many details to smooth out. You coming in?"

"Maybe later. I'm trying to get an interview over at University Hospital with a guy who knows Bekker."

When Daniel got off the phone, Lucas peeked over the windowsill and found a redheaded woman staring vacantly at the front of his house while pretending not to see her dog relieve itself in Lucas' bushes.

"God damn it." He crawled back to the bedroom, found his notebook, sat on his bed and called Webster Prentice at the University of Minnesota. He got a secretary and was switched to Prentice's office.

"You think Bekker killed her?" Prentice asked, after Lucas introduced himself.

"Who mentioned Bekker?"

"Why else would a cop be calling me?" the psychologist said in a jovial fat-man's voice. "Listen, I'd like to help, but you're talking to the wrong guy. Let me suggest that you call Dr. Larry Merriam."

Merriam's office was in a building that from the outside looked like a machine, with awkward angles, unlikely joints. Inside, it was a maze, with tunnels and skyways linking it to adjoining buildings, ground-level exits on different floors. Entire floors were missing in some parts of the structure. Lucas wandered for ten minutes, and asked twice for directions, before he found a bank of elevators that would take him to the sixth floor of the right wing.

Merriam's secretary was short, overweight and worried, scurrying like a Disney churchmouse to locate her boss. Larry Merriam, when she brought him back from the lab, was a balding, soft-faced man in a white smock, with large dark eyes and tiny worried hands. He took Lucas into his office, pressed his fingertips to his lips and said, "Oh, dear," when Lucas told him what he wanted. "This is totally off the record?"

"Sure. And nothing'll come back to you. Not unless you confess that you killed Mrs. Bekker," Lucas said, smiling, trying to loosen him up.

Merriam's office overlooked a parking garage. The cinder-block walls had been painted a cream color; a small bulletin board was covered with medical cartoons. From behind the desk Merriam mouthed silently, *Shut the door.*

Lucas reached back and eased the door shut. Merriam relaxed, folding his hands over his chest.

"Clarisse is a wonderful secretary, but she does have trouble keeping a secret," Merriam said. He stood, hands in his pockets, and turned to look out the window behind his desk. A man in a red jacket, carrying what looked like a doctor's bag, was walking across the roof of the parking garage. "And Bekker is a troubling subject."

"A lot of people seem to be troubled by Mr. Bekker," Lucas said. "We're trying to find an angle, a . . ." He groped for the right words.

"An entry wedge," Merriam said, glancing back over his shoulder at Lucas. "You always need one, in any kind of research."

"Exactly right. With Bekker—"

"What's this man doing?" Merriam interrupted, staring down at the roof of the parking garage. The man in the red jacket stopped next to a midnight-blue BMW, glanced around, took a long silver strip of metal from his coat sleeve and slipped it between the window and the weather stripping, down into the door. "I think, uh . . . Is this man stealing that car?"

"What?" Lucas stepped over to the window and looked out. The man below stopped for a moment and looked up at the hospital building, as though he sensed Merriam and Lucas watching. He wouldn't be able to see them through the tinted glass. Lucas felt a pulse of amusement.

"Yeah, he is. Gotta make a call, just take a minute," Lucas mumbled, reaching for Merriam's desk phone.

"Sure," Merriam said, looking at him oddly, then back down at the thief. "Dial nine . . ."

Lucas dialed straight through to the dispatcher. "Shirl', this is Lucas. I'm looking out a window at a guy named E. Thomas Little. He's breaking into a BMW." He gave her the details and hung up.

"Oh, dear," Merriam said, looking out the window, his fingertips pressed to his lips again. E. Thomas Little finally got the door open and climbed into the front seat of the BMW.

"E. Thomas is an old client of mine," Lucas said. The amusement pulsed through him again, felt good, like a spring wind.

"And he *is* stealing the car?"

"Yeah. He's not much good at it, though. Right now he's jerking the lock cylinder out of the steering column."

"How long will it take a police car to get here?"

"Another minute or so," Lucas said. "Or about a thousand bucks in damage." They watched, silently, together, as Little continued to work in the front seat of the car. Sixty seconds after he got inside, he backed the car out of the parking space and started toward the exit. As he was about to enter the circular down ramp, a squad car, driving up the wrong way, jerked to a stop in front of him. Little put the BMW in reverse and backed away, but the squad stayed with him. A minute later he was talking to the cops.

"Very strange," Merriam said, as the cops handcuffed Little and put him in the backseat of the squad. One of the patrolmen looked up at the hospital windows, as Little had, and waved. Merriam lifted a hand, realized that he couldn't be seen, and turned back to Lucas. "You wanted to know about Michael Bekker."

"Yeah." Lucas went back to his chair. "About Dr. Bekker . . ."

"He's . . . Do you know what I do?"

"You're a pediatric oncologist," Lucas said. "You treat kids with cancer."

"Yes. Bekker asked if he could observe our work. He has excellent credentials in his own field, which is pathology, and he's also developing something of a reputation among sociologists and anthropologists for work on what he calls the social organization of death. That's what brought him up here. He wanted to do a detailed examination of the chemistry we use, and how we use it, but he also wanted to know how we handle death itself . . . what conventions and structures had grown up around it."

"You agreed?"

Merriam nodded. "Sure. There are dozens of studies going on here all the time—this is a teaching and research hospital. Bekker had the credentials and both the studies had potential value. In fact, his work *did* result in procedural changes."

"Like what?"

Merriam took his glasses off and rubbed his eyes. He looked tired, Lucas thought. Not like he'd missed a night's sleep, but like he'd missed five years' sleep. "Some of it's stuff you just don't notice if you work with it all the time. When you know somebody's about to die—well, there are things that have to be done with the body and the room. You have to clean up the room, you have to prepare to move the body down to Path. Some patients are quite clear-headed when they're dying. So how must it feel when a maid shows up and peeks into the room with a bunch of cleaning stuff, checking to see if you're gone yet? The patient knows we must've told her, 'Well, this guy'll be gone today.' "

"Ouch," Lucas said, wincing.

"Yeah. And Bekker was looking at more subtle problems, too. One of the things about this job is that some medical people can't handle it. We treat kids with advanced and rare types of cancer, and almost all of them eventually die. And if you watch enough kids die, and their parents going through it with them . . . well, the burnout rate with nurses and technicians and even doctors is terrific. And they sometimes develop problems with chronic incapacitating depression. That can go on for years, even after the victim has stopped working with the kids. Anyway, having Bekker look at us, we thought, might give us some ideas about how we might help ourselves."

"That sounds reasonable," Lucas said. "But the way you're talking . . . did Bekker do something wrong? What happened?"

"I don't know if anything happened," Merriam said, turning to look out at the sky. "I just don't know. But after he was here for a week or two, my people started coming in. He was making them nervous. He didn't seem to be studying so much the routines of death . . . the structures, processes, the formalities, whatever you'd call them . . . as watching the deaths themselves. And enjoying them. The staff members were starting to call him 'Dr. Death.' "

"Jesus," said Lucas. Sloan had said that Bekker was known as "Dr. Death" in Vietnam. "He enjoyed it?"

"Yeah." Merriam turned back and leaned over his desk, his hands clenched on the desktop. "The people who were working with him said he seemed to become . . . excited . . . as a death approached. Agitation is common among the medical people—you take a kid and he's fought it all the way, and you've fought it all the way with him, and now he's going. In circumstances like that, even longtime medical people get cranked up. Bekker was different. He was excited the way people get with an intellectual pleasure."

"Not sexual?"

"I can't say that. There *was* an intensity of feeling on the order of sexual pleasure. In any case, it seemed to people who worked with him that it was definitely pleasure. When a kid died, he registered a certain satisfaction." Merriam stood and took a turn around his chair, stopping to look down at the parking garage. A patrolman had pulled the BMW back into its parking place and was standing beside it, writing out a note to its owner. "I don't know if I should say this, I could expose myself to some criticism. . . ."

"We're off the record. I mean that," Lucas said.

Merriam continued to look out the window and Lucas realized that he was deliberately avoiding eye contact. Lucas kept his mouth shut and let the silence stretch.

"There's a rhythm to death in a cancer ward," Merriam said eventually, and slowly, as though he were considering each word. "A kid might be an inch from death, but you know he won't die. Sure enough, he improves. Everything backs off. He's sitting up again, talking, watching TV. Six weeks later, he's gone."

"Remissions," Lucas offered.

"Yeah. Bekker was here, off and on, for three months. We had an agreement: He could come in anytime, day or night, to watch. Not much to see at night, of course, but he wanted complete access to the life on the wards. There was some value in that, so we agreed. Remember: He's a university professor with excellent credentials. But we didn't want a guy wandering around the wards on his own, so we asked him to sign in and out. No problem. He understood, he said. Anyway, during his time here, a child died. Anton Bremer. Eleven years old. He was desperately ill, highly medicated . . ."

"Drugged?"

"Yes. He was close to death, but when he died, it came as a surprise. Like I said, there seems to be a rhythm to it. If you work on the ward long enough, you begin to feel it. Anton's death was out of place. But you see, sometimes that *does* happen, that a kid dies when it seems he shouldn't. When Anton died, I never thought much about it. It was simply another day on the ward."

"Bekker had something to do with the death?"

"I can't say that. I shouldn't even suspect it. But his attitude toward the deaths of our patients began to anger our people. Nothing he said, just his attitude. It pissed them off, is what it did. By the end of the three months—that was the trial period of the project—I decided not to extend it. I can do that, without specifying a reason. For the good of the division, that sort of thing. And I did."

"Did that make him angry?"

"Not . . . obviously. He was quite cordial, said he understood and so on. So two or three weeks after he left, one of the nurses came to me—she doesn't work here anymore, she finally burned out—and said that she hadn't been able to stop thinking about Anton. She said she couldn't get it out of her head that Bekker had killed him somehow. She thought the kid had turned. He was going down, hit bottom and was stabilizing, beginning to rally. She was a second-shift nurse, she worked three to midnight. When she came in the next afternoon, Anton was dead. He died sometime during the night. She didn't think about Bekker until later, and she went back to see what time he had signed out that night. It turned out our log didn't show him signing in or out. But she remembers that he was there and had looked at the kid a couple of times and was still there when she left. . . ."

"So she thinks he wiped the log in case anybody ever went back to try to track unexplained deaths."

"That's what she thought. We talked about it, and I said I'd look into it. I talked to a couple of other people, and thinking back, they weren't sure whether he was here or not, but on the balance, they thought he was. I called Bekker, gave him this phony excuse that we were looking into a pilferage problem, and asked him if he'd ever seen anybody taking stacks of scrub suits out of the supply closet. He said no. I asked him if he'd always signed in and out whenever he visited, and he said he thought so, but maybe, at one time or another, he'd missed."

"You can't catch him in a lie . . ." Lucas said.

"No."

"Were there any other deaths? Like this kid's?"

"One. The second or third week he was on the wards. A little girl with bone cancer. I thought about it later, but I don't know. . . ."

"Were there postmortems on the kids?"

"Sure. Extensive ones."

"Did he do them? Do you know?"

"No, no, we have a fellow who specializes in that."

"Did he find anything unusual?"

"No. The fact is, these kids were so weak, they were so near the edge, that if he'd simply reached out and pinched off their oxygen feeds . . . that might have been enough. We'd never find that on a postmortem—not enough to separate it from all the other wild chemical shit we see in cancer cases: massive loads of drugs, radiation reactions, badly disturbed bodily functions. By the time you do a postmortem, these kids are a mess."

"But you think he might have killed them."

"That's too strong," Merriam said, finally turning around and looking at Lucas. "If I really thought that, I'd have called the police. If there had been any medical indication or anybody who actually saw anything or had a reason to believe he'd done it, I'd have called. But there was nothing. Nothing but a feeling. That could simply be a psychological artifact of our own, the insider's resentment of an outsider intruding on what Bekker called our 'rituals of death.' "

"Did he publish?" Lucas asked.

"Yes. I can give you the citations. Actually, I can probably have Clarisse scrounge up some photocopies."

"I'd appreciate it," Lucas said. "Well . . . You know what happened. The other night."

"Bekker's wife was killed."

"We're looking into it. Some people, frankly, think he might have had a hand in it."

"I don't know. I'd kind of doubt it," Merriam said grimly.

"You sounded like you thought he'd be capable. . . ."

"I'd doubt it because if he knew his wife was going to be killed, he'd want to be there to see it," Merriam said. Then, suddenly abashed, he added, "I don't know if I believe that, really."

"Huh," Lucas said, studying the other man. "Is he still in the hospital, working with live patients? Bekker?"

"Yes. Not on this ward, but several others. I've seen him down in the ORs a couple of times and in the medical wards where they deal with the more extreme varieties of disease."

"Did you ever mention to anyone . . . ?"

"Listen, I don't *know* anything," Merriam barked, his soft exterior dropping for a moment. "That's my problem. If I say anything, I'm implying the guy is a killer, for Christ's sakes. I can't do that."

"A private word . . ."

"In this place? It'd stay private for about thirty seconds," Merriam said, running a hand through his thinning hair. "Listen, until you've worked in a university hospital, you've never really experienced character assassination. There are ten people on this staff who are convinced they'll be on next year's Nobel list if only some klutz in the next office doesn't screw them up. If I suggested anything about Bekker, it would be all over the hospital in five minutes. Five minutes later, he'd hear about it and I'd be fingered as the source. I *can't* do anything."

"All right." Lucas nodded. He stood, picked up his coat. "Would you get me copies of those papers?"

"Sure. And if there's anything else I can do for you, call, and I'll do it. But you see the kind of jam I'm in."

"Sure." Lucas reached for the door, but Merriam stopped him with a quick gesture.

"I've been trying to think how to characterize the way Bekker acted around death," he said. "You know how you read about these zealots on crusades against pornography, and you sense there's something wrong with them? A fascination with the subject that goes way beyond any normal interest? Like a guy has a collection of two thousand porno magazines so he can prove how terrible it is? That's how Bekker was. A kind of a pious sadness when a kid died, but underneath, you got the feeling of a real, lip-smacking pleasure."

"You make him sound like a monster," Lucas said.

"I'm an oncologist," Merriam said simply. "I believe in monsters."

Lucas walked out of the hospital, hands in his pockets, thinking. A pretty nurse smiled at him, and he automatically smiled back, but his head wasn't smiling. Bekker killed kids?

The medical examiner's investigator was a fat, gloomy man with cheeks and lips so pink and glossy that he looked as though he might have been playing with an undertaker's makeup. He handed Lucas the file on Stephanie Bekker.

"If you want my opinion, the guy who did her was either a psycho or wanted it to look that way," the investigator said. "Her skull was like a broken egg, all in fragments. The bottle he hit her with was one of those big, thick tourist things from Mexico. You know, kind of blue-green, more like a vase than a bottle. The glass must have been a half-inch thick. When it broke, he used it like a knife, and drove the edges right down through her eyes. Her whole face was muti-lated, you'll see in the photographs. The thing is . . ."

"Yeah?"

"The rest of her body was untouched. It wasn't like he was flailing away, hitting her anyplace he could. You take somebody flying on crank or PCP, they're just swinging. They go after a guy, and if the guy gets behind a car, they'll go after the car. If they can't hit you on the face, they'll hit you on the shoulders or chest or back or the soles of your feet, and they'll bite and claw and everything else. This thing was almost . . . technical. The guy who did it is either nuts and it has something to do with the face, with the eyes, or it's supposed to look that way."

"Thanks for the tip," Lucas said. He sat down at an empty desk, opened the file and glanced at the photos.

Freak, he thought.

The file was technical. To judge from body temperature and lack of lividity, the woman had died just before the paramedics arrived. Stephanie Bekker had never had a chance to resist: she had been a strong woman, with long finger-nails, and they were clean—no blood or skin beneath them. There were no abrasions on the hands. She'd had intercourse, while alive and probably an hour or so before she'd died. No bruising was evident around the vagina and there were indications that the intercourse had been voluntary. She had washed after the intercourse, and samples taken for DNA analysis might not prove valid. The samples had not yet been returned.

The medical examiner's investigator noted that the house had been undis-turbed, with no evidence of a fight or even an argument. The front door had been unlocked, as had a door into the kitchen from the garage. Bloody tracks led into the garage. The outer garage door had also been unlocked, so an intruder could have come through the house from the alley. There was a single bloody handprint on the wall, and a trail of blood from the point where she'd fallen in the initial attack. She'd lived, the medical examiner thought, for twenty to thirty minutes after the attack.

Lucas closed the file and sat staring at the desktop for a moment.

Loverboy could have done it. If the few solid facts of the case had been given him, Lucas would have bet money on it. But this kind of violence rarely came immediately after a successful sexual encounter; not without some pre-liminary crockery-tossing, some kind of mutual violence.

And then there was Bekker. Everybody had a nervous word for the man.

The fat investigator was washing his hands when Lucas left.

"Figure anything out?" he asked.

"Freak," Lucas said.

"A problem."

"If it's not a freak . . ." Lucas started.

"Then you got a *big* problem," the fat man finished for him, shaking water from his delicate pink fingers.

The days were getting longer. In the pit of winter, dusk arrives shortly after four o'clock. When Lucas arrived at City Hall, there was still light in the sky, although it was well after six.

Sloan had already gone, but Lucas found Del in Narcotics, flipping through a reports file.

"Anything good?" Lucas asked.

"Not from me," Del said. He pushed the file drawer shut. "There were meetings all day. The suits were arguing about who's going to do what. I don't think you'll get your surveillance team."

"Why not?"

Del shrugged. "I don't think they'll do it. The suits keep saying that there's nothing on Bekker, except that some dope cop thinks he did it. Meanin' me—and you know what they think about me."

"Yeah." Lucas grinned despite himself. The suits would like to see Del in a uniform, writing tickets. "Is the press conference still on?"

"Two o'clock tomorrow," Del said. "You been out on your net?"

"Yeah. Nothing there. But I talked to a doc at University Hospital, he thinks Bekker might have killed a kid. Maybe two."

"Kids?"

"Yeah. In the cancer ward. I'll use it to jack up Daniel on the surveillance, if I have to."

"Awright," Del said. "Nothing works like blackmail. . . ."

Lucas' answering machine had half a dozen messages, none of them about Bekker. He made two answering calls, checked the phone numbers on the pen register and locked up. City Hall was almost dark and his footfalls echoed through the emptying corridors.

"Davenport . . ."

He turned. Karl Barlow, a sergeant with Internal Affairs, was walking toward him with a sheaf of papers in his hand. Barlow was small, square-shouldered, square-faced and tightly muscular, like a gymnast. He wore his hair in a jock's crew cut and dressed in white short-sleeved shirts and pleated pants. He always had a plastic pocket protector in his breast pocket, filled with an evenly spaced row of ballpoint pens. He was, he professed, an excellent Christian.

An excellent Christian, Lucas thought, but not good on the streets. Barlow had trouble with ambiguities. . . .

"We need a statement on the brawl the other night. I've been trying . . ."

"That wasn't a brawl, that was an arrest of a known pimp and drug dealer on a charge of first-degree assault," Lucas said.

"A juvenile, sure. I've been trying to get you at your office, but you're never in."

"I've been working this Bekker murder. Things are jammed up," Lucas said shortly.

"Can't help that," Barlow said, planting one fist on his waist. Lucas had heard that Barlow was a Youth Football coach and had found himself in trouble with parents for insisting that a kid play hurt. "I've got to make an appointment with a court stenographer, so I've got to know when you can do it."

"Give me a couple of weeks."

"That might be too long," Barlow said.

"I'll come in when I can," Lucas said impatiently, trying to get away. "There's no rush, right? And I might bring an attorney."

"That's your right." Barlow moved in closer, crowding, and poked the sheaf of papers at Lucas. "But I want this settled and I want it settled soon. If you get my drift."

"Yeah. I get your drift," Lucas said. He turned back toward Barlow, so they were chest to chest and no more than four inches apart. Barlow had to move back a half-step and look up to meet Lucas' eyes. "I'll let you know when I can do it."

*And I'll throw you out the fuckin' window if you give me any shit,* Lucas thought. He turned away and went up the steps. Barlow called, "Soon," and Lucas said, "Yeah, yeah . . ."

He stopped just outside the City Hall doors, on the sidewalk, looked both ways and shook himself like a horse trying to shake off flies. The day had a contrary feel to it. He sensed that he was waiting, but he didn't know for what.

Lucas crossed the street to the parking garage.

# 8

Pressure. He opened his fist, felt for the tab in his hand, licked it, felt the acidic cut of the drug as well as the salty taste of his own sweat. Too much? He had to be careful. He couldn't bleed today, he'd be in the car. But then the speed was on him and he stopped thinking about it.

He called Druze from a pay phone.

"We have to risk it," he said. "If I do Armistead tonight, the police will go crazy. Meeting could be tough after this."

"Are the cops still hanging around?" Druze sounded not worried—his emotional range might not reach that far—but concerned. "I mean, Armistead's still on, isn't she?"

"Yes. They keep coming back. They want me, but they've got nothing. Armistead will steer them further away."

"They might get something if they find the guy in the towel," Druze said sullenly.

"That's why we've got to meet."

"One o'clock?"

"Yes."


Stephanie's keepsake photos were stuffed in shoe boxes in the sewing closet, stuck in straw baskets in the kitchen, piled on a drawing table in the study, hidden in desk and bureau drawers. Three leather-bound albums were stacked in the library, photos going back to her childhood. Bekker, nude, stopping frequently to examine himself in the house's many mirrors, wandered through the antiques, hunting the photos. In her chest of drawers, he found a plastic bag for a diaphragm—at first he didn't recognize it for what it was—shook his head and put it back. When he was satisfied that he had all the photos, he fixed himself a sandwich, punched up Carl Orff's *Carmina Burana* on the CD player, sat in an easy chair and replayed the funeral in his mind.

He had been fine, he thought. The tough-guy cop. He couldn't read the tough guy, but he had Swanson beat. He could sense it. The tough guy, on the other hand . . . his clothes were too good, Bekker decided.

As he chewed, his eye found a small movement in the far corner of the room. He turned to catch it: another mirror, one of a dozen or so diamond-shaped plates set in the base of a French lamp from the twenties. He moved again, adjusting himself. His eyes were centered in one of the mirrors and, at this distance, looked black, like holes. His genitals were caught in another plate, and he laughed, genuine enjoyment.

"A symbol," Bekker said aloud. "But of what, I don't know." And he laughed again, and did his jig. The MDMA was still on him.

At noon he dressed, pulled on a sweater, loaded the photos into a shopping bag and went out through the breezeway to his car. Could the police be watching him? He doubted it—what else would they expect him to do? Stephanie was already dead; but he'd take no chances.

Out of the garage, he drove carefully through a snake's nest of streets to a small shopping center. No followers. He cruised the center for a few minutes, still watching, bought toilet tissue and paper towels, toothpaste and deodorant and aspirin, and returned to the car. Back through the snake's nest: nothing. He stopped at a convenience store and used the phone on the outside wall.

"I'm on my way."

"Fine. I'm alone."

Druze lived in a medium-rise apartment at the edge of the West Bank theater district. Bekker, still wary, circled the building twice before he left the car on the street, cut through the parking lot and buzzed Druze's apartment.

"It's me," he said. The door opened and he pushed through into the lobby, then took the stairs. Druze was watching a cable-channel show on scuba diving when Bekker arrived. Druze punched the TV out with a remote as Bekker followed him into the apartment.

"Those the pictures?" asked Druze, looking at the bag.

"Yes. I brought everything I could find."

"You want a beer?" Druze said it awkwardly. He didn't entertain; nobody came to his apartment. He had never had a friend before. . . .

"Sure." Bekker didn't care for beer, but enjoyed playing the relationship with Druze.

"Hope he's here," Druze said. He got a bottle of Bud Light from the refrigerator, brought it back and handed it to Bekker, who was kneeling on the front-room carpet, unloading the shopping bag. Bekker turned one of the shoe boxes upside down, and a clump of snapshots fell out on the rug.

"We'll get him," Bekker said.

"Big, flat, blond Scandinavian face. Head like a milk jug, pale, almost fat. Got pretty good love handles on him, a belly," said Druze.

"We knew a half-dozen people like that," Bekker said. He took a hit on the beer and grimaced. "Most likely he's part of the antiques crowd. That could be tough, 'cause I don't know all of them. There's a possibility that he's with the university. I don't know. This affair is the only thing the bitch ever did that surprised me."

"The bad thing is, antiques people are the kind of people who go to plays. Art people. He could see me."

"Up on the stage, with the makeup, you look different," Bekker said.

"Yeah, but afterwards, when we go out in the lobby and kiss ass with the crowd, he could see me up close. If he ever sees me . . ."

"We'll figure him out," Bekker said, dumping the last box of photos on the pile. "I'll sort, you look."

There were hundreds of pictures, and the process took longer than Bekker imagined it would. Stephanie with friends, in the woods, shopping, with relatives. No pictures of Bekker . . .

Halfway through the pile, Druze got to his feet, burped and said, "Keep sorting. I gotta pee."

"Mmm," Bekker nodded. As soon as Druze closed the bathroom door, he stood, waited a minute, then quickly padded across the front room to the kitchen and opened the end drawer on the sink counter. Maps, paid bills, a couple of screwdrivers, matchbooks . . . He stirred through the mess, found the key, slipped it into his pocket, eased the drawer shut and hurried back to the front room as he heard the toilet flush. He'd been here a few times, waiting for the chance at the key. . . . Now he had it.

"Any more candidates?" Druze asked, stepping out of the bathroom. Bekker was back in the center of the photo pile.

"A couple," Bekker said, looking up. "Come on. We're running late."

There were several large blond men, but this was Minnesota. Twice Druze thought he'd found him, but after a closer look under a reading lamp, he shook his head.

"Maybe you should look at them in person. Discreetly," Bekker suggested.

"They're not the guy," Druze said, shaking his head.

"You're positive?"

"Pretty sure. I didn't get the best look at him, I was on the floor, and he was standing up, but he was heavier than these guys. Fat, almost." He picked up a photo of Stephanie and a blond man, shook his head and spun it sideways back into the pile around Bekker.

"God damn it. I was sure he'd be in here," Bekker said. The photos were scattered around them like piles of autumn leaves; he grabbed a handful and threw them at an empty box, frustrated. "That bitch talked to everybody, took pictures of everybody, never gave anybody a minute's rest. Why wouldn't she have him in here? He's got to be here."

"Maybe he's somebody new. Or maybe she took them out. Have you gone through her stuff?"

"I spent half the morning at it. She had a diaphragm, can you believe it? I found this little plastic pack for it. Cops didn't say anything about that. . . . But there's nothing else. No more pictures."

Druze began scooping the photos together and tossing them into the boxes. "So what do we do? Do we go ahead? With Armistead?"

"There's a risk," Bekker admitted. "If we don't find him, and we do Armistead, he might decide to turn himself in. Especially if he's got an alibi for the time that Armistead gets hit—as far as we know, he's hiding out because he's afraid the cops think he did it."

"If we don't do Armistead pretty soon, she'll dump me," Druze said flatly. "This turkey we're working on now, this *Whiteface,* won't last. And she hates my ass. We're hurting for payroll and I'll be the first to go."

Bekker took a turn around the rug, thinking. "Listen. If this man, Stephanie's friend, turns himself in to the police, they'll tell me, one way or another. I wouldn't be surprised if they have him come look at me, just to make sure I didn't pull something out in San Francisco. Make sure I wasn't the killer and somebody else was out there . . . Anyway, if I can find out who he is, before he has a chance to see you, we can take him. So if we take Armistead, and you stay out of sight, except when you're working . . ."

"And then I'll stay in makeup. . . ."

"Yeah."

"That's what we ought to do," Druze said. "Maybe we can smoke the cocksucker out. If we can't, we can keep working on it. . . ."

"'I'll figure him out, sooner or later," Bekker said. "It's only a matter of time."

"How are we going to talk, if the cops stay on you?"

"I've worked that out."

Bekker's neighbor in the pathology department was working in England. Just before he had left, he and Bekker had chatted about their work and Bekker had noticed, idly at the time, that the other man had an answering machine in his bottom desk drawer, an operation manual peeking from beneath it. Late one night, when the office was empty, Bekker had slipped the old-fashioned lock on his neighbor's door, turned the answering machine on and used the instruction manual to work out new access codes for the memo option. He now gave the touch-tone codes to Druze.

"You can call from any touch-tone phone, leave a message. I can do the same to get the message, or leave one for you. You should check every few hours to see if I've left anything."

"Good," Druze said. "But make sure you clean up the tapes. . . ."

"You can erase them remotely, too," Bekker said, and explained.

Druze jotted the code numbers in an address book. "Then we're all set," he said.

"Yes. We should probably stay away from each other for a while."

"And we're gonna do Armistead like we planned?"

Bekker looked at the troll, and a smile touched his face. Druze thought it might be simple joy. "Yes," he said. "We'll do Armistead. We'll do her tonight."


The stained-glass windows in Bekker's parlor came from a North Dakota Lutheran church that had lost its congregation to the attractions of warmer climates and better jobs. Stephanie had bought the windows from the church trustees, trucked them back to the Twin Cities and learned how to work in lead. The restored windows hung above him, dark in the night, ignored. Bekker focused instead on the coil that was unwinding in his stomach.

A dark exhilaration: but too soon.

He suppressed it and sat on a warm wine-and-saffron Oriental carpet with a wet clawhammer and the pile of paper towels. He'd bought the hammer months before and never used it. He'd kept it in the basement, hidden in a drawer. Bekker knew just enough about crime laboratories to fear the possibil-

ity that a chemical analysis would pick up something unique to the house—
Stephanie's refinishing chemicals, glass dust or lead deposits. There was no
point in taking chances. He washed it with dishwashing detergent, then sat on
the rug and patted it dry with the paper towels. From now on, he would handle
it only wearing gloves. He wrapped the hammer in extra towels and left it on
the rug.

Plenty of time, he thought. His eyes skittered around the room and found his
sport coat hanging on a chair. He got the pill case from its breast pocket and
peered inside, calculating. No Beauty tonight. This needed a cold power. He
put a tab of PCP on his tongue, tantalized himself with the bite, then swallowed. And a methamphetamine, for the action; usually the amphetamines
were Beauty's ride, but not on top of the other. . . .


Elizabeth Armistead was an actress and a member of the board of directors of
the Lost River Theater. She'd once played on Broadway.

"Bitch'll never give me a part." Druze had been drunk and raving, the night
six months earlier when the deal had occurred to Bekker. "Just like that
movie—what was the name? On the train . . . ? She's gonna dump me. She's got
the pretty boys lined up. She likes pretty boys. With this face . . ."

"What happened?"

"The company voted to do *Cyrano*. Who gets the lead? Gerrold. The pretty
boy. They made him ugly and I'll carry a goddamn pike in the battle scenes.
Before this bitch joined up—she supposedly played on Broadway, big deal,
but that's why they took her, she can't act—I used to be something. The next
thing I know, I'm carrying fuckin' pikes."

"What're you going to do?"

Druze had shaken his head. "I don't know. Finding a job is tough. Up on the
stage, with the lights, with makeup, this face is okay. But getting in the door—
people look at me, theater people, and they say, Whoa, you're ugly. Theater
people don't like ugly. They like pretty."

Bekker had asked, "What if Elizabeth Armistead went away?"

"What do you mean?" But Bekker had caught the quick, feral glint when
Druze looked toward him, and he knew the idea was there in the back of
Druze's head. If Armistead went away, things would be different. Just like they
would be for him, if Stephanie went away. . . .


Bekker had kept the coveralls in a sack at the back of his chest of drawers since
he bought them, at a Sears, three months earlier. They were blue, the kind a
mechanic might wear. He pulled them over his jeans and sweatshirt, found the
matching hat in the closet and put it on. Druze knew about costumes and had

put it together for him. This costume said *service*. Nobody would look at him twice.

Bekker glanced at his watch, and the first dislocation occurred, thrilling him: the watch elongated, a Dalí watch, draped over his wrist like a sausage. Wonderful. And the power was coming, darkening his vision, shifting everything to the ultraviolet end. He groped in his pocket for the cigarette case, found a tab of the speed and swallowed it.

So good . . . He staggered through the room, feeling it, the power surging along his veins, a nicotine rush times two hundred. He pushed the power back in a corner, held it there, felt the tension.

The time was getting tighter. He hurried down the steps, checked a window to see how dark it was, then carefully picked up the hammer and slid it into his right-hand pocket. The rest of his equipment, the clipboard, the meter and the identification tag, were piled on Stephanie's desk.

The clipboard, with the paper clipped to it, went with the service costume. So did the meter. Druze had found the meter in an electronics junk store and bought it for almost nothing: it was obsolete, with a big analog dial on top, originally made for checking magnetic fields around power lines. The identification tag was Bekker's old hospital ID. He'd laminated it and punched a hole in one end, and hung it from his neck by an elastic string.

He took a breath, did a mental checklist, walked out through the breezeway to the car and used the automatic garage-door opener to lift the door. He drove the long way out of the alley, then continued through the next alley, watching his mirror. Nobody.

Traveling by back streets, he made it to Elizabeth Armistead's house in a little over eight minutes. He would have to remember that. If Druze suspected, he should know the time of his arrival. He just hoped she would be there.

"She does one half-hour of meditation, then drinks an herb tea, then comes down for the warm-ups," Druze said, prepping him. "She's fussy about it. She missed her meditation once and spent the whole show dropping lines."

Druze . . . The original plan had called for Bekker to phone Druze just before he left the house on the way to Armistead's. As soon as Druze got the call, at a remote phone in the theater's control booth, he would call the ticket office with his best California-cool accent. *My name is Donaldson Whitney. Elizabeth Armistead said that she would put me on the guest list for two tickets. I'm in a rush through town, but I have time for her play. Could you call her and confirm?*

They would call and confirm. They always did. Too many bullshitters trying to get in free. Donaldson Whitney, though, was a theater critic from Los Angeles. Armistead would gush . . . and the ticket people would remember. That was the point of the exercise: to create a *last man* to talk to the dead woman, with Druze already in makeup, onstage, warming up . . . alibied. Druze had suggested it and Bekker had found no way to demur.

He could, however, go early; Druze wouldn't have to know. But the cops would figure it out. . . .

And after doing Armistead, he could call as though he were just leaving his house. Then Druze would make his Donaldson Whitney call, and if Armistead didn't answer the phone when the ticket office called her, well, she simply wasn't home yet. That could hardly be Bekker's fault. . . .

Bekker took it slowly the last few minutes down to Armistead's. He'd cruised her house before, and there were no changes. The lots were small, but the houses were busy. One man coming or going would never be noticed. A light burned in Armistead's house, in the back. Her silver Dodge Omni was at the curb, where it usually was. He parked at the side of the house, under a tree heavy with bursting spring buds, got his equipment, leaned back in the seat and closed his eyes.

Like a digital readout: one-two-three-four-five. Easy steps. He let the power out, just a bit; when he looked, the steering wheel was out-of-round. He smiled, thinly, allowed himself to feel the burn in his blood for another moment, then got out of the car, changed the thin smile for a harassed look and walked around the corner to Armistead's house. Rang the doorbell. And again.

Armistead. Larger than he thought, in a robe. Pale oval face; dark hair swept back in a complicated roll, held with a wooden pin. Face slack, as though she'd been sleeping. Door on a chain. She peered out at him, her eyes large and dark. She'd look good on a stage. "Yes?"

"Gas company. Any odor of gas in the house?"

"No . . ."

"We show you have gas appliances, a washer and dryer, a hot-water heater?" All that from Druze's reconnaissance at an Armistead party. Bekker glanced down at the clipboard.

"Yes, down in the basement," she said. His knowledge of her home had confirmed his authority.

"We've had some critical pressure fluctuations up and down the street because of a main valve failure. We have a sniffer here"—Bekker hefted the black box, so she could see the meter—"and we'd like to take some readings in your basement, just in case. There could be a problem with sudden flareups. We had a fire over on the next block, you probably heard the fire trucks."

"Uh, I've been meditating. . . ." But she was already pulling the chain. "I'm in a terrible rush, I've got to get to work. . . ."

"Just take a minute or two," Bekker assured her. And he was in. He slipped his hand in his pocket, gripped the hammer, waited until he heard the door close firmly.

"Through the kitchen and down the stairs," Armistead said. Her voice was high and clear, but there was an impatient edge to it. A busy woman, interrupted.

"The kitchen?" Bekker glanced around. The drapes had been closed. The smell of prairie flowers was in the air, and spice, and Bekker realized that it must be her herb tea. The power came out now, out of the corner of his head, and his vision went momentarily blue. . . .

"Here. I'll show you," Armistead said impatiently. She turned her back on him, walking toward the rear of the house. "I haven't smelled a thing."

Bekker took a step behind her, began to draw the hammer, and suddenly blood gushed from his nose. He dropped the meter and caught the blood with his hand, and she saw the motion, turned, saw the blood, opened her mouth . . . to scream?

"No, no," he said, and her mouth closed, halfway . . . everything so slow. So slow, now. "Ah, this is the second time today. . . . Got hit in the nose by my child, just a five-year-old. Can't believe it . . . Do you have any tissue?"

"Yes . . ." Her eyes were wide, horrified, as the stream of blood dripped down his coveralls.

They were on the rug in the front room, and she started to pivot, going for the tissue. The power slowed her motion even more and demanded that he savor this. There could be no fights, no struggles, no chances. She couldn't be allowed to scratch him, or bruise him. . . . This was business, but the power knew what it wanted. She was saying, "Here, in the kitchen . . . ," she was pivoting, and Bekker, one hand clenched to his face, stepped close again, pulled the hammer from his pocket, swung it like a tennis racket, with a good forehand, got his back and shoulder in it.

The hammer hit with a double shock, hard, then soft, like knocking a hole in a plaster wall, and the impact twisted Armistead. She wasn't dead; her eyes were open wide, saliva sprayed from her mouth, her hips were twisting, her feet were coming off the floor. She went down, dying, but not knowing it, trying to fight, her hands up, her mouth open, and Bekker was on her, straddling her. One hand on her throat, her body bucking. Evading the fingernails, hitting with the blunt head of the hammer, her forehead, once, twice . . . and done.

He was breathing like a steam engine, the power on him, running him, his heart running, the blood streaming down his face. *Can't get any on her* . . . He brushed his bloodied face with the sleeve of his coveralls, looked back down, her eyes half open. . . .

Her eyes.

Bekker, suddenly frightened, turned the hammer.

He'd use the claw. . . .

# 9

The evening dragged; the feeling that he was *waiting* stayed with him.

He thought of calling Jennifer, to ask for an extra visit with their daughter. He reached for the phone once, twice, but never made the call. He wanted to see Sarah, but even more, he wanted to settle with Jennifer. Somehow. End it, or start working toward reconciliation. And that, he thought, was not a process begun with a spur-of-the-moment phone call. Not with Jennifer.

Instead of calling, he sat in front of the television and watched a bad cop movie on Showtime. He switched it off a few minutes before the torturously achieved climax: both the cops and the crooks were cardboard, and he didn't care what happened to any of them. After the late news, he went back to the workroom and began plodding through the game.

Bekker stuck in the back of his head. The investigation was dying. He could sense the waning interest in the other cops. They knew the odds against the case: without eyewitnesses or a clear suspect who had both motive and opportunity, there was almost no chance of an arrest, much less a conviction. Lucas knew of at least two men who had killed their wives and gotten away with it, and a woman who'd killed a lover. There was nothing fancy about any of the murders. No exotic weapons, no tricky alibis, no hired killers. The men had used clubs: a grease gun and an aluminum camera tripod. The woman had used a wooden-handled utility knife from Chicago Cutlery.

*I just found her/him like that,* they told the answering cops. When the cops read them their rights, all three asked for lawyers. After that, there wasn't anything to go on. The pure, unvarnished and almost unbreakable two-dude defense: Some other dude did it.

Lucas stared at the wall behind the desk. *I need this fuckin' case.* If the Bekker investigation failed, if the spark of interest diminished and died, he feared, he might slip back into the black hole of the winter's depression. Before the depression, he'd thought of mental illnesses as something suffered by people who were weak, without the will to suppress the problem, or somehow genetically impaired. No more. The depression was as real as a tiger in the jungle, looking for meat. If you let your guard down . . .

Bekker's beautiful face came up in his mind's eye, like a color slide projected on a screen. Bekker.

At twenty minutes after eleven, the phone rang. He looked at it for a moment, with a ripple of tension. Jennifer? He picked it up.

"Lucas?" Daniel's voice, hoarse, unhappy.

"What happened?"

"The sonofabitch did another one," Daniel rasped. "The guy who killed the Bekker woman. Call Dispatch for the address and get your ass over there."

A little spark of elation? A touch of relief? Lucas hammered the Porsche through the night, across the Mississippi, west to the lakes, blowing leftover winter leaves over the sidewalks, turning the heads of midnight walkers. He had no trouble finding the address: every light in the little house was on and the doors were open to the night. Groups of neighbors stood on the sidewalk, looking down toward the death house; occasionally one would cross the street to a new group, a new set of rumors, walking rapidly as though his speed alone would prove to watching cops that he was on a mission of urgency.

Elizabeth Armistead was lying faceup on her living room carpet. A bloodstain marked the carpet under the back of her head, like a black halo. One arm was twisted beneath her, the other was flung out, palm up, the fingers slightly crooked. Her face, from the nose up, had been destroyed. In place of her eyes was a finger-deep pit, filled with blood and mangled flesh. Another wound cut across her upper lip, ripping it, exposing white broken teeth. Her dress was pulled up high enough to show her underpants, which appeared to be undisturbed. The room smelled like a wet penny, the odor of fresh blood.

"Same guy?" Lucas asked, looking down at her.

"Gotta be. I caught the first one, too, and this one's a goddamn carbon copy," said a bright-eyed medical examiner's investigator.

"Anything obvious?" Lucas asked, looking around. The house seemed undisturbed.

"No. No broken fingernails, and they're clean. There doesn't seem to have been a fight, and there's no doubt she was killed right here—there are some blood splatters over there by the table. I didn't look myself, but the other guys say there's no sign of a door or window being forced."

"Doesn't look like rape . . ."

"No. And there aren't any signs of semen outside the body."

A Homicide detective stepped up beside Lucas and said, "C'mere and look at the weapon."

"I saw it when I came in," Lucas said. "The hammer?"

"Yeah, but Jack just noticed something."

They went out in the hallway, where the hammer, wrapped in plastic, was being delicately handled by another cop.

"What?" asked Lucas.

"Look at the head and the claw. Not the blood, the hammer," the second cop said.

Lucas looked, saw nothing. "I don't see anything."

"Just like the fuckin' dog that didn't bark," the cop said with satisfaction. He held the hammer up to a lamp, reflecting light from the shiny hammer-head into Lucas' eyes. "The first time you use a hammer, drive a nail or pull one, you start putting little nicks in it. Look at this. Smooth as a baby's ass. The goddamn thing has never been used. I bet the guy brought it with him, to kill her."

"Are you sure it was his? Not hers?"

The cop shrugged. "The woman's got about six tools—some screwdrivers, a crescent wrench and a hammer. One pack of nails and some picture hangers. They're still in the kitchen drawer. She wasn't a do-it-yourselfer. Why would she have two hammers? And a big heavy one like this? And how'd the guy just happen to get his hands on the second one?"

A bright light swept the front of the house and Lucas half turned.

"TV's here," said the first cop. He stepped away toward the front door.

"Tell everybody to keep their mouths shut. Daniel'll issue a statement in the morning," Lucas said. He turned back to the cop with the hammer.

"So he brought it with him," Lucas said.

"I'd say so."

Lucas thought about it, frowned, then clapped the cop on the shoulder. "I don't know what it means, but it's a good catch," he said. "If it's new, maybe we could check and see where they sell this Estwing brand. . . ."

"We're doing that tomorrow. . . ."

"So what do we know about her?" Lucas asked, pointing a thumb back toward the living room.

Armistead was an actress, the hammer-toting cop told Lucas. When she hadn't shown up for a performance, a friend had come to check on her, found the body and called the police. To judge from the body temperature, still higher than the rather cool ambient temperature of the house, she'd been dead per-haps four hours when the medical examiner's investigator had arrived, a few minutes after eleven. There was no sign of a burglary.

"Where's the friend?" Lucas asked.

"Back in the bedroom, with Swanson," the cop said, nodding toward the rear of the house. Lucas wandered back, looking the place over, trying to get a picture of the woman's life-style. The place was decorated with taste, he decided, but without money. The paintings on the walls were originals, but rough, the kind an actress might get from artist friends. The carpets on the floor were worn Orientals. He thought about the rugs at Bekker's house, and stooped to feel the one he was standing on. It felt thin and slippery. Some kind of machine-woven synthetic. Not much of a tie . . .

The bedroom door was open, and when Lucas poked his head in, he found Swanson sitting in a side chair, rubbing the lenses of his wire-rimmed glasses with a Kleenex. A woman was lying faceup on the bed, one foot on the floor.

The other foot had made a muddy mark on the yellow bedspread, but she hadn't noticed. Lucas knocked on the jamb and stepped inside as Swanson looked up.

"Davenport," the Homicide cop said. He put his glasses back on and fiddled with them for a second until they were comfortable. Then he sighed and said, "It's a fuckin' bummer."

"Same guy?"

"Yeah. Don't you think?"

"I guess." Lucas looked at the woman. "You found the body?"

She was redheaded, middle thirties, Lucas thought, and pretty, most of the time. Tonight she was haggard, her eyes swollen from crying, her nose red and running. She didn't bother to sit up, but she reached up to her forehead and pushed a lock of hair out of her eyes. They looked dark, almost black. "Yes. I came over after the show."

"Why?"

"We were worried. Everybody was," she said, sniffing. "Elizabeth would go on with a broken leg. When she didn't show up and didn't call, we thought maybe she'd been in an accident or something. If I didn't find her here, I was going to call the hospitals. I rang the doorbell, and then looked through the window in the door and saw her lying there. . . . The door was locked, so I ran over to a neighbor's to call the cops." A wrinkle creased her forehead and she cocked her head forward and said, "You're the cop who killed the Indian."

"Mmmnn."

"Is your daughter okay? I heard on the TV . . ."

"She's fine," Lucas said.

"Jesus, that must have been something." The woman sat up, a quick muscular motion, done without effort. Now her eyes were jade green, and he noticed that one of her front teeth was just slightly crooked. "Are you going after this guy? The killer?"

"I'm helping," Lucas said.

"I hope you get him and I hope you kill the sonofabitch," the woman said, her teeth bared and her eyes opening wide. She had high cheekbones and a slightly bony nose, the craggy variety of Celt.

"I'd like to get him," Lucas said. "When was the last time anybody saw Armistead . . . Elizabeth?"

"This afternoon. There was a rehearsal until about three o'clock," the woman said. She stroked the side of her cheek with her fingertips as she remembered, staring sightlessly at the bedspread. "After that, she went home. One of the ticket ladies tried to call her an hour or so before the play was supposed to start, but there wasn't any answer. That's the last I know."

"Why'd they call? Was she already late?"

"No, somebody wanted in on a freebee, and she'd have to approve it. But she didn't answer."

"Bucky and Karl are down at the theater, talking to people," Swanson said.

"Did you check Bekker?" Lucas asked.

"No. I will tomorrow, after we've got this nailed down. I'll have him do a minute-by-minute recount of where he was tonight."

"Isn't Bekker the name of that woman who was killed?" asked the woman on the bed, looking between them.

"Her husband," Lucas said shortly. "What's your name, anyway?"

"Lasch . . . Cassie."

"You're an actress?"

She nodded. "Yeah."

"Full-time?"

"I get the smaller parts," she said ruefully, shaking out her red hair. It was kinky and bounced around her shoulders. "But I work full-time."

"Was Armistead dating anyone?" Swanson asked.

"Not really . . . What does Bekker have to do with this? Is he a suspect?" She was focusing on Lucas.

"Sure. You always check the husband when a wife gets murdered," Lucas said.

"So you don't really think he did this?"

"He was in San Francisco when his wife was killed," Lucas said. "This one is so much like it, it almost has to be the same guy."

"Oh." She was disappointed and bit her lower lip. She wanted the killer, Lucas realized, and if she had her way about it, she would have him dead.

"If you think of anything, give me a call," Lucas said. Their eyes locked up for a second, a quick two-way assessment. He handed her a business card and she said, "I will." Lucas turned away, glanced back once to see her looking after him and drifted out toward the living room.

The cop with the hammer was talking to a uniform, who had a middle-aged woman in tow. The woman, wearing a pink quilted housecoat and white sneakers, was edging toward the archway that opened into the living room. The cop blocked her with a hip and asked, "So what'd he look like?"

"Like I said, he looked like a plumber. He was carrying a toolbox or something, and I says to Ray, that's my husband, Ray Ellis, Mr. and Mrs., 'Uh-oh,' I says, 'it looks like that Armistead woman's got troubles with her plumbing, I hope it's not the main again.' They dug up the main here in this street, the city has, twice since we been here, and we only got here in 'seventy-one, you'd think they'd be able to get that right . . .'" She took another crab step toward the arch, trying to get a look.

"You didn't like Ms. Armistead?" Lucas asked, coming up to them.

The woman took a half-step back, losing ground. A flash of irritation crossed her face as she realized it. "Why'd you think that?" she asked. A defensive whine crept into her voice. She'd heard this kind of question asked on *L.A. Law,* usually just before somebody got it in the neck.

"You called her 'that Armistead woman.' . . ."

"Well, she said she was an actress and I said to Ray . . ."

"Your husband . . ."

"Yeah, I said, 'Ray, she don't look like no actress to me.' I mean, I know what an actress looks like, right? And she didn't look like no actress, in fact, I'd say she was plain. I said to Ray, 'She says she's an actress, I wonder what she's really involved in.' " She squinted slyly.

"You think she might be involved with something else?" asked the cop with the hammer.

"If you ask me . . . Say, is that the murder weapon?" The woman's eyes widened as she realized that the cop was holding a hammer wrapped in a plastic bag.

"Before you get to that," Lucas interrupted impatiently, "the man you saw at the door . . . why'd he look like a plumber?"

" 'Cause of the way he was dressed," she said, unable to tear her eyes away from the hammer until the cop dropped it to his side. She looked up at Lucas again. "I couldn't see him real good, but he was wearing one of those coveralls, dark-like, and a hat with a bill on it. Like plumbers wear."

"You didn't see his face?"

"Nope. When I saw him, he was on her porch, with his back to me. I saw his back, saw he had a hat."

"Did you see a truck?"

She frowned. "No, now that you mention it. I don't know where he come from, but there weren't no cars on the street, just Miz Armistead's Omni, which I always notice because Ray had one almost like it, when he was married to his first wife, silver, except it was a Plymouth Horizon."

"Did you see him leave?"

"Nope. I was washing up the dishes."

"All right. Thanks," Lucas said. Nothing. She'd probably seen the killer, but it wouldn't help. Unless . . .

"One more question. Did the guy have plumber's tools or any kind of tools, anything you could see . . . or did he just *feel* like a plumber?"

"Well . . ." She didn't understand the question. "He just *looked* like a plumber. You see him on the sidewalk, you say, 'There goes a plumber.' "

So he might have been a plumber. Or he might have been an actor. . . .

Lucas stepped away, to the arch into the living room. One of the lab cops was videotaping the body and the living room, his lights bleaching out Armistead's already paper-white face. Lucas watched for a moment, then walked outside. The uniform had stretched crime-scene tape around the house and its hedge, and a half-dozen TV cameras were parked just off the curb. He heard his name ripple among the reporters, and the floodlights started flicking on as he walked down the porch steps to the street.

"Davenport . . ." The reporters moved in like sharks, but Lucas shook his head.

"I can't talk about it, guys," he said, waving them away.

"Tell us why you're here," a woman called. She was older for a television reporter, probably in her early forties, about to fall off the edge of the media world. "Gambling, dope? What?"

"Hey, Katie, I really want to leave it to the Homicide people. . . ."

"Anything to do with those guys selling guns . . . ?"

Lucas grinned, shook his head and pushed through to his car. If he stayed to talk, somebody would remember that he was working on the Bekker case and would add it up.

As he drove away, he tried to add it up himself. If the first murder was hired by Bekker, what did the second one mean? There had to be a connection—the techniques were identical—but it was hard to believe that Bekker could be involved. Swanson and the other investigators had been leaning on him: if he had some relationship with this woman, past or present, he'd hardly risk killing her. Not unless he was stupid as well as crazy. And nobody said he was stupid.

Lucas stopped for a red light, one foot on the clutch, the other on the gas pedal, idly revving the engine. The first killing had the earmarks of an accidental encounter. A doper goes into a house in a rich neighborhood, looking for anything he can convert to crack. He unexpectedly bumps into the woman, kills her in a frenzy, runs. If it hadn't been for Bekker's reputation with his relatives, if Sloan hadn't made the call to Bekker's former Army commanding officer, the killing might already have been written off as dope-related. . . .

But this second killing looked as though it were planned: The hammer, newly bought and then left behind. Nothing missing from the house. Not like a doper. A doper would have grabbed *something*. Nothing missing from Bekker's house, either . . .

Lucas shook his head, realizing the red light had turned green, then yellow. He was about to pop the clutch to run the yellow, when a black Nissan Maxima, coming up fast from behind, slid a fender in front of him and stopped. Lucas jabbed the Porsche's brake pedal, and the car bucked and died.

"Motherfucker," he said, and pulled the door latch-handle. The other driver was faster. As Lucas pushed open the door, a tall blonde hopped out of the Nissan and walked through Lucas' headlights, a tight smile on her face. TV3. She'd been around for a couple of years and Lucas had seen her on the Crows case.

"God damn it, Carly . . ."

"Stuff it, Lucas," the woman said. "I know how you worked with Jennifer and a couple other people. I want on the list. What happened back there?"

"Hey . . ."

"Look, my fuckin' contract is up in two months, and we're talking, me and the station," she said. "I'm asking sixty and it's like, Maybe yes, maybe no, what've you done for us lately? I need something: you're it." She posed, ankles crossed, fist on her hip.

"What's in it for me?" Lucas asked.

"You want somebody inside Three? You got it."

Lucas looked at her for a moment, then nodded. "I trust you just once," he said, holding up an index finger. "You burn me, you never come back."

"Fine. And it's the same with me. You ever burn me, or even get close, and I'll deny everything and sue your ass," the blonde said. They were both in the street, face to face. A black Trans Am slowed as it passed around them, and the passenger window rolled down. A kid with carefully coiffed hair and a hammered forehead looked out and said, "What's happening?"

"Cop," Lucas said. "Keep moving."

"We're cool," the kid said, then pulled his head inside, and the car accelerated away.

"So what happened?" Carly asked, glancing after the Trans Am, then turning back to Lucas.

"You know about the Bekker killing?"

"Sure."

"This one's identical. A woman named Elizabeth Armistead with the Lost River Theater, she's an actress. . . ."

"Oh shit, I know her. . . . I mean I've seen her. There's no doubt that it was the same guy?" The woman put a long red thumbnail in her mouth and bit it.

"Not much . . ."

"How was she killed?"

"Clawhammer. Hit her on the back of the head, then smashed out her eyes, just like with Stephanie Bekker." The traffic light was running through its sequence again, and the woman's hair glowed green, then gold as the yellow came on.

"Jesus Christ. What are the chances that the other stations'll have it by the morning shows?"

"I told the people back there to put a lid on everything, pending a release from the chief," Lucas said. "You should have it exclusively, if some uniform hasn't leaked it already. . . ."

"Nobody's talking back there," she said. "Okay, Lucas, I appreciate it. Anything you need from the station, let me know. My ass is in your hands."

"I wish," Lucas said with a grin. The blonde grinned back, and as the stoplight turned red, Lucas added, "There's not much more I can tell you about the murder."

"I don't need more," she said as she turned back toward her car. "I mean, why fuck up a great story with a bunch of facts?"

She left Lucas standing in the street, her car careening around in an illegal U-turn, simultaneously running the red light. Lucas laughed and got back in the Porsche. He had something going, for the first time in months. He was operating again.


And he thought: A copycat? The idea didn't hold up; the murderer's technique with Armistead was too similar to the Bekker killing. There hadn't been enough information in the press to tell a copycat exactly what to do. The killings *had* to be the same guy. The guy in coveralls, the coveralls a way to get inside?

He was edging toward a conclusion: They had another psycho on their hands. But if the guy was a psycho, why had he taken a weapon to Armistead's, but not to Bekker's? He'd killed Stephanie Bekker with a bottle he'd picked up in the kitchen. The Bekker scene made sense as a spur-of-the-moment killing by an intruder, a junkie who killed and got scared and ran. The Armistead scene did not. Yet both by the same guy.

And neither woman was sexually assaulted. Sex, in some way, was usually involved in serial killings. . . .

If Bekker had hired the first killing done, was it possible that he'd set off a maniac?

No. That's not how it worked.

Lucas had worked two serial killers. In both cases, the media had speculated on the effect of publicity on the mind of the killer: Did talking about killers make more killers? Did violent movies or pornography desensitize men and make them able to kill? Lucas didn't think so. A serial killer was a human pressure-cooker, made by abuse, by history, by brain chemistry. You don't get pressure like that from something as peripheral as TV. A serial killer wasn't a firecracker to be lit by somebody else. . . .

Tangled. And interesting. Without realizing it, Lucas began whistling, almost silently, under his breath.

# 10

The briefing room stank of cigarette smoke, nervous armpits and hot electronics. Twenty reporters crowded the front of the room, Lucas and a dozen more cops hung in the back. Carly Bancroft's early-morning report on the second murder had touched off a panic among the other stations. The press conference had started just after ten o'clock.

"Any questions?" Frank Lester's forehead was beaded with sweat. Lester, the deputy chief for investigations, put down the prepared statement and looked unhappily around the room.

"Lester in the lion's den," Sloan muttered to Lucas. He stuck a Camel in the corner of his mouth. "Got a light?"

Lucas took a book of matches out of his pocket, struck one and held it for Sloan's cigarette. "If you were Loverboy, would you come in?"

Sloan shook his head as he exhaled a lungful of blue smoke. "Fuck no. But then, I'm a cop. I know what treacherous assholes we are. I don't even know if I would've mentioned Loverboy in the thing. . . ."

"About Mrs. Bekker's . . . friend, have you done any voice analysis on the nine-one-one tapes?" a reporter asked Lester.

"Well, we've got nothing to match them to. . . ."

"We hear you're calling him 'Loverboy.' . . ."

"Not me, but I've heard that," Lester said grimly.

"Could the killer be going for women in the arts?" a reporter called out. She worked for a radio station and carried a microphone that looked like a Ruger Government Model .22-caliber target pistol. The microphone was aimed at a point between Lester's eyes.

"We don't know," he answered. "Mrs. Bekker would only be peripherally in the arts, I'd say. But it could be—there's no way to tell. Like I said, we're not even sure it's the same perpetrator."

"But you said . . ."

"It probably is. . . ."

From the front row, a newspaper reporter in a rumpled tan suit: "How many serial killers have we had now? In the last five years?"

"One a year? I don't know."

"One? There were at least six with the Crows."

"I meant one series each year."

"Is that how you count them?"

"I don't know how you count them," Lester barked.

"By series," a newspaper reporter called.

"Bullshit." Television disagreed. "By the killers."

From the back of the room, a radio reporter with a large tapedeck: "When do you expect him to hit again?"

"How're we gonna know that?" Lester asked, a testy note creeping into his voice. "We told you what we knew."

"You're supposed to be running the investigation," the reporter snapped back.

"I *am* running the investigation, and if you'd ever worked in a market bigger than a phone booth, you'd know we can't always find these guys overnight in the big city. . . ."

There was a thread of laughter, and Sloan said dryly, "He's losing it."

"What the f f f . . . What's that supposed to mean?" the reporter sputtered. The TV cameraman behind him was laughing. TV people ranked radio people, so laughing was all right.

"What's 'fff' supposed to mean?" Lester asked. He turned away and pointed at a woman wearing glasses the size of compact discs. "You."

"What precautions should women in the Twin Cities take?" She had an improbably smooth delivery, with great round O's, as though she were reading for a play.

"Don't let anybody in your house that you're not sure of," Lester said, struggling now. "Keep your windows locked. . . ."

"Who tipped Three, that's what I want to know," another reporter shouted from the back of the room. Carly Bancroft yawned, tried not very hard to suppress a grin, then deliberately scratched her ribs.

When Daniel had scheduled the press conference, he'd expected the police reporters from the dailies and second-stringers from the television stations. With the Armistead killing, everything had changed. He'd passed the press conference to Lester, he said, in an attempt to diminish its importance. It hadn't worked: media trucks were double-parked in the street, providing direct feeds to the various stations. City Hall secretaries were gawking at the media stars, the media stars were checking their hairsprays, and the TV3 anchorman himself, tan, fit, with a touch of gray at the temples and a tie that matched his eyes, showed up to do some reaction shots against the conference. His station had the beat; he had nothing to do with it, but the glory was his, and his appearance gave weight to the proceedings.

The conference started angry and got angrier. Lester hadn't wanted to do it, and every reporter but one had been beaten on it. By the end, the Channel Eight reporter was standing on a chair, shouting at Lester. When she stood on the chair, the cops around her sat down; she wore a very short black leather skirt.

"I guess you gotta get what you can get," Sloan said, laughing. Lester had fled, and Sloan, Lucas and Harmon Anderson walked together down the hall toward Homicide.

"Department full of fuckin' perverts," Anderson said, adding, "You could see the crack of her ass, if you sat just right."

"Jesus Christ, Harmon, I think that's sexual abuse in the third degree," Lucas said, laughing with Sloan.

"You know why they've got such great voices, the TV people?" Anderson asked, going off in a new direction. "Because they reverberate in the space where most people have brains . . ."

Swanson came slouching down the hall toward them, heavyset, glittering gold-rimmed glasses. "Did I miss it?"

"You missed it," Sloan confirmed. "Anderson got his first look at a woman's ass in twenty years."

"How about Bekker?" Lucas asked.

"Not a thing. We got his ass in here first thing, asked him if he wanted a lawyer, he said no. He said he'd ask if he needed one. So we said, What'd you do? He said he spent the late afternoon working at home, and the evening watching television. We asked what he was watching, and he told us. He was, like, watching CNBC in the afternoon, some kind of stock market shows, and then the news. . . . He went out around nine o'clock to get a bite to eat. We got that confirmed. . . ."

"How about phone calls?"

"He talked to one guy on the phone, a guy from the hospital, but that was late, way after the killing."

"Who called who?" Lucas asked. The four detectives circled around each other as Swanson talked.

"The other guy called in . . ." Swanson said.

"Could have a VCR, tape the shows," Anderson suggested.

"He does have a VCR," Swanson said. "I don't know about taping the shows. Anyway, we got his statement, and shit, there was nothing to say. He didn't know Armistead, doesn't even know if he'd ever seen her on the stage. . . . He was just . . . There wasn't anything there. We sent him home."

"You believe him?" Lucas asked.

Swanson's forehead furrowed. "I don't know. When you're leaning on a guy, like we been leaning on Bekker, scouting around his neighborhood, calling his neighbors, all that . . . and something happened that could clear him, you'd think he'd be peeing all over himself in a rush to prove he didn't do it. He wasn't like that. He was cool. Answered all the questions like he was reading off of file cards."

"Keep up the pressure," Anderson said.

Swanson shook his head. "That ain't gonna work with this guy. I'm starting to think—he's an asshole, but he could be innocent."

They were still talking about it when Jennifer Carey turned the corner.

"Lucas . . ." Her voice was feminine, clear, professional.

Lucas turned in instant recognition. Sloan, Anderson and Swanson turned with him, then moved away down the corridor, furtively watching, as Lucas walked toward her.

"Daniel said you'd be talking afterwards," Jennifer said. She was slender and blonde, with a few thirties wrinkles on a well-kept face. She wore a pink silk blouse with a gray suit, and almost stopped his heart. She and Lucas had a two-year-old daughter but had never married. They'd been estranged ever since their daughter had been wounded.

"Yeah. Didn't see you at the conference."

"I just got here. Where will you be talking? Down at the conference room?" She was all business, brisk, impersonal. There would be more to it than that, Lucas knew.

"Nah. I'll just be around. . . . How are you?"

"I'm working with a new unit," she said, ignoring the question. "Could we get you outside, on the steps?"

"Sure. How've you been?" he persisted.

She shrugged and turned away, heading for the steps. "About the same. Are you coming over Saturday afternoon?"

"I . . . don't think so," he said, tagging along, hands in his pockets.

"Fine."

"When are we going to talk?"

"I don't know," she said over her shoulder.

"Soon?"

"I don't think só," she threw back. "Not soon."

"Hey, wait a minute," he said. He reached forward, hooked her arm and spun her around.

"Let the fuck go of me," she said, jerking her arm away, angry.

Lucas had always worried that women feared him: that he was too rough, even when he didn't mean to be. But her tone cut. He put a hand against her chest and shoved, and she went back against the wall of the corridor, her head snapping back. "Shut up . . ." he snarled.

"You fuck . . ." He thought she was going to swing, and stepped back, then realized that she was frightened and that her hand, coming up, was meant to block a punch. Her wrist looked thin and delicate, and he put up his hands, palms out.

"Just listen," he said, his voice dragging out in a hoarse near-whisper. "I'm tired of this shit. More than tired. I can't stand it anymore. In the past couple of days, I went through to the other side. So I'm telling you: I'm ready to quit. I'm ready to get out. You've been jerking me around for months and I can't deal with it and I won't deal with it. I'm not gone yet, but if you ever want to talk, you better decide soon, because I'll tell you what: You wait much longer and I ain't gonna be there to talk to."

She shook her head, tears starting, but they were tears of anger, and he turned and walked down the corridor. A TV3 producer stepped out into the hallway and looked down toward Jennifer, still flattened against the wall, looked into Lucas' face as he went by, then looked back at Jennifer and said, "Jen, you okay? Jen? What happened?"

As he went out on the steps to meet the cameras, Lucas heard Jennifer answer, "Nothing happened."


All five stations did quick interviews, Lucas standing on the City Hall steps for four of them, suppressing his anger with Jennifer, aware as he talked that it was slowly leaking away, leaving behind a cold hollowness. He did the fifth interview on the street, leaning against his Porsche. When the camera was done, Lucas stepped around the hood of the Porsche to get into the car, looking carefully for Jennifer, half hoping she'd be there, not believing she would be. She wasn't. Instead, a *StarTribune* reporter came after him, a dark-haired, overweight man with a beard who always carried a pocketful of sliced carrots wrapped in waxed paper.

"Tell me something," the reporter said. He waggled a carrot slice at Lucas, in a friendly way. "Between you and me—background, not for attribution, whatever. Are you looking forward to hunting this guy?"

Lucas thought for a second, glanced at the last television reporter, who was out of earshot, and nodded. "Yeah. I am. There's not been much going on."

"After busting the Crows, the other stuff must seem small-time. . . ." The reporter gobbled the carrot stick in two quick bites.

"Nah," Lucas said. "But this is . . . interesting. People are dying."

"Will you get him?"

Lucas nodded. "I don't know. But we'd be better off if we could get to Stephanie Bekker's lover. He knows things he doesn't know he knows. . . ."

"Wait a minute," the reporter said, slipping a slender notebook out of the breast pocket of his sport coat. "Can I attribute this last part? Can we go back on the record just for that?"

"Okay. But just that bit: Mrs. Bekker's friend—quote me as calling him a friend—has actually seen the guy. He might think he's told us about her, calling nine-one-one, sending the note, but he hasn't. A good interview team would find things in his memory that he has no idea are there. And I'm not talking about giving him the third degree, either. If I could get him ten minutes on the telephone, or if Sloan could . . . I think we'd have a hundred-percent-better chance of breaking this thing in a hurry."

The reporter was scribbling notes. "So you want him to come in."

"We want anything we can get from him," Lucas said. He unlocked the Porsche's door and opened it. "Off the record again?"

"Sure."

"Loverboy's our only handle, that's how bad we need him. There's something wrong with this case, and without his help, I don't know how we'll find out what it is."

\*     \*     \*

His anger with Jennifer came back as he drove across town, replaying the scene in the hall. She knew about scenes, knew about drama, knew psychology. She didn't have to be the one who asked him for an interview. She was jerking him around, and it was working. The optimism, the lift of the last few days, was gone. He accelerated out the Sixth Street exit onto I-94. Go home and go to bed, he thought. Think it over. But his eye caught the sign for the Riverside exit, and without good reason, he took it, then turned left at the top of the ramp and headed down toward the West Bank theater district.

Cassie Lasch was sitting on the floor of the ticket lobby of the Lost River Theater. She was wearing jeans and a pink T-shirt and was digging through a gray plastic garbage bag. Lucas pushed through the revolving door into the lobby, and, as she looked up at him, he stopped short.

"The actress," Lucas said. He paused, his eyes still adjusting to the dim light. "Lasch. Cathy."

"Cassie. How are you, Davenport? Want to help? I'm looking for a clue."

Lucas squatted next to her. The weather was too cold for a T-shirt, but the woman seemed not to notice. Her arms were strong, with long, round muscles that carried up to her neck. And she was tanned, as much as a redhead could tan, too smoothly, by artificial lights. A lifter, Lucas thought. "What clue?"

"The cops were here all morning and I forgot to tell them . . ." She stopped rummaging through the garbage for a moment. A tiny scrap of paper was stuck to the side of her jaw, and her red hair had fallen over her eyes. She brushed it back and said, "Nobody asked about the guy who tried to get on the guest list last night. Remember, I told you that the ticket-office lady tried to call Elizabeth about the freebee, and couldn't get her?"

"I remember," Lucas said, nodding. He reached over to her cheek, peeled off the scrap of paper, showed it to her and flicked it away.

"Thanks . . . uh . . ." She'd lost her thought, and she smiled up at him, her crooked tooth catching on her lower lip. Her face was just the slightest bit foxy, and mobile. Freckles were scattered lightly over the bridge of her nose.

"The guest list," Lucas prompted.

"Oh, yeah. This guy says he's some big-time reviewer and wants on the list as Elizabeth's friend. I asked the ticket-takers this morning and they said they didn't give out any freebees last night. Whoever called didn't show up. That could be a clue." She said it seriously, intently, like a Miss Marple with terrific breasts.

"Why is that a clue?"

"Because maybe if he knew Elizabeth, he went over there. . . . I don't know, but he didn't show up."

Lucas thought for a minute, then nodded. "You're right. The list is in here?"

"Somewhere. On a piece of notebook paper from one of those teeny brown spiral notebooks. Probably wadded up."

"So let's dump it out," he said. He picked up the garbage bag by its bottom and shook it onto the lobby rug. Most of the litter was paper, much of it soaked with Coke and 7-Up, and toward the bottom, they found a paper coffee filter full of grounds.

"Ugh. Maybe you shouldn't have done that," Cassie said, wrinkling her nose at the mess.

"The hell with it," Lucas said. "We need the list."

They spent five minutes pawing through the sodden trash, working shoulder to shoulder. She had, Lucas decided, one of the better bodies he'd ever brushed up against. Everything was hard, except what was supposed to be soft, and that looked very soft. Every time she leaned forward, her breasts swelled forward against the thin fabric of the T-shirt. . . .

*Jesus Christ, Davenport, you're ready for the peep shows. . . .*

He smiled to himself and picked up a Styrofoam cup. Inside was a paper wad the size of a marble. He unwrapped it, turned it around. At the top somebody had written "Guests" and, under that, "Donaldson Whitney, LA Times."

"This it?"

Cassie took it, looked at it and said, "That's it. Kelly—the ticket-window lady—said the guy was from LA."

Lucas stood, the cartilage in his knees popping. "Got a phone? Someplace quiet?"

"There's one in the office, but there're a couple of people in there. . . . There's another one in the control booth. What do we do about this garbage?" She looked down at the pile of trash on the floor. The coffee grounds were smeared where Lucas had stepped on them.

He frowned, as though seeing it for the first time, and said, "I don't care. Whatever you want."

"Well, fuck that, I didn't put it there," Cassie said. She flipped her hair and turned away. "C'mon, I'll show you the control booth."

She led him down a hall to the theater auditorium. In the light of day, the place was a mess. Black paint was scaling off concrete-block walls, the seatbacks were stained, the overhead light rack was a tangle of electrical wires, ropes, spotlights, outlets and pulleys. At night, none of that would be visible.

The control booth was at the back of the auditorium, up two short flights of stairs. The booth itself was built out of plywood, painted black on the outside, unfinished inside. A barstool and a secretary's swivel chair sat in front of a control panel. Extension and computer cords were fixed to the walls and floors with gaffer tape. A phone was screwed to the wall to the left of the control panel.

Cassie noticed him looking around and said, "No money for luxuries."

"First time I've been in a theater control booth," Lucas said.

She shrugged. "They mostly look like this, unless the theater's getting government money."

Lucas used his credit card to call Los Angeles, Cassie leaning against the control panel, arms locked behind her back, listening with interest. Whitney was not at his desk, Lucas was told. He pressed, was switched around, and eventually talked to an arts copy editor who made the mistake of picking up a ringing telephone. He said that Whitney was on vacation.

"In Minneapolis?" Lucas asked.

"Why would he be in fuckin' Minneapolis in April?" the copy editor asked crossly. "He's in Micronesia on a skin-diving trip."

"Well?" Cassie asked, when Lucas had hung up.

"Well, what?"

"Was it him last night?"

"Uh, I appreciate your help, Miss Lasch, but this is police business. . . ."

"You're not going to tell me?" She couldn't believe it. She reached out, took hold of his jacket sleeve and tugged at it. "C'mon."

"No."

"No fair . . ." Her eyes were as large as any he'd ever seen, and dark again, with a spark. She tipped her head, a tiny smile on her face. "I'll show you my tits if you tell me."

"What?" He was surprised and amused. *Amused,* he thought, watching himself.

"Out there in the lobby, you were doing everything but feeling me up, so . . . tell me, and I'll give you a look."

Lucas considered. "This is embarrassing," he said finally.

"I don't embarrass very easily."

"Maybe not, but I do," Lucas said.

Her eyebrows went up. "You're embarrassed? That shows a certain unexpected depth. Do you play the piano?"

She was moving too fast. "Ah, no . . ."

"Quick, Davenport, make up your mind. . . ." She was teasing now.

Lucas put her off: "What do you do besides act? You said you don't get the good parts."

"I'm one of the world's great waitresses. I learned in the theater restaurants in New York. . . ."

"Hmph."

"So how about it?" she pressed.

"You'd have to keep your mouth shut," he said severely.

"Sure. I'm very secretive."

"I'll bet. . . . All right: The *Times* guy is in Micronesia, on a skin-diving trip. Micronesia's in the middle of the Pacific Ocean."

"I know where it is, I've been there," she said. "Then there's no way in hell he could have been here last night."

"No." Lucas glanced around. There was no one else in the theater area, and the booth was even more isolated. "So . . ."

"If you're waiting to see my tits, forget it," she said, crossing her arms over her chest.

"Ha. Rat out on a deal, huh?" he said, grinning.

"Of course. When you want to find out something, first you try treachery— that wouldn't work in this case—and then you make weird sex offers," she said calmly. "Usually, you'll find out what you want to know. I learned that from dealing with agents."

"Fuckin' women," Lucas said. "So casual about the way you break a guy's heart."

"You look thoroughly destroyed," she said.

Lucas took a short step toward her, not knowing exactly what he was planning to do. Whatever it was, she didn't back away; but at that moment, a man walked out on the stage below them, and Lucas stopped and looked down. Without a word, and apparently unaware that they were in the booth, the man hit a light switch, stepped to the center of the stage and began juggling. He'd brought a half-dozen baseballs with him, and they spun in a circle, smoothly, without a miss, and then, just as abruptly as he'd begun juggling, he started to tap-dance. Not a simple tap, but a dance almost baroque in its complication, and all the time the balls were in the air.

The man was in blackface. There was something about his head. . . . An effect of the makeup, the wide white-greasepainted lips, the strange flat nose?

Cassie caught Lucas' interest and stepped close behind him and whispered, "Carlo Druze, one of the actors. This is one of his routines."

Druze began to sing, a phony black accent, minstrel-show style, in a shaky baritone, "Way down upon the Swanee River, far, far away . . ."

"We're doing a thing called *Whiteface,* it's like a racial-satire thing. . . ." She was whispering, but Druze apparently heard. He took down the balls in a swift, coordinated sweep.

"I've got an audience?" he called, looking up at the booth.

Lucas applauded and Cassie yelled, "Just us, Cassie and a cop."

"Ah . . ." Was he startled? Lucas wasn't sure. Was there something wrong with his face?

"That was really good, Carlo," Cassie said.

Druze took a bow.

"If only Miz Cassie wuz runnin' d'show," he said, going back to the accent.

"We'll get out of your hair," Cassie said, leading Lucas out of the booth and down the steps toward the exit light.

In the hall on the way back to the lobby, Lucas asked, "Was what's-his-name here last night?"

"Carlo? Yeah. Most of the time, anyway. He was working on the set. He's the best carpenter in the company. And he does great voices. He can sound like anybody."

"Okay."

"He's a tough guy," she added. "Hard. Like his face."

"But he was here?"

"Well, nobody was taking names. But yeah. Around."

"Okay." Lucas followed her down the hall, watching her back and shoulders in the dim light. She looked delicate, like most slender redheads, but there was nothing fragile about her, he realized. "You're a lifter, right?" he said.

"Yeah, some," she said, half turning. "I don't compete or anything. Do you lift?"

"No. I've got some weights in my basement and I've got a routine I do in the morning. Nothing serious."

"Gotta stay in shape," Cassie said, slapping her stomach. They stepped into the lobby, and Cassie stopped suddenly and caught Lucas' arm: "Oh, no," she groaned.

"What?"

"Deep shit," she said.

A man stood over the garbage on the rug. He was dressed all in black, from his knee boots to his beret, and his shoulder-length auburn hair was tied in a stubby ponytail. His hands were planted on his hips, and one foot was tapping in anger. Cassie hurried toward him and he looked up when he heard her coming.

"Cassie," he said. He had a goatee, and his teeth were a brilliant white against the beard. "Did you do this? One of the ticket women said you were looking through the garbage. . . ."

"Uh . . ."

"I did it," Lucas said, his voice curt. Cassie flashed him a grateful look. "Police business. I was looking for information involving the Armistead killing last night."

"Well, are you going to clean it up?" the man asked, nudging a wet ball of paper with the toe of a boot.

"Who are you?" Lucas asked, stepping closer.

"Uh, this is Davis Westfall," Cassie said from behind him. She still sounded nervous. "He is . . . was . . . the co–artistic director with Elizabeth. Davis, this is Lieutenant Davenport of the Minneapolis police. I was showing him around."

"She's been a help," Lucas said to Westfall, nodding at Cassie. "Mr. Westfall . . . Miss Armistead's death would put you in sole charge of this theater, would it not? I mean, in one sense, you'd be a . . . beneficiary?"

"Why . . . that would be up to the board," Westfall sputtered. He glanced at Cassie for support, and she nodded. "But we're a nonsexist theater, so I imagine they'll appoint another female to take Elizabeth's place."

"Hmp," Lucas said. He studied Westfall for another moment, skepticism on his face. "No major disagreements on management?" he asked, keeping Westfall pinned.

"No. Not at all," Westfall said. Now he was nervous.

"But you'll be around?"

"Well, yes . . ."

"Good. And don't move this garbage right away. Our crime lab might want to look at it. If they're not here by . . ."—Lucas glanced at his watch—"six o'clock, you can have somebody pick it up."

"Anything we can do . . ." Westfall said, thoroughly deflated.

Lucas nodded and turned to leave. "I'll show him to the door," Cassie said. "I'll make sure it's locked."

"Thank you," Lucas said formally.

At the front door, Cassie whispered, "Thanks. Davis can be an asshole. I'm at the bottom of the heap here."

"No problem," Lucas said, grinning. "And I appreciate the tip on the guest list. It really could turn into something."

"You gonna ask me out?" she asked.

She'd surprised him again. "Mmm. Maybe," he said, smiling. "But why . . ."

"Well, if you're going to, don't wait too goddamned long, okay? I can't stand the suspense."

Lucas laughed. "All right," he said. As he stepped out on the sidewalk, the door clicked shut behind him. He took another step away, toward the car, when he heard a rapping on the door glass. He turned around and Cassie lifted the front of her T-shirt, just for an instant, just a flash.

Long enough: She looked very nice, he thought. Very nice, pink and pale . . .

And she was gone.

# 11

Bekker walked in circles on the Heriz carpet, orbiting the Rococo revival sofa, watching cuts from the press conference on the noon news. He'd heard shorter cuts on his car radio on the way to the hospital, and had gone back home to see it on television. Most of the press conference was nonsense: the police had nothing at all. But the appeal to Stephanie's lover could be dangerous.

"We believe the man who called nine-one-one is telling the truth. We believe that he is innocent of the murder of Mrs. Bekker, especially in light of this second murder," the cop, Lester, was saying into the microphones. He was sweating under the lights, patting his forehead with a folded white handkerchief. "After discussions with the county attorney, we have agreed that should Mrs. Bekker's friend come forward, Hennepin County would be willing to discuss a guarantee of immunity from prosecution in return for testimony, provided that he was not involved in the crime. . . ."

Lester went on, but Bekker wasn't listening anymore. He paced, gnawing on a thumbnail, spitting the pieces onto the carpet.

The police were all over the neighborhood. They weren't hiding. They were, in fact, deliberately provocative. Stephanie's idiot cop cousin, the doper, had been going door to door around the neighborhood, soliciting information. That angered him, but his anger was for another time. He had other problems now.

"Loverboy," they called him on TV. Who was it? Who was the lover? It had to be somebody in their circle. Somebody with easy access to Stephanie. He had exhausted himself, tearing at the problem.

Fuckin' Druze, he thought. Couldn't find the face. The face had to be there, somewhere, in the photographs. Stephanie took photographs of everybody, could never leave anybody alone, always had that fuckin' camera in somebody's face, taking snapshots. She had boxes, cartons, baskets full of photos, all those beefy blond Scandinavian males. . . .

Could Druze be wrong? It was possible, but, Bekker admitted to himself uncomfortably, he probably wasn't. He didn't seem unsure of himself. He didn't equivocate. He'd looked at the photos, studied them and said no.

"Bitch," Bekker said aloud to Stephanie's house. "Who were you fucking?"

He looked back at the television, at Lester yammering at the cameras. Anger surged in him: it was unfair, they had twenty men, a hundred, and he had only himself and Druze. And Druze couldn't really look, because if he was seen first . . .

"Bitch," he said again, and gripped by the anger, he pounded out of the parlor, up the stairs, into the bedroom. The cigarette case was with his keys and a pile of change, and he snapped it open, popped two amphetamines and a sliver of windowpane, and closed his eyes, waiting for Beauty.

There. The bed moved for him, melted, the closet opened like a mouth, a cave, a warm place to huddle. His clothes: they gripped him, and he fought the panic. He had felt it before, the shirt tightening around his throat, the sleeves gripping his arms like sandpaper, tightening. . . . He fought the panic and stripped off the constricting shirt, slipped out of his pants and underwear, and threw them out into the room. The closet called, and he dropped to his knees and crawled inside. Warm and safe, with the musty smell of the shoes . . . comfortable.

He sat for a minute, for five minutes, letting the speed run through his veins and the acid through his brain. Fire, he thought. He needed fire. The realization came on him suddenly and he bolted from the cave, still on his hands and knees, suddenly afraid. He crawled to the dresser and reached over it, groping, found the book of matches and scuttled back to the closet, his eyes cranked wide, not handsome now, something else. . . . In the semi-dark of the closet, he struck a match and stared into the flame. . . .

Safe. With the fire. His anger grew and darkened. Bitch. Her face flashed, and melted. Pain flared in his hand, and suddenly he was in darkness. Match gone. He struck another one. Bitch. A bed popped up, not their bed, and strange wallpaper, with fleur-de-lis, where was that? The hotel in New York. With the acid singing through him, Bekker saw himself come out of the bathroom, naked, holding a towel, Stephanie on the phone. . . . Pain in his hand again. Darkness. He dropped the match, struck a third. Bitch. Step into the bathroom to shower; when I come out, she's already on the phone, calling her paint stripper or someone. . . .

His mind stretched and snapped, stretched and snapped, cooled, chilled. Pain. Darkness. Another match. He wiped spittle from his chin, staring at the guttering flame. Pain. Darkness. He crawled out of the closet, the first rush going now, leaving him with the power of ice, of a glacier. . . .

And the answer was there, in the acid flash to New York. He stood up, his mind chilled, precise. Pain in his hand. "Am I stupid?"

Bekker walked out of the bedroom, still nude but unaware of it, down to the study, where he settled behind the big oak desk. He opened a deep drawer and took out a gray plastic box. The tape on the front said "Bills: Paid, Current."

"New York, January . . ." He dumped the box on the desk and combed through the stack of paper, receipts and stubs of paid bills. After a minute he said, "Here . . ."

The phone bill. He hadn't called anyone, but there were six calls on the bill, New York to Minneapolis, four of them to a university extension. He didn't know the number. . . .

Mind like ice. Riding the speed, now. He punched the number into the desk phone. A moment later, a woman answered. "Professor George's office, can I help you?"

Bekker dropped the phone back on the hook, heat flushing the ice from his head. "Philip George," he crowed. "Philip George . . ."

There was work to do, but the drugs had him again and he sat for half an hour, rocking in the chair behind the big desk. Time was nothing in the grip of the acid. . . .

Pain. He looked at his hand. A huge blister bubbled from the tip of his index finger. The ball of his thumb was raw, a patch of burned skin. How had he burned himself? Had there been a fire?

He went to the kitchen, pierced the blister with a needle, smeared both the finger and the thumb with a disinfectant and covered the burns with Band-Aids. A mystery . . . And Philip George.

Bekker pawed through the library, searching for the book. No. No. Where? Must be in the junk, must be in the keepsakes, where could she . . . Ah. Here: *Faculty and Staff, University of Minnesota.*

His own face flashed up at him as he flipped through the pages, then the face of Philip George. Bland. Slightly stupid, somewhat officious, he thought. Large. Blond. Fleshy. How could she? The pain bit into his hand, and confused, he looked at his finger again. How . . . ?

"Carlo?"

"God damn, I thought . . ." Druze was shocked.

"I'm sorry, but this is an absolute emergency . . ."

"Have you seen the television?" Druze asked.

"Yes. And nobody has even begun to look at you. Yet. That's why I'm calling. I found our man."

"Who?" Druze blurted.

"A law professor named Philip George. We've got to move—you've seen the television."

"Yes, yes, where are you?" Druze asked impatiently. "Are you okay?"

"I'm a block down the street, in the VGA supermarket," Bekker said. He was using a convenience phone at the newsrack, and a woman customer was heading toward him with a shopping list in her hand. She'd want the phone. "I've checked and I've checked and there's nobody with me. I guarantee it. But I'm going out the back and down the alley. I'll be at your place sixty seconds after I hang up here. Buzz me in. . . ."

"Man, if anybody sees you . . ."

"I know, but I'm wearing a hat and a jacket and sunglasses, and I'll make sure the lobby's empty before I come in. If you're ready for my buzz . . . I'll come up the stairs. Have the door open."

"All right. If you're sure . . ."

"I'm sure, but I need you to say yes, he's the one."

Bekker hung up and looked around. Was he being watched? He wasn't sure, but he didn't think so. The woman customer was using the phone now, paying no attention to him. An elderly man was going through the check-out with a can of coffee, and the only other people in sight were store employees.

He'd taken a quick trip around the store once before he picked up the phone. There was an exit sign by the dairy case. . . .

He got a pushcart and started to the back of the store, checking the other customers. But you couldn't tell, could you? At the dairy case, he waited until he was alone, then left the cart and walked straight out a swinging door under the exit sign. He found himself in a storage area that stank of rotting produce, looking at a pair of swinging metal doors. He pushed through them to a loading dock, walked briskly along the dock and down the stairs at the far end, watching the door behind him.

Nobody came through, nobody looked through. Five seconds later he was in the alley that ran along the back of the store. He hurried down the length of the block, around the corner, another hundred feet and into the outer lobby of Druze's apartment building. He pushed the button on Druze's mailbox, got an instant answering buzz, pulled open the inner door and was inside. Elevator straight ahead, stairs through the door to the right. He took the stairs two at a time, checked the hallway and hustled down to Druze's apartment. The door was open and he pushed through.

"God damn, Mike . . ." Druze's face was normally as unreadable as a pumpkin. Now he looked stressed, uncharacteristic vertical lines creasing the patchwork skin of his forehead. He was wearing a tired cotton sweater the color of oatmeal, and pants with pleats. His hands were in his pockets.

"Is this him?" Bekker thrust the photo of Philip George at Druze.

Druze looked at it, carried it to a light, looked closer, his lower lip thrust out. "Huh."

"It must be him," Bekker said. "He fits: he's blond, he's heavy—he's even heavier in real life than he is in that picture. That photo must be four or five years old. And he wasn't in any of the other photos. And Stephanie was calling him secretly from New York."

Druze finally nodded. "It could be. It looks like him. But the guy at the house, I just saw him like that." Druze snapped his fingers.

"It must be him," Bekker said eagerly.

"Yeah. Yeah, I think it is. Give him a couple of more years . . . Yeah."

"God damn, Carlo," Bekker crowed, his beautiful face absolutely radiant. He caught Druze around the neck with the crook of his elbow and squeezed him down, a jocklike hug, and Druze felt the pleasure of approval flush through his stomach. Druze had never had a friend. . . . "God damn, we beat the police."

"So now what?" Druze asked. He felt himself smiling: What an odd feeling, a real smile.

Bekker let him go. "I've got to get out of here and think. I'll figure something out. Tonight, after your show, come up to my office. Even if they're watching me, they won't be inside the building. Call me before you leave and I'll come down and let you in at that side door by the ramp. If you look like you're unlocking the door, they'd never suspect . . ."

*     *     *

Philip George.

Bekker worried the problem all the way back to the hospital. They had to get to George quickly. He stopped at the secretary's desk in the departmental office.

"Lucy, do you have a class schedule?"

"I think . . ." The secretary pulled open a filing cabinet and dug through it, and finally produced a yellow pamphlet. She handed it to him. "Could you bring it back, it's the only one. . . ."

"Sure," he said distractedly, flipping through the schedule. Pain flared in his hand, and he stopped and looked at it more carefully. He should bandage it. . . .

"Lucy?" He went back to the secretary's desk. "Do we have any big Band-Aids around here? I've burned my thumb. . . ."

"I think . . ." The secretary dug through her desk, found a box of bandages. "Let me see. . . . Oh my God, Dr. Bekker, how did you do this . . . ?"

He let her bandage it, then walked down the corridor to his office, unlocked it and settled behind his desk. Law school, George . . . he glanced at his watch. One-thirty. *George: Basic Torts, MWF 1:10–3:00.*

He would be in class. Bekker picked up the phone, called the law school office and twittered at the woman who answered: "Phil George? In class? I see," he said, putting disappointment in his voice. "This is a friend of his over at Hamline, I'm just leaving town, terrible rush, we were supposed to meet one of these nights, and I'm trying to get my schedule together. . . . Do you know if he has classes or night meetings the rest of the week? . . . No, I can't really wait, I've got a seminar starting right now, and it runs late, then I've got a plane. Tried to call Phil's wife, nobody home . . . Yes, I'll hold. . . ."

The law secretary dropped the receiver on her desk and Bekker could hear her walking away. A minute passed, then another, and then she was back: "Yes, tomorrow night, seven to ten, he has preparation for moot court. The other nights are clear here at the school."

"Thank you very much," he said, still twittering. "You've been very kind. What is your name? . . . Thank you very much, Nancy. Oh, by the way, where is the moot-court prep going to be? . . . Okay, thanks again."

He hung up and leaned back in his chair, making a steeple of his fingers. George would be working late. That could be useful. What'd he drive? It was a red four-wheel-drive of some kind, a Jeep. He could cruise by George's house later on. He lived in Prospect Park and probably left the car in the street. . . .

Druze was sure that Bekker was using, but he wasn't sure what it was. An ocean of cocaine flowed through the theater world, but Bekker wasn't a coke-head; or if he was, there was something else involved. At times he was flying, his beautiful face reflecting an inner joy, a freedom; at other times, he was dark, reptilian, calculating.

Whatever it was, it moved through him quickly. He'd been manic when Druze arrived at the hospital. Now he was like ice.

"He'll be out tomorrow night," Bekker said. "I know that's not much time. . . . He drives a red Jeep Cherokee. Fire-engine red. He'll be parked behind Peik Hall."

He explained the rest of it and Druze began shaking his head. "Happy accident? What kind of shit is that?"

"It's the only way," Bekker said calmly. "If we try to pull him out, set him up, we could spook him. If he thinks we might come after him . . . I can't just call him, cold, and ask him to meet me down at the corner. He's got to be a little afraid—that somebody might figure him out, that the killer might come after him. . . ."

"I just wish there was some other way," Druze said. He looked around and realized he was in some kind of examination room. Bekker had met him at a side door, normally locked, and led him down a dimly lit hallway to a red metal door, and had opened it with a key and pulled him inside. The walls were lined with stainless-steel cabinets, a stainless cart sat against one wall, and a battery of overhead lights hung down at the center of the room. Their voices ricocheted around the room like Ping-Pong balls. The room was cold. "It seems pretty . . . uncertain."

"Look, the hardest thing to investigate is a spur-of-the-moment thing, between strangers. Like when you did that woman in New York. How can the cops find a motive, how can they find a connection? If you try to set something up, it leaves traces. If you just go there, where he is, and do it . . ."

"You know he'll be there?" Druze asked.

"Yes. He's got the moot court. He plays the part of the judge, he *has* to be there."

"I guess it's got to be done," Druze said, running his fingers back through his hair. "Jesus, I don't like it. I like things that can be rehearsed. Your wife, that was no problem. This . . ."

"It's the best way, believe me," Bekker said intently. "Look for his car. It should be in the parking lot right behind the building. There's a lot of foliage around the lot—I checked. If he parks there, try to get close to the car, let the air out of one of his tires. That'll give the students time to get away from the building and it'll keep him busy changing the tire while you come up on him. . . ."

"Not bad," Druze admitted. "But God damn, Michael, I've got the feeling that we've kicked the tarbaby. One foot's stuck and now we've got to stick the other one in, trying to get the first one loose. . . ."

"This is the end and we've got to do it, don't you see? For your own safety," Bekker said. "Get him, dump him . . ."

"That bothers me, too. Dumping him. If I just whacked him, and walked away, who's to know? But if I have to take him out to Wisconsin . . . Jesus, I could get stopped by conservation officers looking for fish, or who knows what?"

Bekker shook his head, holding Druze with his eyes. "If we kill him and leave him, they'll know from his eyes that he must be Stephanie's lover—why else would his eyes be cut? But that'll throw the serial-killer pattern right out the window. And how would the killer be able to find the guy? They're already suspicious, and if we killed him and left him in the lot, they'd be all over me."

"We could skip the eyes. . . ."

"No." Bekker was cold as stone. He stepped close to Druze and gripped his arm above the elbow. Druze took a half-step back, chilled by the other man's frigid eyes. "No. We cut the eyes. You understand."

"Jesus, okay," Druze said, pulling back.

Bekker stared at him for a moment, judging his sincerity. Apparently satisfied, he went on. "If we dump him somewhere remote—and I know the perfect place—nobody's going to find him. Nobody. The cops might suspect that he was Stephanie's lover, but they won't know if he ran because he was afraid, or because he was the killer, or if he's dead, or what. They just won't know. . . ."

Druze left the way he'd come, through the side door. Bekker walked back toward his office, rubbing his chin, thinking. Druze was reluctant. Not in rebellion, but unhappy. He'd have to consider that. . . .

In the elevator, he glanced at his watch. He had time. . . .


"Sybil."

Was she asleep? Bekker leaned over the bed and pulled her eyelids up. Her eyes were looking at him, dark and liquid, but when he let go of her eyelids, she closed them again. She was awake, all right, but not cooperating.

He sat beside her bed. "I have to look in your eyes as you go, Sybil," he said. He could feel himself breathing a little harder than usual: his experiments had that effect on him, the excitement. . . .

"Here we are. . . ." He clapped a strip of tape over her lips, rested the heel of his other hand on her forehead and pulled her eyelids up with his index and ring fingers. Her eyes open, he leaned into her line of vision and said, quietly, "I've taped your mouth so you can't breathe, and now I'll pinch your nose, until you smother. . . . Do you understand? It shouldn't hurt, but I would appreciate a signal if you see . . . anything. Move your eyes up and down as you go through to the other side, do you understand? If there is another side?"

He was using his most convincing voice, and quite convincing it was, he thought. "Are you ready? Here we go." He pinched her nose, holding his fingers so she could see it, even if she couldn't feel it. Sybil couldn't move, but there were muscles that could twitch, and they did twitch after the first minute, small tremors running through her neck to his hands.

Her eyes began to roll up and he put his face an inch from hers, looking into them, whispering, urgent. "Can you see it? Sybil, can you see . . . ?"

She was gone, unconscious. He released her nose, placed his hand on her chest, compressed it, lifted, compressed it again. She hadn't been that close, he thought, although she couldn't know that. She'd thought she was dying. *Had* been dying, would have died, if he hadn't released his hand . . .

She owed him this information. . . .

"Sybil, are you in there? Hello, Sybil, I know you're there."

At two, Bekker was home, MDMA burning low in his mind, under control. The episode with Sybil had, ultimately, been unfulfilling. A nurse had come down the hall, gone into a nearby room. He'd left then, thinking it better not to be seen with Sybil. As far as he knew, he hadn't been. He'd gone from her bedside to his office, popped the ecstasy, hoping to balance the disappointment, turned off the lights and left.

He drove past the front of the house on the way to the alley. As he passed, he saw a man, there, at the end of the street. On the sidewalk. Turning his head to watch Bekker go by. Large. Watching. Familiar.

Bekker slowed, stopped, rolled down the window. "Can I help you?" he called.

There was a long moment of silence, then the man sauntered out into the street. He was wearing a leather bomber jacket and boots.

"Mr. Bekker, how are you?"

"You're a police officer?"

"Lucas Davenport, Minneapolis police."

Yes. The man at the funeral, the tough-looking one. "Is the police department camped on my porch?" Bekker asked. Safe now—the man wasn't a mugger or revenge-bound relative—the sarcasm knit through his polite tone like a dirty thread in a doily.

"No. Only me," the cop said.

"Surveillance?"

"No, no. I just like to wander by the scene of a crime now and then. Get a feel for it. Helps me think . . ."

Davenport. A bell went off in the back of Bekker's mind. "Aren't you the officer that the FBI agent called a gunman? Killed some ridiculous number of people?"

Even in the weak illumination from the corner streetlight, Bekker could see the flash of the cop's white teeth. He was smiling.

"The FBI doesn't like me," the cop said.

"Did you like it? Killing all those people?" The interest was genuine, the words surprising Bekker even as they popped out of his mouth. The cop seemed to think about it for a moment, tipping his head back, as though looking for stars. It was cold enough that their breath was making little puffs of steam.

"Some of them," the cop said after a bit. He rocked from his toes to his heels, looked up again. "Yeah. Some of them I . . . enjoyed quite a bit."

Bekker couldn't quite see the other man's eyes: they were set too deep, under heavy brow ridges, and the curiosity was almost unbearable.

"Listen," Bekker heard himself say, "I have to put my car in the garage. But would you like to come in for a cup of coffee?"

# 12

Lucas waited at the front door until Bekker got the car in the garage and walked through the house to let him in. Bekker turned on the porch light as he opened the door. In the yellow light, his skin looked like parchment, stretched taut over the bones of his face. Like a skull, Lucas thought. Inside, in the soft glow of the ceiling fixtures, the skull illusion vanished: Bekker was beautiful. Not handsome, but more than pretty.

"Come in. The house is a bit messy."

The house was spectacular. The entry floor was oak parquet. To the left was a coat closet, to the right a wall with an oil painting of a British Isles scene, a cottage with a thatched roof in the foreground, sailboats on the river beyond. Straight ahead, a burgundy-carpeted staircase curled up to the right. Off the entryway, a room with glass doors, full of books, appeared to the right, under a balcony formed by the stairs. To the left was the parlor, with Oriental carpets, a half-dozen antique mirrors and a stone fireplace. Beautiful and hot. Seventy-five or eighty degrees. Lucas unzipped his jacket and crouched to press his fingers against the parlor carpet.

"Wonderful," he said. The pile was soft as beaten egg whites, an inch or more deep, and as intricately woven as an Arabian fairy tale.

Bekker grunted. He wasn't interested. "Let's go back and sit in the kitchen," he said, and led the way to a country kitchen with quarry-tile floor. Stephanie Bekker had been killed in the kitchen, Lucas recalled. Bekker seemed unaffected by it, pulling earthenware cups from natural oak cabinets, spooning instant coffee into them.

"I hope caffeine is okay," he said. Bekker's voice was flat, uninflected, as though he daily drank coffee with a cop who suspected him of murder. He must know. . . .

"Fine." Lucas looked around the kitchen as Bekker filled the cups with tap water, stuck them in a microwave and punched the control buttons. The kitchen was as carefully crafted as the rest of the house, with folksy, turn-of-the-century wallpaper, dark, perfectly matched wood, and touches of flag-stone. While the rest of the house felt decorated, Lucas thought, the kitchen felt lived in.

Bekker turned back to Lucas as the microwave began to hum. "I know nothing at all about cooking," Bekker said. "A little about wine, perhaps."

"You're handling your wife's death pretty well," Lucas said. He stepped up to a small framed photograph. Four women in long dark dresses and white aprons, standing around a butter churn. Old. "Are these, what, ancestors?"

"Stephanie's great-grandmother and some friends. Sit down, Mr. Daven-port," Bekker said, nodding at a breakfast bar with stools. The microwave beeped, and he took out the cups, the coffee steaming hot, carried them to the bar and sat down opposite Lucas. "You were saying?"

"Your wife's death . . ."

"I'll miss her, but to be honest, I didn't love my wife very much. I'd never hurt her—I know what the police think, Stephanie's idiot cousin—but the fact is, neither of us was much of a factor in the other's life. I suspected she was having an affair: I simply didn't care. I've had female friends of my own. . . ." He looked for reaction in Lucas' face. There was none. The cop accepted the infidelity as routine . . . maybe.

"And that didn't bother her? Your other friends." Lucas sipped at the coffee. Scalding.

"I don't believe so. She knew, of course, *her* friends would have seen to that. But she never spoke to me about it. And she was the type who would have, if she cared. . . ." Bekker blew on his coffee. He was wearing a tweed jacket and whipcord pants, very English.

"So why not a divorce?" Lucas asked.

"Why should we? We got along reasonably well, and we had this"—he gestured at the house—"which we couldn't maintain if we split up. And there are other advantages for two people living together. You share maintenance chores, run errands for each other, one can take care of business when the other one is gone. . . . There wasn't any passion, but we were quite well adapted to each other's habits. I'm not much interested in marriage, at my age. I have my work. She couldn't have children; her fallopian tubes were hope-lessly tangled, and by the time in vitro came around, she was no longer think-ing about children. I never wanted any, so there wasn't even that possibility." He stopped and seemed to reflect, took a sip of the scalding coffee. "I suppose other people wouldn't understand the way we were living, but it was conve-nient and comfortable."

"Hmp." Lucas sipped his own coffee and looked the other man straight in the eyes. Bekker gazed placidly back, not flinching, and Lucas knew then that he was lying, at least about part of it. Nobody looked that guiltless without deliberate effort. "I suppose a prosecutor could argue that since you had no interest in each other, and it made no difference to you whether she lived or died, her death would be very . . . convenient. Instead of having half of this"—his gesture mimicked Bekker's—"you'd have all of it."

"He could . . . if he were particularly stupid or particularly vicious," Bekker said. He flashed a smile at Lucas, a thin rim of white teeth. "I invited you for coffee because of the people you've killed, Mr. Davenport. I thought you'd likely know about death and murder. That would give us much in common. I study death as a scientist. I've studied murder, both the victims and the killers. There are several men who consider themselves my friends out at Stillwater prison, serving life sentences. From my research I've drawn two conclusions. First: Murder is stupid. In most cases, it will out, as somebody British once said. If you're going to commit murder, the worst thing you can do is plan it and commit it in league with another person. Conflicts arise, the investigators play one against another. . . . I know how it works. No. Murder is stupid. Murder plotted with someone else is idiotic. Divorce, on the other hand, is merely annoying. A tragedy for some couples, perhaps, but if two people genuinely don't love each other, it's mostly routine legal procedure."

Bekker shrugged and went at the coffee. When he extended his perfect pink lips to the cup, he looked like a leech, Lucas thought.

"What's the second thing you know about murder? You said there were two things," Lucas asked.

"Ah. Yes." Bekker smiled again, pleased that Lucas was paying attention. "To plan and carry out a cold-blooded murder—well, only a madman could do it. Anyone remotely normal could not. Serial killers, hit men, men who plot and kill their wives: all crazy."

Lucas nodded. "I agree."

"I'm glad you do," Bekker said simply. "And I'm not crazy."

"Is that the real reason you invited me in? To tell me you're not nuts?"

Bekker nodded ruefully and said, "Yes, I guess it is. Because I thought you might understand the totality of what I'm saying. Even if I had wanted to kill Stephanie—and I didn't—I wouldn't have. I'm simply too smart and too sane." He reached forward and touched Lucas on the arm, and Lucas thought: *The sucker is trying to seduce me. He wants me to* like *him.* . . . "Your fellow officers have been all over the neighborhood, quite deliberately creating an impression. I can feel it in my neighbors. I'm sure Stephanie's crazy cousin, the dope addict, has told you that I had her killed to get this house, but if you ask her friends, you'll find that I never had much interest in it. The house or the furnishings . . ."

"You could sell it—"

"I was coming to that," Bekker interrupted. He made a brushing motion with his free hand, as though batting away gnats. "I'm not much interested in the house or its furnishings, but I'm not totally unappreciative, either. It is a very comfortable place to live. Success in academia is largely political, you know, and the house is a wonderful backdrop for social gatherings. For impressing those who must be impressed. I would keep it, but . . . I'm afraid Stephanie's crazy cousin may succeed in driving me out. If all my neighbors believe I killed her, remaining here would be intolerable. You might tell that to Del, when you see him. That if I sell, it will be only because he drove me out."

"I will," Lucas nodded. "And if the other officers are creating problems for you . . . I have some pull at headquarters. I'll back them off."

"Really?" Bekker seemed surprised. "Would you?"

"Sure. I don't know whether you were involved in your wife's killing, but there's no reason you should be illegally harassed. I'll look into it."

"That'd be wonderful," Bekker said. Gratitude saturated his voice, but a spark of contempt flared in his eyes. "I'm glad I asked you in: I had an intuition that you'd understand. . . ."

They sat in silence for a moment, then Lucas said, "She was killed here in the kitchen. Your wife."

"Oh, yes . . . I suppose she was," Bekker said, looking around vaguely.

*Wrong reaction, asshole.* Bekker had to know where she was killed. He must have thought about it, looked at the spot, carried the image in his head: anyone would, innocent or guilty, crazy or sane. *And that business about a divorce being simply annoying. If you believe that, you're stupider than I think you are. . . .* Lucas waited, expecting more, but Bekker pushed off the barstool and dumped the last of his coffee into the kitchen sink.

"The men you killed, Lucas. Do you think they went anywhere?" His tone was casual.

"What do you mean?" Lucas asked. "You mean, like, to heaven?"

"Or hell." Bekker turned to study him. His voice was no longer casual.

"No. I don't think they went anywhere," Lucas said, shaking his head. "I used to be a Catholic, and when I first started police work, I worried about that. I saw a lot of people dead or dying for no apparent reason . . . not people I killed, just people. Little kids who'd drowned, people dying in auto accidents and with heart attacks and strokes. I saw a lineman burn to death, up on a pole, little bits and pieces, and nobody could help. . . . I watched them go, screaming and crying and sometimes just lying there with their tongue stuck out, heaving, with all the screaming and hollering from friends and relatives . . . and I never saw anyone looking beyond. I think, Michael, I think they just blink out. That's all. I think they go where the words on a computer screen go, when you turn it off. One minute they exist, maybe they're even profound, maybe the result of a great deal of work. The next . . . Whiff. Gone."

"Gone," Bekker repeated. His white eyebrows went up. "Nothing left?"

"Nothing but a shell, and that rots."

"Hah." Bekker turned away, suddenly shaken. "Very sad. Well. I have to get to bed. I have work tomorrow."

Lucas stood, drank the last of his coffee and left the cup on the bar. "I wonder if I could ask something. I'm sure other cops have been all over the house. Could I take a look at the room where Stephanie and her friend were . . . spending time?"

"You mean her bedroom," Bekker said wryly. "I don't see why not. Like you said, the carpets are virtually worn-out from the impact of all the flat feet . . . no offense."

Lucas laughed in spite of himself, then followed Bekker up the long staircase. "I'm down there," Bekker said, when they reached the top. He gestured to the left, but turned to the right. Halfway down the hall, he pushed a door open, reached inside, clicked on a light, stepped back and said, "Here we are."

Stephanie Bekker had slept in an old-fashioned double bed with a rough-cut French frame. The quilt, blankets and sheets were in a heap at the foot of the bed, lying across the frame and partially covering an antique steamer trunk. A dozen magazines on home decorating, antiques and art were piled on the trunk. Near the head of the bed, a Princess phone sat on a bedstand, along with a clock, two more magazines and a Stephen King novel.

A door opened to the left. Lucas stuck his head inside and found a compact but complete bathroom, with a vanity, toilet, tub and shower. A ruby-colored bath towel hung from one of two towel racks. There were traces of fingerprint powder on the vanity, toilet handle, shower handles and towel racks. Lucas turned back into the bedroom, noticed another towel on the red-toned Oriental carpet.

"Just like . . . the night . . ." Bekker said. "The laboratory people said they'd call and tell me when I can clean up. Do you have any idea when that might be?"

"Have they filmed it?"

"I think so. . . ."

"I'll check that, too," Lucas said. He looked at Bekker across the bedroom, measuring him, and asked, "You didn't do it?"

Bekker looked at him now. "No," he said levelly, with the same straightforward, unflinching gaze.

"Well. Nice meeting you," Lucas said.


Outside, the night had turned colder, sliding into frost. The cold air was welcome on his face after the heat of the house. Lucas strolled up the sidewalk, took a right to the alley, looked around and walked down the alley until he was behind Bekker's house. The killer had probably come in this way.

At the side of the house, a light came on, a long narrow shaft gleaming bright at the edge of a curtain. Struck by a sudden impulse, Lucas pushed the gate in the hurricane fence along the backyard. Locked. He glanced around, then vaulted the fence and walked carefully through the dark backyard, feeling with his feet as much as his eyes, wary of loose garbage can lids and invisible clotheslines. . . .

At the side of the house, he moved by inches to the lighted window, put his back to the outside wall, then slowly rotated his head until he could see through the crack.

Bekker was in the study, nude, lurching from one end to the other, chewing convulsively, his face twisted into a mask of pain, terror or religious ecstasy, his eyes turned so far up into his skull that only the whites were visible. He shuddered, twisted, threw out his arms, then collapsed into a leather chair, his mouth half open. For a minute, then two, he didn't move, and Lucas thought he might have had a heart attack or stroke. Then he moved, his arms and legs uncoiling, smoothing themselves into an upright attitude, like that of a king on a throne. Laughing. Bekker was laughing, a mechanical "Ha-ha-ha-ha" choking out of his throat. And still his eyes were looking inward, at God.

Lucas dreamed of Bekker's face. Had to be drugs. Had to be. In the dream he kept arguing that point, that it was drugs; but no drugs were found, and Bekker, lightly restrained by two faceless cops in blue uniforms, would swoop up and screech, *I'm high on Jesus.* . . .

The dream was one of those where Lucas knew he was dreaming but couldn't get out. When the alarm went off, just after one in the afternoon, it was a positive relief. He rolled out, cleaned up and was about to pour a cup of coffee when Del banged on the door.

"You're up," Del said, when Lucas answered.

"Come on in. What's going on?"

"Got some calls on the tip line. Nothing much." He shook a no-nicotine, no-tar cigarette out of a crumpled pack and lit it with a Zippo as they walked through the house to the kitchen. "And Sloan talked to a woman named Beulah Miller this morning—another one of Stephanie Bekker's friends. He asked about the psychologist, and she said, 'Maybe.' "

"But the shrink denies it. . . ."

"So does his wife," Del said. He settled at the kitchen table, and when Lucas held up a pot of coffee, he nodded. "Sloan went back and got her alone. She said he'd had an affair, years ago, and she knew about five minutes after it started. There haven't been any since. And she said that after Sloan went away after the first visit, she went straight back to her husband and asked him. He denied it. Still denies it. And she believes him."

"Has she got a job of her own?" Lucas asked, handing him a cup of hot coffee.

"Sloan thought of that," Del said. "And she does—she's a lobbyist for the Taxpayers' Forum and a couple of other conservative interest groups. She's got a law degree, Sloan says, and she probably makes a pretty good buck."

"So she doesn't need a meal ticket."

"Guess not. Anyway, she suspected that Stephanie was having an affair. They never talked about it, but there were some pretty heavy hints. And she says she thinks they never talked about it because she probably knew the guy, and maybe the guy's wife, and Stephanie didn't know how she'd react. Like she was afraid Miller'd freak out or something."

"So she says it's not her husband, but probably somebody they know. . . ."

"Yeah."

"Did Sloan get a list of possibilities?"

"Naturally. Twenty-two names. But she said some of them were pretty remote possibilities. Sloan's looking at the most likely ones today, the rest of them tomorrow . . . but he got something else you might be interested in."

Lucas raised his eyebrows. "What?"

"Bekker apparently had an affair sometime back, two or three years ago. A nurse. Common talk around the hospital. Sloan got her name and address, went over to see her. She told him to get lost. He pulled the badge, but you know Sloan, he likes people a little too much. . . ."

"Huh. You think . . . ?"

"What I think is, you'd be the perfect guy to talk to her," Del said.

"Why not you?"

"I'd like to come along, but I don't look right to do it by myself," Del said, shaking his long black hair. "I look a little too much like Charlie Manson. People don't let me in the door, even, unless they're assholes. But you—when you put on one of those gray suits, you look like the fuckin' Law."

Cheryl Clark didn't want to let them in.

"This is about a murder, Miss Clark," Lucas said, cool and official, his ID in her face. "You can talk to us, and the chances are about ninety percent that we'll walk away. Or you can refuse to talk, and we'll take you downtown and let you call a lawyer, and we'll talk to you that way."

"I don't have to talk."

"Yes you do. You don't have the right to refuse to talk. You have the right not to incriminate yourself. If you think you're going to incriminate yourself, then we'll go downtown, you can call a lawyer, we'll get you a grant of immunity from prosecution—and then we'll talk. Or you'll go to jail for contempt of court," Lucas said. His voice warmed up a couple of notches. "Look, we don't want to be jerks—if you haven't done anything criminal, I'm telling you, it'd be a lot easier just to have an informal chat right now."

"I really don't have anything to say," she protested. Her eyes skittered past Lucas to Del, who waited at the foot of the stoop, looking at a motorcycle.

"We'd like to ask anyway," Lucas said.

"Well . . . all right. Come in. But I might not answer," she said.


Her apartment was tidy but impersonal, almost like a motel room. A television was the most prominent piece of furniture, dominating one wall, facing a couch. The couch was covered with a thick green baize that might have been taken off a pool table. A sliding door led to a tiny balcony, with a view toward the Mississippi River valley.

"Is that your boyfriend's Sportster outside?" Del asked, friendly.

"It's mine," Clark said shortly.

"You ride? Far out," Del said. "And you smoke a lot of dope?" He stood in front of the balcony doors, looking out at the river. He was wearing a long-sleeved paisley shirt under a jean jacket, and dirty black jeans with a silver-studded black biker's belt.

"I don't . . ." Clark, dressed in her white nurse's uniform, sat rigidly on her couch. Her eyes, sunk deep in her pale face, were underlined by black smudges. She looked at Lucas. "You said . . ."

"Don't bullshit us," Del said, but in a friendly voice. "Please. I don't give a fuck about the dope, just don't bullshit us. You could get a goddamn contact high off these things." He flicked the curtains with his fingers.

"I don't . . ." she started, then shrugged and said, ". . . smoke a lot."

"Don't worry about it," Lucas said to her. He sat on the couch himself, half turned toward Clark. "You had a relationship with Michael Bekker."

"I told the first officer. It was almost nothing." Her hands fluttered at her chest.

"He's under investigation in the murder of his wife. We're not accusing him, but we're looking at him," Lucas said. "You seem like an intelligent person. What we need from you is . . . an assessment."

"Are you asking me . . . ?"

"Could he kill his wife?"

She looked at him for a moment, then broke her gaze away. "Yes."

"Was he violent with you?"

There was a moment of silence, and then she nodded. "Yes."

"Tell me."

"He . . . used to hit me. With his hands. Open hands, but it hurt. And he choked me once. That time, I thought I might die. But he stopped. . . . He'd go into rages. He seemed unstoppable, but he always . . . stopped."

"What about sexual practices? Anything unusual, bondage, like that?"

"No, no. The thing is, there almost wasn't any sex." She looked up at Lucas to see if he believed her.

"He's impotent?" Lucas asked.

"He wasn't impotent," she said. She glanced at Del, who nodded, encouraging her. "I mean, sometimes we did, and sometimes we didn't, but he didn't seem driven so much by sex as . . ."

"What?"

Clark's fear of them had slipped into the background and she seemed to be searching for the right phrase, interested despite herself. "He needs to control things. He'd make me do . . . you know, oral sex and so on. Not because it turned him on, I don't think, but because he liked to make me do it. It was the control he liked, not the sex."

"Did he ever use drugs while you were around?"

"No . . . well, he maybe smoked a little marijuana. You know, though, I think he might have used steroids. He has a very good body. . . ." She dropped her eyelashes. "But he had very small testicles."

"Small?"

"Very small . . . almost like marbles," she said. "You know, he lifts weights, and weightlifters sometimes use steroids. Testicles can shrink with prolonged use of steroids, so I asked him, and he got angry. . . . That was the time he choked me."

"Did you ever see him dance?" Lucas asked.

"Dance? His dance?" Clark pulled back. "You've been watching him. . . ."

"So you've seen it," Lucas said. Del was frowning at him, confused.

"One time, he beat me up," Clark said in a rush, bouncing on the couch. "Not bad, I mean, nothing showed, but I was hurting, and crying, and all of a sudden he started to giggle and jump up and down. I couldn't believe . . . it was like a dance. It *was* a dance, a jig. . . ."

"Jesus Christ," Del blurted. "A jig?"

Lucas nodded. "I've seen it. It's gotta be dope. You should talk to your people, see if he's buying on the street."

Del looked at Clark and asked, "Why'd you go along with him?"

She looked up at him and said, "Because he's beautiful."

"Beautiful?"

"He's beautiful. I'd never had a beautiful man." She looked between them, looking for understanding. After a moment, Del nodded.


They left her ten minutes later.

"She knows something else," Lucas said. "She didn't tell us something, and she thinks it might be important."

"Yeah. But there's no way to tell how important it is." Del scratched his head, looking back at the apartment house door. "And if we squeeze, she'll either crack like Humpty-fuckin'-Dumpty or call a lawyer. . . ."

"Which is worse . . ."

"Yeah."

They were walking along the sidewalk to the car. "Where's your wife?" Lucas asked suddenly. "I heard she split."

"Yeah. More'n a year ago."

"You gettin' laid?"

"Only by Lady Fingers," Del said, with a dry chuckle. "Look at me, man, I'm a fuckin' wreck. I'm stoned half the time and I'm walkin' around with a gun in my armpit. Who'd go out with me? Other'n maybe a couple of hookers?"

"Yeah." Lucas looked at the other man. "You know what? She kind of liked you. Clark did. Talking about bikes and all. I mean, she's a rider and you're . . . like you are."

Del shook his head. "Man, I can do better'n her."

"You haven't been," Lucas pointed out. "And doing better won't tell us what she knows."


"I'd say twelve or thirteen of them are straight-out nutcases, and we didn't want to bother you," the dispatcher said, handing Lucas a stack of call slips. "I've marked those. Six of them wouldn't identify themselves at all. You can judge for yourself, but they're a waste of time. . . . There are a half-dozen you ought to get back to. People who knew the Bekkers or Armistead and say they might have a piece of information for you. None of them thought their information was particularly urgent."

"All right. Thanks."

"That last one, she said it was personal."

Lucas looked at it. Cassie Lasch.

He thought about not calling. An easy way out, if you didn't call for long enough. He went home and ate a microwave dinner, aware of the telephone out on the edge of his vision. He lasted an hour before he picked it up.

"You didn't call," Cassie said.

"I'm working. Give me a little time."

"How much time does it take to call? Where do you live?"

"St. Paul."

"Why don't I come over?" she asked.

"Ah . . ." Lucas felt himself freeze for a moment, an impulse to push her away. He was looking at the kitchen table, piled with newspapers and unopened mail, books, some read, some not, a couple of unopened cereal boxes, a stack of unwashed bowls. . . .

He wasn't doing anything. He was barely alive.

"You know where Mississippi River Boulevard is?"

# 13

Cassie was muscular and intense, and fought him, wrestling across the bed. When they were done, she lay facedown on the extra pillow, while he lay faceup, sweat evaporating from his chest, chilling him.

"Jesus," he said after a while. "That was all right. I was a little worried."

Her head turned. "About what?"

"It's been a while."

She propped herself up on one elbow. "Ah. A little depression?"

"I guess," he said, curiously ready to talk about it. He'd never talked about problems with Jennifer. "I had all the symptoms."

She crawled over him, reaching, switched on the bedside lamp. He winced and turned away from it.

"Look here," she said, showing her wrists to him. There were two whiter lines on the inside of each, parallel, transverse. Scars to be read as clearly as needle tracks.

"What's this shit?" he said. He took her wrists in his hands and stroked the scars with his thumbs.

"What do they look like?"

"Like you cut your wrists," he said.

She nodded. "You win the golden weenie. Fake suicide attempt—that's what the shrinks say. Depression."

"The scars don't look so fake," he said.

"I didn't think so, either," she said, pulling her wrists away. "Are there any cigarettes around here?"

"No. I didn't know you smoked."

"I don't, except after sex," she said.

"Those were pretty heavy cuts. Tell me . . ."

She sat up and pulled her knees under her chin, looking down at him. "This was five years ago. I was never in much danger. A lot of blood, and I had to go to counseling for a few months."

"What's fake about that?" Lucas asked, rolling up on an elbow.

"What the shrinks say is, I was living with this guy and he had a gun, and I knew where it was. And our apartment was on the seventh floor, I could have jumped. And I knew the guy was coming home pretty soon. So they say I really wanted to live and this was just an attempt to draw attention to my condition."

"But the cuts . . ."

"Yeah. The shrinks are full of shit. They can tell you how to talk to someone else, how to deal with personal problems, but they don't know what happens inside your head, unless it's happened to them. I could have jumped out the window. I could have shot myself. But that's not what I thought of. I had this, like . . ."

"Fixation."

"Yeah. Exactly," she said, smiling at him. "See, you *know*. The theater's got a whole oral literature about killing yourself and knives are the way to do it. I fucked it up, did it all wrong—I should have cut myself lengthwise, or at the elbow, but I didn't know that. I could have used little pieces of glass, you get a better cut that way, but I didn't know that, either."

Lucas shuddered. "Glass. I saw that once. You don't want to cut yourself with glass."

"I'll keep that in mind," she said wryly.

"So you cut yourself . . . ?"

"Yep. I just hacked and sat there and bled and cried until my friend came home. They didn't even give me a transfusion at the hospital," Cassie said. "Good thing, too. This was back when there was AIDS in the blood supply. Though who'd ever know, with me fuckin' actors, and all."

"Jesus, that makes me feel good. . . ." He looked down at himself.

"Maybe you oughta run dip it in Lysol . . ." she said.

"Don't have any Lysol—I got some Oven-Off," he said, and laughed. She grinned and patted his leg. "So what were you going to do? Your guns?"

He looked at her for a minute and then nodded. "Yeah. I've got a gun safe down in the basement. It was like they were glowing down there, the guns. Glowing with some kind of gravity, or magnetism, or something. I could feel them wherever I was, pulling me down there. It didn't make any difference if I was on the other side of Minneapolis, I could feel them. I carry a gun, but I never thought about using it. It was the guns in the safe, pulling me down."

"You ever go down? Just to look, or handle them? Stick one in your ear?"

"Nope. I would of felt stupid," Lucas said.

She threw back her head and laughed, but not a happy laugh; an acknowledgment. "I think a lot of suicides are avoided because you'd feel stupid. Or because of the way you'd look afterwards. Like hanging . . ." She gripped herself around the throat and squeezed, crossing her eyes and sticking her tongue out.

"Jesus," he said, laughing again.

She turned serious. "Did you think about it because everything was too painful, or what?"

"No. I just couldn't handle what was going on in my head, this, this *storm*. I couldn't sleep: I'd have these crazy fucking episodes where nine million thoughts would go pounding through my head, and I couldn't stop them. Crazy shit. You know, like the names of people in my senior class, or all the guys on the hockey squad, and all kinds of bizarre shit, and you get crazy because you forget a couple of them."

"That's pretty common," Cassie said, nodding.

"But basically, I thought about the guns because it didn't seem to make any difference whether I lived or died. It was like, Heads I live, tails I die—and if you keep flipping, it'll come up tails, sooner or later."

Cassie nodded. "There was a guy I knew in New York, he used to play Russian roulette with a revolver. About once a year he'd spin that thing, that . . ."

"Cylinder."

"Yeah. Then he'd put the barrel in his mouth and pull the trigger. Right around Christmastime. Said it kept him straight for a whole 'nother year."

"What happened to him?" Lucas asked.

"I don't know. He wasn't that good a friend. He was still alive the last time I was in New York. I could never figure out if he was lucky or unlucky."

"Huh."

She stretched out again, her hands behind her head, and they lay beside each other in comfortable silence for a minute. "Did you have the voice in the back of your head, watching you go through all this shit?" she asked finally.

"Yeah. The watcher. It was like having my own critic back there. My own journalist."

She giggled. "I never thought of it that way, but that's it. Like, the major part of me was hacking away with a bread knife—"

"Ah, fuck, a bread knife?"

"Yeah, the kind with the serrated blade?"

"Ah, Jesus . . ."

"Good brand, too, Solingen . . ."

"God, Cassie . . ."

"Anyway, the big part was hacking away, and this little voice was back there reporting on it, like CNN or something. Kind of skeptical, too."

"Jesus." He reached out and stroked her, from navel to breasts, and back down across her groin to the inside of her knee.

"Pretty gross, huh? Anyway, I'm glad you're getting better."

"I'm not really sure I am. . . ."

"Oh, you are." She patted the bed. "You're here. When you're really depressed, your sex life jumps in a car and leaves for Chicago. I was in this group, as part of the therapy, and every one of the men said so. It wasn't that they couldn't—they just couldn't stand the thought of the complications. Sex is the first thing to go. When it comes back, you're definitely getting better."

The phone rang at eleven o'clock. Lucas woke clear-eyed, rested, already rolling toward the edge of the bed before he was aware of the weight on the other side. He'd slept, and dreamed, and had almost forgotten. . . .

Cassie was lying facedown again, bare as the day she was born, the sheet covering her hips. Her hair had parted on either side of her head, and the light slanting through the venetian blinds played across the sensuous turn of her vertebrae, starting at the nape of her neck, trailing down almost to her just hidden tailbone. He reached down, still aware of the phone, now ringing the fourth time, or fifth, and gently slid the sheet even farther down, onto her legs. . . .

She reached down with one hand and pulled it back up. "Go answer the phone," she grumped, not moving her head.

He grinned and headed for the kitchen, and picked the phone up on the sixth ring. Dispatch. "I've got a call holding from Michael Bekker," the woman said. "Put it through?"

"Yes."

There was a click, a pause, and then Bekker said, "Hello?"

"Yeah, this is Davenport."

"Yes, Lucas. Will you be free tonight, late?" Bekker's voice was low, friendly, carefully modulated. "I've got classes, then a dinner, but I've found something in my wife's papers that I thought was interesting. I'd like to show it to you. . . ."

"Can you tell me on the phone?"

"Mmm, why don't you come over? Somebody'll have to anyway, and I'd prefer it be you. That other policeman . . . he's a bit thick."

Swanson. Not thick at all, although any number of Stillwater inmates had made the mistake of thinking so. . . . "All right. What time?"

"Tennish?"

"I'll see you then."

Lucas hung up and padded back to the bedroom. The bed was empty, and water was running in the bathroom. Cassie was bent over the sink, using his toothbrush. He winced, then reached out and touched her bottom.

"Hi," she said through a mouthful of bubbles, looking into the mirror over the sink. "Done in a minute. Breath like a dinosaur. And I gotta pee."

"I'll run down to the other bathroom," he said. He went down the hall, looked back to make sure she wasn't following, opened a drawer, took out a new toothbrush, peeled the package, removed the brush and hastily stuffed the packaging back in the drawer. He was smiling when he looked at himself in the mirror.

Back in the bedroom, he found the sheets and blankets in a pile on the floor, while she lounged in the middle of the bed.

"Hop in," she said, patting the mattress beside her. "We're right on time for a nooner and we're not even up yet. Ain't it great?"

After Cassie left, in a cab, he spent the rest of the day fooling around, unable to focus much on the case, making call-backs, driving around town, checking the net. He walked past Bekker's house again, and spoke to a neighbor who was raking the winter gunk from his lawn. Stephanie had once had a cocker spaniel, the neighbor said, and when Bekker had had to walk it in the winter, he'd take it up to the corner and then "kick the shit out of it. I saw him out the window, he did it several times." The neighbor's wife, who had been splitting iris bulbs, turned and said, "Be fair, tell him about the shoes."

"Shoes?"

"Well, yeah, the dog had bad kidneys, I guess, and he used to sneak up to Bekker's closet and pee in his shoes."

Lucas and the neighbor started laughing at the same time.

In the evening, an hour before Cassie went on at the Lost River, she and Lucas walked down the block for a cup of coffee. They sat across from each other in a diner booth, and Cassie said, "Ultimately, you're not flaky enough for me. But it'd be nice if we could keep it together for a couple of months."

Lucas nodded. "That'd be nice."

At five after ten, he walked up the steps to Bekker's. Lights blazed from several of the ground-floor windows, and Lucas resisted the temptation to go window-peeking again. Instead he rang the bell, and Bekker came to the door, wrapped in a burgundy dressing gown.

"Is that your Porsche?" he asked in surprise, looking past Lucas to the street.

"Yeah. I have a little money of my own," Lucas said.

"I see." Bekker was genuinely impressed. He knew the price of a Porsche. "Well, come along."

Lucas followed him into the study. Bekker seemed skittish, nervous. He would try something, Lucas decided.

"Scotch?"

"Sure."

"I've got a nice one. I used to drink Chivas, but a couple of months ago Stephanie . . ."—he paused on the name, as if calling up her face—"Stephanie bought me a bottle of Glenfiddich, a single malt. . . . I won't be going back to the other."

Lucas couldn't tell one scotch from another. Bekker dropped ice cubes into a glass, poured two fingers of liquor over them and handed the glass to Lucas. He looked at his watch, and Lucas thought it odd that he would be wearing a watch with a dressing gown. "So what'd you find?" Lucas asked.

"A couple of things," Bekker said. He settled behind the desk, leaned back with the scotch and crossed his legs. They flashed from the folds of the dressing gown like a woman's legs from an evening dress. Deliberately, Lucas thought. *He thinks I might be gay, and he's trying to seduce me.* He took a sip of the scotch. "A couple of things," Bekker repeated. "Like these."

He picked up a stack of colored cardboard slips, bound together with a rubber band, and tossed them across the desk. Lucas picked them up. They were tickets to shows at the Lost River. He thumbed through: eight of them, in three different colors.

"Notice anything peculiar about them, Lucas?" Bekker asked. Using his first name again.

"They're from the Lost River, of course. . . ." Lucas rolled the rubber band off and looked at the tickets individually. "All for matinees . . . and there are eight tickets for three different shows. All punched, all different shows."

Bekker mimed applause, then held up his glass to Lucas, as if toasting him. "I knew you were intelligent. Don't you find you can always tell? Anyway, the second woman who was killed worked for the Lost River, correct? I went to a couple of evening performances with Stephanie, but I had no idea she was going in the afternoons. So I began to wonder: Could her lover . . . ?"

"I see," Lucas said. A connection. And it seemed to let Bekker out.

"And I also found this," Bekker said. He leaned forward this time, and handed Lucas several letter-sized sheets of paper. American Express account sheets, with various items underlined in blue ballpoint ink. "The underlined charges are for tickets at the Lost River. Six or seven times over the past few months, on her personal card. A couple of them match with the matinee dates and the charge amount is right. And then, on four of the days, there's a dining charge, and none less than thirty dollars. I'd bet she was taking somebody to dinner. That restaurant, the Tricolor Bar, I've been there once or twice, but not in the afternoons. . . ."

Lucas looked at the papers, then over the top of them at Bekker. "You should have shown these to Swanson."

"I don't like the man," Bekker said, looking at him levelly. "You, I like."

"Well, good," Lucas said. He drank the last of the scotch. "You seem like a pretty reasonable guy yourself. Pathology, right? Maybe I'll call you on one of my games; you could consult."

"Your games?" Bekker glanced at his watch again, then quickly looked away.

*What's going on?* "Yeah, I invent games. You know, historical strategy games, role-playing games, that sort of thing."

"Hmph. I'd be interested in talking sometime," Bekker said. "Really."

# 14

Bekker shut the door behind Lucas and dashed upstairs, leaving the lights out. He went to the window over the porch and split the curtains with an index finger. Davenport was just getting into his Porsche. A moment later the car's lights came on, and in another minute it was gone. Bekker let the curtain fall back into place and hurried to his bedroom. He dressed in dark blue slacks, a gray sweatshirt and navy jacket, loafers. He gobbled a methamphetamine and went out the back, through the garage, and got in the car.

A neighborhood restaurant had a pay phone just inside the door. He stopped, dialed, got the answering machine on the second ring—a message was waiting. He punched in the code, 4384. The machine rewound, paused, then Druze's voice blurted a single syllable.

Druze hunched over the wheel, the weight of the night pressing on him.

*Like the tarbaby. One foot stuck, then you have to kick with the other one, then you have to punch him, and your fist gets stuck. . . .*

This would be the last for him. He'd talk Bekker out of the third killing. There was no need for a third. Not now. He'd seen them on television, and the cops were convinced: one killer, a psycho.

Druze was orbiting a red-brick university building, Peik Hall, watching. Lots of lights, big orange sodium-vapor anticrime lights, walk lights, globe lights outside the entrances to the university buildings. Lots of trees and shrubbery, too. Good cover. And nobody around.

The night was cold, with heavy broken clouds darting across the sky, a full moon sailing between them; and it smelled of coming rain. A good night for beer and brats and television in the Riverside Avenue taverns with the theater crowd. Druze could never be one of the happy crowd, throwing darts or chattering, but he could sit on his stool at the end of the bar, feeling a little of the reflected warmth. Anything would be better than this—but he had nobody to blame for this but himself. He should have gone after the fat man. . . .

Druze was wearing the ski jacket again, but this time as much for conceal-ment as for protection from the weather. He wouldn't want George to recog-nize him prematurely.

George's Cherokee was parked in a small public parking lot tucked behind an older building adjacent to Peik Hall. Pillsbury Drive, a cross-campus road, ran past the end of the lot. After ten o'clock there was little traffic—but there was some. Every few minutes or so, a car went past, and the road was smooth enough that you couldn't hear it coming.

One other car was parked in the lot, across from George's. Druze circled the campus complex as long as he dared, then parked his Dodge wagon beside George's Jeep, leaving a full parking space between them. He sat for a moment, watching, then got out, listened a few seconds more. The lot was poorly lit, with most of the light coming from a bowl-shaped fixture on the back of the building.

No people around, unless they were hiding in the bushes. Druze started toward the sidewalk that led past the building, stopped next to a bush of bridal wreath and listened again, ten seconds, twenty. Nothing. He walked back to the Jeep, squatted, took a tire-pressure gauge out of his pocket, reversed it and used the spike to let the air out of the Cherokee's left rear tire. George had to approach from that side; he should see it.

The hissing air sounded like a train whistle in Druze's ears, and it seemed to go on forever. But it didn't. In less than a minute, the tire was flat. Druze stood, looked around again and wandered away.

*The parking meters. Jesus Christ.*

He walked back and plugged the university's twenty-four-hour parking meters. He'd have to remember to look for the campus cops. They checked the parking lots once or twice a night. A ticket would be a disaster.

Druze didn't feel anything when he killed—revulsion, sorrow, empathy. He didn't fear much, either. But tonight there was an edge of apprehension: it came as he almost walked away from the meters. Suppose he came back, killed George and only then noticed a ticket on his windshield? They'd have him. Or, like Brer Rabbit with the tarbaby, he'd be chasing around the campus, hunting down the cop with the ticket book. He'd have to kill him to get the book. And then . . .

That'd be impossible. That was a nightmare, not a rational possibility. Druze shivered and hunched his shoulders. He hadn't expected to get this tangled.

A woman student, carrying books, walked by on the other side of the street, looking resolutely away from him. He went out to University Avenue, keeping an eye on the lighted windows in Peik. Bekker had scouted the building, told him which ones to watch. . . . A black kid in a red jacket hurried by, on the other side of the street. Another kid, white, wearing a white helmet and a daypack, zipped past on Rollerblades.

Druze sauntered now, moving into actor mode, one hand in his pocket, on the handle of the antique German knife-sharpening steel. The steel was as heavy as a fireplace poker, but shorter, eighteen inches long, tapering like a sword, with a smooth hickory handle. He'd shoved the point of the steel right through the bottom of his pocket. The handle was big enough for the steel to hang there on its own, cold down his leg, out of sight. He'd practiced drawing it. It came out smoothly and swung like a pipe wrench, with better balance. It would do the job.

Druze moved off University Avenue and walked across a lawn outside Peik. He was doing a lot for Bekker, he thought, and then: But not only for Bekker. This is for me, I'm the one he'd recognize. . . .

At five minutes after ten, three students carrying books came out the front door of Peik Hall. They stopped on the steps for a moment; then one of the men went left, the man and woman right. Another minute passed, and another knot of students came out of the building, talking, and walked away together. A bank of lights went off in the target windows, then another. Druze drifted out toward University Avenue again, then down Pillsbury, toward the parking lot.

He walked to the far end of the lot, stepped between two bushes, waited, waited. . . .

Two men walked into the lot, from along the side of the building. He could hear their voices, at first like a faraway typewriter, clacking, then as human speech:

". . . Can't figure out how they won it, given the way the company failed to warn anybody about the gas-tank leaks . . ." The speaker was the shorter of the two men.

"Juries. You have to keep that in mind, always. There's no absolutely good way to predict what they'll do, even with the best screening program. In this particular . . . Oh, shit." The conversation stopped. Druze started back up the sidewalk toward the building. If there were two of them, he'd have to forget it. "Look at the goddamn tire. It's only three months old. . . ."

"You want me . . ." the other man offered. A student, Druze thought.

"No, no, I can change it in two minutes," George said, peering down at the tire in disgust. "But it pisses me off, excuse the expression. I should be able to drive over railroad spikes with those tires. . . . Now, there's a case for you, Mr. Brekke. Sue the goddamn tire company for me. . . ."

"Glad to . . ."

There was more talk and a clatter of tools as the slender student stood and watched the heavyset professor dismount the spare from the Jeep. Druze, feeling something almost like relief, thought the student would stay. But after watching for a couple of minutes, the man looked at his watch and said, "Well, my wife will be wondering . . ."

"Go on. This'll just take a minute."

The student was gone, rolling out of the lot, never looking toward Druze's bush. Druze let him go, heard his car accelerate down University. . . . The professor had his jacket off, his shirtsleeves rolled up, and he grunted and cursed in the night. The flat came off, the spare went on. He seemed to know what he was doing, working without wasted motion. With a series of quick twists, the spare was lugged down.

Druze took a deep breath, got a grip on the sharpening steel with his right hand and stepped into the parking lot, jingling his car keys with his left hand, moving slowly.

The professor popped open the back of the Jeep, leaving the keys in the lock—everything was moving slowly for Druze now, everything was in needle-sharp focus—lifted the flat, holding it carefully clear of his trousers, and heaved it inside the Jeep.

Druze was ten feet away, checking, checking. Nobody around. Nothing coming on Pillsbury, no cars: The professor, a big, beefy blond man, slamming the back of the Jeep, now turning at the sound of Druze's keys . . . The keys would be a soothing sound, suggesting that Druze was headed for the last car in the lot. . . .

"Flat tire?" Druze asked.

The professor nodded without a flicker of recognition, although Druze was less than a long step away. "Yeah, damn thing was flat as a pancake."

"Got it under control?" Druze asked, slowing. He looked around a last time: Nothing. The handle of the sharpening steel was cool in his hand.

"Oh yeah, no problem," George said, pulling on his jacket. His hands were black with grease from the lug nuts.

"Well . . ." Druze drew the steel behind his leg and stepped on, heading for his car, then pivoted and swung the steel one-handed, half overhead, like a whip, or a machete chopping sugarcane. The steel crashed through the side of George's head, two inches above his right ear. The professor bounced off the Jeep and down. Druze hit him again, but it was unnecessary: the first blow had crushed the side of his head. A sudden stench told Druze that George's bowels had relaxed. Neither he nor Bekker had thought about the stink the body could make in the car.

No reason to be furtive now: if anyone came in the next thirty seconds, it was over. Druze grabbed George under the arms, dragged him to the station wagon. The building lights, which had seemed remote and inadequate a few moments before, now seemed bright as stadium lights. Druze snatched open the wagon's back door and threw the body on the black plastic garbage bags that covered the floor behind the front seat. A short-handled spade was on the floor below the bags. When George's body hit the floor, it landed on the tip of the blade, and the handle popped up, tearing the bags. Druze swore and pushed the handle down, but now the body rolled. . . .

George was heavy, and his legs were still sticking out of the car. Druze struggled, half frantic, trying to bend the legs; then he grappled with the overweight torso, pulling on the sport coat lapels, not seeing the bloody twisted head, trying to lift the torso farther into the car while he pressed the feet in behind. The spade bounded up and down like a teeter-totter, obstructing everything. Druze was sweating heavily by the time he finished.

*Never been scared* . . . He was scared now. Not badly, but enough to identify the emotion, a feeling that went back to the days of the burning. The hospital baths, where they peeled the dead skin . . . those had scared him. The transplants had scared him. When the doctor had come to check his progress, that had scared him. He hadn't been scared since he'd left the hospital. But he felt it now, a distant tingle, but definitely there. . . .

When George was fully inside the car, on the floor behind the front seat, Druze covered the body with more black plastic garbage bags and then folded the back seats down over it. The seats didn't quite cover it, but to anyone looking casually inside, the wagon would appear empty.

He slammed the door, went back to the Jeep, got the keys out of the back door, shoved them between the curb and the front tire, then checked the meter: ten minutes. Druze took more quarters from his pocket, put in two hours' worth, then went back to the wagon. Nobody around. Nothing but the lights of Minneapolis, over across the river, and the distant sound of an unhappy taxi horn on Hennepin Avenue.

What if the wagon wouldn't start? What if . . . The wagon turned over, and he rolled it out of the lot, took a right. Met no cars. Turned onto University Avenue, let a breath out. Past the frat houses . . . Checked the gas gauge for the hundredth time. Full. He drove down Oak Street, then left, and then onto I-94, and pointed the car east toward Wisconsin.

The drive was eerie. Quiet. He had the feeling that the car was standing still, with the lights zooming by, like a nightmare. A cop crossed the overhead ramp at Snelling. Druze kept his eyes glued on the rearview mirror, but the cop continued south on Snelling, and out of sight.

He crossed the Fifth Street exit, past Highway 61, and exited at White Bear Avenue. Drove into a Standard station, called the number Bekker had given him, got the answering machine and spoke a single syllable: *"Yes."*

Back on I-94, fifty-five miles per hour all the way, ignoring the signs for sixty-five, through the double bridge across the St. Croix River at Hudson, out of Minnesota and up the Wisconsin side. The interstate mileage signs started on the western ends of each state, so he could count the ascending numbers as he moved deeper into Wisconsin, ten miles, twelve. He took the exit specified by Bekker, heading north.

Four-point-two miles, three red reflectors on a sign at the turnoff. He found it, right where Bekker had said, took the turnoff and bumped down a dirt track. Two-tenths of a mile. The track ended at a simple post-and-beam log cabin, a door in the center, a square window on either side of the door. The cabin was dark. In the headlights, he could see a brass padlock hanging from a hasp on the door.

Beyond the cabin, Druze could see moonlight on the lake. Not much of a lake; almost like a large pond, rimmed with cattails. He turned off the car lights, got out and walked down to the water, his feet groping for the path between the cabin and the water. There was a dark form off to his left, and he stepped next to it, trying to figure out what it was. Boards, on a steel frame, tires . . . a rollout dock. Okay.

On the opposite side of the lake, he could see a single lighted window but not the house around it. There was no sound but the wind in the trees. He stood for a moment, listening, watching, then hurried back up to the car.

George was easier to handle this time, because Druze didn't have to move so quickly or quietly. He got a flashlight from the glove compartment, then grabbed George by the necktie and the crotch, and hauled him out of the wagon. He threw the body over his shoulder like a sack of oatmeal and carried it down past the end of the track, as Bekker had said, past the tire swing hanging from the cottonwood. He flicked the light off and on, as he needed to spot footing; he was walking diagonally away from the cabin across the lake, so the light wouldn't be visible at the other house.

Blackberry brambles, dead but still armed, plucked at his clothing. Through the brambles, Bekker had said. Just go straight on back, nobody goes out there. Bekker and Stephanie had explored the place three years earlier, when she had been looking for a lake cabin. They'd seen the "For Sale" sign on the way back from another lake, stopped to look, found the cabin vacant, stayed for ten minutes, then moved on. The cabin was primitive: an outhouse, no running water, no insulation. Summer only. Stephanie hadn't been interested, and nobody in the world knew they had been there.

Druze pushed through the brambles until the ground went soft, then dumped the body. He flicked the light on, looked around. He was on the edge of a bleak, rough-looking tamarack swamp. Bekker was right. It could be years before anyone came back here. Or never . . .

Druze walked back to the car, got the spade and went to work. He labored steadily for an hour, feeling his muscles overheat. Nothing fancy, he thought; just a hole. He dug straight down, a pit three feet in diameter, the soil getting heavier and wetter as he dug deeper. He hit a few roots, flailed at them with the spade, cut through, went deeper, covering himself with muck. At the end he had a waist-deep hole, flooded ankle-deep with muddy water. He climbed out of it, beaten, grabbed the body by the necktie and pantleg, and dumped it headfirst into the hole. There was a splash, and he flicked the light on. George's head was underwater, his feet sticking up. His socks had fallen down around very white ankles, Druze noticed, and one shoe had a hole in the sole. . . .

He stood for a moment, resting, the clouds whipping overhead like black ships, the moon sliding behind one, then peeking out, then going down again. Cold, he thought. Like Halloween. He shivered, and started to fill the hole.

No one saw, no one heard.

He backed the car out, not turning on the headlights until he was down the track. He was in St. Paul before he realized he'd forgotten to cut George's eyes. Fuck his eyes. And fuck Bekker.

Druze was free of the tarbaby.


Two campus cops cruised past George's Jeep and flashed the meter. More than an hour on the clock.


*"Yes."*

The single syllable was in his ear, like stone, so hard. George was dead.

Bekker, standing in the hallway outside the restaurant entrance, dropped the phone in its cradle and danced his little jig, bobbing up and down, hopping from foot to foot, chortling. Caught himself. Looked around, guilty. Nobody. And they were clean. There were details to be tidied away, but they were details. After he got rid of the Jeep, there'd be no way to connect him to anything. Well: there'd be one way. But that was a detail.

He glanced at his watch: not quite midnight. Druze should be in Wisconsin by now. Bekker walked out to his car, drove to the hospital, parked. Took the cigarette case from his pocket, opened it in the gloom, popped one of the special Contac capsules, inhaled. The coke hit him immediately, and he rode with it, head back, eyes closed. . . .

Time to go. Nobody was following, but if someone was, he could handle it. He and his friends. He walked through the hospital lobby and took the stairs. Down, this time. Used his key to get into the tunnel and walked through the maintenance tunnel to the next building. Everybody did it, especially in the winter. But the cops wouldn't know.

Careful, he told himself, paranoia . . . there were no cops. The dope was in his blood . . . but what was it, exactly? He couldn't quite remember. There had been some amphetamines, he always did those, and a lick of the PCP; he'd had some aspirin, a lot of aspirin, actually, for an incipient headache, and his regular doses of anabolic steroids for his body and the synthetic growth hormone as part of his antiaging trip. All balanced, he thought: and for creativity, a taste of acid? He couldn't remember.

He walked out of the next building, pulling his collar up, the brim of his hat down. Peik Hall was three minutes away. He got close, walked behind a building onto Pillsbury, down the street, pulling on his driving gloves. The Jeep was there, right where it should be. He stooped, found the keys, unlocked the door and got inside. This was the risky part. Fifteen minutes' worth. But if he got the car to the airport, the cops might be bluffed into thinking that George had taken off on his own. . . .

The campus cops came back ten minutes later. The Jeep was gone. One of the cops saw something round and flat winking up at her in the headlights, and she said, "Something over there?"

"Where?"

"Right there. Looks like money."

She got out, stooped and picked it up. Lug nut. She tossed it in the back of the squad car.

"Nothing," she said.

Bekker took the Jeep out the same way Druze had driven, down to I-94, but westbound, to I-35W, south on I-35W and then on the Crosstown Expressway to the airport. He dropped the Cherokee in the long-term parking garage and left the ticket under the visor. Back on the street, he flagged a cab, keeping his hat down against the wind and against identification.

"Where to?" the cabbie grunted. He wasn't interested in talking.

"The Lost River Theater, on Cedar Avenue . . ."

From the Lost River, it was a twenty-minute walk to the hospital. He went in the way he'd come out, walked up to his office and sat for ten minutes. He remembered to call the answering machine and, using the touch-tone buttons, ordered it to reset. He waited a few more minutes, impatient, then turned off the lights in his office and went back down to his car.

At home, Bekker stripped off his clothes as he walked up the stairs, dropping them wherever they came off. Stephanie would have been outraged; he smiled as he thought about it. He crawled into his closet and took two tabs of phenobarbital, two more of methaqualone, two of methadone, a heavy hit of acid, five hundred mikes. The warmth was incredible. The drugs unwound as they always did—color sequences, clips from life, fantasies, the face of God—then shaded unexpectedly from yellows and reds through pinks into purples; and finally, the fear growing in his throat, Bekker watched the snake uncurl.

The snake was huge, scaleless, more like an eel than a snake, no mouth, just a long cold form unwinding, curling into him.

And George was there.

He didn't say anything, George: he simply watched and grew. His eyes were black, but somehow bright as diamonds. He closed on Bekker, the eyes growing larger, the mouth beginning to open, a forked tongue deep inside. . . .


Bekker had killed three whores in Vietnam. He'd done it carefully, confident that he'd never be exposed; he'd worn an enlisted man's uniform, the Class A greens of a spec-5 killed in a Saigon traffic accident, the uniform dumped at Bekker's doorstep in a black satchel that had been with the dead man in his jeep.

Bekker had strangled the three women. It hadn't been hard. They'd been specialists of a sort, unsurprised when he let them know that he wanted to sit on their chests. More surprised when he pinned their hands. Definitely surprised when he clamped his powerful fingers on their throats, crushing the cartilage with a powerful pinch of his thumb and forefinger . . .

The first one had looked straight into his eyes as she'd died, and it was there that Bekker had had his first hint that she'd seen something beyond.

And she was the one who'd come back.

She'd preyed on him, haunted him, followed him with her black eyes. For six weeks he'd doped himself, screaming through the nights, afraid of sleep. He'd seen her in his waking hours, too, in the shiny reflections from his instruments, from mirrors, in panes and fragments of glass. . . .

She'd faded, finally, beaten down with drugs. And Bekker had known instinctively that the physical eyes made the difference.

For the next woman, he'd been prepared. He'd pinned her, choked her and, with a stainless-steel scalpel, cut her eyes as she'd died. And slept like a baby.

The third one had died quickly, too quickly, before he could cut her eyes. He had cut them dead, but he still feared that she would follow him into his dreams: that it was necessary to cut the *living eyes*.

But it was not. He'd never seen that one again.

He'd cut the eyes on the old man dying of congestive heart failure, and the old woman with the stroke—they'd delivered those two right to him, in the pathology department, and he still had the taped description of the cutting of the old woman's eyes. And he'd cut the eyes of the boy and the girl from Pediatric Oncology, although he'd had to take a good deal more risk with those. The girl he'd gotten to just before they moved her body out of the hospital. For the boy, he'd had to go to the funeral home and wait his chance.

That had been a bad two days, waiting, the boy out there. . . .

But in the end he'd cut them all.

He hadn't been able to cut George.

And George was here now, coming for him.

Deep in his closet, naked, his arms wrapped around his knees, his eyes wide and staring into the beyond, Bekker began to scream.

# 15

"You're sure?" Lucas asked Swanson. "It's Loverboy?"

Swanson scratched his belly and nodded. "It's gotta be. I went over to Bekker's as soon as I heard. Shook him out of bed. This was about three hours ago, six A.M., and he looked terrible, and I said, 'For the lover, how about Philip George from the law school?' He went like this"—Swanson mimed Bekker's perplexed look—"and he said, quote, If you told me so, I wouldn't be . . . shocked, I guess. I mean, we knew him. Why? Is it him? Unquote. Then I told him about George. He seemed kind of freaked out."

"You got the time George disappeared? It's nailed down? Exactly?"

"Yeah. Within five minutes, I'd bet," Swanson said, nodding. He was unshaven, holding an empty Styrofoam coffee cup, his eyes glassy from fatigue and caffeine. He'd been roused out of bed at five o'clock, after four hours' sleep. "There was a guy with him, a student, when George started changing the tire. The student was supposed to get right home to his wife, she's pregnant, due anytime, so he was anxious. Anyway, he's got a clock on the dashboard of his car. He said he looked at it going out of the lot, and remembers it was ten-fourteen. He remembers that close. . . ."

"What about this shrink Shearson's been looking at?"

Swanson shrugged. "I always thought that was bullshit, but Daniel wanted him covered."

"Sonofabitch," Lucas said in a black fury. Del was leaning in the doorway, listening, and Lucas bolted past him, out of his office, took a turn down the hallway, then almost trotted back, his face white. "The cocksucker was using me as an alibi. You know that? I'm Bekker's fuckin' alibi. . . ."

"If George is dead," Swanson said. "That's a pretty big if. And if Bekker had something to do with it . . ."

Lucas poked Swanson in the gut with his index finger. "George is dead. And Bekker did it. Believe it." Lucas turned to Del. "Remember when you said the San Francisco alibi was a little too convenient?"

"Yeah?"

"Well, how about this? He invites an investigating *cop* over for a drink, to talk, *he tries to fuckin' seduce me, man,* precisely when the main witness is being taken off. How's that for a motherfucking coincidence?"

Del shrugged. He didn't say "I told you so," but his shoulders did.

Lucas turned back to Swanson, remembering his odd characterization of Bekker. Bekker had looked fine the night before: sleek, even. Beautiful. "You said he looked terrible? What do you mean?"

"He looked fucked up," Swanson said. "He looked like he was a hundred years old. He ain't getting no sleep."

" 'Cause he was working a fuckin' murder. That's why. 'Cause he had a murder going down last night," Lucas said. "All right. We're gonna take him down. One way or another"—this time he poked Del—"the motherfucker falls."

Sloan was coming down the hall, rolling an unlit cigarette around between his lips, his hands deep in the pockets of his trench coat.

"Bekker did it?" he asked.

"Fuckin' absolutely," Lucas said grimly.

"Huh," Sloan said. He shifted the unlit cigarette. "You think he killed George before or after he drove his Jeep out to the airport?"

Lucas looked at him blankly: "Say what?"

"Airport cops listed the bulletin for his Jeep, found it in the long-term ramp. Long-term. Like he ain't planning to come back."

Lucas shook his head. "Bullshit. If George is the one, he ain't running. He's dead."

"We don't know that for sure," Sloan said. "He coulda took off for Brazil. He could of cracked, decided to split."

"Who's talking to his wife?" Lucas asked.

"Neilson, but I'm going over later," Sloan said.

"I tell you, the motherfucker is dead," Lucas said, settling back in his chair. "How's he gonna leave a lug nut in the parking lot? How can you forget to put on a lug nut? You've got the bolt sticking out at you, you can't forget. The flat tire was a setup."

"How old is the Jeep?" Del asked Sloan.

Sloan shrugged. "New."

"See?" Lucas said with satisfaction. "Flat, my ass."

They were still arguing when Harmon Anderson leaned in the door, a piece of white paper in his hand. "You'll never guess," he said to Lucas. "I'll give you two hundred guesses and betcha a million bucks you don't get it."

"You don't got a million bucks," Swanson said. "What is it?"

Anderson dramatically unfolded the paper, a Xerox copy, and held it up like an auctioneer at an art sale, pivoting, to give everybody a look.

"What is it?" Del asked.

The Xerox showed a painting of a one-eyed giant with a misshapen head, half turned, peering querulously over a hill, a naked sleeping woman in the foreground.

"Ta-da," Anderson said. "The Bekker killer, as seen by Mrs. Bekker's lover. A cyclops, is what it is."

"What the fuck?" Sloan said, taking the paper, frowning at it, passing it to Lucas.

"We got it in the mail—actually, this is a copy, they're looking at the original for prints," Anderson said.

"Is the original in black and white?" Lucas asked.

"Yeah, a Xerox. And there's a note from Loverboy. We're sure it's for real, because he goes over some of the stuff he said in the first letter. Calls him a troll, not a giant."

"Jesus," said Lucas, rubbing his forehead, staring at the face of the giant. "I know this guy from somewhere."

"Who? The troll?"

"Yeah. I know him, but I don't know from where."

The other three cops looked at Lucas for a moment; then Sloan said skeptically, "You been talking to any gruff billy goats lately?"

"When was it mailed?" Lucas asked.

Anderson shrugged. "Sometime yesterday, that's all we know."

"Anybody know where this painting comes from?" Lucas asked.

"Not as far as I know . . . We could check it out."

"I mean, if it's from a book, maybe he got it out of the library or something," Lucas suggested.

Sloan and Swanson looked at each other, and then Sloan said, "Right. See, this guy is really freaked out after witnessing this killing, and he's got about a hundred cops on his ass, so he goes down to the library and says, Here's my card, just go ahead and put me in your permanent computer records so Lucas Davenport can come in here. . . ."

"Yeah, yeah, it's weak," Lucas said, waving Sloan off.

"It's not fuckin' weak, it's fuckin' limp."

Lucas looked at the photocopy. "Can I keep this?"

"Be my guest," Anderson said. "We only got as many as you can make on a Xerox machine."

Bekker, straight, the morning sun slashing into him, went out to a phone booth and called Druze.

"You didn't do the eyes," he said, when the receiver was picked up.

There was a long silence, and then: "No. I forgot."

"Jesus, Carlo," Bekker groaned. "You're killing me."

Lucas went home at noon, driving through a light, cold drizzle, darker clouds off to the west. He spent five minutes building a turkey sandwich with mustard, put it on a paper plate, got a Leinenkugel from the refrigerator, went and sat in the spare bedroom and stared at the wall.

He hadn't been in the room for months, and dust balls, like mice, half hid under the edge of the guest bed. On the walls were pinned a series of paper charts, laying out possibilities and connections: traces of the Crows case. Most of what he needed to find the men was on the charts, organized, poised, waiting for the final note. He closed his eyes, heard the gunfire again, the screams. . . .

He stood, exhaled and began pulling down the charts, pushing the pins back into the wall. He looked over the names, remembering, then ripped the papers in halves, in quarters, in eighths, and carried them to the study and dumped them into his oversized wastebasket.

The drawing pad was still there, and he sat down, opened it, chose with some care the precisely right felt-tip marker and began to make lists as he ate the turkey sandwich.

*Bekker,* he wrote at the top of the first sheet. And under that: *Drugs, Times and Places. Friends?* At the top of a second he wrote *Killer.* And below that:

Looks like troll
Knows Bekker
Could be dope dealer?
Is he paid? Check Bekker accounts
Theater connection?
Do I know him?

On the Bekker sheet, he added:

Cheryl Clark
Vietnam killings
Cancer kids

On a third sheet he wrote *Loverboy,* and underneath:

Cleaned drain
Changed sheets
Xeroxed note
Philip George?

He carried the new charts to the bedroom, pinned them on the wall and stared at them.

Why had the killer gone after George, if indeed he had? If George had known him, why hadn't he said so when he called 911? And if he hadn't known him, why would the killer worry about it? Maybe they worked together, or moved in the same social circles? That didn't fit with the drug thing . . . unless George was a user? Or maybe George was involved with Bekker? What if Bekker, a doctor, was dealing, and a junkie knew that, came into his house . . . but then, why Armistead?

He stood, speculating, trying to come up with something he could hold on to and work with. He found it right away. He thought about it, got his jacket and called Dispatch. As he dialed, he looked out the window: still raining. A cold, miserable slanting spring rain, out of the northwest.

"Could you get in touch with Del and have him meet me at the office?" he asked when Dispatch came on. "No big rush, this afternoon sometime . . ."

"He's sitting in a bar," the dispatcher said. "He's taking calls there, if you want the number. . . ."

"Sure." Lucas took a piece of paper from his shirt pocket, the Xerox of the painting of the one-eyed giant, and scribbled down the number. When he called, a bartender answered and put Del on. He could meet Lucas at four o'clock. As they talked, Lucas looked at the giant peering at the sleeping woman. The creature had a nearly round head, like a basketball, and thin, wide twisting lips. Where . . . ?

When he finished talking to Del, Lucas pulled out the phone book and called the rare-book room at the university library.

"Carroll? Lucas Davenport."

"Lucas, you haven't been coming to the games. Zhukov is about to go after the Romanians north of Stalingrad. . . ."

"Yeah, Elle told me. She said you needed Nazis."

"No fun for the Nazis from here on out . . . ."

"Listen, I need some help. I've got a picture of a one-eyed giant. He's looking over a mountain at a sleeping woman and he's got a club. It's a painting and it's kind of crude. Childlike, but I don't think a kid did it. There's something good about it."

"It's a one-eyed giant, like a cyclops from *The Odyssey?*"

"Yeah, exactly. Somebody said it's a troll, but somebody else said that technically it's a cyclops. I'm trying to figure out what book it came from, if it came from a book."

There was a moment of silence, then the book expert said, "Damned if I'd know. An expert on *The Odyssey* might, but you'd have to get lucky. There are probably about a million different illustrations of cyclopses."

"Shit . . . So what do I do?"

"You say it's crude but good. You mean slick-crude, like a *Playboy* illustration, or . . ."

"No. The more I look at it, the more I think it might be famous. Like I said, there's something about it."

"Huh. Well, you *could* take it over to the art history department. There's a good chance that nobody will be there, and if there is somebody there, he might not talk to you unless you've got a fee statement."

"Hmpf. Okay, well, thanks, Carroll . . ."

"Wait a minute. There's a painter, over there in St. Paul—actually, he's a computer genius of some kind—and he comes in here to look at book illustrations. He's pretty expert on art history. I've got a number, if you want to give him a ring."

"Sure." Lucas heard the receiver being laid on a desk, then a minute of silence, then the receiver being picked up again.

"The guy is a little remote, out in the ozone, like painters get. Use my name, but be polite. Here's the number. . . . And come on back to the games. You can be Paulus."

"Jeez, I don't know what to say. . . ."

When he got the book expert off the line, Lucas dialed the number. The phone rang five or six times and he was about to hang up when it was answered. The painter sounded as though he'd been asleep, his voice gruff, cool. An edge of wariness entered it when Lucas explained he was a cop.

"I got your name from Carroll over at the U. I've got a question that he said you might be able to help on. . . ."

"Computers?" Wary. Lucas wondered why.

"Art. I've got this picture of a giant, a painting, weird-looking. Kind of strong. I need to know where it came from."

The artist didn't ask why. Again, Lucas thought that was odd. "Is the giant biting the head off a dead body?"

"No, he's . . ."

"Then it's not Goya. Has the giant got one eye?"

"Yeah," Lucas said. "Big mother, one eye, looking over a mountain . . ."

"At a nude woman in the foreground, lying on the mountainside. Like one of those saints on a Catholic holy card."

"That's it," Lucas said.

"Odilon Redon. The painting's called *The Cyclops*. Redon was French, mostly did pastel. Painted the cyclops around the turn of the century. The nude's got her back to the cyclops, so you're looking right at her . . ."

"Yeah, yeah, that's it. What kind of book would that be in? I mean, obscure, or what?"

"No, no, there are any number of books on Redon. He's in vogue right now. Or was. The library would have something. He's not exactly a household name, but anybody who knows about painting would know about him."

"Hmph. Okay. So probably a book."

"Or a calendar. There are dozens of art calendars around, and art postcards and art appointment books. Depends on what size it is."

"Okay, thanks. That's about what I needed. You say that you'd have to know something about art. . . ."

"Yeah. If you want some kind of index, I'd say maybe one percent of the people walking around on the sidewalk would know about Redon, would know his name. Of those, one in five could tell you a picture he painted."

"Thanks again."

"Always delighted to help the police," the artist said. He sounded like he was smiling.


Del was not smiling. Del was twisting his hands.

"Jesus Christ, it's not hard," Lucas said, squatting beside him. Del sat in the metal folding chair on the visitor's side of Lucas' desk. "You just tell her you've been thinking about her. You say, 'I want to apologize for the way I acted, you seem like a really nice woman. You got nice eyes.' Then she'll ask, sooner or later, 'What color are they?' And you say, 'Hazel.' "

"How do I know they're hazel?" Del picked up the phone receiver in one hand, holding down the hang-up button with the index finger of the other.

" 'Cause they are," Lucas said. "Really they're brown, but you make it sound nice when you say hazel. She knows she's got brown eyes, but she likes to think they're hazel. She'll think you care more if you say hazel. . . . Christ, Del, when was the last fuckin' time you asked a woman out?"

" 'Bout twenty-two years ago," Del said, his head hanging. There was a moment of silence; then they both started to laugh. Del said, "Ah, fuck me," and started punching phone numbers. "Does it have to be tonight?"

"Sooner the better," Lucas said, moving behind the desk. He wanted to be where Del could see his face, in case he needed coaching. The phone rang six times and Del reached out to hang up, when Cheryl Clark answered.

"Ah, is this, ah, Miss Clark?" Del stuttered. Twenty-two years? Lucas shook his head. "Ah . . . this is the cop who was over there with the other cop, I'm the one with the headband. Yeah, Del. Listen, uh, this is got nothing to do with the investigation, you know, but, uh, I been thinking about you, and I finally decided to call. . . . I don't know, you seemed like a pretty nice chick, uh, woman, you know, shit, you had real nice eyes. . . . Uh, huh . . . yeah, kind of, if you'd like to, I was wondering if you'd be interested in a cup of coffee. Un-huh, okay." He turned away from Lucas, hiding his eyes, his voice dropping. "How about Annie's over on the West Bank? Uh, huh. I'll pick you up, is that okay? Uh. Forty-one. Yeah. Yeah. Uh, why, they're hazel, really pretty, you know. . . . Yeah. Okay. Listen, about six-thirty? Get something to eat, a couple burgers? Okay?" By the time he hung up, Del's face was running with sweat.

"Forty-one?" Lucas asked, grinning. "Who the fuck is forty-one?"

"Get off my ass, Davenport," Del said, collapsing in his chair. "I fuckin' did it, okay?"

"All right," Lucas said, turning serious. "Now what'll you talk about?"

"How the fuck do I know? Bekker, of course . . ."

"No. Not about Bekker . . ."

"But why . . . ?"

"This woman has been used all of her life. She's the type, and she'll be very sensitive to it. She lets herself be used because that's the only way she can find relationships. She keeps hoping for something real, but she doesn't believe it's going to happen," Lucas said. He was leaning on the desk, talking rapidly, eyes narrowed, voice urgent, trying to impress his student. "If you come on to her about Bekker, she'll *know*. She'll know we're trying to manipulate her. You'll offend her right down to the soles of her feet. What you do is, you never mention Bekker. You do what all divorced guys do—talk about your ex-wife. Pretty soon she'll start to hint. Wanna know about Bekker? No. You don't want to know about Bekker. You want to talk about you, your ex-wife, her, and how miserable it is to get a relationship going with anyone decent. You say, Fuck Bekker, I don't wanna hear about that shit, that's work. Take her out a couple of times, and she'll start talking about him all on her own. She won't be able to help herself. Just don't push."

"Don't push," Del said. His eyes were like marbles.

"Don't push," Lucas confirmed, nodding.

Del leaned back in his chair, studying Lucas as though he were a felon, and one he'd just met. "Jesus Christ," he said after a minute, "you are a cruel sonofabitch, you know that?"

Lucas frowned at the tone. "Are you serious?"

"I'm serious," Del said.

Lucas shrugged and looked away. "I do what I've got to do," he said.

\*     \*     \*

He met Anderson on the way out to the car.

"I sent Carpenter down to the library after you called," Anderson said. "He found a book on this Redon dude, and that's the picture all right, but the library's picture was bigger than the one we got. He could only find it in one book, and that hasn't been checked out for two months."

"That's something," Lucas said.

"Yeah? Exactly what?" Anderson asked.

As Lucas drove home, a hard rain began to fall and lightning crackled overhead. A good night for trolls, he thought.

*Bekker, God damn it.*

# 16

---

The rain was steady and cold, driving, slicing through his headlights, the wipers barely able to keep up. Miserable night. A half-dozen black beauties gave him the edge he needed, a couple of purple egg-shaped Xanaxes cooled his nerves.

Not enough, maybe. The flapping of the windshield wipers was beginning to grate on him, and he had to bite his tongue to keep from shouting at them. *Fwip-fwip-fwip,* a torture . . .

Red light. He caught it at the last second, jammed on the brakes and nearly skidded through the intersection. The driver of the car one lane over looked at him, and Bekker had to choke down the impulse to scream at him. Instead of screaming, he went into his pocket, pulled out the cigarette case, tongued a yellow oblong Tranxene and snapped the case shut. He no longer tried to track his drug intake: he was guided by internal signals now, running with his body. . . .

And he was all right; he'd eaten half a handful of downers over the day, and they'd held him together like the skin of a balloon, containing the pressure. But only for a time. The snake was waiting, off in the dark. Then, when it was time to meet Druze, the black beauties pulled him up, out of the downers. He'd be afraid to drive with those downers in his blood. But with the black beauties, driving was a snap. . . .

The traffic light changed and Bekker went through, gripping the steering wheel with all his might.

They'd agreed to meet at an all-night supermarket on University Avenue, a place where the parking lot was usually full. Tonight there were only a few cars in front of the store, and one of them was a baby-blue St. Paul police cruiser.

When he saw it, Bekker nearly panicked. Did they have Druze? How did they get him? Had he and Druze been betrayed? Had Druze gone to the police . . . ? No, wait; no, wait; no, wait; wait-wait-wait . . .

There he was, Druze, in the Dodge, waiting, the windows steamed. No cops near the squad car. Must be inside. Bekker parked on the left side of Druze's car, killed the engine and slipped out, watching the lighted entrance of the supermarket. Where were the cops? He opened the back door of his car, got the shovel off the floor, locked the door. He was wearing a rain suit and a canvas hat, and had been out of the car for no more than fifteen seconds, but the water poured off the brim of the hat in a steady stream.

Druze popped the passenger door on the Dodge as Bekker stepped over. He was breathing hard, almost panting. He scanned the rain-blasted lot, then hurled the shovel on the floor of the backseat, on top of Druze's spade, and clambered into the car. With the door shut, he took off the canvas hat and threw it in the back with the shovel. Druze was shocked when Bekker turned toward him. Bekker was beautiful; this man was gaunt, gray-faced. He looked, Druze thought, like a corpse in a B movie. He turned away and cranked the starter.

"Are you all right?" Druze asked, as he put the car in gear.

"No. I'm not," Bekker said shortly.

"This is fuckin' awful, man," Druze said. He stopped at the curb cut, waiting for a stream of traffic to pass. His burned face was flat, emotionless, the scarred lips like cracks in a dried creek bed. "Digging up the dead."

"Fuck it—fuck it," Bekker rasped. A bolt of lightning zigzagged through the sky to the east, where they were going. "We gotta."

"I can't get the tarbaby out of my head," Druze said. "We can't shake this guy, Philip George." In other people, anger, fear, resentment flowed like gasoline. In Druze, even the violent emotions moved like clay, slowly turning, compressing, darkening. He was angry now, in his muted way, listening to Bekker, his friend. Bekker picked it up, put his hand on Druze's shoulder.

"Carlo, I'm fucked up," Bekker said. He said it quickly, the words snapping off after the last syllable. "I'm fuckin' crazy. I can't apologize for it. I don't want it. But it's there. And honest to God, I'm dying."

Druze took it in, not understanding, took the car onto the entrance ramp for I-94. "I mean, have you tried Valium or whatever?"

"You stupid shit . . ." Bekker's anger burst through like napalm, but he instantly backed off, humbling himself. "I'm sorry. I tried everything. Everything. Everything. Everything. There's only one way."

"Dangerous . . ."

"Fuck dangerous," Bekker shouted. Then, quiet again, straining to see through the rain as they accelerated off the ramp and into traffic, his voice formal, that of a man on an emotional seesaw: "A snake. There's a snake in my brain."

Druze glanced sideways at Bekker. The other man seemed to be sliding into a trance, his face rigid. "We were supposed to stay away from each other. If they see us . . ." Druze ventured.

Bekker didn't answer. He sat in the passenger seat, twisting his hands. Six miles later, coming back from wherever he was, he said, "I know. . . . And one of them's no dummy. I had him in for coffee."

"You what?" Druze's head snapped around: Bekker *was* losing it. But no: he sounded almost rational now.

"Had him in for coffee. Found him in front of my house. Watching. Lucas Davenport. He's not stupid. He looks mean."

"Tough guy? A little over six feet, looks like a boxer or something? Dark hair, with a scar coming through his eyebrow?" Druze quickly traced the path of Lucas' scar on his own face.

Bekker nodded, his head cocked to one side: "You know him?"

"He was at the theater after you did Armistead," Druze said. "Talking to one of the actresses. They looked pretty friendly."

"Who? Which one?"

"Cassie Lasch. Played the maid in . . . you didn't go to that. She's a second-stringer. Good-looking. I could see this guy coming on to her. She lives in my building."

"You work with her much?"

"No. We're both part of the group, but we've never talked much or anything. Not personally."

"Could she pipe you into what Davenport's thinking?"

"I don't know. She might pick something up. If the guy's smart, I don't need him checking on me."

"You're right," Bekker said, looking at Druze as the Dodge's interior was swept by the lights of an oncoming car. "What was her name again? Cassie?"

"Cassie Lasch," Druze said. "A redhead."

Lightning crashed around them as they crossed the St. Croix River into Wisconsin and headed up the bluff. When they passed the Hudson turnoff, the thunderhead opened. Rain swept across the road, shaking the car, and Druze was forced to slow as they pushed into the dark countryside. By the time they reached the exit to the lake, they were down to forty miles an hour, the last car in an informal convoy.

"What a fuckin' night," Druze said. Lightning answered.

"I couldn't make it another twenty-four hours," Bekker answered. "Is he deep?"

Deep? Ah, he meant George. "More than two feet, anyway," Druze said. "Probably closer to three."

"Should be quick . . . Won't take long," Bekker said.

"You weren't here last night," Druze said sourly. "We're talking about a peat bog. This is gonna take a while."

They missed the turnoff to the cabin. Druze had slowed further on the blacktopped county road, driving thirty, then twenty-five, watching for the reflectors that marked the turn . . . but they missed them, went a mile too far, had to come back. They saw only one other vehicle, a pickup, passing in the opposite direction, a man with a hat and a face that was a blurred oval hunched over the steering wheel.

They found the track coming back, turned and picked their way between the high bushes. The rain was tapering off; the thunderhead, still spitting out long chains of lightning, had moved to the north. The cabin popped up in the headlights like a mirage, congealing out of darkness, suddenly, and close. Druze parked in front of it, killed the headlights and said, "Let's do it."

He took a gray plastic raincoat from the backseat and pulled it on. Bekker wore sophisticated foul-weather gear, with a hood like a monk's cowl.

"Take my hat," he said to Druze, snagging it out of the backseat and passing it to the other man.

They got out, the ground firm underfoot, sandy rather than muddy. As the rain slowed, a wind seemed to increase and moaned through the bare birch trees overhead. Past the cabin, perhaps two or three hundred yards across the lake, Bekker could see a blue yard light and, lower, the yellow rectangle of a lighted window.

"This way," Druze grunted. His pantlegs below the rain suit were already wet, and he felt the first tongue of water inside his athletic shoes. He put the spade over his shoulder and, with the flashlight playing on the ground, led the way through the brambles, back to the edge of the tamarack swamp. The ground changed from high and sandy to soft, and finally to muck.

"How much . . ." Bekker started.

"We're here." Druze shined the light on the ground, and Bekker could just pick out an oval pattern of raw earth.

"I kicked some shit over it before I left," Druze said. "In two weeks, you wouldn't be able to find it if you tried."

"We'll do that again before we leave. Maybe get some leaves on it," Bekker said vaguely. Rain ran down his face and collected in his eyebrows, and he sputtered through it. He was disintegrating in the water, falling apart like the wicked witch, Druze thought.

"Sure," Druze grunted. He jammed the flashlight into the branches of a bare bush and scooped up a shovelful of muck. "Dig."

Bekker worked frantically, shoveling, talking to himself, spitting in the rain, digging like a badger. Druze tried to be more methodical but after a few minutes simply tried to stay out of the way. To the north, the thunderhead was still rumbling, and another burst of rain put a half-inch of water in the hole.

"I can't tell . . ." Bekker said, gasping between words, "I can't tell . . . if the water's from the rain . . . or if it's coming up . . . from below."

"Some of both," Druze said. The flashlight caught a lump that looked different, and Druze prodded it with the tip of his shovel. The blade hit something resilient. "I think I got him."

"Got him? Here, let me . . ."

Bekker motioned Druze aside and knelt in the hole, holding the blade of his shovel like a scoop, working like a man in a frenzy, throwing the muck out in all directions. "We got him," he said, breathing hard. A hip, a leg, a shoulder, the sport coat. "Got him got him got him . . ."

Druze stood back, holding the light, while Bekker cleared the mud away from the top of the body. "Shit," he said, looking up at Druze, his pale face the color and consistency of candle wax, "He's facedown."

"I just kind of dumped him . . ." Druze said, half apologetically.

"That's okay, I just have to . . ."

Bekker tried to free the body by pulling on the sport coat, but there was still too much dirt around it and it held George as firmly as if he were frozen in concrete.

"Suction or something," Bekker grunted. His rain suit and his face were covered with mud, but he paid no attention. He straddled what he could see of the body, put his hands around George's neck and tried to pry the head free. "Can't fuckin' get it," he said after a minute.

"We have to clear away."

"Yeah." Bekker went back to the shovel, still using it as a scoop, a pan, and dug around the body, trying to loosen the arms, which were apparently sunk in the mud below. He got the left one first, the hand white as chalk, the fingers rigid and waxy as candles. Then Bekker got part of the left leg and turned his face up to Druze and said, "If you could help just here."

Druze squatted on the rim of the hole, reached in, grabbed George's belt. "Get his head," he said. "Ready? Heave."

George came partway out of the hole like an archaeological artifact on the end of a crane cable. Not stiff, but not particularly loose, either, his legs still anchored in the muck, his head hanging forward . . .

"There," Druze said, and with a heavy pivoting motion of his shoulders he managed to flip the body onto its side, the legs rolling out of the muck below. Mud caked the nose and mouth, but one eye socket was clear. As the rain washed away the last of the soil, they could see the dead white orb of an eye looking up at them.

"Jesus," Druze said, stepping back.

"I told you!" Bekker screamed. His hand groped in his pocket and came out with a screwdriver. "I told you, I told you, I told you . . ."

He held the corpse's head by the hair and drove the screwdriver first into one eye socket, then the other, over and over, ten times, twenty, thirty, with furious power, screaming, *"I told you,"* until Druze grabbed him by the collar and jerked him out of the hole, hollering, "Enough, enough, enough . . ."

They stood looking at each other for a moment, the rain still driving down, Bekker gasping for breath, staggering, Druze afraid he was having a heart attack, and then Bekker said, "Yeah . . . that should be enough."

He took the flashlight from Druze, squatted next to the hole and with an almost gentle hand turned George's head. The eyes were deep bloodless holes, quickly filling with mud.

Bekker looked up, and a long flash of lightning from the distant storm lit him up as clearly as a fly on a television screen. His face was beautiful again, clear, the face of an angel, his white teeth flashing in a brilliant smile.

"That should do it," he said. He let George's head go, and the body flipped facedown into the watery hole with a wet, sucking splash.

Bekker stood up, turning into the rain, letting it wash him. He was bouncing, Druze thought: *Jesus, it's a dance.* And as Bekker danced, the rain slowed, then stopped. Druze was backing away, frightened, fascinated.

"Well," Bekker said a moment later, his labored breath squeezing through the hysterical smile, "I suppose we should fill the hole, should we not?"


The grave filled quickly. The last they saw of Philip George was his right foot, the sock pulled down around the hairless, paper-white ankle, the shoe already rotting with water. Druze beat the surface down with the shovel, then kicked some leaves and brambles over the freshly turned soil. "Let's get the fuck out of here," he said.

They hurried back to the car, and Druze had to jockey it back and forth to turn in the narrow track in front of the cabin. Bekker, his voice clear and easy now, said, "Check the answering machine. Three, four times a day. Call from public phones. When George turns up missing, the cops are probably going to sit on me. If I've got to talk to you . . . the tapes are the only way. And listen, don't forget to press number three, and reset the tape."

"I meant to ask you about that," Druze said, as he wrestled the Dodge onto the blacktopped road. "If you reset the tape, isn't the message still there . . . ?"


Across the lake, the yellow rectangle burned in the cabin window. A woman in a pink robe, her hair in curlers, sat under the light reading an old issue of *Country Living.* She was facing an old-fashioned picture window, positioned to look over the lake, when Druze and Bekker got back to the car.

"Richard," she called to her husband, and stood and looked out the window. "There are those headlights again. . . . I'm going to call Ann. I really don't think they were planning to come up tonight."

# 17

---

Lucas punched the Porsche down the country highway, hissing along the wet blacktop, past woodlots of unleafed trees and the sodden, dark fall-tilled fields. The day was overcast, the clouds the color of slag iron. A deer, hit by a car, probably the night before, lay folded like an awkward, bone-filled backpack in a roadside ditch. A few hundred yards farther along, a dead badger had been flung like a rag over the yellow line.

He'd been to two hundred murder scenes, all of them dismal. Were murders ever done in cheerful surroundings, just by accident? He'd once gone to a murder scene at an amusement park. The park hadn't yet opened for the season, and although it made a specialty of fun, the silent Ferris wheels, the immobile roller coasters, the awkward Tilt-A-Whirls, the Empty House of Mirrors were as sinister as any rotting British country house on a moor. . . .

He crested a low hill, saw the cop cars parked along the road, with an ambulance facing into a side road. A fat deputy sheriff, one thumb hooked under a gunbelt, gestured for him to keep moving. Lucas swung onto the shoulder, killed the engine and climbed out.

*"Hey, you."* The fat deputy was bearing down on him. "You think I was doin' aerobics?"

Lucas took his ID out of his coat pocket and said, "Minneapolis police. Is this . . . ?"

"Yeah, down there," the deputy said, gesturing at the side road, backing off a step. He tried a few new expressions on his face and finally settled for suspicion. "They told me to keep people moving."

"Good idea," Lucas said mildly. "If the word gets out, you're gonna get about a million TV cameras before too long. . . . How come everybody's parked out here?"

Lucas' collegial attitude loosened the deputy up. "The guy who answered the call thought there might be tracks down there in the mud," the fat man said. "He thought we ought to get some lab people out here."

"Good call," Lucas said, nodding.

"I don't think we'll see any television," the fat man said. Lucas couldn't tell if that made him happy or unhappy. "Old D.T. put a lid on everything. D.T.'s the guy running the show down there."

"Hope we can keep it on," Lucas said, heading toward the side road. "But if they do turn up, don't take any shit from them at all."

"Right on." The deputy grabbed his gunbelt in both hands and gave it a hitch.

*        *        *

The side track was two hundred yards long. At the end of it, Lucas found a nervous gray-haired woman and a pipe-smoking man sitting on the narrow porch of a cabin, both in cable-knit sweaters and slickers. Beyond the cabin, in a tangle of brush and brambles, Swanson was standing in a pod of people, some in uniform, others in civilian clothes.

Lucas walked past the cabin and gingerly into the scrub, staying away from a long strip of yellow police tape that outlined the original track into the raspberry bushes. Halfway back, a uniformed deputy, working on his hands and knees, was pouring casting compound into a footprint. He looked up briefly as Lucas went by, then turned back to his work. He'd already poured some casts farther along the trail.

"Davenport," Swanson said, when Lucas pushed through to the end of the track. Two funeral home attendants in cheap dark suits were waiting to one side, a carry litter with pristine sheets for the uncaring body set carefully by their feet. Two more men, deputies, were working in a muddy foxhole, excavating the body with plastic hand trowels, like archaeologists on a dig. The body was half uncovered, but the face was still down. Swanson stepped away from the group, his face gloomy.

"It's for sure? George?" Lucas asked.

"Yeah. When they went into the hole, they got his foot, and the deputy stopped the digging and called for help. When they started again, they got to his hip, took his billfold out of his pocket. The same guy who found him recognized the name and called for help again. The clothes are right. It's him."

Lucas stepped off to the side to get a better look at the hole. A foot stuck up awkwardly, like a grotesque tree shoot struggling for the sun. A sheriff's deputy in a ball cap and a raincoat came over and said, "You're Davenport?"

"Yeah."

"D.T. Helstrom," the deputy said, sticking out a bony hand. He was a thin man, with a dark, weathered face. Smile lines creased his cheeks at the corners of his mouth. "I've seen you on TV. . . ."

They shook hands and Lucas said, "You were the first guy out here?"

"Yes. The couple back there on the porch . . . ?"

"I saw them," Lucas said. He moved away from the hole with Swanson and Helstrom as they talked.

"They saw some lights over here last night. We have a lot of break-ins in these lake cabins, so I came by and checked it out. There was nothing at the cabin, but I could see somebody had been through the bushes. I went along . . . and there was the grave."

"They didn't try to hide it?" Lucas asked.

Helstrom looked back along the track and cracked a thin grin. "Yeah, I guess, in a city way. Kicked some shit over the grave. Didn't try too hard, though. They must have figured that with the rain, hell, in a couple of weeks there'd be nothing to find. And they were right. In a week, you couldn't find that hole with three Geiger counters and a Republican water-witcher."

"We're both saying 'they,' " Lucas said. "Any sign of how many?"

"Probably two," Helstrom said. "They left tracks, but it was raining off and on all night, so the prints are pretty washed out. We've got one guy in gym shoes, for sure, 'cause we can still see the treads. Then there are prints that don't seem to have treads on them, on top of the treaded prints—but we can't be sure, because the rain might have taken them out. . . ."

"Car?" Swanson asked.

"You can see where the tires were. But I followed it all the way out to the road, and the tread marks were gone."

"But you think there were two," Lucas said.

"Probably two," Helstrom said. "I looked at every track there is, marking the ones to cast; I couldn't swear to it in court, but I'd be willing to bet on it in Vegas."

"You sound like you've done this shit before," Lucas said.

"I had twenty years in Milwaukee," Helstrom said, shaking his head. "Big-city police work can kiss my ass, but I've done it before. We're taking the body over to Minneapolis, by the way. We've got a contract with the medical examiner, if you need the gory details."

Swanson was looking back toward the hole. From where they were standing, all they could see was the foot sticking up and the two men working in the hole, getting ready to move the body. "Maybe we got us a break," he said to Lucas.

"Maybe. I'm not sure how it'll help."

"It's something," Swanson said.

"You know what I thought, when I first dug him up?" Helstrom asked. "I thought, *Ah! The game's afoot.*"

Lucas and Swanson stared at him for a moment, then simultaneously looked back to the hole, where the foot stuck up. "Jesus," Lucas groaned, and the three of them started laughing.

At that instant, one of the deputies, pulling hard, got the body halfway out of its grave. The head swung around to stare at them all with empty holes where the eyes should have been.

"Aw, fuck me," the deputy cried, and let the body slump back. The head didn't turn, but continued looking up, toward the miserable gray Wisconsin sky and the black scarecrow twigs of the unclothed trees.


He thought about it on the way back, weighing the pros and cons, and finally pulled into a convenience store in Hudson and called TV3.

"Carly? Lucas Davenport . . ."

"What's happening?"

"You had a short piece last night about a guy disappearing, a law professor?"

"Yeah. Found his car at the airport. There's a rumor flying around that he was Stephanie Bekker's lover . . ."

"That's right—that's the theory."

"Can I go with . . . ?"

". . . and they're taking him out of a grave in Wisconsin right this minute. . . ."

*"What?"*

He gave her directions to the gravesite, waited while she talked to the news director about cranking up a mobile unit, then gave her a few more details.

"What's this gonna cost me?" she asked in a low voice.

"Just keep in mind that it'll cost," Lucas said. "I don't know what, yet."

Sloan was working at his desk behind the public counter in Violent Crimes when Lucas stopped by.

"You've been over in Wisconsin?" Sloan asked.

"Yeah. They did a number on the guy's eyes, just like with the women. Did you talk to George's wife yesterday?"

"Yeah. She said it's hard to believe that he was fuckin' Stephanie Bekker. She said he wasn't much interested in sex, spent all his time working."

"Huh," Lucas said. "He could be the type who gets hit hard, if the right woman came around."

"That's what I thought, but she sounded pretty positive."

"Are you going to talk to her again, today?"

"For a few minutes, anyway," Sloan said, nodding. "Checking in, see if she forgot to tell me anything. We got along pretty well. That Wisconsin sheriff called her with the news, she's got some neighbors over there with her. Her brother's going out to identify the body."

"Mind if I tag along when you go?"

"Sure, if you want," Sloan said. He looked at Lucas curiously. "What've you got?"

"I want to look at his books. . . ."

"Well, shit, I'm not doing much," Sloan said. "Let's take the Porsche."

Philip George had lived in St. Paul, in a two-block neighborhood of radically modern homes nestled in a district of upper-middle-class older houses, steel and glass played against brick and stucco, with plague-stricken elms all around. Three neighborhood women were with his wife when Sloan and Lucas arrived.

Sloan asked if he could speak to her alone, and Lucas asked if he could look at George's books.

"Yes, of course, they're right down there, in the study," she said, gesturing at a hallway. "Is there anything . . . ?"

"Just wondering about something," Lucas said vaguely.

While Sloan talked to George's wife, the neighbor ladies moved into the living room and Lucas walked through the study, a converted bedroom, looking at books. George had not been an adventuresome reader. He owned a hundred volumes on various aspects of the law, a few histories that appeared to be left over from college, a dozen popular novels that went back almost as many years, and a collection of Time-Life books on home repair. No art books. Lucas didn't know much about art, but he knew that most of the work on the walls was of the professional-decorator variety. Nothing remotely like Odilon Redon.

On the way back to the living room, Lucas scanned the framed photographs hung in the connecting hall. George at bar association meetings, accepting a gavel. George looking uneasy in new hunting clothes, a shotgun in one hand, a dead Canada goose in the other. In two photos, one black-and-white, the other color, he was singing in different bars, arms outstretched, beery faces laughing in the background. Overhead in one, a banner said "St. Pat's Day Bad Irish Tenor Contest"; in the other, a cardboard sign said "Bad Tenors."

Annette George, tired, slack-faced, was sitting at the kitchen table talking to Sloan when Lucas returned from the tour. She looked up, red-eyed, and said, "Anything?"

"Afraid not," Lucas said, shaking his head. "Was your husband interested in art at all? Painting?"

"Well, I mean . . . no. Not really. He thought maybe he'd like to try painting sometime, but he never had the time. And I guess it would have been out of character."

"Any interest in a guy named Odilon Redon?"

"Who? No, I never heard of him. Wait, the sculptor, you mean? He did that *Thinker* thing?"

"No, he was a painter, I don't think he did sculptures," Lucas said, now confused himself.

She shook her head. "No . . ."

"There're a couple of photographs in the hall, your husband singing in bad-Irish-tenor contests. . . ."

"Yes, he sang every year," she said.

"Was he good? I mean, was he a natural tenor, or what?" Lucas asked.

"Yes, he was pretty good. We both sang in college. I guess if he had an art form, that was it."

"When he sang in college, what part did he sing?" Lucas asked.

"First tenor. I was an alto and we sang in a mixed choir, we'd stand next to each other. . . . Why?"

"Nothing. I'm just trying to picture him," Lucas said. "Trying to figure out what happened."

"Oh, gosh, the things I could tell you," she said, staring vacantly at the floor. "I can't believe that he and Stephanie . . ."

"If it helps any, I don't believe it, either," Lucas said. "I'd appreciate it if you'd keep that under your hat for the moment."

"You don't believe?" she asked.

"No, I don't . . ."

Later, when Sloan and Lucas were leaving, she asked, "What am I going to do? I'm fifty. . . ."

One of the neighbor ladies, looking at Lucas as if the question were his fault, said, "Come on, Annette, it's all right."


Sloan looked back from the sidewalk: she was still standing there, looking through the glass of the storm door. "What does that mean, about the art? And the Irish-tenor contest?" he asked, turning to Lucas. "And do you really think there's somebody else . . . ?"

"Have you ever heard an Irish-tenor contest?" Lucas asked.

"No . . ."

"I did once, at the St. Pat's Day parade. The guys are *tenors,*" Lucas said. "That's a fairly high voice—and especially a first tenor. You must've heard guys singing 'My Wild Irish Rose'? Like that. Our guy on the nine-one-one tape, I don't see how he could sing in a tenor contest. Not unless he had a terrible cold or something."

"Didn't sound like he did," Sloan said, eyes narrowing.

"No. He sounded like a baritone, or even a bass."

"And George wasn't interested in art, or what's-his-name . . ."

"Redon," Lucas said absently. "And this artist I talked to, he said you'd probably have to know a little about art to pull that picture out of your head. It's not one you see every day. As far as I could tell, the Georges don't have an art book in the house."

Sloan looked back at the house. Annette George was gone. "Well, if George wasn't the guy, then the real lover's in the clear. Everybody in the world's assuming that he was the guy."

"Now think about this," Lucas said, moving slowly down toward the car. "If this guy's a serial killer, why'd he go to the trouble of burying George? He didn't care about burying the other two. And dragging a body around the countryside, that's a hell of a risk. What's he hiding about George?"

"And why didn't they bury him the same night he disappeared, instead of waiting? That's even more of a risk," Sloan added.

"It's fucked up. I'm beginning to wonder if we really know what's going on," Lucas said. They'd reached the car and he leaned on a fender. "We keep looking at Bekker, because we *feel* like he's the guy. But it doesn't make sense from his point of view."

"Tell me," Sloan prompted.

"If Bekker's behind it, why was Armistead murdered? He claims he didn't know her, and we've got no indication that he did. Her friends certainly didn't know Bekker, because they'd remember his face. And if the killer hit George just for the thrill of it, why leave the others but bury George?"

Sloan nodded and sighed. "Like you said, it's fucked up."

"Interesting," Lucas said.

"Gimme the keys," Sloan said. "I wanna drive this piece of shit."


On the way back to City Hall, Lucas told Sloan about the gravesite, and about the deputy's line: *"The game's afoot."*

"Cracked us up, Swanson and me," Lucas said.

"That ain't bad," Sloan admitted. He had a weakness for wordplay. *"The game's afoot."*

They were headed west on I-94, and Lucas, in the passenger seat, was looking blankly at a billboard advertisement for South Dakota tourism. Afoot? "Jesus," he said. "When they dusted for prints at Bekker's place, did they do the floor outside her bathroom? The bathroom that opens off her bedroom?"

"Fuck if I know," said Sloan. "Why?"

"Footprints," Lucas said. "The lover, whoever he is, might have wiped all the handles and stuff, but I bet the sonofabitch didn't wipe the floor. And if he didn't, we might still be able to get prints. I mean, since the game is a foot . . ."


Cassie came over and cooked Italian, humming in the kitchen, brewing tomato sauce, dancing around and sucking on the wooden spoon as she worked in the spices. She was wearing a fuzzy sweater that clung to her, and Lucas moved around behind her, handling her, stroking her stomach.

"Christ, the muscles are unbelievable," he said.

"I pray to Jane Fonda every morning. . . ."

"Mama's Got a Squeeze Box" came up on the radio and she tried to give him a quick dance lesson. He failed.

"You got the same problem as all large white men: you're afraid to shake your ass," she complained. "You can't dance if you don't move your ass."

"I feel ridiculous when I try to move my ass," Lucas said. He gave it a tentative shake.

"Yeah," she said, nodding, "you do look kinda weird. We could work on it. . . ."

"Maybe I could take banjo lessons or something. . . ."

The phone rang while they ate, and Lucas stepped into the kitchen to pick it up.

"This is Mikkelson," said a deputy medical examiner. "Things are getting strange outside."

"What'd you find?" Lucas asked.

"All kinds of shit. There was fresh blood and fresh fecal matter in George's clothing when he went into that grave. It mixed with the mud before it started to congeal, so it hadn't congealed yet when he went into the hole."

"Which means he wasn't killed until last night . . ."

"That's what you'd think, but that'd be wrong," the medical examiner said. "The holes in his eyes were filled with mud, too, but the holes were made after all the blood had pooled into his chest and arms, a long time after he was killed."

"That doesn't compute," Lucas said, confused.

"Only one way," the deputy M.E. said with evident relish. "They had to bury him and then dig him up to do the eyes. We've got some more tests going, but from the tissue evidence, I'd say that's what they did."

"Why?"

"Shit, Lucas, I'm a goddamned doctor, not a fuckin' psychic. But that's what happened. And there's something else, too—some people from your lab brought me over a bunch of footprints from the Bekker house?"

"Yeah?"

"Not a match in the bunch. Not even close."

# 18

"I need help," Daniel said. "Political help. You know how the city council gets. They think the voters are stupid, they think the voters are gonna run them out of office if we don't catch the guy today. They're getting pissy."

"You got a couple of bad columns, too," Lucas said. They were sitting in Daniel's office, under the watchful eyes of Daniel's political mug shots.

"Yeah, well, what do you expect?" Daniel said. He looked in his cigar humidor, then slammed the lid. "Column-writing is the only job I know where sarcasm passes for intelligence. . . . God damn it, Davenport. I need something, and I don't care what it is."

"Stick full-time surveillance on Bekker," Lucas suggested.

"All right," Daniel said, grasping. "Why?"

"To settle him, one way or another. Tag everybody he talks to, track everywhere he goes. If he's involved, he hired a really strange-looking dude for the killing. We need somebody on the team with enough brains to break off Bekker, if he has to, and go after a likely-looking killer. And we ought to get a court order, tap his phones both at home and at work. We either clear him or we hang him."

"What do you think? Is he the guy?" Daniel asked with genuine curiosity.

"I don't know." Lucas shrugged. "He's the only thing we've got, but everything points somewhere else."

"All right, I'll get the surveillance going," Daniel said. "I can give that out to a couple of people, that we've got a guy being watched. That'll cool some of the council fever. But it'd be nice if we got a little decent PR for a change."

"I was talking to a snitch a few nights ago, and he said a mutual acquaintance came into a bunch of TV sets—maybe a couple hundred of them, a boxcarload from over in St. Paul. Then I talked to another guy and he says Terry—this is Terry Meller, you remember him? No? He's a longtime semi-bad dude—he says Terry is working out of a rental warehouse off Two-eighty. He says the TVs are stuffed in there, and probably a bunch of other shit. We could get the ERU and a warrant, call up the TV and the papers. . . ."

"I could tell the ERU guys to armor up some of the reporters—we got some extra vests . . ." Daniel said, brightening. The Emergency Response Unit always got airtime. "Give them some good film."

"We won't lose the Bekker story, but we'll look good on this other thing," Lucas said. "And there'll be film. . . ."

"Get a warrant," Daniel said enthusiastically, poking a finger at him. "I'll get the ERU started and some Intelligence guys over to look at the warehouse. Stop down at Intelligence when you leave and give them the location."

"I've got a new friend at TV3, by the way," Lucas said. "She kind of owes me. . . ."

"You feed her that break on George's body?" Daniel asked, looking sideways at Lucas.

Lucas grinned and shrugged. "Maybe something slipped out. But since we're not going to kill the Bekker story, anyway, I want to tell her that I'm going off the reservation. I want to tell her I don't think George is the lover, and I want to make it seem like there's a little controversy between me and the department. Good guy, bad guy, the department being the bad guy. That'll get us better play, and the other stations will come after it, and the papers . . ."

They'd talked about the possibility that Loverboy was still alive, but Daniel was skeptical. "You really think he's still out there?"

Lucas' forehead wrinkled. "Yeah. I know there are some problems with that—like, why was George killed and dumped if he wasn't the lover? I can't figure that out. I mean, he should have been her lover. They knew each other, they were the right age for each other. . . . I don't know. . . . By the way, has Shearson got anything on this shrink he was looking at? Stephanie's other friend?"

"He thinks there's something."

"He ain't exactly the sharpest knife in the dishwasher. . . ."

"Hey, he's okay," Daniel said mildly. "You don't like him because he wears better suits than you do."

"Yeah, but with golf shirts . . ."

"Look," Daniel said. "We know that Bekker didn't kill either George or his wife, not in person. . . ."

"Yeah. And I was sure that he set me up as an alibi on George, but now . . . God damn it, this thing is getting on top of me. And Loverboy's the key. If he's still out there, I want to get to him. Maybe I can make some kind of appeal. Or drop a hint that I'm closing in on him, and that he'd be better off talking to me now—that if he doesn't come in, we'll find him anyway and pack him off to Stillwater on a charge of accessory to first-degree murder."

"I don't know," Daniel said. He rubbed his developing five-o'clock-shadow fuzz with the back of his fingers. "My inclination is not to do that."

"Your inclination?"

"Yeah. That's my inclination. But you're an adult. Your ass is in your own hands," Daniel said. Lucas nodded. Daniel was in politics. If Lucas went public and was wrong, Daniel had planted a little ambiguity around the decision process.

"Okay," Lucas said. "And you can tell the mayor we're watching a guy and hustling after Loverboy. . . ."

"He's no dummy, the mayor," Daniel said.

"Yeah, I know, but all he wants is something to feed to the sharks, and that's something."

"Good enough. I'll get Anderson to pull some guys for a surveillance team and we'll get on Bekker by tonight."


Lucas stopped at Intelligence, gave the duty officer the address of Terry Meller's TV warehouse, went to his office and called Carly Bancroft, then talked to the department artist and got a quick sketch done. A half-hour later, he met Bancroft at a Dairy Queen in the Skyway.

"I've got another piece of story for you," he said, nibbling around the edge of his chocolate-dipped cone. "Some of it's points for me—you'd owe me more—but some of it's part of your paycheck. Call it a wash. But I want to get it on the air."

"Let's hear it," she said.

"Everybody's assuming that Philip George was Mrs. Bekker's lover and the killer took him out to protect himself."

"Yeah, that's what we're saying," she said.

"I don't think that's right. In fact, I'm pretty sure it's wrong," Lucas said. "I think the guy's still out there. The Loverboy."

She took a lick of her vanilla softie and nodded. "That's an okay story if we can put your name on it. What else?"

"You've got to hint that I'm closing in on the guy—that I'm talking to people and that I've got an identikit picture I'm showing around. I'll show it to some-body you can interview, and they'll know they're supposed to talk to you. They'll describe the guy for you, but I'll refuse to show you the picture."

"That's all fine. What's the payoff part?"

"I want you to report it as though you got it from a third source. You must use my name, but you can't quote me directly and you can't say I'm the source of the story. You have to say that I've refused comment. . . ."

"That's lying," she said.

"Right. Lying," Lucas agreed. "You have to indicate that you got the story from a secret source in the department, but definitely not me. Suggest that there's an interdepartmental difference of opinion and I've been ordered to keep my mouth shut. And then you've got to do a little background on me, say that Davenport has secret sources that not even other cops know about."

"I don't understand what all this means," she said, a tiny wrinkle appearing between her eyes. "I'd like to know where I'm going, in case I'm going off a cliff."

Lucas finished the chocolate part of the cone, took two licks of the vanilla ice cream, reached back and dumped the cone in a wastebasket. "I do think the guy's out there. I want him to feel threatened, but I don't want to be the threatening guy. I want him to come to me," Lucas said.

She nodded. "All right. We can play it like you said."

"And not a bad story," Lucas said.

"Speaking of which"—she glanced at her watch—"I've got to run."

"What's happening?"

"Some big bust going down somewhere—I don't know exactly what it is, but I'm going in with the ERU."

"Sounds good," Lucas said.

"Sounds like bullshit, but I get to be in the movies," she said. "Film at ten."

Elle Kruger's lips moved silently as she walked slowly along the sidewalk, down the hill past the college duck pond, head bowed. Her hands counted through the large black beads of the rosary hanging down her side. Lucas, who'd missed her at her office, followed fifty feet behind, idly checking out the coeds—most were sweet and blonde and large, as though punched from a German Catholic cookie cutter—waiting until Elle had worked her way through the last decade.

When she'd finished, she released the beads, straightened up and lengthened her step, continuing her stroll around the pond. Lucas hurried after her, and she turned and spotted him coming when he was still fifty feet away.

"How long have you been back there?" she asked, smiling.

"Five minutes. The secretary said you'd be down here. . . ."

"Has something happened?"

"No, not really. I'm puzzled, trying to hack my way through what's happening with this Bekker case."

"A strange case, and getting stranger, if the papers can be trusted," she said, but with an upward inflection, making the statement into a question.

"Yeah. Maybe." He was reluctant to commit himself. "Tell me this: We've got this guy who kills two women, completely destroys their eyes. Then he kills another guy, takes him out and buries him in Wisconsin, and he's spotted purely by chance—some neighbors see his car lights and think he might be a burglar. Turns out he probably buried the body the night before, and he came back for the sole purpose of hacking out the eyes. . . ."

". . . Doesn't want to be watched by the dead," Elle said crisply.

"I was wondering if it might be something like that," Lucas said. "But I was also wondering—would it necessarily have to be sincere? If there was some kind of manipulation going on, could he be doing it for some other reason?"

"Like what?"

"Publicity? Or a deliberate effort to tie the murders together?"

She shrugged. "I suppose he could, but then why go back and hack the eyes out of a man whose body you're trying to hide, and don't expect to be found?"

"Yeah, there's that," Lucas said, discouraged. He thrust his hands into his jacket pockets.

"So it's probably real, and it has implications," she said, looking up at him.

"Like what?"

"He hacked the eyes out of all three people he's killed—at least, all three that we know about. And he did it instantly: he killed the first one, Bekker, and did her eyes at the same time. How did he know that the first one would watch him after she was dead? It would suggest . . ."

"That he's killed before and was watched." Lucas slapped his forehead with the heel of his hand. "Damn it. I missed that."

"He's a very dangerous man, Lucas," Elle said. "In the psychological literature, we'd refer to him as a *fruitcake*."

\*    \*    \*

Restless, Lucas drove to the Lost River. The door was locked, but he could see a woman inside, painting. He rapped on the glass door, and when she saw him, he held up his badge case.

"Cassie around?" he asked when she opened the door.

"There's a rehearsal going on," the woman said. "They're all out on the stage."

Lucas walked through the hall to the theater. The lights were up and people were walking or standing around the stage or the low pit in front of it. Two or three more were sitting in the seats, watching and talking. Half of the whites were in blackface, with wide white-greasepainted lips, while two blacks were in whiteface. Cassie saw him and raised a tentative hand, said something to the artistic director, and they both walked over.

"Just looking around, if that's okay," Lucas said. "Would it bother you if I watch?"

"Not much to see," the artistic director said, his greasepainted lips turning down. "You're welcome to stay, but it's mostly people talking."

"We'll be another hour or so . . ." Cassie said. Her green eyes were like lamps peering through the dark paint.

"How about some French food? I mean, later, if you're not doing anything."

"Sounds great." She stepped away and said, "About an hour."

Lucas walked halfway up the rising bank of seats and settled in to watch. *Whiteface* was a brutal but cheerful attack on latter-day segregation. A dozen set pieces were combined with rewritten nineteenth-century show tunes. There were frequent halts to argue, to change lines, to choreograph body positions. Twisting through the set pieces, the troupe kept up a running vaudeville: juggling, tap and rap dancing, joking, banjo-playing.

One manic set involved the two black actors as professional golfers, trying to sneak through a segregated southern country club. Cassie, in a play within a play, took the part of a white southern college belle in blackface, trying to sort out her relationship with a black radical in whiteface.

In a darker piece, a burly man in a wide snap-brimmed felt hat robbed white passersby in a park. Although he was obviously in blackface, none of the victims, when they were talking to the cops, could ever get beyond the blackness, even though they *knew* . . .

When that segment was over, there was a brief, sharp argument about whether it violated the pace and feel of the rest of the show. The two black actors, who were used as arbiters of taste, split on the question. One, who seemed more involved in the technical aspects of playmaking, thought it should go; the other, more interested in the social impact, insisted that it stay.

The artistic director turned and looked up into the seats.

"What do the police think?" he called.

"I think it's pretty strong," Lucas said. "It's not like the rest of the stuff, but it adds something."

"Good. Let's leave it, at least for now," the director said.

When they were done, Lucas sat with Cassie and a half-dozen other actors while they cleaned the paint off their faces. The man who played the mugger was not among them. On the way out, Lucas saw him on the stage, working on a dance he did late in the show.

"Carlo," Cassie said. "He works at it."

They ate and went to Lucas' house. Cassie flopped on the living room couch.

"You know what the worst part of being poor is? You have to work all the time. You're rich, you can take six weeks to veg out. That's what I need: about six weeks of daytime TV."

"Better'n watching the news, anyway," Lucas said. He lifted her legs, sat down on the couch and dropped them in his lap. "At least with the soaps, you *know* you're getting bullshit."

"Hmph. Well, we could get really philosophical about the media and have an intelligent conversation, or we could go fool around," Cassie said. "What'd you want to do?"

"Guess," Lucas said.

Later in the evening, Del called. "Sorry about the other day . . ."

" 'S okay," Lucas said. "What's happening?"

"I've been out with Cheryl twice and she's starting to talk," he said. "I keep telling her I don't want to hear it, and she keeps talking."

"Told you," Lucas said.

"Asshole," said Del. "I actually kind of like her. . . . Anyway, she thinks Bekker might be on some kind of drug. Speed or coke or something. She said he'd sometimes act nuts, he'd be fuckin' her and he'd go a little crazy, start raving, spitting. . . ."

"Sex freak?"

"Well, not exactly. The sex, I guess, was pretty conventional, it's just that he'd kind of lose control. He'd come after her with this really ferocious rush, and then afterwards, it was almost like she was a piece of furniture. Didn't want to hear her talk, didn't want to cuddle up. Usually he'd bring something to read, until he got it up again, and then he'd start freaking out all over."

"Hmph. That's not exactly the worst thing I've ever heard. . . ."

"Well, I'm gonna see her again tomorrow."

"Is there any way we can let Bekker know you're seeing her?"

Del sounded surprised. "What for?"

"Maybe push him a little? We got the surveillance running, so there shouldn't be any problem for her."

"Well . . . yeah, I guess we could work something out. Maybe I could get her to call him, let it slip somehow. . . ."

"Try," Lucas said.

# 19

The phone rang at three in the morning.

Cassie lay on her back, barely visible in the light from a streetlamp filtering through the blinds, the sheet pulled up around her throat, clutched there with two fists, as though she were dreaming sad dreams.

Lucas tiptoed into the kitchen and picked it up.

The dispatcher, with an overlay of personal concern: "Lucas, this is Kathy, at Dispatch. Sorry to wake you up, but there's a guy on the phone, says he's a doctor, says it's about your daughter. . . ."

His heart stopped. "Jesus. Patch him through."

"I'll push the button. . . ."

There was a moment of electronic vacancy, then the sound of somebody breathing, waiting.

"This is Davenport," Lucas snapped.

There was no immediate response, but the feeling of a presence, a background sound that might have been a distant highway.

"Hello, God damn it, this is Davenport."

A man's voice came back, low, gravelly, atonal, artificially clipped, the words evenly spaced, as though a robot were reading from a script: "There is nothing wrong with your daughter. Do you know who this is?"

Lucas had listened to the tapes. Loverboy. "I . . . yes, I think so."

"Give me your phone number." The voice was from *Star Wars*, from Darth Vader. No contractions. No sloppy constructions. Scripted and pared to the bone. "Do not make a call. I will call you back within five seconds. If your line is busy, I will be gone. I have a pencil."

Lucas gave him the phone number. "You're gonna call . . ."

"Five seconds." There was a click and Lucas said, "Kathy, Kathy? Are you still on the line? God damn it." The dispatcher was gone, and Lucas hung up. A second or two later, the phone rang once.

Lucas snatched it up. "Yeah."

"I want to help, but I cannot help directly," the voice grated, still on the script. "I will not come out. How can I help?"

"Did you send us a picture? I gotta know, just for identification."

"Yes. The cyclops. The killer does not look like the cyclops. The killer feels like the cyclops. His head looks like a pumpkin. There's something wrong with it."

"Not to say you're lying, but that sounds like the one-armed man, in that TV show a long time ago," Lucas said, letting a tint of skepticism color his voice. Reaching for control. Cassie came into the kitchen, sleepy, rubbing her eyes, drawn by the tone of his voice.

"Yes, *The Fugitive,*" Loverboy said. "I thought of that. Where did you get an artist's drawing of me?"

*Loverboy had seen Carly Bancroft on TV3.* "Let me ask the questions for a minute, okay? If you get spooked, I don't want you ditching me before I get them out. Do you know of any connection between either of the Bekkers and Philip George?"

"No." There was a moment of hesitation, and then, off the script, voiced a notch higher, inflection: "I've speculated . . ." He changed his mind, and his voice, in midsentence: "No." The robot control again.

"Look," Lucas said. "You've got a conscience. We've got a fuckin' monster out there killing people and he might not be done yet. We need every scrap we can get on the case."

"Get Michael Bekker."

"We don't know he's involved."

Back on script, all inflection gone: "He is a monster. But he did not kill Stephanie personally. I did not make that mistake."

"Look, give me the connection between you and George, if you think there is one," Lucas said, going soft. "If you want to stay out there, and you get caught later, I'll testify that you were feeding me information, that you helped, okay? Maybe help you out."

Another pause. Then: "No. I cannot. You have thirty more seconds."

"Hold on . . . why?"

"Because you may trace the call. I budgeted two minutes. You have twenty-five seconds left. . . ."

"Wait, wait, we've got to set up some way for me to reach you. . . . If I need you, bad . . ."

"Put an advertisement in the *Tribune* personals. . . . Say you are no longer responsible for the debts of your wife. Sign it 'Lucas Smith.' I will call about this time. Two minutes. Look at Bekker. Stephanie was scared of him. Look at Bekker."

"Gimme one more question, one more," Lucas pleaded. "Why's Bekker a monster? What'd he do to Stephanie . . . ?"

*Click.*

"God damn it," Lucas said, looking at the phone.

"Who was it?" Cassie asked, moving up beside him. Her soft fingers trickled down his spine, warm, reassuring.

"Stephanie Bekker's lover," Lucas said. He poked a seven-digit number and the other end was picked up instantly: Dispatch.

"This is Davenport. Let me talk to Kathy."

"How's your daughter?" the woman asked a second later.

"That was all bullshit," Lucas said. "But it's okay, the guy had to get through to me. I'll need the tapes on your part of the call, so you might want to mark them."

"Well . . . there aren't tapes," the dispatcher said. "He came in on the nonemergency line, the thirty-eight."

"God damn it," Lucas said. He scratched his head. "Listen, write down what you remember he said and give it to Anderson in the morning. Write down everything you remember, what his voice sounded like, the whole nine yards."

"Heavy-duty?" she asked.

"Yeah. Very heavy."

When Lucas hung up, Cassie said, "I think . . . ," but he waved her away and said, "Shhh . . . I've got to remember . . ." She followed him into the bedroom and he flopped onto the bed, lay back and closed his eyes. Remember. Not the words. The feel of the other man. The voice was deep, the words well paced, the sentences clear. When he was off script for a moment, he'd used the word "speculated." He watched TV3.

And, Lucas thought, he looked like George. That's what he had *speculated,* Lucas was sure of it. Lucas had done the same thing: the phony identikit photo he was circulating was a simplified sketch of Philip George.

What else? Loverboy had not gone to the funeral, because he wasn't sure whether George was there. He had done research on Lucas. He knew that Lucas had a daughter and did not live with her. After the Crows case, there'd been quite a bit of press attention to Lucas, to Jennifer and their daughter, so the research wouldn't have been difficult—he might, in fact, simply be operating on memory. But just in case, a check of the libraries again, the newspaper files? He'd talk to Anderson about it.

Lucas opened his eyes. "Sorry, I just had to try to get it down. . . ."

"That's okay—that's how I remember lines," Cassie said.

"He's a smart sonofabitch," Lucas said. He stood up, found his underpants on a chair and pulled them on. "I've got to make a few notes."

She followed him down to the spare bedroom, looked at the charts hanging from the wall. "Wow. Mr. Brainstorm."

"Pieces of the puzzle," he said. A sheet of paper, folded in quarters, was lying on the bed. As Cassie looked at the charts on the wall, he unfolded it. The photocopy of the cyclops painting. "The thing is, we know Bekker is goofy, but everything points in some other direction. . . ."

Cassie was still looking up at his charts, but somber now.

"Do you do this for all your cases?" she asked.

"The big complicated ones, yes."

"Have you ever had all the clues up there, posted, but not been able to figure them out until too late?"

"I don't know—I've never thought about it. You hardly get all the information you need to make a case, unless it's simple open-and-shut: you catch a guy red-handed, or five witnesses see a guy kill his wife," Lucas said. "If it's more complicated than that . . . I don't know. I've sent people to prison who claimed to be innocent and still claim they're innocent. I'm ninety-nine percent sure they're not innocent, but . . . you can't always know for sure."

"Wouldn't it freak you out if there was a key piece of information up there, you just didn't see it, and somebody got killed?"

"Mmm. I don't know. You can't blame yourself because a psycho kills people. I'm not Albert fuckin' Einstein."

"So what're you going to do next?" Cassie asked, still wide-eyed.

Lucas tossed the folded Xerox of the cyclops back on the bed. "What any good cop would do at three in the morning. Go back to bed."


Lucas set the alarm for seven. When it went off, he silenced it, slipped out of bed, leaving Cassie asleep, and went to the kitchen to phone Daniel. He caught the chief at breakfast and told him about the call from Stephanie's lover.

"Sonofabitch," Daniel sputtered. "So you're right. But why'd they kill George?"

"He said he didn't know. Actually, he said he'd speculated about it, but didn't want to talk about it. But I know what he was thinking: that he looks like George. And when you sort through all the implications of that, it points at Bekker," Lucas said, and explained.

Daniel listened and agreed. "Now what? How do we get to the guy?"

"We could maybe invent a crisis, put an ad in the paper, stake people out all over town, wire up my line, and when he calls—bam, we're tracing. We might get him."

"Hmph. Maybe. I'll talk to some of the techs about it. But what happens if he calls from Minnetonka?"

"I don't know. The thing is, he's smart," Lucas said. "If we fuck with him, he might just go back into the woodwork. I don't want to risk chasing him away. He can put the finger on a suspect, if we ever come up with one."

"Okay. So let's keep this tight between us," Daniel said. "I'll order a tap on your line and we'll monitor calls. I'll talk with Sloan and Anderson and Shearson and see if we can come up with some kind of pressure that'll get to him to call back."

"I could do that. I figure . . ."

"No. I don't want you chasing Loverboy. I want you focused on the killer or the killers—Bekker and whoever he's working with."

"There's not much there."

"You just keep pushing. Keep moving around. I got all kinds of guys who can do the pony work. I want you on the killer before he does it again."

# 20

Not knowing the nature of neighborhood friendships around Bekker, and afraid to ask, the surveillance team decided not to seek a listening post among Bekker's neighbors.

Instead the team keyed on the intersections around the front and back of his house. From two parked cars, they could watch the front door directly, and both ends of the alley that ran behind his house. The cars were shuffled every hour or so, both to relieve the tedium and to lessen the possibility that Bekker might grow suspicious of one particular car.

Even so, a jogger, a woman lawyer, spotted one of the surveillance cars within an hour of the beginning of the watch on Bekker and reported it to police. She was told that the car belonged to an undercover detective on a narcotics study, and was asked to keep it confidential. Later that same day she saw a second car and realized that Bekker was being watched. She thought about mentioning it to a neighbor but did not.

The surveillance began in the evening. The next morning, four tired cops took Bekker to work. Four more monitored him in the hospital, but quickly understood that a perfect net would be impossible: the hospital was a warren of passageways, stairs, elevators and tunnels. They settled for containing him within the complex, with occasional eyeball checks of his location. While he was pinned, a narc stuck a transmitter under the rear bumper of his car.

The discovery of George's body was a sensation and a shock. Bekker watched, aghast, a TV3 tape of khaki-clad deputies marching through the brambles near the lakeside cabin, horsing out a litter. The body was covered with a pristine white sheet, wrapped like a chrysalis. A blonde newscaster, with a face as stylistically and cosmetically appropriate for the scene as a Japanese player's is for Noh, intoned a dirgelike report, with the gray skies hanging theatrically in the background.

Bekker, not a watcher of television, found a newspaper TV guide and marked the newscasts. The other stations were on the story, although none had TV3's film.

The next evening, fearing more bad news, he was nonplussed to find himself watching a seemingly interminable story about the recovery of a boxcar full of television sets from a warehouse someplace in Minneapolis. Television sets? He began to relax, switching channels, found television sets everywhere, and television reporters in flak jackets. . . .

If anything important had happened, surely he wouldn't be seeing television sets. . . .

He nearly missed it. He was switching through the channels when he found the blonde again, back in the studio and out of her flak jacket. She delivered another body blow: Davenport, she said, did not believe that Philip George was Stephanie's lover, believed that the lover was still at large, and was circulating an identikit picture of the man. Davenport, she said, was a genius.

"What?" Bekker blurted, staring at the television, as though it could answer him. Could Davenport be right? Had they missed with George? He needed to think. Nothing ephemeral. Needed something to reach him, something to focus. He opened the brass case, studied it. Yes. He lifted it to his face and his tongue flicked out, picking up the capsule the way a frog picks up a fly. Focus.

The flight was not a good one. Not terrifying, like the snake, but not good. He could manage it, though, steering between the shadows where Davenport hid. Goddamned Davenport, this case should be done, he should be free. . . .

Bekker came back, the taste of blood on his lips. Blood. He looked down, found blood on his chest again, stirred himself. He'd been away again. . . . What had happened? What? Ah . . . yes. The lover. What to do? To settle, of course.

He staggered to his feet and wandered toward the stairs. To the bathroom, to wash. He went away, came back a few minutes later, his hand on the banister leading up the stairs, his eyes dry from staring. He blinked once. Druze had been uncharacteristically moody on the trip to Wisconsin, the trip to cut George's eyes. Hadn't really understood the necessity of it. Was he pulling away? No. But Druze had changed . . . didn't have moods.

*Need to involve him again.* Bekker's eyes strayed to the phone. Just one call? No. Not from here. He must not.

He went away once more while he groomed himself and dressed, but he could not remember the content of the trip—if there was any content—when he returned. He finished dressing, took the car out, drove to the hospital. Inside the building, he took the stairs down, hurrying, not thinking.

The quickness of Bekker's move confused the surveillance team. One of the narcs was behind him by ten seconds, walked straight down the hall past the elevators and the staircase door, which were in an alcove. And Bekker was gone. Perhaps the elevator had been waiting, ready to go? The narc hurried back outside and told the team leader, who had a cellular telephone and punched Bekker's office number into it.

"Can I speak to Dr. Bekker?" The team leader looked like a mail clerk, short hair, harried, gone to a little weight.

"I'm sorry, Dr. Bekker hasn't come in yet."

"I'm downstairs and I thought I saw him just a minute ago."

"I sit right here by the door, and he's not in."

"We've lost him," the narc told the rest of the team. "He's got to be in the building. Spread out. Find him."

Bekker hurried down the steps to the tunnel that led to the next building. He stopped at a candy machine, got a Nut Goodie, then hurried on through the tunnel to a pay telephone.

Druze was not at his apartment. Bekker hesitated, then called information and got the number for the Lost River Theater. A woman answered and, after Bekker asked for Druze, dropped the telephone and went away. Not knowing whether she was looking for Druze or simply had been exasperated by the request, Bekker stood waiting, for two minutes, then three, and finally, Druze: *"Hello?"*

"You heard?" Bekker asked.

"Are you at a safe phone?" Druze's voice was low, almost a whisper.

"Yes. I've been very careful." Bekker looked down the empty hallway.

"I heard that they found the body and that this cop, Davenport, doesn't think George was the lover. . . . And it's not a game they're playing. He's got some good reason to think so."

"How do you know that?"

"Because he's been seeing one of the actresses here, Cassie Lasch. She was the one who found Armistead, and she and Davenport struck up some kind of relationship."

"You mentioned her. She lives in your building. . . ."

"Yeah, that's the one," Druze said. His words were tumbling over each other. "Cassie was telling us this morning that the lover's still out there. I think Davenport's talking to him, but doesn't know exactly who he is. And something else. The cops have supposedly got some kind of picture of me. Not a police drawing, it's something else."

"Jesus, can that be right?" Bekker rubbed his forehead furiously. This was getting complicated.

"Somebody asked Cassie why we wouldn't have seen it on television, if that's true," Druze said. "She said she hadn't seen the picture, but she knew about it and that there was something weird about it. And she was positive about the lover, by the way. She was being mysterious, but I think she knows. I think they're sleeping together, she's getting pillow talk. . . ."

"Damn." Bekker gnawed on a fingernail. "You know what we've got to do? We talked about doing a number three before George came along? I think we've got to do it. We've got to do somebody that doesn't make any sense for either one of us. Somebody completely off the wall."

"Who?"

"I don't know. That's the whole point. Somebody at random. The god-damned shopping-mall parking lots are full of women. Go get one."

There was a moment of silence and then Druze said, "I'm really hanging out there, man."

"And so am I," Bekker snapped. "If there is some kind of drawing of you—if Stephanie's friend sent them something—and if this actress person sees it, then we've got serious trouble."

"Yeah, you're right about that. She sees me every goddamned day and night of my life. . . ."

"What's her name again?" Bekker asked.

"Cassie Lasch. But if we do her . . ."

"I know. We couldn't do it now, but later, next week. . . . If we can get the cops to go hounding off somewhere, maybe she could have an accident. Something unrelated. What floor is she on? High up?"

"Six, I guess. And she did once try to commit suicide. . . ."

"So maybe if she went out a window . . . I don't know, Carlo. We'll work something. But we've got to get the cops going somewhere else. Something not related to the theater or to the university or antiques . . ."

"So . . . are you serious? A mall?" Druze sounded confused, uncertain.

"Yeah. I am. Pick one out on the edge of town. Burnsville would be good. Maplewood. Roseville. You're bright, figure out some way. . . . Pick somebody who looks like she's on a big shopping trip. Get her at her car. Then dump the car with all the packages. Be sure you do the eyes. The thing is, we'll want it to look like it's totally random. . . . You know what? Maybe you could cruise the lots. See if you could get somebody with Iowa plates or something."

"I don't know. . . . I gotta have time to think about it."

"If the lover's out there, we don't have time," Bekker urged. "We've got to lead them away from us, at least until we can pinpoint the guy."

"Jesus, I wish . . ."

"Hey. We had to get rid of them. We deserved to be rid of them. Now we just have to clean up a little bit. Okay?"

Silence.

"Okay?" Bekker demanded.

"Okay, I guess. I gotta go. . . ."

\*     \*     \*

Druze was getting sticky: Bekker would have to move on him.

On the way back to his office, Bekker stopped at a men's room and urinated. He went to a sink and was washing his hands when a student came in, looked at him, then casually moved to a urinal. A heavy canvas bookbag hung from his shoulder.

The student looked a little odd, Bekker thought. The jeans and cardigan were okay, the oxford-cloth shirt was all right. . . . He glanced at the student again as he went out.

It was the shoes, he thought, pleased that he'd picked it out. The kid must have just gotten out of the army or something. You didn't see students wearing that kind of black, shiny-toed, oxford anymore. Not since Vietnam, anyway.

In the restroom, the student listened to Bekker's heels hitting the concrete floor, moving away, then took the radio out of his bag. "I got him," he said. "He was in the can. He's on the basement level, on his way up the west stairs."

At the elevators, another student was waiting to go up, reading one of the free entertainment newspapers. He had shoes like the kid in the restroom. A new trend? A signal to buy oxford stock? On the other hand, neither of the kids looked exactly like fashion trend-setters. . . .

Back to the office, or up to see the patient? Bekker glanced at his watch. He had time, and nobody coming to see him. A small thrill pulsed through him. Might as well do some serious work.

Bekker rode up to Surgery, nodded to a nurse, and went into the men's locker room, peeled his clothes off and dressed himself in a lavender scrub suit. Technically, he didn't need a scrub suit; he wouldn't be going into Surgery or Burns, where they were most useful. But he liked them. They were comfortable. And he liked them like surgeons liked them, for the aura. . . . When he was wearing a scrub suit, people always called him "Dr. Bekker," which they sometimes forgot when he was in the Path area.

With his face, and with the aura of the suit, sometimes he simply went down and relaxed in the cafeteria, let the public look at him. . . .

Not today. When he was dressed, he pulled paper shoe-covers over his loafers, got his clipboard from the locker and headed up another flight of stairs, his heart pounding a bit. It had been a few days since he'd talked to Sybil. He really had to find more time.

At the top of the stairs, he pushed through the fire door and walked down the hall to the nurses' station.

"Dr. Bekker," a nurse said, looking up. "You're earlier than usual."

"Had a little extra time." He put on a smile. "Any changes?"

"No, not since you were last here," the nurse said, not managing a smile. "Changes" was Bekker's euphemism for "death." It had taken her a few of his visits to catch on.

"Well, I think I'll wander down," Bekker said. "Anywhere I shouldn't go?"

"Room seven-twelve, we have a radiation treatment there—we're keeping that clean."

"I'll stay away," Bekker promised. He left her at the desk, plowing through the endless paperwork that seemed to afflict nurses. He stopped at two rooms, for show, before heading to Sybil's.

"Sybil? Are you awake?" Her eyes were closed as he stepped into the room, and they didn't open, but he could see that a drip tube leading to her arm was working. "Sybil?"

Still her eyes didn't open. He glanced down the hallway, then stepped up to her bed, leaned forward, placed his fingertips on her forehead, pulled up an eyelid with his thumb and murmured, "Come out, come out, wherever you are. . . ."

The television behind him was tuned to TV3, a game show that apparently involved some kind of leapfrog. He didn't notice; Sybil had opened her eyes and was looking frantically around the room.

"No, no. There isn't any help, dear," Bekker crooned. "No help anywhere."

Bekker spent an hour at the hospital. He was picked up by the surveillance team as he left through the lobby.

"He's got a funny look on his face," the narc said into her purse. "He's coming right at me." She watched Bekker go down the sidewalk, past the bench where she was reading a car issue of *Consumer Reports.*

"What's funny?" the crew chief asked, as the net closed around Bekker again.

"I don't know," the narc said. "He looked like he just got laid or something."

"A look you know well," said a cop named Louis, normally in uniform, but pulled for this job.

"Shut up," the crew chief said. "Stay on his ass and don't spook him. We're doing good."

Halfway across the campus, Bekker did a little jig. He did it quickly, almost unconsciously, but not quite—he caught himself and looked around guiltily before moving on.

"What the fuck was that all about?" the narc asked.

"Potty-mouth," said Louis.

"Shut up," said the crew chief. "And I don't know. We oughta get some video on this guy, you know? I woulda liked to have some video on that."

The crew took him home, where another crew picked up the watch. Louis, who liked wisecracks, went back to police headquarters, where he bumped into the police reporter for Channel Eight.

"What's happening, Louis?" the reporter asked. "Workin' on anything good?"

Louis chewed a lot of gum and tipped his head, a wiseguy. "Got a thing going here and there," he said. "Hell of a story, if I could only tell ya."

"You look like you been on surveillance," the reporter suggested. "All dressed up like a human being."

"Did I say surveillance?" Louis grinned. He liked reporters. He'd been quoted several times at crime scenes.

The reporter frowned. "Hey, are you working that Bekker thing?"

Louis' smile faded. "I got no comment. Like, really."

"I won't fuck you, Louis," the reporter said. "But there's a hell of a leak around here somewhere, and TV3 is kicking ass."

Louis liked reporters. . . .

# 21

Anderson tossed two manila file folders on Lucas' desk.

"Surveillance report, and summary interviews from the theater people and Armistead's friends," he said.

"Anything in them?" Lucas asked. He was leaning back in his chair, his feet on a desk drawer. A boom box on the floor was playing "Radar Love."

"Not much," Anderson said, with a flash of his yellow teeth. He was the department's computer junkie. He dressed like a hillbilly and had once been a ferocious street cop. "Bekker mostly hung around the university, his office, the hospital. . . ."

"All right, I'll take a look," Lucas said, yawning. "If we don't break something soon . . ."

"I'm hearing about it from Daniel," Anderson said, nodding. "That goddamned warehouse raid saved our asses, but there's nothing going on today."

"How many TV sets did we get?"

"One hundred and forty-four: twelve dozen. Hell of a haul. Also thirty Hitachi VCRs, six Sunbeam bathroom scales, about thirty cases of Kleenex man-size bathroom tissues, some water-soaked, and one box of Lifestyles Stimula vibra-ribbed rubbers, which Terry said were for personal use only. Wonder if they work?"

"What?"

"Vibra-ribbed rubbers . . ."

"I don't know. I use Goodyear Eagle all-weathers myself."

Anderson left, and Lucas picked up the surveillance folder and flipped through it. Bekker had done a jig: Lucas spotted it immediately and thought back to the night he'd met Bekker and the frenzied dance he'd seen through the window. What was he doing in the hospital? Might be worthwhile checking again . . .

The folders yielded nothing else. Lucas tossed them aside, yawned again, feeling pleasantly sleepy. Cassie was a little rough, a little muscular in her lovemaking. Interesting.

And different. He watched her, comparing her with Jennifer, finding the differences. Jennifer had a tough veneer, developed over years as a reporter. Lucas had the same shell. So did most social workers.

"When you see too much shit in one lifetime, you've got to find a way to deal with it," Jennifer had said once. "Reporters and cops develop the shell as a defense. If you can laugh at a crazy rapist, you know, 'the B.O. Fucker' and all those cute names you cops develop, well, then you don't have to take it so seriously."

"Yeah, right, pass the joint," Lucas had said.

"See? That's exactly what I'm talking about. . . ."

Cassie had no shell. Everything that happened to her, she felt. Psychiatry, she thought, was normal. Most people were screwed up, but it helped to talk about it, even if you had to pay somebody to listen.

Occasionally, when he'd been with Jennifer, Lucas had had a feeling that they both yearned to talk, to let it out, but couldn't. Talking would have made them too vulnerable and, each of them knowing the other, the vulnerability would have been used. . . .

"Hey, you get beat up. People use you, you get played for a sucker," Cassie had said, when he told her about that. "Big fuckin' deal. Everybody gets beat up."

And Lucas had once again found himself trying to dissect his episode of depression: "I've fooled around with a lot of women, ever since I was a teenager. I slowed down a lot after I started dating Jen—slipped up a couple of times, bad, but we were making it until . . . you know. But the thing is, when she walked . . . I just stopped. Fell off the cliff. The real pit was last fall, around Thanksgiving, I'd just gotten back from seeing this woman in New York and she'd pretty much called off our relationship. I thought I was crazy. Not crazy crazy, like in the movies. Crazy where you don't get out of bed for two days. You don't pay the mortgage, because you can't get yourself to write a check."

"I once didn't pay my taxes for that reason. I had the money, but I couldn't deal with the government," Cassie had said, not laughing.

"I was down there for three or four months, and when I started feeling like I was moving again, I was afraid of looking at a woman. Any woman. I was afraid that things wouldn't work out, and I'd go back in the pit. I'd rather be celibate than go back in the pit. I'd rather do anything than go back in there. . . ."

"You had it bad," Cassie had said simply. "That's when you need somebody with really big boobs so you can curl up and put your head between them and suck on your thumb."

Lucas had started laughing, trying to get his head between Cassie's breasts. One thing led to another. . . .

Daniel walked into Lucas' office and shut the door. "We got a problem."

"What?"

Daniel ran a hand through his thinning hair, his face caught between anger and confusion. "Tell me the truth: Have you been feeding stuff to Channel Eight?"

"No. I've been working a woman from TV3. . . ."

"Yeah, yeah, I know about that. Nothing going to Eight?"

"No. Honest to God," Lucas said. "What happened?"

Daniel dropped into the visitor's chair. "I got a call from Jon Ayres over at Channel Eight. He says he has a source who tells them that we've got a suspect under surveillance and we're about to make a bust. I denied it. They said they had it pretty solid. I still denied it and told them that false stories could damage our investigation. The guy got huffy, we passed some more bullshit, and he said he'd think about it. . . ."

"That means they're going to use it," Lucas said urgently. "You've got to call the station manager."

"Too late," Daniel said. He pointed at the wall clock. Twelve-fifteen. "It was the lead story on the noon news."

"Sonofabitch," Lucas groaned.

"I know, I know. . . ."

Del stopped by late in the day. "We hit it off and now I can't shut her up about Bekker. She's *insisting* that I investigate him. The problem is, she doesn't know much."

"Like nothing?"

"She thinks he might be on some kind of speed. He gets weird. And here's something: He does have a thing about eyes."

"He does?" Lucas leaned forward. This *was* something. "What?"

"Remember how she told us that he liked to humiliate her? Force her to do blow jobs and so on? When she was doing them, he'd always make her hold her head so he could look in her eyes. Used to say something about the eyes being the hallway to the soul, or something like that . . ."

" 'These lovely lamps, these windows of the soul . . .' " Lucas quoted.

"Who said that?"

"Can't remember. I once took a poetry course at Metro State, I remember it from that."

"Well, he's apparently got a thing for them. He still scares her, when she sees him around the hospital."

"Does she have any idea what he's doing now?"

"No. Want me to ask?"

"Yeah. You'll be seeing her again, huh?"

"Sure, if you want me to pump her some more," Del said.

"I wasn't thinking about that," Lucas said. "I was thinking . . . you look pretty good."


Bekker learned about the police surveillance from Druze. He half expected a call, to warn of a third killing, and every few hours he checked the answering machine.

"TV report on Channel Eight says the cops are doing surveillance on a suspect," Druze said without identifying himself. "I've been watching and I don't think it's me." And he was gone.

*What?* Bekker couldn't focus, and played it again.

"TV report on Channel Eight . . ."

Surveillance? Bekker reset the tape, his mind working furiously. If they *were* watching Druze and had seen him make this call, would they be able to trace it? He thought not, yet he wasn't sure. But it was unlikely that they would be watching Druze—how would they get to him? The alleged picture? Perhaps.

It was more likely that *he* was the one being watched, if it wasn't just some kind of TV fantasy. The image of the student in the men's room came to him, and the second one at the library. . . .

Not military shoes, he said to himself. Cop shoes . . .


# 22

The weather patterns were seesawing across the state, Canadian cold and Gulf heat. Druze felt as if he was breathing water. Thunderstorms prowled western Minnesota; TV weathermen said they'd be into the metro area before nine o'clock. From the interstate, Druze could see lightning to the north and west. The storm was too far away for the thunder to be heard.

Maplewood Mall was the northeastern shopping anchor for St. Paul, out in the suburbs. Low crime, high affluence. Boys in letter jackets, teenage girls trying out their new slinks.

Druze cruised the parking lot, watching the shoppers. He wanted a woman leaving the mall. Forties, so she'd fit the profile. If he could get her at the right place, he wouldn't have to move her. Do it right in the parking lot, leave her there. The quicker she was found, the quicker the cops would be turned.

He stopped at a cross-drive and a woman walked in front of his headlights; she wore a cardigan, slacks and high heels, held a purse with both hands, a determined look on her face. A little too old, Druze thought, and not in the right place.

He parked, got out and sauntered toward the mall. A bronze rent-a-cop car rolled slowly through the lot, and Druze headed inside. He'd worked on his face with Cover Mark cosmetics and wore a felt hat with a snap brim, so he wouldn't be particularly noticeable from a range of more than a few feet. Not unless they saw the nose. He pulled the hat farther down on his forehead.

Druze was worried. In the beginning, when he and Bekker had worked through the plan, it had seemed simple. Bekker would take Armistead, and Druze would take Stephanie Bekker. Both he and Bekker would get what they wanted—Bekker his freedom, Druze his security. Both would have solid alibis. If the pressure on Bekker got too great, Druze could take a third. No problem. But then the lover came along. . . .

Was George the right one? He looked like the man in the hall, but the man in the hall had been wearing only a towel, his thinning hair had been wet, his face contorted. Druze had seen him only for an instant. Had he been heavier than George? Now, at this distance, Druze just wasn't sure. He'd looked at too many pictures of people who were almost right. Contaminated with information, he thought.

Bekker . . . He was no longer sure of Bekker. They'd met after a show, in a theater café, Bekker there with Stephanie and some kind of doctors' group from the university. Bekker had been out on the edge of the group, left alone. Druze had come in, also alone, looking for a drink. He'd seen the beautiful man immediately, couldn't take his eyes away: Bekker had so much. . . .

Bekker had been equally fascinated. He'd made the first approach: *Hello there, I think I saw you on the stage a few minutes ago. . . .*

And later, much later, after they were . . . friends? was that right? . . . Bekker had said, "We're the opposite sides of the same coin, my friend, trapped by our looks."

But it hadn't been their appearances that held them together. It had been something else: the taste for violence? what?

\*    \*    \*

He stood next to the atrium rail in the mall, looking down to the lower floor. Shoppers strolled down the length of the mall, some still in careful winter dress, dark, somber, protective, gloves sticking out from coat pockets. Others, the younger ones, had shifted with the Gulf winds, going into summer, T-shirts under light nylon windbreakers, a few of them in shorts, surfers for the boys, tennis shorts for the girls.

He started picking out women. Forties. Somebody attractive. Somebody who might catch the eye of a psycho. There were dozens of them, singles, twos and threes, tall, small, heavy, slender, scowling, laughing, intent, window-shopping, strolling, paying cash, checking receipts, holding up blouses. . . . Druze unconsciously flipped his car keys in the air with one hand, picked them out of the air with the other, tossed them back to the first, and did it again.

And he chose: Eenie meenie minie moe . . .


Nancy Dunen couldn't believe the price of jeans. She never believed. Every time she came in, she thought the last time must have been an aberration, a nightmare. The twins always managed to wear out the back-to-school jeans, bought in September, at the same time in the spring. Two twelve-year-olds, four pairs of jeans, thirty-two dollars a pair . . . she stared blankly into the middle distance, her lips moving, as she calculated. A hundred twenty-eight dollars. My God, where would it come from? Maybe Visa would have a sense of humor about the whole thing.

She held the pants up, checking for flaws in the fabric. Noticed the feminine cut. Twelve years old, and they were getting curves in their pants already. Must be hormones in the breakfast cereal.

A man meandered past the open front of the store. Something wrong with his face, though it was hard to tell exactly what it was. He was wearing an old-fashioned brown felt hat, with the brim snapped down. She was looking past the pants when she saw him; she felt the light *clink* of eye contact, turned away as the man turned away, and she scraped at a knot in the denim with a fingernail. Good eye, Dunen, she thought. She put that pair of jeans back, got another.

Nancy sometimes thought she might be pretty, and sometimes she was sure she wasn't. She kept her dark hair cut short, skimped on the makeup, stayed in shape with a three-time-a-week jog around the neighborhood. She didn't spend a lot of time worrying about whether she was pretty or not, although she claimed she had the best forty-three-year-old butt in the neighborhood. She was settled in her body, in her life. Her husband seemed to like her, and she liked him, and they both liked the kids. . . .

She took the jeans to the cashier's counter, groaned when she saw the Visa charge slip, folded it, dropped it in her purse.

"If my husband finds it, he'll wring my neck," she said to the girl behind the counter.

"Yeah, but . . ." The blonde salesgirl tossed her hair with a smile and made a piano-playing gesture with her hand as she put the jeans in a bag. Husbands can be handled, she was saying. "They're nice pants."

Nancy left the store and, bag in hand, window-shopped at a women's store, but she kept moving. The man with the hat was behind her on the escalator, heading toward the same exit. She noticed but didn't think about it. Let's see, I was out the exit by the cookie stand. . . .

A burly high school kid with a letter jacket and a white-sidewall haircut held the door for her. He was wearing an earring and looked at her butt, and she smiled to herself. When she was growing up, in the fifties, there were older boys with sidewalls, but they'd have cut their own wrists before wearing an earring. . . .

Nancy stepped over a curb and stopped at her car, and fished in her purse for her keys. The man with the hat went by. She almost nodded—they'd sort of looked at each other a few times in the mall—but she didn't. Instead, she popped open the car door, dumped the jeans in the backseat, climbed in and started the engine. She should make it home by eight. What was on TV tonight?

Druze had been ready, the knife-sharpening steel in his pocket, the same one he'd used on George. He had cleaned it meticulously, kept it in his kitchen drawer. And it was ready when he needed it. He followed the woman out of the mall, into the parking lot, ready to close on her, watching for other walkers, for cars turning down the rows, checking the lights. He was ready. . . .

The woman stopped at the first car in the lot, a white Chevy Spectrum. Propped the bag between her hip and the car, began digging in her purse. They were absolutely exposed to the mall. If he moved on her, he would be seen. He glanced back: people on the sidewalk, at the doors, coming, going . . . Shit.

He felt stupid. If he picked a woman inside, there was an excellent chance that she'd be parked somewhere in the open, where he couldn't get to her. Or even that she'd be picked up at the curb by a husband or son. He'd have to wait outside. He went by Nancy Dunen, unconsciously flipped his keys in the air with one hand, picked them out with the other. The woman glanced vaguely at him, then went back to her purse. He never looked back, he heard the door slam and the engine start. . . .

Druze went back to his car, moved it to the edge of the lot, tried a parking space, found he couldn't see out of it, tried another. Good. He parked, turned off the lights and waited. He was parked at an acute angle to a side entry. People wouldn't naturally look at this area, but he could watch them coming through.

He waited five minutes. Nothing. Then a couple crossed the lot, walking toward the cluster where Druze was parked. A single woman followed them by twenty yards. The couple reached their car; the man walked around to the passenger side to open the door, then opened the trunk to put their packages inside. The single woman reached the cluster as the man closed the trunk and popped open the driver's-side door. By that time, the single woman, unaware that she was being watched, and not more than thirty feet from Druze, was already getting into her car. She backed out at the same time as the couple, and they were gone.

Damn. She would have been a good one, Druze thought. A little young, but that was okay. He slouched in the seat, the hat brim pulled down. People walked in and out of the lighted doors. Eenie meenie minie moe . . .

Kelsey Romm was wearing a scarlet blouse and jeans, with white gym shoes, her hair long, her lipstick dark. She worked part-time at Maplewood and part-time at a convenience store in Roseville, and on weekends at a Target. Sometimes the workload made her sick to her stomach; sometimes her legs ached so bad that she couldn't bend them to sit down. But full-time jobs were hard to find. Economics, her Maplewood boss told her. You could patch to-gether a bunch of part-time employees and avoid all benefits, he said. And it made scheduling easier. It wasn't his fault, he said: he didn't own the store. He was only following orders.

She got the same story at the other places. If she didn't like it, there were plenty of high school kids looking for jobs. It wasn't as if she needed a lot of skill. Scan a code, and a number came up on the cash register. Scan another, and the machine told you the change. Kelsey Romm needed the work. Two kids, both in junior high. Two mistakes, running wild, the girl already into alcohol and who knew what else. She didn't even like them much, but they were hers, no doubt about that.

Kelsey Romm walked with her head down. She always walked with her head down. You didn't see things that way. She didn't see Druze, either. She walked to the car, an '83 Chevy Cavalier, brown, a beater, air didn't work, radio didn't work, tires were going bald, the brakes sounded like they had air in them, the front-seat latch was broken. . . .

She stuck her key in the door lock. She saw the man at the last minute and started to turn her head. The steel caught her behind the ear, and the last thing Kelsey Romm saw in her life was the entrance to the Maplewood Mall, and a kid leaning on a trashcan.

If you'd told her this was the way it would end, she would have nodded. She would have said, "I believe it."

*    *    *

Druze saw her hurry through the entrance and knew instinctively that she'd be coming all the way out. He cracked the car door, so it would open silently. She had her head down and came straight across the lot, heading for the row behind Druze's car. That was fine. That was good. He got out and sauntered down the row, flipped his keys in the air with one hand, picked them out with the other, did it again. There were still a few people on the sidewalks outside the mall, a kid standing by the entrance, looking the other way. This could work. . . .

She came on, paying no attention to him, turned in at an old Chevy. He'd seen where she was going, and made his own move, cutting between the cars. If she had her keys in her hand, he thought, he might be too late. He put his own keys into his pocket, got a grip on the sharpening steel and stepped a little more quickly. She started digging in her purse as she turned in at her car, her head still down. Like a mole, Druze thought. Digging. He was close now, could see the shiny fabric of her shirt, glanced around, nobody . . .

And he was there, swinging, the steel whipping around, the woman cocking her head at the last minute.

The steel hit and bit and she went down, bouncing off the car as the professor had; but the woman made a noise, loud, like the caw of a crow, air from her lungs squeezing out. Druze looked around: he was okay, he thought. The kid by the garbage can might be looking at them . . . but he wasn't moving.

Druze stooped, pulled open the woman's purse, found her keys, unlocked the door, picked her up and shoved her into the Chevy. The car had bucket seats with an automatic-transmission console between them, and she lay humped over the seats, in an awkward, broken position. Druze stood straight, checked the lot again, then got in with her, touched her neck. She wasn't breathing. She was gone.

He used a screwdriver on her eyes.


Bekker was Beauty tonight, a little sting of amphetamine, just a taste of acid. His mind was moving, a facile, glittering thing, a mink of an intellect, and it worked through the problems in what seemed like no time at all . . . although time must have passed . . . it was light outside when he came home, and now, it was dark . . . How long . . . ? He went away again.

Cheryl Clark had called him at his office.

She wanted to come back, he thought. Knew his wife was gone now. Was trying to ingratiate herself. Had news: A cop had been coming around to see her. They wanted to know about his love life, his personal habits. She thought he should know, she said.

Maybe he would see her again. She'd grown tiresome after a while, but there'd been a few nights. . . .

His mind was like liquid fire, the taste of the MDMA in his mouth, under his tongue. What? More? He really should be more temperate. . . .

When he came back—came back long enough to know that he would be okay—he'd found the solution to the surveillance. So simple; it had been there the whole time. He had a friend with the authorities, did he not?


The surveillance net picked up Bekker as he left the alley, headed down to Hennepin Avenue and took Hennepin to the interstate. He went to the library, parked and went inside. The net was with him. Looked at a book in the reference section. Headed back to the car. One of the cops in the net looked at the book, a cross-reference directory for St. Paul. He noted the pages: if he'd had time to scan the names, he'd have found Lucas Davenport listed about halfway down the second column. . . .

Across the Mississippi and then south. Nice neighborhood . . . Damn St. Paul addresses, the numbers had nothing to do with the streets. Started at 1 and went however high they needed to go . . .

Davenport's house was not particularly impressive, he thought when he found it, except for the location. One-story rambler, stone and white siding, big front yard. Nice house, but not terrific. Stephanie wouldn't have given it a second look. Lights in the windows.

He rang the doorbell, and a moment later Davenport was there.

"Officer Davenport," Bekker said, nodding, pleased to see Lucas. He had his hands in the pockets of his hip-length leather coat. "You said you would see that I'm not harassed. Why am I followed everywhere?"

Davenport, perplexed, stepped out on the porch. His face was like a chunk of wood, and Bekker stepped back. "What?"

"Why am I being followed? I know they're out there," Bekker said, flipping a hand at the street. "This is not paranoia. I've seen your officers watching me. Young men in college clothes and police shoes . . ."

Davenport's face suddenly tightened, seized by some sort of rictus, Bekker thought. He stepped close and gripped Bekker's coat at the lapels. He lifted and Bekker went up on his toes.

"Put me down . . ." Bekker said. He was strong, but Davenport held him awkwardly close and his arms were bent. He tried to push Davenport away, but the cop held him, shaking, apparently gripped by rage.

"You never come to my house," Davenport rasped, his eyes wide and crazy. "You hear that, motherfucker? The last guy that came to my house, I killed. You come to my house, I'll kill your ass just like I did him."

"I'm, I'm sorry," Bekker stuttered. Davenport was not the cool, rational cop who had walked through Stephanie's bedroom. His eyes were straining open, his head cocked forward on a tense neck, his hands hard as stones.

Davenport shoved Bekker back, releasing him. "Go. Get the fuck out of here."

Bekker staggered. Down the sidewalk, ten feet from the porch, he said, "I just wanted the surveillance pulled, I don't want to be hectored. . . ."

"Call the chief," Lucas said. His voice was cold, brutal. "Just stay the fuck away from my house."

Davenport stepped back inside and shut the door. Bekker stood on the walk for a moment, looking at the door, not quite believing. Davenport had been friendly, he'd understood some things. . . .

Bekker was in his car when his own anger caught him.

Treated like a Russian peasant. Kicked down the stairs. Thrown off. He pounded his palms on the steering wheel. Saw himself striking out, the edge of his hand smashing under Davenport's nose, blood rolling down his dark, bleak face; saw himself kicking, going for the balls . . .

"Fuckin' treat me like that, fuckin' treat me like a . . . a . . . Fuckin' treat me, you can't, you better think about it . . . Fuckin' treat me . . ."

As Bekker drove away from Davenport's house, the net still in place, a teenage boy strolled up to Kelsey Romm's car and peeked inside. Was she fuckin' somebody? What was she . . .

He'd been leaning on a trashcan outside the mall entrance, waiting for something to happen, somebody to show up, when he saw something happen. He didn't know what. There was this guy. . . . He had gotten a videocassette for his birthday, a movie, *Darkman,* his favorite flick. And this guy looked like Darkman, no bandages, but the hat was right. . . . And something happened.

He saw the guy duck inside the car. He was in it for a moment or two; then he got out, went to another car and drove away. It never occurred to the kid to look at the license plate. And he was not the kind of kid who knew his cars. He was just a kid who hung out and watched *Darkman* in the afternoons, after school. . . .

The car with the woman didn't move. When the other car, the Darkman car, was out of sight, the kid considered for a moment, then ambled across the sidewalk, down the long rows of cars. What was she? Was she, like, a hooker, giving blow jobs in the backseat? That'd be something.

He got close, he peeked. . . .

"Aw, Jesus . . . Aw, Jesus . . ." The kid ran toward the mall, his arms milling. Halfway there, he began screaming, "Help . . ."

Lucas, still hot from Bekker's visit, was working on Druid's Pursuit when the watch commander called.

# 23

A thunderstorm was rolling across Minneapolis when Lucas left his house, lightning crackling through the clouds, storm-front winds lashing the elm branches overhead. He went north, up Highway 280, the lights of downtown Minneapolis to the west, barely visible through the advancing rain. The storm caught him just before he turned east, a few drops splatting off the windshield, and then a torrent, a waterfall, hailstones pecking on the roof, small white beads of ice bouncing off the road in his headlights. He turned east on I-694 and the rain slackened, then quit altogether as he outran the storm front.

From the highway, the mall was screened by an intervening block of buildings, but he could see red emergency lights flashing off window glass. The White Bear Avenue exit was jammed. He put the Porsche on the shoulder and worked his way to the front. A Minnesota highway patrolman ran toward him, and Lucas hung his badge case out the window.

"Davenport," the patrolman said, leaning in the window. "Stay behind me and I'll make a hole in this line."

The patrolman jogged along the shoulder, leading the Porsche to a roadblock. The street was a nightmare tangle of shoppers trying to get out of the mall, gawkers trying to drive past the murder scene, and the normal traffic on and off the interstate. The patrolmen had given up trying to control the crush and had settled for getting as many people out of the mall as possible. At the roadblock, the patrolman leading Lucas said something to the others, and they stopped traffic, directed a car out of the way and let Lucas slip through to the parking lot.

"Thanks," Lucas yelled as he went through. "I came through that storm—it's a bad one, with hail. If you got rain gear . . ."

The patrolman nodded and waved him on.

Television vans and reporters' cars were lined up on the perimeter of the lot, a hundred yards from a battered brown Chevy. All four doors on the car were open and emergency lights bathed it in a brilliant showroom illumination. Lucas left his Porsche in a pod of squad cars and walked toward the Chevy.

"Davenport, over here." A cop in a short blue jacket, who'd been talking to another cop in a sweater, called to him, and Lucas walked over.

"John Barber, Maplewood," said the cop in the jacket. He had pale blue eyes and a long lantern jaw. "And this is Howie Berkson. . . . Howie, go on over and tell that TV bunch it'll be another twenty minutes, okay?"

As Berkson walked away, Barber said, "C'mon."

"Any question whether it's the same guy?" Lucas asked.

Barber shrugged. "I guess not. One of your people is running around out here . . . Shearson? He says the technique is the same. Wait'll you see her face."

Lucas went and looked, and turned away, and they started a circle around the car. "Looks like him," he said sourly. "A copycat couldn't get up that much enthusiasm for it. . . ."

"That's what Shearson said. . . ."

"Where is he, by the way?" Lucas asked, looking around the lot.

Barber grinned. "He said it looked like we had it under control. I heard he's looking at shirts over in the mall."

"Asshole," Lucas said.

"That's the feeling we got. By the way, we found a kid who saw the guy."

"What?" Lucas stopped short. "Saw him?"

"Don't get your hopes up," Barber said. "He was a hundred yards away and wasn't paying too much attention. Saw the guy's car, too, but doesn't have any idea about make or model or even color . . . Didn't get anything. Says the killer looked like a guy from some comic-book movie."

"Then how do you know he saw . . ."

"Because he saw the woman walking out toward her car. He wasn't paying any attention to her, just hanging out, but a minute later, he saw a man by her car, it looked like he was helping her inside. Then, a couple of minutes later, he really doesn't know how long it was, he sees the guy walking away. And the woman never backs the car out. So the kid thinks—he told us before his mother got here—he thinks this woman is a hooker maybe, doing blow jobs in her car, or maybe she's dealing dope. That's the way his head works. And he kind of casually strolls by to take a look. . . ."

"So he saw the guy for sure."

"Seems like it," Barber said.

"Let me talk to him."


The kid was a slender, ragged teenager with skateboard pads on his knees, fingerless gloves, dirty blond shoulder-length hair and a complexion that was going bad. He wore a long-billed hat with the bill turned down and to the side, covering one ear. His mother hovered over him, throwing severe looks alternately at the kid and the police.

"You got a minute?" Lucas asked the kid, when Barber walked him up.

"I guess so, they won't let me go nowhere," the kid answered. He brushed his hair out of his eyes, the same gesture Cassie used, half defense, half necessity.

"We would like to go home sometime," his mother said, spotting Lucas as an authority. "It's not like . . ."

"This is pretty important," Lucas said mildly. To the kid, he said, "Why don't we take a walk down the mall. . . ."

"Can I come?" asked the kid's mother.

"Sure," Lucas said reluctantly. "But let your boy tell the story, okay? Any help you give him . . . isn't help."

"Okay." Her head bobbed: she understood that.

"So what does this guy feel like?" Lucas asked, as they started down the length of the mall.

The kid's forehead wrinkled. "Feel like?"

"What kind of vibrations did he give off? The Maplewood cop, Barber, says you couldn't see him too clearly, but you must've gotten some vibrations. Barber said you thought he looked like some comic-book guy. . . ."

"Not a comic-book guy, a comic-book *movie* guy," the kid said. "Did you ever see the movie *Darkman?*"

"No, I haven't."

"You oughta. It's a great movie. . . ."

"His favorite," his mother clucked. "These kids . . ."

Lucas put his index finger on his lips and she shut up, her face reddening.

"See, there's this guy Darkman, who gets his face all fuck . . . uh, messed up by these hoods," the kid said, glancing at his mother. "He tries to put his face back together with this skin that he makes—"

"Whoa, whoa," Lucas said. "There was something wrong with his face? The guy in the parking lot?"

"I couldn't see that much, he had this hat. But he moved like Darkman. . . . You gotta see the movie," the kid said with wide-eyed seriousness. "Darkman moves like . . . I don't know. You gotta see it. This guy moved like that. Like, I couldn't see if there was anything wrong with his face, but he *moved* like there was. With his face kind of always turned away."

"Did you see him jump the woman?"

"No. I saw her walking out, then I was looking at something else, then I saw him. Then he got in her car, and then he got out, and then he moved away like Darkman. Kind of glided. With that hat."

"Glided?"

"Yeah. You know, like, most guys just walk. This guy kind of glided. Like Darkman. You gotta see the movie."

"All right. Anything else? Anything? Did you see him talk to anybody, did he do a little dance, did he do anything . . . ?"

"No, not that I saw. I just saw him walking. . . . Oh yeah, he was juggling his keys, that's all."

"Juggling his keys?"

"Yeah. Toss them up, then go like this . . ." The kid mimed a man throwing his keys up, made a quick little double step, snagged them with his off hand.

"Jesus," Lucas said. "Just once?"

"Naw, he did it a couple, three times."

They'd stopped walking outside a cutlery store. In the window, a two-foot-long model of a Swiss Army knife continuously and silently folded and unfolded. "What do you do for a living, kid?" Lucas asked. "Still in school?"

"Yeah."

"You got a good eye," Lucas said. "You might make a cop someday."

The kid looked away. "Naw, I couldn't do that," he said. His mother prodded him, but he went on. "Cops gotta fuck with people. I couldn't do that for a living."

Lucas left the kid and his anxious mother with a Maplewood cop and used a pay phone to call Cassie. She was supposed to be off, but there was no answer at her apartment. He tried the theater, but no one answered the phone.

"God damn it." He needed her. He went back outside and found Shearson and Barber standing at the mall entrance. Shearson had a sack under his arm that might have contained a necktie. Rain swept across the lot beyond them, and the floodlights around the death car had been turned off.

"Find everything you needed?" Lucas asked Shearson, tapping the sack with a finger.

"Hey, I'm out here on my own time," Shearson said. He was wearing a dark cashmere knee-length coat over a pearl-gray suit, with a white shirt, a blue tie with tiny crowns on it, and black loafers. His breath smelled of Juicy Fruit.

"You talk to the kid?" Barber asked.

"Yeah. I'd like to get a stenographer over to his place tomorrow, take a statement," Lucas said. "He told me the guy was juggling his keys, and doing a little dance step when he caught them. I'd like to get him on record for that."

"Give us a call with questions . . ." said Barber.

"You get something?" Shearson asked, eyebrows up.

"I don't know," Lucas said. He trusted Shearson about as far as he could spit a rat. "What's happening with this shrink you've been looking at?"

"He's the Loverboy, all right," Shearson said. "He's hiding something. There aren't a lot of loose ends to pull on. I think we oughta just sit back for a couple days. Until something new comes up. But Daniel's got me covering him like whip on cream."

"Okay . . . Well, I gotta get one last look at this car," Lucas said.

Barber went with him, the two of them hurrying through the rain with a kind of broken-field lope, shoulders hunched, as though they could dodge the raindrops.

"Your buddy's got a great wardrobe," Barber said, tongue in cheek.

"And he'd lose an IQ contest to a fuckin' stump," Lucas said.

The body was being moved out of the car, wrapped in sheets. Another Maplewood cop came over and said, "Nothing in the car that looks like a weapon. Nothing but paper—ice cream bar wrappers, candy wrappers, Ding Dong wrappers. The woman lived on junk."

"All right," said Lucas. To Barber, he said, "Can you keep me up-to-date?"

"I'll fax you everything we got in the morning, first thing. We don't need this clown killing people out here."


Lucas hadn't expected much from the scene itself. If a killer had no relationship with the victim, no apparent motive, no rational method of operation, the only things left to find were witnesses or traceable physical evidence. Because a serial killer could pick the time and place, he could pick a situation that minimized his exposure to witnesses. And evidence left behind—semen, in sex-related cases, or blood or skin samples—didn't help until after the killer was caught.

This attack had been almost perfect. Almost . . .

The storm was dying as Lucas headed west. There was another thunderstorm cell far down to the south, but from I-35W he could see distant jetliner landing lights, going into Minneapolis–St. Paul International from the south, so he knew the storm must be well out downstate.

By the time he got to Cassie's apartment, the rain had diminished to a barely perceptible drizzle. He went into the entry and rang the bell for her apartment, but there was no answer. He continued up the street to the theater, but the windows there were dark.

Damn. He needed her.

And he found her. She was sitting on his porch steps, a gym bag between her feet.

"How long have you been here?" he asked from the car, as she strolled out to the driveway. "How'd you get here?"

"About twenty minutes—I came on the bus. I would have broken in, but the woman next door keeps watching me out her window," Cassie said, grinning. She tipped her head toward a lighted window in the next house. An elderly woman peeked out a lighted window in a side door, and Lucas waved at her. She waved back and disappeared.

"She keeps an eye out," Lucas said. "Besides, you'd need a sledge to get through the doors. . . . Let me get the car inside."

Cassie waited behind the car as he put it in the garage next to his battered Ford four-by-four.

"Sweatsuit and shoes," she said, holding up the gym bag as he dropped the garage door. "I thought we could run along the river."

"In the rain?"

"You could see it going over on the TV radar," she said.

"Okay," he said. He took her elbow in his hand and kissed her on the mouth. "Did you hear?"

"Hear what?" she asked, puzzled by his somber tone.

"We had another killing. Out in Maplewood."

"Oh, no," she said, pressing her fingertips to her lips. "Is it a theater person?"

Lucas shook his head. "Not as far as we know. It's a woman who worked at the mall. They're checking, but she doesn't seem like she'd be a playgoing type. Certainly didn't look like an actress."

"Jesus . . . Like he just picked her out at random?"

"Eenie meenie minie moe," Lucas said. "And I've got something to ask you . . . later."

"What's the mystery?"

"I can't tell you. I want your brain to be fresh. Let's run."

Cassie set the pace along the river until Lucas, puffing, slowed her down. "Take it easy," he said. "Remember, I'm *old*."

"Six years older than me," she said. "At your age, you ought to be able to run a marathon under four, just to be in fair shape."

"Bullshit," he grunted. "If you can run a marathon under six, you're in great shape, for a normal human being, anyway."

"See, you're not hurtin'," she said. "You can still talk." But she slowed the pace and they stopped at a scenic overlook, walked in circles for a minute, then took off again, this time running away from the river.

"I have to stop at a video store," Lucas said. "I want to pick up a movie."

"A movie?"

"A kid at the mall saw the killer. Said he looked like Darkman, in the movie. You see it?"

"No. Heard about it. Supposed to be pretty bad."

"So we watch it for a few minutes."

When they got back to the house, Lucas leaned against the garage door, gasping for breath, dangling the plastic bag with the videocassette in one hand. "I gotta do this more often," he said. "How far do you think we ran?"

"Three miles, maybe. Enough to crack a sweat."

"I hate to tell you, but I cracked a sweat about two hundred yards out," he said.

"Better take a shower," she said in a low voice. She was standing next to him, and she slipped a hand under his sweatshirt and lightly drew her nails from his nipples to his navel. Lucas shivered and moved against her.

"We've got serious business here," he said, patting her on the butt with the plastic bag.

"Hey—what difference does it make if we look at it now or an hour from now?"

He seemed to think about it, stroking his chin. "Hmm. An argument with a certain persuasive force . . ."

"So let's take the shower. . . ."


Lucas, still damp from a second shower, wearing jeans and a T-shirt, popped the cassette into his VCR and turned on the television.

"What are we looking for?" she asked.

"I want to see if this Darkman character brings anybody to mind. Don't study him—just let it percolate."

The movie unwound, Cassie sitting on the floor in front of the TV. "I see why the kid called it a comic-book movie," she said a few minutes into it, when Darkman was blown through his laboratory window by an enormous explosion. "It's all bullshit."

"Doesn't bring anybody to mind?"

"Not yet." She stood up. "Is that peach ice cream still in the freezer?"

"Sure."

She sat with the ice cream, sucking on the spoon, watching intently. During a scene in which Darkman did a macabre dance, an oil funnel on his head, she frowned and shook her head.

"What?" Lucas asked.

"Run that again."

He stopped the movie and reran the dance scene.

"Don't tell me yet," he said.

"Okay. Keep going."

He watched her as the movie continued and she got more and more into it. At the end, she said, "Junk, but some parts were strong."

"So what'd you see?"

She studied him for a moment and then said, "You know, I'm your basic 'Off the Pigs' sort of person."

"Yeah, yeah . . ."

"Me and the people I hang out with."

"Uh-huh."

"And I really hate the idea of police creeping around and monitoring people and all that . . ."

"Come on, come on . . ."

She looked at the blank TV screen, wrinkled her forehead and said, "Darkman reminds me of a guy at the theater. I mean, he's completely different. He's built different, he looks different, but he sort of has . . . the aura of Darkman. He moves like Darkman, sometimes."

"Okay. Don't move."

He hurried back to the spare bedroom, looked around and spotted the Xerox of Redon's *Cyclops* still lying on the bed.

"Close your eyes," he told her, when he got back. "I'm going to hold a paper in front of your face. I want you to look at it for a second, no more, then close your eyes again. You're trying for a momentary impression. . . . Open your eyes when I say 'Open.' "

"Okay . . ."

He held the Xerox in front of her face and said, "Open."

Her eyes opened but didn't close again, and after a little more than a second, he whipped the paper behind his back.

"Jesus," she whispered. "I feel like a fuckin' Judas."

"Who is it?"

"It could be Carlo Druze. You saw him the first day you were at the theater. He was the guy practicing onstage."

"I *knew* it," Lucas said. The thrill of it ran down his spine, and he shuddered. "He's the goddamned juggler, right? The guy you never see without makeup. I knew I'd seen him."

"I feel like . . ."

"Fuck that," he barked. "You saw your friend Elizabeth. You want to look at this woman up in Maplewood? We think he used a screwdriver on her. . . ."

"No, no . . ."

"Are there any good photos of him at the theater? Publicity stuff, anything?"

Cassie nodded, but tentatively. "He's a very scarred man. He doesn't like photo sessions. Sometimes he uses cosmetics to cover up . . . but he's most comfortable in stage makeup. That's how you usually see him in the publicity shots. Full makeup. I don't know if there'd be any raw photos. . . ."

"Can we get in?"

She hesitated. "I could get us inside the building, but the office is locked. And letting you go through the files . . . I don't know."

"C'mon, Cassie," Lucas said, a little less harshly. He reached out and touched her. "You can keep the plans for the fuckin' revolution. I just need a photo of the guy. . . ."

"All right," she said. Then, following him back to the bedroom, she added, "I feel like a shit for saying this, but I keep thinking of more things. . . . Carlo didn't like Elizabeth and she didn't like him."

Lucas, pulling on a shirt, said, "Was she planning to fire him?"

Cassie shrugged. "Who knows? The feeling was, she didn't like him because of his looks. As an actor, he's not bad."

Lucas stopped and looked at her: "Could Druze do this? Is he capable of it? Killing people?"

She shivered. "Of all the people I know . . . yeah, I'd say he's the most likely. But not with passion. I don't understand the eyes. If he wanted to kill somebody, he'd just do it, and walk away."

"Huh. Interesting," said Lucas. He put on a sport jacket, then dug through the bottom drawer of his bureau, found a leather wallet and stuck it in his jacket pocket. "Let's go look."

On the way across town, Lucas said, "When I saw him that time at the theater, I asked you where he was when Armistead was killed. You told me he'd been around all afternoon."

"Yeah . . ." Her forehead wrinkled. "He was around. But people come and go all the time. Run across the street for a cinnamon roll, down Cedar for a cheeseburger. Nobody notices. The theater's only ten minutes from Elizabeth's house."

"But your impression was that he'd been around. . . ."

"Yeah. I really can't remember, though. . . . A cop interviewed him the day after, maybe he'd know."

"But if he killed Armistead, how does the phony phone call fit?" Lucas asked. "We figured the killer was calling to find out if she was at work. . . ."

"Maybe . . . this sounds stupid, but maybe somebody was just trying to get a free ticket?"

"That's usually what fucks up an investigation, trying to find a reason for everything," Lucas admitted. "But the call was odd. I still think . . . I don't know." They parked in front of a rock bar and looked across the street at the theater's dark windows.

"I don't like this," Cassie said nervously, looking up and down the street. "People come in and out of here all the time. And if anybody found out, I'd lose my job. For sure."

"I doubt it," Lucas said, smiling at her. She didn't like his smile. There was an edge of cruelty to it. "Things can be arranged."

"Like what?"

He looked past her at the front of the theater. "You'd be surprised how many building, zoning and health violations you can find in a place like that. I doubt an old theater could survive, if somebody really wanted to tote them all up."

"Blackmail," she said.

"Law enforcement."

"Sure," she said, with distaste. "I don't think I could live with that."

She got out of the car and led the way across the street. The theater was dark, but as she opened the door with her key, she called, "Hello? Anybody here?"

No answer. "This way," she said in a hushed voice. They crossed the lobby in the weak light from the street and started down a hallway. Cassie patted the left wall, found a light switch and turned on a single hall light. Lucas followed her to a red wooden door. She tried the doorknob and found it locked. "Damn it. I was hoping it'd be open," she said.

"Let me look," Lucas said. He took a small metal flashlight from his jacket pocket, knelt at the lock, shined the light into the crack between the door and the jamb, turned the knob as far as he could, then turned it back.

"Can you open it?"

"Yeah." He took the wallet, a trifold, from his pocket. He opened it, laid it flat on the floor and slipped out a thin metal blade.

"What're you doing?"

"Magic," he said. He put the blade in the crack between the door and the jamb, and rotated the blade downward; the bolt slipped back. "Shazam."

The office was small, untidy, with lime-green walls, a metal desk with a phone, four chairs, a bulletin board and file cabinets. A faint smell of mildew and old cigarette smoke hung in the air. As Lucas put his lock set back into his pocket, Cassie stepped to one of the file cabinets and pulled open a drawer. Hundreds of eight-by-ten photos were jammed into manila folders. She took out two, a bulging pair, and laid them on the desk.

"He'll be in these," she said. She started going through them, tapping Druze's face wherever she found it. "Here . . . here . . . here he is again."

"He's good at avoiding the camera," Lucas said. He took several of the photos and held them under the light. Druze was always in stage paint or makeup. Sometimes his face was obscured by a hat; at other times by a hand gesture.

"Here's the best one so far," Cassie said, flipping a photo out to Lucas.

*Troll,* he thought. Druze had a round head, too large for his body. And although he was wearing makeup, there were obvious changes in his skin texture, as if his face had been quilted together. His nose was shortened, ruined.

"That's the best," Cassie said, finishing with the pictures. "But, ah . . ." She glanced at another file cabinet.

"What?"

"If we can get this other cabinet open, we could look through the personnel files. There may be a straight headshot. . . . The cabinet's always locked."

"Let's look," Lucas said. He glanced at the lock on the cabinet, took a pick out of the wallet and had the lock open in less than a second.

"That's fast," Cassie said, impressed.

"For office file cabinets, you get more of a master key than a pick," Lucas said. "I'm not that good with the picks."

"Where do you get them?" she asked.

"I know a guy," Lucas said. He pulled open the top drawer and found a file labeled "Druze." Inside was a block of what once had been eight wallet-sized photos, headshots, straight on, no makeup. Two of them had been cut away with scissors. "Passport shots. And he *does* look like the cyclops, kind of," Lucas said. He went to the office desk, found a pair of scissors in the top drawer, cut out one of the photos and showed it to Cassie.

"Uh-huh." She glanced at it, then went back to the file she was holding. "What's that?"

She looked up, a piece of notebook paper in her hand, a sad smile on her face. "It's *my* file. There's a note from Elizabeth. It says my work has to be evaluated in case financial circumstances worsen."

"What does that . . . ?"

"She was going to fire me," Cassie said. A tear trickled down her cheek. "Fuckin' theater people, man . . ."

Lucas used the pick to lock the cabinet. The office door locked from the inside, then simply pulled shut. On the way out, they turned off the lights.

Cassie had taken Armistead's note, and when they were back in the car again, she reread it under the dome light. "I can't believe it," she said. "I can't believe she'd do this."

"Well, she's gone—things have changed," Lucas said. "I've seen you act, and you're good. . . ."

"But she was supposed to be my friend," Cassie said, wadding up the note. "We talked together. We were always talking about what we wanted to do."

"Your friends . . . are sometimes different people than you think they are. Most of your friends are halfway made-up. They're what you'd like them to be."

"Do you mind if I sit here and cry for a couple of minutes?"

"C'mon," said Lucas, "that'd really bum me out." He put an arm around her shoulder and kissed her on the forehead, and she grabbed his jacket lapel and buried her face on his shoulder. "C'mon, Cassie . . ."

He stroked her hair and she cried.

# 24

Daniel, looking from the photograph to Lucas, was stunned. "We got him? Like that?"

"Maybe," Lucas said. "He fits what we know about the killer. He looks right, he acts right, and my friend says he's something of a sociopath. He had reason to kill Armistead. And Bekker gave me those tickets, which suggested that his wife had something going at the theater. . . ."

"We've had two guys full-time on that and as far as they can tell, nobody ever saw her there—or remembers it, anyway," Daniel said. He looked at the photo again. "But this guy *looks* like the cyclops."

"And we've got those American Express charge slips. . . ."

"Yeah, yeah." Daniel scratched his head, still looking at the photo of Druze. "I think we need to put a team on him. . . ."

"We'll do that, definitely. Since we pulled the team on Bekker . . ."

"The problem is, if Druze saw that story, he might have thought we were watching *him*."

A thin smile creased Daniel's ruddy face. "So for the past two days he's been slinking around with his back to the wall, seeing spies."

"I was thinking . . ."

"Yeah?"

"You could accuse Channel Eight of damaging the investigation, saying they tipped an unnamed suspect to the surveillance and the police have been forced to pull the surveillance after the suspect confronted a departmental officer . . . that being me."

"Yeah. Hmm. It'd back off the TVs a little, too," Daniel said. The grin flicked across his face again. "I'll have Lester do it. He'll enjoy it."

"And if there's a political kickback, you can always blame it on him," Lucas said, grinning himself.

"Did I say that?" Daniel asked innocently, his hand over his heart. "About this guy, Druze . . . maybe we could get some video on him, walking at a distance, show it to this kid out in Maplewood."

"Yeah, good," Lucas said.

"We oughta do that today," Daniel said. He walked around his desk, staring at the photo as if it were a talisman.

"I still think Bekker's in here somewhere," Lucas said. "If Druze and Bekker are talking, maybe we can come up with some phone records."

Daniel nodded. "We can do that, too. All right. Make a list for Anderson, tell him to do it," Daniel directed. "Now, how're you planning to get this picture to Stephanie Bekker's lover?"

Lucas shrugged. "I haven't got that figured. . . ."

"Try this," Daniel said. He sat behind his desk, opened his humidor, stared into it and snapped it shut. "I've been thinking about it. Channel Two still goes off the air sometime after midnight. We ask them to go back on at, say, three o'clock, with the photo. Just for a minute. Nobody'd see it, unless they were accidentally clicking around channels. And the lover would be safe. He could get it on any TV in the metro area, cable or no. And if he's got a VCR, he could record it."

"Great. Have you got any clout with Two?" Lucas asked. Channel Two was the educational station.

"Yeah. Shouldn't be a problem."

Lucas nodded. "Sounds perfect. I'll have an ad in the *StarTribune* tomorrow morning. When he calls me, I'll try to talk him in. If he won't come, I'll tell him when to watch."

"Until then, we treat Druze as though he was the one. And let's get with the other people on this, so everybody knows what we're doing. . . ." He leaned over his desk and pressed the intercom button. "Linda, get Sloan in here, and

Anderson, and the point guys on the Bekker case, everybody who's around. Half an hour . . ."

"We've really got nothing on him yet, it's all speculation," Lucas reminded him.

"We stay with him," Daniel said sharply. "I want to know every step he fuckin' takes. I got a feeling about this guy, Lucas. I get strong vibrations."

"I'm thinking—" Lucas said. He was thinking of cracking Druze's apartment: an informal survey without a warrant.

Daniel stopped him in midsentence. "Don't say it. But, uh, it would be nice to know some things . . ."

Lucas nodded, bent over Daniel's desk, opened the humidor and peered inside. Three cigars. He snapped it shut.

"What?" Daniel asked.

"I always wondered what you really had in there. . . ."


The investigation file on Druze was thin. Nothing on NCIC—Anderson had run him against the federal computers as soon as Daniel called the meeting. Druze had been interviewed by Detective Shawn Draper after the Armistead murder, and the interview had been summarized in a half-dozen tight paragraphs. Subject said he was in theater at the time of the murder. Cited several incidents that placed him there. Brief cross-checks with other actors confirmed those incidents. . . .

Daniel, Anderson, Lester, Sloan, Del, Draper, Shearson and three or four other detectives sat in Daniel's office, plotting out the surveillance, while Lucas sat in a corner reading the file. Draper, a large, sleepy man in a knit suit, slumped on a folding chair behind Anderson.

"You interviewed him, Shawn," Lucas said during a break in the discussion. "Did you think, in person, that he looked at all like the cyclops picture? Was there anything . . . ?"

Draper scratched an ear. "Naw . . . I wouldn't say so. I mean . . . he looked fucked up, but he wasn't. . . . Naw."

"Was he solid for an alibi on Armistead?"

"When the chief called about the meeting, I went back and looked at my notes. He really had the evening nailed down, after about seven or seven-thirty. Earlier than that, it was sketchy."

"We think she was killed, what, about seven?" Lucas asked.

"Give or take," Sloan said.

"So he could have done her, then come back and tried to make himself obvious around the place. . . ."

Anderson jumped into the exchange. "Yeah, but he didn't try to cover himself that much for the actual time of the murder. If I'd been doing it, I would have done something to establish myself *before* I went over. Then I would have gone over, done it and come back as fast as I could, maybe with a bunch of doughnuts or something, and established myself again," he said.

"Well, he didn't," Draper said shortly. "He was solid later, but not earlier."

"Hmph," Lucas grunted.

"What?" asked Daniel.

"I'm still trying to fit that phone call in. . . ."


The *StarTribune* classified-advertising manager said he would see to the ad himself. *Not responsible for the debts of Lucille K. Smith, signed Lucas Smith*. It would appear the next morning.

"This is critical," Lucas said. "Keep your mouth shut, but this is the most important ad you'll run all year."

"It'll be there. . . ."


Lucas called Cassie from the lobby.

"What're you doing here? Oh Gawd, the apartment is a wreck. . . ." Cassie buzzed him through the door. She met him, flushed, at her apartment door.

"Looks nice," Lucas said as he stepped inside. The apartment was small, a kitchen nook opening directly off the living room, a short hall with three doors leading off it, a bathroom, a closet and the single bedroom.

"That's because I just stuffed four days' clothes in a closet, two days' dishes in the dishwasher, and did about a month's worth of cleaning." She laughed, stood on her tiptoes and kissed him, took in the briefcase he was carrying. "What're you doing? You look like Mr. Businessman. I was about to leave for the theater."

"I was over at the U and thought I'd stop by," he said. "You have to leave right away?"

She nodded and produced a sleepy-eyed pout. "Pretty soon. Since I read Elizabeth's note, I thought I'd be on time for work."

"Ah . . . well."

"We could take a quick shower . . ." she offered.

"Nah. If we started a shower . . . And I've got to get back to work, anyway. See you after?"

"Sure. We'll be done before eleven."

"I'll take you someplace expensive."

"Shameless sweet-talker, you." She caught his ear and pulled his head down and kissed him again.

"See you. . . ."


*       *       *

He was in.

Druze's apartment was three floors below, and Lucas hadn't wanted to risk raking the lobby locks. That Cassie lived in the same building was not quite pure luck: several other Lost River players lived there, drawn by its proximity to the theater and the low rent. Lucas took the stairs down, emerging a few doors away from Druze's apartment. The hall was empty. Lucas stepped back into the stairwell, took a handset from the briefcase and called the surveillance team leader. At his last check, Druze was at the theater.

"Where is he?"

"Still inside." The team leader didn't know where Lucas was.

"The instant he moves . . ."

"Right."

The theater was less than a block from the apartment. If Druze had to run home for something, Lucas wanted adequate warning. He called Dispatch and gave the dispatcher Druze's telephone number.

"Patch me through . . . let it ring as long as necessary. The guy may be outside mowing the lawn," he said.

"Sure . . ." Jesus, he thought. He had just made the whole dispatch department an accessory to a felony. He put the handset under his arm, so he could hear it if the dispatcher called back, and stepped into the hall. Sixteen doors, spaced alternately down the hall. Plasterboard walls, aging rug. The power rake would clatter, but there was no help for it. He walked down to Druze's apartment and heard the phone ringing. Five times, ten. Nobody. He tried the door, just in case—it was locked—and took the rake from the briefcase. The rake looked like an electric drill, but was smaller, thinner. A prong stuck out of the tip; Lucas slipped it into the lock and pulled the trigger.

The rake began to clatter, a sound like a ball bearing dropped into a garbage disposal. The clatter seemed to go on forever, but a second or two after it started, Lucas turned the lock and the door popped open.

"Hello? Anybody home?" The phone was still ringing when he stepped inside. "Hello?"

The apartment was neat, but only because there was almost nothing in it. A stack of scripts and a few books on acting were piled into a small built-in bookcase, along with a tape player and a few cassettes. A couch was centered on a television, the remote left carelessly on the floor next to the couch. In his years in the police department, Lucas had been in dozens of cheap boarding-houses and transient apartments, places where single men lived alone. The rooms often had an air of meticulous neatness about them, as though the inhabitants had nothing better to do than arrange their ashtrays, their radios, their hot plates, their cans of Carnation evaporated milk. Druze's apartment had that air, a lack of idiosyncrasy so startling it became an idiosyncrasy of its own. . . .

The telephone was still ringing. Lucas got on the handset and said, "Betty? About that call—forget it."

"Okay, Lucas." A few seconds later, the ringing stopped.

The bedroom first. Lucas didn't know exactly what he was looking for, but if he saw it . . .

He went rapidly through the closets, patting the pockets of the sport coats and pants, checked the detritus on the dresser top, pulled the dresser drawers. Nothing. The kitchen went even quicker. Druze had little of the usual kitchen equipment, no bowls, no canisters, none of the usual hiding places. He checked the refrigerator: nothing but a head of lettuce, a bottle of A.1. sauce, a chunk of hamburger wrapped in plastic, an open box of Arm & Hammer baking soda and a red-and-white can of Carnation. Always a can of Carnation. Nothing in the ice cube trays. Nothing in the bottom drawer of the stove . . .

Druze did have a nice blunt weapon, a sharpening steel. Lucas took it out of the kitchen drawer, swung it, inspected it. No sign of hair or blood—but the steel was exceptionally clean, as though it had been washed recently. He took a piece of modeling clay from the briefcase, held it flat in his hand, and hit it once, sharply, with the steel. The steel stuck to the clay when he pulled it out, but the impression was good enough. He put the steel back into the kitchen drawer, and the clay, wrapped in wax paper, into his briefcase.

The living room was next. Nothing under the couch but dust. Nothing but pages in the books. In a cupboard under the built-in bookcase, he found a file cabinet, unlocked. Bills, employment records, car insurance receipts, tax forms for six years. Check the front closet. . . .

"Damn." A black ski jacket with teal insets. Just like ten thousand other jackets, but still: the lover had seen a jacket like this. Lucas took it out of the closet, slipped it on, got a Polaroid camera from his briefcase, put it on the bookcase shelf, aimed it, set the self-timer and shot himself wearing the jacket—two views, front and back.

When he'd checked the photos, he rehung the jacket. He'd been in the apartment for fifteen minutes. Long enough. He went to the door, looked around one last time. Down the stairs. Out.


"Lucas?" Daniel calling back.

"Yeah." He was sitting in the Porsche, looking at the Polaroids. "Did you get in touch with Channel Two?"

"We're all set," Daniel said. "If he calls you tomorrow night, we can go on the air an hour later. Four o'clock . . ."

"Can I get another picture on?"

"Of what?"

"Of a guy in a ski jacket . . ."

* * *

Later:

Daniel paced around his office, excited, cranked. Lucas and Del sat in visitors' chairs, Sloan leaned against the wall, Anderson stood with his hands in his pockets.

"I've got a real feeling," Daniel insisted. Lucas had cut his own face out of the ski jacket photos before he gave them to Daniel. Daniel and Anderson had looked at them, and agreed that it could be the jacket Stephanie Bekker's lover had described. "Almost certainly is, with what we know," Anderson said. "It's too much of a coincidence. Maybe we ought to pick him up and sweat him."

"We've still got to get him with Bekker," Lucas protested.

"What we've got to do is *turn* him against Bekker, if they're really working together," Daniel said. "If we sweat him a little, we could do that."

"We don't have much to deal with," Sloan said. "With the politics of it, with four people dead, the goddamn media would have our heads if we dealt him down to get Bekker."

"Let me deal with the politics," Daniel said. He picked up one of the Polaroids and looked at it again, then up at Sloan. "We could do this: We charge him with first-degree murder, but deal down to second degree with concurrent sentences if he gives us Bekker. Then we tell the press that even though he's getting a second, we're asking the judge to depart upward on the sentence, so it's almost as good as a first. . . ."

Sloan shrugged: "If you think you can sell it."

"I'd make us look like fuckin' geniuses," Daniel said.

"It'd still be nice if we could get something solid," Lucas pressed. "Can we cover his phones, at least? Maybe watch him for a few days before we move? See if we can get him talking to Bekker, or meeting him?"

"We couldn't get a warrant for the phones, not yet, there's just not enough," Daniel said. "If Stephanie Bekker's friend comes through, if he confirms this . . . then we get the warrant. And we'll want to put a microphone in his apartment."

"So everything depends on Loverboy," Lucas said. "He's got to call back tomorrow night."

"Right. Until then, we stay on Druze like holy on the pope," Daniel said, running his hands through his thinning hair. "Jesus, what a break. What a fuckin' break . . ."

"If it's true," Anderson said after a moment.

Bekker stood in the bay window, looking past the cut-glass diamonds in the center, out at the dark street, and decided: he had to move. Tomorrow. The cigarette case rode low in his pocket and he opened it, and chose. Nothing much, just a touch of the power. He put a tab of PCP between his teeth and sucked on it for a moment, then put it back in the case. The acrid chemicals bit into his tongue, but he hardly noticed anymore.

The drug helped him concentrate, took him out of his body, left his mind alone to work. Clarified the necessary moves. First the woman, then Druze. Get Druze to come with a last-minute call. The best time would be around five o'clock: Druze always ate at his apartment before walking over to the theater, and the woman would most likely be around at the same time.

No luxuries here, Doctor. No studies. Just do it and get out.

He paced, his legs seemingly in another country, working it out in his mind. If everything went right, it'd be so simple. . . . But he ought to check the gun. Go to Wisconsin, fire a couple of shots. He hadn't fired it in years, not since a trip to New Mexico. He'd bought it originally in Texas, a casual purchase from a cowboy in El Paso, a drunk who needed money. Not much of a gun, a .38 special, but good enough.

As for the shot . . . he'd have to risk it. If she had a radio . . . Maybe four o'clock would be better. They should be at home then, and the people in the apartments adjoining the woman's would be less likely to be there.

He paced, working it out, working himself up, generating a heat, the light dose of PCP flipping him in and out of otherwhen.

At midnight, pressed by the needs of Beauty, he threw down two tabs of MDMA. The drug roared through him, hammered down the PCP, and he began to dance, to flap around the living room, on the deep carpets, and he went away. . . .

When he returned, breathing hard, he found himself half stripped. What now? He was confused. What? The idea came. Of course. If something went wrong tomorrow—unlikely, but possible; he was confident without being stupid about it—he would have missed an opportunity. Excited now, his hands trembling, he pulled his clothes back on, got his jacket and hurried out to the car. The hospital was only ten minutes away. . . .

He was stuck in the stairwell for five minutes.

He'd gone to his office first, done another MDMA for the creative sparkle and insight it brought, and a methamphetamine to sharpen the edge of his perceptions. Then he went to the locker room and changed into a scrub suit. The clean cotton felt cool and crisp against his skin, touching but not clinging to his chest, the insides of his arms, his thighs, like freshly starched sheets, the pleasure of its touch magnified by the ecstasy. . . .

He left then, alternately hurrying and restraining himself. He couldn't wait. He crept up the stairs, not quite chortling, but feeling himself bursting with the joy of it. He was careful. If he was seen, it wouldn't be a disaster. But if he was not, it would be better.

At the top of the stairs, he opened the door just a crack, enough so that he could see the nurses' station fifty feet down the hall. He held on to the door handle: if anyone came through unexpectedly, he could react as though he were about to pull the door open. . . .

The nurse spent five minutes on the telephone, standing up, laughing, while he watched her through the crack and cursed her: the drugs were working in his blood, were demanding that he go to Sybil. He held back but wasn't sure how long he could last. . . .

There. The nurse, still smiling to herself, hung up the phone, sat down and pivoted in her chair, facing away from Bekker. He opened the door and quickly stepped through, across the hall, to where her line of vision was cut off. He moved away silently, the surgical moccasins muffling his footsteps, down the hall to Sybil's room.

Her television peered down from the ceiling; it was tuned to the word processor. He frowned. She wasn't supposed to be able to use it. He stepped next to the bed and bent over in the dim light. The processor console sat on a table to the left side of her bed. He reached out, rolled her head: she was wearing the switch. Looking up at the screen, he used the keyboard's arrow keys to move a cursor to the *Select* option, then pressed *Enter*. A series of options came up, including a dozen files. Nine of the files were named. Three were not: they had only numbers.

He was moving the cursor to select the first of the files when he realized that she was awake. Her eyes were dark and terrified.

"It's time," he whispered. The drugs roared and he moved closer to her bedside, peering down into her eyes. She closed them.

"Open your eyes," he said. She would not.

"Open your eyes. . . ." Her eyes remained closed.

"Open your . . . Sybil, I really need to know what you see, there at the end; I need to see your reactions. I need your eyes open, Sybil. . . ." He rattled a key on the keyboard. "I'm looking at your files, Sybil. . . ."

Her eyes opened, quickly, almost involuntarily. "Ah," he said, "so there is a reason I should look. . . ."

Her eyes were flashing frantically from Bekker to the screen. He moved the cursor to the first numbered file and pushed *Enter*. There were two letters on the screen: *MB*.

"Ah. That wouldn't stand for 'Michael Bekker,' would it?" he asked. He erased the letters, moved to the next file. *KLD*. He erased them. "A little message here? Do you really think they would've understood? Of course, with a few more days, you might have been able to squeeze out some more. . . ."

Bekker went to the final file. *ME*. "Got the 'me' done, anyway," he said. He backspaced over the letters, and they were gone.

"Well," he said, turning back to her. "Can I convince you to keep your eyes open?"

She closed them.

"Time," he said. "And this time, we're going all the way. Really, truly, Sybil. All the way . . ."

He stepped to the doorway and glanced down the hall. Nobody. Sybil's eyes followed him across the room and back, dark, wet. Bekker, his eyebrows arched, placed his palm over Sybil's mouth and gently pinched her nose with the thumb and index finger of the same hand. She closed her eyes. With the index and middle fingers of the other hand, he lifted her eyelids. She stared blankly, unmoving, for fifteen seconds. Then her eyes skewed wildly, from side to side, looking for help. Her chest began to tremble and then her eyes stopped their wild careen, fixed beyond him, and began to shine.

"What is it?" Bekker whispered. "Do you see? Are you seeing? What? What?"

She couldn't tell; and at the end, her eyes, the shine still on them, rolled up, the pupils gone. . . .

*"Hello?"*

Panicked, he let go of her nose, backed away from the bed, the hair rising on the back of his neck. He was trembling violently, unable to control himself. She was so close. So close.

*"Hello-o-o?"*

He staggered to the door, barely able to breathe, peeked out. He could see a corner of the nurses' station, but nobody there. Then a woman's voice, two rooms down the hall toward the nurses' station. The nurse: "Did you call me, Mrs. Lamey?"

Bekker chanced it, crossed the hall in three long strides and went out through the internal door. He let the door close of its own weight, let it slide shut with a barely audible hiss, then started down the stairs two at a time. Just as the door shut, he heard the nurse's voice again.

*"Hello?"*

She must have seen or heard something, or sensed it. Bekker fled down the stairs, the moccasins muffling his footfalls. He opened the door on his floor, stepped through and from far above heard another, more distant *"Hello?"*

Ten seconds later he was in his office, the door locked, the lights out. Breathing hard, heart beating wildly. Safe. A Xanax would help. He popped one, two, sat down in the dark. He would wait awhile, get his clothes. The MDMA bit him again, and he went away. . . .

Lucas went to pick Cassie up at the theater, and waited while she scrubbed her face, watching again for Druze. And again, Druze was somewhere else.

"How's the play going?" Lucas asked.

"Pretty good. We're actually making some money, which is the important thing. It's kind of funny, has its message. That's a good combination in Minneapolis."

"Sugar pill," Lucas said.

"Something like that."

They ate a midnight snack at a French café in downtown Minneapolis, then went for a walk, looking in the windows of art galleries and trendoid restaurants. Two of them featured raised floors, and the younger burghers of Minneapolis peered down at them through the windows, their fat legs tucked under tablecloths almost at eye level.

"I kept looking at Carlo, I couldn't help it," Cassie said. "I'm afraid he's going to catch me and think I'm coming on to him or something."

"Be careful around him," Lucas said. "If he comes to your apartment, tell him you're in the shower, still wet, or something. Or that you've got me in there. . . . Keep him out. Keep the door shut. Don't be alone with him."

She shivered. "No way. Though . . . there's a funny thing about this. Before I saw those pictures, I might have said, 'Yeah, Carlo could kill somebody.' Now, it's hard to believe that somebody you know could be doing this. Especially the business about the eyes. Carlo doesn't seem out of control; I mean, he could be crazy, but you feel like it would be a real cold crazy. Not a hot crazy. I could see Carlo strangling somebody and never showing any expression: I just can't see him in some kind of frenzy. . . ."

"Could he fake it? Could he be cold enough to do the eyes without feeling it?"

She thought for a moment, then said, "I don't know. Maybe." She shivered again. "But I'd hate to think *anybody* could be that cold. And why would he, anyway?"

"I don't know," Lucas said. "We don't know what's going on, yet."

At Lucas' house, in the bedroom, Cassie lay on top of him, a compact mass of muscle. She reached down and grabbed an inch of skin at his waist. "No love handles. Pretty impressive for a guy as ancient as yourself."

Lucas grunted. "I'm in awful shape. I sat on my ass all winter."

"Need a workout?"

"Like what?"

"No sex until you pin me for a three-count?"

"Aw, c'mon . . ."

"You c'mon, wimpy . . ."

They wrestled, and after a time, but not too long, she was pinned.


Beauty arrived home at about the same time. The night's work had been both frightening and exhilarating. A disappointment in some ways, true, but then again: he could go back. He still had Sybil to do. As Lucas and Cassie made love, Bekker ate two more MDMAs and danced to *Carmina Burana,* bouncing around the Oriental carpet until he began to bleed. . . .

# 25

Lucas heard the first newspaper hit the front porch. That'd be the *Pioneer Press*. The *StarTribune* should be ten minutes later. He dozed, half listening, drifting from dream to linear thought and back to dream, dream editing reality, Jennifer and the baby, Cassie, other faces, other times. He inserted the *thwap* of the *StarTribune;* but the dream logic wouldn't buy it, and he woke up, yawned and stumbled out to get the paper. At five-thirty it was still dark, but he could see the heavy gray clouds groaning overhead and smell the rain heavy in the air.

*Not responsible . . . Lucas Smith.*

He glanced at the comics and went back to bed, falling facedown across the sheets. Cassie's perfume lingered on them, although she'd insisted on going back to her apartment.

"We're getting close on the play. I shouldn't fool around late and get up late. I have to work," she'd said as she dressed.

The perfume was comforting, a sign of society. He slept on her side, dreaming again, until the telephone rang. Startled, he thought, *Loverboy,* and rose through his dreams and snatched at the telephone, almost knocking the lamp off the bedstand.

"Davenport."

"Lucas, this is Del . . ."

"Yeah, what's happening?" He sat up, put his feet on the floor. Cold.

"I'm, uh, over at Cheryl's. We were talking last night, and she told me that Bekker has been creeping around her ward. He's been seeing a woman patient almost every day—and the thing is, this woman can't communicate."

"Not at all?"

"Not a thing. Her mind's still okay, but she's got Lou Gehrig's disease and she's, like, totally paralyzed. Cheryl says she's got maybe a week or two to live, no more. Cheryl can't figure Bekker—he's not exactly the social type. Anyway, I thought it might be something."

"Hmph. I got a guy over there. I'll give him a call," Lucas said. "Are you on Druze today?"

"Yeah, I'm about to go over."

"I may see you."

Lucas hung up, yawned, glanced at the clock. After ten, already: he'd slept more than four hours after looking at the paper. He dropped back on the pillow, but his mind was working.

He got up, called Merriam, was told the doctor wasn't in yet, left a message and went off to shave. Merriam called back just as he was about to leave the house.

"There's a woman there, I'd like you to check," he said. "Her name is Sybil. . . ."


Lucas stopped at Anderson's office first.

"Where's Druze?"

"Still bagged out at his apartment."

At his own office, the answering machine showed two messages. *Loverboy?* He punched the message button as he took off his jacket.

*"Lucas, this is Sergeant Barlow. Stop and see me when you come in, please."* God damn it, he had no time for this. If he could slip out without encountering Barlow . . . The machine clicked and started again.

*"Lieutenant Davenport, this is Larry Merriam. You better come over here right away. I'll leave a note at the desk to send you up. Pediatric Oncology. I'll be out in the ward. Talk to the duty nurse and she'll chase me down."*

Merriam sounded worried, Lucas decided. He put his jacket back on and was locking the office door when Barlow came down the steps at the end of the hall and saw him.

"Hey, Lieutenant Davenport, I need to talk to you," he called.

"Could I stop up later? I'm kind of on the run. . . ."

Barlow kept coming. "Look, we gotta get this done," he said, his mustache bristling.

Lucas shook him off: "I'm up to my ass. I'll get back to you as soon as I can."

"God damn it, Davenport, this is serious shit." Barlow moved so that he was between Lucas and the door.

"I'll talk to you," Lucas said, irritated, letting it show. They stared at each other for a second; then Lucas stepped around him. "But I can't now. Talk to Daniel if you don't believe me."

Barlow hadn't been good on the street. He was a control freak and didn't deal well with ambiguities—and the street was one large ambiguity. He'd done fine with Internal Affairs, though.

IA usually went to work on a cop only if there was a blatantly public foul-up, and that was okay with most of the cops in the department, outside of a few hothead brother-cop freaks. Better IA, the feeling went, than some outside board full of blacks and Indians and who knows what, which seemed to be the alternative.

The department had barely managed to fight off a city council proposal that would have formed a review board with real teeth. The study commission on that—the commission Stephanie Bekker had served on—had gone a bit too far, though, had given the impression that it wanted to get on the cops a little too much. That hadn't gone down well with voters scared by crime. . . .

So a gross screw-up in public would get you an IA investigation. A cop could find himself a target also if he got too deep into drugs, or started stealing too much. Screwing off and getting your partner hurt, that would do it too.

But IA didn't worry much if a pimp got slapped around in a fistfight. Especially not if he'd pulled a knife. Half of the cops on the force would've shot him and let it go at that, and they would have been cleared by the board. And if the fight had taken place during an arrest on a warrant charging a violent crime, and if the victim of that crime was scarred for life and still around to testify, to be looked at . . .

Where was Barlow coming from? Lucas shook his head. It didn't compute. Anderson was going in the door and Lucas was going out, when Lucas hooked him by the arm.

"You think . . . the guys in the department would like to see me fall? Get taken off by IA?" Lucas asked.

"Are you nuts?" Anderson asked. "What's happening with IA?"

"They're on me for the fight with that kid, the pimp. I can't figure out where it's coming from."

"I'll ask around," Anderson said. "But when the guys decide somebody ought to fall, it's no big secret. You know that. And nobody's talking about you."

"So where's it coming from?" Lucas asked.


Barlow stayed in the back of Lucas' mind all the way to the university campus. He dumped the car in a no-parking zone outside the hospital, stuck a police ID card in the window and went inside. Pediatric Oncology was on the sixth floor. A nurse took him down through a warren of small rooms, past a larger room with kids in terry-cloth robes, sitting in wheelchairs and watching television, into another set of hospital rooms. They found Merriam sitting on a bed, talking to a young girl.

"Ah, Lieutenant Davenport," he said. He looked at the girl in the bed. "Lisa, this is Lieutenant Davenport. He's a police officer with the Minneapolis Police Department."

"What's he doing here?" she asked, cutting straight to the heart of the matter. The girl was completely bald and had a very pale face and unnaturally rosy lips. The chemotherapy aside, Lucas thought, touched with a cold finger of fear, she looked a lot like his daughter would in ten years.

"He's a friend of mine, stopping to chat," Merriam said. "I've got to go for a while, but I'll be back before they start setting up the procedure."

"Okay," she said.

Outside, in the hall, Lucas said, "I couldn't do this." And, "Do you have kids?"

"Four," Merriam said. "I don't think about it."

"So what happened?" Lucas asked. "You sounded a little tense."

"The woman you called about. I went down to see her. She has amyotrophic lateral sclerosis . . ."

"Lou Gehrig's disease . . ."

"Right. She's almost completely incommunicado. Her brain works fine, but she can't move anything but her eyes. She'll be dead in a week or two. And Bekker is trying to kill her."

"What?" Lucas grabbed Merriam by the arm.

"This absolutely defeats me: a goddamn doctor," Merriam said, pulling away. "But you have to see for yourself. Come along."

Lucas trailed behind him as they went down a flight of stairs.

"I went down to find her this morning and stopped to ask at the nursing station," Merriam said over his shoulder. He pushed through a door at the bottom of the stairs. "The duty nurse had worked overnight, and was working an extra half-shift because somebody was sick. Anyway, I mentioned that I was there to see Sybil and asked if Dr. Bekker had been around. The nurse said— you'll have to take this with a grain of salt—she said she didn't see him but she'd *felt* him. Late last night. She said it occurred to her that dirty old Dr. Death was around, because she shivered, and she always shivers when she sees him."

"She calls him 'Dr. Death'?"

" 'Dirty old Dr. Death,' " Merriam said. "Not very flattering, is it? So then I went down to talk to Sybil. She's going by inches, but the nurses say she's got an inch or two left. . . ."

Merriam led him past the nurses' station and down the hall, past an exit door and three or four more rooms, then glanced inside a room and turned. Sybil lay flat on her back, unmoving except for her eyes. They went to Merriam, then to Lucas, and stayed with him. They were dark liquid pools, pleading.

"Sybil can't talk, but she can communicate," Merriam said simply. "Sybil, this is Lieutenant Davenport of the Minneapolis Police Department. If you understand, say yes."

Her eyes moved up and down, a nod, and stayed with Merriam.

"And a no," Merriam prompted.

They moved from side to side.

"Has Dr. Bekker been coming here?" Merriam asked.

*Yes.*

"Are you afraid of him?"

*Yes.*

"Are you afraid for your life?"

*Yes.*

"Have you tried to communicate with your eye switch?"

*Yes.*

"Did Dr. Bekker interfere?"

*Yes.*

"Is Dr. Bekker trying to kill you?" Lucas asked.

Her eyes shifted to him and said, *Yes.* Stopped, and then again, *Yes,* frantically.

"Jesus Christ," said Lucas. He glanced at Merriam. "Has he been interested in your eyes? Said anything about . . ."

Her eyes were flashing up and down again. *Yes.*

"Jesus," he said again. He leaned across the bed toward the woman. "You hang on. We'll bring in a camera and an expert interrogator, and we're going to get you on videotape. We're going to slam this asshole in prison for so long he'll forget what the sun looks like. Okay?"

*Yes.*

"And excuse the 'asshole,' " Lucas said. "My language sometimes gets away from me."

*No,* her eyes said, sliding from side to side.

"No?"

"I think she means, Don't apologize, 'cause he is an asshole," Merriam said from beside the bed. "That right, Sybil?"

She was like a piece of modeling clay, unmoving, still, except for the liquid eyes:

*Yes,* she said. *Yes.*


"I'll have somebody here in a half-hour," Lucas said, when they were outside her door.

"You'll have to talk to her husband, just to make sure the legalities are right," Merriam said. "I'll see the director about this."

"Tell him the chief is going to call. And I'll have one of our lawyers talk to her husband. Can they get all the information from here at your desk?"

"Sure. Anything you need."

Lucas started away, then stopped and turned.

"The kids you think he killed. Did he go after their eyes? I mean, was there anything unusual about their eyes?"

"No, no. I was there for the postmortems, their eyes weren't involved."

"Hmph." Lucas started away again, stopped again.

"Don't let anyone close to her."

"Don't worry. Nobody gets in there," Merriam said.


Lucas called Daniel from a pay phone and explained.

"Sonofabitch," Daniel crowed. "Then we got him."

"I don't know," Lucas said. "But we got something. The lawyers will have to figure out if it'll hold up in court. And it doesn't tie him to these other things."

"But we're moving," Daniel insisted. "I'll send a tape unit over there right now, and Sloan to talk to her."

"Can we put a guy on her door?"

"No problem. Around the clock. You think we should stick a surveillance team on him again?"

Lucas considered, then said, "No. He'll be hyperaware of anything like that. We've got Druze going. . . . Let's see what happens."

"All right. What are you doing?"

"I got a couple more ideas. . . ."


A male duck cruised a female across the college pond, as Elle Kruger and Lucas climbed the sidewalk toward the main buildings. Spring, but a cold wind was blowing. Well off to the west, over Minneapolis, they could see darker clouds, and the blurring underedges that said it was raining.

"The eye fixation could have been created by some kind of traumatic incident, but that seems somewhat unlikely," Elle said. "It's more likely that he's always had a feeling of being watched, and this is his reaction. . . ."

"Then why weren't the kids cut up?"

"Lucas, you're missing the obvious," the nun said. "No good for a gamer."

"All right, tell me the obvious, Sister Mary Joseph, ma'am," he said.

"Maybe he didn't kill the children."

Lucas shook his head. "Thought of that. But Merriam gets these vibrations, and it fits with what he's doing with this Sybil, and the interest in the eyes fits with these other killings. Could be a coincidence, but I doubt it."

"As I said, it is *possible* that he developed the fixation between killings."

"But not likely."

"No."

They walked with their heads down, climbing the hill, and Lucas said, "Would it make any difference when he did the eyes? I mean, could he do them later?"

Elle stopped and looked up at him. "Well. I don't know. This woman who died at the mall—her eyes weren't done until after death."

"Neither were George's, the guy they dug up in Wisconsin. He probably wasn't done for twenty-four hours. . . ."

"That's your answer, then. He does it after death, but apparently it doesn't have to be right away. What are you thinking?"

"Just that if a kid dies and there's going to be a postmortem, you might not want to do the eyes right away. Especially if you had another shot, later."

"Like at the funeral home?"

"Sure. Anytime after the postmortem. He's a pathologist, he's right there with the bodies. He could do the eyes there, right in the hospital, or at the funeral home during a visitation. Who watches a dead body?"

"Do they do anything with the eyes at funeral homes? Would anybody notice?" Elle was doubtful.

"I don't know," Lucas said. "But I can find out."

"What time is it?" she asked suddenly. "I've got a four-o'clock class."

Lucas looked at his watch. "It's just four now."

# 26

Bekker checked the time as he got out of the car: just four o'clock, right on schedule.

The apartment building was a block away. He had the clipboard under his arm, and the flower box. The gun weighed heavily in one pocket; the tape was much lighter in the other. He walked with his head down against the drizzle.

The rain had arrived just in time, and was a blessing, Bekker thought. The rain suit made perfect sense, and the hood would cover his entire head, with the exception of a narrow band from his eyebrows to his lips. He walked heavily: the PCP always did that, stiffened him up. But it made him strong, too. Focused him. He thought about it, then took the brass cigarette case from his pocket and popped another pill, just to be sure.

He had taken elaborate measures to make sure he hadn't been followed, driving through the looping streets of the lake district, waiting, doubling back, taking alleys. If he was being watched, they were doing it by satellite.

Walt's Appliance faced Druze's apartment building from across the street. The sales level was a rectangular space, four times as deep as it was wide, with wooden floors that creaked when a customer walked among the ranks of white kitchen appliances. The washers, dryers, refrigerators and stoves carried brand names that sounded familiar at first, less familiar after some thought. Walt kept the lights off, unless a customer was on the floor; the interior was usually illuminated only by the weak light from the street, which filtered through the dusty windows with the fading advertising signs.

Like his merchandise, Walt was nondescript. Too heavy. Not so much soft-spoken as noncommittal. A few strands of fading brown hair were combed sideways over a balding head, and plastic-framed glasses perched on the end of a button nose slowly withering with age, like an overripe raspberry. Walt had been a beatnik in the fifties, kept a copy of *Howl* in his desk drawer. Read it more now, rather than less.

He was happy to cooperate with the police, Walt was: genuinely happy. He'd never used the loft anyway, except to store leftover samples of carpet and rolls of cracking vinyl, the remnants of a brief fling with the flooring business. He provided an inflatable mattress, an office chair, a collapsible TV tray and a stack of old *Playboy*s. The watchers brought binoculars, a Kowa spotting scope, a video camera with a long lens, and a cellular telephone. They were happy, warm, out of the rain. Pizza could be delivered, and there was a bakery just down the street.

Another team, not so lucky, watched the back entrance of the apartment building from a car.

The watcher at Walt's sat in the chair, facing the street. The TV tray was at his side, on it a Coke in a paper cup. The spotting scope was on a tripod in front of him. The other cop lay on the mattress, reading a *Playboy*. The watcher saw Bekker lurching through the rain, looked at him through the scope, dismissed him, never even mentioned him to the cop on the mattress. He couldn't see Bekker's face because of the hat, but he could see the oblong lavender box under his arm, the kind used to deliver roses all over the metro area. You recognized them even if you'd never gotten flowers, or given them.


Bekker checked the mailboxes, found her apartment number, used Druze's key to open the lobby door and took the elevator to the sixth floor. Her apartment was the last one on the hall. On impulse, thinking of the gun in his pocket, he stopped one door down the hall and knocked quietly. No response. He tried again. Nobody home.

Good. He slipped a hand in his breast pocket, found the tab of PCP, popped it under his tongue. The taste bit into him. He was ready. He'd primed himself. His mind stood aside, ferocious, and waited for his body to work.

His hand—nothing to do with his mind anymore, his mind was on its own pedestal—knocked on the door and lifted the box so it could be seen from the peephole. There *were* flowers in the box. If there was somebody with her, he could leave them, walk away. Druze? He'd still have to do Druze, but the package wouldn't be nearly as nice.

Bekker stood outside Cassie's door, waiting for an answer.


Four o'clock. Lucas left St. Anne's, heading west toward the rain. Maybe meet Cassie, he thought. Maybe time to catch her before the play. But yesterday she'd almost kicked him out. And then there were the questions about the handling of dead bodies. . . . He knew a funeral director, down on the south side of town. He could ask about the eyes of the children, although the idea disturbed him.

Old Catholic background, he thought. Killing people wasn't so bad, but you didn't want to mess with the dead. He grinned to himself, stopped at a traffic signal. Left, he could take the Ford bridge into south Minneapolis, go to the funeral home. Right, he could cut I-94 and be at Cassie's in ten minutes.

The lights at right angles turned yellow, and Lucas took his foot off the brake, ready to let out the clutch. Still undecided. Left or right?

"Flowers?" She was smiling, her face completely unaware as she took the box, showing no hint of apprehension. Bekker's body glanced up and down the hall, then drew the pistol and pointed it at her forehead.

"Inside," he snapped, as her eyes widened. "Keep your mouth shut, or I swear to Christ I'll blow your fuckin' brains out," Bekker's body said, his mind applauding. Bekker's body shoved her back with the left hand, holding the pistol with the right. She clutched the box in both hands, her mouth opening, and as she stepped back, he thought for an instant that she was about to scream. "Shut up," he snarled. Saliva bubbled at his lips. "Shut the fuck up."

He was inside then, pulling the door closed behind himself, the gun no more than a foot from her forehead. "Back up, sit on the couch."

She dropped the box and he noticed the muscles in her arms. He wouldn't want to fight her. She backed up until her legs touched the couch, and she half stumbled and sat down. "Don't hurt me," she stuttered. Her face was pale as paper.

"I won't, if you pay attention," Bekker's body said. His mind still floated, directing traffic. "I just need a place to hide for an hour or so."

"You're not with Carlo?" Cassie asked, shrinking back into the couch.

The question caught him, but the drug covered for him. His body was disassociated now, worked by his mind like a puppet on strings, his hands numb. "Who?"

"You're not with Carlo?"

"I'm not with anybody, I'm just trying to hide until the cops get off the street," Bekker said. His body was stiff as marble, betraying nothing, but his mind was working feverishly: *They knew about Carlo.* Christ, were they watching him? They must be. Bekker gestured with the tip of the barrel. "Lie down on the floor. On your stomach. Put your hands behind you."

"Don't hurt me," she said again. She slipped off the couch onto her knees, her eyes large. She was getting old, Bekker's mind thought: she had tiny wrinkles around her eyes and on her forehead.

"I'm not going to hurt you," his body said woodenly. He'd thought about this, what to say. He wanted her reassured, he wanted her to go along. "I'm going to tape your hands behind you. If I were going to hurt you, if I were going to rape you, I wouldn't do that. . . . I wouldn't put your hands under you. . . ."

She wanted to trust him. She turned, looking over her shoulder, and lay down. "Please . . ."

"The gun will be pointing at your head," he said. "I tried your neighbor first, but she wasn't home—so I know I could get away with a shot, if I had to. . . . I don't want to risk it, but I will if you try to fight. Do you understand what I'm saying?"

"Yes."

"Then put your face down on the floor, straight down, and cross your hands. I'll be taping with one hand. The gun's still pointing at you."

She did it: the marvelous power of the gun. She rolled, her hands behind her, and he awkwardly turned a wrap of the two-inch plastic packaging tape around her wrists, then another, then a third.

"Don't move," he said. He didn't say it viciously, but his tongue was thick, slurring the words. That was more frightening than if he'd been screaming at her. . . . He did her ankles, more quickly now that her hands weren't a threat, but still staying clear of a possible kick. When they were tight, he slipped the gun in his coat pocket and went back to her hands, added more tape, tighter now.

"You're hurting me," she said.

He grunted. No point in talking anymore. He had her. He walked around the couch, put one knee across her back to hold her flat, and slapped a palm-sized strip of tape across her mouth. She fought it, but he held her by the hair and wrapped more tape, tangling her hair across her face, plastering it to the sides of her head.

"That should do it," his body said, more to his mind than to her. The bottom part of her face had been encapsulated, leaving her nose and eyes uncovered. He put the tape in his pocket, grabbed her under the arms and dragged her to the bedroom. When she started struggling, he backhanded her across the nose, hard. "Don't do that."

In the bedroom he laid her facedown on the bed and taped her feet to the endboard. He wrapped another length around her neck, once, twice, and led it to the headboard.

"I'm going in the front room to watch television, see if the cops have figured me out," he said. "I want you quiet as a mouse; you're not hurt yet, but you will be if you cause me any trouble."

He closed the bedroom door and turned on the television. Now the tricky part.

Cassie tried to fold her body against the tape. If she could get enough pressure, she might pull free. . . . If she could get up on her feet, even hobble, there were scissors in the bureau, and she might be able to cut the tape. And if her hands were free, she could push the bureau in front of the door and hold him off—throw something through the window, if necessary, scream for help. . . .

But when she tried to fold herself, the tape around her neck threatened to strangle her. She pulled as long as she dared, then released the tension. The tape on her mouth kept her from gasping for the needed air and she strained to get it through her nose, her vision going red for a moment. No good.

She lay still for a moment, calculating. Nobody coming over? No. If Davenport dropped in, like he had the day before . . . Fat chance. She'd have to do it on her own. She tried rolling, rocking back and forth. She was at it for a minute, two minutes, got over on her back, then another half-turn. Was the tape ripping? She couldn't see. She pulled her arm in close to her body and tried to roll again. . . .

Bekker left Cassie's apartment door unlocked and padded down the hall to the stairs. On the way, he wrapped his right hand in a handkerchief. Druze was three floors down and the cops knew something. Bekker didn't know how they knew, but they did, and they'd be watching.

A camera in the corridor? Unlikely. If the cops were secretly watching Druze, they wouldn't do anything that might call attention to themselves. His mind equivocated: the woman had seen him, so he'd have to do her. But he hadn't exposed himself to any watching cops yet, and he might be about to do that. His mind worked at it, and finally told his body to go ahead. To risk it. There was no other way, if the cops were this close to Druze. He opened the door and peeked out: the third-floor corridor was empty. He pulled up his rain hood, hurried to Druze's door and, about to knock, reconsidered. If the apartment was bugged . . .

He scratched on the door. Heard movement inside. Scratched again. A moment later, the door opened a crack and Druze peered out. Bekker put a finger over his lips for silence and gestured for Druze to step into the hallway. Druze, frowning, followed, looking up and down the hall. Bekker, finger back on his lips, pointed to the door of the stairwell.

"I can't explain it all right now, but we got a problem," he whispered when they were on the stairs. "I talked to Davenport and he said they had a suspect but no evidence. I asked how they were going to catch him, and he said, 'We've got to catch him in the act.' And the way he said it, it sounded like a pun he was making to himself. . . ."

"Aw, shit," Druze said, worried. "What happened to your hand?"

"She bit me. Anyway, I thought I'd come over here, early enough to catch the girl, like we'd talked about. . . ."

"We hadn't talked about it for sure . . ." Druze said.

"Something had to be done and I couldn't risk calling you on the phone," Bekker said. "You may be bugged."

"We don't even know it's me."

"We do now. I went up to her apartment, stuck a gun in her face and taped her up. I was planning to wait until you were at the theater, whack her on the head—you know, do it so they couldn't separate that injury from the injuries in a fall—and then pitch her right out the window. You'd have an alibi, and nobody knows about me."

"What happened?"

"The first thing she said was, 'You're not with Carlo?' " The honesty was there in his voice.

"Aw, God damn it," Druze said, running his fingers through his hair. "And you think the apartment may be bugged?"

"I don't know. But if this woman goes out the window while you're at the theater, that's one more piece of evidence on your side. . . . They'll know you're not involved, anyway. . . ."

There was something wrong with the reasoning, but Druze, shocked, couldn't figure it. And Bekker said, "Come on up to her apartment. You scare her. We need to find out what the cops know. . . ."

"God, I kind of like her," Druze said.

"She doesn't like you," Bekker answered harshly. "She thinks you're the killer."

Bekker led the way quickly up the stairs, feeling the gun bang against his legs. All clear. In the apartment, he gestured at the bedroom and Druze walked back. Cassie was still facedown on the bed, but she had been struggling against the tape, which had been twisted between her legs and the bed.

"Turn her over, so she can see you," Bekker said, moving to Druze's right side. Druze stooped and grabbed Cassie's near shoulder and hip, to roll her over.

His mind was clear as ice, his body moving with the precision of an industrial robot. Bekker pulled the pistol from his pocket—his mind watched it in slow motion, guiding each small movement of the drawing gesture—with the handkerchief-wrapped hand.

In a single move, Bekker's body put the muzzle an inch from Druze's temple. Druze sensed the movement, started to turn his head, his mouth opening.

Bekker pulled the trigger.

Dropped the gun.

Recoiled from the blast . . .

The blast, confined in the small bedroom, was terrific, stunning. Bekker jerked back as Cassie arched up, twisting frantically at the tape.

Druze simply collapsed, the gun disappearing beneath him.

Cassie's sweater was speckled with Druze's blood and small amorphous shreds of bone and brain tissue.

Bekker's robot-controlled body touched Druze's. Dead. No question of it.

The drugs sang in his blood and he went away. He sighed, and came back: Jesus. He'd been gone. How long? He glanced at his watch. Four-twenty. Cassie was staring at him from the bed, her hands working frantically behind her back. He hadn't been gone long, a few minutes at most. He listened. Anybody coming? Not so far. No knocks, no sound of running feet . . .

He looked at Druze on the floor. He'd have to leave him like that, there might be some kind of blood pattern from the shot or something. He couldn't do the eyes, of course. He worried about that, but there was nothing to be done. If Druze was going to take the blame . . .

Cassie.

She'd stopped fighting the tape, but her back was arched, her head turning, trying to see him. He had to hurry: he still had to stop at Druze's apartment, to leave the photos. He started into the kitchen, when a door slammed down the hall, and he stopped. Listened.

Was that a movement? Out in the hall. He strained, listening. The hall was carpeted, would muffle steps. He waited a minute, then a few more seconds.

He couldn't wait longer. He still had to visit Druze's apartment. He patted his chest, confirming that the pictures were there. He'd cut the eyes out. . . .

He'd have to be careful. If the cops had bugged Druze's apartment and realized he was gone, but hadn't left the building, they might be on the way. Maybe he shouldn't try it. If he were caught in the apartment . . . that didn't bear thinking about.

Bekker, the PCP pounding in his blood, went into the kitchen and got a bread knife, the sharpest he could find.

And there again . . . Movement? Somebody in the hall. He froze, listened. . . . No. He had to move.

He didn't do it well, and he didn't do it quickly, but he did it: he cut Cassie's throat from ear to ear, and sat with her, holding her green eyes open with his fingers, as she died.

# 27

Lucas spent ten minutes at the funeral home with a cheerful, round-faced mortician who wanted to talk golf.

"Damn, Lucas, I already been out twice," he said. He had a putter and was tapping orange balls across a plush carpet toward a coffee cup lying on its side. "It was a little muddy, but what the hell. In another two weeks, it'll be every morning. . . ."

"I need to know about the eyes. . . ."

"So don't talk to me about golf," the mortician complained. He putted the last ball, and it bounced off the rim of the cup. "Nobody wants to talk golf. You know how hard it is to talk golf when you're in the funeral business?"

"I can guess," Lucas said dryly.

"So what exactly do you want to know?" the mortician asked, propping the putter against an easy chair.

They were in a small apartment above the funeral home, where the night man stayed. A lot of people die at night, the mortician said, and if you're not there, they might call somebody else. To the average, unknowledgeable member of the general public, one funeral home was as good as another.

"What about the eyes? Do you leave them in or take them out, or what?"

"Why'd we take them out?" the cheerful mortician asked, relishing the conversation. Lucas was uncomfortable, and he could see it.

"I don't know, I just . . . I don't know. So you leave them in?"

"Sure."

"Do you sew the eyelids shut or glue them shut or anything?"

"No, no, once they're shut, they stay that way."

"How about the viewings? Is there always somebody around?"

"Well, there's always somebody *around,* but not necessarily *right there.* We go by judgment. If we see a street person going into the viewing room, we'd go with him, of course—we don't want to get any rings stolen, or whatever. But if the guy looks straight, if he's a member of the family, then we pretty much let him go. We might check every couple of minutes, but a lot of people, when they're saying good-bye, don't like funeral-home people standing around staring at them. They feel like they're being rushed, you know, like when a salesman stands right next to you in a department store. But it's judgment. One time this whole family warned us about a particular guy, one of the grandfathers. The deceased had this gold plate, probably worth a couple hundred, and this old guy was a thief. So we hung on him. He was kneeling there praying, and he kept looking at us and then praying some more. . . . He must've prayed for half an hour. The family members said that was the longest prayer of his life, by about twenty-nine minutes."

"But theoretically, if somebody wanted to get in and touch a body, or look at its eyes . . . he could do it. If you didn't have some warning."

The funeral home man shrugged. "No theory about it—sure he could. No problem. But what can you do to a dead man in two minutes?"

Lucas kept a handset stashed under the seat, and Del caught him halfway back into the loop.

"Something's happened with Druze," Del said. "He's gone. The surveillance guys swear there was no way he got out of the building, but he doesn't answer his phone and he's late for rehearsal."

"What do you think? Check his apartment?"

"I don't know. I thought we'd wait a while longer. . . . We've been calling every two or three minutes, so it's not like he's on the can."

"Keep watching. I'll come on up."

He didn't think of her, not right away. The traffic was heavy on Minnehaha Avenue headed north and he was stuck for three blocks behind a dump truck that resisted all of his attempts to pass. Cursing, he finally got around it, and got the finger from a scowling, long-haired truck driver. He hit three red lights in a row, and then she popped up in his mind. Same building. A chill ran through him, and he picked up the handset and called through to Del.

"I have a friend in that building. She's an actress with the same theater Druze is at," he said. "Would you call her?"

"Sure . . ."

Lucas could see the apartments along I-94, six blocks from the theater, when Del called back. "No answer."

"Shit." Lucas glanced at his watch. She should be at the theater. "Could you call the theater, ask for her?"

He was on Riverside, hurrying now, weaving through traffic. He jumped a light, scared a drunk and a student, saw the apartment building ahead.

"Lucas, we called, and she hasn't shown up."

"Ah, Jesus, listen, I gotta check on her. We've been talking about the case. . . ."

"I'll meet you out in front. I've talked to the manager a couple of times."


Del was walking across Riverside when Lucas arrived. Lucas dumped the car and met him on the sidewalk.

"Anything?"

"No. I called the manager, she should be . . . There she is."

The manager was holding the lobby door, and Del introduced Lucas. "This is not official," Lucas said. "She's a personal friend of mine, she's had some serious problems, and she hasn't shown up at work. We're worried."

"Okay. Since you're the police."

They rode up to the sixth floor in silence, listening to the elevator rattle against the sides of the shaft, watching the numbers click on the counter. There was nobody in the corridor outside Cassie's apartment. Lucas knocked on her door. Nothing. Knocked again.

"Open it," he said to the manager, stepping back. She fitted her key to the lock and pushed the door open. Del shoved past Lucas. An odor filled the small front room. . . .

"You stay right fuckin' here, Lucas," Del shouted. He grabbed him by the collar and pulled him out of the doorway, and held the woman back with the other hand. "You stay right fuckin' here. . . ."

Del headed for the bedroom. Lucas pushed past the bewildered woman, right behind him.

*Cassie.*

Her face was turned away. He *knew,* but he thought *Maybe she's* . . . But the blood was all over the bed, and when he stumbled up to it, and saw her eyes . . . and the huge red gash under her chin, cutting through layers of tape . . . and Druze on the floor beside her, blood everywhere . . .

Somebody moaned, a long, horrible, low-pitched sound, and he realized that it was coming from his own throat, and he reached out and touched her. . . .

"Cassie . . ." He screamed it, and Del pivoted, grabbed him by the jacket and pushed him away like a linebacker working a blocking sled. Del himself screamed, "No, no, no . . ."

The manager, hands clenched in front of her, looked through the bedroom door and then staggered backward, still looking, her mouth hanging open. She ran to the doorway and began retching, and screaming, and retching again, and the stink of vomit overlay the smell of the butchery inside the bedroom. . . .

Lucas strained against his friend, and Del said, "Stay the fuck out, Lucas, stay the fuck out, we need to process, Lucas she's dead, Lucas she's dead. . . ." He pushed Lucas into a chair and picked up the phone.

"We got another one. We need everything you got, apartment six-forty-two. We got two of them, yeah, it's Druze. . . ."

He looked at Lucas, who was back on his feet, ready to go after him. But Lucas walked away from the bedroom and did something that frightened Del more than any effort to look at Cassie: he stood staring at a wall from a distance of no more than a foot, expressionless, unmoving, his eyes open.

"Lucas?" No answer. "Davenport, for Christ's sakes . . ."


"You want to go to the hospital?" Sloan asked.

"What for?" Del had pulled him off the wall, stuffed him into the elevator, guided him to the lobby and held him there.

"Get some dope."

"No."

"You're totally fucked, man. You can't be like this," Sloan said. He was driving the Porsche, while Lucas slumped beside him in the passenger seat.

"Just get me home," Lucas said. The storm was back in his head, the storm he'd feared. Cassie's face. The things he could have done, might have done, that she might have done. Going around, thousands of options, millions of intricate possibilities, all leading to life or to death . . . Sybil's face popped into his head.

"We saved the life of a woman who's gonna die in a week . . ." he moaned.

"But we maybe got Bekker, the lawyers are looking at the tapes right now."

"Fuck me," Lucas said, dropping his chin on his chest. He had to cry, but he couldn't.

And then he said, "I went to a funeral home. If I'd come here . . ."

And then he said, "Every fuckin' woman I see gets hurt. I'm a goddamned curse on their heads. . . ."

And then he said, "I could've saved her. . . ."

"I gotta make a call," Sloan said suddenly, taking the car into a convenience-store parking lot. "Just take a minute."

Sloan called Elle Kruger, looking back over his shoulder at Lucas in the passenger seat of the Porsche. All he could see was the top of Lucas' head. The nun's phone was answered by a woman at a switchboard; Sloan explained that he was calling on a police emergency. The woman said she'd try to find Elle, and began switching. A moment later, she came back on to say that the nun was at dinner, and a friend would get her. She told Sloan to hold on.

"Lucas?" Elle asked when she picked up the phone.

"No, this is his friend Sloan. Lucas has a problem. . . ."

When Sloan returned to the car, Lucas' eyes were closed, and he was breathing slowly, as though he were sleeping. "You okay?" Sloan asked.

"That fuckin' Loverboy. If he'd come in, he could've looked at the picture of Druze the minute I found it, and we could've busted him. But we had to go through this newspaper-ad bullshit. . . ."

"Let it go," Sloan said. "Nothing we can do about it now."


Elle was waiting at Lucas' house with another nun and a small black car.

"How are you?" she asked.

He shook his head, looking down at the driveway. Meeting her eyes would be impossible, too complicated.

"I'll call my friend, get a sedative for you."

"I've got this stuff going around in my head . . ." he said. And the guns: he could feel the guns in the basement. Not heavy, not like last winter, but they were back.

"Let me call my friend." Elle took his arm, then his hand, and led him toward the door like a child, while Sloan and the other nun followed behind.


Lucas woke the next morning exhausted.

The sedatives had beaten him into a dreamless sleep. The storm in his head had dissipated, but he could feel it just over the horizon of consciousness. He slid tentatively out of bed, stood up, swayed, opened the bedroom door and almost fell over the couch. Sloan had pushed it up against the door and was struggling to get up.

"Lucas . . ." Sloan, in a T-shirt and suit pants, with a blanket wrapped around his shoulders, looked tired and scared.

"What the fuck are you doing, Sloan?"

Sloan shrugged. "We thought it might be a good idea, in case you sleepwalked. . . ."

"In case I started looking for my guns?"

"Something like that," Sloan admitted, looking up at him. "You look like shit. How do you feel?"

"Like shit," Lucas said. "I gotta get some dead kids dug up."

The blood seemed to drain from Sloan's face, and Lucas smiled despite himself, smiled as a widow might smile the day before her husband is buried. "Don't worry about it. I'm not nuts. Let me tell you about Bekker. . . ."

# 28

Daniel prowled around his office with his hands in his pockets. He'd pulled the shades but hadn't turned on the lights, and the office was almost dark.

"Homicide is satisfied," he said. "You know I don't clear murder cases on the basis of politics—and there's every indication that we got him. You got him. Bekker is something else."

Lucas was also standing, propped against a windowsill, arms crossed. "If Bekker kills another one and carves her eyes out, then what'll you do? The goddamned press'll be down here with pitchforks and torches."

Daniel threw up his hands in exasperation. "Look, I know this actress woman and you . . ."

"Doesn't have anything to do with it," Lucas said. His head still felt like a chunk of wood. Cassie did have something to do with it, of course. Revenge wouldn't be enough, but it would be something. "Druze may have killed her, but Bekker was behind it."

"Have you talked to the lab people since you came in?"

"No . . ."

"They looked at that jacket in Druze's closet. There was blood on the back of it. You can't see it, because the fabric was black and the blood was soaked in. But it was there, and they've done some preliminary tests. The blood is the same type as Stephanie Bekker's. . . ."

Lucas nodded. "I think Druze killed Stephanie, all right. . . ."

"And George. We got a taxi routing from the airport to the Lost River Theater the night George was done."

"What about Elizabeth Armistead? I'm not so sure about that one. I asked that night, or the next day, and everybody agreed Druze was at the theater most of the afternoon."

Daniel jabbed a forefinger at Lucas: "But maybe not every minute. He could've been gone half an hour and that would have been enough. And the woman who saw the guy at Armistead's said he was in some kind of utility-man getup. That sounds like an actor to me—we've got Homicide guys over at the theater right now, going through their wardrobe."

"What about the phone call?"

"Come on, Lucas. That so-called phone call doesn't make sense no matter how you cut it. And the kid out in Maplewood is pretty sure that Druze is the guy who did the Romm woman." Daniel took a manila folder from his desk and handed it to Lucas. "They found these in Druze's apartment."

Lucas opened the folder: inside were photographs of Stephanie Bekker and Elizabeth Armistead. The eyes had been cut out. "Where'd they get these?"

"Druze's file cabinet. Stuffed in the back."

"Bullshit," said Lucas, shaking his head. "I went through the file cabinet. These weren't there."

"Maybe he carried them with him."

"And puts them in the file cabinet before he goes upstairs to blow his brains out?" Lucas said. "Look, take this any way you want: as a continuing homicide investigation or just covering your political ass. We've got to stay with Bekker. We can tell the press that the case is cleared, but we've got to stay on him. We can start by exhuming these kids."

"What do we say about that?" Daniel asked. "How do we explain . . ."

"We don't say anything. Why should we say anything to anybody? If we can convince the parents to keep quiet . . ."

Daniel walked around the quiet office, head down, rubbing his hands. Finally he nodded. "Damn, I'd hoped we'd finished with it."

"We're not finished until Bekker falls. You saw the tapes with Sybil, for Christ's sake. . . ."

"And you heard what the lawyers said. A dying woman, maybe paranoid, loaded with drugs? C'mon. I believe her, Merriam believes her, Sloan does, so do you—but there's no way a judge is going to put that in front of a jury."

"Dying declaration . . ."

"Oh, bullshit, Lucas—she didn't make it while she was dying, for Christ's sake. . . ."

"You know what Cassie couldn't understand about the killings? The eyes. She said Druze would never do the eyes. You know what my friend Elle says about them? The shrink. She says he *has* to do the eyes. So if Bekker is nuts, and he kills somebody else . . . Jesus, can't you see it? He'll do the eyes again, and your balls will be hanging from a pole outside the City Hall door."

Daniel pulled on his lip, sighed and nodded. "Go ahead. Talk to the kids' parents. If they say okay on an exhumation, do it. If they say no, come back here and we'll talk. I don't want to go for a court order."


Lucas met Anderson in the hallway.

"You've heard?" Anderson asked.

"What?"

"The lab guys say that Druze didn't have much in the way of nitrites on his hands. He may have had a handkerchief on the gun, but still . . ."

"So what are they saying?"

"Maybe he didn't kill himself. The M.E. says the whole scene is a little weird, the way he did it, the way he must have been standing when he pulled the trigger. Can't figure out how the gun got underneath him, either. The muzzle was three or four inches from his temple when he pulled the trigger, and with the shock of the bullet and the recoil, he should have gone one way and the gun another. Instead, it beat him to the floor."

"The M.E. still working on him?"

"Oh, yeah. They've got samples of everything. I don't know, it's getting curiouser."


Lucas sat in his office, thinking it over, feeling the rats of depression galloping just below the surface of his mind. If he stopped concentrating, they'd be out. He forced his mind into it: Did Druze kill Cassie? Despite the questions, it seemed likely. In most murders, the most obvious answer is correct—and in any crime investigation, there are always anomalies. The gun shouldn't have beaten Druze's body to the floor, but maybe it did.

One of the rats slipped out: If only Cassie had identified him a day earlier and Loverboy had called with a definite identification . . .

Fuckin' Loverboy . . .

Lucas frowned, picked up the phone and called Violent Crimes. Sloan was at home, they said, trying to get some sleep. Lucas called, got him out of bed.

"Last night, when I was doped up. Did anybody call?"

"No."

"Hmph. What time did we identify Druze for television and release the news that it was part of the series . . . ?"

"This morning—I mean, they had Druze's name last night, midnight or so, but just the name. We didn't release the serial-killing business until this morning."

"Huh. Okay, thanks." He let Sloan go, dialed TV3 and got Carly Bancroft. "This is Lucas. Did you make Druze's name on the news last night?"

"No, we had it for the wake-up report," she said. "I could have used a little help. . . ."

"I was . . . out of shape," Lucas said. "What about the other channels? Did they have it?"

"Not as far as I know. We picked up the news release on morning cop checks. Nobody was bitching about getting beat, and they would have, on something like this. When can you talk to us? You found them, right? What—"

"I really can't talk," Lucas said. "I'll call you later."

He hung up and sat in his chair, rubbing his temples. Loverboy hadn't called.

Jennifer's car was in the driveway when he got home. He rolled past it slowly as the garage door went up, and parked and walked out of the garage as she got out of her car.

"How are you?" she asked. She was wearing a black turtleneck under a cardigan, with gold loop earrings visible under her short-cropped blond hair.

"What do you want?" His voice was so cold that she stepped back.

"I wanted to see how you were. . . ."

"Did Elle put you up to this?" Jennifer had her back to the car door and he loomed over her. His hands were in fists, inside his jacket pockets.

"She said you were in trouble."

"I don't need your help. The last time I needed your help, I got my head pushed under," he said. He turned away, walked back into the garage.

"Lucas . . ."

His mind was moving like a freight train, all the facts and suppositions and memories and plans and possibilities flying like boxcars just behind his eyes, unsuppressible. Jennifer. Green eyes. Full lips. Sarah, a bundle, squealing when he tossed her in the air. Jennifer and Sarah together in the delivery room, up at the lake cabin, Jennifer skinny-dipping in the moonlight, Sarah starting to crawl . . .

He was at a branch, he felt, when ten thousand things were possible, but he couldn't deal with that, with all the branches. . . .

"Just . . . go away," he said.

He tried, but couldn't sleep. Too many suppositions. Finally, glancing at the clock, he called the Minneapolis Institute of Arts and asked how late the gift shop was open. He had just enough time.

He hurried, trying not to think. Just keep moving. Don't worry about the guns. They sit there in the basement and they glow, and fuck 'em, let 'em glow.

The gift shop was empty, except for a bored saleswoman who was dressed so well that Lucas guessed she was a volunteer.

"Can I help you?" she asked.

"Yeah. I'm interested in a dude named Odilon Redon. What've you got? Got any calendars?"

Five minutes later he was back in the car, looking for a scrap of paper. He finally found a receipt from a tire store. He turned it over, flattened it against the Porsche owner's manual on his leg and started a new list.

And later, afraid of the bed, he sat in the spare bedroom with a bottle of Canadian Club and stared at his charts.

The Killer One chart was complete: Druze. A troll, powerful, squat, odd head, murdering Stephanie. No question about that anymore. If he was working with Bekker, must have killed George, because Bekker was with Lucas. Could have killed Cassie. Could have killed Armistead. Could have killed woman at the shopping center—but why? She was entirely out of the pattern. Not at home; not with the academic/art crowd . . . And where did the photos come from, with the missing eyes?

Killer Two: Did he exist? Was it Bekker? Some tracks at the site of the George killing suggested a second man. How would Druze have found George if Bekker hadn't fingered him? (Possibility: He'd watched Stephanie's funeral?) Why would he have driven George's Jeep to the airport? How could he have killed Armistead? Why the phone call—a coincidence, somebody trying to get in free?

The answers were in the pattern, somewhere. Lucas could feel it but couldn't see it.

He took the tire store receipt from his pocket. At the top he'd written "Loverboy."

He looked at it, closed his eyes and let the circumstances flow through his mind.

At six in the morning, he phoned Del. "I gotta come over and talk to you," he said. Del had an affinity for speed.

"Jesus Christ, man, what're you doing up at six o'clock? You're worse'n me. . . ."

Lucas drove across town with the breaking dawn, another cool, overcast day. The drive-time radio programs had started, and he dialed past the jock talk to 'CCO, half listening as he put the car on I-94 toward Minneapolis.

Del met him at the door in a pair of slightly yellowed jockey shorts and a sleeveless T-shirt that Clark Gable would have approved of. When Lucas told him what he wanted, Del shook his head and said, "Lucas, you'll kill yourself."

"No. I just need to stay awake for a while," Lucas said. "I know what I'm doing."

Del looked at him, nodded, went to the bedroom and came back with an orange plastic vial. "Ten hits. Heavy-duty. But don't try to stretch it too far."

"Thanks, man . . ." Lucas said.

A woman's voice came from the back. "Del . . . ?"

"In a minute," Del said. He smiled thinly at Lucas. "Cheryl. What can I tell you?"

The speed brightened him up. He turned south, looking at the clock. Almost seven. Sloan would be up.

"How're you feeling?" Sloan's wife asked as she opened the door.

"Everybody wants to know," Lucas said, grinning at her. She was a short woman, slightly plump, motherly and sexy at the same time. Lucas liked her. "Is Sloan out of bed?"

She turned her head. "Sloan? Lucas is here."

"Out on the porch," Sloan called back.

"Does Sloan have a first name?" Lucas asked as he went past the woman.

"I don't know. I never asked," she said.

Sloan was sitting on the sun porch, smoking a cigarette and eating a cherry Moon Pie. A Coke sat on a side table by his hand.

"A real lumberjack breakfast," Lucas said.

"Don't talk loud," Sloan said. "I'm not awake yet."

"I need you to sweet-talk some people for me," Lucas said. Sloan was the best interrogator on the force. People told him things. "I've got the names and addresses. . . ."

"What for?" Sloan asked, taking the slip of paper.

"Their kids died," Lucas said. "We want to dig them up. We want to do it today."

# 29

Beauty danced and bled and danced and bled and danced until he fell down on his back, his arms thrown wide, his legs spread, a kind of crucifixion on the huge Oriental rug in the dining room. There were no dreams of eyes. There were no dreams of anything. There was nothing at all.

\*       \*       \*

The pain woke him.

Daylight filtered past the blinds and his body trembled with cold, his muscles tight and shaking. He sat up and looked down, thought that somehow he'd gotten muddy, then realized that his chest was caked with dried blood. When he tried to stand, flakes of the blood broke away and fell on the carpet.

Something had changed. He felt it. Something was different, but he didn't know what. Couldn't remember. He tried to find it, but his mind seemed confused and he could not. Could not find it. He went to the bathroom, turned on the water for the tub, watched it pour, the water swirling, and he began to sing just like Mrs. Wilson had taught them in the fifth grade:

*"Frère Jacques, Frère Jacques, dormez-vous, dormez-vous? . . ."*

In the tub, the blood dissolved, pink in the water, and Beauty bathed in it, patted it on his astonishing face, and sang every song that a fifth-grader knew. . . .

The mirror was steamed over when he got out of the tub. He was annoyed when this happened, because he could not look into his face, he had to open the bathroom door, had to wait until the cool air cleared it. He always tried to rub the steam away with a towel, but he could never quite clear the mirror. . . .

He opened the door and the cold air flooded around him, and the stimulation almost brought the memory back. Almost . . . The first streak of condensation ran down the mirror. Bekker picked up a towel and wiped. Ah. There he was. . . .

The face was far away, he thought, puzzled. He wasn't that far away. He was right here. . . . He reached out and touched the glass, and the face came closer, and the horror began to grow.

This wasn't Beauty. This was . . .

Bekker screamed, stumbled back, unable to tear his eyes from the mirror.

A troll looked back. A troll with a patchwork face, the wide eyes staring, measuring him. And it all came back, the apartment, the gun, and Druze going down like a burst balloon.

"No!" Bekker screamed at the mirror. He grabbed the hair on both sides of his head, pulled at it, welcoming the pain, trying to rip the troll from his consciousness.

But the eyes, cool, cruel, floated in the mirror, watching. . . . Bekker ran into the hallway: another of her mirrors, mirrors everywhere, all with eyes. He stumbled, fell, crawled down the hall, scampering, naked, his knees burning from the carpet, down to his bedroom like a weasel, groping in panic for the brass cigarette case.

The eyes were everywhere, in the shiny surfaces of the antique bedstand, in the window glass, on the surface of the water in a whiskey tumbler. . . . Waiting. No place for Beauty. He gobbled three bloodred caps of Nembutal 100 mg pentobarbital and the green eggs, the Luminal 30 mg phenobarbital, three of them, four, six. And then the purple eggs, the Xanax 1 mg alprazolam. Too much? He didn't know, couldn't remember. Maybe not enough. He took an assortment of eggs with him, squinting through half-closed eyes, avoiding the shiny surfaces, and whimpering, he crawled into his closet, behind the shirttails and the pantlegs, with the shoes and the odors of darkness.

The Nembutal would be on him first; there was a mild rush as they came on, a Beauty rush. Bekker didn't want that. He wanted the calming effect, the sedation; even as he thought it, the rush dwindled and the sedation came on. The Luminal would be next, in an hour or so, smoothing him out for the day, until he could make plans to get at Druze. The Xanax would calm him. . . .

Another voice spoke in his mind, far away, barely rational: Druze. Find Druze.

Bekker looked into his hand, half cupped around the pills. He would find Druze if the medicine held out.


Lucas waited.

The second house was on a slight rise above the street, a greening lawn, neat, flower beds still raw with the spring. A Ford Taurus station wagon was parked in the driveway, the husband's car. He'd arrived just a minute after Sloan and Lucas. Lucas waited in the car while Sloan went inside.

The speed was beginning to bite. Lucas felt sharp and hard, like the edge of a pane of glass; and also brittle. He sat listening to Chris Rea on the tape player, singing about Daytona, his hand beating out the rhythm. . . .

Sloan came straight out the door and across the lawn, the paper in his hand.

"We're clear," he said. "The woman was okay, but I thought her husband was going to freak out."

"As long as we got it," Lucas said.


The machinery of exhumation was fussily efficient. A small front-loader took off the top five feet of dirt and piled it on a sheet of canvas. Two of the cemetery's gravediggers took off the last foot with shovels, dropped hooks onto the coffin and pulled it out, a corroding bronze tooth.

Lucas and Sloan followed the M.E.'s van back downtown and, as the coffin was unloaded, walked inside to talk to the medical examiner.

When they found Louis Nett, he was pulling a gown over his street clothes.

"Have you heard about the other one?" Lucas asked. The second child had been buried in the suburban town of Coon Rapids.

"It's on the way," Nett said. "If you guys want to hang around, I can give you a read in the next couple of minutes . . . depending on the condition of the body, of course."

"What do you think?" Sloan asked.

"Well, she was done by the Saloman Brothers. They're pretty careful, and she hasn't been down that long. I think there's a good chance, as long as the coffin is still tight. If it leaked, you know . . ." He shrugged. "All bets are off."

"We'll wait," Lucas said.

"You can come watch . . ." Nett offered.

"No, no," Lucas said.

"Well, if you don't mind . . . I think I might," Sloan said. "I've never seen one of these."

The medical examiner's office looked like the city clerk's office, or the county auditor's, or any place except one that dealt with the scientific dismemberment of the dead. Secretaries sat in front of smudged computer screens, each desk marked with idiosyncratic keepsakes: china frogs, pink-butted babies, tiny angels with their hands held in prayer, Xeroxed directives from the higher-ups, Xeroxed cartoons from the lower-downs.

In the back room, they were taking apart a long-dead teenage girl.

Lucas looked at one of the cartoons, cut from *The New Yorker*. It showed two identical portly, vaguely Scandinavian businessmen with brush mustaches, conservatively dressed with hats and briefcases, stopped at a receptionist's desk, apparently in Manhattan. The receptionist was talking into an intercom, saying, "Minneapolis and St. Paul to see you, sir . . ."

He turned away from the cartoon, dropped on a couch and closed his eyes, but his eyes didn't want to be closed. He opened them again and stared at the wall, fidgeted, picked up a nine-month-old magazine on bow-hunting, read a few words, dropped it back on the table.

The clock over a secretary's empty desk said four-fifteen. Nett said it shouldn't take more than a couple of minutes. At four-thirty, Lucas got up and wandered around the office, hands in his pockets.

Sloan came back first. Lucas stood up, facing him.

"You called it," Sloan said.

Something unwound in Lucas' stomach. They had him. "The eyes?"

"Cut. Nett says with an X-acto knife or something like it—I figure it was a scalpel. Something that really dug in."

"Can they take photos or something . . . ?"

"Well . . . they're taking the eyes out," Sloan said, as though Lucas should have known. "They put them in little bottles of formaldehyde. . . ."

"Aw, Christ . . ."

# 30

The day started with an argument.

"I didn't become a psychologist so I could advise you on ways to destroy a mind," Elle Kruger snapped.

"I don't need any ethical qualms dumped on me. I had enough of that in school," Lucas answered. "I need to know what'll happen, what you think'll happen. If it won't work, say so. If it will . . . we told you what he's doing. You want this *monster* creeping around hospitals, snuffing kids? Because you've got a Catholic qualm?"

"That is an extremely offensive phrase," the nun said angrily. "I won't have it."

"Just tell me," Lucas said.

They argued for another fifteen minutes. In the end, she relented.

"If he's the man you think, it could be effective. But if he's as intelligent as you say and if he's thinking clearly, he may see right through it. Then you're ruined."

"We have to push," Lucas said. "We need some control."

"I've told you what I think: It could work. You'd want to just give him a flash, so later he wouldn't be sure if he actually saw it or just imagined it. You can't let him experience the . . . materiality . . . of the image. You wouldn't want to send him a photograph, or anything like that. If he has something solid in his hand, if he can sit and contemplate it, he'll say to himself, *Wait. This is real. How did this go from my mind to reality?* And then he'll be onto you. So you have to deal in images, the more ethereal the better. You need a will-o'-the-wisp."

"A will-o'-the-wisp," Lucas said. "That will do it?"

"There are no guarantees with the human mind, Lucas. You should know that, after last winter."

They stared at each other across her desk until he stood up and started away.

"What're you going to do?" she called after him.

"I'm going to push him," he said.

"God, I need video, I can't stand this." Carly Bancroft sat in the passenger seat of Druze's Dodge, working out of a professional makeup kit. The car was muggy inside, with the two of them working so close. The smell of sweat was pushing through her perfume; Lucas was sure he didn't smell any better.

"You'll be able to talk about it," Lucas said. "That'll be a hell of a story."

"I don't work for a fuckin' newspaper. I don't need words, I need pictures," she said. Lucas had refused to let her bring in a cameraman. She had a thirty-five-millimeter Nikon in a shoulder bag but insisted she felt naked.

"This isn't even supposed to be a story. . . ."

"Stop talking while I work around your mouth."

He felt silly, sitting with his head cranked back, while the reporter worked on him. Lucas tipped the visor mirror down and looked at himself as she painted the side of his face. "It's pretty crude," he said tentatively, trying not to move his lips.

"It's just fine," Bancroft said. "This isn't cosmetic makeup, it's stage makeup. You're lucky I took theater crafts. Hold still, dammit, I've got to shorten your nose."

She'd started by scouring his face with a cleansing cream, then wiped most of it off with tissue. When she finished, his skin still felt oily.

"Supposed to," she said. "That's your base."

His hair was already as dark as Druze's had been, but she added a blue-gray tone to his beard area, and under his nose, to give him a heavier shadow. Using a powder puff, she put on a transparent powder to set the makeup.

Most of the time was spent blending a series of blue and reddish tones, to give his face the patchwork effect. Additional cosmetics made his face rounder; not quite Druze's pumpkin, but it was the best they could do. A bath towel wrapped around his chest gave him Druze's bulk. The whole process took twenty minutes.

Then they waited.


"On his way," Sloan said with a voice like static.

"Give me the hat . . ." Lucas said. Bancroft passed him a felt snap-brim and he put it on his head. He picked up the handset, pressed the transmit button and asked, "Where is he?"

"He's coming. Two minutes. You ready?"

"Ready," Lucas said. To Bancroft, he said, "Get in the back, in case something weird happens. You try to peek over the door and I'll pull your goddamned head off. And don't stick that fuckin' camera up, either."

"Tell me what happens," she said, as she climbed agilely over the seat. Lucas got a flash of long legs and then her blue eyes.

"You just stay out of sight. . . ."

"Can't I just peek?"

"Two blocks," said Sloan. "We can see the light. It's red. . . ."

"Changing now," said another voice. "Tell me when. . . ."

"It'll be a goddamned short green light," Lucas said to Bancroft. "Get the fuck down."

"Last corner, Lucas. Roll now," said Sloan. Lucas pulled away from the curve, topped a low rise and headed downhill to the light. He could see

Bekker's car rolling toward the traffic light, signaling a left turn. The light went yellow, then red, on command from the surveillance car.

Lucas pulled up to the light, stopped, stared through the tinted windshield at Bekker. They didn't think he'd be able to see Lucas' face from this distance, but they weren't sure. Lucas could see Bekker. The traffic light for the cross street went yellow. "Here we go," Lucas said. "Stay down."

Bekker, still signaling a left turn, pulled into the intersection, the surveillance car right on his tail to block any possible pursuit. Lucas moved slowly through the intersection, and as he passed Bekker's car, he looked left, out the window. The coat collar was up, the hat was pulled down, his face was shaded. . . .

His eyes caught Bekker's, and Bekker's head snapped around as though jerked by a wire. Lucas accelerated through the intersection and up the hill.

"He's killed the fuckin' car, I think, he's rolling through the intersection, he can't get the car started," Sloan called.

"He saw me," Lucas called back. To Bancroft, he said, "You can sit up."

"I need some fuckin' video," she moaned. "Davenport, you're killing me. . . ."


Bekker, shocked, sat in his car and cried, tried to start it, sent it bucking in first gear, killed it again, started again. . . .

Bekker didn't think of pursuit. He knew who it was he'd seen.

He'd sat in the closet for a day and a night, alternating between sleep and a half-waking state. He had no idea how many pills he'd taken, or the dosages, but finally, seeing daylight again and the cigarette case empty, and hungry, he crawled out of the closet. The eyes waited in the glass. He stood up, stumbled toward the bathroom, his body racked with pain. He'd gotten cramped in the closet, he hurt everywhere. In the shower, he stood in scalding water, the pain driving the pictures out of his mind. . . .

Out of the shower, he dressed, took a careful black cap, amphetamine, just enough to keep him going, went to the car, saw the eyes in the rearview mirror, tilted the mirror away, started down the street. There was a deli less than a mile away. He was caught by a red light. A station wagon across the street . . .


"Is he going on?" Lucas asked.

"Yeah, he's still going," Sloan said. "He's moving slow, though. I think there's something wrong."

"He's freaked out," Lucas said. "I told you he knew Druze."

"Something definitely wrong," Sloan said. "He's turning around. He's going back out to Twelve. . . ."

The net stayed with Bekker as he drove toward downtown.

"Could be heading for the hospital," Sloan called.

Lucas stuck a borrowed police light in the window of the Dodge and raced for the university campus. Bancroft, who'd crawled back into the front seat, pulled a safety belt over his lap and snapped it. "You drive as bad as a camera-man," she said, buckling herself in.

"Don't have a lot of time," Lucas said. "You know where to take the car?"

"Yes." She sounded taut and he grinned. "You'll be all paid off after this."

"I'll be paid off and a half," she said. "If the station knew I was doing this . . ."

"What?"

"Now that I think about it, I don't know what they'd do. If I had video, they'd probably be lined up outside the station with their lips puckered. . . ."

Lucas hopped out of the car on Washington Avenue, at the base of a foot-bridge. If Bekker followed his usual route to work, he'd drive beneath the footbridge; but from the roadway, there was no quick way up to it. If he stopped his car and climbed up as quickly as he could, Lucas would still have time to duck into a chemistry building at the end of the footbridge.

"Where is he?" Lucas asked on the handset. He hurried along the sidewalk toward the entry to the footbridge.

"He's coming up to the exit, so you got time," Sloan said. "There he goes, he's off."

Lucas climbed the footbridge, looked west across the Mississippi.

"Davenport . . ." He heard Bancroft, on the other side, and turned to look over the rail. She was standing on a wall by the student union, the Nikon to her face. He waved her off and went back to the other side of the footbridge.

"On Washington," Sloan said on the handset. A passing student, a slender, long-haired kid in an ankle-length coat with an ankh on a chain around his neck, looked at him curiously and said, "Can't be Cyrano, with that nose."

"Fuck off, kid," Lucas said. He shaded his eyes as he looked down Washing-ton Avenue toward the river.

"On the bridge," Sloan called on the handset.

"Okay," said Lucas, on his own set.

"Cop?" asked the kid.

"Go away," Lucas said. "You could fuck up something important and I'd have to throw your ass in jail."

"That's a good argument," the kid said, walking hastily away.

Bekker's car was on the bridge, pacing the traffic. Lucas squatted on the far side of the footbridge, out of sight, until Bekker was less than a hundred feet away. He should get just a flash. . . . Now.

Lucas stood up and peered over the bridge. Bekker saw him, swerved. Lucas was gone, hurrying toward the chemistry building.

"He saw you, he's on the side, he's on the side," Sloan called.

"Is he coming?"

"Naw, he's still in his car. . . ."


Bekker sat at the side of the road, his head on the steering wheel. He was afraid to sleep, waiting to move. And now here was Druze, coming back. . . .

He made a U-turn and drove back across the Mississippi, left his car in a dormitory parking lot and walked to the library. A loose net stayed with him, watching. Inside, Bekker scanned an index for the *StarTribune,* looked up the appropriate issue and wrote down the details about the death of a tramp.

From a phone booth, he called the medical examiner.

"I'm trying to locate my father, who . . . had some mental problems," he said. "We weren't close, I was adopted by another family, but I've heard now from an old friend of his that he died and was buried by Hennepin County last year. . . . I was wondering if you could tell me which funeral homes you use, so I could find out where he's buried."

The county used four funeral homes, selected on an annual bid basis. Walker & Son, Halliburton's, Martin's and Hall Bros. He called them in order. Martin's took his last quarter.

"Martin's . . ." The voice low and already consoling.

"I'm calling about the funeral for a Carlo Druze. . . ."

"That's Friday."

"Will there be a viewing?"

"Uh, well, there usually is, but I'd have to check. Can you hold?"

"Yes . . ."

The woman was gone for three or four minutes. When she returned, she asked, "Are you a member of Mr. Druze's family?"

"No . . . I'm from the theater. . . ."

"Well, Mr. Druze's mother made some tentative arrangements which did not include a viewing, but now we understand that several theater people *will* be coming, so we're planning a viewing from seven to nine o'clock tomorrow night in the Rose Chapel, with burial at Shakopee. We will have to contact his mother again for approval."

"Tomorrow night, from seven to nine . . ." Bekker closed his eyes. The burial was sooner than he'd expected, or dared to hope. Druze had died two days before, and he would be buried in another two days. Bekker had been afraid that it would be a week, or even more, before the body was released. He could hold out for a week, he thought, with the right medication. Longer than that, and he'd have to let go, he'd have to go down and face Druze in the territory of dreams.

But now that would not happen. Tomorrow night and it would be over.

# 31

Bekker saw Druze twice more, or thought he did: he couldn't decide, finally, whether he was seeing Druze or an image within his own eye.

He saw him two blocks from his house, a dark thing drifting around a corner. Bekker stood, his mouth open, the newspaper in his hand, and the figure disappeared like a wisp of black fog. He saw him again at midafternoon, passing in a car half a block away. Bekker's eye was caught first by the car, then by the obscured dark form behind the driver's-side glass. He could feel the eyes peering out at him. . . .

He was eating Equanil like popcorn, with an occasional taste of amphetamine; he was afraid to sleep, was living out of his study, from which he'd removed all the glass. If he could spend the day staring at the carpet . . .

He had trouble thinking. He would be all right after Druze was done. He could clear himself out for a while, go off the medications. . . . What? He couldn't remember. Harder to think. The units of thought, the concepts, seemed bound in threads of possibility, the threads tangled beyond his ability to follow them. . . .

He struggled with it: and time passed.


The funeral home was a gloomier place than it had to be, dark red-brown brick and natural stone, with a snaky growth of still-leafless ivy clinging to the stone.

Bekker, shaky, anxious but anticipating, black beauties nestled in his pocket, drove past once, twice. There were few cars on the street but several in the funeral home driveway. As he was making his second pass, the front door opened and a half-dozen people came out and stood clustered on the steps, talking.

Older, most of them, they were dressed in long winter coats and dark hats, like wealthy Russians. Bekker slowed, eased the car to the curb, watched the people on the steps. Their talk was animated: an argument? He couldn't tell. After five minutes, the cluster began to break up. In ones and twos, they drifted out to their cars and, finally, were gone.

Bekker tried to wait but couldn't. The pressure to move . . . and there was nobody in sight. He didn't much credit the funeral home receptionist's comment that theater people were expected, but you never knew with theater people. He climbed out of the car, looked around, walked slowly up the driveway to the funeral home. A car cruised past and he turned his head. A man watching him? Druze again? He wasn't sure. He didn't care. In five minutes, he'd be done. . . .

The net was with him:

"He's out of the car, looking at the door," the close man said, driving on by. He didn't look at Bekker, who was walking slowly up the driveway.

There was no place to hide in the Rose Chapel, but the other rooms were worse. Lucas finally decided he could drive a nail through the top panel of one of the double doors, then pull the nail and have a hole large enough to peep through. The manager wouldn't let him use a nail, but did loan him a power drill with a sixteenth-inch bit. When Lucas, standing in the dark behind the doors, pressed his eye to the hole, he could see the entire coffin area.

"Go up there, bend over him," he told Sloan. Del was leaning against the wall, faintly amused. Sloan stood over the coffin and looked back at the doors. The hole was invisible.

"Put your hand on his head, or over it, or something," Lucas called from behind the doors. Sloan put his hand over Druze's head. A moment later, the doors opened.

"Can't see your hand," Lucas said. He looked around the room. "But I think any other arrangement would look wrong."

"Yeah, with the alcove like that," Sloan said, nodding toward the coffin.

Del grinned. "We could, like, put, you know, a spring with a clown under his eyelids, and when Bekker pulls it open, see, it pops up. . . ."

"I like it," Sloan said. "Motherfucker'd have a heart attack. . . ."

"Jesus," Lucas said, glancing toward the body. "I think we'll settle for the hole in the door."

"He's moving," said the voice on the handset.

Sloan looked at Lucas. "You cool?"

"I'm cool," Lucas said.

"So'm I," Del said. He unconsciously dropped his hand back to his hip, where he kept a small piece clipped to his belt. "I'm cool, too."

The receptionist came from Intelligence and spent his nights working under-cover. "No problem," he said. "I could win a fuckin' Oscar, the work I do." There were two squads immediately available, and the surveillance team coming in with Bekker.

"He's here," the radio burped ten minutes later. "He's going past."

Bekker rambled through the neighborhood, looking it over, and made another pass at the front of the funeral home before he stopped.

"He's out of the car, looking at the door," the radio said.

"Everybody . . ." Lucas said.

A finger of joy touched his soul. In five minutes . . .

Bekker wore a trench coat and a crushable hat, with leather driving gloves. The scalpel, a plastic tube protecting the point, was clipped in his shirt pocket. The funeral home door, he thought, looked like the door on a bad ski chalet. . . .

The funeral home was overly warm. An antique mirror, like those collected by Stephanie, surprised him just inside the door. He flinched, jerked his eyes away, but found them drawn back. . . .

Druze was gone. Beauty looked back at him. Beauty looked fine, he thought, but tired. Unusual lines crossed his wide brow, gathered at the corners of his eyes. A different look, he thought, but not unattractive. French, perhaps, a world-weariness . . . like the actor with the home-rolled cigarette. What was his name? He couldn't concentrate, his own image floating in front of him like a dream. And then a gathering darkness behind his image, and . . .

He pulled his eyes away. Druze was there, still waiting.

"Buchanan?"

"What?" Bekker jumped. He'd been so engrossed in the mirror that he hadn't heard the funeral home receptionist until the man was virtually on top of him.

"Are you here for Mr. Buchanan?" The receptionist seemed ordinary, a thin man in a conservative coat and flannel slacks, a man with no particular relationship to death, although he worked in the middle of it. No imagination . . .

"No . . ." Bekker said, "ah, Mr. Druze?"

"Oh, yes. That would be the Rose Chapel. Down to your right . . ." The receptionist pointed like a real estate man giving directions to the third bedroom, the one that was a little too small.

"Thank you."

The funeral home was quiet, all sounds smothered by plush drapes and heavy carpets. To quiet the weeping, Bekker guessed. As he stepped into the Rose Chapel, he glanced back at the receptionist. The man had turned away and seemed about to go down to the next room, when a phone rang in the entry. The receptionist stopped, picked up the receiver and launched into a conversation. Good. Bekker stepped into the chapel.

Lucas stood out of sight, heard the Intelligence guy ask the question, heard Bekker say, "No . . . ah, Mr. Druze?" A moment later the phone rang. Worried that Bekker might arrive and yet develop cold feet, they'd worked out the diversion of the telephone, with Sloan calling from a back room. If Bekker could hear the receptionist talking, he'd be encouraged to act.

The Rose Chapel was small, with fifteen dark wooden chairs facing the coffin. The plaster walls were a pale shade of rose; the woodwork an antique cream. A closed pair of double doors was straight ahead of Bekker, apparently leading to the depths of the funeral home; they were sized to take a coffin on a gurney.

The coffin itself was to Bekker's right, on a dais within a plaster alcove. Roses were molded into the plaster, and individually hand-painted. The dais was covered with a rose-colored drape, a deeper shade than the walls. Bekker could see the side of Druze's head and his heavy shoulders under a dark suit.

Beauty was pushing through now, anxious for the celebration, moving him. He could hear the receptionist talking, faintly, far away, and he moved to the front. His hand went to his pocket, found the scalpel. He pulled the tube off the end and moved next to the coffin.

Druze's head was large, he thought. Not just a pumpkin, but a big pumpkin. His face had been liberally worked with makeup, so the patchwork of skin grafts was barely visible. The nose, of course . . . not much you could do about that. He frowned. Too bad. Druze actually had been something of a friend. A man you could talk to. But he had to go; Bekker had known that from the beginning. Murder was something you didn't share, except with the dead.

Lucas pressed his eye to the hole in the double doors. He couldn't see Bekker as he came in, couldn't see his beautiful face as he went by. Bekker paused, just for a moment, in front of the coffin, looking down. Lucas could hear the receptionist muttering in the hall, and then, suddenly, Bekker was on Druze, bending over, the hand out of sight, but working over him. . . .

Bekker glanced back over his shoulder, then reached across Druze's face with his left hand and lifted his eyelid. The eye beneath was intact, but dull, dry, a piece of leather, staring sightlessly and unflinchingly at the ceiling. His heart pounding, the pressure in his veins, the murmur of the receptionist's conversation providing him with the necessary security, Bekker plunged the point of the scalpel into Druze's eyeball, and then turned the handle, like a corkscrew. He felt some of the weight leave him, a pressure gone from his shoulders.

Quickly, quickly, his mouth open, panting, he did the second eye, looking over his shoulder, twisting the knife. . . .

And he was free. He felt it, almost as if he were being lifted from the floor. He did a little step, Beauty coming on, and looked back at Druze.

The eyelids were open, wrinkled and pulled up, like fragments of dead leaves. His heart beating hard and with joy, Beauty reached out to smooth them down, round them carefully, the scalpel still in his hand. He stepped back.

"Cut his eyes, Mike?"

The voice broke on him like a bucket of ice water, crashing down, snatching his breath away, each word hurting, a sharp stone: CUT HIS EYES, MIKE?

Bekker whirled, the scalpel still in his right hand.

Davenport was there, leaning in the double doors, wearing a dark leather jacket, a pistol in his hands, pointed not at Bekker but to one side. He looked wired, his eyes wide, his hair dirty, his face unshaven. A thug. Another man came in from the left, and then a third, Stephanie's dope-addict cousin, Del. The receptionist was behind them.

". . . 'Cause if you cut his eyes, Mike, we got you for the kids, too. We just dug them up today and the medical examiner says they were done with a knife just like that one, a scalpel. Is that a scalpel, Mike?"

Bekker stood speechless, the words bouncing through his brain, GOT YOU FOR THE KIDS, TOO, and Davenport moved in on him. One of the other cops, a thin man, said, "Be cool," but Bekker had no idea what that meant.

Lucas moved in on him, the pistol in his hand. Bekker was startlingly beautiful in the soft light coming off the rose plaster, a violent contrast to the leathery patchwork face of the man behind him.

Lucas' mind was pure ice: he could do anything when his mind was like this, he thought. Some of it was the speed. He'd been up three days now, but felt awake and in control, sharp, as sharp as he ever had. He reached Bekker, brushed past him, ignoring the scalpel, stretched past him, lifted Druze's eyelids with his left hand, just as Bekker had. Bekker turned away.

Lucas, ice, stepped away from the coffin and glanced at Sloan.

"Cut them right through. Want to take a look?"

Lucas was crowding Bekker with his hip, and Bekker tried to move back, letting the scalpel slip from his fingers as he moved. It bounced off the deep carpet, the blade pointing at him like a steel finger.

"Got them both—really did a job," Sloan said, bending over Druze's body.

"What I want to know," Lucas said to Bekker in a conversational tone, "is why you killed Cassie Lasch. Why'd you have to do that? Couldn't you just have done Druze? Just gone in there, stuck the gun in his ear and pulled the trigger? You could have stashed the photos anyway and we'd have gotten the point. . . ."

Bekker's mouth was open, but no sound came out.

"I need an answer," Lucas said.

"Cool," said Sloan, catching his coat sleeve.

"Fuck cool," said Del, moving up on the other side of Bekker. He put his face four inches from the other man and said, "I knew Stephanie longer than you did, Mike. Loved that girl. So you know what?"

Bekker, caught between Lucas and Del, shrinking back against the wall, still didn't answer.

"You know what?" Del screamed, his eyes wide.

"Hey, now," said the Intelligence cop. He had Del by the coat.

"What?" Bekker croaked, half under his breath.

"I'm going to beat the snot out of you, m'boy," Del said. His right hand came around in an arc and hit Bekker in the nose. Bekker slammed against the wall, his nose broken, blood gushing down his chin. He put his arms up, crossed his face.

"Wait," Sloan yelled. He tried to step around Lucas, but Lucas pushed him; and before Sloan could recover, Del hit Bekker twice more, once with each hand, evading Bekker's feeble block. Bekker's head snapped back twice more, the back of it knocking the wall like a judge's gavel, and another cut opened on his eyebrow. The Intelligence cop was on Del's back, and Sloan wrapped him from the front and pushed him away. Bekker was moaning, one hand cupping his nose, a high, dying sound: "Eeeee . . ."

"That's enough, that's enough!" Sloan screamed. They hauled Del back, and Bekker dropped one of his covering hands.

"No, it's not," Lucas said quietly. He was less than an arm's length from Bekker. Sloan and the Intelligence cop were struggling with Del but looking toward Lucas.

The pistol came around like a whip, the front sight leading the arc.

" 'Member Cassie, motherfucker?" Lucas said, the words as much a groan as a scream. Saliva sprayed into Bekker's face, and Lucas had him by the throat with his left hand. Bekker had time only to flinch before the sight sliced across his cheek and the side of his nose. A ragged furrow opened in its wake. Bekker grunted from the impact, a pain like fire ripping through his face.

Lucas, precise, quick, moving with the easy coordination of a speed-bag man, hit Bekker with the gun a dozen times, leading with the sight.

Ripped his forehead, twice, three times, opened his eyebrows, carved bloody canyons across his nose, the left cheek, then the right, sliced through his lips, his hands a blur . . .

Sloan hit Lucas in the back, wrapped up one arm. Lucas flailed with the pistol, a last wild swing ripping across Becker's chin, opening the flesh as effectively as a chainsaw.

Lucas, mind blank, focused, could barely feel Sloan's arms binding him, barely feel the Intelligence cop sweeping him off his feet, barely feel the uniforms barreling into the room, pinning him.

Even as he went down, his eyes were focused on Bekker, his hands straining. Sloan had the pistol, was twisting, his thumb under the hammer. . . .

Lucas was aware of weight on his chest, and Sloan, then of Sloan looking away, looking back up at Bekker, who was sliding a bloody path down the plaster walls. Sloan was looking at Bekker's face, and Lucas heard Sloan say, "Oh Christ, ah Christ, ah sweet Jesus . . ."

The doctor's face was a mask of blood and curling, wounded flesh. Even Druze might have turned away, had he been alive to see it.


In ten minutes, the world was moving again.

Lucas sat on a hard wooden bench in the entry, Sloan next to him.

Del was down the hall, his hands in his pockets. The Intelligence man, two uniforms and the paramedics were with Bekker. When they brought him out, on a gurney, one of the paramedics held a drip bottle above him, the line plugged into one of Bekker's arms. He was conscious. One of his eyes was puffed nearly shut, but the other was open.

He saw Lucas, recognized him, and a noise came through his ruined lips.

"What?" Lucas asked. "Hold it. . . . What'd he say?"

The paramedics stopped and looked down. Bekker, struggling, one eye open, blood running into it, tried to sit up, put the words together. . . .

"You should have . . ." He lost it for a moment, then came back, a red bubble of blood on his lips.

"What?" Lucas asked. He stooped over and the blood bubble burst.

"You should have . . ."

"What, what, motherfucker . . . ?" Lucas shouted down at him, Sloan on his arms again.

". . . killed me . . ." Bekker tried to smile. His lips, cut nearly in half, failed him. "Fool."

# 32

Lucas sat outside Daniel's office, six feet from the secretary's desk. She had tried talking to him but eventually gave up. When the secretary's intercom beeped, she tipped her head toward the office door and Lucas went inside.

"Come in," Daniel said. His voice was formal, his office was not. Papers were scattered across the top of his desk and an amber cursor blinked on his computer screen, halfway down a column of numbers. A veil of cigar smoke hung in the room. Daniel pointed to the good guest chair. "What a fuckin' week. How are you?"

"Messed up," Lucas said. "I'd only known Cassie for a few days, and I don't think we would have lasted . . . but shit. She was pulling me up. I was feeling almost human."

"Are you going back over the edge?" Daniel's face was questioning, concerned.

"Christ, I hope not," Lucas said, rubbing his face with his open hands. He was exhausted. After the arrest, he'd gone home and crashed, slept the night and the day through, until he was shaken out of bed by Daniel's call. "Anything but that."

"Hmm." Daniel picked up a dead cigar, rolled it between his fingers. "You've heard about the answering machine."

"No, I've been out of it. . . ."

"One of the crime-scene guys—you know Andre?"

"Yeah . . ."

"Andre was going through Bekker's office, and a secretary said she'd seen Bekker coming out of the next office down from his. She thought he was just doing some housekeeping for his neighbor, who's off in Europe on a fellowship. Anyway, Andre gets on the phone and calls this guy in Europe, tells him what happened, gets his okay, and they check out his office. There's an answering machine in his desk and it's turned on. Andre pushes the button and the tape just stops; it's been rewound. But when he pushes it again, it starts running, and it's a message from Druze to Bekker, telling him it's done. . . . We went back to the phone company, checked it, and the call came in a half-hour after the woman was killed at Maplewood. There's another fragment of conversation under that, just a few words, but it's Bekker."

"So that ties it," Lucas said.

"Yeah. And there are a couple of other things, coming along."

"What about Loverboy?" Lucas asked.

"I pulled Shearson off the shrink. Shearson thinks he's the one, but we'll never know. Not unless he just comes out and tells us." Daniel rolled the cigar between his palms. He looked more than unhappy.

"What's wrong?" Lucas asked.

"Shit." Daniel backhanded the cigar butt at the wall, where it bounced off the black-and-white face of Robert Kennedy and fell to the floor.

"Let's have it," Lucas said.

Daniel swiveled his chair to look out the window at the street. Spring was definitely coming, the days stretching toward summer. The street was sunlit, although the temperatures hung in the forties. "Lucas . . . God damn it. You beat up Bekker. His fuckin' face . . . And remember that pimp, that kid, Whitcomb? His goddamn attorney has been back to Internal Affairs—Whitcomb's family don't believe a word of that pimp story, they think their little boy fell into the hands of a bad cop. They're talking about the courts. . . ."

"We've handled it before . . ." Lucas suggested.

"Not like this. You've been in fights. These people . . . Shit, these people didn't have much of a chance."

"Whitcomb is a fucking violence freak," Lucas said, leaning forward. "Has his attorney looked at the girl he worked over?"

"Yeah, yeah. Whitcomb's a criminal—but you're not supposed to be. And now there are rumors about you going into Druze's apartment. Too many people know about it. If you tried to deny it at a hearing, you'd be perjuring yourself. And there's more. . . ."

"Like what?"

"A guy from Channel Eight was talking about making a formal complaint that you gave special privileges to one of the reporters from TV3. That wouldn't be any big deal, normally, except that Barlow picked it up, and decided that you fed her confidential investigatory material."

"You could quash that," Lucas said.

"Yeah. That. Or any one of the others. But the whole bunch . . ."

"Cut to the action," Lucas said. "What're you telling me?"

Daniel sighed, turned back and leaned over his desk. "I can't fuckin' save you."

"Can't save me?" Lucas said it quietly, almost pensively.

"They're gonna hang your ass," Daniel said. "The shooflies and a couple of guys on the council . . . And I can't do a fuckin' thing about it. I told them that you'd maybe had some psychological problems, they were straightening out. They said bullshit: If he's nuts, get him off the street. And you've killed a few guys. You see that *Pioneer Press* editorial? *Our own serial killer . . .*"

"Jesus Christ," Lucas said. He levered himself out of the chair and took a turn around the office, looking at all the black-and-white mug shots, the smiling sharks, a lifetime of politicians. He stopped at the color, the Hmong tapestry, the Minnesota weather calendar. "I'm gone?"

"You could fight it, but it'd be pretty bad," Daniel said. "They'd be asking about the break-in, about the fight with Whitcomb and about Bekker's face. . . . I mean, Jesus, you look at a picture of the way Bekker used to be, and his face now. Jesus, he looks like Frankenstein. On top of it all, you haven't gone out of your way to win any popularity contests."

"There are some people in the press. . . ."

"They'll turn on you like rats," Daniel said. "Nothing gives an editorial writer more satisfaction than seeing somebody else booted out of his job."

"I've got friends. . . ."

"Sure. I'm one. I'd testify for you . . . but like I said—and I'm a politician, I know what I'm talking about—I can't save your ass. As a friend, I tell you this: If you resign, I can turn it all off. I can short-circuit it. You walk away clean. If you decide to fight it, I'll stand with you, but . . ."

"It wouldn't do any good."

"No."

Lucas stared bleakly at the weather calendar, then nodded and turned to face Daniel. "I knew I was getting close to the end of my string," he said. "Too much shit coming down. I just kind of wish . . ."

"What?"

"I wish I'd dumped Bekker. Damn it. . . ."

"Don't talk like that. To anybody," Daniel said, pointing a finger at Lucas. "That can only bring you grief."

"When do I go?"

Daniel tipped his head. "Soon. Like now."

"Do you have a sheet of department paper?" Lucas asked.

Lucas hunched over Daniel's desk, writing it out in longhand, two simple sentences. *Please accept my resignation from the Minneapolis Police Department. I've enjoyed my work here, but it's time to pursue new interests.* "Twenty fuckin' years," he said, as he dotted the *i* and crossed the *t*s in *interests*.

"I'm sorry," Daniel said. He had turned his back again, and was staring out the window. "The retirement'll be there, of course, if you care. . . ."

"Fuck retirement. . . ." Lucas looked at his hand, found that he was holding a square of pink paper, a receipt from a tire store. On the back was a list, with the word "Loverboy" at the top. He crushed it into a tight little wad and tossed it toward the big plastic basket that stood in an alcove behind Daniel's desk. The paper wad rimmed out, and they both watched it bounce across the rug. "I dated the letter tomorrow—I've got some official things to clean up. And I want to slide some of my files over to Del."

"Okay. Del . . . I know he pounded on Bekker, but he doesn't have the history . . ."

"Sure. If there's a problem, if Internal Affairs gets on his case, tell them to talk to me. I'll take the heat for it."

"Won't happen. Like I said, I can contain it, if you're not around to goad them. And I can do something else, I think. I can take your resignation and put you on reserve. . . ."

"Reserve? What the fuck is that?"

Daniel gestured helplessly. "It's nothing, right now. But maybe, if you get out clean, let things cool down, we could get you back. . . . If not full-time, in some kind of consultant capacity . . ."

"Sounds like bullshit," Lucas said. He looked at Daniel for a moment, then said, "You could do more than contain it . . . but you can't, can you?"

Daniel turned, uncertain. "What?"

"You can't have me around. I'd . . ." He looked at Daniel for another long minute, then shook his head and said, "I'm outa here."

Daniel, still confused, said in a rush, "Do something, Lucas. You're one of the smartest guys I've ever known. Go to law school. You'd make a great attorney. You got money: see the world for a while. You've never been to fuckin' Europe. . . ."

As Lucas was going out the door, he stopped, and he turned back again to look at Daniel, who was standing behind his desk, his hands in his pockets. Lucas looked for a long three seconds, opened his mouth to say something, then shook his head and walked out, pulling the door closed behind him.

From the chief's office he went down to the evidence room, signed for the box on Bekker and started through it. The physical evidence was there—plaster casts of the footprints at the Wisconsin burial site, the pieces of the bottle used to kill Stephanie Bekker, the hammer used to kill Armistead, the notes from Stephanie's lover.

Tape pickups had been used to preserve the lover's footprints from the floor of Stephanie Bekker's bedroom. They'd been sealed in plastic bags, with a label stapled to the top of the bag. They were gone.

After checking out of the evidence room, Lucas got his jacket, locked his office and walked up the stairs to the street level, out past the bizarre but strangely interesting statue of the Father of Waters, and onto the street.

Where to go? He waited for the pull of the guns, down there in the safe in the basement. They'd be glowing, wouldn't they, like a luminescent brand of gravity. . . .

"Not a lot left, fuckhead," he said aloud to himself as he wandered toward the corner.

"Hey, Davenport." A uniformed cop was calling from the door to City Hall. "Somebody looking for you."

"I don't work there anymore," Lucas shouted back.

"Neither does this one," said the cop, holding the door open and looking down.

Sarah, in a pink frock and white shoes, toddled through the door looking for him, her face breaking into a happy smile when she spotted him. She had a pacifier in one hand, waved it and gurgled. Jennifer was a step behind, her face flushed with what might have been embarrassment. The whole scene was so blatantly contrived that Lucas started to laugh.

"Come here, kid," he said, squatting, clapping his hands. Sarah's face turned determined and she came on full-steam, dashing toward a soft landing in Lucas' hands.

"So we start talking, if it's not too late," Jennifer said as Lucas tossed the kid in the air.

"It's not too late," Lucas said.

"The way you were the other night . . ."

"I was full of shit," Lucas said. "You know about . . . ?"

"Sloan heard rumors, and called me," Jennifer said. She poked her daughter in the stomach and Sarah clutched Lucas' neck and grinned back at her mother. "I think Sarah's got a future in the TV news business. I coached her on going through the door, and she did it like a natural. She even got her lines right."

"Smart kid . . ."

"When do we talk?"

Lucas looked down the street toward the Metrodome. "I don't want to do anything today. I just want to sit somewhere and see if I can feel good. There's a Twins game. . . ."

"Sarah's never been."

"You wanna see a game, kid? They ain't the Cubs, but what the hell." Lucas lifted Sarah to straddle the back of his neck and she grabbed his ear and him with the pacifier. What felt like a gob of saliva hit him in the part of his hair. "I'll teach you how to boo. Maybe we can get you a bag to put on your head."


When Lucas had gone, Daniel gathered his papers together, stacked them, dropped them into his in tray, shut down the computer and took a lap around the office, looking at the faces of his politicians. Hard decisions. Hard.

"Jesus Christ," the chief said quietly, but aloud. He could hear his heart beating, then a rush of adrenaline, a tincture of fear. But now it was ending, all done.

He stepped back toward his desk, saw the paper wad that Lucas had fired at the wastebasket. He picked it up, meaning to flip it at the basket, and saw the ballpoint ink on the back. He smoothed the paper on his desk.

In Davenport's clear hand, under the heading "Loverboy":

—Heavyset, blond with thinning hair. Looks like Philip George.
—Cannot turn himself in, or even negotiate: Cop.
—No hair in drain or on bed: Cop.
—Called me through Dispatch on nontaped line: Cop.
—Extreme voice disguise: Knows me.
—Served with S. Bekker in police review board study.
—Knew Druze was the killer.
—Didn't call back after advertisement in newspaper and pictures on TV: Already knew Druze was dead and that he was S. Bekker's killer.
—Had Redon flower painting on calendar; same calendar at Institute of Arts has cyclops painting for November; changed it for weather calendar.
—Assigns fuck-up to chase phony Loverboy.

Then there was a space, and in a scrawl at the bottom, an additional line:

*—Has to get rid of me—that's where IA is coming from . . .*

"Jesus Christ," Daniel said to himself.

He looked up, across the office at the weather calendar, which hung on the wall amid the faces of the politicians, all staring down at him and the crumpled slip of paper. Stunned, he looked out the window again, saw Davenport tossing a kid in the air.

Davenport knew.

Daniel wanted to run down after him. He wanted to say he was sorry.

He couldn't do that. Instead he sat at his desk, head in his hands, thinking. He hadn't been able to weep since he was a child.

Loverboy wished, sometimes, that he still knew how.